'I'M YOUNG, VERY WELL OFF, AND VERY MUCH IN LOVE WITH YOU,' SHE REPLIED. 'WE HAVE THE PERFECT COMBINATION.'

'The perfect combination for calamity.' He held her away, the strength of his grip betraying his tension. 'We're indulging in madness.'

'Then walk away,' she said softly. 'Walk away right now and don't look back! Pack your things and book your passage but stay away from any place where we might meet. While you're waiting for the ship to sail, play your recording of the Rachmaninov and don't even think of me. Fly out to the back of beyond in Australia and forget we ever stood together in a mystical garden on top of a hill in Hong Kong. When you've done all that, the madness will have passed.'

He looked down at her in challenge. 'And what will you be doing all that time?'

'You musn't care about that, either.'

'Then the madness will never end.'

ABOUT THE AUTHOR

Elizabeth Darrell spent her early childhood in Hong Kong immediately before the outbreak of the Second World War, where her father was stationed with the Royal Engineers. Before her marriage to a senior civil servant she served as an officer in the WRAC. She is the author of five acclaimed novels, including *At the Going Down of the Sun* and *And in the Morning*; the *Reader's Digest* magazine has praised her 'storytelling genius ... masterfully blending history and imagination'. Elizabeth Darrell is currently working on a new novel to be published next year. Under the pen name Emma Drummond she has written ten historical novels.

ELIZABETH DARRELL

CONCERTO

A SIGNET BOOK

SIGNET

Published by the Penguin Group
Penguin Books Ltd, 27 Wrights Lane, London W8 5TZ, England
Penguin Books USA Inc., 375 Hudson Street, New York, New York 10014, USA
Penguin Books Australia Ltd, Ringwood, Victoria, Australia
Penguin Books Canada Ltd, 10 Alcorn Avenue, Toronto, Ontario,
Canada M4V 3B2
Penguin Books (NZ) Ltd, 182–190 Wairau Road, Auckland 10, New Zealand

Penguin Books Ltd, Registered Offices: Harmondsworth, Middlesex, England

First published by Michael Joseph 1993
Published in Signet 1994
1 3 5 7 9 10 8 6 4 2

Printed in England by Clays Ltd, St Ives plc

Chapter One

Rod Durman was worried, overtired and deeply frustrated. An outbreak of cholera was threatening to become a major epidemic and, if it did, every doctor in Hong Kong would be working flat out to bring it under control. He was getting too little sleep already, studying well into the small hours in preparation for the coming selection board for a post in the tropical medicine department of Queen Mary Hospital, where he was presently a member of the general staff. Success would gain him what he had long wanted; failure could put it beyond his reach while he remained in Hong Kong. At this particularly difficult time his wife, Celeste, was in one of her impossible moods.

The day was overcast and unpleasantly humid, so he returned to his office already literally and metaphorically hot under the collar after a conference at which opinions had been aired in too personal a manner. The chairman had stopped just short of calling him a liar; the meeting had broken up with professional reputations frayed and nothing decided. Rod knew it was typical of charitable establishments like the Halburton Clinic. He and three other doctors gave their services free during their off-duty time and worked damned hard for Chinese patients in the four-ward clinic founded by a consortium of the colony's influential residents. These men who provided the cash had no medical knowledge, so it was practically impossible to see eye to eye with them on any issue.

With his temper barely under control, Rod found it swiftly igniting on reading through a report he had compiled on a

1

complicated case for which he required a second opinion. He had sent it to be typed before the conference and it was waiting in his in-tray on his return. He saw it as the last straw. Getting to his feet so violently that he knocked the chair on to its side, he went along the corridor like a maddened bull ready to charge. The door of the small typing room slammed back against the wall as he entered, making the two female occupants look up sharply.

'Which of you has the initials S.R.C.?' he demanded.

'I,' said the one sitting at a desk by the window.

He advanced on her, holding out the report. 'If you are responsible for this appalling work you deserve to be lynched.' He flung the typed papers down with such force they splayed out and some slipped to the floor, where they fluttered around in the downdraught from the circling fan like newly landed fish.

The girl sat as if mesmerized, colour tinting her cheeks. 'I'm afraid I have no idea who you are, or what this is all about.'

It was said quietly, but her cut-glass English accent fuelled Rod's rage. He knew the type all too well. Poor little rich girls: daughters, and wives of young men in the colonial administration, who did nothing but gossip, play games and flirt with European playboys who had as much money and as few morals as they.

'It's about my report on the medical condition of a patient suffering from acute malnutrition, cirrhosis, and attacks of inexplicable amnesia. The bloke is seriously ill! *Your* attacks of amnesia apparently occur the moment you sit at that typewriter and try to remember how to use it. There are fifty-two errors in that report. *Fifty-two!*' He attempted to control his anger, but failed. 'That fancy English school you went to failed to teach you how to spell, even when the bloody words are there for you to copy. Luckily for that poor bastard, this report on his case can be done again by someone with shorter fingernails and a few brains instead of feathers inside her head. If I made just *one* mistake in *my* work, he could die. We're dealing at this clinic with people's lives, S.R.C., not someone's hairdo or golf handicap. If you must salve your conscience by fooling yourself you're doing something useful for several hours a week, go and do it where nobody can suffer from your inadequacy.'

The girl's long hair cloaked her face as she bent to retrieve the pages on the floor, so her voice was muffled as she said she would do the report again.

'Don't waste your time,' he told her savagely. 'Give it to your friend here. She might make a better job of it.'

Back in his office, Rod stood looking out over Stanley Bay while he rode out his wrath. No one but Celeste raised it to such an extent, as a rule, but it had been a bastard of a day and he had to return to her at the end of it. She was playing up because he spent each evening refreshing his knowledge on tropical diseases. She knew how important it was to him, and that the study would end after the selection board, but she resented a profession that occupied so much of his time and dedication. Her punishment always took the form of sexual provocation. It was starting to get to him. A man of strong passions, Rod was still susceptible to Celeste's animal attraction. She knew, and gave him no peace until he surrendered to it.

In some curious way, that girl with the initials S.R.C. had made him aware of his deplorable vulnerability in that direction. She was the complete opposite of his dark, sensual wife: a cool blonde with clear, guileless, green eyes, who would doubtless sail through life untouched by passion. She was a little different from most of her kind. Her hair hung straight to her shoulders with no hint of Marcel waving, and her skin was unusually pale. A new arrival, perhaps, but certainly a young woman with her feelings well under control. In an expensive dress of some pale-green silk material, with gold earrings, and a heavy gold bracelet on her right arm, she had looked as self-assured as they come. 'Daddy' no doubt made everything in life come right for her. Time she found out it was no picnic.

Turning back to his desk, he picked up a fat file and tried to concentrate on its contents. A child of eight was suffering repeated attacks of sickness leading to fainting, with no obvious cause. She had been admitted yet again and was awaiting his examination. Taking the file with him to the ward, Rod was soon lost in work he loved and to which he

3

was deeply committed, frustration forgotten as he attempted to solve a puzzle which had existed too long. After his examination, he discussed the case with Wah Boon, a Chinese orderly whose father ran a practice in Kowloon. Although Chinese methods were mostly dismissed by Western doctors as quackery, Rod saw merit in some of their treatments and went so far as to support the application of needles to specific parts of the anatomy to ease muscular or spinal pain. His opinions made him unpopular in certain quarters, but he was prepared to support any treatment with proven success if it cured a patient.

After arranging to visit Wah Boon's father, a long-standing acquaintance, to ask his opinion on the little girl's condition, Rod returned to his office and wrote up his own findings on examining her. Only as he prepared to leave, on the arrival of a young Scots doctor who would take night-duty, did he notice a thick pile of typewritten sheets in the in-tray. Reading through them he found no mistakes, despite the initials S.R.C. at the bottom of the last page. His mouth twisted. Who did she think she was fooling? The other girl had done the work, that much was obvious, and they had conspired to make it seem otherwise. He slipped the report into an envelope, addressed it to the specialist and took it out to his car intending to deliver it right away. It meant a detour, but he wanted the man's assessment as soon as possible.

When he caught himself taking his usual route, and had to double back to reach the road leading to the specialist's home, Rod realized just how tired he was. Dangerously tired. Only a fool would ignore the signs. Why was he asking for second opinions on two of his cases? How had he come to lose control so swiftly this afternoon? Where were he and Celeste heading? He seemed to be losing his grip on himself just when the chance of gaining what he had worked for was within reach. Hong Kong was a small community medically, so members of the selection board would soon hear that he was under par and bang would go his hope of specializing in the subject which most fascinated him.

Two miles from the district where he rented an apartment,

he pulled to the side of the road giving a view of the busy harbour. Switching off the engine, he got out to sit on a stone bench. For some moments he gazed listlessly at a mass of vessels plying the deep waters which made this island colony so important to the British. The largest of passenger liners and merchant ships could navigate alongside the wharves, so East–West trade was conducted on a large scale by companies dating back to the early part of the last century, when Hong Kong was seized as part of a growing empire. Amid huge ships from neutral nations of the world was a fleet of junks, sampans and dhows which also used the harbour, trading in everything from ivory to opium with unbelievable possibilities lying between the two. Vice, slavery, poisons all formed part of the illegal trading practised since the colony's inception. It would never be stamped out. A vast network of Triad gangs ensured that the lucrative dealings continued. Rod had come across victims of Hong Kong's underworld activities too often to have illusions about an island seen by many as a carefree, sunwashed playground.

These blinkered souls still saw it as such despite the war raging across Europe, and the presence of the Japanese only thirty-five miles from the border with China. Admittedly, they had been there for almost eighteen months without showing signs of aggression towards the British colony. The military garrison had been greatly augmented two years ago, in 1939, and the British women had been compulsorily shipped to Australia, along with their children. This had caused anger because American, French and other European women had remained with their husbands, and periodic vain attempts were made to have the evacuation order reversed. Quite a few had managed to stay in Hong Kong by promptly volunteering as nursing aides, or by persuading their employers to claim that their services were indispensable. Wives of a number of influential Englishmen had considered themselves exempt from the order, and the Governor had turned a blind eye, much to the fury of the self-styled 'bachelor husbands' deprived of their families during long months of perfect peace in the colony. Inevitably, romantic liaisons sprang up between lonely men and women eager to console them, so Hong Kong spawned scandals as never before.

Some younger Englishmen had returned to fight for their country; the rest had been recruited into the Hong Kong Volunteer Defence Corps or the Naval Reserve and trained in their spare time whilst continuing to enjoy life as before. Air-raid shelters had been built for the military garrison, warning sirens had been placed around the Island, mock blackouts were practised but, as months passed with no sign of aggression from the Japanese, these all became emergencies from the past. The good life continued; confidence was restored.

The greatest concern to the British when the Japanese halted a few dozen miles from the border, was an influx of over three-quarters of a million Chinese refugees from tyranny. Overcrowding was so great in the Chinese quarter, many were forced to live on the streets, putting such strain on sanitation that epidemics followed one after the other. Landlords – many of whom were controlled by Triads – quadrupled their rents. Those unable to pay were evicted and replaced by three times as many tenants willing to hand over meagre savings for one room in a sordid tenement. Fake cures for the ailments of the East were peddled to those who believed Western medicine was sorcery by 'foreign devils', and the markets in drugs and prostitution had swelled to uncontrollable levels. All this had added to the problems of those responsible for health in Hong Kong. Medical resources had been stretched to the limit; doctors had laboured exhaustively to minimize the acute danger to life presented by the lack of facilities for such a drastic increase in population.

Although some of Rod's countrymen had returned to Australia to don uniform in aid of the Commonwealth, he was dedicated to saving life rather than taking it so had stayed in Hong Kong during the critical period brought about by the arrival of the refugees. He believed he was serving humanity his own way. Many who remained in the colony, however, had done so because they were overfond of the good life.

Rod sighed heavily. It could have been a good life here for

him if his marriage had survived its many hazards. Divorce was the obvious step to take, but a doctor had to guard his reputation more closely than most and he knew Celeste would make the split messy and damaging. She was happy enough with the present situation, revelling in an abundance of clothes and parties, secure in her married state. Even if a reasonably decent end could be put to their relationship, Hong Kong had a tiny, insular European community and Celeste was almost certain to scar him by reflected scandal as a divorcee.

Frowning down at the spread of masts, sails, prows and funnels below, Rod recalled the black-haired, passionate girl who had taken him by storm when he was a medical student. Half-Italian, Celeste was beautiful, sensuous and highly provocative. A fellow student had brought her to a beach party, but she made it plain with whom she wanted to leave. Rod had been twenty-two, she eighteen. He had slept with her on their second date, and married her a month later. Both sets of parents had been upset, but they were so crazy about each other no wrath could touch them.

Despite getting little sleep and finding concentration difficult, Rod managed to qualify and took a job in the Northern Territories as one of a Flying Doctor team. Celeste hated the isolation, the lack of excitement and the Outback mentality of the people. Using pregnancy as an excuse to go to her parents in Sydney, Celeste flatly refused to return when she miscarried two months later. With cracks already apparent in a relationship based on physical attraction, Rod gave up work he found satisfying to become the junior partner in a Sydney practice. His sacrifice brought them no closer in understanding, and he grew resentful in a post he did not enjoy.

By the time her second pregnancy miscarried Celeste had made clear three things: she hated the smell of antiseptic whenever Rod took her in his arms, she was sick to death of things medical, and she had no intention of becoming a mother – natural or adoptive. When the chance came along to join the staff of a hospital in Hong Kong, Rod seized it eagerly in the hope that the marriage could still be saved. The island colony gave him an opportunity to study Oriental diseases, which furthered his interest in tropical medicine. It also offered Celeste as many parties as she could desire, beautiful clothes and every outlet for a temperament geared to excitement. With individual fulfilment came growing incompatibility. Rod became more and more dedicated to healing; Celeste found excitement increasingly heady. All that remained of the marriage was physical attraction, which flared briefly, then died to leave them both further disillusioned.

Staring into space on that roadside bench, Rod wondered how he could contrive to be alone until the day of the selection board. Would Celeste jump at an offer to visit her family in Sydney? Oh no, she was having too much fun here. Besides, the figures on his bank statement seemed permanently to be printed in red. He sighed again. A good night's sleep would help. For the sake of his patients his present tense state must be eased. He would forget books this evening, take a shower, have a light meal, listen to soothing music then get to bed early. He might take a sedative to ensure complete relaxation.

The moment he entered the apartment, Rod sensed his wife's mood. Music filled the rooms – bouncy, modern dance tunes that Celeste loved and he found irritating. The aroma of her favourite perfume hung in the air, and their boy, Lim, was setting out dishes of hors-d'oeuvres on the long glass-covered bamboo sideboard. He came forward, smiling, to take Rod's bag.

'You late, Doctor. Work too hard, much too bad. Missy say not good for you.' He turned towards the closet, saying over his shoulder, 'I make you good cup tea while you take shower. I already put out clothes. You plenty time. Flends not come for two hour. Dinner leddy in thirty minutes. Missy say not too much tonight. Cookee make fish and plenty good soup for you.'

Rod's temper smouldered again. With no more than a mumbled word to the efficient Chinese who had served them for over two years, he made for the bedroom, switching off the gramophone as he passed. Celeste turned swiftly from the full-length mirror at his forceful entry, her expression hardening as she saw his.

'What's this about friends coming in two hours' time?' he demanded. 'I don't recall inviting anyone for this evening.'

'No, sweetie, I did. We owe hospitality to so many, I thought it was time something was done about it.'

He advanced, growing even more incensed. 'I owe nothing to anyone, much less plates of expensive bits of fish and chicken to wash down with far too many drinks.' Two yards from her he noticed the clinging silk sheath she wore. 'Is that another new dress?'

Smiling wickedly, she closed on him. 'You *noticed*, darling. Things must have gone well today.' Her arms encircled his neck. 'It slips off very easily and we have half an hour before dinner.'

'I'm in no mood for your games,' he snapped, disentangling himself. 'As it happens, it was a pig of a day. Two difficult cases, another row with the management, and a set-to with –' He broke off, unwilling to relate the story of the cool blonde who had caused him to lose control this afternoon.

Celeste's dark, expressive eyes mocked him. 'My, my, not only the day was a pig, apparently. Before long you'll upset someone with real influence, who'll send you out of that clinic on your backside. It's the only way you'll give up work that is unpaid and brings out the worst in you.' She looked him over assessingly. 'Are you *sure* you're in no mood for games? We always have such fun when you're angry.'

Before he could respond, a tap on the door heralded Lim with a tray. While he arranged cup and saucer with fussy precision, then poured strong tea for his employer, Rod tugged off his tie and began unbuttoning his limp shirt. Celeste enjoyed rows; they appealed to her need for excitement. He found them degrading. They were intelligent adults in a difficult situation. Shouting abuse at each other was no solution and merely reduced them to the level of petulant children. That thought led to recollection of how he had treated the volunteer typist. Self-disgust swept through him. He was a man of thirty with impressive qualifications; a doctor in whose hands people had often to place their lives. This hopeless marriage was turning him into a boor; an aggressive lout.

9

Lim departed, but Rod left his tea cooling in the cup as he continued undressing with movements that betrayed his tension. The apartment was attractive and airy, and, if this bedroom was overly feminine with its pink and cream décor and frothy bedlinen, Celeste had used her flair for style to impressive advantage in the other rooms. On the fourth floor, with a splendid view across a strip of dazzling cobalt sea to one of the emerald offshore islands, this rented home could be the ideal place in which to relax and plumb the delights of marriage to an exciting, sensual woman. Instead, it had become a cockpit. They were already raw and bleeding. Would it end with one crowing over the total destruction of the other?

He took a shower with the intention of cooling both body and temper before tackling Celeste again, yet he knew her well. She was charged up for an evening of cocktails and high jinks; certainly in no mood for him to plead his cause with success. Towelling down, he returned to the bedroom to find that she had left it for the central room which opened on to a wide veranda. He stood in the connecting doorway, a towel around his waist, thinking of evenings when they had been swept by the old magic. Sitting out there with a drink beside them, the warm night whispering seductively, the lights spread below looking like reflections of the stars so vivid in this southern hemisphere, they had known fleeting rapport. Afterwards, the frothy bedlinen had been thrown aside during lovemaking which both indulged in with passionate abandon. There would be none tonight even if he had the energy. Celeste was lost in the prospect of a party, standing in the centre of the room while swaying to the rhythm of a dance tune produced by the gramophone. Her superb body, outlined by close-fitting gold silk that tightened across her hips as she moved to the beat, left him untouched by desire but increased his anger. He strode across to stop the music once more, and tried to keep his voice down as he answered her protest. 'I can't talk to you above that.'

'Then don't talk to me, sweetie. Get some clothes on, instead. You're provoking me rather too much. One tweak and that towel would be at your feet.'

'One slap and you might calm down,' he retaliated, instantly back to the state he had been hoping to avoid. 'You'll have to phone all the people you've invited and cancel your shindig. I need to get some sleep – now, tonight! I saw the danger signs this afternoon and, with a cholera epidemic threatening, it's absolutely essential that I get back on form for it.' He appealed to her: 'Try to understand, Celeste. I'm whacked out, and it's dangerous. I might make mistakes which could have fatal consequences. Postpone it until next week, if you really feel you have to entertain a crowd of social parasites, but I want the place to myself tonight.'

Her narrow face grew hostile. 'It's always what *you* want, isn't it? You and the bloody hospital! *I have to go, Celeste, it's a matter of life and death. You'll have to attend the party alone, there's an emergency at the clinic. Don't arrange anything this weekend, it's my turn to visit the islands. Stop playing that music, I'm trying to study. Cancel your party, I need to sleep,*' she cried in derisive tones. 'If you hadn't stayed up into the God-awful hours of the morning for the past fortnight reading about germs and bacteria, you wouldn't be asleep on your feet snapping the heads off everyone in sight. *Those* are the parasites that are driving you to insanity, not the social kind, Rod. You're *pathetic!*'

She swung round and started the gramophone once more. Raucous music echoed back from the walls until he put an end to it very forcibly by snatching the record from the turntable and hurling it across the room. Celeste was as startled by his action as he. They gazed at each other in silence for several moments before he said quietly, 'Sorry. As I told you earlier, it's been a pig of a day. I really do need to rest tonight.'

'And I need more stimulating company than I've had recently,' she retorted, magnificent eyes flashing. 'I can't cancel at this late hour, and I won't. Go back to the Queen Mary and admit yourself to one of the wards. You don't want rest, you want a straitjacket, sweetie.'

Well into the hurling of abuse he had deplored a little earlier, Rod heard himself say, 'I pay the rent on this place, so I'm entitled to call the tune. Get on that phone and tell your friends the party's off.'

11

'No!'

'Do as I bloody well say!'

Her full mouth curved into a satisfied smile. 'All right, darling. I'll tell them you're cracking up and liable to throw things, so we'll all go to the Peninsula Hotel instead . . . and send the bill to you.'

He knew he could not win; he never did when she had this particular bit between her teeth. But he had one last try. 'It won't get paid. We're in the red again. I'm almost glad, because I shall be fully justified in telling your dressmaker and the big stores to serve you at their own cost. That'll curb you, if my words won't.'

Her smile broadened. 'And have the whole of Hong Kong knowing that Dr Durman keeps his wife so short of money she can no longer leave her apartment? That vulnerable reputation of yours would suffer more than I.' She changed mood dramatically, approaching to run a finger softly over his chest and tease at his nipples. 'A party is just what you need to get rid of that black mood. Relax, soften up with a drink or two, and show everyone that you can be a real charmer when you choose to be.'

He stepped back abruptly, to launch a fresh attack. 'You think this can be solved by suppressing emotions with alcohol? I'm not in a black mood, Celeste, I'm fighting for the survival of something not worth saving. Sure, my reputation is vulnerable enough for you to ruin me professionally, if that's what you want. But you'd be finished in Hong Kong too, so I know you won't go that far. You need me, but I could get along far better without you if there was a way of doing so without harming my future. I can't see one at present, so we're stuck with each other. For God's sake, let's make it as painless a union as possible. I allow you to spend money on clothes and entertainment as fast as I can earn it. In return, you allow me to put in a great many hours on work I love, leaving you alone.' He stepped further away from her as she advanced. 'Last week you put us in the red again with bills from Lane Crawford and Madame Tong, which landed me in an awkward meeting with Charters at the bank. I smoothed him down. Now I'm asking you to compensate by postponing tonight's party.'

She was close to him again. 'Until when?'

'Well ... the selection board is to be held in a couple of months,' he said, thrown by her apparent surrender. 'I'll need to study until then, and ...'

'And after that there'll be something else, some other medical demand I have to bow to. No, Rod, if you're suggesting give and take, you're madder than I guessed. Between you, the hospital, the charity clinic, and that floating dispensary you help to run, I find it's me doing all the giving,' she said heatedly.

'And all the taking,' he returned with bitterness. 'How long do you think we can go on living as we are, with debts piling up in every direction?'

'Play me "Hearts and Flowers",' she cried. 'You spend two days a week and every fourth weekend working for charity. If you ran a private practice instead, like some of your colleagues, you'd be raking in the dollars. You're a fool, Rod; a character from a novel. No one dedicates himself to mankind for no reward these days. Who do you imagine you are? Christ?'

Her words touched on the principal cause of friction between them. His commitment to healing was absolute; she saw it as weakness. 'You think medicine is a money-making concern like trading or banking, and condemn me for not hauling in the shekels at the expense of some poor bastard's misery,' he said with growing vehemence. 'Well, I warn you, one of these days *you'll* need help when you're doubled up with pain or have difficulty breathing. But if you're lucky enough to be spared a serious illness, old age will get you. When that lovely, lithe body of yours cracks with arthritis and the muscles begin to sag, when you have to hide those teasing eyes behind thick lenses, you'll cry out for someone to help you walk and minimize your incontinence. Your doctor will be the most important man in your life then – and the only one who'll show any interest in you, believe me.'

He had now touched *her* sensitive spot, and she reacted in typical manner. 'Before that happens I mean to *live*. I'm going to use what nature gave me before it's taken away again. You can waste your youth by incarcerating yourself in fortresses of sickness, but I want to have fun. To hell with your sermons! Money is there to be spent. You never need any, so I'll continue to buy the pleasures I enjoy and Charters at the bank can go to hell.' She reached out swiftly and tugged the towel from his waist. 'Get dressed! Dinner is in fifteen minutes.'

Rod stared at her slim, shapely back as she went to retrieve the record he had thrown across the room and knew an impulse to do the same with her. It appalled him and served as another warning. Was he close to cracking up? The dance music sounded even louder through the closed door – an additional frightening fact. He found himself shaking as he stared at his reflection in the long mirror. Dark shadows under his eyes, mouth pulled taut at the corners, a muscle jumping in his left cheek. Apart from those tell-tale signs he looked perfectly fit, but his professional knowledge told him he was heading for trouble. He stood indecisive for more than a minute. It was out of the question to attempt sleep, even sedated. Celeste's lively friends were certain to walk in. They always claimed freedom of the entire apartment, especially the women. He would have to go out for the evening, perhaps visit Wah Boon's father to discuss the case of the small girl with fainting fits. Yet that would add further weight to his overburdened brain and increase his tiredness. Perhaps he *should* admit himself to one of the private rooms at the hospital, where he would find complete rest. But he would then betray his condition and lose his chance at the selection board.

Putting on the underclothes Lim had laid out, Rod turned to the wardrobe for a less formal shirt and trousers. In so doing, he caught sight of a large card propped on the nearby chest of drawers. He had forgotten the charity concert; put it from his mind because he had not intended to go there. The price of two tickets was the most important participation in such events. These charity affairs were attended by too many VIPs who gave too many speeches. Celeste would have enjoyed the opportunity to rub shoulders with Hong Kong's upper set, but Rod knew it would go to her head and had avoided the danger. The tickets now provided the solution he sought. His seat was certain to be near the back, so he could sleep through the performance without being spotted by any guest of distinction.

Clad in dinner jacket and black tie, he scooped up the keys to his car and left the bedroom.

Celeste looked across from the glossy magazine in her hands and gave him admiring scrutiny. 'God, you're wasted in the corridors of healing! You'll be the most desirable man in the room tonight.' She smiled and stood up. 'Delia Wright lusts after you. She told me . . .' Breaking off as he headed past her, she asked, 'Where are you going?'

Rod turned in the open doorway. 'Does it matter? You've got what you wanted.'

It was still hot in the evening streets busy with people. He cursed under his breath as he drove around rickshaws, braked to avoid jaywalkers and inched past a procession complete with a long silken 'dragon' swaying from side to side, leaping and prancing. He was deafened by crashing cymbals; firecrackers exploding alongside the car set his nerves jumping. Laughing Chinese faces pressed against the windows momentarily as he was forced to stop by a meandering rickshaw. Beads of perspiration stood on his brow and his heartbeat raced as he accelerated and almost hit a tram. When he reached the concert venue, he sat for a while in his parked car to calm himself down.

The concert was in aid of a school for deaf Chinese children. Owing to the tender age of some performers chosen to add emotional strength to the cause, the usual format had been reversed. The items were starting earlier and would be followed by champagne and a buffet. Entering a fan-cooled hall, Rod's heart sank on glancing at the expensive programme. He had not known the diverse style of the evening. Aside from items by the orchestra of the military garrison, there would be songs from a Chinese soprano, mime performed by the Kowloon School of Acting, a poetry reading by a boy genius, a lion dance given by a travelling troupe . . . Rod stopped reading. Some hope of sleeping through that lot!

His seat was four rows from the back of the hall and cooled by a fan immediately overhead. The usual mixture of dinner jackets, military scarlet and feminine glamour was gathered there, and several doctors waved acknowledgement as he took the seat on the aisle leaving an empty one between himself and a distinguished Chinese accompanying a woman with many gold bracelets in figure-hugging jade brocade. Rod settled back in the seat feeling completely drained. After sitting through the concert he would suffer the boredom of the reception merely to have something to eat. Alcoholic drinks were out tonight, or he might be in real trouble.

When the lights dimmed, his lids drooped. They shot up again when a loud, rattling drum roll heralded 'The Thieving Magpie' overture played by an energetic military orchestra. He enjoyed the piece, which was followed by a movement from the 'Dolly' Suite. The diminutive daughter of the military bandmaster then played a simple piano waltz, raised by a cushion on the stool in order to reach the keys. When a bespectacled youth marched out to read several poems that made no sense whatever to Rod, sleep finally triumphed.

He awoke to hear the dramatic opening bars of a piano concerto by Rachmaninov being played with such fire he was driven to sit up, immediately alert. In a long dress of sapphire-blue taffeta, her blonde hair in a chignon, the pianist seemed totally lost in the music. Her hands raced unerringly across the keys, and the movements of her slim body suggested she had become one with the passionate mood she was creating. Rod had an excellent recording of the concerto which he had had no time to hear lately, but this live performance contained a magical quality he found enthralling. It was surprising, because the woman was playing accompanied by a recording of the orchestral part of the concerto. The method was used in practice, never in performance, but the recording was amplified, and the soloist so gifted the experiment succeeded. Lights shone on golden hair to suggest a halo, and her vivid dress began to dazzle Rod so that he saw nothing but the pliant figure whose pale arms waved back and forth over the keyboard. When the second movement began, the woman's fingers caressed the keys with such sensitivity, Rod felt his scalp tingle in response to the yearning she conjured from the score. With

16

the final, flamboyant movement under way, he was so caught up in the spell being cast in that hall that his throat began to constrict with emotion as the main theme was played in a manner that suggested to him a curiously angry defiance on the part of the pianist. He had not been so moved by music for years, and he was not the only one. When the last note echoed into silence, several moments elapsed before a single voice shouted 'Bravo', and the audience rose applauding. When his neighbour turned to smile and nod at him, Rod realized it had been his own voice he had heard.

The pianist appeared to require time to emerge from the depths of her performance. She remained seated, staring at the keyboard until awareness returned. When she finally stood, supporting herself by a hand on the piano, she was visibly overwhelmed by her reception. Despite loud demands for an encore, she soon left the stage and did not reappear even though the applause continued for several minutes. People began to leave their places as the hall filled with the less musical sound of loud conversation, and Rod took another look at his programme which had slipped to the floor whilst he had dozed. The pianist was named as Sarah Channing. It meant nothing to him, but he had been out of touch with the concert world since leaving Australia. Why would a performer of such calibre be in Hong Kong? Was she *en route* to temporary wartime headquarters in his homeland? Many European artists had fled before the Germans invaded their countries, and who could condemn them? When the madness and killing ended such people would assist the return of sanity.

Growing aware that he was the only one left in the hall, Rod pocketed the programme and made his way to the gallery where guests were paying more attention to their supper than to the exhibits hanging on the walls. Although he had had no dinner Rod was under the spell of the evening and no longer hungry. The crush was so great it would have been a test of dexterity to hold a glass and a plateful of food without losing either. Champagne corks were popping above the clamour of conversation. He was not lured by the sound. Whisky was his drink, but not tonight. The Chinese steward had failed to hide his astonishment when asked for soda water, neat, and Rod tried not to grimace whilst drinking it.

His mind was full of visions of a woman producing glorious sounds with the suppleness of her fingers and the passion of her nature, when a loud voice accosted him. A senior consultant from his hospital was making for him, pushing between two women in colours that clashed atrociously. Sir Kingston Dailey would be a member of the selection board. It was highly unusual for a medical 'god' to approach a junior doctor at a social gathering, so Rod was puzzled.

Tall, thin, with a mop of greying ginger hair, Sir Kingston came up to nod a greeting. 'Surprised to see you here, Durman. Not your kind of thing, surely.'

'On the contrary, sir. I used to queue each week for symphony concerts in Melbourne.'

Gingery-grey eyebrows rose. 'You have such things down there?'

'Only for those with two sheep to barter for a ticket,' Rod responded smartly, used to slurs on his nation's cultural life.

Sir Kingston appeared to be in a mellow mood. His momentary frown was followed by a shout of laughter. 'That's good. Very good!' He indicated Rod's glass. 'What are you drinking?'

'Soda water.'

'*What*? Puss piss, man! I thought Australians could drink anyone under the table and then shout for more. Boy, bring two double whiskies,' he demanded of a passing steward.

Rod was unsure what to make of his senior's fulsomeness. He had either imbibed a great deal in a short time, or there was an ulterior motive in his unusual tolerance of a lowly member of staff in a newly built Government hospital. Both surmises were shown to be true when Sir Kingston smiled and confessed that he had been intending to corner Rod for a chat.

'Ah, here's our whisky. Drink up, man. drink up!'

Rod knew he could not refuse on the grounds of suspecting himself to be on the verge of cracking up, so he did as ordered while the other continued in confidential tones.

'I know you give your services to the Halburton Clinic

18

and also help to man that floating dispensary funded by Wang Chua. Indeed, I understand it was your prompt treatment of the old devil's great-grandson when he was hit by a tram that prompted his philanthropic gesture.'

Rod nodded, the swift injection of whisky in a room growing very warm making him slightly muzzy.

'Splendid!' Watery blue eyes smiled into his. 'You're just the man.'

'Just the man for what?' demanded Rod suspiciously.

'A little project I hope to get off the ground later this year. Funds are short, unfortunately, so each participant must be a volunteer. But it's such a worthy scheme, you know.'

Rod groaned inwardly. Whenever anyone trotted out that line they expected unreserved co-operation. The consultant outlined plans for a scheme whereby a team of volunteers from military and civilian hospitals would monitor the health of those living in sampan colonies around the Island and Kowloon.

'There's another cholera epidemic threatening. It's those wretched people who start them, Durman ... *and* all the other deadly infections that sweep the colony. If we can treat them at source it'll save a great many lives.'

Rod had heard the concept aired many times. 'It's an impossible task, sir. Those communities are forever on the move. We'd never keep track of the people we initially monitored. The idea is excellent in principal, but hopeless to implement.'

'I know the difficulties, man,' Sir Kingston snapped. 'I won't accept "impossible", however. I shall call together my volunteers early next month to thrash out details. I can count on you? Splendid, splendid!' he cried, before Rod could answer. 'Let's drink to your generosity. Whisky, boy!'

While his companion endeavoured to outshout others calling for drinks, Rod caught the eyes of two colleagues standing nearby with their wives. Each made the gesture of spreading butter on bread. Rod smiled sourly and waggled his glass at them, but how wrong they were. He was not a man to indulge in such tactics. He believed in gaining what he wanted by merit, not flattery. It was Sir Kingston doing the buttering-up.

Having ensured delivery of two more stiff whiskies, the consultant turned back to ask slyly, 'After that place in Tropical Diseases, aren't you?'

'Yes. I wouldn't use that as an ulterior motive for anything I do,' Rod said pointedly. 'I've been wanting to specialize for several years.' He was surprised by his own lack of enthusiasm. A piano concerto had reawoken him to something of which he had lost sight for too long. He was at this instant attuned to passionate cascading melody rather than the cries of the suffering. Visions of filthy sampan colonies threatened to banish those of an enigmatic, graceful woman who had reached him through the genius of Rachmaninov.

'. . . the kind of man we want,' Sir Kingston was saying. 'Young, sound qualifications, plenty of general experience. Willing to offer your skills without financial reward. Rare, these days. Yes, in most respects the kind of man we want. A word of advice, though. It won't do to be involved with Chinese quackery, or to be heard advocating Oriental cures. The Queen Mary is a Government hospital practising Western medicine. You are qualified in that field, and the hospital is glad to have you on the staff. But you are known to have friends who favour therapies and potions not recognized by us, and you've been overheard arguing their merits. I suggest you very swiftly change your attitude and find more acceptable friends among your Western colleagues. If not, seeking an interview with the selection board will be a waste of everyone's time . . . and you might be invited to offer your services to the Tung Wah hospital, where the remedies of the Orient are freely dispensed.'

'And are curing patients quite successfully,' Rod put in firmly. 'No doctor worth his salt should dismiss known curatives without at least investigating their properties very thoroughly. If Oriental medicine were as dangerous or as ineffective as some claim, the Chinese race would have died out long ago.'

Sir Kingston studied him shrewdly. 'That's another thing you should curb. It's a wise man who knows when to keep his own counsel.'

'And a wiser one who defends his beliefs when they hold merit, sir. Where would we be now if the giants of medical discovery had allowed themselves to be shouted down?'

'*They* were men of genius, Durman.'

'And compassion. I share their belief in not allowing a patient to suffer if there's even an outside chance of helping. If some bloke can prove to me that a mixture of Brylcreem and turps will cure where other remedies have failed, I'm prepared to investigate his claim, not laugh it off.'

'Lord help your patients,' said Sir Kingston sharply.

'It's when He doesn't that I'm prepared to consider *anything*.'

After a long moment the consultant gave a faint, reluctant smile. 'Your heart may be in the right place, Durman, but you'll have to decide whether you want a good, solid career in medicine, or whether to chance being a genius and end up committing murder. You could have the first without difficulty if you heed my advice between now and the selection board.'

Rod tossed back the whisky in one draught, aware that he had just been told the post in Tropical Diseases could be his very easily. He felt no surge of excitement, because he was not prepared to compromise along the lines suggested. A curious detachment had overtaken him. Tension had been replaced by a pleasant sensation of immunity to words and circumstances. There was no longer tightness in his stomach, nor did his pulse race. Such inner peace had been for so long a stranger he felt almost lightheaded. In this unusual state he grew aware that Sir Kingston had turned away to greet a man as tall and thin as himself, with grey hair, a trim grey moustache and dark-rimmed spectacles.

'Ah, Peter, tried unsuccessfully to push through the crowd surrounding you and your daughter half an hour ago. Good to see you, but why have you kept us all in ignorance of her tremendous talent, man? Will you have a whisky?' The strident voice called again for drinks, before adding, 'Now, I want to meet that young lady. Rescue her from those two harpies in puce and bring her over. Want to offer congratulations. I'm thinking of staging some kind of show in aid of a new project I mean to set up. Would she consent to play, do you think?'

Rod stood forgotten as the man named Peter moved off to where the woman who had taken an audience by storm was being bombarded with effusion from two of the colony's most competitive hostesses. Detaching his daughter with expertise, he brought her to meet Sir Kingston, who saw in her another volunteer for his impossible project. Rod was surprised by her youth, and put her age at no more than twenty, despite the sophisticated chignon usually worn by more mature women. Her face was faintly familiar. He wondered if she had ever been a patient at the Queen Mary. It was possible, for she was pale and shadows beneath her eyes hinted at a past illness. Standing silent and unsmiling beside her father, she showed no sign of the fire and passion evident during her performance. In fact, she looked positively exhausted as Sir Kingston showered her with whisky-laden compliments.

Rod frowned. The girl was clearly not up to the demands of socializing. She should be allowed to rest after a perform-ance to which she had given so much emotional power. He was studying her in clinical fashion when she turned her head and caught sight of him. For a moment or two she gazed as if mesmerized, while faint colour crept into her cheeks. Rod then knew, with a sense of astonishment, where he had seen her before. Sir Kingston followed her glance and complicated the situation.

'Miss Channing, may I present one of my junior colleagues who was as enchanted by your dazzling virtuosity as was everyone present? Durman, this young lady is the daughter of the President of the Channing Mercantile Banking Corporation.'

Rod shook hands with one of the business monarchs of Hong Kong, and told himself he had this afternoon inexcus-ably insulted Sarah R. Channing, volunteer typist at the Halburton Clinic, daughter of a man much admired for his philanthropic work and a girl who most certainly did not have feathers instead of brains. The two knights embarked on a business conversation leaving her gazing at Rod as if he were about to fly at her throat. Never good in situations requiring tact and a certain amount of oil on troubled waters, Rod searched for a way to extricate himself and relieve her of the distress his presence was causing. Then he saw her start to sway, and reacted swiftly. Taking hold of her arm, he put his own behind her for support, and began leading her through the crowd creating increasing heat and noise in a room with few windows.

'Lean on me,' he told her. 'Breathe deeply. You won't pass out, I promise.'

Forcing a path between laughing, elated groups who hardly noticed their identity, Rod headed for the hall where the concert had taken place. The girl was shaking now. He practically carried her forward until they reached the empty seats before the stage. There he sat her down and pushed her head below her knees. Taking off his dinner jacket, he wrapped it around her before squatting down to speak in soothing tones.

'Let yourself go limp. There's no one here but us. I've seen more women faint than you've had birthday parties.' He smiled reassuringly, although she could not see him. 'I've known blokes do it, too. Show some of them a hypodermic syringe and even sheep-shearers can pass out.'

She raised her head slowly and straightened, clutching his jacket around her with white-knuckled hands while she gazed at him with lingering apprehension.

Holding up his arms in a sign of surrender as he stood, he said, 'It's all right. The beast is now chained.' It brought no reaction, so he asked, 'Have you had anything to eat this evening? No? Stay right there and I'll see what I can snatch from beneath the snouts of the ravening horde.'

The heat hit him on re-entering the gallery, and his opinion of Sir Peter Channing dipped considerably as he spotted the man still talking to Sir Kingston, with several others of their ilk. How could he have permitted his daughter to be mobbed after such an exhausting performance without giving her a chance to recover with a drink and something sustaining? How could he now be so unconcerned over the whereabouts of the girl? Piling a plate with the most nutritious tit-bits remaining on the tables, Rod stopped a passing steward and commanded him to bring brandy for someone feeling ill. With that also in his hands he returned to Sarah Channing, who was looking much less afraid.

'Take a few sips of brandy, then eat,' he ordered, putting the plate and napkin on her lap after handing her the glass. 'You'll feel a new woman after you've tucked all that away.'

Sitting on the chair next but one to hers, he studied her with a frown. He had been all wrong about S.R.C. this afternoon. She was no cool, assured, pampered social butterfly. He had just witnessed her mastery of a particularly passionate and complex concerto; watched her fuse personal emotions with sounds that compelled and entranced. This girl was two people: one who had this afternoon taken on the chin a verbal attack more suited to an Outback drover, the other this vulnerable, hesitant artist. He preferred the earlier version – expensive simplicity, with shining hair hanging free and eyes unafraid to meet his. Which was more truly representative of the banking monarch's daughter?

As she drank, he said, 'I apologize for raving at you today. I'm not usually so brutally bad-tempered.'

She glanced up with that same cool gaze of this afternoon, disconcerting him with her sudden change of approach. 'Aren't you? Marion said you had a reputation for eating people alive. Once I knew that I was able to appreciate your basic point of view. A medical report is a vitally important document. I shouldn't have undertaken it when I was in a state of nerves about tonight.' She sipped the brandy again. 'Was my second copy acceptable?'

'You didn't do it!'

'I took it slowly, checking each paragraph as I went. Marion read it through before we sent it along to your office.' Offering the plate, she said in her 'cut-glass' accent, 'Do help me out. You brought enough for a sheep-shearer.'

Rod's sense of being in company with a female chameleon increased. It was an intriguing experience for a man used to tackling people head on. 'Let's get this straight. You stayed at the Halburton doing that report again when you were due to play the Rachmaninov tonight?'

'I had to give it my full attention, which actually calmed my nerves.' She waggled the plate. 'Please take some of this.'

Choosing a vol-au-vent and a smoked salmon sandwich, Rod put both on the seat between them as he studied the girl wrapped in his jacket, her long hair now drawn back from a face as yet unlined by experience, her blue shoes kicked off in relaxed fashion.

24

'Why is a concert pianist working as a volunteer typist at a charity clinic?'

'Why are you? Anyway, I'm not a concert performer yet, Dr Durman. Tonight was the first time I've performed before a very large public audience. Once I began to play I forgot where I was. It came as a shock when I heard clapping and realized I was surrounded by people. I longed to escape, but someone shouted "Bravo" at the top of his voice and prolonged the applause.'

'That was me, I'm afraid.'

'You?'

'Don't look so astonished.' He smiled. 'I may eat people alive, but I'm house-trained and have civilized habits.'

After a moment's hesitation, she smiled back. It was full of warmth and candour. 'You're really very nice beneath that aggressive approach.'

'You have me confused,' he said, again victim of her swiftly changing moods. 'I was so whacked tonight I fell asleep during the poetry, and awoke to the sound of someone playing quite superbly a piece of music that happens to be a favourite of mine. I took you for another artist escaping war torn Europe. Now you say you've never played to an audience before.'

She shrugged off his jacket and held it out. 'Thank you. I've got over the shivers.'

'Eat up the rest of that stuff,' he ordered as he put it on, 'or you'll get them back again.'

'You haven't eaten yours,' she pointed out.

'You're the patient, not me. Do as I say.'

She bit into a finger of pheasant pie, then referred to his earlier point. 'I always took part in end-of-term concerts, but only ever played études or studies to an audience of parents and teachers. I've performed concertos in front of examiners, of course, but tonight was altogether different.' She gave him tentative appraisal before adding, 'Rachmaninov embodies so many of my own deep feelings. When I heard applause and returned to reality, I instantly regretted playing it before total strangers. When they crowded round me afterwards I felt . . . exposed. That's why I made such a fool of myself just now. As a doctor, can you understand that?'

25

'I can understand it as a man,' he said. 'So you're not a professional artist?'

'Gracious, no. It takes *years* of training. It was my intention to go to Paris or Vienna on leaving Cheltenham, but the war has prevented that.'

'Hong Kong is no substitute, believe me.'

She glanced at the plate in her lap for a moment, as if uncertain how to continue. Then she looked up, to say, in slightly defensive tones, 'I didn't choose to come here. Father was concerned about my safety in England.'

'I see. How about your mother?'

'She died when I was four, so I was sent home to Ellie . . . my grandmother.'

'You were born here?'

'All I recall of Hong Kong are childish things – favourite toys, birthday parties, how to wind the amah around my little finger.'

'What do you think of the place now?' he asked, and received an unexpected reply.

'The place is all right, it's the people I find difficult to accept. The Europeans, I mean. They're totally out of touch with the rest of the world. All that concerns them is making money, or making merry. The military contingent talk very importantly about being ready to defend the Island against any invader, but none of them thinks for one moment that Hong Kong will ever come under attack. It's all just so many words. And all these people here tonight have no idea what food rationing is like . . . or how it feels to hear bombs exploding all around them, night after night.'

Here, at last, was a slight return of the fire Rod had witnessed in the performing artist. He deliberately fanned the flames. 'You've been through all that?'

'We live in the Cotswolds, far from any establishment of interest to German bombers, but I was in London for examinations and master classes often enough to know what it's like to be marked down for destruction by an enemy determined you'll have no sleep. You can't imagine what people are going through in England; how courageous they are,' she told him almost defiantly. 'Rationing affected everyone but we were luckier in the country because we could grow vegetables and keep poultry for meat and eggs. There were also pheasants and rabbits to shoot. But we couldn't provide our own sugar, tea, coffee, oranges, bananas ... oh, so many things you long for when you can't have them. Things everyone in Hong Kong takes for granted.'

'Is that why you've joined us, Miss Channing?'

'Certainly not!' she cried. 'I've already told you that I didn't choose to come here.'

Rod studied her shrewdly before saying, 'I'd credit you with too much determination to bow to the wishes of a father you've seen little of.'

'I haven't,' came the prompt reply. 'I bowed to the wishes of someone who has been both parents to me and a wonderful, beloved friend. To do as she advised was my only opportunity to show my gratitude for all she has done for me over the years.'

'Ah, how frequently we do the unacceptable for the sake of someone we love,' said Rod with feeling. 'Tell me about the dweller in the Cotswolds, who shoots rabbits and pheasants.'

The girl's smile quenched her fire. '*She* didn't. It was Robert who took out the guns.'

'Who is Robert?'

'Lord Frampton's gamekeeper. He was wounded in Ypres so couldn't be called up this time. Ellie and he are special friends, so a rabbit or pheasant would sometimes appear on the back doorstep after a clear, moonlit night.' Her smile softened. 'Ellie's everyone's special friend.'

Rod's vision of a dear old lady in a rocking chair, who dispensed advice, recipes and old-fashioned cures, was rapidly shattered by her next words.

'My mother died two months after my grandfather. Poor Ellie was heartbroken, but I turned up on her doorstep as unexpectedly as one of the pheasants so she set about doing something to keep herself from grieving. A woman in the village used to write stories for her grandchildren, and Ellie suggested that if she did illustrations for them they could be offered to a publisher.' Lost in a world she had left with great reluctance, Sarah became immensely animated. 'It was just as they portray such things in novels and films, although it rarely happens in real life. Afraid that her work would be considered too similar to that of Beatrix Potter, Ellie took the first three stories to London, believing she would return with them. She was dumbfounded when they were accepted, but she's so gifted an artist she shouldn't have been. Robert became a friend through her work. He would take her to spots known only to him where she could sit and sketch foxes, badgers or hares at play. Later, of course, she extended her scope and spent many hours studying animals in zoos all over the country.' Her eyes shone with fervour as she added, 'You'll have realized by now that Ellie is, in fact, Eleanor Fairlie.'

Rod nodded obligingly. He had never heard the name. Nor had he any knowledge of a woman called Beatrix Potter, whose work was similar to that of this girl's unusual granny. However, he was learning more about Sarah Channing and was additionally intrigued. 'You weren't tempted to follow in her footsteps?'

'Gracious, no! I'm even hopeless at drawing matchstick men.'

'Your artistic talent has surely come from your granny's branch of your family.'

'I suppose so. The Channings are all steeped in banking.'

'All?'

'There are dozens of them dotted all over the world. All incredibly formal and dreary, I'm afraid.' She chuckled. 'Ellie once did a sketch of a family get-together and gave them all the heads of borzois. You know what long, long muzzles they have and how terribly pompous they can look? We have two. *They're* absolute darlings, but we could see the resemblance between them and the Channings.' Sobering again, she added, 'I miss Sasha and Vlad so much.'

'You miss it all, I'd guess,' he said quietly.

She looked down at the plate once more. 'That's where I belong.'

'So why did your grandmother send you out here?'

The question seemed to prompt confusion, and when the reply came, Rod was certain it was only half an answer. 'If I had stayed in England I would have been called up into the forces, or drafted into factory work. Ellie agreed with Father

28

that it would be better for me to join him, at last, so that we can get to know each other.' Her brow furrowed and she appeared to be looking beyond him, as she added, 'It's only until the war is over. Then I'll go back.' Her eyes focused on Rod again, and she seemed close to tears. 'Poor old England!'

He took the plate from her unresisting hands. 'The old country has survived centuries of triumphs and reverses. She'll be right at the end of all this. But you, young woman, have had more than enough for one day. Come on, it's time you impressed upon your father that you need to leave this carnival and get to bed.' His hand beneath her elbow coaxed her to her feet. When she was facing him, he smiled. 'You might be a damned awful typist, but you are a sensational artist, Miss Channing. I'm no good at expressing sentiments, but the pleasure you have given me tonight more than justifies the redoubtable Ellie's wisdom in sending you to safety in Hong Kong. Give us time. We might grow on you.'

'You're not included in my disparagement,' she said with sincerity. 'You are doing something very worthwhile here . . . and you're the first really genuine person I've come across since my arrival. I know I'm a damned awful typist, but you'll discover that I'll soon be a damned good one. I'd hate to upset you again. It's a very daunting experience.' Sudden diffidence was evident as she added, 'I much prefer you as you are tonight.'

She walked away, a slender figure in an old-fashioned evening dress, carrying a pair of blue shoes in her left hand. At the door she turned back with composure regained. 'Thank you for rescuing me before I collapsed at Father's feet, embarrassing everyone in sight. I'm immensely grateful. How dreary for you to have missed the fun because you're a doctor.'

'On the contrary,' Rod heard himself say,' the fun only began when you almost passed out.'

He left the building by a side door, drove his car straight and true to a nearby hotel, and booked a room for the night. He slept soundly until nine a.m. without the aid of a sedative.

Chapter Two

Echoes was a house epitomizing early colonial grandeur. Built on three floors with white columns and wide, balustraded verandas, it occupied a place along the favoured mid-levels of Victoria Peak. Higher up, frequent mists invaded homes; lower down the noise and squalor of Victoria itself intruded. Along the mid-levels the air was reasonably pure, scented by the freshness of damp undergrowth and warm breezes from the ocean. The altitude allowed residents breathtaking views of lush emerald slopes reaching to deep sapphire waters. When flame-of-the-forest trees came into full bloom to provide blazing red swathes among the vegetation, new arrivals could be excused for thinking Hong Kong a jewel colony. They quickly discovered the gem had many flaws.

Channings had occupied Echoes for the past sixty years, filling it with furniture and carpets brought from Europe in the great merchant vessels of companies they represented. In the way of foreign settlers, they surrounded themselves with the trappings of their own culture, shipping out porcelain, glass, cutlery, linen, paintings and all the usual adjuncts to gracious living beloved by Europeans. The only concessions to their true surroundings were ceiling fans, mosquito nets, and blinds to keep the sun from ruining the colours of rugs and fabrics.

The English anywhere abroad try to cultivate gardens from even the most barren of soils. In Hong Kong it was possible to have flowering shrubs, lawns of clipped coarse grass and dramatic trees to provide shade. Echoes had all these in addition to a circular driveway at the front entrance, where water shimmered in a pool lined with Italian mosaic. Fish had been installed there by various owners. Each time, they had been eaten by unseen predators and never replaced. Sir Peter Channing had given up the struggle on losing a number of valuable carp soon after his arrival in 1919.

The present president of the Far-Eastern branch of the family bank had served with a Guards regiment during 1914–18, earning several commendations for outstanding leadership. His friends attributed his courage to a disinterest in life after the death of his young wife within six months of his impetuous marriage. Although a mature thirty-year-old, Captain Peter Channing had been unable to accept his loss at a time when *husbands* were dying by the thousands to be mourned by their widows. During the last months of the war, however, he met the daughter of a country parson, who drove a London taxi with skill, enthusiasm and a great deal of merriment, and embarked on a second impetuous marriage.

Frances Channing had been the ideal wife for a man with business ambitions. Fair, full of *joie de vivre*, and amiable enough to earn general popularity, she was defeated by Hong Kong's climate. The difficult birth of a stillborn son lowered her resistance so much she could not survive a severe attack of malaria. Her daughter Sarah was sent to England but, due to family pressure to produce a male heir, the twice-widowed knight selected a third wife. Alannah Channing was herself widowed, and an American. She was also barren. Six months after the medical verdict, divorce ended a union neither cared to continue. Sir Peter's intimates accepted that there would be no more wives for a man now wedded to banking. In consequence, they were surprised when the daughter of whom he rarely spoke was brought to live at Echoes with him, a man who appeared to have buried finer feelings along with Frances and her stillborn child. How would the girl settle in a house on the mid-levels with a relative stranger?

Sarah could have given the answer if she had been asked. The first few weeks had been terrible. Aching with homesickness, Sarah had been met on the Swedish merchant ship

31

that had brought her from Durban to Hong Kong by a father who had shaken hands by way of greeting, saying in polite tones that he trusted she had had a comfortable voyage. The shock of seeing a dark-haired woman of around forty-five, in a stylish silk dress and matching hat, climbing the gangplank with Sir Peter's hand beneath her elbow had been considerable. There had been no mention of a close female companion, but infrequent letters to Sarah had contained little about her father's personal life. Olivia Lord had offered the warmth and friendliness lacking in his greeting, but her presence had only compounded the trauma of arrival at an alien place where Sarah had no wish to be.

They had all been driven to an enormous mansion on a hill topped by mist, to eat lunch at a long table that could seat twenty-four. Pleading an important business meeting, Sir Peter had then departed leaving his daughter in the hands of an enigmatic stranger. Resistant to circumstances that had been forced upon her, Sarah found the woman, who appeared on close terms with Sir Peter, so completely the opposite of the beloved grandmother in England that she could not accept Olivia's hope of becoming friend and confidante.

After two months she still found it impossible. Wealthy, poised, always dressed in expensive flamboyant style, and in a position to introduce a banking president's daughter to Hong Kong society, the accountant's widow aroused no rapport in a girl whose life was pledged to music. Sarah was still unsure of Olivia's relationship with Sir Peter. She claimed to be no more than a kind of social secretary; arranging all lunch or dinner parties for him, and acting as his hostess at Echoes. Sarah understood that he was at a grave disadvantage without a wife, yet Olivia treated Echoes as a second home. Servants obeyed her without question; she came and went as she pleased. She had asked if Sarah wished to take over the household's organization, but the continuing numbness caused by severance from all she loved had made her decline. So Olivia remained virtual mistress of Echoes whilst living in an apartment at the top of a prestigious block several miles away.

Efficient and devoted Olivia most certainly was, and these

virtues constituted grounds for the continuing distance between Sarah and a woman too eager to take over the life of a second Channing. It was not only a sense of personal unease, but also a divergence of personalities that made Sarah resistant to Olivia's urge to create someone in her own image. On discovering, to her horror, that the trunks brought halfway across the world contained little more than piles of sheet music and carefully protected gramophone records of the classics, Olivia had swept her unwilling protégée, with Sir Peter's assent, to a series of dressmakers, exclusive stores and beauty parlours. Two months later, and eight weeks wiser, Olivia had accepted that she was fighting a losing battle. Sarah retained her straight, shoulder-length bobbed hairstyle and would wear only simple dresses in pastel shades, with the minimum of jewellery.

There were other problems. Determined to introduce Sarah to the younger set frequenting the clubs that provided the limited European-style entertainment on that small island off the coast of China, the older woman discovered that, despite having attended one of Britain's most prestigious girls' schools, Sir Peter's daughter was unresponsive in company. She preferred to spend her days in musical practice, or in solitary contemplation of recordings she had brought with her, and she made clear her aversion to those who flirted and frolicked through indolent days. Olivia had not arranged further visits to clubs or tea-dances, and Sarah hoped the matter was settled. It was not as if her father cared whether or not she roistered around with the pampered playboys and girls on Hong Kong. So long as she did nothing to ruffle his smooth waters he was unconcerned how she passed her days.

On the first floor of Echoes was a large salon decorated in ivory and *eau-de-Nil*, where a Steinway had been neglected to the extent of being played only by visitors for the amusement of dinner guests. After skilful tuning, Sarah had used the instrument with dedication and delight, swamping her unhappiness with floods of glorious sound for long periods. Six days after the concert, she again tackled the Rachmaninov concerto. The usual emotions beset her as the composer's genius almost reduced her to tears. After two attempts at the difficult second movement she shook her head, deciding to take a rest before continuing. Her back was aching, her hands were much too damp, and her head felt heavy.

Walking to a small table where a jug of iced barley-water stood, Sarah poured some into a glass and took it out to the veranda. The day was humid and overcast; the air very still. She crossed to the balustrade from where she could look down into a stony gorge at the bottom of a sheer drop beyond the limits of the garden. Her father said her music would be drowned by the thunder of water racing through it during the rainy season, or after a typhoon. It was now dry and boulder-strewn, silent save for the call of birds echoing through the great scar. The house had been named because of the sounds in that gorge throughout the year. Sarah had yet to know it in its tempestuous mood. Would it be more awesome than now?

She gazed down the fern-covered sides to the bottom, which was only visible when she stood on her toes to hang over the stonework. The desolate depths held terrible fascination for her. The brooding emptiness, the harsh, alien cries of unseen birds seemed to speak of her own present feelings. Her father was stiff and formal, unable to bridge that absence of fifteen years. She was the same. Olivia was an inexplicable thorn in her side, and she felt unable to accept that people could swim, dance, play cricket and lose their shirts on a race while Europe was in flames. Anger burned within her whenever she came into contact with them, and it was impossible to stay silent. They did not even understand why. Worst of all, there was no one to guide her musically. Practice was essential – there was no problem there – but she would make no progress without advice on technique, timing and interpretation.

Turning her back on the silent, sullen landscape Sarah gazed instead at the brooding magnificence of Echoes and longed for a Cotswold cottage whipped by blustery winter showers, where smoke bellowed from the hearth on wintery nights and carpets rose with the force of draughts beneath doors. There were dogs sleeping before the log fire, and squirrels waited on windowsills for nuts to be hung from the fir tree. All the treasures of childhood lay in a room with pansy-patterned wallpaper ... and there was dear, wonderful Ellie. Within Noon Cottage there was love and sincerity. Sarah had yet to find it in Hong Kong.

Tears again threatened as she recalled Ellie's response to her father's letter. *You must go, my dear. You are a Channing and should take your place in the family. It's time you discovered there are people in this world.* Sarah had not understood that last sentence. She had departed from a small south coast town in November drizzle in a flying-boat heading for South Africa, still not understanding. Now she did.

Channing money had sent her to a renowned school, and Ellie had taught her a set of values that made her self-reliant, capable and true to her beliefs. Passionate dedication to music had occupied time used by fellow pupils to forge friendships, have fun and indulge in adolescent flirtations. The emotions of puberty had, in Sarah, found expression in powerful, stormy études, uninhibited cascades of notes to thrill her senses, or dreamy heartbreaking melodies that touched unawakened responses to an unidentified pain. Although she felt relaxed with Ellie's friends in the village, there had been but one beloved companion of youth for Sarah. Through music she spoke to those around her. Face to face with them, words and warmth were suspended.

After the concert she had been physically and emotionally exhausted, unable to receive compliments graciously whilst regretting her attempt to confound those for whom she had scant respect. The plan had rebounded. No true artist would have performed a technically difficult work, full of fire and poignancy, accompanied by a recorded orchestra. She had advertised herself as a musical braggart, besides betraying emotions that should never have been put on public display. The flattery heaped upon her could only have been for the daughter of Channing Mercantile.

On the point of realizing she might exacerbate her misery by fainting, Sarah's eyes had met those of a man who already believed her to be more than feeble. It had seemed the last straw when he took her arm and marched her away to seclusion, administering rough treatment to stave off faintness. Returning with food and brandy, he had then revealed a bedside manner that was still forceful but surprisingly charming. It had encouraged her to confide in him things she had suppressed since arriving in Hong Kong, and her whole concept of the man had changed dramatically. Here was someone who understood her sentiments, who listened to her account of life in wartorn England with sympathy and who genuinely appreciated music. It had been difficult to believe he was the same man who had earlier slayed her with words then stormed out leaving her stunned by his ferocity.

Leaning back against the stonework as she sipped her drink, Sarah smiled in reminiscence. How foolish of him to hold up his hands and say: The beast is now chained. She had not been apprehensive of *him*, merely of passing out at his feet to earn further disparagement. How foolish of *herself* to have so misjudged him. His fury at the Halburton, although more aggressive than any other she had suffered, had been justified. A detailed medical report containing a number of Latin words was not a beginner's work.

The Englishwomen who had avoided compulsory evacuation had all justified their exemption by claiming they were indispensable. Some had become involved in charity work, others in first-aid classes. Neither were taken too seriously. Sarah had bought a typewriter and taught herself to use it after offering her services to the Halburton Clinic on one afternoon a week. Clearly, she needed to improve if the work was as involved as the report for Dr Durman. She intended to fulfil her vow to him to become a damned good typist.

That one afternoon at the Halburton did not satisfy Sarah's need to compensate for what she should have been doing at home, either in the services or in a munitions factory. Ellie maintained that one gifted pianist for the future was a better offer for her country than two more hands packing shells into boxes, but the future was a long way off and England was desperately concerned with the present.

Denied the opportunity to do what her conscience told her she should, Sarah had decided to use the gift she possessed in some beneficial way. A charitable group founded by several Europeans and Chinese with interest in the arts had welcomed her offer to give basic tuition to promising children whose families were unable to afford piano lessons. Sarah now had five pupils to coach during Tuesday mornings and Thursday afternoons. This delightful work salved her conscience, in part. When she was more proficient at typing she would spend a second day at the Halburton Clinic. Her colleague Marion was a cheerful girl married to a young naval officer. She was the nearest to a friend Sarah had, but they met only in the little typing room. There, they were on common ground.

Finishing the barley-water, Sarah returned to the keyboard telling herself she spent too much time in introspection and not enough creating Ellie's 'better offer' for her country. An hour passed in trying to perfect a Chopin waltz, but she was still dissatisfied when her concentration was broken by Olivia's voice from across the room.

'My dear girl, you must have played that a dozen times. Do you never tire of hearing the same thing over and over again?'

Sarah turned reluctantly, knowing she would not be allowed to continue until after lunch. 'It wasn't the same thing over and over again, Olivia. Each version was slightly different.' She stood up and flexed her shoulders. 'I haven't got it right yet.'

Olivia smiled through the tall roses she was arranging in a black and pink porcelain vase. 'I'm learning so much from you. I thought a composer wrote musical notes and expressions, which told a performer how to play the piece as he meant it to be played. I believed it was a simple business of following instructions, so to speak.'

'So it is, if one wishes merely to do as one is told, but every composer wills the artist to understand heart and soul of those black marks on sheets of white paper. The truly great interpreter not only understands, but *feels* the heart and soul of any work. I'm still trying where that extravagant waltz is concerned.'

Sarah crossed to where the roses gave a dual splash of colour, in reality and in reflection in the polished table. 'You're an artist with flowers. They always look so spectacular.'

'Well, thank you, Sarah. Peter never notices my arrangements.'

'He'd notice if they were missing,' she said quietly.

Olivia concentrated on placing the last rose. 'You're beginning to know your father. I'm glad.'

'Oh, I don't think that small fact constitutes *knowing* him.' She perched on the arm of a chair. 'Can anyone claim to do that . . . apart from you?' Olivia gave a faint smile, but said nothing as she studied the arrangement from several feet away. Sarah pursued the subject. 'Your husband must have been an exceptional person to grow close enough to become Father's friend. You've said often enough that he treats everyone as a business acquaintance.'

'Derek had much in common with Peter.'

Olivia had said that often enough too. It was all she was now prepared to say on the subject, because she deftly began a discussion on the dinner party she was arranging for the next evening. Sarah let the details float over her head as she took in every detail of the other's oyster-coloured shantung costume and elegant rose-patterned blouse. Had she such flair that her wardrobe contained clothes to suit every flower arrangement? The two-tone shoes and matching handbag undeniably came from a store famed for its leather goods, and Olivia's passion for jade was reflected in a superb flamingo pendant and in a heavy ring on her scarlet-tipped right hand. Not for the first time Sarah reflected that her father must pay his social secretary an enviable wage.

The apartment Olivia occupied had been acquired after the death of Derek Lord, a man reputedly from humble origins. It was impressively furnished and housed a valuable collection of jade pieces to which she was continually adding by crossing to Macau for shopping trips. It was an expensive hobby for a working woman. Olivia always laughed off such a description, claiming that what she did for Sir Peter was to help a dear friend and to occupy her own time usefully. Sarah might have found it easier to accept Olivia if her father married the woman. As it was, the situation was awkward and unsettling for her.

'I know tomorrow is your day at the Halburton Clinic,' Olivia was saying, 'but do ensure that the tyrant who kept you so late last week understands that you are working there as a volunteer. He has no right to treat you as if you are a paid secretary.'

Sarah found herself smiling again at her recollection of 'the tyrant' claiming that the beast was chained. 'It was my own decision to stay and finish his report. As you say, I'm a volunteer, and it was important to him.'

Olivia's dark eyes studied Sarah with impatience. 'Please volunteer your presence at Echoes tomorrow in plenty of time to dress for an evening that is important to Peter.'

'Why, who is coming?'

Visibly annoyed, Olivia tried to keep the bite out of her voice. 'I told you only five minutes ago.'

'Sorry, I was still thinking about the Chopin, I suppose.' She rose from the arm of the chair and circled the table to reach Olivia. 'I'm certain there'll be no reason for me to remain at the Halburton later than four-thirty.' Trying very hard not to compare this immaculate, efficient, enigmatic person with another who dressed in tweeds that were invariably covered in borzoi hairs, and who embraced the whole world with her smile, Sarah forced herself to add, 'I'll bear in mind that it's important to Father.'

As she walked off to seek solitude in her room before preparing for lunch, Olivia called after her. 'He was very proud of you during last week's concert.'

Sarah looked back, slowing her pace. 'Was he? He's never been keen on the career I've chosen. He once told Ellie that a Channing shouldn't do for payment what most women of our class do to entertain their dinner guests.'

For a moment Olivia seemed at a loss, then she said, 'He sent for you so that you could get to know each other. Why won't you at least try to meet him halfway?'

'It took him fifteen years to issue the invitation,' Sarah said from the doorway. 'Don't expect miracles from me, Olivia.'

Justification for Sarah's attitude must surely have been obvious during the light meal, even to a woman who knew and understood Sir Peter. Encountering his daughter for the first time that day, he nodded a greeting as he took his place at the table and merely asked if she was well before turning to Olivia to speak of a business lunch he would like arranged for the following Tuesday.

'Can't have it here, or at the club. Sir Dougal Craig insists on his comprador being present, and Masterson will be accompanied by several Chinese contractors who will enable him to estimate the size of the loan he wants from us. Saves time to sit around a table with all interested parties. I'll leave the venue to you. Nothing too grand, but well enough to suit the bank's reputation.'

Olivia smiled as she broke bread for her soup. 'No ostentation, just quiet, expensive good taste. From all I've heard of Sir Dougal, his attention to shrewd dealing far outweighs his attention to what is put on the table before him. He has a reputation for shovelling food down his throat while his beady eyes and great flapping ears miss not even the slightest nuance of tone or expression.'

'You liken him to an elephant, Olivia,' Sir Peter said drily. 'Just as they can put down their huge feet with great delicacy, so Craig can drop quietly into the discussion an ultimatum of heavy significance just when everything is about to be settled.'

'But you hold the purse-strings,' she pointed out.

'Mmm, but there are other considerations here. This particular elephant is the rogue in an important herd. Can't afford to anger him. If he ran amok it could cause the bank a deal of damage.'

Olivia's eyebrows rose significantly. 'Not that old problem stirring after all this time?'

Sir Peter drank the last of his consommé and laid down the heavy engraved spoon. 'Not as yet, but rising dust could conceivably uncover it.'

'Then I suggest you invite wives and have dinner rather than lunch. Women always soften the atmosphere, and Lady Craig is notorious for holding the limelight, which will make Sir Dougal less of a rogue. He might not be dominated by the effusive Eunice but he's certainly matched by her. In addition, his comprador's wife is one of the most striking Chinese women I've ever seen. Her manners are exquisite and he's certain to respond to her Oriental charm.' She dabbed her scarlet mouth with a napkin. 'I really think that's the best plan, Peter.'

'What an astute woman you are! I'll leave it in your hands.' After nodding his readiness for the next course to the white-coated boy standing patiently by the serving table, Sir Peter added, 'Take Sarah along. Show her how it's done. Time she became involved in such things.'

'I think she has no wish to become involved in them,' said Olivia, as if Sarah were not present. 'All my invitations to do so have been declined.'

'Why is that?'

'I really couldn't say.'

'Perhaps *I* can,' put in Sarah, causing them both to turn her way. 'Olivia is very efficient in that area. She also so obviously enjoys doing it there seems little point in my assistance. I rarely have the time, in any case.'

Her father's pale eyes behind the spectacles were devoid of recognizable expression as he studied her while they were all served with salmon puffs, green peas and asparagus by the soft-footed boy. 'What keeps you so busy?'

'Some charity work, and a great deal of practice. It's essential even though I have no tutor out here to advance my studies.'

'You would have been unable even to practise if you had remained in England to be recruited for war work.'

The comment was snapped out with some anger. Sarah responded swiftly. 'I know that, Father. I wasn't complaining, just stating a fact.'

He sighed, cut into his salmon puff, then glanced back at her. 'Do you intend to do nothing more than shut yourself away with the Steinway, day after day?'

'That's the pattern of a musician's life.' At his frown, she added, 'Just as arranging your social events is the pattern of Olivia's.'

Olivia bit into asparagus with relish before saying, 'You must remember, Peter, that your daughter has spent her life in a remote village with the sole company of an elderly woman engaged in drawing furry animals for children. Don't expect too much of her.'

'On the contrary, Olivia, I think Father is expecting too

little of me if he rates arranging a dinner party above perfecting the performance of a difficult piano concerto.' Into the silence following her cool defence came a mental reminder of a doctor who had charmed her into confiding in him. A smile broke through as she used his words. 'I might have lived in a remote village all my life, but I'm house-trained and have civilized habits.'

Olivia's mouth tightened in irritation, but Sir Peter finished his meal as if the conversation had not taken place, then accepted coffee from his servant and began a discussion concerning his plans to promote a Chinese clerk to a position normally held by a European member of staff.

'Integration has to come, Olivia. Can't stop it. So many of them are gaining university degrees or other professional qualifications these days. Good thing, on the whole. I'm glad to see it. Just so long as we keep hold of the reins. It's our colony, after all.'

Sarah drank her coffee in silence, lost in thoughts of what the forthright Dr Durman would make of these two people. She wished he were there. Something told her he would make short work of Olivia, if not of the controlled Sir Peter Channing.

Unlike the previous Friday, it was pleasantly cool with sunshine and a gentle breeze. Time passed swiftly as Sarah tapped the typewriter keys, taking extra care when copying Latin terms. She was disappointed that there was no work from Dr Durman. She had hoped to impress him with her skill after devoting time to practice on this other keyboard during the week, so it was with curious reluctance that she finished a long official letter at four-fifteen and faced an empty tray.

'Goody, that's the last blinking page,' exclaimed the red-haired girl from the other desk as she gathered up a sheaf of papers and fastened them with a paper-clip. 'I reckon I deserve a medal for coming in today when Bill's ship's due back at any moment. It'll be a rush getting a hairdo and manicure in before it's time to go to the jetty.' She lowered the report to her desk in dreamlike fashion and her eyes shone with excitement. 'Six whole days without him. Six lonely nights. I can't believe he'll be kissing me in two hours' time. I've forgotten what he looks like, forgotten the sound of his voice. It'll be like falling in love all over again. Oh Sarah, he's so *wonderful*.'

These wild, romantic comments meant little to Sarah. She did not understand how six days could be an eternity to people madly in love and had withstood entire afternoons devoted to euphoric descriptions of William Bennett's good looks, his fascinating personality, and his ability to make his wife's toes curl up with delight whenever he kissed her. Even so, Sarah liked Marion Bennett, possibly because the girl talked incessantly and required few return comments.

As she watched her companion apply lipstick and powder her nose, she caught herself wondering if Bill Bennett was fortunate to be so openly adored, or if he found his wife's eagerness embarrassing. How would she, herself, behave if she ever loved a man? Love for Ellie was deep, and Sarah expressed it without reservations. She wrote letters filled with affection for the grandmother she still missed most acutely, but she had no idea whether or not she would gush and giggle, like Marion, if she ever found romantic love.

Marion glanced at the clock and uttered an impatient cry. 'Sarah, I've finished my work. Be a *dear* and do the necessary until four-thirty so that I can slip away to the hairdresser. I've just *got* to look beautiful for him when he walks off his ship.'

'You already look beautiful,' Sarah said smiling. 'If you get any more so your husband will be so bowled over he'll fall into the harbour. You don't want that, do you?'

'Thanks, you're a darling,' Marion declared, taking for granted Sarah's agreement to tidy up. 'I'll do the same for you when you can't wait to meet your lover.'

The mood remained as Sarah cleared the two desks, covered the typewriters, then collected the pages in both in-trays to take along to the main office. It was empty, so she left the work and returned for her things before leaving. Yet she lingered in that office containing the essence of Marion's urgency for reunion with someone who governed her every thought and action, reluctant to leave for Echoes and a dinner party with people who aroused no response in her.

Sudden longing for Ellie swept through her. Longing for her real home with all its beloved comforts. Longing for Sasha and Vlad, the borzois who made no secret of their love for her when she threw her arms around them and told them they were Russian princes turned into dogs by a sorceress. She had lost all that and gained no compensation.

When she eventually walked outside to sunshine and a caressing breeze, Sarah stopped on the path to gaze at the sun-sparkled bay beyond the clinic. The sands were invaded each weekend by parties of Europeans, who hired the mat-sheds as changing rooms and frolicked in the sea. They brought picnic hampers and gramophones and beach quoits, and stayed all day. The beach was now empty save for a coolie bowed beneath the weight of two laden buckets dangling from a pole across his shoulders. The sea was innocent of swimmers; the only other signs of life were aboard a cluster of distant fishing-boats. The hutted village of Stanley huddled below scrub-covered slopes, at the top of which were some impressive summer houses owned by wealthy merchants. As these were set among trees, they did not intrude upon a scene Sarah found more attractive when beach parties were absent and the ethnic charm was apparent.

As she watched the coolie plodding barefoot over the sand with his burden, an unbidden sense of rapport touched her with chilly fingers. A lone person on a featureless expanse of sand. What were his thoughts and feelings? Did anyone care?

'Too quaint for you?' enquired a deep Australian voice.

She spun around to find him a few feet away. In crisp white shirt, striped tie and fawn trousers, with his jacket over his arm, his physical strength was suddenly very apparent. Reminded of his aggression last week she wondered about his present mood, but he seemed docile enough as he studied her. She was immensely glad to see him and smiled a greeting. 'I told you it was not the place but the people I found hard to accept.'

'So you did . . . and I told you not to be too harsh in your judgement. They're probably all as homesick as you are.'

'No, they're having a good time.'

'On the surface, perhaps, but underneath their gaiety the story could be vastly different.'

She pushed back strands of hair blown over her face by the breeze that came in from the sea. 'You appear to know a lot about people's hidden feelings. Are you a psychoanalyst?'

'Nothing half so clever, just an ordinary bloke who comes into contact with his fellows when their barriers are down.'

'As mine were on the night of the concert.'

'Were they?'

He had neatly turned the table inviting her confidence, yet sudden reticence led her to turn away along the path, asking over her shoulder, 'Are *you* homesick, Dr Durman?'

'Not exactly.' He fell in step beside her. 'Australia will always be a special place – I had some good times there – but I don't believe in looking back when I'm moving forward. I might miss a stage of my life that'll be even better than the last.'

'*More* psychology . . . delivered in your bedside manner?'

He studied her shrewdly for several moments. 'I thought you said I was excluded from your disparagement of the human race, Miss Channing.'

'I did – and you are. I didn't say I disparaged the whole human race, just this particular cross-section of it,' she protested, coming to a halt. Then she smiled again. 'I'm sorry if I was rather sour just now, but your words sounded like a reprimand for my wanting to be in England.'

'Did they? Now you know why I'm not a psychoanalyst. I say all the wrong things.' He shook his head. 'I was speaking purely for myself when I said I didn't look back . . . but you know that saying about wearing the cap if it fits, don't you?'

'Also the one that proclaims home is where the heart is,' she countered lightly.

'Now, look here, if you're going to argue with me in proverbs, I'm surrendering now. You're certain to know more of them than I do, and I'm a bad loser.'

'Is that when the beast is unchained?'

His expression darkened. 'That won't happen again. I'd had a hell of a day, and . . . well, I'd had a hell of a day. Let's leave it at that.'

45

'I know exactly what you mean,' she offered, sorry that her teasing remark had upset him. 'I have days when my fingers seem twice as fat and half their length. Passages I normally manage with ease become completely unplayable. Instead of giving up, I persevere and make things even worse because I'm then too angry to concentrate. In the end, I fling music across the room and slam the lid over the keyboard. Then I burst into tears.'

'Good Lord! Last week I had you cast as a cool blonde well in control of herself. How wrong first impressions can be. You're quite as dangerous as that Durman bloke.'

She laughed, and he put a hand beneath her elbow to lead her across the car park. 'You know, it's never easy to start afresh. New country, different circumstances, everybody a stranger. Hong Kong has a lot to offer if you know where to look. It would be a pity to miss it because your eyes are turned constantly towards England. Every experience – even a bad one – is an education.'

He halted beside a dark-blue car, unlocked the door and put his medical bag and jacket on the back seat. As she watched him, Sarah caught herself saying, 'I don't think you're an "ordinary bloke", at all. You give the same brand of advice as Ellie, and she's quite exceptional.'

He glanced across at her. 'You followed hers. Do the same with mine.'

Loath to let him drive away leaving her to face a boring evening, she continued the conversation. 'I'll try, but it would be easier if you wore tweed skirts and had grey curls all over your ears.'

'And drew pictures of baby kangaroos?' He laughed. 'Sorry, you'll have to take me just as I am.'

Out of the blue, his casual, joking comment touched her in a startling way. In place of the mature, friendly doctor she suddenly saw a man of great physical impact, with thick dark hair and amber eyes alive with amusement in a tanned face that betrayed his moods without deceit. His medical guise had cloaked someone of disturbing attraction, she now realized, and the revelation kept her silently gazing until his smile faded into a questioning look.

'I shouldn't detain you,' she murmured, still recovering

from the impact of a moment before. 'You must have urgent things to do.'

Leaning on the open door, he shook his head. 'Nothing that won't wait. Now the cholera scare is over, I'm going to see a friend who lives on a hill more often than not wreathed in mist. It's clear today, so the view will be magnificent.' After a brief scrutiny of her face, he asked, 'Care to come? It'll give you proof of what Hong Kong has to offer.'

Longing to accept, yet mindful of her father's dinner party, she played for time. 'How would your friend react to an uninvited guest?'

'Come and find out.'

His smiling challenge was irresistible. 'I'll just tell Ming he won't be needed.'

Elated as she had not been for many months, Sarah ran to where the Chinese chauffeur waited beside a large black car. Ming never questioned anything. His life was ordered by phrases like 'Pick me up at three', or 'Drop me at the council building and come back in two hours', so he found it easy to drive off leaving his employer's daughter in a remote area of the Island without learning her subsequent plans.

Sarah settled in the passenger seat of the blue car with no sense of guilt, conscious only of the man beside her. Their first encounter had shown him to be a person capable of hot passion; their second had revealed his understanding and gentleness. Today, he was different again – intriguingly different. As he took the car in a tight sweep to gain the road leading around the coast, Sarah found pleasure in watching his large brown hands moving on the wheel. The solitary coolie on the beach plodded on, forgotten. Breeze through the open windows lifted her hair and caressed her throat, adding to her sense of release. Her sigh of pleasure caused her companion to glance her way.

'Regretting your impulse?'

She shook her head. 'I'm going to enjoy every minute of my outing.'

'Ah ... you don't yet know what you'll have to do to reach my friend's house.'

'Tell me!'

'And spoil my fun?' He pointed to a rock formation standing a little way offshore. 'Do you know why that's called Slaughter Rock? No? In the colony's early days, merchant ships were frequently stopped and boarded by pirates demanding money in exchange for a free passage to the harbour. If this was refused, a hostage was taken and held to even higher ransom. Legend has it that failure to pay for his release led to the poor devil being disembowelled alive on those rocks, and left there as a warning to others with miserly tendencies.'

Sarah studied the spot as they passed. Yellow sand, clear cobalt sea breaking around pale grey stone. So beautiful and so peaceful, yet those sands had long ago been violated by the boots of men dragging a terrified victim, and that sea had been stained by blood running from a living corpse.

'Your father must know plenty of tales concerning pirates, as he's closely allied to many of the old merchant companies.'

She turned from the coastal scene. 'You might find grisly tales enthralling, Dr Durman. I don't.'

'Your Ellie's animal stories have made you too sentimental, Miss Channing.'

'My grandmother's talent would charm even *you*.'

Laughter lit his eyes as he glanced her way after completing an S-bend. 'I'm a hardened character, not easily charmed.'

'Ellie would manage it with ease. She wins over everyone she meets.'

With his attention back on the road, he said, 'You could probably do the same, if you stopped disapproving of those around you.'

Unable to deal with that, Sarah sought refuge in pursuing his previous comment. 'What turned you into a hardened character?'

'Life. When you reach my advanced years you'll be the same.'

Sarah smiled. He could not be more than thirty and looked fitter than many younger men. His present vigour had not been apparent at the concert, and she could not believe that it was only the new way she was seeing him today that brought it to the fore. Something else must have wrought the change in him. It intrigued her.

'Tell me about your youth in Australia ... if you can remember that far back,' she added drily.

He shook his head. 'The purpose of this outing is to teach you a little about Hong Kong, not about me, Miss Channing.'

'Just now, you told me a horrible tale concerning piracy and torture which has hardly endeared the place to me. As I've placed myself in your hands without knowing where you're taking me, don't you think I'm entitled to know a little about my guide? And my name is Sarah.'

He appeared to be considering her argument as he drove through the last inhabited area to an isolated stretch along the eastern coast. 'Fair enough. But if I'm to leave out the grisly parts, my youth will sound unbearably boring.'

'When I start to yawn you'll know it's time to talk about something else ... and do I have to continue calling you Dr Durman?'

'I thought the English were hot on observing protocol and only used first names after knowing each other for years.'

'What do the initials R.J. stand for?' she demanded.

He sighed. 'All right, you can have a potted autobiography, but you'll have to concentrate on the main lesson after that. Roderick James was born on a sheep station called Dalgara. Dad was delighted with a third son, but Ma wanted a girl for company. We had our early schooling over the wireless, like all children on isolated stations. As each of us reached eleven we went to boarding school in Melbourne, and everything changed. Jack and Cliff couldn't wait to get back to Dalgara, but it hadn't the same pull for me. We had all grown up with sheep, but I knew I wanted something else for the future. I used to mix in during the holidays, of course. We'd be out all day – often all night, too – and meet up back at the house. Ma's a real good cook. We'd eat a gargantuan meal, then sit outside yarning beneath the stars. Before turning in, my brothers and I would swim in the tank and horse about as boys do.' He frowned at his memories. 'They were good times, yet they didn't satisfy me any more as they did the other two. One day, Jack didn't

49

ride in on time. We found him out on the boundary caught in a dingo trap. The doctor took so long getting to us, Jack bled to death. I suppose that's when I decided what to do with my future.'

Sarah's imagination struggled to conjure up visions of all he described, but it proved impossible. It was too different from her girlhood in a Cotswold village. 'It must have been a blow to lose your brother. Mine died at birth, so I never knew him as such.' After a moment or two, she asked, 'Do I call you Roderick?'

'Not if you value your life.' Lightness was back in his voice. 'The short version is safe to use, but that's enough about the guide. You're on this trip to learn about Hong Kong.'

'No more tales of disembowelment,' she warned.

'Oh, they did other things like beheading, flogging and locking villains up in a cangue.' He glanced at her. 'Any idea what that is?'

'No, but it's certain to be horrible.'

'The victim has head and hands fastened into a kind of portable stock, and has to walk around like that until punishment ends.'

'I knew it would be unpleasant,' she declared. 'Can't you tell me something more cheerful?'

'There are a number of colourful festivals throughout the year, which are celebrated with great zest and dedication. They're mostly concerned with religion and the Chinese calendar, of course.'

As the car wound its way along a tortuous road that appeared to lead into the heart of a hill, he told Sarah about the Springtime festival of Ching Ming, when families visited the graves of ancestors to offer gifts of food and to polish their bones.

'If that's too grisly a notion for you, you'll surely enjoy the Dragon Boat Festival. Everyone turns out for that. Long, narrow vessels, with prows resembling dragons' heads and sterns fashioned like ridged tails, race against each other with much excitement and banging of drums. During the race, dumplings are scattered on the water.'

Sarah was fascinated. 'Dumplings? What's the reason for that?'

'The story goes that a one-time official at the Emperor's court became so ashamed of the cruelty and corruption around him that he vowed to put an end to it. Failure led him to put an end to himself instead. He jumped into the sea and his restless spirit lurks beneath the surface. The dumplings are to appease the spirit so that it may rest.' He cast her a questioning glance. 'Is that tale suitable for your delicate ears?'

'Perfectly,' she told him, trying not to smile. 'Do you know any more like that?'

'So many I haven't time to relate them all now. We're nearly there.'

The car began climbing a steep track that grew progressively more bumpy and stony. Sarah let Rod concentrate on negotiating the bends and prayed no one was presently on the way down. On each side stretched unbroken trees and scrub, making it impossible to see the view. It occurred to her then that she had jumped into this man's car in the most trusting fashion, without any notion of where he was taking her. Who was this friend of his?

Around the next sharp bend a space large enough to accommodate a car had been carved from the hillside. Rod drove into it, switched off the engine, then turned to her. 'My word, you look scared to death, girl. I warned you at the outset that this would be a test of stamina.'

'You didn't,' she protested. 'I was promised a wonderful view, rarely to be seen, and proof of all Hong Kong has to offer. So far, I've only been regaled with bloodthirsty tales during a hair-raising drive up a primitive track never meant for cars.'

The smile lit his eyes with a warmth that made nonsense of her attempted disapproval. 'Afraid that I'm really a white-slaver about to sell you to the highest bidder in this mountain lair?'

It was impossible to maintain her stand in the face of such teasing charm. 'If you are, the population will be coming here to deposit dumplings for *my* restless spirit every year.'

He got out, laughing, and walked round to help her from the passenger seat. 'I'll vindicate myself in less than ten minutes. The view really is magnificent ... when we've climbed up those.' He pointed to where a flight of stone steps rose through dense scrub that hid the upper section from view. Who would live in such an isolated spot? As she turned to him with the question on her lips, he took her arm and began walking. 'Come on, they won't be bringing dumplings, I promise. There are fifty-nine steps. If you can't manage them all in those shoes, I'll carry you up the last stretch.'

The air of mystery increased as Sarah climbed. She was acutely aware of the man behind her who, she was certain, really would carry her if she flagged. It was a long ascent, but she tackled it with determination to reach the top unaided. When the end came in sight, the undergrowth began to thin giving a hint of what was to come. Seven steps from the top a clearing revealed just how high they were, and Sarah took the rest of the flight eagerly. Breathless, legs aching, she stood gazing at verdant slopes to left and right, cut by the road they had travelled and edged by water silver-gilded as the sun died and the moon began its reign. The glittering straits snaked between a series of islands projecting like dark icebergs from a frosted sea and, beyond them, it was possible to see a distant purple mountain range rising to a pale mauve sky. 'Oh!' she breathed, spellbound.

'Those mountains are in China,' he said from very close behind her. 'It's only possible to see them on days like this. Glad you came?'

She nodded, still gazing at the scene. 'It's *magical*. The colours; that spectrum! I'm glad it's visible only occasionally. That makes it particularly special, and seeing it a true privilege.'

They stood in silent accord for a moment or two, then Rod murmured, 'You're an impossible romantic, Sarah.'

She spun round to face him. 'So are you! First the Rachmaninov, now a breathtaking silvered view of China. You react exactly as I do to things of beauty. This *is* magical, isn't it?'

Her voice faded into a listening silence as she gazed at him in instant recognition of something that had happened before she was prepared for it. There, on the peak of a dusk-washed foreign hill, she saw in his dark eyes a message that could not be mistaken, even by her inexperienced senses. It overwhelmed her; held her motionless; all the passion she expressed in music now centred on this awareness that took her by storm. It was echoed in his expression, in the way he stood oblivious of their surroundings while the moment went on and on. But he had greater command of himself than she, and broke the spell with an obvious effort.

'My friend is Chinese. I shall have to ask his permission to bring you in to his home. It's a formality I must observe.'

He turned to walk towards a house Sarah had been too enchanted to notice; a large, powerful man who looked out of place among the Oriental delicacy surrounding him. Pools and fountains, small arched bridges, willows, banyans and red-stemmed figs were enhanced by a profusion of flowering shrubs whose perfume hung in the clear, balmy air. Wind chimes produced tinkling music with strings of mother-of-pearl discs, and the splashing of fountains added to the entrancing harmony. The house beyond these gardens was set on two levels, roofed with blue tiles that flared at each corner and overhung a wide veranda running around the property. The walls were inset with large heavily-carved wooden panels that slid back to allow the breeze into the rooms.

Still beneath the influence of undeniable emotion Sarah saw it all through eyes attuned to enchantment. How had Rod become the friend of someone who lived in such isolation? Was the owner some kind of healer? She had heard of miraculous results Western medicine could not achieve – or explain. Rod was a different person today. Had he received here some kind of ethnic cure for whatever had ailed him on the day he had flung the report back at her?

Rod reappeared to beckon her, and Sarah picked her way along winding paths and over tiny bridges pursuing this supposition. Perhaps her host was some kind of Oriental magician who had cast a spell this afternoon. If so, it lingered despite Rod's almost abrupt comment that she had been extended a gracious welcome to take tea.

The interior was as unexpected as the outside of the house. Bare brickwork walls were hung with portraits of ancestors and with silk banners embroidered with Chinese characters. Ornate octagonal lanterns hung from silken ropes above heavy, carved blackwood furniture polished to a sheen resembling glass. The floor was paved with marble slabs, and marble shelves bore a collection of outsized porcelain jars. Tall blackwood cabinets were stuffed with books and parchments yellowed by age. In the silver light of dusk it could well be the home of a mystic, Sarah thought. But all such notions fled when Rod took her forward to meet an old man in a long gown of black shantung, who was sitting in one of the hard wooden chairs.

'May I present Miss Sarah Channing, who works with me at the Halburton Clinic?' he asked.

'You are welcome in my house, Miss Channing,' said her host in very good English. 'I apologize for the need to climb so many steps, but if I laid a road my peace would be disturbed.'

Rod told Sarah, 'Wang Chua is the venerable head of a prestigious trading family. He has ten sons, four daughters, thirty-six grandchildren, and one hundred and twenty-two great-grandchildren. His generosity has funded a number of projects, including a floating clinic that visits the offshore islands every weekend.'

'You have a house to suit every mood, sir,' Sarah told her host with sincerity. 'I perfectly understand your reluctance to provide easy access to it.'

After indicating that she should sit in one of two matching chairs joined together like a divided settee, Rod settled beside her on the hard polished seat. 'Miss Channing is a gifted pianist,' he explained. 'I knew she would appreciate the peace and beauty here.'

Wang Chua's broad, wrinkled face broke into a smile as he nodded the head covered in profuse grey hair topped by a black round hat. 'I know of her great gift with music, Dr Durman. I live high above the world, but little occurs below these heights that is not conveyed to me by my family. It gives me sorrow not to receive the boon of attending one of your performances, Miss Channing, but my ears have heard so many evil sounds they wish only to be bombarded by the gentle beckoning whisper of paradise.'

Tea was brought by a servant in a blue gown and soft felt

slippers. He poured it into minute handleless cups of wafer-thin porcelain, which he placed on matching plates to offer the guests. Sarah grew increasingly enchanted. The house was filled with mysterious music as breezes invaded it to set mother-of-pearl chimes in motion and the wooden shutters moved gently against each other. Octagonal lanterns swayed on their silken ropes, suggesting rather than producing a soothing whisper of sound to complement the symphony. In addition, she sensed echoes of unidentifiable voices, songs without words, swirling around the vaulted rooms. Perhaps it was mere fancy, perhaps the altitude. Perhaps Wang Chua really was a healer, and the tea contained a potion to produce sensations of serene well-being.

Time passed, and darkness produced further enchantment. Lanterns were lit by soft-footed servants so that the gardens took on an exotic, tantalizing beauty beneath moonlight. Wang Chua was a charming host, showing Sarah some of the treasures he had collected during his colourful life, and explaining to her the stories depicted by carvings on an immense wooden chest. 'The tales of an ancient heritage are put upon things we have in our houses, Miss Channing,' he told her with a smile. 'We pass furniture to our children, and they to theirs. It is one way of ensuring that legends are never forgotten. Books are such fragile things. Chairs and tables last a greater time.'

When Rod expressed appropriate regret at the necessity to leave, Wang Chua nodded understanding and began to lead the way through a series of rooms on the far side of the house. Sarah was by now beyond being surprised, and walked beside Rod in a mood of continuing serenity, happy to go wherever she was conducted. It was only gradually that she grew aware of a distinct change in Wang Chua, so the first part of his conversation with Rod had gone unheeded. What she then heard was incomprehensible to her, but evidently not to Rod for he looked deeply troubled.

'How long can you let this continue? They'll never give up. Next time it will be even worse.'

The broad face that had easily smiled now wore an implacable expression. 'They will stop when they see they have no power against the House of Wang.'

'They never stop,' Rod said harshly, halting by an arched doorway. 'An entire police department is helpless against them. They have *enormous* power, my friend. Your guards will be no match for them if they decide to make you their target, which they will if you insist on fighting them. This hill is no protection.'

'No!' the elderly Chinese said emphatically. 'They have taken enough – a son, two grandchildren, junks, warehouses, an entire fortune. I will not allow them to begin again.'

'You have no choice. This was their warning. Next time, it will be more than a ring that they send you. It'll be the finger it was on. I've seen their victims.'

With a lightning change of direction, Wang Chua asked, 'Have you been successful in your application for the post in Tropical Diseases?'

Rod seemed resigned to the other's tactic. 'The selection board doesn't meet until next month. So you even heard about that?'

'Of course. As I told Miss Channing, little occurs on this island that I do not hear about.' The smile returned as Wang Chua included Sarah in the conversation once more. 'Is Sir Peter in good health?'

'You know Father?' she asked in surprise.

'We have not met for many years. You resemble your mother. I thought so when Dr Durman brought you through the garden. Thank you for visiting me. Now I understand why the mist moved away today.' He gave a slight bow, then turned back to Rod. 'I am told you will be successful with the selection board. You are welcome here at any time, Doctor.' With another bow he turned to walk back through the connecting rooms, to vanish within the house of silent sounds.

Rod took hold of Sarah's arm, drawing her attention from the sudden departure of their host. 'They're waiting to take us back to my car.'

Following the direction of his nod, she saw servants with two sedan-chairs at the foot of a short flight of steps. Still bemused, Sarah allowed Rod to help her into one of the chairs so that she could be carried on the shoulders of two blue-clad servants down a rough path illuminated by moon-light. The undulating motion of the chair suspended from two long, pliant poles was hardly reassuring on a steeply sloping track between dense trees, so Sarah gripped the sides of the chair in anticipation of being tossed from the fragile seat. The men were sure-footed, however, and came to a halt beside Rod's car some minutes after setting off. They bowed politely before taking up her empty chair and melting into the forest as if they had never existed.

Left alone with someone whose magnetism enveloped her again in the soft, beguiling darkness, Sarah was out of her depth. They were silent until they were in the car and descending the track, headlamps revealing the steepness of the incline. 'I hope you have good brakes,' she said on a nervous laugh.

He grunted, and negotiated several tight bends before asking, 'Did you enjoy your visit?'

Sarah was bewildered. Where was the person who had brought her up the hill; the man who had awoken her with a long burning glance at its crest? He sounded politely matter-of-fact.

'I enjoyed it very much. Thank you for bringing me.' When silence fell again, she said desperately, 'You proved your point about what Hong Kong has to offer . . . and there was nothing grisly up in that house.'

'Don't you believe it. You probably made little sense of our conversation on parting, but it concerned the fact that one of Wang's nephew's children has been abducted and held to ransom. He refuses to pay it, and has been sent a ring given by him to the boy. They'll send the finger next, then a whole hand. That's the way they operate.'

'Who?' she asked, the magical elements of the evening fast evaporating.

'Triads. You must know about the gangs? They terrorize, practise extortion and organize every branch of crime in Hong Kong. Your father certainly will have been their victim at some time during his years here. Wang stood out against them twenty years ago, and they murdered three members of his family before he gave in. They took almost everything he owned. He began again and has built up a powerful trading company, so the Triads are out for more from him. The longer he refuses their initial demands the more they will maim, kill or rape his relatives. Or they'll set fire to his junks and warehouses, sink those vessels already at sea. The police can do nothing. Their men are afraid of becoming victims themselves, if they've not already been corrupted by threats to their own loved ones.' They were back on the coast road heading for the lights of Victoria. 'Wherever there are people who have immense wealth, there will be others determined to take it from them by vicious means. I've never had a desire for riches. Coming to Hong Kong has underlined that. I've treated the victims of criminal greed too often.' Into the silence that had fallen, he said quietly, 'Don't do with anyone else what you did today, even if you know the man well. As the daughter of Sir Peter Channing, you are eminently suitable to hold to ransom.'

She shivered in the warm evening breeze. 'Do you still maintain that Hong Kong has much to offer?'

'Of course. You extol the virtues of Britain even though right now there's too little to eat, not enough coal, dark, dangerous streets, and an enemy dropping bombs nightly. You should take the rough with the smooth here too, Sarah.'

She found the transition to reality unwelcome and disturbing. 'Oh, we're now back to psychoanalysis. This has merely been a medical experiment, has it?'

He shook his head, saying calmly, 'It was an impromptu offer to show you something other than the European scene you find unacceptable. I hoped it would help. You can't fight Hong Kong any more than Wang can take on the Triads. Try to get that into your head and you'll be a lot happier.'

They were silent after that, until they reached the centre of Victoria, when Rod said, 'I suppose the Channing residence is on the mid-levels.'

'I can take a taxi from here,' she said quickly, only now remembering the dinner party. Official cars would be arriving at Echoes. She could not turn up looking as she must with a companion dressed equally casually. Olivia would be

58

furious enough without adding fuel to her fire. Rod continued towards Victoria Peak, as if she had not spoken, so she said again that she would take a taxi up to her home.

In the midst of busy traffic, he risked a swift glance in her direction. 'Have I upset you so much?'

'What do you mean?'

'Why the sudden cold shoulder?'

All at once, the magnetism was back. She surrendered to it willingly. 'It's not a cold shoulder, simply a matter of tact. Father is having a dinner party for some important people this evening. I was supposed to have come straight from the clinic to prepare for it. My late arrival might cause some unpleasantness.'

'You mean the dusty, ancient car of a lowly hospital doctor would offend the gleaming limousines rolling into your driveway?'

It was basically what she had thought but his words upset her. 'Put like that it sounds terrible.'

'Yes, doesn't it!' He swerved around a tram, surprising her with evidence of sudden anger. 'In my profession you soon realize that *all* people are important people, right down to the emaciated, toothless coolie who rakes through rotting rubbish in sampan colonies looking for his next meal.'

As he set his car at the winding road leading to the mid-levels in the manner of a Roman charioteer going to war, Sarah caught herself saying, 'Sorry, I didn't mean to unchain the beast again.'

Half a minute of labouring engine roar and crashed gears later, Rod also apologized. 'I tend to see everyone in medical terms, and get hot under the collar on that particular subject.' A hint of anger was still in his dark eyes as he added, 'Can we forget about the beast now? It emerged for one day only. I explained that to you earlier on.'

'If you'll forget my ridiculous *faux pas*.'

He nodded. 'Is there an entrance to the house other than the front door?'

'Several ... but the front door is where I'd like you to drop me, if you don't mind.'

He smiled momentarily. 'Attagirl!'

They arrived at Echoes soon afterwards. Rod whistled

through his teeth when he saw the house, and joined the small queue of cars circling the driveway to deposit passengers on the front steps. Sarah took advantage of the delay to thank him for taking her to Wang Chua's house.

'I'd never have seen it otherwise. There's one thing I don't understand, though. If the old man has been a recluse for years, how did you ever become his friend?'

'It's a long story,' he replied, watching dinner-jacketed men, and women in elaborate gowns, climb the few steps to an impressive colonnaded entrance. 'In short, I happened to be passing when one of his great-grandsons was hit by a tram. After giving emergency treatment, I drove him to the nearest hospital where they virtually brought him back to life. Chinese hold many strong beliefs, one of which is that a debt of gratitude is for life. Hence, his home and fortune are at my disposal while he remains there.'

Sarah's brow creased. 'He would give you anything you asked for?'

'In effect, yes. In *fact*, he knows I accept that it is merely symbolic.'

'But he would not refuse if you *should* ask?'

'He would lose face by doing so. "Face" is terribly important to Chinese people. They frequently commit suicide when it is lost.'

'We once felt that way about honour, didn't we? Pistols at dawn, a bullet through the temple behind a locked door. Death before dishonour.' She sighed. 'That same spirit is alive today in Spitfires, in tanks and at sea, I suppose.'

'Of course. Isn't that why you're so disparaging of your countrymen here?'

'Oh dear, now you're back to your old tricks.'

'You can't teach an old doctor new ones.'

As there was only one car ahead, Sarah said impulsively, 'I thought you'd stopped being a doctor and become ... a friend.'

He pulled up at the foot of the steps, got out and walked round to open the door like the official chauffeurs were doing. When she was standing with him there was no mistaking the look that had also been in his eyes in that dusk-time garden. His words made a mockery of it, however.

60

'If you heed my advice you'll find an attractive substitute. A whole bunch of them.'

Knowing she would not, Sarah watched him drive away, missing him before he was out of sight.

Chapter Three

In the lofty hall, guests were being attended by servants trained to treat their European administrators with respect. None of the formally clad diners were Chinese. Sir Peter employed a comprador who held a very privileged position in the bank and a number of Chinese clerks. He served on several committees with Chinese worthies; he entertained Chinese businessmen to lunch or dinner in plush hotels. He did not invite them to Echoes. There was a fine line of protocol maintained by Hong Kong Europeans obliged to live cheek by jowl with their ethnic neighbours, and it was rarely crossed. There were occasional eccentrics; flamboyant characters who 'went native' and opened their doors to those with whom they felt more fulfilled. There were others who married across that line. If these misfits were influential or wealthy – usually each went hand in glove – they were tolerated on a strict racial basis but never admitted to the élite circle of Hong Kong's European giants.

The coolie class served their white masters, as they had others over the centuries. Middle-class Chinese struggled for recognition in the professions and business; wealthy taipans ran mammoth trading companies in aloof rivalry. All three groups accepted the situation whilst thinking their private thoughts.

As soon as Sarah entered, the handsome Sikh steward who had headed staff at Echoes for twelve years came across to her. 'Miss Channing, Sir Peter has been greatly concerned. I have orders to inform him of your safe return without delay. Are you unharmed?'

Sarah frowned at the uniformed Indian who stood almost a foot and a half taller than she. 'What an extraordinary question! I'm a little later than expected, that's all. Tell my father I shall join him as soon as I am able.'

The man's fierce gaze softened. 'I rejoice that all is well.'

'All is *very* well,' she murmured, smiling as she mounted the side staircase. Rod had put her under an obligation to amend her opinion of these people flocking to be wined and dined by her father. She would try to do that, for *him*, but she knew there would be no substitute recipient of the wealth of feelings she had discovered this afternoon. They were two of a kind, she knew that instinctively, but he did not move in the same social circle so her only chance of seeing him was at the clinic on Fridays. Love on one day a week! He had shown reservations, which she had foolishly strengthened by offering to take a taxi from Victoria, so she must make it obvious to him that Sir Peter Channing's daughter made her own decisions on whom she wished to know.

A young Chinese named Ai Bee acted as maid to Sarah. Usually full of smiles, the girl today greeted her mistress with downcast eyes and an expression of abject misery. However, with the need for speed uppermost in Sarah's mind, she rushed straight to the bathroom to shower with no more than a few words to the girl concerning the dress she would wear. Only on returning to the dressing room did Sarah realize that something was seriously affecting Ai Bee. Wrapped in a huge towel and very conscious of time flying past, she tackled the slender girl in evening uniform of black figured-silk cheongsam. A disturbing story unfolded. The chauffeur Ming, Ai Bee's uncle, had been dismissed without a reference. This constituted such terrible loss of face it brought shame on the niece employed on his recommendation. After she had helped her mistress to bed tonight, Ai Bee would go home and not return.

Sarah was perplexed, but not all her questioning could get from the maid why Ming had been so treated.

'Whatever he has done, Ai Bee, makes no difference to your position here,' she said eventually, knowing dinner must be served very shortly. 'I have been completely satisfied with your efficiency and pleasant nature. There's absolutely no need for you to leave.'

The girl doubled forward, misery a physical pain. 'I unworthy servant. Go tonight.'

Unable to stay and reassure her in the depths of her self-effacement, Sarah speedily dressed, brushed her damp hair, then snatched up the pleated silk bag on a silver chain handle that Ellie had given her. She hurried down the stairs, her ice-blue chiffon dress floating out behind her. The hall was now empty of guests. A nearby buzz of conversation punctuated by laughter told Sarah they had all been fortified with drinks so that they would not notice the clock showing eight-twenty. Olivia, standing near the door, looked daggers at Sarah as she entered, but Sir Peter appeared from the crowd with such alacrity it suggested he had been watching the staircase.

'Father, I'm sorry I'm –' Her apology was cut off by his abrupt statement that he would like a few words in private, and she found herself crossing the hall to a small office he sometimes used. Once inside the room he turned, surprising her with his expression.

'Have you any idea of my feelings when Ming returned without you? He merely said that you sent him away after talking to a man by a blue car. He did not know the man or what you were going to do after he left. I sacked him on the spot, of course.'

'But Ming wasn't at fault,' Sarah protested, before Sir Peter continued with hardly a pause.

'I imagined any number of appalling possibilities when I telephoned the Halburton. A Chinese receptionist confirmed that you had left the clinic, and said several of the helpers owned blue cars. He had noticed them parked outside but could not say to whom they belonged.' Pausing to control himself, he then asked, 'Where, in God's name, have you been? Why did you send Ming back here without even a message for me or for Olivia?'

Taken aback by a strength of feeling he had never before displayed, she murmured, 'There was no need for anxiety.'

'There was *every* need,' he retorted heatedly. 'You are a young woman of considerable wealth in your own right. *I* am a respected influential banker of even greater wealth. There are vicious people in this colony who regard such as we as targets for extortion. You are in Hong Kong, Sarah, not a sleepy village among the Cotswolds. Why do you imagine I send you everywhere in cars driven by my own chauffeur, or in company with Olivia?'

Sarah was shaken at his implication, coming so swiftly after Rod's unexpected warning. Because she was unable to handle this suggestion of real concern from a parent who had previously held aloof, she took refuge in aggression. 'I've been puzzled by Olivia's role in this family. I hadn't realized she is employed as my bodyguard.'

Sir Peter was unable to handle such a response from a daughter who was a relative stranger. He strove for words during the strained silence that followed, then brushed his moustache with a nervous hand before letting it drop heavily to his side in a gesture of resignation. 'Perhaps I should have spoken to you earlier of the dangers to be found in this restless society.'

'You have never had the time, Father,' she said quietly.

'No . . . no.' He sighed deeply. 'When I asked you to join me here I had no idea you were . . . that you had been so . . . so *protected* by your grandmother. I thought Cheltenham would have given you greater maturity, sophistication that would allow you to settle into your new life without difficulty. Olivia is a friend and invaluable assistant to me. What nonsense to call her your bodyguard!' He frowned at her. 'When we both accepted that you could not adjust to our ways easily, she did her utmost to help and advise you. I understand you rejected both help and advice, while making no effort to mix with those whom she went out of her way to introduce to you. Several people have been somewhat offended by your coolness, to say nothing of your tendency to speak of little but the war and England's sacrifice. And now tonight. Allowing that you might not know the risks prevalent in this colony, don't you think mere courtesy demanded that you should send a message explaining where you were going and that you might be late?'

'Yes, of course. I apologize for being so thoughtless.' When another uncomfortable silence fell between them,

Sarah continued, 'I'm sorry you are disappointed in me, Father, but you should no more judge me by Hong Kong society than I should judge them by people at home. I realize how wrong I have been to do so and hope to change my tactics, although it's unlikely that I shall immerse myself in the social round Olivia enjoys. I'm a musician, Father, and they are notorious for preferring isolation. I need to practise every day and, when I'm not actually playing, I *think* through the bars I'm finding difficult to perfect. I mean to make music my life's work, as you have made banking. I'm aware that you don't approve, but I hoped you would consider a professional career as a concert pianist of greater worth than years wasted in party-going before marriage to a suitable candidate for the Channing fortune. If Mother was anything like Ellie, she would have approved of my determination to use my talent to the full ... And it wasn't protection Ellie gave me, it was love.'

Her father's long face grew pensive as he studied her for a few moments. Then he said, 'I suppose I must admire your dedication to music, even if I find it difficult to understand, and perhaps I overlooked your maturity in seeking sophistication.'

'Perhaps,' she agreed, feeling her way carefully in this very personal conversation – the first they had shared. 'There are no Triad gangs in England, but we had bombs and blacked-out streets and trains running late, if at all. We grew used to delays, or people failing to turn up when they should. Time took on a different perspective. It's difficult to forget all that, but I suppose I shouldn't bombard with the details those people who have never experienced it.' She hesitated, before adding, 'But it is *their* country too. Have they forgotten that?'

She had gone too far. Fragile understanding evaporated as Sir Peter looked beyond her to where his guests were still waiting for their meal.

'Olivia is signalling that it is now eight-thirty. We can no longer delay dinner.' He left the office with his usual confident pace causing Sarah to hurry beside him across the mosaic hall. As he strode toward the reception room, he asked almost casually, 'Where *did* you go, and with whom, by the way?'

Some of the afternoon's magic returned to offset a curious

feeling of having won then lost. 'I was taken to the home of a fascinating man named Wang Chua, who lives on a high hill giving a view stretching as far as a mountain range in China. It was breathtaking.'

Stopping abruptly, her father challenged her in sharp tones. 'Wang Chua is a recluse. No one is allowed up that hill, save members of his prodigious family. He has repeatedly refused to see me, *and* several of my acquaintances.'

Sarah also stopped. Aware that their voices were echoing in the airy hall, she spoke quietly. 'I was taken there by a doctor who was instrumental in saving the life of one of Mr Wang's relatives. That entitles him to visit whenever he pleases. I was accepted because he introduced me as his friend. It was an opportunity I didn't want to miss, but I had no idea the visit would last so long.'

Sir Peter probed further. 'Who is this doctor – the one who presumably owns a blue car?'

'You were introduced to him at the concert by that tall man with gingery hair, who was fond of whisky. I believe he holds an important post at Queen Mary Hospital.'

'Sir Kingston Dailey . . . but who is this man who knows Wang Chua?' he demanded with surprising impatience.

Sarah wished she had not been obliged to mention Rod. Their relationship was of such uncertain quality. It should have been allowed to develop before being revealed to others. Why was her father making such a fuss just as his censure was virtually over? A moment ago, dinner had been of prime importance.

'He's an Australian, also on the staff of Queen Mary's. I've done some typing for him at the Halburton.'

'He has a name, I take it.'

The comment was snapped at her with such force she felt resentment rising. She was no child and, until four months ago, whom she knew and what she did was of no interest to her distant parent. Surely he was not going to play the heavy father over this.

'Why is it so important?' she asked. 'It was an impromptu invitation from a doctor making a courtesy call on someone who sponsors a floating clinic he helps to man. He behaved like a perfect gentleman, Father.'

'So I should damn well hope!' A moment later he underwent a lightning change of mood. 'Olivia has taken immense trouble with the arrangements for this evening. If we keep our guests waiting any longer, your thoughtlessness will become downright discourtesy.'

Putting his hand beneath her elbow, he led Sarah to the reception room, as if the subject of her companion had been forgotten. Yet she had the curious sensation that it had not, and returned a caustic reply when Olivia issued her own reprimand under cover of general movement to the dining room.

'How could you do this after my particular request to be punctual? There are some very important people here tonight.'

'*All* people are important, Olivia, right down to the emaciated, toothless coolie who rakes through rubbish in sampan colonies looking for his next meal.'

Sarah walked past the elegant woman in oyster satin with jade accessories, telling herself Rod Durman was well able to take care of any situation, so her vague worries were unnecessary. She then set about the task of getting through an evening certain to be an anticlimax after the afternoon, determined to follow the advice of 'an ordinary bloke' whom she regarded as anything but.

Alex Tennant was bored. The evening was a blueprint of so many others; most of the male guests were stuffed shirts and their partners the type of women who deserved them. The food was perfectly cooked, perfectly served with the perfect liquid accompaniment. Conversation was well-mannered, cultured and informed, but he had heard it all a hundred or more times at similar events. He was certain these people all owned a publication entitled 'Things to Say at Deadly Dull Dinner Parties'.

There had been a promise of excitement at the start of the evening, when he had spotted from a window the Channing girl climbing from a dusty blue saloon hobnobbing with the sleek limousines inching around the drive encircling a fish pool empty of life. She had looked in no hurry to join her papa's guests – not that Alex could blame her for that – and

68

her reluctance to part from the dark-haired bruiser driving the car had been interestingly apparent. Father Channing had collared his errant daughter the moment she descended the stairs in a cloud of blue froth, and hauled her off for a parental wigging which had delayed dinner to the extent of inviting speculation on what the girl had been up to. Papa and butter-wouldn't-melt-in-her-mouth daughter had then joined the assembled company as if nothing were amiss. *He* had worn an expression resembling a cat sighting cream, and *she* looked like one who had already had it.

Although his hopes of scandal to enliven the evening had been dashed, Alex was still interested in the change in Sarah Channing tonight. It was so subtle as to be almost unnoticeable, but he knew women rather well and had a particular score to settle with Sir Peter's aloof daughter. Rumour had it that she had no time for Hong Kong society, but she had clearly found time enough for some muscle-bound brute from the *hoi polloi* this afternoon. Resentment vied with curiosity. Alex had been successful with the female sex since puberty. Too successful, perhaps, for he now had little real respect for those who succumbed to his strategy. Like these dinner parties, they had become boring; using the same coy phrases, doing the same things with the same insincerity. If they were willing, he took what they offered as he took the welter of other pleasures Hong Kong provided, but his life was really no richer for any of it.

After their initial meeting Alex had classed the Channing girl an aloof prude with little or no personality. However, Sir Peter was a close associate of his benefactor, in addition to being their banker, so he decided that conquest of the man's colourless daughter might be wise. His fortune on the racetrack and gaming-table fluctuated drastically, making it essential to keep his banker sweet. Saintly Sarah could be instrumental in that. He had soon discovered she was some-what less than saintly. His usual line in seductive patter had been countered by disapproval so strong, it became clear the girl was more passionate than he guessed. There was none for him, nevertheless. Far from thinking him an exciting daredevil when he told her he piloted a super-charged seaplane painted scarlet and decorated with dragons, she had made cutting comparisons with young men in Britain who were flying and dying in defence of their country. She had been disparaging about his interest in racing, too, claiming that the sums he bet on horses and frequently lost should more profitably be given to the war effort.

'If you decline to take up arms yourself, you might at least give some of the wealth you throw away at the racetrack to help buy weapons for those who have,' she told him.

Her heated remark had stung him into retorting, 'I'm an officer in the Hong Kong Volunteers.'

'As the Germans are unlikely to advance this far, you're playing pretty safe, Mr Tennant.'

He hit back – something he rarely did these days. 'Isn't this a case of pot and kettle? I heard somewhere that girls at home are driving ambulances, manning guns and guiding damaged aircraft safely home. Why have you run out on your chums when things are at their hottest?'

The effect on her of his taunt had been more than gratifying and, on the few occasions that they had been in the same company since then, they avoided each other. Alex had only come to Echoes tonight because he was badly in the red and his allowance was not due until the end of the quarter. Reginald Jay, Alex's boss and reluctant benefactor, had suggested it would be prudent to accept the invitation whilst also indulging in an activity known as 'drawing in one's horns' for the next few weeks. Small wonder boredom had set in. Yet, as Alex watched Sarah during the dessert course, he found interest in her reviving.

She possessed the classic natural look found in English girls of her class when he had been a man about town. It was now old-fashioned. Girls permed their hair into waves and curls, painted their nails as red as their lips, and dressed provocatively. Beside them Sarah had appeared pale and lifeless . . . until this evening. The fall of smooth blonde hair gleamed in light from candles as she moved her head, hinting of sensual pleasure to be found by stroking it, and her mouth touched by pale pink lipstick had softened from its disapproving line. As she smiled at something her neighbour said, the truth hit Alex. Some man had succeeded in

70

bringing her to life where he had failed. Who was the nobody in an ancient blue car? Almost certainly a fortune-hunter. The Channing girl might have taken the bait, but would not be landed. Papa had surely got wind of what was going on just now. The blighter would be sent packing, and that would be the time for Alex to make his own move. Girls on the rebound from an aborted infatuation were known to be grateful for a shoulder to cry on. Alex would enjoy seeing Sarah Channing in tears.

The Victorian custom of gentlemen taking port and cigars at the dinner table, after the ladies withdrew to gossip in genteel isolation from such masculine degeneracy, continued in modified version in Hong Kong. Although women now drank and smoked alongside them, the period immediately after dinner provided an opportunity for men of affairs to talk business or politics while women exchanged tittle-tattle on subjects dear to *their* hearts. Alex always suspected he would prefer spicy feminine conversation to dull discussions on finance and administration. Tonight reinforced that belief.

The male guests gathered on the veranda where they could form into convenient groups, then easily re-form to pursue their interests. As they downed their drinks and puffed at Havanas they believed they held the world in the palms of their hands. Alex wandered to the balustrade and stood with a whisky in one hand, a de Reske in the other, gazing moodily at the spread of lights giving night-time romance to a city festering with poverty beneath the walls of commerce. He hated it. Shipping held no attraction for him; cargo manifests and trade routes were too sober for his wild nature.

His mother's schoolfriend had married the shipper Reginald Jay before he amalgamated with Julian Frobisher to form the present mercantile company. She had persuaded her husband to take on the Tennants' black sheep of a son four years ago, and Alex conceded that they had both been very decent and kept gossip to a minimum. Scandal was rife in Hong Kong with a new one swiftly superseding the last, so Alex had occupied the limelight for only a short time. Even so, society refused to take him seriously. He knew it never would. *Alex Tennant? Oh, he's a divine dancer, plays an acceptable game of tennis, looks graceful on a diving-board, and is a handsome addition to any gathering . . . but lock up your daughters!* He flicked the glowing cigarette stub over the balustrade and tossed back the rest of his whisky as memories swamped him.

Maurice Tennant, self-made millionaire, had built his steel empire on the graves of those he had ruined. Despite reluctant admiration for his dedication to work, which had taken him from orphanage to boardroom, Alex's father bred universal dislike in every walk of life. His abrasive tongue, outsize ego and determination to amass money at any cost had inspired particular hatred in Britain's newspaper barons. Miriam de Boucher, daughter of a respected legal family, had been overwhelmed by the aggressive courtship of a man used to getting what he wanted. Having made her his wife, Maurice pursued the next challenge and forgot her.

Nine months after the wedding, Alex had been born to a doting, possessive mother and a father determined to rear a son in his own image but with all the advantages lacking in his own orphaned boyhood. Those early years still resembled a nightmare. Harsh, demanding, never satisfied, his father drove Alex to impossible standards, thrusting him into social circles where he was disliked and resented because of his parent, and forcing from him behaviour that was foreign to his gentler creed. Maurice Tennant believed in physical punishment for failure and in dominance of free spirits in order to mould them into unyielding strength.

Even now, Alex could feel the thin cane cutting into the flesh of his buttocks again and again. Only when he resorted to tears had the punishment ended. To spare himself pain, Alex used to begin crying as soon as the beatings started. This brought additional harshness, laced with contempt for his weakness of character. Those years of abuse, both physical and verbal, the solitary hours in a locked room and humiliating visits to people who knew well how to make him aware of his unworthiness to be among them, had bred hatred of his father, and driven him to seek the comfort and indulgence offered by his gentle mother. Yet she was so in awe of her husband she would never openly defend her small son either at home or in company.

Entry to a top public school brought escape from parental cruelty, but it taught Alex the additional pain of being a mongrel among thoroughbreds. Only a mediocre sportsman and certainly not academically gifted, he found favour in neither set and was constantly bullied by boys who thought the son of an ill-bred steel manufacturer unfitted to their ranks. For the first few months Alex felt he had moved from one purgatory to another.

Yet everything changed when it became apparent that young Tennant possessed the third essential quality for success in a school of adolescent boys. The local girls adored him, and fought over the prize of his virginity. He swiftly surrendered it to an experienced waitress. Alex then trod the risky path of sexual conquest beneath the noses of the school authorities, and it was some time before he was found out and duly dealt with. But his daring exploits in this delightful direction finally brought him friends. He was welcomed in their homes during vacations as Miriam de Boucher's son. Maurice Tennant was tactfully overlooked.

By the time he reached manhood, Alex had acquired polish, self-assurance and the knowledge that his blond good looks were irresistible to most members of the female sex. Then the blow had fallen. Instead of accompanying his friends to university and four more years of vague study sweetened by love affairs, Maurice ruled that Alex was to go into the steel business, starting at the bottom.

Alex would never forget the day he had been given that news. He had flatly refused to dress in overalls and go off at dawn each morning with a sandwich box under his arm. He had told his father that he had no interest in steel and intended to plan his own future. Son and father had then brought out the hatred of twenty years, flinging angry accusations at each other until Miriam became hysterical. Maurice had lost control and hit her. When Alex lunged at him in her defence, his father had knocked him down saying that he would either take his place at Tennant's Steel Works, or cease to be his son with every advantage of that position.

A generous allowance from his paternal grandmother had financed Alex during the next two years, but the plan for his future remained elusive. There were a great number of women willing to help the days pass in pleasant indolence, and he told himself he would get down to the problem soon. Then he had been introduced to Colin Weatherly, rich, handsome and reckless. Life had become high-powered in every sense. Alex was persuaded to buy a fast car and an even faster boat, which entailed borrowing a large sum from Colin. The maintenance for these powerful machines cost more than Alex's allowance would stand, so he borrowed more from his friend. Expenses mounted; so did his debt to Weatherly.

In the summer of 1937 things came to a head. Colin lost heavily on a horse and called in his loan, but Alex had backed the same horse and could not pay his rent, much less the debt. After drowning his sorrows in gin, Alex proposed a further wager in a mood of bravado. He and Colin would race their boats around the Isle of Wight. If he lost, he would surrender both his boat and sports car to Colin but halve the debt. If he won, the debt would be wiped off. It was madness, because Colin's powerful vessel could attain a speed well in excess of any Alex could hope for, but he believed he was the better navigator.

The affair ended in tragedy and the Press had the full story from an anonymous telephone caller. They pilloried Maurice Tennant's son in an orgy of malice. Even when the coroner recorded a verdict of accidental death on Colin they continued the vendetta against Alex, ferreting out the most trivial details of his life to enlarge them by innuendo into evidence of upper-class decadence.

Hounded by reporters, shattered by guarded suggestions that he had engineered Weatherly's death in order to keep the powerful machines he prized, and haunted by the memory of Colin careering drunkenly into a tug at uncontrollable speed, Alex went to pieces. In that wretched state he allowed his mother to arrange his escape. He had a reputation as a playboy and found acceptance only in that guise. Social excesses kept ghosts at bay and alcohol dulled all his senses into a semblance of peace.

A burst of loud laughter brought Alex from his depressing introspection to survey the men sharing the veranda with him. They had all made successful careers in this colony, some in administration and others in commerce. They all expected continued success before retirement to a country estate in Britain with a knighthood or comparative recognition for their services. Hong Kong was their life's blood. Alex regarded it as his prison. A self-imposed prison, he supposed, for he made little effort to break out, tied as he was by the conditions set by the de Boucher family. If he left Hong Kong within five years, the quarterly allowance would cease. Used to a certain style of living, the thought of relying only on what he could earn appalled him. Even so, he was honest enough to admit that the stronger reason for remaining here was that he could think of nothing better. These people surrounding him were all fired by enthusiasm for what they did. Nearby was the Military Attaché, a senior director of Jardine's, a high official in the Hong Kong Police and a bishop. Each was a man exuding confidence and expertise. Tonight's host was an energetic banker, and even his unlikeable daughter had a deep commitment to music. Alex envied them that elusive driving passion.

Having come back to the subject of Sarah Channing, he realized that his recent restlessness had been provoked by that girl's derision at their several meetings. For the first time since arriving in Hong Kong, someone had *not* accepted that he was an inveterate indolent charmer. She had said that he should be fighting for his country, which suggested that the Channing girl believed him capable of doing so.

Subconsciously, he had begun to question his own lack of determination. If the Japanese *had* attacked eighteen months ago, his future would have been changed by fate, taking the responsibility from his shoulders. As it was, the weight still rested firmly there. It was starting to bother him.

When the company reassembled, Sarah was asked to provide music. Much as Alex disliked the girl, he freely admitted that she became a different person at the keys of a piano. Alex caught himself once more envying her passion for something she did superbly. Yet she appeared unaware of the still, silent audience during a fiery piece Alex thought might have been written by Liszt. Enthusiastic persuasion for an encore led her to embark upon the dreamy 'Clair de

Lune', but she concluded the musical interlude with a Chopin waltz after which she covered the keyboard very firmly.

Alex thought it curious that, after being showered with compliments from guests not easily roused to genuine appreciation, the girl stood apart beside a long window, looking almost drained of her earlier vivacity. Even more curious was the fact that the assembled company was now prepared to forget the daughter of their host. After the passionate flow of melody, she retired into her shell and became invisible to those around her. It was a reasonable assumption. That shining blonde hair blended with the yellow satin brocade curtains at the window from which she was now staring, and her pastel blue dress lost the little colour it contained beside the vibrant blue-green wall-covering.

Boredom began to evaporate. Sarah Channing was the only intriguing person present. Alex once again wondered about the man who had prised out a little of her hidden self earlier that day, and started across the Persian carpet, drink in hand, to pursue a little diversion in this dull party. She jumped nervously and spun round when he spoke.

'Recovering from the demands of music? I'm not surprised. You should be performing on a concert platform, not as an after-dinner entertainer.'

She looked irritated by his approach. 'I'm not yet ready for that. There's still a great deal to learn.'

'Including how to accept a compliment gracefully.'

'I do, when it's genuine,' she said sharply.

'What makes you think mine wasn't?'

'I've heard a great deal about you, none of which suggests that you're an authority on music. Quite the reverse.'

Leaning negligently against the wall, he tut-tutted. 'You shouldn't believe all you hear about people. For instance, I've been told you have no time for men *not* wearing a uniform, yet you arrived home rather late this afternoon in company with a prizefighter in mufti.'

Faint colour touched her cheeks; her eyes sparkled with aggression. 'He's a dedicated doctor who spends his off-duty time in charity medical work. I find that more than admirable.'

'Dear me, yes. *Most* admirable.'

The mouth that had been softened by smiles during dinner tightened again. 'How do you come to be here this evening? Are you a business acquaintance of Father's?'

'It depends on how you regard the term "business acquaintance",' he replied easily. 'Channing Mercantile handles my personal account as well as that of Frobisher–Jay. I suppose it could be called a business association with Sir Peter, but I imagine I was invited as an appendage of the Jays, who are close friends of my mother. She's Miriam de Boucher.'

'So I have heard.'

'Without being impressed, clearly.'

'There's little about you that I find impressive.'

'Ah, I must get myself a stethoscope.'

She bridled. 'Do you ever take *anything* seriously?'

He knew he was rousing that elusive personality to some kind of life, even if the beefy doctor brought out her better traits. He continued the experiment. 'Of course I do. My bank balance . . . and the gee-gees.'

'Perhaps the first would benefit from neglect of the latter. I've heard Happy Valley is your second home.'

He countered that in customary sleepy fashion. 'What did I tell you just now concerning things you hear about people? As soon as I have that really big win, I mean to buy it and make it my *first* home.' He offered his gold cigarette-case. She shook her head, so he lit a de Reske and exhaled before asking, 'Hasn't it ever occurred to you that almost every prominent European and Chinese in Hong Kong patronizes the races? I'm not there in the stands alone, you know.' He made an elegant gesture with his hand. 'Most of these stuffed shirts go to Happy Valley for a flutter. You've been here long enough to know Hong Kong is hardly a mecca of entertainment. We have to do whatever we can to console ourselves for being far from home.'

When accompanied by a forlorn expression, this was one of his most successful lines. To his surprise, even without the forlorn expression, it had some effect on the resistant girl beside him.

'If you're homesick, there are other ways of trying to

forget it. I miss England dreadfully, too. Teaching music to Chinese children twice a week, and working for a day at the Halburton Clinic, helps me forget my unhappiness.'

'I know nothing about medical matters,' he murmured, telling himself the 'dedicated doctor' seeking an advantageous match must also work at the Halburton. The mystery was gradually unravelling.

'Neither do I. I do the typing.' She smiled reflectively. 'Rather badly, I'm afraid.'

He smiled back in his most persuasive manner. 'Perhaps you should stick to the keyboard you finger so well.'

'As you stick to what you do so well?'

He took advantage of her softer mood. 'You should come to the races one day. It's not compulsory to place bets. There's a great deal of excitement in just watching.'

The soft fall of hair swung as she shook her head. 'I don't believe horses were meant to race each other, whipped on by jockeys. I prefer to cross Cotswold country on a crisp autumn day, letting the animal race the wind as it pleases.'

'So you ride?'

'Of course, don't you?'

'Of course.' He signalled a white-coated boy to bring his tray of drinks. 'We could go out together. I know a fellow who owns stables.'

He had misjudged the moment. She retreated. 'I haven't time.'

'You don't go to the Halburton every day.'

'I practise each morning and afternoon. That's more important than anything.'

'Even having fun?'

Her expression was more potent than words, and Alex revised his strategy while taking two glasses from the boy's tray and handing her one. Perhaps moonlight would help. It invariably did. 'Shall we escape to the veranda? It's growing very close in here.'

Without waiting for a response, he put his hand beneath her elbow and guided her to where shuttered doors folded back to the evening. He sensed that she was unused to masculine wiles. Was she in fact completely inexperienced where men were concerned? Could such a phenomenon exist today? If so, the doctor was surely batting on a sticky wicket. Too much medical heroism would have her falling into his arms, and his bed, before he had time to take stock of the consequences. Hong Kong would then have a juicy scandal to liven the coming lethargic summer days.

Sarah moved away from his guiding hand as they encountered the relative darkness outside, so he quickly reverted to the subject of music. 'Do you really practise morning and afternoon . . . every day?'

She walked to where moonlight flooded the stone balustrade and he only just heard words spoken to the hillside as he moved to join her. 'It's necessary so that one's fingers don't stiffen up, if nothing else. But constant practice is essential, first in learning a new work, and then in keeping it in one's memory. There is always room for improvement, although it's impossible to reach perfection. No, that's not exactly true. An artist might give a supreme performance just once in an entire career.'

'That sounds like an awful lot of work for very little reward.'

She continued staring at the faint shape of the slopes some hundred yards distant. 'I guessed you'd say something like that; that you'd never understand.'

'But the good doctor does?'

Silence greeted that probe for several moments, then she asked, in deliberately conversational tones, 'Did you know this house gained its name from sounds heard in the gorge out there? I'm told the roar of water after a typhoon is so tremendous it's impossible to hear anyone speak indoors.'

'I well believe it,' he murmured, wondering why his approach had no effect on this girl. 'I've seen the gorge from the air. It's formidable.'

Turning to face him, she said, '*There's* one obvious means of relieving your homesickness. Go back and offer your flying skill to the RAF. It might mean an awful lot of work, but I guarantee the reward will be more than sufficient – even for you.'

'Slow death in a blazing cockpit? No thanks,' he snapped, annoyed by her return to this subject in perfect romantic circumstances.

79

'If everyone thought that way, our country would have fallen long ago. I thought you were an inveterate gambler, Mr Tennant, but I see now that you'll bet only on someone else's chances, not on your own. It suggests that you have no belief in yourself. That means you'll die the slowest death of all.'

She walked back to the noise and heat indoors leaving him alone with the moonlight and nocturnal echoes from the gorge.

Two days after the dinner party at Echoes, Alex took the ferry to Kowloon, where his seaplane was moored. He had spent the morning with others like himself who had been recruited into the Volunteer Corps. For a year they had been drilling, exercising, practising on the rifle range, and making then revising defence plans none of them believed would ever be necessary. Even the professional troops of the garrison acknowledged that the colony was severely under-manned, with insufficient artillery and air cover comprising only three obsolete bombers and a couple of marine aircraft. They worried about it, but the war was going so badly elsewhere they accepted that a colony under no threat from the enemy could not expect reinforcements.

Alex felt the entire business of dressing in uniform and going through the motions of soldiering was slightly farcical. Regular members of the Volunteers were men who enjoyed the occasional excitement of military training, but he found no rapport with things martial. As the ferry plied its route across a waterway busy with junks, sampans, barges, tugs and dhows, Alex looked back at Victoria Peak and reflected that Sarah Channing might have been quite amenable this morning if she had seen him in khaki. Why were so many women bowled over by a uniform? It had to be discarded for the most satisfying part of the relationship, leaving the wearer looking much the same as any man.

Pushing away recollections that had flitted in and out of his mind since Friday evening, Alex concentrated on the pleasure to come. A fast car was relatively wasted on an island with few roads, and he believed he would never again want to possess a powerful boat, so his penchant for speed was now satisfied by *Dragonfly*, his powerful stream-lined floatplane. It was seen by many as an extravagance fitting for his preferred style of life, yet it was the one activity he indulged in because it gave him a sense of true satisfaction. When he climbed into that tiny cockpit, switched on the engine, then skimmed the water before rising to circle in an endless deserted sky, he could be a different person.

He took a rickshaw from the pier to his mooring, eagerness mounting. An overalled figure was already scrambling from the scarlet machine, and Alex returned the man's wave of greeting as he strode along the narrow jetty. 'Hallo, Jim, how is she?'

'Fine. Raring to go. I came over yesterday because I was a bit worried about the port strut. That storm last week didn't do it no good. Guess it bashed into the jetty a bit hard. Told you we should've protected them floats a bit more.'

'Is it all right now?' Alex asked, studying the delicate strut from float to fuselage.

'Quite okey-dokey.' The man grinned. 'I wouldn't let you go up unless everything was tickety-boo. Got my reputation to think of.'

Alex grinned back. 'I know. The best engineer on the station.'

It was a joke they shared. The Flight was so small there was no competition. Jim Maiden was an RAF corporal, a passionate enthusiast for marine aircraft. His wife had taken their three children back to England eighteen months ago when panic evacuation had been under way, but they were now in greater danger in their London home. Jim missed them. He was worried about their safety, and looked after *Dragonfly* to help ease that worry, besides earning a nice supplement to his wages for the future – if they had one. He was a genius with few opportunities to exercise his talent, so it was with pleasure that he looked after a superb machine on which no expense was spared.

Surprising camaraderie existed between these two men of such different type and background. It was rooted in the common interest of *Dragonfly*, yet they also felt easy in each other's presence. Jim was always respectful to someone he regarded as a 'toff', but knew little of Alex Tennant's private life. He took on face value the owner of a craft he had no desire to possess. Jim's eyes were not on the sky. He loved tinkering, putting things right; his passion was nuts and bolts. Alex found the engineer good company. Perhaps with Jim Maiden he dropped the pose that had almost taken over his personality; perhaps the relief of communing with someone of down-to-earth values and intelligence allowed Alex to experiment with another persona.

For more than half an hour they fussed over the little machine that was dancing on the sparkling water, checking every aspect and preparing her for flight. It was a perfect day for it. Clear sky, light breeze, sunshine that browned arms and faces, and just enough movement on the water to aid take-off. Alex enjoyed listening to Jim as the man pointed out various aspects of the engine he had cleaned and then run several times.

'It should sound sweet, you see, and I can soon tell if there's a problem, no matter how small. I *hear* trouble.'

Alex glanced at Jim's square, grimed face as they stood on the bobbing step looking at the shining tubes and pistons that were mostly a mystery to him. 'You're a gem. They should make you a general, at least.'

'We don't have no generals . . . but I'd say no to being an air-marshal. They don't get the chance to fuss around engines. I'd hate that.'

They returned to the jetty and Alex went to the small matshed to strip to his underpants before donning the white overalls he wore to fly. When he walked back to his aircraft, breeze ruffling his hair and sun burning his face, instead of the usual sense of well-being he was troubled by a return of recollections from Friday.

Go back and offer your flying skill to the RAF . . . The reward will be more than sufficient – even for you.

He must have been frowning, for Jim asked what was wrong. 'Nothing. Just someone walking on my grave,' he murmured, fitting the leather helmet over his thick fair hair.

'Not just yet, they won't,' Jim said with a wag of his head. 'That machine's fit for Churchill himself to fly in. Safe as houses, it is.'

Alex had complete confidence in Jim. As he climbed in and lowered himself on to the narrow seat, a girl's voice accused him of having no confidence in himself. The engine burst into action, drowning it, and he nodded to Jim who detached the anchor. He was away, bouncing over ripples with gathering speed until he gently brought the stick towards him and lifted into that other element. Up over masts and sails, still climbing, then he was circling above Victoria Peak commanding a view of which he never tired. Hong Kong lay below in a shape resembling a camel with no front legs, an emerald gem far distant from that other green island whose adventurers had discovered and laid claim to it a hundred years ago. To the right was Lantau Island, larger and more sprawling than Hong Kong, but lacking the virtues of a prize possession for imperialists. Around and between the two was a series of greenish-brown islets breaking through the sea with a collar of white waves.

He banked and headed back over a mainland that had its own offshore islands. Apart from Kowloon, with wharves, cranes, great white houses of commerce and a small residential area, the scene was one of dark wooded hills, paddy fields, rivers, reservoirs and tiny walled villages clustered around the temples of worship for those living within walking distance. It was nevertheless important territory, one of the prime reasons being the abundance of water. Hong Kong Island could not meet the demand, especially since the influx of refugees eighteen months before, so had to rely on mainland supplies. As Alex overflew one of the vast reservoirs, he thought of a conversation this morning concerning plans for water rationing in the event of the mainland falling into enemy hands. It did not bear thinking about. Thank God the Japanese apparently had no designs on Hong Kong.

In an instant he was back on the veranda at Echoes. How would he measure up if he followed her advice and returned to England? His father had never been satisfied with a boy who invariably failed to reach his exacting standards, his headmaster had had little time for a pupil whose greatest merit was his success with village girls, his friends ... He cast away that train of thought with a surge of anger.

Self-analysis invariably resulted in black depression which could only be banished by an injection of excitement, preferably of the risky kind. Gambling, parties, a new woman – all these helped. But he was presently able to indulge in the best of all antidotes to gloom.

Smiling savagely, Alex pushed the throttle away to begin a series of manoeuvres designed to boost his spirits and cause heads to tilt back to watch the daring display of aerobatics. As he swooped, soared and banked in dangerously sharp turns the savage smile remained. Corporal James Brian Maiden would be cussing in hearty style down on the jetty, but Alex was not doing it to aggravate Jim. It was his way of telling the world that he did not give a damn for it. As the engine roared gamely in response to his demands, and the slim fuselage began to shudder with the strain of manoeuvres that had first sea, then sky, then green-clad hills circling dizzily beneath its racing scarlet floats, Alex's smile began to harden. What he would give to swoop over those puffed-up bastards who considered him a subject of derisory amusement.

No sooner had the idea arrived than he acted on it. Losing height, he headed for those beaches around the Island which attracted revellers on weekends like this. Repulse Bay, with its famous hotel set among green lawns and extensive flower gardens, was his first target. The beach was as busy with human dots as the hotel terrace. He overflew the area first at several thousand feet, then turned and dived at speed, flattening out low enough to create minor panic below the long cylindrical floats. He began to laugh. That would shake them out of their smug superiority!

Swooping heavenward at the end of the bay, he went on to the next broad sandy beach to repeat his demonstration of disdain for public opinion. Panic again ensued as he roared low over picnics, ball games, and courting couples. His laughter increased. If they were terrified of Alex Tennant, dubbed by them 'The Red Baron', how would *they* measure up if the Japs ever attacked?

He flew around the Island frightening Europeans and Chinese alike, arriving finally at Stanley Peninsula, the last of the spots favoured by those seeking relaxation and enjoyment on a lovely Sunday afternoon. Above the bay stood the twin white buildings of the Halburton Clinic. They provided the final spur to Alex's defiance. The doctor who was considered 'more than admirable' might be spending some of his free time there today. Perhaps he should have a demonstration of skill equalling any his forceps might produce.

Pushing down *Dragonfly*'s nose, Alex plunged towards the two small buildings, laughter vanishing on the heels of bravado. So intent was he on creating hell he forgot the hilly terrain of the area. After racing no more than feet above the flat rooftops of the clinic, he found himself hurtling towards the long range of fir-clad hills on the far side of Stanley Bay. Banking violently to port in a desperate bid to avoid the promontory, he soon realized *Dragonfly* was travelling too fast to clear the end of the heights. The next minutes were a nightmare as he struggled to straighten and climb above the barrier looming ahead. Beads of perspiration stood on his face; his hands grew clammy on the stick. His heart was now pounding and the pulse in his temples sounded like thunder inside his head.

Jim Maiden's devoted care now paid off as Alex demanded of the machine a performance beyond its power. He fought to rise above the treeline, never forgetting the floats well below his cockpit, entreating help from a God he had never worshipped. Divine help, or outstanding skill, brought off the impossible. With treetops mere inches from the bright red floats, *Dragonfly* cleared the danger and laboured on over the sea towards Lamma Island. Alex was shaking. He felt sick, and weak in all his limbs. His brain was numb. The little seaplane flew on while he slowly recovered. His mind returned to normal first, and it began to tell him something quite extraordinary. He had executed an amazing piece of flying back there; a last-minute escape from certain disaster. Only a highly talented pilot could have done it.

He began to sense power, a strong feeling of pride in what he had done. Maybe the nickname 'The Red Baron' was not in the least derogatory. He banked gently and headed for the jetty in Kowloon feeling wonderfully peaceful. Then the peace was broken by that girl's voice. *Why don't you go back and offer your skill to the RAF?* His sense of well-being evaporated fast. Damn Sarah Channing! She was beginning to get under his skin. Because of her taunts he had damn near killed himself this afternoon.

Chapter Four

Sampan owners lived, slept, gave birth and died on the long, flat vessels from which they traded for a meagre livelihood. Crammed upon them were families of several generations, their few personal possessions, cooking pots and an ancient burner, a chicken or two, and a mangy dog to warn off thieves. Sampans held small cargoes of rotting vegetables bought cheaply from floating restaurants, limp fading flowers discarded by stall owners, low-grade coal difficult to ignite, lengths of tawdry cloth, second-hand pots and pans, cheap tin trays, or bric-à-brac that failed to sell in Victoria's curio shops. These were peddled or bartered to people of poor coastal villages. The acres of boats linked by perilous floating walkways rang with loud chatter, the cries of babies and the barking of rival guard-dogs. This community spirit continued when sampans were on the move, families calling the latest news to each other across wide stretches of water.

On a wild night early in May, fire sprang up in one sampan and rapidly spread to adjacent craft. The high wind whipped flames across the plank walkways to catch at other boats until they formed a conflagration. Many people cut off from the fire jumped overboard only to drown beneath the bouncing, closely packed hulls. Panic brought more deaths as others pushed and clawed their way along the flimsy thoroughfares offering access to shore, careless of the fate of those they knocked aside in the surge for safety.

When disasters of this nature occurred in Hong Kong, medical resources were pooled to deal with casualties. Rod raced to the scene with army doctors and other civilians able to be contacted. Tents were erected as first-aid posts, but the medical men were severely hampered by the gale and darkness. The doctors' worst difficulty, however, was in preventing victims from escaping. Sampan Chinese were superstitious, independent and loath to mingle with those on land. They distrusted European medicine and preferred to suffer rather than submit to the potions of 'foreign devils'.

Several hours passed while firemen fought to master the blaze, and a fleet of ambulances took away the dead and suffering. Rod shared a tent with an army captain and a Eurasian who understood much of the lore of sampan colonies. Burns were tricky. The bad cases were too ill to care what was happening, but those brought in by orderlies who had caught them before they staggered away under cover of darkness were sullen, aggressive or terrified. They frequently had to be held whilst treated, losing no opportunity to shout abuse as they left with dressings on their limbs, or to spit at the feet of their benefactors. Mothers had to be restrained whilst their children received treatment for minor burns or cuts. These little ones, their great, staring black eyes filled with pain and fear, aroused Rod's greatest compassion. Although destined not to be a father, he always delighted in contact with children, and these were incredibly stoical.

There was a lull after tending three children with minor cuts to their hands, and Rod flexed his aching back as the last was taken out into the night. 'That lad's mother will have the dressing off before he's gone ten yards,' he remarked to his companions, who were also taking a breather. 'We've been wasting our time on half of them tonight.'

'Quite possibly,' agreed the young army captain.

'If it was your child, would you allow a Chinese healer to slap on one of *his* concoctions then leave it intact?' asked the Eurasian, whose father had been Dutch. 'It's not so much a question of lack of trust as an inborn suspicion of each other that goes back a long way.'

The military doctor grimaced. 'Foreign devils and slit-eyed yellow bastards. It'll take years before we stop regarding each other as such.'

Rod looked at the two men in crumpled, stained shirts, their faces pale and weary in the harsh light of oil lamps suspended from a bar across the tent. 'We shouldn't be regarding them as anything but patients. It's time we put aside long-standing prejudices and shared our medical knowledge. We have a lot to learn from each other, but, whereas the Chinese have joined with us in certain areas, we are still firmly opposed to their methods.'

'I ask you again, Durman, if you would allow a Chinese healer to treat your child,' said the Eurasian.

'If he was the only person on hand, yes. Wouldn't you?'

'That goes without saying,' came the reply.

'You're both talking a lot of nonsense,' put in the military captain. 'You'd treat the child yourselves.' He stretched. 'God, I'm tired. What I need is a plate of sandwiches, not psychoanalysis.'

Rod sank wearily on to a bench, immediately reminded of Sarah. He had created a hell of a problem. What had happened on that hill was as disturbing as it had been sudden: a moment of incredible serenity, a breathless dusk and a young woman who had turned to him with dawning recognition in her eyes. How dangerously near he had been to instinctive response! She had often been in his thoughts after the concert. He had fooled himself that the invitation to visit Wang Chua was for the reason he had given her. He was a mature, experienced male who should have damn well faced the fact that Sarah Channing had got to him from their first encounter – yes, even when he had let fly at her over the report. Her youthful composure had appealed to him even as it added fuel to his rage.

The coldness left inside him by the death of his marriage had been warmed by each successive meeting. Therein lay the danger. Responsibility for quenching the springing flame lay squarely on his shoulders, yet compulsion to fan it into a conflagration was strong. Celeste had been ablaze from the start. Her fire had swiftly consumed him before dying to embers which now ceased even to glow. A passionate man, he longed to explore the depths of Sarah's hesitant, emerging personality. He had gone out of his way to avoid meeting her at the Halburton, but that was the coward's solution. He would have to set things right, by one means or another, and try to put her out of his mind.

His introspection was broken by the arrival of several more reluctant patients to whom he gave treatment they silently resented. It was not until four a.m. that he was able to leave the site, where survivors crouched in misery to gaze at the wreckage of their community. They must feel that their goddess T'ien Hai had deserted them tonight, yet they would continue to lay offerings at her temple nearby. The Chinese always accepted their fate. Centuries of oppression had made them a patient, uncomplaining race.

Celeste was asleep when Rod let himself into the apartment. He took a shower, raided the refrigerator for a thick cheese sandwich and a glass of milk, then settled in his bed knowing that he could sleep for as long as he wished. It was the dawn of a Sunday morning on which he was not due to man Wang Chua's floating clinic. He closed his eyes, at peace with the world. After Sir Kingston Dailey had hinted that the post in Tropical Diseases could be his, after both his requests for second opinions on cases had brought confirmation of his own findings, confidence had returned. He had been sleeping well, and enjoying his work. His quick temper was now easier to control, which improved relations with his colleagues, and he had returned to his favourite sport of water polo. He had been picked for the team to challenge the army next week, but his fellows knew a professional emergency might arise and always nominated a reserve.

Celeste had been more reasonable since the night of the charity concert. It had been so unlike him to stay in a hotel, she had maybe realized that her behaviour had been selfish or, at the very least, inconsiderate. Her mild repentance, plus the fact that he spent less time refreshing his memory of tropical medicine, had created a calmer atmosphere between them. She had even sat quietly, buffing her nails or flicking through a magazine, while he played some of the classical records he had not heard for a long time. Every time he played the Rachmaninov concerto he recalled the passion and tenderness of Sarah's performance when he had feared he was going to pieces, and regret flooded him. Despite his determination to put her out of his mind, he now drifted into slumber with the echo of her music in his ears, and the memory of that moment of recognition in a silent Eastern garden.

He came from the depths of sound sleep on a surge of physical desire. A woman's naked body was against his, teasing, arousing, demanding. His hands moved automatically to caress her firm, supple lines, and desire doubled as her tongue probed his mouth in challenge. When he would have rolled towards her she stopped him with familiar, outrageous actions, and he was soon groaning in mounting delight. Still lethargic with the aftermath of sleep, he reached a climax very quickly and swore under his breath. She laughed – a taunting, beckoning sound designed to spur him to further effort. She eventually surrendered to his strength and remained beneath him during a passionate wrestling match from which they both would emerge the winner. Some time passed before they were satisfied and lay quietly. As he stared at the ceiling, Rod acknowledged that it had been too long since he had enjoyed sexual release. The sensation of well-being presently flooding him provided the final cure for his threatened breakdown. He was fully in control of himself again.

Celeste stirred beside him, then moved to lie across his chest and plant small kisses on his heated skin. He stroked her back with a gentle hand, lost in recollection of their first years together. How wildly in love they had been; how certain that it would remain that way.

'You've always been at your best in the morning,' Celeste murmured against his shoulder, 'and you've just surpassed yourself, darling.'

Rod smiled reflectively, but said nothing. He did not care to spoil his drowsy happiness with conversation. A tap on the bedroom door disturbed it, however, because Celeste left him abruptly to wrap herself in a vivid kimono before jumping into her own bed just as the door opened to admit Lim with breakfast on a trolley.

'Velly good morning,' he greeted them cheerfully. 'Sun up, all light with the world.' He pushed the trolley between the two beds then crossed to fold back the shutters and prove his statement. Rod closed his eyes against sudden brightness, but Lim still addressed him. 'Doctor come home late. Not good. Missy say blekfast not too soon. Ten clock in bedloom. Doctor now leddy for eggbacon. Cookie make how you like. Make hot tea, toast. Thank you.'

The click of the door told Rod the boy had departed. Part of him longed to maintain his comatose state; the other was tempted by the smell of his favourite breakfast. Spoons clinked against saucers as tea was poured; then he heard the metallic ring of covers being removed from serving dishes.

'Come on, darling, you must be hungry after all that spent energy.' Celeste's tone was as honey-sweet as it could be when she was happy. Rod opened his eyes to meet a dazzling smile. She was beautiful enough for any man, with her black hair tousled, her eyes glowing with the aftermath of loving, and her full breasts pushing against the yellow and black silk kimono. Desire flared again briefly until she indicated a plate full of fried eggs and bacon beside a cup of steaming tea. Hunger triumphed over lust. Pulling on a bath-robe he sat on the side of his bed, facing her, while he buttered toast and began on his breakfast. They had not done this for months. He supposed the fault was mainly his. Too often a telephone call took him from bed, or he was on early duty, or it was his weekend to take the floating clinic to the islands. There were often times, of course, when Celeste had been partying until dawn and was hung-over all the next day, or she had arranged to join an early swimming party and departed before he awoke. They had been living separate lives since coming to Hong Kong. He had believed it must continue that way. Had Celeste finally realized where they were heading and decided to do something before it was too late?

Munching toast, he said, 'We should do this more often.'

'You're rarely here to do it,' she retorted, then softened her accusation by adding, 'but when you are, it's really something.'

'It used always to be like that.'

She wiped butter from the corner of her mouth with a flame-tipped finger, making even that gesture seem sensual. 'We were very young and hungry for each other. It was the only thing that mattered then.' She put down her knife and fork to give him a direct look. 'You qualified and became the world's great healer. That's when the rot set in.'

Some of the morning's pleasure faded as he sensed that

they could easily rake up bitterness again. 'Other women manage to accept their husband's profession.'

'They're not like you, sweetie. God's gift to medicine.' She averted danger by smiling in her most placatory fashion. 'Don't let's have a row and spoil everything. I want to enjoy today.'

He nodded, knowing something *had* gone from this morning, and attacked his breakfast again. 'So do I, after the rigours of last night. God knows how many were drowned.' A glance at her face told him he was off on his hobby-horse. 'Sorry.' He ate in silence for several moments, then said, 'I'm playing water polo this afternoon. Come and watch. We could go on from there to Repulse Bay and have dinner.'

'Will the bank balance stand it?'

'To hell with the bank balance. We haven't had a night out together for weeks.'

'Whose fault is that?'

He threw down his knife and fork. 'All right, let's forget it.'

Immediately contrite, she scrambled across to his bed and slung an arm around his neck, causing the kimono to gape and reveal one of her breasts still swollen from their lovemaking. 'We've grown so used to quarrels it's almost impossible to have a normal conversation. Of *course* we'll go to Repulse Bay for dinner, darling.'

He no longer wanted to. Even breakfast had lost its appeal. 'What's behind all this, Celeste? You're as wound up as a clockwork toy.'

She returned to her own bed and faced him, exuding such electric excitement he had again to admit that she was a superb creature when aroused.

'The most astonishing invitation came in yesterday's mail. I can still hardly believe it. I had to keep reading it in case it was a mistake. But it was there, clear as crystal. "Dr and Mrs R.J. Durman".' She giggled. 'I even searched the telephone book and rang all the medical centres asking if they had an R.J. Durman on their staff. Only then did I believe it really was for us. Sweetie, for once you've done us a good turn with your damned dedication.'

He had no idea what she was on about and said so. Celeste returned to his side, too elated to keep still, and kissed his mouth with insistent persuasion. 'You've clearly impressed him with your skill in some way. Thank you, darling. Thank you. Thank you.'

Each expression of gratitude was punctuated with a kiss, but he had lost all inclination of desire and put her away from him. 'Out with it. When you're in this state I know you're about to tell me something I won't like.'

Laughing, she pushed a hand through her hair and told him he was wrong. 'Not this time. You'll *love* it. It's our passport to where I've always wanted to be ... and it'll get you that place in Tropical Diseases. It's certain to. Oh, darling, I never dreamed your bloody profession would put us up there with the really big wigs. But it has, it has!'

Rod tried to make sense of her extravagant words. 'Calm down and put all of this into some form I can understand. What's all that about an invitation?'

She grabbed his hands, gazing at him with life fairly fizzing from her eyes. 'To the Chamber of Commerce ball. Sir Peter Channing would be delighted if Dr and Mrs Durman would join his party for dinner at Echoes before the ball.' She pumped their linked hands up and down to add weight to what she was saying. 'Rod, whatever it was you did to impress the man, I can't thank you enough. We'll never look back after this ... and I'm going to have the most sensational new dress for it. You'll get the recognition you want, and I ...' She laughed breathlessly. 'And I'll enjoy the swankiest of Hong Kong's social events. Delia Wright will be emerald with envy.'

Rod could hardly believe what she had said. It seemed totally out of character for Sarah to make such a move, yet only she could be responsible for the invitation. A secretary would have sent the cards out so it was unlikely that Sarah would know of Celeste's existence. To find out in such a manner would be particularly distressing for her ... and for himself. He released his hands, saying, 'We'll have to decline, I'm afraid. That sort of affair is right out of our league.'

Celeste's expression slowly hardened. 'What d'you mean, it's out of our league?'

He sighed. 'People who go to those events are knights or millionaires. We don't belong with them.'

'We will, after this.'

'No, Celeste.'

She got to her feet in fighting mood. 'Oh *yes*, Rod. We may never have another chance like this. I don't give a damn if they're knights, earls or even princes. I'm *me*. I've been invited to join them and I'm bloody well going to.' She tugged the belt tighter around her waist with a furious gesture. 'My God, how often have I heard you trot out your opinion that a coolie is as important as a magistrate? Well, I'm no coolie, sweetheart, but Sir Peter Channing and his fancy guests will welcome me with open arms.'

Rod stood to confront her. 'You know damn well that opinion refers to people in need of medical help. This is entirely different.'

'And about time! You've been working your guts out for no reward. Someone has finally noticed and means to give you a leg up. What did you do to impress the Channing bloke?'

It was difficult, so he hedged. 'Nothing. I've met him once, that's all.'

'When?'

'At a concert. We exchanged only a few words.'

Her eyes widened. 'You've never been a great orator. Those few words must have been sensational to prompt an invitation to dinner at his posh place on the mid-levels. Whatever did you say to him?'

'Good evening, so far as I recall.'

'Oh, come on, Rod,' she snapped.

'I was introduced to him by Sir Kingston Dailey, who had just roped me in for a crazy scheme he has concerning sampan colonies and epidemics. I suppose they continued discussing it after I left them . . . but there's nothing in that to prompt an invitation of this kind. There's only one explanation. Men like them flatter men like me when they want something. I'm doing more than enough already. That's why we're not going.'

'Yes, we are,' she contradicted fiercely. 'I posted an acceptance last night.'

*

Rod was prevented by an emergency at the Queen Mary from going to the Halburton on Friday, so all through the next day he prayed for another that would keep him from attending the ball. There was none and, in any case, Celeste declared that she would go on her own if he was called away to save lives. Her excitement had built during the week until he longed to shake some sense into her. He could hardly tell her *why* they had been invited to join a group of people certain to make the Durmans well aware of their true place in Hong Kong society. Celeste was unlikely to be jealous – she flirted enough herself – yet he hesitated to reveal Sarah's search for friendship to a woman who found no difficulty whatever in becoming part of any group. She would never understand artistic temperament, or the pain of loneliness.

There had been no choice but to hire a car and driver to take them up to Echoes and on to the hotel where the ball was to be held. It was no limousine, but expensive enough to make Rod wince when quoted the price. He dared not consider what it would cost him in drinks at the ball, buying rounds for Sir Peter's other guests. Celeste had spent several sessions with her dressmaker during the week. He had no notion what the dress would be like, but it was certain to cost more than any other she had. As he waited on the veranda in dinner jacket and stiff shirtfront, with a collar that rubbed his neck, gloom settled over him. This was what overtook a man old enough to know better, who fell victim to the oldest lure in the book. He should have left the girl to be driven home by her chauffeur, and thereafter forgotten her.

Lim came to tell him the car had arrived, so he went to hurry Celeste. Although he had no wish to be the first arrival, neither did he want to get there so late they drew unwelcome attention. When he walked in to the pink and white bedroom and saw his wife, he knew they would get it whatever time they arrived. The gleaming white dress fitted her like a second skin as far as her knees, then flared out in a froth of lace and diamanté around citrus-yellow shoes with spiky heels. Her back was bared by a deep vee plunging from neck to hips. Long citrus-yellow gloves reached beyond her elbows, and four-inch shimmering earrings echoed that vivid colour. A black crushed-velvet cloak lay across a chair beside a black moiré bag studded with diamanté. Rod took a deep breath. Never had Celeste's Italianate beauty been so apparent. She looked stunning, but it was a costume for an elaborate stage musical rather than the Chamber of Commerce ball.

She spun around, afire with excitement. 'What do you think?'

'It's every bit as sensational as you promised but you can't possibly wear it tonight,' he told her emphatically. 'As we're tight for time you'll have to make it snappy.'

'Make *what* snappy?'

'The change of dress.'

'I'm changing nothing.'

His temper flared. 'For God's sake, Celeste! These affairs are very formal. The women'll be pretty well covered up in frocks nowhere near as elaborate as that. They're sticky about convention and dress accordingly.'

Celeste's black eyes fired with anger. 'What you mean is that they're a parcel of frumps.'

'If that's how you care to interpret it.'

'Then I'll bloody well shake them up. Believe me, the Chamber of Commerce will get an injection of life tonight.' She picked up the cloak and bag as she spoke, then approached to confront him. 'If we're tight for time, hadn't we better get moving?'

'Yes, sure,' he replied, with the almost savage decision to let her make a fool of herself, if she was determined on it. He could rest assured that they would never receive another such invitation, and Sarah Channing would look elsewhere for a friend after tonight.

They were silent during the journey to Echoes, but Celeste could not help an exclamation on first seeing the house. As they entered, Sir Peter detached himself from a trio of men in expensive dinner jackets and came to greet them. Urbane and well practised in the social arts, the tall, slim banker could not entirely hide his reaction to the sensual young woman on his threshold. The lean face with its clipped moustache schooled itself swiftly, however, and a smile appeared on cue. 'Ah, Dr Durman. I'm glad your professional demands did not prevent your coming this evening.' He shook hands with Rod, then turned to Celeste with a hint of a bow. 'Mrs Durman, so good of you to come. Allow me to introduce you to Mrs Lord, who will see that you are served with a drink while you meet my other guests.'

A dark-haired woman in a striking gown of ebony crêpe highlighted by unusual jade jewellery appeared at Sir Peter's elbow but, despite her smile, she made no secret of her close scrutiny of Celeste as introductions were made. She led them into the room, saying, 'I imagine you're not already acquainted with Sir Peter's friends, Mrs Durman. They're all extremely cultured people, and I am afraid I had to guess what your interests might be when making the seating plan. I have put you next to Professor Colin Bragg, whose hobby is collecting butterflies. As an Australian, I thought you'd have a love of nature and outdoor life. You *are* Australian, aren't you?'

'That's right,' Celeste agreed sweetly. 'And what are you?'

Rod knew immediately that his wife was out to put down this woman who behaved as if she were Lady Channing, but Mrs Lord ignored the jibe and called one of the servants with trays of drinks.

Then she turned to Rod. 'I gather that you were introduced to Sir Peter at the charity concert, Doctor, which I hope means you have an interest in music. You'll be seated next to the Honourable Martha Clive at dinner. She's an expert on Indonesian flutes.'

The boy arrived with his tray and Rod took two glasses, handing one to his wife. 'I must tell her something about the Aboriginal didgeri-do. She'll find that fascinating.'

Mrs Lord smiled too widely. 'Do let me introduce you to Judge and Mrs Arthur. They've visited Australia on several occasions, so you'll have something in common.'

As she led the way towards a group of four elderly people, Rod saw Sarah standing silently in a circle of chattering younger guests. At that moment she turned her head and caught sight of him. His worst fears were realized when her expression revealed her delight far too clearly. She left the group and came forward glowing with an intimacy that betrayed the stage their relationship had reached. Even as he condemned himself, Rod responded to her appeal yet again.

Ten feet from him, Sarah noticed Celeste at his side. Her sense of shock was evident, but she could not alter direction without creating the speculation she must avoid. Mrs Lord compounded the situation by drawing Sarah forward.

'I believe you know Sir Peter's daughter, Doctor. Does your wife?'

'I haven't had the pleasure,' Celeste murmured silkily, as she took in Sarah's pale face and shocked eyes. 'I imagine you're one of Rod's patients, Miss Channing. You don't look at all well.'

Avoiding Rod's eyes, Sarah came forward slowly with hand outstretched. 'How do you do, Mrs Durman. I'm quite well, thank you. Your husband and I met at the Halburton Clinic, where I work in the office one day a week. We both feel it's important to do something useful.'

Rod was impressed. Shades of the renowned Ellie! It was a hell of a situation, yet she was handling it with classic dignity, her cool English voice and manner, the simple dress in chartreuse shot silk, her lack of ostentation contrasting sharply with Celeste's vibrant, vivid presence. He thought of the cool clarity of moonlight after the beating force of the sun, and yearned for the tranquillity Sarah radiated.

'How commendable,' purred Celeste, glancing swiftly at Rod before turning her attention back to Sarah. 'But you really shouldn't let it wear you out. Rod comes home whacked on so many occasions and falls straight into bed. He has no *fun*. I thought he'd forgotten how to enjoy himself . . . but perhaps I'm wrong. Do you get much work done at the Halburton, Miss Channing?'

'A great deal, Mrs Durman, but nowhere near as much as you must have to cope with. The wife of the doctor in my home village said his profession was just as much hers, because she barely had time for a life of her own. That must be doubly applicable out here.'

Celeste merely smiled. 'And what do *you* do on the six days you *don't* go to the clinic?'

Rod spoke quickly. 'Miss Channing is training to become

a professional classical pianist. She needs to practise for long hours every day.'

Celeste turned her dark, calculating glance on him. 'Mrs Lord should have sat you two together tonight. You could have talked about those old records of symphonies you've dug out recently and play *ad infinitum*.' She faced the hostess who had witnessed the little scene without interrupting. 'What a shame Sir Peter's daughter didn't tell you Rod's interest in music lies more in pianos than flutes. It would have saved all that worry over the seating plan.'

Mrs Lord was a match for anything, apparently. 'It would certainly have been easier had I known more about your husband, Mrs Durman ... and I would have moved you from the side of Professor Bragg and put you next to Ramsay Knight of the Diplomatic Corps. Now, do let me introduce you to the Judge and his wife.'

Throughout the next two hours Rod covertly watched Sarah. Conversation appeared to flow around rather than to her, but her quietness appealed to him as much as her grace of movement. He recalled the elegance of her arms and body whilst playing the Rachmaninov, and his thoughts lingered on her composure this evening when confronting Celeste's spicy attack: a surprisingly swift recovery from initial shock on realizing the truth. Not once did she glance his way, so it was impossible to judge her mood. Her background stood her in good stead this evening. Celeste, in a similar situation, would have created a scene leaving no one in ignorance of a potential subject for gossip. He must try to take Sarah aside later in the evening to offer her an explanation. It would be difficult, but he could not leave things as they were.

During the short drive to the hotel from Echoes, Celeste talked incessantly about the rather sweet fuddy-duddies she had charmed, to the annoyance of the laced-corset brigade around them. During dinner, she had learned that Olivia Lord had been married to Sir Peter's accountant and that she now arranged the banker's social calendar as well as acting hostess at Echoes.

'It all sounds very fishy to me,' she added, 'although the dear old gents didn't hint at hanky-panky between the black widow and that cold fish Channing. She's sure not what she makes out to be, take my word on it. I can spot a hundred-carat bitch a mile off, and she's one. Mrs Lord is no lady, but she badly wants to be.' Taking her compact from the black bag, Celeste powdered her nose with the aid of its mirror. 'That girl hasn't been out here long – but I expect you already know – and people expected her to take over from our Olivia. You can see why she didn't, can't you? That woman could eat her for breakfast, and she's probably got Daddy on a tight rein too.' Pausing to put away the compact, she then said, 'You never told me you had that girl working at the clinic.'

'Whenever I talk about my work you walk away yawning, or start a row,' he reminded her stiffly.

'If I didn't know only too well that your reputation means the sun and moon to you, I'd warn you to watch your step. Little Miss Muffet has a crush on you. Oh, don't look so innocent! It stands out a mile. You are the saviour of suffering humanity – something you both agree on absolutely – and she's at the impressionable age. That you're also a sexual knockout completes the impact on a schoolgirl straight from an English convent.' She sighed contentedly. 'Life's a bitch, and she'll learn the way we all did. Thank God I'm past the stage of worshipping imaginary heroes! Love 'em all a little and yourself the best, is my motto. Life's too short for self-sacrificial passion. Look where it got us.'

'There's never been much self-sacrifice on your part,' Rod said bitterly, glad the driver was shut off by a partition. 'Sarah has the wrong idea about the life of *this* doctor's wife.'

'Sarah? So you know her that well, do you?' Her eyes narrowed speculatively. 'Watch it, Rod, or you could make a bloody fool of yourself and lose all you value so much.'

He was now angry enough to rise to her bait. 'Don't judge me by those amoral pranksters you spend so much time with. If I were the type to play around, I'd have been struck off long ago.'

She smiled maddeningly. 'Maybe the temptation has never been there before. But I'd be most put out if you succumbed to the pale prune-in-the-mouth Sarah, sweetie. If you're going to ruin yourself, think of my pride and pick someone of my calibre.'

Their car swept into the hotel entrance behind that of Judge and Mrs Arthur, who hurried inside on seeing them. Celeste laughed as she gathered her cloak around her ready to get out. 'Another saucy devil being dragged away from me! Isn't it a hoot? Oh, I *am* enjoying myself.'

There was no doubt that she was. Immune to veiled disapproval, Celeste was sailing through the evening like a fast tea clipper amidst traditional junks. Her entrance was as effective as she had hoped. Those already in the ballroom nudged each other and nodded in Celeste's direction as Sir Peter conducted his party to the tables reserved for them at the far end of the ballroom. The band was playing a quick step, and those couples on the dance floor glanced over their shoulders to watch the progress of the new arrivals. Rod's surmise had been correct. Even the younger women present wore the type of dresses favoured by Australia's élite in photographs of the Melbourne Cup ball. Many of the younger men, however, could not take their attention from a sight they greatly appreciated. Rod had once revelled in other men's envy. Now it left him curiously uncomfortable.

For more than an hour, Rod shunted around the dance floor a succession of women whose manners were as stiff as the corsets he felt beneath his right hand. Sarah had pointedly ignored him throughout, and he decided it was time he abandoned social duty to put things right between them. People must have noticed her attitude and started to speculate. The music began again so Rod advanced with determination, interrupting a conversation between Sarah and the flute expert to invite her to dance. She coloured faintly, but he stood his ground as she looked set to refuse.

'You've partnered everyone else, Miss Channing, and so have I.'

His message got through to her, and she walked with him to the dance floor.

'I'm not a very good dancer.'

'That makes two of us,' he said, taking her in his arms.

Her uncorseted body was firm and warm beneath his hand; her hair shining and scented like gardenias. He drew

102

her closer, realized what he was doing, then held her away again. She was physically resistant and kept her gaze on a point beyond his head. They must be creating more speculation now than *not* dancing together. It was impossible to say what he must. The band was too loud and bouncy, and they were too noticeable out there beneath the bright lights.

'Would you mind sitting this one out?' he asked.

'No, I'd be delighted.' She moved from his hold immediately, and made for the seat she had just vacated.

He was not having that. Seizing her elbow he led her with deliberation towards the doors to the terrace, schooling his expression to one of normal sociability as he said firmly, 'I think we should talk and outside is the best place for that. After inviting me here, your other guests will soon catch on to your deliberate avoidance of any contact between us and start speculating. Neither of us wants that.'

They broke through to a broad lamplit area where a tall fountain in the gardens beyond rose in a shower of shimmering drops gilded by the lights. Coolness wafted to them as they reached the balustrade, but the noise of the cascading water was muted by the vivid night and provided a soothing background harmony. He released her. 'This is much better, isn't it?'

Putting several feet between them, Sarah said coldly, 'I would never have presumed upon our slight acquaintance to invite you to Echoes, I assure you.'

Rod then knew she was deeply hurt, and he was angry with Celeste for putting them both in this difficult position. As a result, he spoke vigorously. 'Don't put on that aloof English pose with me, or we'll get nowhere!'

Suddenly passionate, she said, 'I don't need your bedside manner, Dr Durman. A few minutes' first aid after the concert, plus a visit to your Chinese friend, doesn't entitle you to know everything I think and feel. Right now, it's probably as well you don't.'

'Oh, really?' he retorted sharply. 'Maybe it would do me good to hear your opinions. I might then understand what's going on here tonight.'

'I don't know what you mean.'

'Think about it! The only time I met your father was at

103

the concert. I'm not big-headed enough to imagine that brief encounter created such a favourable impression he couldn't wait to put me on his list of close acquaintances. If you didn't send the invitation, who did – and why?'

'I've no idea.'

They stood facing each other, knowing anger was their only defence against what they truly felt. Rod recovered quicker than she. He sighed. 'Look, I'm sorry this has happened. I'm only here because Celeste accepted the invitation before telling me. She threatened to come alone if I cried off.'

'I see.' She turned away, and it was a moment or two before she said, 'It never occurred to me that you might be . . . well, I suppose I just didn't think. It was something of a shock when I saw you together. There's no reason why you should have mentioned that you were married, of course, but some of the things I said that day now seem very embarrassing.'

'I'm not easily embarrassed.' He drew her to a corner of the terrace away from a couple who had come to stand just a few yards from them.

She waited for him to continue, her face highlighted by moonlight against the darkness of trees beyond the terrace, her fine hair gently ruffled by the movement of air created by the surging waters of the fountain. He was hopelessly charmed.

'It's not what you must think, Sarah. I don't make a habit of this kind of thing.'

'What kind of thing?' She was not making it easy for him.

He tried again. 'You charmed me with Rachmaninov when everything seemed to be falling apart around me. I was immensely grateful for that. I believed I invited you to visit Wang Chua in an attempt to help you, in return. You were well aware of what happened on that hill. I wasn't prepared for it. That's why I've handled the situation so badly.'

She was looking at him in a way that undermined his determination, but he battled on. 'I tried to cool the atmosphere before I dropped you at Echoes, then made sure we didn't bump into each other at the Halburton.' He gave a faint rueful smile. 'I told you I don't normally go around mucking up people's lives. If I did, I'd have known the plan would end in catastrophe.'

She moved closer. 'I'm not absolutely sure what you're trying to tell me, but I think it explains your sudden change of mood that day. I was afraid it was something I'd said or done.'

'It was. You'd highlighted the danger of where we were heading. I should have told you there and then that I'm a thirty-year-old married cynic in a demanding profession, and that you're a sensitive romantic with a brilliant musical career ahead. It's impossible for us to be friends, much less . . . anything else. I'm more sorry than I can say that I was the handy doctor when you almost passed out at the concert.'

'I'm not,' she told him softly. 'I'll never forget that enchanted garden on top of a hill.'

'You must, Sarah,' he insisted, longing to touch her, take her hand. 'In a place like Hong Kong it's all too easy to let these things happen, but they don't bring lasting happiness and it would ruin us both, in the long run.'

'I know. You must be careful about your private life,' she said, with the frankness he so admired. 'Dr Barnes is twice your age, but there were whispers concerning the number of times he gave a lift to the butcher's schoolgirl daughter. No one else was able to run a car due to petrol rationing, and it's a three-mile walk to the village school. The gossips preferred to forget that he also offered lifts to a number of villagers, including Ellie.'

Rod hardly knew how to follow that. This was not a parallel case. He was not taking all and sundry on excursions to his Chinese friend, and Sarah was no village schoolgirl. As he stood there continuing to acknowledge something he should deny, Sarah said, 'I'll change my day at the Halburton, if that would help.'

'That's not necessary,' he replied swiftly. 'The help you give there is more important than any other consideration. This is a small island, so we're likely to meet up occasionally. As we move in different social circles it won't be too often. This kind of evening won't happen again, Sarah.'

She turned to gaze at the fountain for a moment, then

said, 'I'm sorry I behaved so badly earlier. When I saw her with you I could hardly take in the implications, and I thought . . .'

'I know damn well what you thought! There are too many married men out here doing what they shouldn't with any available girl.'

She turned back swiftly. 'That constituted the greatest shock. I couldn't believe it of you, and yet –'

A voice broke across her words to say, in lazy cultured tones, 'Ah, finally tracked you down! I've been looking everywhere to ask you for a dance.'

Rod swung round to find an immensely attractive young man standing a few feet away. Slim, elegant, blue-eyed and blond, he looked the epitome of every adolescent girl's dream. Yet closer study highlighted dark circles beneath those boyish eyes, lines of bitterness tugging at the mouth, and a twitching muscle in his jaw. Rod recognized the same signs of mounting stress he had seen in himself on the night of the concert. But this product of wealth and privilege was more likely to be driving himself into the ground with social excesses than with overwork.

Sarah was very obviously shaken by the interruption. 'I've been out here for the length of a waltz, that's all. How is it you didn't have a partner for it?'

The man offered a smile that would have been charming if it had not held a touch of cynicism. 'Most of the women are built like battleships, and the belle of the ball is so closely surrounded a fellow can scarcely get a foot in.' He looked at Rod. 'Your wife has pepped up this dreary annual affair and injected some pizazz into it. You're a lucky man.'

Sarah said coldly, 'We were just discussing how some people like to be unpleasant whenever they have the chance. Do you count yourself among them?'

The man laughed. 'Not *all* the time . . . but it's far more amusing than going around wearing a halo and saying all the right things.' He offered his hand to Rod. 'I'm Alex Tennant.'

His grip was surprisingly strong for such a languid personality, Rod thought. 'The name's Durman. I am a doctor.'

'How very commendable! Miss Channing is a great admirer of industry . . . but I expect you already know that.'

'I know she puts in a lot of time perfecting what is already a remarkable talent. I was lucky enough to hear her performance of Rachmaninov's Second a few weeks ago. Were you there?'

'Cole Porter's more in my line. I heard her play a piece by Liszt at Echoes recently. I think it was that day you gave her a lift home after being detained at the Halburton.' He brushed away a fluttering moth attracted by a nearby lamp. 'I understand you also work at the clinic.'

It was then that Rod realized this suave young man was sharper than his appearance suggested. Like the hapless Barnes in a Cotswold village, he was being told that he had been caught out with a young girl.

'Where do *you* work, Tennant?'

Leaning negligently against the stonework, Alex took out a gold cigarette-case to offer Rod. 'No? However do you keep going without nicotine?' He lit a de Reske and pocketed the gold engraved box. 'I go almost every day to the offices of Frobisher–Jay, but you know the words of Count Danilo in *The Merry Widow.*' He began to sing in a reasonable tenor:

> I'm seated at my desk by one
> Among the urgent files galore.
> A little furtive drinking done,
> I'm back at home for drinks at four.

Rod studied him shrewdly. 'You have no interest in shipping?'

'None whatever.'

'Why not change to something else?'

Alex smiled lazily. 'And ruin a very pleasant routine?'

'You'll ruin your health if you're not careful. I suggest you have a check-up with your doctor pretty soon. He'll tell you to concentrate more on shipping and less on sipping.'

Tapping ash from his cigarette, Alex looked from Rod to Sarah and back again. 'So you're holding surgery out here, dispensing medical advice to Miss Channing. And there was I thinking all manner of things. Shame on me!'

Rod's volatile temper rose. 'I don't like your attitude, Tennant.'

'Ah, that's more like it, Doc,' said Alex, straightening. 'An

Australian who preaches against drink seemed highly suspect. Now you look ready to punch me on the nose, I feel reassured. But you should consult a colleague about that temper of yours. It could get you into trouble in high-class company like this.'

Rod turned to Sarah who was looking even paler than usual. 'Perhaps you'd like to go inside while I sort out this man's problem.'

'His only problem is the determination to continue making a mess of his life,' she said. 'If he can ridicule any worthwhile person he meets along the way, the happier he'll be.' Giving Alex a contemptuous look, she began walking away. 'And to think young men at home are dying in order to make the world safe for people like him!'

Rod stepped into his path as Alex made to follow her. 'Let's get a few things straight, shall we?'

'I don't think so.'

'I *do*.'

The other man was watching Sarah with a surprising suggestion of regret.

Rod put two and two together and found the result unwelcome. The fact that he should not fanned his anger. 'She made pretty plain her opinion of you. I suggest you keep clear of her for the rest of the evening.'

'Is that your professional advice?' Alex asked with slightly less poise.

'It's man-to-man advice, Tennant. There are enough women in Hong Kong willing to pander to your vanity without making a nuisance of yourself with Sarah Channing.'

'Are you speaking as her doctor, or as an interested party?'

Rod ignored that and launched a full attack. 'I've met idle bastards like you before, and they all end up destroying themselves. As a doctor, I have to put personal feelings aside and treat as equals all those who need my help. I meant what I said a moment ago. You're heading for a breakdown. For God's sake pull yourself together before it's too late ... and find for amusement a woman who likes Cole Porter.'

'And leave the way clear for you?' Alex asked, with what

seemed almost to be genuine anger. 'You're well out of line *and* depth with Channing's daughter. Apart from professional misconduct hovering in the background, you've a wife who's pretty much your social level. Just because you can't control her, you've no right to look among your peers for consolation. There are numerous whores to provide that, and you're in a position to know which are listed as safe.'

Holding on to his control with difficulty, Rod gave his parting shot. 'Contrary to your impressions of Australians, we don't knock down everyone we don't like. As you said, this is high-class company, so I'll leave that pleasure to another well-dressed well-spoken pretty-boy like yourself. I hope you hit the ground at a hundred miles an hour, and I hope I'm called out to deal with what remains of you.'

Knowing he could take no more of an event he had hoped to avoid, Rod re-entered the ballroom to collect Celeste and leave. He could not miss her. She was in the centre of a group of younger men urging one of their number to imitate Rudolph Valentino in the tango that had just been announced. Celeste, a wonderfully sensual dancer, was seeking an extrovert partner for the number which was certain to make any eyes that had not popped do so now. Rod crossed quickly to prevent the final straw in a difficult evening. His wife looked up at him in delight.

'Sweetie, you're just in time to watch this. Miles is rather bashful but they say he's sensational in the tango.'

He ignored the enthusiastic circle around her. 'We're leaving, Celeste. Get your cloak and we'll say our thanks to Sir Peter.'

'I can't,' she said firmly. 'I've promised to show them how the tango *should* be danced.'

'Another time,' he insisted through clenched teeth.

Celeste was no meek wife used to doing a husband's bidding. He was rarely with her when she was enjoying herself, anyway, and tonight was a highlight for her. Flushed with excitement and wine, although well in control of herself, she simply refused to do as he wanted. 'I want to stay. My friends want me to stay. Don't you?' she demanded of those encircling her, and received a chorus of yeses. 'You go home, Rod, or to the hospital, or wherever. Send the driver back for me.'

She turned to her blushing prospective partner and the laughter began again. Short of dragging her off like a caveman choosing a mate there was nothing Rod could do. With the first notes of the tango in his ears, he headed for the bar and a couple of double whiskies to calm him down. It was hot, crowded and noisy in the long, narrow room, but he pushed his way to the counter and ordered both whiskies, slamming the money down on the polished surface to relieve some of his anger. The recent escape from stress had come to an end tonight. He was as taut as a bow-string. The second drink did nothing to relax him, and a shout of wild laughter from the ballroom tightened his nerves further. He was about to order a third whisky when a hand fell on his arm. Through the smoke haze he saw Sir Peter smiling at him. The man's urbanity seemed unbearably irritating.

'Ah, Durman, guessed I might find you here,' he said in soothing tones. 'Wanted a quiet word with you.'

'You won't get it here,' Rod pointed out. 'The volume of everyone's voice rises by the minute.'

'Mmm, it's rather noisy, I grant you. Perhaps we could step out to the vestibule.'

Rod followed him through the red-nosed throng, then beyond the heavy glass doors leading to the comparative peace of the potted-palm-dotted entrance to this famous old hotel which had been patronized by so many giants of colonial growth over the past hundred years. Various thoughts went through Rod's mind about the subject of this quiet word. Surely not a 'hands off' concerning Sarah. There was no justification for that. A caution about Celeste's behaviour? No, Channing was too lofty to indulge in such a thing. Medical advice? More probable. Perhaps something he preferred not to discuss with his own doctor.

Sir Peter came to the point without preamble once they stopped beside a tall palm. 'You took my daughter on a visit to Wang Chua's remote stronghold recently.'

Rod frowned. 'Yes, I did. She knows very little about the ethnic side of the colony, so I thought she'd find it interesting.'

'Yes, doubtless, but I confess I was astonished when she spoke of her visit. The old reprobate has refused a meeting with me on numerous occasions. Claims to have retired from the business world and become a recluse.'

'So he has,' Rod told him, wondering what this was all about. 'His many offspring are running the House of Wang now. The old man must be well into his eighties, you know.'

The irritating smile reappeared. 'But still has his fingers on the pulse of their enterprises.'

'Undoubtedly.'

'That's why I wanted a word with you.' Sir Peter paused while a couple in evening dress crossed the mosaic floor towards the lift. 'Sarah said she was given an audience because you introduced her as your friend. She also claimed Wang Chua is under an obligation to you.'

'I treated his great-grandson after an accident.'

Sir Peter nodded. 'A *heavy* obligation. The thing is this, Durman. The bank has been after some of his assets for a long time. One of our clients is very keen to acquire them – at an attractive commission. I'm certain he could be persuaded to let them go if I laid the conditions before him in person. All my written messages have been ignored, and it's impossible to call on him uninvited because he is surrounded by guards. Now, if you were to be my go-between, introduce me as one of your friends – he has met my daughter, and received her most graciously – I could tie up the deal to everyone's benefit in a very short time.' He laid a hand on Rod's shoulder. 'I'd make it worth your while, naturally.'

Rod's ethical hackles rose alarmingly. Now he had the reason for the invitation. Flatter a nobody who can get something previously out of reach, then bribe him with promises of money or position to do exactly what you want. He saw red and turned on his devious host.

'My God, you people stop at nothing, do you! Did you really imagine this shindig would make me putty in your hands? Is your head so far in the executive clouds you see everyone in your own image? Wang Chua is a respected and valued friend. I'd never consider betraying his trust so that you can indulge in business skulduggery. You've got the wrong man, Channing. I may be on the bottom rung but you can keep your reward for treachery. I can't be bought.'

Chapter Five

During the next six weeks the Durmans were inundated with invitations from members of Hong Kong's élite. Cocktails, beach picnics, garden parties, exclusive lunches and high jinks at Happy Valley racecourse were all available for Rod and Celeste to enjoy. He was astounded, but Celeste saw their sudden popularity as proof of her claim that the Channing invitation would open doors previously closed to them. She seized every opportunity offered. Never had her beauty been so marked by total happiness, her vivacity so primed by elation.

Celeste was rarely at home. Rod passed his wife as he entered, and she left the apartment dressed in expensive clothes he had not seen before. She no longer cared that his work mainly prevented his accompanying her. There was always Monty or Giles or Randy or Alex to substitute as a partner. His query confirmed that the Alex referred to was the same he had clashed with on the terrace with Sarah, but Celeste was canny enough to need no warning about men like him.

It was a particularly unsettling period for Rod. Concern over this unwelcome development was balanced by relief at his wife's absence as the date of the selection board advanced. Despite Sir Kingston's guarded suggestion that the post was certain to be his, Rod resumed his study of the subject in the solitude of an empty apartment. He had initially been constantly interrupted by telephone calls from Celeste's former playmates, but they soon caught on to the fact that they had been superseded and left him in peace.

The peace was misleading. It was around but not within him. He had walked out on Sir Peter Channing and still deeply resented the way that the man had cashed in on that impulsive decision to take Sarah on the visit to Wang Chua. Certain she knew nothing of her father's calculated attempt to coax the old man into selling assets coveted by a client willing to pay Channing Mercantile a highly lucrative commission, Rod felt that her innocence had been exploited. He now had double the regret over taking her to that hilltop retreat. Alex Tennant's interruption at the ball had left the situation with Sarah up in the air. Yet what else could have been said that night concerning a dangerous attraction he must determinedly crush? Small wonder inner peace was elusive.

Fate intervened to undermine his determination. He met Sarah on three consecutive Fridays, despite his vow to avoid her. On the first occasion she entered the building somewhat breathless, practically cannoning into him as he came from his office at the clinic. He steadied her with hands on her arms, delighted with the flesh contact.

'I know I said we'd be certain to bump into each other, but you've taken my words too literally.'

She laughed, suddenly radiant. 'I'm late for work. Our new chauffeur must tell the time by the sun. When it's cloudy, he's all at sea.'

Seeing her again reminded him of that cool, soothing quality he found so beckoning. In a dress of peppermint green linen with touches of white, she looked youthful, fresh and unbearably out of reach. 'My prescription for what ails you will cost you nothing, madam. Learn to drive the car yourself. We didn't have chauffeurs in the Outback.'

The smile in her eyes faded as she asked, 'How are you, Rod?'

'Busy. What about you?'

Her hand pushed silky hair back with a graceful movement. 'The same. I've had a stroke of luck and found someone to give me tuition. It's *so* important. Practice is all very well, but unless I have the benefit of advice from someone with greater experience I can't grow as a pianist.' Her smile returned. 'You look bemused. The practitioner

113

trying to understand the artist. You seek a second opinion sometimes, don't you? It's the same thing.'

Knowing he should cut the conversation short, he ignored better judgement and said, 'A good simile. I'm glad you've found help – but here, in Hong Kong? It's hardly a cultural centre. Who is this person experienced enough to advise the brilliant Sarah Channing?'

'Thanks,' she said softly. 'I know that's no throw-away compliment. You're one of the few sincere people out here. My tutor is an elderly Dutch gem-merchant forced to abandon his distinguished career as a concert pianist after an accident to his hands. His name is Jakob Myburgh. He lives in the same apartment block as Olivia and I'm very annoyed with her for not telling me about him when she knew I was desperate for tuition.'

A picture of the supercilious Mrs Lord entered Rod's mind. 'A very self-absorbed woman, that. Not the type to do anyone a good turn unless there's a reward attached to it. So how did you hear about the old man?'

'Alex Tennant lives in the neighbouring apartment. I happened to mention the subject and he arranged a meeting very quickly.'

'*Tennant!*' he said sharply. 'I thought you hated the hide of that poisonous layabout.'

Her eyes widened with surprise at his vehemence. 'I've never had much time for him, but I've been practising what you preached and trying to adopt a more generous attitude when he approached me. What good advice you gave! It was worth the effort.'

'I wouldn't trust him too far, if I were you,' Rod warned, annoyed by his own reaction to her words. He had no right to be jealous of any man free to enjoy friendship with Sarah.

'Don't worry,' she replied, with obvious understanding. 'I have no intention of encouraging his company. But I'm grateful for his introduction to someone who enjoys our musical classes as much as I do.' When a door was opened along the corridor, she stepped away from him swiftly, saying, 'Marion will think I'm never coming. I'm later than ever now.'

'Look after yourself,' he said. 'Musicians are vulnerable in a place like Hong Kong.'

'Yes ... aren't they,' she breathed, everything about her telling him something he ought not to rejoice over as he turned away towards the main part of the clinic, where a colleague was heading.

The second time he met Sarah on her day at the Halburton they were forced to exchange polite conversation for the benefit of the red-haired Marion, whose husband had come to collect her at the end of the afternoon and stayed to chat with Sarah. They discussed the inadequacy of the Royal Naval presence in Hong Kong, then the failure on almost all fronts of the war against Germany. Marion soon tired of depressing topics and, clearly anxious to drag her personable husband off to domestic togetherness, brought the foursome to an end without much finesse. Left alone, Rod and Sarah could say little due to the general departure of the permanent clinic staff who called loudly to each other in Chinese as they walked to the village of Stanley. Rod asked how the musical tuition was going; Sarah enquired about the progress of Sir Kingston Dailey's plan to monitor sampan dwellers. After she had described a particularly hectic session with the temperamental Jakob Myburgh, and he had recounted how Sir Kingston's many 'volunteers' had been unanimous in voting the scheme unworkable, they were conspicuously alone in the car park and reluctantly departed.

On the next Friday they spent an hour together with others at a general staff meeting. Rod found it curiously difficult to concentrate on what was an important discussion, when Sarah was sitting with a notebook taking down every word he said. All they managed that day was a formal greeting, and comments on how hot it was for the patients when the breeze off the sea dropped. After the meeting dispersed they walked together through the corridor, almost touching, but two people following them made personal conversation impossible.

In his saner moments Rod knew he should arrange to change his Friday duty, but he had never put his personal life before his professional one and would not do so now. As time passed, the impact of each meeting would lessen, until they could face each other unemotionally. Nonsense was made of that belief when, after no sight of each other for several weeks, they came face to face in Queen's Road. Sarah was leaving the building where she gave lessons to children sponsored by the Anglo-Chinese arts charity, and he was entering it for a meeting on how best to improve the Island's water supply strained to the limit by the refugees who were continuing to steal across the border from Japanese occupation and oppression.

Rod climbed from a rickshaw at the foot of the steps and looked up to see Sarah coming down them, with an expression of such vivacity it would be clear to anyone watching her, as he was, that this was no meeting of mere acquaintances.

'Whatever are you doing here?' she asked, coming to a halt one step up from him.

'I could ask the same of you.' He found it strange to have her almost eye to eye. 'Why aren't you at home practising scales?'

Her smile was wide and delighted. 'What a greeting! I swear you growl only to support your reputation for eating people alive. It doesn't impress me. I know the real Rod Durman.'

'Do you?'

She was instantly serious, searching his face with a questioning gaze. 'Don't I?'

'I played my recording of Rachmaninov's Second last night, but the soloist is less sensitive than you in several of the more romantic passages,' he told her, enjoying the way shadows of palm fronds played over her face and bare arms as the breeze touched them. 'I shall never forget going to sleep as a Chinese boy recited poems that didn't rhyme, and waking to discover a girl in blue weaving magic I'd forgotten existed.'

'And I'll never forget standing with you in an enchanted garden on top of a hill.'

'Perhaps you should.'

'Can you?'

There was only one answer to that and she already knew it. He veered away from it by attempting to diffuse the personal element in their words. 'Wang Chua hasn't fol-

116

lowed your example in taking my advice, by the way. The Triads issued another warning last week. His first son's house was burnt to the ground. By luck or mistiming, no one was in it.'

She frowned. 'Poor Mr Wang. What a terrible choice to be forced to make. I suppose he must surrender eventually, but I share his belief in putting up a fight against those who use threats. We have to stand by our right to personal freedom.'

He studied her gentle features, that betrayed ancestry far different from his own, and her slender figure in a tailored dress of lilac and cream. It was all easy on his eye and spirit. 'You're a fraud, Miss Channing,' he said softly. 'You came at me like a sweet, romantic dreamgirl but underneath you're a real tough nut.'

'And you came at me like an unchained beast, when you're really a dedicated, gentle, caring man unaware of the impact you make on those around you.'

They were back to the impossible again, having made what amounted to veiled declarations of their deep feeling for each other. There, on a flight of white stone steps in the heart of Victoria, with well-dressed citizens passing them in ascent or descent, and with occupied rickshaws bowling along the dusty road, they would soon attract speculative eyes reading into their prolonged intense interest in each other a truth that could damage them both.

'Sarah, there's no future in this,' he said quietly. 'We agreed on that at the ball.'

'I know,' she sighed. 'Perhaps I really should change my day at the Halburton.'

'And also never go out in case we meet?'

'Then what do you suggest?'

'How the hell do I know? Deeper concentration on our professional interests ... and a swift end to this meeting before tongues start wagging.' He mounted the step to stand beside her. 'Take care of yourself, and don't become too tolerant of that bloke Tennant.'

He ran up the remainder of the flight but could not resist turning at the top. She was standing beside a chauffeur-driven car, looking up at him. They made no gesture of farewell, but he turned away in the belief that they would behave like passing acquaintances from now on.

Because of pre-occupation with his work and deepening frustration over a love that was out of reach, Rod was hardly aware of the change in Celeste. Her zest had acquired an edge of wildness; her flamboyance was almost out of hand. The stores she now patronized were happy to extend credit to a beautiful woman who paraded their most sensational merchandise in all the right venues. To such customers accounts were sent half-yearly, so the Durman bank account did not reflect their financial situation.

One evening, when Rod yet again returned to an empty apartment filled with the essence of French perfume, it struck him that he and Celeste were still leading separate lives but had reached the stage of no longer caring. How could they continue a marriage in which neither gave to or expected to receive anything from the other? Three months ago that might have suited him very well. Tonight, it highlighted the loneliness he had experienced since meeting Sarah. Instead of studying, he sat on the veranda drinking, wondering what to do about his future.

Lim came to him after a while, soft-footed and solicitous. 'You want eat something, Doctor? Not good sit in dark all alone, not have dinner. Cookie make chicken vegables. Keep hot, wait you call me serve. Have now? You leddy eat dinner?'

Rod left his seat and walked inside with an empty glass. Too much alcohol on an empty stomach had made him maudlin. The first priority was to secure the Tropical Diseases post, which would give his professional status a valuable boost, then tackle his difficult private life. He put a hand on the boy's shoulder. 'You're a good lad. I'll have dinner now, but no fuss over serving it. I'll be looking at my books while I eat.'

The Chinese was affronted. No servant of any standing would serve dinner in less than immaculate style.

Rod recognized his slip and gave a weary smile. 'All right, Lim, go ahead and serve dinner with your usual excellence. The books can wait.'

He did not study that evening. After a solitary dinner, he

returned to the veranda with his troubled thoughts. Resolution was repeatedly blurred by memories of Sarah and he was still undecided when he finally turned in alone.

An ageing Anglo-Portuguese doctor known for a successful research programme on bacteria was chosen by the board members to fill the vacant post in the Department of Tropical Diseases. Rod was stunned. He heard the news with a disbelief that was swiftly followed by a sense of failure deeper than he had ever known. His interview had gone very well; he had answered correctly all the questions they had thrown at him. Sir Kingston had been unwilling to meet his gaze even during direct questioning, but Rod had put that down to discretion. Now he knew why the old devil had felt awkward in his presence. The decision had clearly been made before the interviews, and Sir Kingston had been forced to go along with it. What had occurred to change everything? Short of tackling the consultant – which was out of the question – he would never know. The third applicant shrugged his shoulders and claimed that it was not the end of the world, but Rod knew it was the end of his hopes. There would be no second chance of it in Hong Kong.

For the very first time in his professional career Rod considered giving up medicine. Celeste was right. He worked his guts out for the minimum financial reward, then gained no academic ones. He was in a fool's game and would be better off raising sheep with his brother at Dalgara. Anger built inside him until he could contain it no longer. Tugging off his white coat, he left the hospital and took off in his car through the centre of Victoria. There would be no consolation in an empty apartment. He could not go to Sarah, so he headed for the place she had visited with him. The hill was wreathed in mist after two days of heavy rain, but the warmth of her presence would still be there. He also hoped Wang Chua would have heard, perhaps through his mysterious channels of communication, what had gone wrong today.

The atmosphere at Echoes was oppressive. Despite circling

fans the rooms seemed stifling in a midday temperature in the top nineties. Humidity was high, making the heat more difficult to bear; mist had descended as far as the mid-levels to hang in the clefts and valleys, adding to the gloom.

After two hours of determined practice on the second movement of Tchaikovsky's Piano Concerto in B flat, Sarah was glad to close the lid over the keys and go to her room to change for lunch. Her loose cotton dress stuck to her back, strands of hair clung to her damp face and neck, her body ached and her head felt as if it were stuffed with rags. She was reasonably pleased with her progress on the test piece Jakob Myburgh had given her, but throughout her practice period she had competed with the roar of water down the ravine. It was quite as deafening as she had been told, and she had heard her own performance as if it were a sound at the end of a long tunnel. At a more advanced stage she would have been unbearably frustrated, but perfecting her fingering was most important now. *Hearing* her interpretation would be the priority later.

Her bedroom was at the front of the house. It had a view envied by many but it was not possible to see into the depths of the ravine, as it was from the guest room above that in which the piano stood. Sarah was glad of the fact. That deep gash instilled in her inexplicable apprehension when filled with no more than birds and reptiles. She had no real wish to watch a torrent tumble through it, carrying rocks, plants and possibly living debris to join the brown foaming waters racing downhill through the especially constructed nullahs leading to the sea. Yet she was drawn to the outside by the thunder of headlong water, and stood gazing at the upper stretches visible from the corner of her balcony. Mist swirled spasmodically, first covering then revealing the stony scrub-covered drop that formed the far side of the gorge. Sarah was just able to make out the bouncing, splashing froth topping the cascade which, with the echoing roar, was enough to fuel her imagination. Echoes was now living up to its name with a vengeance.

When engrossed in music she forgot all else. Now, the familiar anguish returned to riot through her like water through the ravine. To think of that startling woman sharing Rod's life brought jealousy so intense it frightened her. He insisted that they concentrate on work and dismiss emotion. She could not; she did not want to. She longed for his dark strength, the sound of his voice, the smile that denied his words. There was a compulsive joy even in the pain of loving him. Without that there would be a void so dark and fathomless she dared not contemplate it. She would return to the lonely, dismal life before that fatal concert, except that it would be far, far worse after glimpsing heaven.

She turned away with a sigh to make her way downstairs to the dining room, where lunch was served at one p.m. each day except Sunday. The whole house resounded with the boom of tumbling water, drowning all other sounds including that of the gong to announce the meal. Sarah reached the door of the small parlour leading to the dining room unheard by the pair drinking sherry just inside the doorway. She pulled up at the mention of Rod's name, then listened motionless as her father and Olivia continued their conversation in voices raised above the outside roar.

'Durman was turned down by the selection board yesterday. Sir Kingston saw to that in return for an extension of his overdraft.'

'So you've achieved your object, Peter.'

'Absolutely. When Durman refused to persuade Wang Chua to hear my business proposition – in the most offensive way, mark you – I knew that wife of his was my ideal weapon. I *will not* be bested by a junior doctor built like a Bondi Beach lifeguard, with manners to match. That deal is worth a fortune to all concerned.' He sipped his sherry. 'I knew that dreadful creature would run wild given her head, creating the kind of gossip to ruin any man's chances of advancement out here. My long-suffering friends more than fulfilled their obligations to me by issuing invitations to the Durmans. They can be relegated to their own level now, thank heaven.'

Olivia's smile turned malicious. 'I'd love to see her when she realizes she's been dropped like a hot cake, wouldn't you?'

Sir Peter took her empty glass to place on a nearby table.

'My dear, I have no desire ever to see Celeste Durman again. Or her pugnacious husband.'

'After this slap in the face, the man will surely think twice before again taking on someone with friends in the right places,' said Olivia, as they moved towards the dining room.

'Perhaps ... but my friends can't get me an interview with Wang Chua, more's the pity.'

Their words were thereafter drowned, but Sarah was already retreating in shock as comprehension rushed in to turn her cold in the midday heat. Her mind cried out that it was not possible; that her father was too honourable to dabble with dirty tricks. The words she had overheard tumbled through her brain as she slowly backed across the hall, the sense of shock increasing as her distressed senses unravelled the truth.

Reaching the foot of the stairs, she turned and ran up to the privacy of her room, where she faced the fact that she was responsible for depriving Rod of the post he had been sure of winning. By telling her father about Wang Chua, she had set in motion a chain of circumstances foreign to her understanding of behaviour. Guilt was twofold. Not only had Rod's career been damaged, his exuberant wife had been deliberately humiliated by people who owed her father a good turn.

Deafened by a cataract as turbulent as her emotions, she rode out a tide of bitter regret over what she had done. It was imperative to see Rod, confess the entire disgusting story. It would not gain him the promotion he so badly wanted, but he would know the failure was not his own. She could not wait until Friday at the Halburton; she did not know his address. Going to the telephone, she asked the operator to put her through to Queen Mary Hospital. Within seconds she heard Rod's voice on the end of the line and her courage almost failed. She was still so shocked it was not easy to speak. His second, very testy, demand to know who wanted him prompted her response, but instinct made her cautious.

'It's Ellie's granddaughter. I must see you.'

He was immediately concerned. 'What's happened? Are you all right?'

'Yes – but I must talk to you. It's *very* important.'

'Where are you?'

'At home. We can't meet here,' she added swiftly. 'Can you come to the first station of the Peak Railway?'

A short silence. 'I'll be there in fifteen minutes.'

The receiver went down, cutting him off, and she was left facing the prospect of the most unpleasant thing she had yet had to do. Ellie would go resolutely to meet it, and so must she. Leaving the house without being seen, Sarah took a path leading to the steep track up which trams had climbed since 1888 to provide the easiest means of reaching the various levels of the great hill. With mist so low today it was not possible to see the descending tram until it loomed from greyness fifty yards off. Climbing aboard, she sat on the wooden seat facing three curious Chinese whose stares seemed to accuse her during the brief journey to the lower station. Leaving the tram, and her silent companions, she walked back and forth in agitation. How would she begin to tell him? What would his reaction be?

One tram approached from below and rattled past on its way to the crest. Rod would still be driving through Victoria. Fifteen minutes, he had said. Ten had already passed. He might be on the next tram. He *would* be on the one after that, surely. She could still hear water tumbling through the gorge, distant now because the track veered away from that gash as it neared the foot of the Peak. Had they missed her at Echoes yet? How could she continue living there after this? A downward tram filled with chattering children passed, then she saw the tiny shape of the next starting up and swallowed nervously. Exactly fifteen minutes had passed since his voice had spoken in her ear.

He jumped from the open carriage and came to take her hands, searching her face with eyes further darkened by incomprehension. 'What's wrong? You sounded afraid.'

'Did I?' Face to face with him, knowing he had come without hesitation, she sensed the full extent of feeling between them. She was silenced by it.

Conscious of other passengers walking close by, Rod took her elbow to lead her beside the track beyond the point which gave access to lower levels of the hill. The path developed into no more than a rough stony way, deserted save for a few lizards.

They stopped. Rod said, 'You're shaking! For God's sake tell me what this is all about.'

Now they were alone in a relatively wild area, she felt stronger. 'I'm sorry. Ellie wouldn't be very proud of me.'

'Damn Ellie,' he said explosively.

'It's not her you should damn, it's me.'

He shook his head. 'I don't think I could ever do that.'

'You did once – when I typed your report badly.'

'I didn't know you then.'

'You won't *want* to know me after today.'

'Let me be the judge of that.' He traced her cheek with his finger. 'Come on, out with it.'

Where to begin? At the start of it all, she supposed. 'Remember our visit to Wang Chua?'

'Will I ever forget it!'

'Father was extremely angry because I sent the chauffeur back without a message telling where I was going or who I was with.'

'I didn't know you'd done that. No wonder he was mad.'

'Yes. *I* know why now. I didn't, at the time . . . and as I'd lived for fifteen years without his concern for my safety, it didn't occur to me that I might be creating anxiety so great poor Ming paid for it with his job.'

'That was a bit harsh, wasn't it?'

Giving him a frank look, she said, 'Father suggested that Ming was some kind of bodyguard. He was really furious . . . about being late for his dinner party too. I was obliged to tell him where I had been, and his anger then changed direction. After doubting the truth of what I said, he grew interested in you. Too interested.' She sighed. 'I thought he suspected your intentions as a gentleman – how very old-fashioned of me! – and was surprised that he dropped the subject abruptly when I got on my high horse over his questioning. I see now that I had given quite enough information for him to trace and contact you.'

She shivered as a thread of mist reached and engulfed them momentarily. Rod took off his jacket to drape around her shoulders, holding it by the lapels so that she was gently

124

imprisoned by him. The gesture made matters worse. Her next words burst from her in accusation.

'Why didn't you tell me Father had asked you to use Wang Chua's debt of gratitude to help him with a business deal?'

'Can't you guess? That entire evening had been impossible. Celeste was out of hand; the other guests were trying to pretend we weren't there. Then that obnoxious Tennant bloke began jumping to all the right conclusions.' He shook his head wearily. 'I'd had it up to the neck by the time Sir Peter slapped me on the back and told me the reason for it all. I saw red. Firstly, I don't go along with all that "old boy" stuff, Secondly, I don't abuse someone's trust for financial advantage and, thirdly, I don't think much of a man who'll use his daughter for business ends.' He frowned. 'I'd had a few drinks at the bar so I don't remember my exact reply, but I walked out after it and took a rickshaw home. I'm pretty sure your father got my message.'

Recollection of that recent conversation washed over her again. She put a hand up to his holding the jacket around her. 'I have just had confirmation of that. He was talking to Olivia – they didn't know I was listening. Oh, Rod, I'm so, *so* sorry.'

'For what?'

There was only one way to tell him. 'Father asked all his friends to send out invitations so that your wife would ... cause gossip among people of influence. Sir Kingston Dailey was then easily able to persuade the selection board members to turn you down on the grounds of social unsuitability.' Watching his expression, she added brokenly, 'I've never really known my father, but I only believe this of him because he discussed it in my hearing. You know how we compared Chinese "face" with our own conception of honour? I thought ... *naturally*, I thought my father an honourable man.' She gripped his clenched hands with her own in distress. 'It's an unforgivable, immature way of repaying a slight. Your wife was used in the most disgusting manner; pressure was put upon men who should have more integrity than to ruin someone's career as a favour to a friend. The Channings have robbed you of so much. I'm deeply ashamed.'

His arms slid around her shoulders to draw her against him in comfort, and they remained silent for some time. When he eventually spoke, his voice was rough with an emotion she could not name. 'That deal must have been more lucrative than I guessed. Now you know why I've never been a social climber. I expect people to take me on merit, not on how bloody tricky a game I can play. The bastard!'

Sarah arched back in his embrace to ask, 'What did he expect to gain by it? He's lost all chance of meeting Wang Chua now.'

'And I've lost all hope of promotion. He'll see that as true justice.'

'What about your wife? She's done nothing to deserve such treatment.'

'Celeste was an instrument,' he said bitterly. 'I guess she'll now be cold-shouldered by those she's been mixing with. I warned her she was out of her league with that lot.'

Near to tears, Sarah whispered, 'I'm so dreadfully sorry I let out about Wang Chua. None of this would have happened if –'

He cut her short. 'Please don't torture yourself. This kind of nastiness isn't peculiar to Hong Kong society. There are those in your home village out to ruin *their* doctor's reputation.'

'That's different,' she cried. 'Village gossips are simple, incurably rural people. They invent scandal to enliven their dull routine. Father and his associates are intelligent, cultured and worldly. What they've done is monstrous! Setting aside the petty personal revenge of one man who couldn't get his own way, you have a team of responsible people deliberately turning down the best applicant to fill an immensely responsible post. Perhaps you'll now understand why I have a poor opinion of those I've encountered out here.'

The next tram clattered upward along the track ten feet above, making them aware of the fact that they were being watched by several rows of fascinated onlookers.

Rod swore explosively. 'Christ, is there *anywhere* on this damn island where you're not up against walls of staring faces?' He practically pushed Sarah along the narrow path until a projecting slope hid them from view of the railway. Bushes and spreading ferns were hung with the silvery dampness of mist, intensifying the humidity, but still Sarah shivered within the folds of Rod's jacket. He stood as if trying to gain control of himself for a moment or two, then turned to her, grim-faced. 'When I heard the news yesterday I walked out and drove up to see Wang Chua. It seemed the only place to go. Like many Chinese, he's sensitive to mood and has an almost uncanny ability to read minds. After the usual exchange of polite greetings, he said: "So you have come to say goodbye to your old friend." Only then did I realize that he was right.'

'Goodbye?' Sarah grew even colder. 'Where are you going?'

He avoided a direct answer. 'I believe I once told you that it was important to be selected yesterday because I'd decided to specialize.' She nodded, and he went on: 'I didn't give you my reason for that decision; why I intended to abandon general medicine to become one of the white-coated élite.' Perching on a rock protruding from a mass of ferns, he studied her sombrely. 'I married Celeste before I qualified. It was an irresponsible and headstrong decision, but that was what we both wanted. We've paid for our mistake. The marriage has been over for several years – even longer than that, if I'm honest – but Hong Kong's a small community and I've guarded my professional standing from scandal or malicious speculation. Within acceptable bounds, we've been living separate lives.'

'Under the same roof?' Sarah asked, hating to talk about his life with the flashy Celeste.

'More often than not, we aren't. That's been the root of the problem. My work is highly demanding; she needs a constant playmate. That saying "Never the twain shall meet" certainly applied to the Durmans.' He sighed heavily. 'I thought I'd compensate for the failure of my private life by gaining laurels in my profession. I was knocked for six when they turned me down yesterday.'

'But you now know why,' she said urgently. 'It's not personal failure. You mustn't feel that it is.'

'Oh, I'd stopped doing that by the time I reached Wang Chua's. It was there I saw that I had no reason to remain in Hong Kong. What you've just told me confirms that. Your father and his pals have attached to the Durman name the very unpleasantness I've striven to avoid. It will ensure that my career will stagnate here.' His faint smile contained bitterness. 'Sir Peter may well have done me a good turn. I can move on – alone.'

The day was growing blacker by the minute. Her initial shock was being compounded by all Rod told her. She had run to him from the unacceptable revelation of her father's duplicity, only to learn that the one shining light in the gloom of her loneliness was about to be extinguished. Bleakness chilled her as she asked where he meant to go.

'Back home. I'll probably return to the Flying Doctor Service until the divorce is settled. It'll take quite a while, but when you're the only doctor for hundreds of miles people don't give a damn about your private life. So long as you can mend a broken arm, deliver a baby or give anti-snake-bite serum you're accepted, warts and all.'

Hurt and bewildered, Sarah hit out. 'You're going to let these deplorable snobs drive you away to obscurity?'

He got to his feet. 'It's my own decision.'

'No, it isn't! You're conceding defeat.'

'I'm being realistic.'

'You're not going to attempt to fight back?'

'With what?'

Caught out, she changed tack. 'So you're abandoning your hope of specializing.'

'For a while,' he retorted, her attack plainly getting to him. 'Haven't you temporarily abandoned *your* professional plans?'

'I have no choice,' she flung at him.

'Neither have I,' he flung back. 'Life can be a bastard, Sarah. These things happen.'

'So you simply shrug them off, run away and start again?'

'If that's still possible, yes.'

'I see.' She backed away, fighting the storm rising within her. 'Well, good luck! I hope all your plans work out successfully; that you deliver all their babies and cure all the snake bites and . . .' She turned and fled.

He stopped her before she had gone ten yards, and she could no longer hold back her tears as he kissed her with all the anger they had just ignited. There had never been passion like it before in her life, but she responded instinctively until Rod finally lifted his head to murmur unsteadily, 'You've unchained the beast again.'

'Have I?' she asked, revelling in the way his every feature glowed with life. 'That's how this all began.'

His palm cradled her head against his chest, and he said into her hair, 'And that's how it must end. I'm ten years older than you, practically broke and about to leave for Australia.'

'I'm very young, very well off, and *very* much in love with you,' she replied. 'We have the perfect combination.'

'The perfect combination for calamity.' He held her away, the strength of his grip betraying his tension. 'We're indulging in madness.'

'Then walk away,' she said softly. 'Walk away right now and don't look back! Pack your things and book your passage but stay away from any place where we might meet. While you're waiting for the ship to sail, play your recording of the Rachmaninov and don't even *think* of me. Fly out to the back of beyond in Australia and forget we ever stood together in a mystical garden on top of a hill in Hong Kong. When you've done all that, the madness will have passed.'

He looked down at her in challenge. 'And what will you be doing all that time?'

'You mustn't care about that, either.'

'Then the madness will never end.'

Alex had had a night on the tiles, and felt worse than usual as he sat at his desk drinking the concoction his secretary always mixed for him on such occasions. The temperature was rising by the minute. He cursed the rule refusing to allow the staff of Frobisher–Jay to wear shorts for business. It was acceptable dress for military and administration personnel, but both partners in the merchant shipping company had adhered to old-fashioned standards where their employees were concerned.

After glancing at his watch to find that only an hour had passed since his late arrival this morning, Alex sank back in his chair and closed his eyes. After a difficult cocktail-time scene last night with a girl trying to keep alive an affair that had died several months ago, he had gone on the town with some of his cronies. Alex could not recall how they had all come to be in a sampan singing the 'Eton Boating Song' when a police launch came alongside. It had been a splendid night out, so why did he have this feeling amounting to guilt? No one had been hurt by their antics. A few stuffed shirts might have been affronted, but they were easily upset. The money he had spent was his own; the girls he had cuddled were the kind one paid for their generosity. Girls with smooth beautiful faces and black almond eyes full of excitement. So different from those pale classical features and straightforward accusing green eyes that bothered him at all the wrong times.

He would see Sarah tonight. She was due to play at a concert being given in the grounds of Flagstaff House to welcome Hong Kong's new governor, Sir Mark Young. The Hong Kong Volunteers were to parade with the regular garrison. It was an affair designed to impress, so everyone was expected to be on best behaviour. It was the kind of evening Alex detested, and the presence of that girl who had disturbed his careless, lethargic life here would provide the additional thorn in his side. Yet it was a strangely enjoyable pain she inflicted.

His thoughts were interrupted by a knock on the door. Opening his eyes, he saw one of the clerks enter with a fat file to present to him.

'The Bolton Rochas details on the main godown, sir,' he said with a wide smile.

Alex made no attempt to take the file, so the man's smile faded. 'You asked for them yesterday afternoon, sir,' he explained, black eyes blinking nervously behind thick lenses. 'You had left the office when I brought them up from the record room, so I've just been down again.' He thrust the file across the desk. 'I hope I am not too late, sir.'

Raising himself, Alex took the thick folder. He did not recall asking for it; could not think why he would have done. 'Thanks, Chang,' he murmured. 'I've been so busy I'd forgotten all about it. Leave it with me for a day or so. I'll get round to it when I can.'

The young Chinese left, shutting the glass-panelled door carefully behind him. On the glass was Alex's name in black lettering. An important official of the Frobisher–Jay shipping company who could not remember what he did in this office from day to day, while the Frobisher half faced German tanks in the desert. Would he be happier doing that? *Why don't you go home and offer your flying skills to the RAF?* That voice gave him little peace. He got to his feet swiftly, intending to fetch a drink from the side table, but his hand caught the edge of the file and knocked it to the floor. The contents spilled across the room in a slither of documents and letters. Alex swore as he trod over them to pour himself a gin and tonic, before turning to survey the mess. After a long pull at his drink, he put the glass on his desk and squatted to scoop the scattered papers into a manageable heap.

On the point of cramming them into the file willy-nilly, a letter heading caught his eye and stilled his hands. Anything concerning the Channing family was of present interest to him. Pulling the single page from the rest, Alex read what appeared to be a reply to a request for a loan from the managing director of Bolton Rochas – rather a large loan. The letter, signed by Sir Peter Channing, was worded in a manner that gave no true indication of whether or not the loan was being considered by Channing Mercantile. As Julian Frobisher senior had bought up the godowns, offices and goodwill of Bolton Rochas just before amalgamation with Reginald Jay, Alex supposed the application must have failed. Yet the letter in his hand made references to 'further evidence of assets and securities which might influence a decision for additional discussion on the subject'. Alex had heard enough about business methods from his father to sense curious undertones here. Channing Mercantile was too large a bank to flirt with a potential customer in this manner, and the applicants would surely have fired their big guns concerning security at their initial approach. What 'further evidence' could they supply?

Settling himself on the floor, Alex began searching through the papers fanned out around him. Half a dozen letters from Channing Mercantile were easily identified by their unique letter heading, but discovering Bolton Rochas correspondence on the subject meant going through the entire file. After scanning the six letters he had retrieved he was driven to do just that. With the papers piled on his desk, he sat on the swivel chair to sort through them, his gin and tonic forgotten. During the next half-hour all he discovered was his reason for requesting the file from Chang yesterday. Their insurers wanted details of the last fire officer's report on three of the older godowns before renewing their policy.

Setting aside that report, Alex continued his search for the other half of what he felt was rather a mysterious transaction. Channing Mercantile had approved the loan, and Alex was curious about their change of mind after initial coolness. He even forsook the midday meal known by old colonials as tiffin so that he could continue his search. By mid-afternoon he had looked at every item on his desk and sifted out several long letters from the managing director of Bolton Rochas, named Colin Bolton-Sneed. There was no mention of a Rochas. He had presumably died or sold out.

Putting all the letters in chronological order, Alex then read through an entire transaction on paper. Finally, tucked between the papers of Bolton-Sneed's last communication, he found a handwritten memo that must have lain there undisturbed for years. It puzzled him so much he picked up the telephone and asked for the number of one of his cronies who was a stockbroker. After commiserating on his hangover, Alex got to the point.

'Tell me about Bolton Rochas, Giles.'

'What's to tell, old boy? Went down the river seven years ago.'

'I know that. It was before my time, which is why I want to know the story,' Alex said impatiently.

'The old, old one of course. The big boys grew even bigger and began squeezing out the rest. Bolton Rochas borrowed

132

heavily from Channing Mercantile to buy two huge modern merchant ships and challenge the big boys. Confidence in them rose very swiftly. Shares went to exciting levels. We could scarcely keep up with them.'

'And?'

'And completion of the ships was delayed by strikes, a couple of their godowns were destroyed by fire, Gabriel Rochas took his money out and went home. Collapse of company.'

Alex whistled through his teeth. 'What happened to Bolton-Sneed?'

'Married an American heiress and left for Honolulu.'

'You're joking!'

'Stockbrokers never joke, old boy. Old man Frobisher bought up the usable assets and Channing Mercantile was repaid.'

'And the shareholders?'

'Sweet F.A., old sport. It's like Happy Valley here. You takes your choice and puts your shirt on it. Some you win, some you lose.' There was a slight pause, then the voice said, 'Caused a bit of a rumble at the time, of course, because those who bought shares after Channing's hefty loan made a small fortune by selling when they reached the top limit just before the crash. There were whispers of inside knowledge – all the usual suspicions in such cases – but nothing was ever proved. It seldom is . . . and the fat boys grow even fatter.'

Alex contemplated that for a moment or two, then asked, 'Was there a title involved in the affair?'

'A title? Don't know what you mean, old boy.'

'I found a couple of references to M'lord. Wondered who it could have been.'

'No idea. Only Lord I know of was Derek, Channing's accountant at the time.'

'Husband of the poisonous Olivia?'

'The same.'

Alex glanced again at the handwritten memo. Yes, M'lord could possibly be Mr Lord. In which case . . . 'Thanks again, Giles,' he murmured, and put down the telephone.

A further fifteen minutes studying all the relevant papers

from a file that had probably remained unopened like all others inherited with Bolton Rochas's offices gave Alex a curious sense of shock. Without that memo which never should have been filed, the letters merely indicated a sudden change of mind on behalf of Sir Peter Channing over the loan of a very considerable sum of money. The memo of a telephone call from Derek Lord suggested that he had audited their accounts and 'sorted out the earlier difficulties to everyone's advantage'. Two days after the date of the memo, Channing Mercantile had agreed to the loan. For the first time in his business life Alex took a great interest in the Frobisher half of his company, which had bought up what little had been salvaged from the Bolton Rochas crash.

The evening was following expected lines. Officers of Hong Kong's regular garrison, augmented by those of the Volunteers, had given a reassuring suggestion of military strength to the man taking up at a time of war a post in the British colony far from any friendly shore. Men of wealth and influence, whose ladies rigidly upheld colonial traditions of good breeding and utter confidence in themselves, had gathered to represent the mercantile worth of the island known to Chinese as Fragrant Harbour.

Cocktails had been enjoyed inside the house by the military contingent, whose talk had been of the two Canadian battalions that had set sail for Hong Kong as reinforcements. There were mixed feelings on the subject. Some felt aggrieved that men with little or no battle experience should be sent to help defend a vital garrison; others stated plainly that they had deterred the Japanese for over eighteen months and needed no boys from the backwoods to help them do it.

A huge marquee had been erected in the grounds and guests began arriving for the concert in a constant flow. Alex sat near the back with the stockbroker, Giles, and a young banker named Bunny, both of whom also wore the uniform of the Volunteers. Beneath the buzz of conversation Alex asked Bunny a question he had been pondering for several hours. 'What does a bank require to know about a company before approving the loan of several million dollars?'

Bunny's lean face showed concern. 'Not *that* much in the red, are you?'

'No, it's nothing to do with Frobisher–Jay, I'm just curious.'

'In the middle of a concert?'

'The thing hasn't started yet. If you flannel about much longer it will have,' Alex said impatiently. 'Answer the question.'

'Keep your hair on,' his friend retaliated. 'If it's *so* badly important to know right this minute, I'll put it in a nutshell. Assets, securities, prospects. What the cash is to be spent on, and proof of the company's soundness. In short, a very good study of its accounts.'

'By the bank's accountant?'

'Possibly, or by a reliable impartial body.'

'Thanks.'

'May I now doze off before this dreary musical interlude gets under way?'

'You may,' said Alex, pleased with what he had heard.

'Wake me when they all head for the supper tent.'

During the first part of the concert given by the garrison band and orchestra, Alex mused on what he had learned that day and vowed to investigate further. Had he, by chance, stumbled on a case of people who live in glass houses? He gazed out at the night where bats and huge moths dived and weaved around arc-lights, and thought of his father's greed for money and power. Was Sir Peter Channing another of the breed . . . and was his disturbing daughter aware of the fact?

When Sarah came on to the raised platform three-quarters of an hour after the start of the concert, Alex gazed in appreciative surprise. A clinging dress of smoke-grey chiffon, highlighted by a huge deep pink flower at her waist, revealed a shape Alex had not before noticed. With that soft hair fastened into a pleat at the back of her head, she looked a mature, willowy and very desirable woman. Alex knew a sensation foreign to him as he scanned the audience for a man he was certain had produced this exciting version of a personality he had found elusive. Was Durman still playing around with her?

He was certain of the answer when she began to play. She fairly fizzed with exuberance during a Chopin impromptu and followed it with a polonaise so lively she almost bounced up and down on her seat in time with it. The applause was highly enthusiastic, but the biggest surprise of all was the final item of the concert – a medley of popular songs of the day arranged by Jakob Myburgh for the piano and military band. Alex sat enchanted as the girl who could thrill an audience with the classics awoke in them even more emotional fervour by playing the sentimental ballads of their wartorn homeland.

With an unspoken pecking order when it came to moving from the main marquee to the other in which supper was set, it was fully twenty minutes before Alex entered with his friends, more intent on drinking than eating. Sarah was standing beside her father in a group containing Sir Mark Young, Major-General Maltby – Military Commander in Hong Kong – and several prominent members of the colony's trade and administrative bodies, with their wives. As usual, Sarah stood silently while those around her chatted, but Alex saw a distinct difference tonight from that other occasion when she had appeared almost to fade into the décor of her home. Silent she might be, yet she exuded such vibrance the eyes of each person in the group were constantly drawn to her. Throughout the next hour, Alex found his own were similarly compelled.

For once, the conversation of his companions bored him. The moment he saw Sarah temporarily isolated with Jakob Myburgh he broke from the group and walked across to them, greeting his Dutch neighbour in friendly manner.

Thin, stooping, prone to waving his arms in emphasis of words and opinions, the ageing Myburgh smiled with satisfaction. 'So, are you not proud of yourself for bringing together an old man with music in his head and a very talented young lady who has it also in her fingers? Tonight she has shown a hint of the brilliance to come. You heard, you saw, my friend.'

'If there's any credit to be allocated, it's yours. All I did was to speak of you to Miss Channing.' He laughed. 'And my reward is to have the peace of my apartment disturbed by scales, chords and irascible ravings from you.'

'Ah, you clearly have no soul, no artistry,' scolded the Dutchman.

'Some of us have to keep our feet on the ground, sir.'

Myburgh gave a sly grin. 'So that is why you are forever in the sky with that red machine?'

'I see I no more have your championship than your pupil's,' said Alex with a glance at Sarah. 'She also disapproves of my aerial exploits.'

A bony, deformed hand rested on his khaki sleeve. 'Then I leave you to impress her with some other aspect of your youthful charm. So lovely a young woman does not want the company of an old man and his irascible ravings on an evening like this.' Taking Sarah's hand to his lips in an old-fashioned Continental gesture, he then winked at Alex before walking away.

Sarah watched his retreat, murmuring, 'I'm really indebted to you. His guidance is invaluable.'

'I'm glad.' When she turned to him, Alex asked, 'Dare I risk complimenting you on your performance tonight? I know you rate my knowledge of music deplorable but, as a Cole Porter *aficionado*, you might allow me to judge your final item as extremely impressive.'

'I didn't play anything by Cole Porter, so far as I'm aware.'

'I wish you would.'

She shook her head. 'My heart isn't in that kind of music.'

'Where is it?'

'Oh, with the passion of Rachmaninov, the tragedy of Tchaikovsky, the flamboyance of Liszt, the fire of Chopin. You wouldn't understand.'

'You're very fond of saying that. As you hardly know me, I dispute your right to do so.' He held up a hand as she made to speak. 'No, you're going to plead that you've heard what others say on the subject. Don't you know by now that people react differently to those they meet? Give me half a chance and you might be surprised.'

'I doubt it, Mr Tennant.'

'Alex.'

She gave him her distinctive cool, appraising gaze. 'You

137

certainly *look* different tonight. I didn't immediately recognize you.'

'Ah! This uniform disguises the fact that I'm a worthless gambler determined to continue along a dissolute path while others die for my sake,' he said with soft deliberation. When colour appeared in her pale cheeks, making her glow of vitality even more attractive to him, he added, 'I'm not the only villain masquerading as a hero tonight, so don't be too hard on me.' Then he smiled. 'I've been ordered to impress you with my youthful charm, but you'll need to be receptive to it if I'm to succeed.'

After a moment of uncertainty, she smiled back. 'Why do you persist in trying to cultivate my friendship when, so gossip has it, you have more than enough female conquests to your credit?'

'I find you intriguing,' he said frankly.

'I'm afraid I don't feel that way about you,' she told him with equal frankness.

'Perhaps that's the secret of your fascination.'

'The one heart you can't win?' Her smile returned with a trace of warmth. 'You'll have to do better than that. I've read it in far too many novels to take such a concept seriously.'

'So you read when you're not spending all those hours in practice! And you ride across Cotswold country, letting the horse have his head.'

'You remembered that?'

'Of course. What else do you like to do?'

'The kind of things you'd find dull.'

'How do you know? Ah! Don't repeat that you've heard what everyone in Hong Kong says about me. I've already reprimanded you on that score,' he said, enjoying the soft line of her throat now revealed by the swept-back hairstyle and the gentle swell of her breasts beneath grey chiffon. 'Tell me everything about yourself and we might find we have several things in common.'

'I doubt it.'

Although still resistant, Alex felt that she was softening towards him. He intensified his campaign. 'What do you think of modern art?'

'It's . . . much of it is incomprehensible to me.'

'And to me. Do you swim?'

'Not very well.'

'Neither do I. Have you ever been in an aircraft?'

'Yes. A flying-boat from England to South Africa.'

'What did you think of the experience?'

'It was exciting.'

'Yes, isn't it. Do you eat ice-cream?'

She began to laugh. 'Stop it! I refuse to submit to an inquisition.'

'But don't you agree that it has revealed how very much attuned we are; what a splendid basis we have for close friendship?'

He had misjudged the moment. Her laughter faded. 'The one heart you can't win? I think you know how many hours a day I spend in practice. In addition to my classes with Jakob Myburgh, I teach Chinese children twice a week and work in the office of the Halburton Clinic every Friday. I haven't time for close friendships.'

'Except with the brawny doctor. He didn't rate an invitation tonight, of course.'

Pique had prompted the comment, but her response was more than he had bargained for and suggested that the liaison had progressed since the night of the Chamber of Commerce ball. 'Now you're reverting to type,' she said coldly. 'You asked for half a chance just now. I wouldn't give you a hundredth part of that.'

The temper normally swamped by resignation rose swiftly, as pique deepened to a more dangerous emotion. 'You've always condemned me for what you think I am, but I never play a double game. That's what *he*'s doing. Is it that you can't or won't see it? This isn't a Cotswold village, you know. Many people here have too much time and too little to occupy it. All you'll get from your philandering doctor is a reputation that'll attract a cluster of other married men eager to cash in on a tried certainty. Stick to Chopin and Liszt. Their music sustains your romantic view of life, and the men themselves are dead. You can create heroes of *them* and never be disillusioned.'

As Alex was about to turn away he was prevented by the

arrival of Sir Peter and a handsome young diplomat known to be seeking a wife with enough personal wealth to shore up his family's fortunes. Sir Peter glanced from his daughter to Alex with a frown. 'Is something amiss?'

'No, sir,' Alex said swiftly. 'Sarah and I were discussing life here, and in England. Over there, they're suffering attack and privation, while we're holding out against the Oriental enemy at the door.' He forced a smile. 'I'm glad we have Canadian reinforcements coming shortly. We Volunteers are only part-time soldiers, bearing the responsibility over and above that of our regular professions.' He nodded to the hopeful young man at Sir Peter's side. 'Evening, Hobart. On a night like this you must feel particularly galled by the embarrassing medical problem that prevents you from joining our trusty band of warriors.'

Hesketh Hobart blushed to his ears, mumbling an incomprehensible reply as he handed Sarah a dish of peaches and cream he had brought her from the buffet. Well into his stride, Alex embarked on something he had not planned before the exchange with Sarah, which had upset him more than he wished to own. The Channings had no cause to condemn him when their own house was in evident disorder.

'Made the cocktail hour by the skin of my teeth, sir,' he said, in easy conversational manner. 'Had to look into a matter concerning Bolton Rochas. The affair was before my time, so I was tempted to read up all the documents in a file we inherited when the company collapsed. They made fascinating reading.'

'Mmm, but it's history now,' said Sir Peter, looking bored. 'A familiar story in this part of the world.'

'So I was told by my stockbroker friends. Last desperate attempt to shore up a crumbling company, share prices soar on false expectation, company then folds. Shareholders lose every penny, but those who sold at a premium just before the crash make a fortune. My father would applaud their business acumen. I'd describe it rather differently ... but I'm immune to the lure of sharp dealings. I prefer to make money on the speed of a horse rather than by some poor devil's misfortune.'

'Indeed? Every man to his taste,' said Sir Peter, glancing pointedly across the marquee to indicate his lack of interest in the subject. 'Must have a word with Sir Brian Clunes before he leaves.'

'I noticed that you were involved in the affair, sir,' Alex put in quickly.

The grey head turned back instantly. 'I?'

'Channing Mercantile advanced the loan that gave Bolton Rochas its final gasp of life.'

'Ah ... possibly. It happened some years ago. Can't remember every transaction.'

It was said smoothly enough, but the man's demeanour had been shaken, Alex would swear. He continued the attack. 'This was an inordinately large sum, sir. One you would surely remember.' After a swift glance at Sarah's face, he added, 'Must have been quite a blow when the company nevertheless collapsed – especially after your accountant's approval of their books and records. I'm no expert on the subject, but I was surprised by the speed at which they folded after such an injection of dollars.'

The grey-haired banker was now visibly angered by Alex's words. 'By your own admission, you are no expert on the subject, Tennant. Perhaps you shouldn't attempt to discuss such things with those who are. It might also be more expedient to concentrate on your future rather than on events that are over and done with.' He turned his attention on Sarah. 'I'll have a brief word with Sir Brian, then we'll take our leave.'

Sarah quickly gave back to Hesketh Hobart the untouched peaches and cream. 'I'd prefer to leave now. I'll send the car back for you immediately.' She nodded at the confused young man on her left. 'Goodnight, Mr Hobart.' Then she walked away without further word, the soft chiffon of her dress rippling from the swift pace she adopted. Alex was left with the surprising conclusion that her anger had been suddenly redirected against her father.

Chapter Six

A typhoon hit Hong Kong during the first week of October. Warning signals were systematically hoisted to notify its speed of approach and growing ferocity, and the colony steeled itself during the evening and early part of the night. Emergency services stood by to cope with casualties and extensive destruction, knowing these tropical storms could never be harnessed.

Staff at the Queen Mary Hospital prepared extra beds and brought from stores additional supplies in readiness for a flow of injured and dying. Doctors who had been on duty all day snatched a few hours' sleep on the premises before being called back to their wards.

Rod was shaken awake by a Chinese orderly at two-thirty a.m. He dressed, splashed himself with cold water to drive away remaining drowsiness, then made his way to those wards he normally served. Wind was already buffeting windows with devastating force as he hurried along corridors, wondering how much glass would be left when the typhoon moved on. None, he suspected. Shutters were being closed over them by Chinese workers, but slatted wooden covers would be as vulnerable as glass in a gale capable of demolishing stone buildings.

They were certain to lose their electricity supply. An emergency generator would give adequate lighting, but lamps were being assembled in case of total breakdown. Their work would be really tricky if that happened. As Rod reached his wards he considered his intended departure from Hong Kong, and told himself this was the last typhoon he was likely to experience.

As a swan song it excelled. General power was lost within minutes of the storm's arrival. Hong Kong was plunged into darkness, and communications were lost as telephone lines came down across the Island and Kowloon. Rain descended in thunderous walls of water that soon filled the nullahs with racing cascades, which then swept through the streets as they overflowed. The tempest flattened hillside hovels, crumbling tenements in Wanchai's narrow, festering streets, and many trees, lamp posts, telegraph poles and billboards in its path. Mammoth waves bore ships to founder on beaches or rocks; sampan colonies were devoured by the greedy sea.

The wards of hospitals could contain no more by the time dawn arrived, so extra beds were set up in corridors, waiting rooms and in stores – any space that would accommodate the suffering. So great was the demand on doctors, many Chinese orderlies found themselves giving injections, applying splints, stitching up small wounds and performing other services generally restricted to European practitioners. As many of these young men had qualified at medical school they rose to the occasion magnificently, knowing they would again be denied responsibility once the emergency was over.

Along with his colleagues, Rod worked night and day with only short breaks for food. On the second night they were reduced to working by the light of lamps. Stories of extensive destruction filtered through to the medical staff as rescue workers continued bringing in casualties. Yet there were signs that the typhoon was moving on. This hope was boosted by a definite lightening of the sky which would aid their work.

Rod returned from a ten-minute break for strong tea, sandwiches, and a swift wash, wending his way through corridors packed with beds until he reached a Chinese orderly tending a man with multiple cuts on face and body.

'You take a break now, Kai. I'll carry on here.'

The Chinese glanced up, shaking his head. 'There is something not right here, Doctor. He has lost much blood, but this should not account for some convulsive paroxysm. Three times I have seen this.'

'Tetanus?' Rod suggested, knowing Kai was qualified to practise Western medicine.

'I thought this, at first, but it is different.' The round face assumed an expression of shame. 'I cannot make diagnosis.'

'Then it must be something unusual. In which case, I'll be just as stumped.' He gave a weary, encouraging smile. 'We can't know everything.'

Bending over the bed, Rod checked for signs of tetanus. There were none until the paroxysms Kai had mentioned began again. There was no doubt that the patient must have been in the grips of an illness when the typhoon struck, causing a great number of lacerations to a lean, tough body. Its condition suggested that he ate reasonably well and lived in a healthy environment. Some affliction had struck him swiftly, it seemed.

Rod was intrigued. 'There must be other recognizable symptoms,' he murmured, studying the patient's torso with frowning concentration. 'Let's clean him up a little more thoroughly before I begin to put sutures in those larger wounds.'

'He is bleeding very badly beneath those pressure dressings,' Kai warned.

'That might be the least of his worries. I want to get to the bottom of this other business first.'

Taking a handful of swabs, Rod began cleaning all remaining blood smears from the body in a search for clues. There appeared to be none. He was about to confess that he was also baffled, when the patient started to convulse once more and flung out an arm in his frenzy. In his armpit was evidence that shocked Rod to the core. 'Christ! We've got to get this bloke out of here. *Now!* Fetch a stretcher, Kai, and run all the way.'

The Chinese went without question, leaving Rod to examine the patient's groin and mouth for what he feared to find. The significant pink blisters were there. Excitement mingled with apprehension. He had seen this deadly fever only once before. It had wiped out a cattle baron and his family up in the Northern Territories, but the Aboriginal general hand who had incubated it during his walkabout from the swamplands survived. Rod had been isolated for a month in a medical outstation for fear of starting an epidemic. When he had been flown back to the Flying Doctor centre, Celeste had gone, leaving a note informing him that she would be in Sydney until their child was born and its father decided to return to civilization.

Kai arrived with two stretcher-bearers. His expression was eloquent, but he made no attempt to waste time with questions as he instructed the men to remove the patient with utmost speed. 'Where do we put him, Doctor?' he then asked in English. 'The hospital is full.'

'We'll have to use some place outside. Anywhere will do so long as we isolate him with the utmost urgency,' said Rod. 'If this develops further, it'll bring a greater death toll than the typhoon.'

They made their way through the confusion, Rod forcing others to allow them passage, the tone of his voice sufficient to bring immediate compliance. He was trying to marshal thoughts in a brain dulled by overwork and lack of rest. The typhoon was definitely moving on; day was advancing. Although rain was still falling heavily, it should be safe enough to venture into the open with the stretcher. This was one of those decisive moments doctors had sometimes to face. Did he risk a life in order to save many more? There was no doubt in his mind in this case. He had seen two small children die in the grips of this particular fever early in his career and had never forgotten. This one man – probably a seaman plying to and from the East Indies, where fevers were rife – must take his chances without endangering the lives of others.

True to their national characteristics, the stretcher-bearers unhesitatingly carried their burden into rain and gusting wind when told to do so, and deposited the patient in an empty ambulance bay as if it were not in the least unusual. Only when they departed did Kai ask the burning question above the thunder of rain on the roof. 'You have made diagnosis?'

'Luckily, I saw this once in Australia,' Rod told him, easing his sodden shirt from his back. 'It's relatively rare, and it's bloody fortunate that you drew my attention to the paroxysms or the consequences could have been catastrophic. This fever has three stages. The first is barely noticeable, even to the victim. Spasmodic flushing and the occasional twitch of a limb. The second stage comes anything from a week to a month later. High temperature and quite severe convulsions, with the development of pinkish blisters in mouth, groin and armpits. When those blisters turn black and start to suppurate, the third and highly dangerous stage has arrived. Thank God we've isolated this bloke before that happens.' He sighed heavily. 'Neither of us dare hang around here. It's too risky. I propose giving him a shot, then leaving a CONTAGIOUS sign on the door until a team from Tropical Diseases can deal with him. We just have to hope he's still alive when they get here.'

While he worked throughout the remainder of that day and the next night, Rod's thoughts often wandered to that tragedy seven years ago when he had flown to an isolated mansion in cattle country to answer a call for help over the airwaves. He had failed to save those who had summoned him, but they had died knowing that a medical stranger and a far distant team were doing all they could. The only other time a patient had died on him had been when a boozy old prospector had staggered into a nest of scorpions. People living in isolated areas of that vast country mostly received the attention they needed and made a complete recovery. They were uncomplicated, friendly people, like his own family. Rod felt right with them; Celeste had thought them dull and clannish. So he had gone to her in Sydney.

Suddenly, in the aftermath of that typhoon, he knew what he wanted for the future. Out there in the heart of his homeland was the work he most enjoyed. To hell with specializing, seeking medical prestige! He had no wish to mingle with the likes of Sir Kingston Dailey or to abandon his beliefs in a bid to conform to their standards. Those weekends he spent around the offshore islands with Wang Chua's clinic always pleased and fulfilled his urge to aid the helpless. He now realized those weekends were a substitute for the Fying Doctor job he had sacrificed for Celeste.

Towards late afternoon on the third day a move was made to give staff time for enough sleep to recoup their strength. The real emergency was over, so staff were divided into shifts during which they could go home for a rest and a decent meal. Rod walked through the stifling corridors half asleep, but feeling wonderfully relaxed. The stress and unhappiness of recent years was about to end. A new life beckoned; a new love promised to fulfil it for as long as the sands in passion's hourglass ran.

'Ah, Durman, I believe congratulations are in order,' said a loud voice beside him. Sir Kingston, looking weary and worn, produced a tired smile. 'Saved us from a nasty epidemic with your sharp observation at a time when it could easily have been overlooked.'

Rod came to a halt beside the man who had practically promised, then robbed him of, a post he had once wanted very badly. His temper rose swiftly. 'It was the sharp observation of Kai Sung-li that saved us from an epidemic. But you won't offer him congratulations because he's not one of us. Instead, you'll probably advise him to transfer to the Tung Wah hospital. When are you people going to recognize the worth of those you administer and give them the respect they deserve? Your Kingdom may have come in Hong Kong, but it's now well and truly on its way out.'

Sir Kingston was too exhausted to react as he undoubtedly would have done in normal circumstances. He merely appeared confused. 'I believe I once warned you about speaking your mind, Durman. I'll allow that you're overtired and not entirely in control of your tongue, but watch yourself in future, or you'll be asked to leave.'

'That's no problem,' snapped Rod. 'I'm not waiting to be asked. If the senior staff of a hospital allow themselves to be manipulated by bankers when selecting applicants for major posts, I want no part of their organization. Medicine is about saving lives, not doing social favours for someone who stoops to exploiting a gullible woman to gain petty revenge for having his nose put out of joint by her husband. You make me sick, the whole lot of you!'

He walked out into a smitten community and saw little of the devastation around him. When he reached his apartment he found the block swarming with those eager to make money before the next man. Windows were being replaced, roofing was being repaired. Waving aside Lim's offer of food, and hardly interested in the information that Missy was visiting friends, Rod took a shower and crawled between the sheets well on the way to oblivion.

He awoke at six the following morning. Celeste was asleep in the other bed. He lay watching her for a while with a faint sense of sadness. She had every hope of making a fresh start with a man who would give her all she needed to make her happy. That their love had died so swiftly could not be blamed on either of them. It had happened and could never be reversed. He hoped she would make their parting painless; hoped they would not go their separate ways hating each other.

On leaving Sarah at the Peak Railway he had committed himself to asking Celeste for a divorce before flying home, where Sarah would follow a week later. In Australia, she could pursue her career until he became a free man. It might be several years before the divorce became absolute, during which time she could decide whether or not the love that had hit her so suddenly was the abiding kind. Rod would walk out of her life if he thought it best for her, but his desertion would leave her desolate in the house of a father she now loathed. Her only course, then, would be to return to England where music would have to be sacrificed for war work, and where she would be exposed to danger.

For himself, he saw only a girl who had charmed him from growing desperation at a time when his life had reached stalemate. A concerto had restored his sanity; her kindred spirit promised the return of confidence, self-respect and personal as well as professional fulfilment. He was no fool in love, however. Sarah was destined for a musical career incompatible with the life of an Outback doctor. At this moment, she was young, lonely and inexperienced. Time would possibly diminish what was now fervent, generous love for him, but he was selfish enough to want it for as long as it thrived.

They had parted on the understanding that Rod would be in touch as soon as he had tackled Celeste, who would be told nothing of Sarah's part in his plans. Unfortunately, the typhoon had prevented him from advancing the situation or from making contact with Sarah. He hoped that she guessed all medical staff had been fully occupied over the last few days. Unlike Celeste, Sarah would understand priorities.

Invigorated by a shower and dressed in shorts and a cool shirt, Rod ate breakfast at the rattan table and thought about the best way to persuade Celeste to set him free. He was prepared to produce the usual hotel bills for a charge of adultery, and to pay three months' rent on the apartment while she worked out her new life. If she refused to release him, he would have to trump up some kind of charge against her. It would be difficult and messy, and he hoped it would not come to that.

He was on the veranda, enjoying the first sunshine since the typhoon hit the area, when he heard his wife tell Lim to bring her a large straight gin. Turning into the sitting room he found her there, dressed in a satin wrap with poppies splashed over a white background. She looked unwell. Dark rings beneath her eyes emphasized a face drawn and unhappy. The life in her was drastically subdued this morning. Rod guessed she had become aware of the fact that her new top-drawer friends had dropped her practically overnight. It did not bode well for the announcement that he was about to leave her.

Celeste glowered as he approached. 'So you're home at last . . . and, my God, you're dressed as if to stay for a while. Don't tell me Hong Kong can actually manage without you for an entire morning.'

As she took the glass from Lim, Rod told him they would not want anything for an hour or so. The boy understood that message, and went out with a sunny smile that hardly suited the mood between his employers.

'Gin first thing in the morning won't help the way you're feeling,' Rod said firmly.

'How the hell do you know how I'm feeling?'

'By the sight of your face. Gin will make the situation even lousier. Take some of that stuff I brought you from the chemist instead.'

Celeste drank from the glass with deliberation, then gave a hollow laugh. 'You're always so damned righteous, you men. *We know best!* Well *I* know best what I want this morning, and it's gin, gin, gin.'

'Fair enough,' he said, his heart sinking. She was in the worst possible mood for what he had to say.

Celeste moved across the room to top up the glass, then took a generous gulp before coming up to him. Rod then saw that she looked even worse than from a distance. She had clearly taken the cold-shouldering badly. He felt momentary anger against Sir Peter and his unprincipled friends, but the initial sense of rage for what they had done to him had faded beneath the brilliance of beckoning freedom.

'You look disgustingly fit after saving the colony from extinction,' Celeste said above the glass of gin. 'What's made you so perky?' She tipped it and swallowed. 'If you sent Lim away so that you could exert some of that smug vigour on rolling me, sweetie, you haven't a hope.'

'I packed Lim off because I want to talk to you,' he said, keeping hold of his control.

'How coincidental, darling,' she murmured, running her finger around the empty glass to collect any liquid remaining. '*I* want to talk to *you*. God knows, this is the first chance I've had for over a week.'

Determined not to let her take the initiative, he led straight in with, 'I didn't get the job in Tropical Diseases.'

She lifted her shoulders in a careless shrug. 'I told you not to waste all that time studying night after night. A fat lot of good it did you.'

He decided against telling her why he was turned down, because she would want to know how he learned about it. It would also complicate the real issue of divorce. 'I'd banked a lot on that chance. It came as quite a blow.'

She gave another hollow laugh as she tossed the empty glass on to the settee. 'Not half as big a blow as I had last week. I'm pregnant again.'

It was as if she had kicked him in the stomach. He tried to tell himself she had somehow found out his intentions and was lying to spoil them, but memories of that morning a couple of months ago when she had awoken him to instinctive desire were as damning as the disgust on her face.

'Who confirmed it?' he demanded hoarsely.

'Bill Charlton, of course. He seemed to think you'd be delighted.' She flopped into a chair and tipped back her head in a gesture of anguish. 'He took *my* delight for granted. Why do men always imagine every woman's greatest desire is to be impregnated and go through the disgusting business of morning sickness, swollen belly, nights ruined by a leaping foetus, and endless hours of agony to produce a little screaming demon who will drag her down to the level of a slave for the next twenty years of her life?'

Rod stood icy cold in the growing heat of morning. The love that had slowly turned to dislike now became outright hatred as he faced the consequences of her announcement.

Celeste glared at him. 'I've just retched my heart out because of you. Don't lecture me about gin! The bloody thing'll miscarry like the others, but I want to hasten the event by any means. Delia Wright says jumping down a flight of stairs works wonders, but, knowing my luck, I'd break a leg instead.' She raked him with a look. 'Bill Charlton had the wrong idea. I've never seen anyone look less like a delighted potential father than you do, sweetie.'

Through the waves of shock, Rod heard himself say tonelessly, 'Gin will only make you sicker, and you could kill yourself as well as the child with Delia Wright's suggestion. For God's sake, pull yourself together and behave like a responsible woman.'

She came up from the chair in a fury. 'Don't preach at me! You're not my damned gynaecologist!'

'No, I'm just your husband and that's damned enough for any man!'

Rod sent a note through to Sarah at the Halburton Clinic that Friday, asking her to meet him on the beach when she finished at four-thirty. He thought the beautiful isolation of Stanley Bay would provide the best setting for what he must say to her. Not normally a person to shirk unpleasant duties, it had nevertheless taken him two days to undertake this one. For probably the first time in his life he felt completely defeated, and could not bounce back from it.

Celeste was convinced that she would miscarry at three to four months, as she had with the two previous pregnancies, but he knew it was very possible that she would not. One morning hour had tied them in the most unequivocal

151

way possible. Whatever he felt for Celeste he could never abandon his child, and that entailed a lifetime's commitment. He still meant to return to Australia. If Celeste's hopes were realized, he would be free to go alone. If not, he would do his best for the child and try never to resent it. Whatever the outcome of the pregnancy, that brief promise of happiness with a girl as serene and beckoning as moonlight on a dark night had been extinguished.

As four-thirty loomed on that Friday afternoon, Rod tried to concentrate on a case report concerning a pregnant girl who claimed she had been raped by a devil. It was a familiar story. Youngsters barely into puberty were waylaid by vicious toughs disguised by face masks of the villains in Chinese folklore. The girls were so terrified they allowed themselves to be subjected to all manner of perversions, believing that the 'devils' would punish their entire family if they so much as struggled. Such cases had always angered and sickened Rod, but he saw this as one of the unalterable alien facets of a place he could not wait to leave, and this time remained unmoved.

He left the clinic early and took a flight of overgrown steps leading directly to the shore at that end of the bay never used by beach parties. The beauty of the clear waters fringed by soft sands, with a hilly backdrop standing against a brilliant sky, left Rod cold. All he could see was Celeste in a gaudy wrap, drinking gin and telling him his world was no more than a large cage. He walked on, the only other figure in view a coolie bowed beneath the weight of baskets filled with fish heads, which hung from a pole across his shoulders. Rod felt as burdened and resigned as that yellowed old man.

When he reached the limits of the bay, he stood gazing at distant islands like a prisoner without a boat viewing freedom so near and yet so far. He was so lost in that tragedy he did not hear Sarah approach.

'I must have lived through two whole lifetimes during the past nine days. That *wretched* typhoon! How dreadfully inconsiderate of it to arrive just as we're about to change the world.'

He turned to discover just how devastating his farewell

was going to be. Her face was blushed by love; her eyes glowing with laughter and excitement.

'You can't imagine my impatience. It's one of my worst failings, I warn you.' Her wide, loving smile faded as she studied his face. 'I'm so sorry. You've been working non-stop for days, and this whole business must be difficult for you. How thoughtless of me to ramble on about my own feelings – but I've never been in love before.' The smile returned briefly. 'I now know how Marion feels about her Bill, because I've been as restless as she since that day beside the Peak Railway. Father's beginning to notice my hostility – surprising when he has never been perceptive where I'm concerned – and Olivia has twice questioned my response to her. I can't bring myself to tell them I've discovered their abominable secret, so the atmosphere at Echoes is growing unbearable. With the constant thunder of a torrent through the gorge to contend with, and workmen hammering all over the house, I've even been unable to settle to serious practice. See what a disturbing effect you have on me, Roderick James Durman.'

He had to prevent her from any more words she would later find humiliating. 'I'm afraid I've something to tell you which makes what we planned impossible.'

'Then we'll make a new plan.'

'That's not what I meant.'

A shadow of apprehension crossed her face. 'Your wife won't give you a divorce? That makes the situation wretched for you. I'm sorry, Rod, but you foresaw that possibility.'

'Yes, I did ... but she presented me with one I didn't foresee. She's pregnant.'

The impact of his words was completely deflected by her mistaken conclusion. 'Then you have grounds for divorcing *her* – perfect grounds.'

Came the moment he had delayed for two days, and the words almost stuck in his throat. 'The child's mine, Sarah.'

For several moments she gazed up at him like an animal he had just cruelly snared. 'Yours? How can it be yours?' she demanded with an effort. 'You're living separate lives, you said. You have been for some years. She means abso-lutely nothing to you ... *you said!*'

He had to suffer her laboured condemnation in silence. What could he possibly say to ease her pain and disillusionment? She began backing away, paler than ever.

'What other lies have you told me? Were you sincere in *anything* you said? What did you hope to gain from me? Adoration from someone searching for a hero? Well, you got it, didn't you? You played your part to the hilt, right down to the white coat as pure as your ideals.' She backed further. 'Alex Tennant was right about you. Because I had no respect for him I dismissed his assessment of what you really are. My judgement of people must be hopeless, because *you're* the one who deserves no respect.' Fighting for control, she added, 'You once told me never to do with anyone else what I did with you on the day we went to Mr Wang's. I now understand your warning. What a fool I've been!'

Rod watched her turn away from him, a slender dignified figure in pale yellow, hair flying in the breeze, legs striding across the sand with increasing speed as she walked out of his life. She would have forgiven him any transgression but this one, giving proof of recent sexual intimacy with a wife he had claimed meant nothing to him. That was why he had had no option but to deliver the blow he guessed she would be unable to accept. Someone as sensitive and romantic as Sarah would take a long time to recover from it. The damage he had just inflicted on a member of the Channing family more than cancelled out what Sir Peter had done to the Durmans.

Alex lay sweating on a hillside and cursed as heartily as his friends, who were equally averse to spending their free time doing something for which they had no enthusiasm. His eyes ached as they scanned the scrub-covered rocky slopes looking for any sign of men wearing broad red armbands over their khaki – the supposed enemies today. It reminded him of games played by small boys wearing papier mâché caps and wooden swords. When an 'enemy' was sighted, both boys stood up, said 'bang-bang', then argued over which of them was obliged to pretend he was dead. How could an exercise of this nature prepare men for the real thing? Only the most earnest, dedicated or experienced among them managed to conjure up the life-or-death flavour in what they were doing here. Unfortunately, the men Alex was supposed to lead all lacked his sense of the absurd. As the majority were Chinese or Indian, he accepted that they felt strongly about defence of their island home, particularly as a number of them had branches of their families in China and had heard first-hand stories of Japanese atrocities.

For two more hours Alex clambered about the hillside trying to look as if he believed in what he was doing. At the end of that time he had 'killed' or captured many of the opposing group. Much to his own amazement he seemed to have an aptitude for stalking and outwitting an enemy.

As he was driven back to Kowloon in a military convoy, Alex's thoughts dwelt on the potentially scandalous affair linked to Sarah's father. He believed he had uncovered damning evidence concerning the Bolton-Rochas crash. A complete study of the files his firm had inherited from the company had led to further questioning of Giles on the subject of the rise and fall of shares prior to eventual collapse. Discreet enquiries of acquaintances in banking, including a junior director of Channing's, then prompted an investigation that combined business with pleasure. Women could be persuaded to betray even the closest secrets and the truth was so near he was prepared to do almost anything to gain it.

The facts he now possessed added up to a very unsavoury story – one he could not prove because certain of his informants would never publicly repeat information. In any case, he had no real desire to go that far. The deed was done, long over ... and his own father had committed worse, far worse. Accusations against residents of this most exclusive colony would surely bring retaliation on Maurice Tennant's son. Finding the truth had given Alex great satisfaction, however. He appeared to be a black sheep among quite a flock of them.

As far as he could deduce, Colin Bolton-Sneed had suspected that his company could not survive against the giants and contrived the means to emerge with enough money for luxurious survival. The placing of substantial orders for two new ships and an injection of cash from a bank as big as Channing's invoked confidence in investors. Before this news was made public, certain people bought up shares through friends or under cover of a false identity, which they sold at a premium when the stock-market demand reached its zenith shortly before the staged crash.

Bolton-Sneed had almost certainly known the ships would not be delivered in time. Alex suspected the fires in the godowns had also been set by men paid by Bolton-Sneed, for he had proof of the purchase of a majority of shares by the sister-in-law of the American who had married the man and left for Honolulu at the vital moment. The sale of those shares had realized a considerable fortune for the Bolton-Sneeds, plus a nice commission for the sister-in-law.

Finding definite evidence against Sir Peter Channing had proved difficult, but the accountant, Derek Lord, had carelessly used his Chinese mistress as a proxy to purchase shares for him. There could be little doubt that Sir Peter had used a fictitious company to make his pile, in return for recommending the loan to a firm whose accounts were falsified by Derek Lord for the purpose. Olivia had inherited her husband's ill-gotten gains, which made her a partner in crime to Sir Peter. It amused Alex, more than anything else, to have discovered the unique link between the pair that was so pure yet so binding. Each relied on the other's discretion, so they had discovered the best way of ensuring it without legal ties neither wanted. Alex was certain Sarah had no knowledge of all this – it had happened long before she arrived – and he filled many quiet moments by imagining himself telling her that her father did not live up to her rigid standards. For now, he intended to keep his knowledge to himself. It might be useful one day.

On arrival back in Kowloon, Alex left the rest of the weary psuedo-soldiers and took a rickshaw to Kai Tak. Jim Maiden was there with *Dragonfly*, as arranged, but the RAF man was looking rather worried as Alex paid the coolie and approached him.

'What's up, Jim? Something wrong with the engine?'

'No, Mr Tennant, she's fine. It's that weather over there.' He pointed towards Lantau. 'Don't look too good to me. Better not take her up now.'

Alex clapped him on the shoulder, grinning. 'You're always such a prophet of doom. A slight rattle in the nose, a splutter in the tanks or a cloud on the horizon and you advise me to stay on the ground. It's obvious you're no pilot.'

'More bravado than sense, most of them,' was Jim's observation. 'That's why so many crash. Won't listen to them who knows best.'

'Good thing, or powered flight would still be unknown to man.' He studied the dark barrier of cloud over Lantau, then dropped his gaze to the beautiful red machine riding the ripples. He had been looking forward to taking her up this afternoon – a reward for the silly antics of the day. Admittedly, the exercise had finished later than scheduled so night would curtail the flight. Would darkness arrive before the bad weather? He decided to risk it, and went off to change his dusty khaki for white flying overalls, leaving Jim scowling in disapproval.

It was wonderful to be airborne. Speed in the air exceeded the elation of it on water or land, he had discovered. After crawling through undergrowth housing all manner of verminous creatures, the pleasure of swooping and gliding through the heavens, master of himself and his machine, was greater than usual. As he overflew the New Territories, away from the coming bad weather, he looked down on the terrain where he had just fought a mock battle. If he ever had to face an enemy he would prefer to do so in an aircraft than on the ground. He would be responsible only for his own life, not those of others under his command. Into his mind came that voice which disturbed him so frequently. *You have no belief in yourself. That means you'll die the slowest death of all.*

Sudden anger brought the desire to be reckless. She admired a lecherous bruiser from the Outback because of his romantic profession, but he never had to take risks with his own life. Dispensing pills and applying bandages was child's play. Could the dark, brooding doctor tempt fate by pitting himself and machine against the elements? Alex doubted it. The fellow got by on the kind of mentality that relied on muscle-power and the awe in which medical men are

157

generally held. Sarah Channing had set her dawning sexual sights on all the wrong attributes.

Jealousy of Rod Durman led Alex to indulge that desire to be reckless. Flying over sea beyond the border with China, he looked down on the coastal belt now occupied by Japanese troops and was disappointed that it looked little different from the New Territories. A few miles further on, however, his attention was fully taken by a sight that *was* different and quite unexpected. He leaned from the cockpit to get a better view. In a tiny inlet was a concentration of small boats moored in precise fashion, their design unlike the usual sampans or assortment of poor fishing-craft. The neat arrangement of these grey vessels aroused in Alex a sense of curiosity he was driven to satisfy.

Circling seaward, he then dived towards the shore in a manoeuvre that enabled him to flatten out very low over the inlet. The sea changed from blue to green, then to muddy brown beneath the scarlet floats as Alex alternately watched his altimeter and the scene passing below. *Dragonfly* shot past too swiftly, so he began to climb in preparation for another pass in the opposite direction. The import of what he believed he had discovered made the back of his neck tingle. Why would the Japanese have twenty or more fast launches moored in an area boasting nothing more than paddy fields and the usual crumbling villages?

All at once, the sensation of crossing hostile country invaded him and set his pulse racing. He was now aware of the roar of *Dragonfly*'s engine shattering this rural tranquillity, betraying his presence. He wished he could muffle it. The seaplane was designed for speed, however, and he had always revelled in the thunder of powered propulsion. The second dive increased that thunder until the excitement of what he was doing overcame apprehension to set him laughing exultantly. As the mud-coloured ribbon of water grew nearer and clearer, Alex concentrated thoughts and actions. *Dragonfly* swooped down on the series of small jetties, alongside which boats were tied in fours, as Alex hung over the side of the cockpit to take a better look at them. He saw machine-guns fore and aft of each, and his excitement trebled. So far as he was aware, the Hong Kong garrison knew nothing of this armed armada moored very close to the border. Engrossed with this discovery, Alex continued flying low towards the mouth of the inlet knowing he must report what he had seen on his return to Kai Tak.

It was a moment or two before he grew aware of a curious rat-a-tatting on the fuselage to his right, and leaned out to discover the cause. Almost instantly there was a thump on his arm, a burning pain and a red stain that began to spread very quickly over his white sleeve. Thought was momentarily suspended as Alex stared at it. Then came the astonishing truth. It was no longer a case of boys saying 'bang-bang' and arguing over who should pretend to be dead. Somewhere along the banks of this inlet was a machine-gun post. The weapon had just been fired at him by someone using real bullets; someone who intended no argument over which of them should be dead.

Instinct took over as Alex, shocked and in pain, put his aircraft into a climb that took him in a wide turn over the sea and on a course for Kowloon. Knowing he should tie something around his arm to stanch the flow of blood, Alex glanced at his feet hoping Jim might have left a rag or cloth of some kind on the floor of the cockpit. There was none, but he saw holes in the fuselage. *Dragonfly* had caught the brunt of that attack designed to bring her down. Alarm touched him briefly. No one knew where he was – even Jim Maiden – and this area was occupied by people who had just advertised their attitude towards intruders.

For probably the first time in his life Alex knew no one was going to help him out of an appalling situation. If *Dragonfly* had sustained serious damage he would only know when she began to fail. Then he would have to fight for survival any way he could. Heart pounding, he flew on in the expectation of hearing the engine cut out or of seeing a float drop to the cobalt depths below. *Dragonfly* roared on reassuringly as minutes and miles slowly passed. He was losing blood at a dismaying rate, however. His right sleeve was saturated and a sticky pool was forming at his feet. He would need medical attention as soon as he reached Kai Tak.

When Alex crossed the border of the New Territories he

felt little sense of relief. He was still alone over the sea. If *Dragonfly* suddenly fell apart, he would plummet into it a mile off the coast and drown before anyone could reach him – supposing that anyone actually saw it happen. His right arm had grown numb and useless, so he was flying the machine left-handed. His attempt to estimate how long it would be before he reached Kowloon failed. His brain was too weary to cope with mathematics. Coldness had crept into every part of his body in that open cockpit; his teeth were chattering and he was shivering uncontrollably. When he studied the coastline it seemed blurred, dancing up and down before his eyes so that he could not identify landmarks. He had no idea where he was.

It was growing dark. How much of that darkness was due to oncoming night and how much to his condition, he was unsure. It frightened him. How would he see well enough to land on a shifting sea? Several minutes later, the problem no longer bothered him. Slumped in his seat, too frozen to move, he did not care who or where he was. All he could hear was a faint voice telling him he would die the slowest death of all. She was wrong. It would be swift. All he had to do now was to close his eyes.

He never did, because from the vague dusk ahead a massive dark-green wall materialized. The shock of it set up a reflexive action. Pulling on the stick with his left hand, Alex watched the tree-clad hill swing away dizzily until there was only greyness ahead once more. Swift movement dispelled the numbness in his arm to bring a return of grinding pain. This served to prod his brain into some kind of cohesive thought that told him he must get down now, or never. Peering over the edge of the cockpit like a man intoxicated, Alex made out what could have been a finger of land stretching into a dark shifting expanse of sea. It offered his best chance. Plenty of water for *Dragonfly*'s floats, but a peninsula that must support life of some kind – people who might help him.

Even as he pushed the stick forward he felt in his heart that no one *could* help him. It was tricky enough to land on choppy water in decent light, totally alert. How could he possibly do it now? As the alternative was hardly more attractive, Alex continued his descent, wondering if Colin Weatherly had felt this way on realizing he could not avoid hitting that tug in the Solent. Perhaps it was true justice that his own death should also be a watery one.

Unable to gauge his height above the sea, Alex had to pray for heavenly guidance. It grew warmer as he flattened out a little, but it seemed darker down here and he lost all hope of a safe landing. All he could do was continue in a shallow descent until he hit the sea, or stalled and pitched forward. Then he could sleep.

It came suddenly. A shuddering thump, a stomach-churning lift, then another thump which brought the sound of tearing wood as the machine was wrenched so fast in a circle Alex was thrown against his right arm. His yell of pain was all part of the frightening melody around him while *Dragonfly* performed a crazy dance to it. The engine laboured in deafening bursts as the aircraft did everything save capsize, until Alex's brain told him to switch off. When the roar died away there was the sinister silence of sea and encroaching night all around him, plus the dread certainty that *Dragonfly* was slowly sinking. Already she was tilting to port, which suggested that the float was damaged.

He knew he must get out or be dragged under by the wreckage, but his strength had deserted him. So had his will. It seemed so much easier to stay where he was and drift off to sleep before the sea closed over his head. Poetic justice for the death of a friend who had crashed and died in a madcap race.

Yet, when Alex felt water seeping in by his feet, inborn desire for survival set him struggling to escape his sinking coffin. Grasping, clawing, sobbing with effort and the agony of his wound, he inched his way from the narrow cockpit knowing he would sooner take the slender chance of defeating the sea than be dragged under with no chance whatever.

Falling heavily into the heaving surface, Alex clung to the tilting float with his left hand and faced facts. He could not swim with a useless right arm. All he could do was support himself by the wreck for as long as it was there, then try to float in the hope of being washed up by the flow of the tide.

The undulating motion did nothing to ease waves of giddiness invading him, and his hopes began to wane. The slowest death of all, she had said. Should he simply let go and slip under?

Strong hands came beneath his armpits; a voice commanded him to go limp and make no attempt to struggle. A hand moved to beneath his chin urging him on to his back. The voice told him again to relax and float. Perhaps Colin Weatherly had come to claim and drag him down to hell. No, it was not Colin's voice ... and he was staying above the surface. Through fading consciousness Alex heard splashing, and the voice continually encouraging him. It was quite pleasant to abandon effort and be guided along by that one hand under his chin, so he closed his eyes in the confidence that all would be well.

When he next opened them he was in a tiled room lying on a narrow bed, wrapped in a number of blankets. A man stood beside the bed, filling a syringe from a small bottle. His dark hair was plastered to his scalp; a blanket was draped over his saturated shirt and trousers. His expression was grim.

Aware that Alex had regained consciousness, Rod Durman glanced down at him. 'Our ambulance will take you to the Queen Mary, where they'll see to your arm. I'll give you a shot of morphine to get you through the journey.' He concentrated on administering the painkiller, then glanced back at Alex with undisguised dislike in his dark eyes. 'I told you to ease up on the booze and pull yourself together. Perhaps you'll now take my advice.'

Jim Maiden came to the Queen Mary Hospital twice the next day. Alex was hazy with drugs the first time, but managed to impress upon the RAF corporal details of the boats he had seen along the coast. That same evening, when Jim returned, Alex was feeling more himself and anxious to hear what message his friend had regarding the sinister discovery. It astonished him.

Settling on a chair beside the high, white-covered bed, Jim came straight to the point. 'They ain't best pleased with you, Mr Tennant. I know,' he added quickly, seeing Alex's expression, 'it's not something that should be ignored. The thing is this; the Flight has strict orders not to overfly territory beyond the border, nor to do anything what might be construed as aggressive action.' He grimaced. 'Those was the OIC's very words . . . more or less.'

'But those boats are there for a purpose, and it's not to catch fish!' Alex cried.

Jim nodded. 'That's obvious. But the OIC's hands are tied, see. The fact that you were shot at emphasizes our orders. Good thing *Dragonfly* bears no marks to identify her as British-owned, or we'd be up the creek.'

'Don't you mean up the inlet?' Alex was disgusted and deeply disappointed. 'So your pilots aren't going to take a photo reconnaissance?'

Jim shifted awkwardly on the chair. 'They'd give their eye-teeth for the chance, but they'd be court-martialled.'

'So nothing's going to be done?'

'Oh, yes. A report's been sent to General Maltby, and someone's going to come and ask you what you saw.'

'I've already *said* what I saw,' Alex fumed. 'And if they're not going to take it seriously there's no point in repeating it.'

Jim turned red. 'They're taking it seriously, Mr Tennant, but they don't much like . . . well, *amateurs* nosing about over the border and stirring up trouble.'

'The OIC's very words?' asked Alex bitterly. 'When those boats land on the beaches here they won't give a damn that I'm an amateur so long as I can fire a rifle.' He fought to control his anger. 'They mean to take Hong Kong, Jim. I shared the general view until yesterday. Those fast armed launches are only a fraction of what is probably being assembled in China ready for an invasion.'

'Nah!' Jim shook his head. 'They'd have come long ago if they meant to.'

Alex lay back against his pillows, suddenly weary, unable to pursue a conversation that had little obvious evidence to support it. Just because he had suffered a real attack from someone bent on killing in earnest, was he exaggerating the incident out of all proportion? The shock of what had happened was now overtaking him. Was he imagining large-scale attack from an army simply because he had drawn nervous reaction from a single soldier who was alarmed by a swooping scarlet aircraft?

'So that's the end of *Dragonfly*,' he murmured.

'More or less,' Jim agreed. 'Someone at Stanley went out with a motor-boat and towed the wreck back to shore. It's on that beach just below the Halburton Clinic. Good thing they saw you come down. That doctor bloke was just getting into his car, apparently, and went into the water like billy-o. One of our officers says he's a powerful swimmer. Plays water polo . . . when he ain't busy, which isn't often. Bit of a sparky cove, it seems. Don't mind who he takes on, regardless of rank. But he's a pretty good doctor, by all accounts.'

'And rather too fond of women.'

Jim looked interested. 'Really? I never heard that about him.'

'Your officer was too keen on singing his praises, that's why.' Alex decided to change the subject. 'Well, thanks for all your splendid work on *Dragonfly*, Jim. It was fun while it lasted.'

The man looked crestfallen. 'You won't be getting another?'

'Shouldn't think so.'

After Jim left, Alex was settled for sleep by a brown-haired nurse who, despite being extremely shapely, aroused in him no desire to try his luck. There were more serious things on his mind, and the wound in his arm was starting to throb again. He lay filled with uncertainty in the dimly lit ward waiting for the sedative to help him sleep. He had spoken without thinking when he told Jim he would not replace *Dragonfly*. He had made no conscious decision on the matter yet. What he had experienced put a fresh light on everything. Life had suddenly become valuable; a commodity to be used wisely. The revelation sobered and alarmed him. When sleep came it was plagued by dreams and images that gave him no peace.

A pink-faced lieutenant with milk-fair hair and surprised blue eyes came to see Alex on the following morning. The interview proved to be very brief, and the young officer's face was poppy-red as he left the ward. After asking the patient for a concise description of the boats he *believed* he *might* have seen during a flight over an *unknown area* of the Chinese coast, the young man read a pompous lecture regarding the ill-advised actions of civilians which endangered the situation and damaged the standing of those whose profession required them to guard the safety of Hong Kong and her residents.

Alex recognized the boyish subaltern as one of the 'enemy' he had captured during the exercise on the day of his flight, and made a to-the-point comment about the fellow's ability to guard the Island or its inhabitants. He finished by saying he *believed* he *might* kick him in an *unknown area* of his bumptious person if he did not get going pretty smartly.

Hot on the heels of one unwelcome visitor came another. Rod Durman, in a white coat with the requisite stethoscope around his collar, walked down the ward and stopped at the foot of Alex's bed. He looked strained and hollow-eyed as he nodded a greeting. 'I've just been told by a cocksure little bastard who needs a good kick up the arse that you've mucked up the defence plans for this colony by flying over enemy territory and getting shot at. Is that right?'

Alex glared at him. 'How did you imagine I got two bullets in my arm?'

'I didn't think too hard about it. In a place like Hong Kong, men with too much money and time to waste often get shot at, or have their throats slit. I see them when they're brought in. My concern is treating their injuries, not how they came to be inflicted.' He glanced at the chart at the end of the bed, then looked up to say, 'I suppose I owe you an apology.'

Alex fought a battle with himself, then said, 'I suppose I owe you my life.'

'That makes us about quits,' said Rod off-handedly. 'That machine of yours – or what's left of it – is littering the beach below the clinic at Stanley. The local kids have been all over it for the past two days. Shouldn't think there's anything worth salvaging.'

'Don't worry. My mechanic quickly rescued any important gadgets.'

'You have your own mechanic?'

Alex imagined a slight sneer in the question and bridled. 'It was a figure of speech, that's all. He's an RAF fellow who has a passion for fiddling about with aircraft.'

They studied each other warily for a moment or two, then Rod said, 'You must have something of a passion for flying. It took a bit of doing, bringing that thing back with a crook right arm and losing blood fast. Any man who can carry that off must know his way around a plane.' After a brief pause, he added, 'Why don't you give up shipping and go into aviation? They're crying out for pilots, you know.'

The words touched an open wound, causing Alex to hit back. 'I don't need advice from you ... of all people. I suppose she put that notion into your head.'

Rod stiffened immediately. 'Who is *she*?'

'You know damn well! You also know that what you're doing is out of line and pretty bloody despicable. She's inexperienced, and ridiculously romantic when it comes to ideas of nobility. You're playing on her weakness quite ruthlessly, you bastard!'

As Rod stepped back and into a ray of sunlight from the window, Alex saw naked pain on a face working with anger. 'Don't make me regret being on hand when you ditched in the sea, Tennant.' He turned, the tails of his white coat flapping around powerful legs as he strode back up the ward.

When Alex left hospital he felt little inclination to slip back into his old routine. He tossed away all the invitations awaiting him, and twice declined to go on a binge with his pals. The one person with whom he now felt at ease was Jim Maiden. Together, they inspected the wreck of *Dragonfly* and carefully disconnected any parts that were undamaged, storing them temporarily in a rough earthen cavern below the Halburton until they could arrange for a boat to take it all across to Kai Tak.

A summons by the commanding officer of his Volunteer unit resulted in Alex being told yet again that his flight over enemy territory had been not only irresponsible, but dangerously provocative. Alex pointed out that everyone kept referring to 'enemy territory' when the Japanese were supposedly not Britain's enemy. So, either it was perfectly permissible to fly over friendly country, or the Japanese must be regarded as a hostile nation and the import of those boats in the inlet must be taken seriously. He got nowhere with his argument and departed in frustration to sit in his apartment, gazing at the nearby mainland with moody dislike. The urge to leave Hong Kong was growing. He had never been happy here. His mood deepened to remind him that he could not actually pinpoint a phase in his life when he had been. Delight and excitement he knew well. Satisfaction, perhaps, even elation, in its inebriated form, but never true, deep happiness. Lately, those states he had enjoyed no longer contained the same appeal.

On his first day back in the office, all Alex could think of was the Bolton Rochas affair, which smacked so much of his own father's activities that his depression deepened further. He had none of Maurice Tennant's love of power over others; business held no attraction for him. Maybe he *should* get out of shipping and into aviation. The Pan American Clipper from Kai Tak would get him to Australia or New Zealand very quickly. With so many of their young men away fighting, it should be easy enough to be taken on by a civil airline. It would mean foregoing the generous allowance from his mother's relations, but life was reputedly easy in the Antipodes and civil aviation paid well, besides carrying an aura of glamour that should compensate. A smart apartment, plenty of admiring women, sunshine – a fresh start. He continued to swing moodily in his revolving chair, totally uninspired by the prospect. What in hell *did* he want? As if by way of an answer, Chang knocked and entered to announce that Miss Sarah Channing would like to see him urgently, and was waiting in the visitor's room.

Astonishment kept Alex in his chair for some moments, then he got up telling his clerk to show Miss Channing in. Surely she had not come to fire up in defence of her two-timing doctor, who had repeated to her that accusation made in hospital. She could not be *that* infatuated, and Durman was not *that* despicable. Yet what other reason would bring her here?

Dressed in an expensive coffee-coloured two-piece with cream trimming, Sarah again reminded Alex of that very English brand of beauty found in women who were rarely conscious of it. Yet he was taken aback by the dark shadows beneath her eyes and by her obvious air of unhappiness. Circling his desk, he held the chair while she sat, trying to marshal his thoughts in this unexpected situation. When he returned to face her, the formal enquiry after her health died on his lips. Instead, he went straight to the point. 'I imagine you've come here only as a last resort.'

Her eyes widened. 'How did you know?'

'You've always made it clear my company is most unwelcome.'

'Oh . . . I see.'

He was disturbed by her lack of vitality. Even before Durman had come upon the scene and released her reluctant personality, Sarah had been self-possessed. She now seemed unsure; nervous even. In a surprising rush of sympathy, Alex sat on the corner of the desk and smiled encouragement. 'You have a problem which I might be able to help you with?'

'I need to get back to England as soon as possible,' she told him with a hint of desperation. 'I've tried all the other shipping companies, without success. Could you check your lists to see if there's a vacant cabin on any of the merchant lines? I know they sometimes take passengers. I came out on a Swedish cargo ship from Durban. It doesn't have to go all the way. I could get another from India, say, to South Africa, then fly from there.'

'Is there family trouble at home?' he asked.

She would not answer that. 'Would you check for me?'

'Of course.' He pressed the buzzer to summon Chang. 'Have you forgotten the Clipper? You could fly all the way to the United States via the Pacific. It would only take a week to cross the Atlantic from there.'

'I don't want to do that,' she said, too quickly. 'Please look at your lists. You're my last hope.'

'The story of my life,' he murmured, more and more certain that she was in some kind of desperate situation. Could the truth about her father's part in the Bolton Rochas crash have somehow begun circulating? Recalling the strain on Rod Durman's face, it seemed far more likely that *that* affair had come to a head in the most devastating fashion, forcing the girl to leave Hong Kong before . . . Sudden anger swept through him. Surely it was not as serious as *that*. It was one thing to play around with pert young women who knew the score; quite another to take advantage of someone whose ideals blinded her to the obvious. Durman should face the music, not let the poor girl go through this alone. When Chang went off to fetch the sailing schedules, Alex pursued his theory.

'I would have thought Sir Peter could have sorted something out for you.'

She pushed back her hair with a nervous movement. 'I want to make the arrangements myself.'

He aimed at the bull's-eye. 'Does he know you're planning to leave?'

'Until I know a sailing date there's no point in telling anyone.'

Chang returned with the papers, giving Alex time to put two and two together to make a sum he found unacceptable. If Sarah did not manage to get away before the truth became obvious, she would be pilloried by the snobs and martinets of this colony until her heart was broken. She was the type of girl who protected her seducer's identity, allowing him off scot free. Durman should be exposed and ruined.

'*Is* there a cabin available?' Sarah's urgent question brought him from his thoughts and set him scanning the lists. When he glanced up, he was smitten by her expression and no longer wished to score points by revealing that her father was not the pillar of respectability she believed him to be. Betrayal by one man she had put on a pedestal was more than enough to crush all her idealistic attitudes.

'There's a single cabin, as yet unreserved, on a small Indonesian freighter leaving for Singapore next week. From there, I'm afraid it goes east to Sumatra, Java and the smaller islands.'

'Is that all?'

Filled with compassion for someone who, with the fight

driven out of her, appealed to him in unexpected fashion, he said gently, 'That's all for November. We shall receive new schedules at the end of the week. Of course, they've been greatly reduced since the war began, but I'll let you know if there's anything suitable, if you'd like me to.'

She made no attempt to go. It was as if she wanted company – even his. He supposed she had few friends in Hong Kong so, in cryptic fashion, their relationship provided a tenuous link in the wilderness.

'I could go to Singapore next week, then try the shipping companies there for an onward passage.'

'I suppose that might be a solution,' he agreed. 'It depends on what you want most – an early departure from here or a quick voyage home.'

She appeared thrown by that so, after waiting in vain for her answer, he continued. 'You could be stranded in Singapore for weeks. Channing's has a branch there, so you'd be looked after all right, and it's a very exciting place. On the other hand, by waiting here for a couple of weeks you could get a faster ship heading west.'

Although she was gazing at him he had the feeling that she saw something else, and his compassion deepened. 'If I were you, I'd take the Clipper to Australia and across the Pacific.'

'No!' It was surprisingly emphatic. 'I want to take the usual route home.'

'There's no longer a usual route home – hasn't been for almost two years.' He saw her indecision. 'Look, why don't I reserve for you the cabin to Singapore before it's taken up by somebody else. Then, when the new schedules arrive, I'll look for a better prospect and cancel the other. Either way, you're almost sure to be leaving Hong Kong before Christmas.'

She gave a long sigh as she looked at him almost helplessly. 'I hated coming here . . . but you've been marvellous. It's very good of you to take so much trouble over this.'

'It's my job. I don't really drink all the time I'm here, you know. People expect it of me, so I go along with the belief.'

'You shouldn't.' She got to her feet, clutching the cream leather bag under her left arm so tightly her knuckles showed white. 'I'd like to apologize for some of the things I've said to you. I had no right to judge you.'

He left his desk to approach her. 'None of us has the right to judge others, but we all do. It's such fun.'

On the point of saying more, she changed her mind and made for the door. Alex moved swiftly to open it for her, probing one last time.

'I suppose you heard about my crash last week. Your doctor friend pulled me out of the drink before I drowned – a heroic rescue. It seems I had the wrong idea about him.'

'Oh, that's *dreadfully* easy to do,' she said bitterly, telling him he was on the right track. 'Goodbye, Mr Tennant.'

'Please call me Alex,' he said.

'It's rather too late now, isn't it?'

He watched her walk the length of the airy sun-splashed office and knew regret that it *was*. Four days later he sent her, by hand, a note telling her he had cancelled the passage to Singapore and booked a cabin for her on a South American freighter calling at Cape Town, which sailed on December 10. He did not add that he had booked a second cabin for himself.

Chapter Seven

Alex's note reached Sarah just before noon. She regretted the twelve-day delay, but felt that Cape Town would be an ideal port from which to arrange the rest of her journey home. Now departure was certain she could make her plans. The first task was to write to Ellie warning of her return. The freighter was due to reach Cape Town on January 19, so Sarah was unlikely to be in England until February even if she were lucky enough to get a seat on an Imperial Airways flying-boat. In contrast with the usual long, loving letters full of thoughts and feelings, Sarah wrote a brief account of her travel plans in the hope that it would arrive at Noon Cottage before she did. A single sentence at the end explained to Ellie that the experiment had failed, so it was better to return than to prolong a situation that could never improve. A note to Alex Tennant thanking him for his efforts on her behalf was quickly penned and put with the other envelopes to post.

With that done, Sarah sat at the writing desk facing the prospect of two more weeks in Hong Kong. If it had not been for the war she could have left almost immediately on one of the many liners that used to ply to and from the Orient, and nurse her wounds on the high seas. As it was she could not run away from the deepest pain she had known – deeper even than that she'd felt on parting from Ellie. The knowledge added to her distress, for her grandmother's love was true and enduring, not to be compared with a passing passion that allowed a man to kiss one woman, then go home to bed another. The thought of Rod indulging in the most intimate lovemaking possible with his flamboyant, sensuous wife brought the white-hot fire of jealousy. It swamped cool reason, which told her she could not have been wrong about his sincerity. Surely there had been pain as acute as her own in his expression that afternoon on the beach. Yet that woman was carrying his child. Or was she? Had he told her the surest lie to ensure his extrication from a difficult situation? Time would show whether or not Celeste Durman was pregnant, but Sarah had no intention of waiting to find out. Either way, it would prove heartbreaking. She would discover that Rod was either a liar or a prospective father. Better by far to be on the other side of the world by then, with music the only love in her life.

During her session with Jakob Myburgh that afternoon, he cast doubts for a second time on that resolution. After thirty minutes' work on a difficult study in F, her tutor threw up his hands in despair.

'No, no, you have pork sausages for fingers and mashed potato inside your head. Think, think! *Con*centrate! This you did last week. This *same* you did.' He sang the passage in his quavering tenor to demonstrate what his damaged hands could not. 'And did I not tell you this instead?' He sang again, emphasizing how they had agreed it should be interpreted.

Sarah nodded. 'Yes, I'm sorry. I had forgotten.'

'Forgotten? *Forgotten!*' he snorted. 'And will you forget when you are before several hundreds of people who are hoping to hear *music* coming from a young lady's fingers? Again! Again!'

Walking away with a pained expression, he stood in an attitude that suggested his ears were preparing for punishment. Sarah normally found his tutelage invaluable and amusing. Today, his attitude invoked despair of her own ability. Her fingers now felt like pork sausages; her concentration diminished further. Two minutes later she stopped playing and stood up. 'You're right, I do have mashed potato inside my head today. I apologize for wasting your time, maestro.'

The wiry old man pursed his lips while studying her, then

nodded and beckoned her to the further end of the long room. 'We shall have some tea and talk of other things. Come! Come!' He moved off to sit in an antique chair by full-length windows giving a view of Happy Valley. After ringing a small enamelled bell on the table, he pointed to a matching chair. 'Sit there, miss. One beauty resting upon another.'

Sarah tried to summon a smile, but failed. Had her talent vanished on the wings of a lost love? Beneath the silent scrutiny of hooded eyes in the face of a man whose own brilliance and musical hopes had been tragically destroyed by a road accident, she found it possible to confess her fears. 'I seem to have lost something. Whereas music has always been a joy within me, it has become . . .' She hesitated.

'Yes?'

'A challenge.'

His features registered satisfaction. 'Then you are on the verge of becoming a true artist, at last. Music should always be a challenge; it should torment, weary and persecute those who believe themselves equal to interpreting it. If it has been a joy to you, you have been no more than a mere piano-player, my dear. This is the moment when you must decide whether you wish to entertain dinner guests or to enthral millions in concert halls across the world.'

Sarah was silent while an Indonesian servant in a colour-ful batik sarong brought tea and small cakes to place on the table. He poured the tea into delft cups before retiring. Sarah remained silent, so Jakob revealed his perception by taking up a new angle on the subject.

'It has been clear to me for several weeks that you have become a victim of that irritating state known as "being in love". Possessing substantial talent does not make any of us immune, I regret to admit. Artists frequently suffer more than others – I once considered suicide in my youth; she was so very lovely – but they have greater powers of recuperation, you see. There is the challenge you spoke of.' He offered the plate of cakes. 'It takes two to create the harmony of love, and there is little to be done if one's partner grows tone deaf. A dedicated artist is alone in creating perfect harmony. It is not easily attained; perhaps it will be for ever elusive. *But . . .* it is there to be sought for the length of one's life.'

174

He took a cake, bit into it and munched in silence for a while, apparently lost in reflection. 'The lovely object of my unrequited passion married a nobleman soon after my temptation to suicide. She had ceased to be seekable when I was twenty-two.' He gave a wry smile. 'See how foolish we are to become embroiled in romantic notions? I can no longer recall her voice, but the greatness and power of music is a force that still rules me.' Leaning back in his chair he studied Sarah's expression. 'You are thinking of my useless hands. Yes, I believed my life would end because I could no longer play. Then I discovered that I had *ears*, my dear.' He gave a brief shout of laughter. 'My hands are splendid for cake-eating, my eyes are good for valuing gem stones, but my *ears* – oh, my ears are my greatest possession.' He put his deformed hands up to them. 'When the rest of Jakob Myburgh is worn out, these will continue to hear Brahms, Beethoven, Wagner, Tchaikovsky, Mahler. And if *they* ever wear out, those glorious melodies are in my head where I shall still hear them.' His hands dropped to rest on his knees, as he concluded gently. 'Of what value is transient love against such riches?'

Sarah came close to tears for the first time since Rod's farewell. This elderly man, who had given so much of his time in return for the pleasure of helping someone to achieve what had been stolen from him on the brink of a brilliant career, had suddenly become a friend. There was an age gap of over fifty years, a difference of nationality, and a tutor–pupil relationship between them, yet the bond of music had overcome all these to create understanding and allow her to say what she could not to her father. 'I'm not considering suicide. I'm running away. I was more foolish than that young Dutchman, because my love was already unseekable when I met him.'

Jakob wagged his shaggy, brindled head whilst clicking his tongue in sympathetic admonishment. 'My poor young friend.'

'I'm sailing for home in two weeks' time.' She managed a smile. 'I shall miss you.'

He sat forward with a remarkable agility to impress his words upon her. 'Never mind about *miss*. Remember all I have told you, seek what is there to be sought, and give your heart to a love that will remain constant until death. Pour your passion into your work; give your all to the whole world. When you realize the full majesty of your talent, you'll find there is more than enough to go around.'

Father and daughter dined with Olivia at the long gleaming table so often surrounded by rich, influential or titled members of the colony. Olivia was leaving for another trip to Macau at the weekend, and Sir Peter had been occupied in a series of meetings with the bank's shareholders so had avoided an evening engagement. Throughout the light meal the older pair chatted amiably on subjects ranging from how slowly repairs to typhoon damage were being made, to details of the Hong Kong Police Federation fancy-dress ball. Neither one commented on Sarah's silence, or attempted to draw her into their conversation.

Relations had been strained for some time in this grand old house. Sir Peter had accepted his daughter's hostility with a mixture of disinterest and deepening resignation, but Olivia was not a woman to be treated with dumb insolence by anyone, even a Channing.

Three exchanges, during which Sarah had countered the other woman's acid challenge with a brand of cool dignity learned from Ellie, had resulted in unspoken agreement *not* to speak unless it became imperative to do so. Olivia's underlying tendency to rule, plus the kind of aggressive superiority practised by those who knew inferiority, all came to the fore and confirmed Sarah's suspicion of the woman's initial proffered friendship. Olivia had eventually slipped up badly by saying that she had no intention of being treated with contempt by a young inexperienced girl who had made no effort to fill the rôle expected of her at Echoes. Sarah's reply had silenced her.

'I've never been certain what *your* rôle at Echoes is meant to be, Olivia, but you appear to have filled it to overflowing. There's hardly room for any other . . . and you're not even a Channing.'

Her afternoon with Jakob Myburgh had given Sarah the determination to confront these people so close to each

176

other, yet so distant from her. The Dutchman's kindness had emphasized what was lacking between herself and the man who had once loved her mother enough to create a child within her – a child who had inspired no paternal fondness. When her father and Olivia walked through to the airy room opening to the terrace, where coffee was served when no guests were present, Sarah followed and took the cup handed to her by Foo before walking to gaze from the open doorway. There was rain in the offing. The moon had a fuzzy halo around it, and the lights of Victoria were shimmery-bright below. The sound of ships' hooters seemed louder than usual. A mournful sound at the best of times, she felt, and tonight, the wailing blasts highlighted the desolation in her heart. It was goodbye to Hong Kong, where she had never felt at home but where she had finally learned there were people in the world. Ellie had wanted that, but she had surely not foreseen a love so deep and painful that to leave this island would amount to leaving behind the girl she had been for almost twenty years. The spirit of that girl would remain here for ever, and no one would come with dumplings to appease it.

Foo departed leaving the coffee tray on the table beside Olivia. She and Sir Peter were momentarily silent as they sipped from delicate cups decorated in pink, green and gold, so Sarah turned to face them across a room containing the accumulated treasures of several generations of rich bankers.

'Father, I suppose I should have asked you this when I first arrived, but I imagined the answer would become obvious. If it did, I didn't recognize it. Will you now tell me why you sent for me?'

Sir Peter's thin face showed irritation mingled with surprise that she had actually spoken after so long a silence. 'You've been in Hong Kong for almost a year. What a foolish question.'

'Then give it a foolish answer. It'll be better than none.'

Olivia set down her cup and saucer and leaned back, smoothing the skirt of her turquoise dinner gown. 'Your father has had a particularly demanding series of meetings, and this is one of the few evenings in which he can relax.

Don't you think you should spare him another bout of the unattractive mood you've been in lately?'

Sarah gave her a cool look. 'Please don't interrupt, Olivia. Your chance to be eloquent will come in a moment.'

Sir Peter bristled. 'Don't be impertinent, Sarah!'

'I'm not the child of four you sent away to England, Father. I believe I am entitled to speak as I choose in my own home to someone who is only a guest here!' When he made to say something, she continued swiftly: 'I was unable to question your motives sixteen years ago when I was banished. Now I do, and would like a reply, please. Why was I summoned here?'

'What is this all about?' he demanded testily.

'*Why*, Father?'

After a glance at Olivia's tight expression, he realized she intended offering no further assistance and said, in weary tones, 'Your time at Cheltenham had come to an end. It had always been my intention that you should come out here at that point. It so happened that the situation in Britain made it even more imperative that you should. I could not have you dressing up in uniform, being sent to the firing line. Or even working in a factory in some city being bombed daily.'

'Mother drove a taxi in London during your war. Why should you think I'm incapable of emulating her?'

His expression hardened. 'The circumstances were altogether different. Your mother was in no real danger.'

'They bombed London, didn't they?'

'Where is all this leading, Sarah?' he demanded, getting to his feet.

'It's leading to the reason why you sent for me, when it's more than obvious that you have no real interest in your daughter as a person. You shook my hand when I arrived, and have kept me at hand-shaking distance. Only once have you spoken to me as a father, and that was to say how disappointed you were in me.'

His frown suggested that he did not remember the occasion, then light dawned. 'The night of an important dinner party! If you recall, you had sent Ming back with no indication of where you had gone, or with whom. I was deeply worried.'

'About my safety ... or a possible demand for ransom from the Triads?'

Sir Peter gave a thin smile. 'One ties in with the other. You should know that after almost twelve months here.'

'Yes, I suppose I should ... but you have never talked to me about the darker side of this community.'

'Running a huge banking corporation is no easy task. If you were my son, you would be at my side, learning about the problems and responsibilities of such an organization. As it is, you cannot be expected to understand the demands on my time.'

She rose to that. 'If it is never explained to me, of course I can't understand. You have never attempted to take me into your confidence.'

'Because you are constantly hunched over the keyboard of a piano, showing little interest in anything else.' Despite his usual outward self-assurance, there were signs of growing inner anger. 'As a Channing you are destined to follow a pattern set by this family. I saw to it that you were given the best possible education, and Olivia was ready to launch you into the social environment to which any child of mine automatically belongs. You would have none of it. After almost twelve months you remain aloof in company, you make little attempt to ingratiate yourself with those whose acceptance is important, and you continue to pursue the notion of becoming a performing musician. There has been absolutely no attempt on your part to accept your responsibility towards me, and the family.'

'I'm sorry,' she said coldly. 'After almost twelve months perhaps you'd be good enough to tell me what that is?'

Her tone and manner appeared to fan his smouldering anger. He could conceal it no longer. 'Your hostility over the past few weeks hasn't passed unnoticed either by me or by Olivia. We have no idea what has prompted it. It is now verging on insolence, which is inexcusable. You have been offered every advantage in life and are expected to play your part in return.' He moved across to study a portrait of past presidents of the bank, hanging against a wall covered with ivory silk. 'I had no sons to take my place and, in turn, produce their own sons to inherit a proud tradition. If your brother had survived, you could have played your piano with my blessing.' He swung back to face her. 'Your husband will automatically become my heir; he will receive a wedding present of the Channing Mercantile Banking Corporation, Far-Eastern Branch. He will receive a fortune along with my daughter, so it is vitally important that he be the right man.' He let out his breath in a gusty sigh. 'The only way to ensure that was to bring you to Hong Kong so that you mixed with the finest applicants for the honour and privilege. It was essential that you also gained the necessary poise and the knowledge of how things are done out here, so that you would play your rôle with ease.'

'I see,' she said, her dislike of him deepening. 'You lied to Ellie when you wrote that you wanted us to know each other and grow close. The lie masked a calculating plan to marry me off to someone of your choice who would substitute for your lost son – my brother. For that reason alone I was obliged to leave someone I love dearly, and the only home I remember?'

'Be sensible! I couldn't risk your making a foolishly emotional wartime marriage with some soldier or airman from an unsuitable background.'

Her composure crumbled to allow impassioned words to pour from her. 'I'm determined to pursue a musical career in spite of your scathing comments about "piano-players". It will dominate my life to the extent of excluding marriage, so your precious bank will have to look elsewhere for an heir. I have no part to play in return for being given every advantage, as you claim. Is it an advantage to lose one's mother at the age of four and be sent away across the world to a strange relative? Is it an advantage to be regarded by one's father as an object of barter for acquiring a suitable successor? Is it an advantage to receive no love or praise from the one surviving parent? Your life is governed by material things, Father. You deride my musical ability because you're unable to place monetary value on it. You despair of me because the standards taught me by Ellie are based on humanity rather than on the Hong Kong dollar. You move around in your saintly social enclave, each member of which believes in his own consequence whilst practising the kind of underhand tricks soldiers and airmen from an unsuitable background would never consider.'

Taking a deep breath to steady herself, she said, 'I hardly know how or why I have remained here so long – perhaps for Ellie's sake, because she doesn't believe in giving up easily – but I've had enough of this life you regard with great satisfaction. I'm leaving Hong Kong and going home.'

'What nonsense,' he said dismissively. 'It's out of the question.'

'I had a note from Alex Tennant this morning.'

Her father looked up sharply. 'Tennant? I thought you had little to do with him.'

'I've never much liked him, but he's proved to me how wrong one can be about people. I sail with the *San Maritino* on the tenth, and I don't believe Ellie will condemn my decision. I know what you did, Father – you and Olivia. When I recovered from the shock of it, I realized I couldn't stay with two people who would stoop to such measures to ruin others' lives without a qualm. I've never had reason to love you, Father, but even respect has now died. I can't leave quickly enough.'

Sir Peter stared at her with dawning dismay. 'Who else knows of it?'

'Only one,' she said, thinking of her distress for Rod at the Peak Railway, and the plans they had made. 'Apart from your accomplices, of course.'

'Can he be relied upon to keep silent?'

'I wouldn't rely on *anything* where he's concerned, but he'd gain nothing by spreading the story. The damage has been done.' Bitterness welled up in her anew. '*I* won't mention it to anyone, particularly to Ellie. I'll invent an excuse for my return that will leave your integrity intact.' She turned towards Olivia, who was looking pale and strained. 'Your part in the affair was equally contemptible. I'm sure you think you've got away with it scot free, but this island is small and word gets around. It's my earnest hope that a great number of people will soon share the distrust I've had of you from our first meeting. I might well have failed to fulfil expectations, but I have faithfully followed the standards taught me by a woman who shows you

181

up as the ruthless social climber you are beneath those jade ornaments. I wish you well of Echoes and of my father. Your self-seeking devotion to them both deserves that reward.' She turned back to Sir Peter. 'Until I leave on the *San Maritino* please exclude me from any social engagements you may have. I think we've reached a point of no return tonight!'

When she was almost at the door, her father said, 'What you have heard is only one side of the story. You should take into account my reasons for what I did.'

She turned back. 'I know your reasons . . . and my interest in the affair is well and truly over. Goodnight, Father.'

'No, stay!' He approached her, once again the assured man of business. 'That screen of music you hide behind distorts your view of reality. Allow the accused to speak in his defence.'

'There *is* no defence for what you did,' she cried.

'The voice of inexperience which is unfit to judge. People often act because they have no choice.'

On the point of declaring that he had taken his revenge on the Durmans out of pure pique, Sarah was silenced by her father's next words.

'When a man has wealth, he is in constant danger from others who want a share. They use various means to lay hands on it, from marriage to criminal threat, with deception, business acumen and kidnapping in between. I've been exposed to several of the more minor versions, but some years ago I inadvertently upset a prominent Chinese merchant whom I was unaware had connections with the Triads. They turned their attention on me so rapidly I was unprepared. Their demands increased until I saw financial ruin in sight. It was at that desperate point that Colin Bolton-Sneed approached me with a proposition that offered a way out. I seized it without hesitation, but it was necessary to involve Derek Lord, who had to juggle the accounts.' He sighed. 'The rest you already know. Yes, some people went under – it's the luck of this game we all play – but I, and the bank, survived until the Triads found a fresh victim. I made very little personal gain because most of it was paid over to Chinese hiding their criminal connections behind a façade of respectability, but Derek acquired a fortune beyond his dreams. The fool let it go to his head, and died of cholera caught from frequenting a Chinese area. Olivia inherited a sizeable sum, and we consequently formed a comfortable relationship that assured our silence on the affair as well as providing mutual benefits.'

Sir Peter rubbed his brow with a weary hand. 'For the first five years I lived in dread of this coming to light, then I believed we were safe. But ever since Tennant mentioned at your last concert that he had studied the Bolton Rochas affair and found it fascinating reading, I've been uneasy about him. And so has Olivia. Can you *truly* assure me that he will keep his counsel after telling you about it?'

Sarah stared at the face before her and knew she would never want to see it again once she escaped from this island colony. If he had seemed a stranger before, he was a monster now.

'Alex Tennant told me nothing except the sailing date of the *San Maritino*,' she said, in a voice that was starting to shake. 'I was referring to your destruction of Dr and Mrs Durman's standing in Hong Kong ... but it seems your capacity for dirty tricks is boundless. What else ought you to confess before I leave?' She began to back away from him. 'You should have married Olivia. Together, you'd have produced a child perfectly equipped to continue your ruthless reign of Channing Mercantile, and I could have been a "piano-player" without ruffling your deep, dark waters.'

Having given the hospital authorities their required two months' notice of his resignation, Rod did his best to fulfil his duties at the Queen Mary despite personal anguish as 1941 neared its close. He expected to be in Australia for Christmas, either alone or with a hostile, pregnant wife. He had exchanged days with another doctor at the Halburton, kept away from Victoria and refused all social invitations in a bid to avoid the pain of meeting Sarah. He knew she still attended the clinic at Stanley on Fridays, which suggested that she had decided to remain in Hong Kong. Was that very English trait of dignity in the face of humiliation responsible for her decision? Was she still trying to repay the love and caring of the grandmother who had sent her here by refusing to leave now the going was rough? Or perhaps he was mistaken about the depth of her feelings, and she had coolly written him off as a necessary lesson in life.

He was not as fortunate. Only now was he aware of how much he had lost. The future seemed bleak and lonely whichever way he looked at it. The surge of certainty that had filled him after the typhoon had vanished beneath the crushing weight of Celeste's announcement. She would never accept life in an Outback town. As he had no taste for general practice it would mean another hospital post in a big city ... and a resumption of life as it had been before a concerto penetrated the hard protective shell he had grown to bring to life a man he had almost forgotten. The loss of Sarah hit him harder than he had thought possible. He had been fooling himself in believing he could easily let her go if and when she discovered that passion had cooled beneath the demands of music.

Although their brief relationship had never been physical, Rod was now plagued by acute sexual desire for the girl he could not have. Walking along the sands at Stanley, he would recall how her silky hair lifted in the breeze and long to crush it in his hands, feel it against his bare skin. When driving along the coast road, he would suddenly remember that moment in Wang Chua's garden when she had turned and recognition had touched them both. Why had he held back from drawing her into his arms and exploiting her sense of wonder? He yearned for that opportunity again, the opportunity that would never come. During wakeful nights, with Celeste sleeping in the other bed, thoughts of having Sarah alongside him in eager surrender aroused such desire it became torment. Her clear, guileless eyes, her precise accent, her soft laugh all haunted him ceaselessly as he ticked off the days and prayed that Celeste would miscarry and free him from a marriage that had turned into a life sentence. Time and again he told himself he had been a fool not to have brought it to an end long ago. The professional reputation he had guarded so jealously counted for nought now, but he had gained nothing in the losing of it.

The full cost of meeting Sir Peter's daughter extended to his finances. On checking at the bank on the amount necessary to get him out of the red, he was staggered. The sale of his car and Celeste's few pieces of decent jewellery would nowhere near settle it, and he then fully realized the extent to which she had spent in order to keep up with Sir Peter's obliging friends. Knowing he had no alternative, Rod sent a cable asking his father for a large loan. The money was transferred without delay. He was able to settle his debts, leaving enough for two air tickets on the Clipper departing the second week of December. He prayed, with only the faintest sense of professional guilt, that he would need just one of them.

His prayer was not answered. The expected miscarriage had not taken place by the start of December. Instead of attending a meeting to discuss a scheme that would not be implemented until after his departure, Rod took a rickshaw to the Pan American office on the fourth day of the month to confirm and pay for both bookings on the Clipper the following week. It represented the sealing of his fate, blackening his mood so much he walked to a nearby hotel and ordered a double whisky at the bar. From the window he had a clear view of the mansions of the mid-levels, so he tortured himself by gazing in the direction of Echoes while downing his drink and several more.

After half an hour he could stand it no longer and left the bar stool to make his way to the foyer. He was halfway across it when the revolving door spilled into the hushed elegance of the hotel a dark-haired woman in a striking cherry-red costume, who was closely followed by a doorman carrying a number of boxes and packages bearing the names of Hong Kong's leading stores.

She led the way to the desk and said to the uniformed attendant, 'Look after these while I have lunch with my friends. Sir Peter Channing's chauffeur will collect them when he comes for me at three.'

As she turned, she caught sight of Rod, hesitated, then headed for the doors of the restaurant with no gesture of recognition. The slight caused Rod's temper to soar instantly. He walked with great deliberation directly into her path, forcing her to stop on the central motif of the marble floor beneath a trio of fans unmoving on this cool December day.

'Good morning, Mrs Lord.'

She assumed an aloof expression. 'Have we met?'

'Unfortunately, yes.'

His aggressive tone unsettled her. She sidestepped. He was ready and moved with her. 'You can't have forgotten the meeting. It was arranged at the request of your pal, Sir Peter Channing, who thought he could buy an introduction to a Chinese friend of mine.'

'I am late for a lunch appointment,' she said coldly, 'and, from the smell of your breath, you have spent too long at the bar. Kindly allow me to pass.'

He remained solidly in her path. 'Here's another reminder of the occasion. You asked my wife if she was Australian, and she asked what you are. I now know the answer to her question.' He raised his voice. 'I wonder how many of these smug sycophants surrounding us are aware of the kind of dirty tricks you and Channing indulge in.'

Olivia Lord sidestepped again, but there was no escape from him. Rod was grimly gratified by the attention he was commanding from a number of people unused to such behaviour within these hallowed colonial portals. The crisscross of patrons had stilled; muted conversation had faded into a silence in which his angry tones were clearly audible.

'I'm not sure what goes on between you two, or why your dubious relationship is accepted by those who look down their supercilious noses at a respectably married woman who happens to be rather exuberant in dress and manner. Judging by the sample of what you and the slimy Sir Peter will stoop to when things don't go your way, I'd guess you've got some kind of hold on each other that neither of you dares to break.'

White about the mouth, his prey looked around her in desperation.

'They're not going to come to your rescue, lady,' he told her savagely. 'This is the most entertaining encounter they've ever seen here. The whole of your blustering, bumptious set will be agog with the details by tonight – all highly elaborated, of course. But the worst you'll suffer is a few scarcely hidden nudges when you appear and the cold shoulder from Sir Peter bloody Channing for a few days. Unfortunately, I'm in no position to ruin you financially, or to blight your career. I imagine you and your banking partner have that side of your liaison well and truly sewn up. You're both equally calculating and ruthless, so it would take someone with those qualities in greater strength to break you. Given time, you'll fall out and bring each other down, but I won't be around to enjoy it.' He took a gusty breath to steady his rage. 'You might well have ruined my chances in Hong Kong, but you're the loser, lady, not me. You're stuck with this place, and with Channing, until it falls around your ears. When it does, it's going to hurt more than being turned down by a selection board. You're going to be *flattened!*'

He became aware of the manager approaching, followed at a safe distance by a red-faced, white-moustached stalwart in a morning suit. Olivia was shocked and shaking, her face ashen against the dark upswept hair and the large earrings of carved jade that matched a sensational necklace. She seemed incapable of moving away from him, or from the stares of the crowd that had gathered in the pillared vestibule.

The manager arrived beside Rod and coughed discreetly. 'Ah, pardon me, sir . . .'

'*Doctor*,' corrected Rod, rounding on him and intimidating the slender Frenchman with his physique. 'Mrs Lord is suffering from a sickness common in Hong Kong. I've been warning her of the dangers. The cure is in her own hands. Unfortunately, like all these self-satisfied people waiting to see if you can throw me out, she'll not heed my advice. When they all collapse, they'll still be wondering how it happened. Now, did you have something to say to me?'

'No, sir . . . Doctor,' the man said diplomatically. 'But perhaps I can be of assistance in obtaining a rickshaw or a taxi for you?'

'No, thanks, but Mrs Lord might be grateful for it. She won't be waiting for Sir Peter's chauffeur to pick her up at three. I think she's no longer up to eating lunch with her friends.'

He strode across the gleaming marble, past the bemused onlookers and out to where a pale winter sun shimmered on the foul waters of the harbour. He stood for a while as rage was gradually filtered into a surprising homesickness. It swept him with such force that he suddenly knew how Sarah had felt about 'poor old England' when he had tried to persuade her that Hong Kong had much to offer. He had not bargained for how much.

He walked slowly, possessed by memories of Dalgara and the happy days of his childhood until Jack had died and sent him in search of a means to compensate. Whisky had made him maudlin; that outburst with Olivia Lord had revived the pain of losing Sarah. Dalgara appeared as a haven from the past eight years, and he longed for it as never before. As he walked he saw everything around him through the eyes of a man raised in a green wilderness where the only sounds were the cries of sheep, the shouts of drovers and the drone of occasional light aircraft flying in. These streets were noisy and odorous: the rattle of trams; the pounding of bare feet as rickshaw-boys passed; the nasal cries of street vendors; pungent aromas from roadside satay-stands, the smell of poverty and sickness emanating from narrow side streets, the stench of dried-out nullahs. Rod suddenly hated it to the point of wishing he could fly out tomorrow. He was due to take Wang Chua's floating clinic to the islands, and he wondered if the pleasure of this monthly duty would also have gone.

When he arrived home it was immediately apparent that Celeste had been drinking. Still under the influence of drowning his own sorrows, he waved Lim away with a curt request to come back in fifteen minutes then crossed to where his wife sat staring at the wall, an empty glass on the table beside her.

'What do you hope to gain by soaking yourself in gin?' he demanded harshly. 'I've told you often enough it won't induce a miscarriage.'

'Go to hell!' she said in a monotone, continuing to stare at the wall.

'Oh, for God's sake pull yourself together! You're not the first woman to have an unwanted child. I don't want it, either, but it damn well exists through our selfishness and we owe it the best chance we can give it.'

She turned towards him a face devoid of its attraction; eyes swollen and red from weeping, lower lip puffy from the pressure of her own teeth.

'How typical of the righteous Dr Durman! Do your best for the child; do your best for your husband's career. What about *me*? I'm in this world, too. I'm entitled to the best, as well. *This* isn't it. Constant retching, swollen, painful breasts, an aching back and a waistline expanding by the minute. That's the price *I'm* paying. Men indulge their lust and it costs them nothing.'

'Doesn't it?' he flung back bitterly. 'I don't give a *damn* about your needs. You've always made sure you had your share of the good things. And if you're talking about lust, there's been more than enough of it indulged in by you. Neither of us pretended love inspired our occasional hectic intercourse. It was a case of satisfying a need – as it was that morning. You were wound up with excitement, and I was half asleep when you began the game. Don't throw at me that tired old cry that men are beasts and women the helpless victims! You thrive on sexual excitement and we've explored most avenues of it during the last eight years because of your eagerness.' He walked round to stand before her. 'Pregnancy lasts only nine months. The sickness will end; you'll get your figure back. Knowing you, it'll be no time before you're whooping it up with a brainless crowd. But my payment for that morning is far greater than you'll ever know. I've lost all hope of freedom from a marriage you gave up on within the first year.'

A wild light appeared in eyes that had been lifeless a moment ago, and she stood up to grip his arm so tightly her nails dug into his flesh. 'You can have your freedom. We both can. There are places in the Chinese quarter. Freda Grainger's amah went to one and was back at work within two days.'

As it dawned on him what she was suggesting, Rod sobered swiftly and turned cold. But she was in full flow and words tumbled from her. 'You can have a divorce. I'll make it easy for you. We'll *both* have the chance of a fresh start – go our separate ways with no ties or regrets.'

He threw off her hands with a violent movement. 'For Christ's sake, you don't know what you're saying.'

The wildness remained in her eyes. 'I don't need your permission, you know. It's my body . . . and Freda gave me the address.'

Shocked, sensing that she was presently desperate enough to do what she threatened, he gave her the truth in raw tones. 'Those people use butchers' tools that aren't disinfected from the last victim. There's no anaesthetic; no aftercare. The abortion will be agonizing and there's a strong chance of bleeding to death afterwards. The very least penalty will be an infected womb and permanent internal damage. Is *that* what you're prepared to suffer rather than have this child?'

Her expression spoke volumes as she shook her head. Then her urgency took another direction. '*You* could do it, Rod. You know how to do it safely and avoid any pain. You could get what you need from the hospital and do it here. We'll give the servants a couple of days off, so no one will be any the wiser. Bill Clinton knows my history, and all my friends are expecting me to miscarry. They'll believe that's what happened.' She seized his arm again, all her wildness returning. 'Think of *freedom*, Rod. Think how easily we can get out of this bloody awful situation!'

As he stood appalled into silence by what she was asking him to do, she added further persuasion. 'You've always been dedicated to helping others with your knowledge and skill. *Now help us!* Get rid of this weight around our necks so that we can live our lives as we both want. We're still young, and there's so much out there to do. We can't let this ruin it for us. We *can't*!'

Sickened and repelled, Rod took her by the shoulders to emphasize his words. 'You're too late, Celeste – years too late. We *both* rushed into this marriage and have suffered the consequences. We *both* participated in the act that created this child, so we must also suffer the consequences of that. Because we've ruined our own lives, we've no justification for ruining a third. You've got to go through with this pregnancy, whether you want to or not. Do you understand? There *is* no way out. Even if I could ignore medical ethics I'd never, under any circumstances, abort my own child.'

She began laughing hysterically. 'The noble doctor! What makes you so sure it's yours? The other two miscarried at three months. This little bastard is alive and kicking at the fourth. I know, I felt it move this morning. Oh God, I threw up!' She pulled away from him as her laughter became indistinguishable from tears. 'There was a party. We all drank too much and the men began fooling around. It was fun. Everyone was having a wonderful time. It seemed the natural thing to do when someone suggested it. We all changed partners two or three times, but I'm the only one who . . .' She caught her breath on a sob. 'I don't know whose baby this is, but it's a damn sight tougher than the two you gave me. *Now* will you get rid of it?'

Rod was swept by the urge to seize her by the throat. Her words completed his destruction, and he could take no more. Before he lost all control and did something terrible he turned and lunged blindly for the door.

The lives of the people on the many small offshore islands had been largely untouched by time. Their stone and brick dwellings, with roof tiles shaped like sticks of barley-sugar and door-gods protecting the entrances, followed the style of their ancestors' houses. Furniture within the dim rooms was basic, with a god-shelf and pictures of family elders from many generations. The communities were often closely inter-related.

They subsisted by tilling the land, keeping a few animals, fishing and working at natural crafts like boat-building, making fishing-nets and baskets. Clannish and suspicious of intruders, many were illiterate, knowing and caring little about the land mass of China or what might be beyond. It had taken them a long time to accept the visits of Wang Chua's floating clinic; even longer before they would use it. There were still those among the elderly who preferred ancient remedies and warned against accepting treatment from 'foreign devils'. But young mothers whose children had been successfully cured, male providers restored to fitness and able to work again, and those whose constant

191

pain had been relieved by Western drugs spoke in favour of the launch manned by British doctors with Chinese assistants, and confidence gradually grew.

Despite the December chill, Rod stood on the narrow deck of the boat as it rode a choppy, blue-grey sea. He had always enjoyed his duty weekend visiting islands too far from the mainland to be easily served by it – there could be no greater contrast to a normal hospital routine – but today he relished only this escape to the wide sea and tiny circles of primitive existence. The sky was a cool, clear blue and the wind contained a reminder of winter that penetrated his thick jacket and pullover. But it was nothing to the inner coldness that had been with him since Celeste's bombshell. He had not been back to the apartment for two days. A phone call to Lim had brought the boy to the Queen Mary with a suitcase, and his replies to Rod's questions suggested that Celeste was not very well. That meant she was still drinking.

During those past two days Rod had drunk quite a bit himself. He had absolutely no idea what to do now. As a person, he wished his wife to the devil. As a doctor, he was afraid of what she might do. His conscience gave him no peace. A back-street abortion by a Cantonese crone could leave him with a death on his hands, and yet he now hated Celeste with a frightening force – a force that would rejoice at her destruction. Running through his dark, vengeful thoughts, however, was the possibility that the child *was* his. Did he have a duty to that outside chance? No other man would accept responsibility of fatherhood. Could he simply leave Hong Kong and not once feel guilty of abandoning an unborn child to a doubtful fate? If he walked out on Celeste without a forwarding address, would he rest at night or be forever plagued by the unknown? He could not find the answers to those questions; he could not begin to see a way through the tangled forest his life had become.

When the launch arrived at the first island and he was brought a baby with a deformed foot, two small brothers with a rash, and an adolescent girl with a nasty gash on her arm, Rod found his concentration wandering back to the unanswerable problem. He also found it difficult to summon a smile for the several young men who habitually came to the jetty to help tie the boat up. The relationship was important because it established goodwill and encouraged others to trust the foreign doctors, but none of it now mattered to Rod. He would soon be leaving all this and meant never to return.

At the second island, they were presented with a problem in the form of a young unmarried woman with a swelling in her breast. Rod diagnosed a tumour, and his young assistant agreed that she should go back with them on the launch for admission to hospital. It took a long time for Chin Sung, Rod's pharmacist and interpreter, to impress upon the patient's family the urgency of her condition and that her life was at risk. Eventually, they agreed to let her travel to Hong Kong when the launch called on its return journey. Rod merely nodded when they asked for assurance that he would be caring for their daughter throughout, and Chin Sung did not question him when they headed north again. He was an intelligent man who ought to further his studies and qualify, but he was content and had no aspirations to become a doctor. Rod had always believed it a waste of ability: today he thought differently. Contentment was an enviable state. A man should hold on to it.

It was late in the afternoon before they reached a tiny island supporting one poor village inhabited by a clan that had only recently allowed them to tie up there. It had been seen as a breakthrough by the four doctors regularly manning the clinic, although they had yet to be presented with a patient. With night already creeping across the sky and the wind rising to add further chill to the air, the low-lying area of land some distance from neighbouring islands looked particularly desolate. The youth in tattered, baggy trousers and loose smock who had made a habit of coming to stare at them as they rode offshore during their early visits, then beckoned them in two months ago and took them on a tour of the minute kingdom in which he lived, was nowhere to be seen. In fact, Rod would imagine the island to be uninhabited if he had not visited it before. As the boat slid alongside a plank jetty kept in good repair by people whose livelihood was gained from fishing, a curious sensation of unease caused Rod to confide it to Chin Sung.

'There's something odd about this place, don't you think?' Where's Po Hin? Why is it so quiet? Not a bark, a quack or even a wail of a baby. What do you make of it?'

Chin Sung's broad face showed apprehension. Superstition played a great part in the lives of Chinese, so they were swiftly alarmed by signs and atmospheres that were unexpected. 'There's bad *fung shui* here, Doctor. Best we go. Come back next time.'

Rod considered his words. *Fung shui* was difficult to translate into Western concepts. The nearest equivalent was propitiousness, although the Eastern version was flavoured by the power of devils and spirits. Nothing was built by Chinese until a *fung shui* man was consulted. He alone could tell whether or not the site was favourable and would not upset evil forces. Bridges had been moved, railways diverted and entire villages resited because of bad *fung shui*. Rod had always respected the belief as a foreigner tolerant enough to give the benefit of the doubt when another race produces evidence to support the claim, but he had never been personally influenced by it. As he stood on the heaving deck looking across at an expanse of green scrubland rippling beneath the force of the wind, he suddenly shared Chin Sung's apprehension and shivered.

'Best we go,' Chin Sung repeated. 'No one here takes our medicine. No use to stay.'

Commonsense returned at his words. Rod translated his sense of foreboding into medical terms and decided he must go ashore in case his help was needed. He clapped his assistant on the shoulder by way of encouragement.

'The *fung shui* has been all right before. Unless the island's moved it can't have changed. Po Hin may be ill and unable to meet us. There could be an epidemic to explain the unusual silence. We can't leave without attempting to offer help, if it's needed.'

The two-man Chinese crew were clearly frightened and shared Chin Sung's reluctance to stay in the vicinity, so Rod weighed up his options. If he obliged his assistant to accompany him ashore, would the crewmen go, leaving them stranded? If he explored the village alone, could he depend on Chin Sung's ability to prevent the others from casting off the launch? He decided on the latter. The young pharmacist was an earnest and loyal assistant. Rod trusted him to exercise those qualities now.

'I'll walk to the village just to check that all's well. No need for you to come.' He forced a grin to suggest that he was making a joke. 'Don't let these characters shoot off the moment I'm out of sight, will you?'

The Chinese gave no return grin, he merely nodded and continued to look scared.

Rod took up his bag, then thought better of it and left it on the seat when he walked along the jetty to the shore. The advancing night sky gave the island a brooding appearance and *fung shui* took on a new meaning as Rod actually felt the presence of evil for the first time in his life. A path led through head-high bushes as far as the collection of crumbling stone houses comprising the village, which also had a tiny temple, numerous shrines and a miniature reservoir for water collected from typhoon rains. It took Rod two minutes to reach the first of the crude shelters, and his sense of foreboding deepened when he found it unoccupied.

Turning his collar up against the biting wind, he went on to the rest of the community. Deserted! There were no pigs rooting in the coarse grass, no poultry pecking hopefully around the dwellings, no children playing games. Fires were smouldering in the shallow pits outside doors guarded by protective gods, but no women were cooking there. Nets hung over broken walls, but the fishermen were not mending them in the usual manner. Old people wizened beyond their years, who normally sat yawning or giving sudden staccato advice from their seat on a stone or chunk of wood, were nowhere to be seen.

Rod's scalp began to crawl. It was inexplicable, and ominous. An entire island community had apparently disappeared. The smouldering fires pointed to very recent departure, yet no boats had been seen in the vicinity during the launch's approach. There was no way of leaving this place save by sea, so how else could everyone have vanished? Not only the people, but the livestock. He knew nothing of the area beyond the village. It gave the appearance of being no different from the scrubland through which he had just come, but Rod felt violently unwilling to explore it alone. *Fung shui* was one thing; this situation was something altogether more difficult to explain.

He walked briskly, pushing through the overgrown sections of the path with a sensation of evil at his back. Chin Sung had been right. Better to have given the island a miss and gone on to the other one where they normally tied up for the night. Even so, dogged devotion to his profession made him decide to take the launch right round the island before heading off into fast-gathering darkness, just to satisfy himself that there had been no kind of disaster that demanded his limited help. It was with relief that he saw the launch still tied up to the jetty. He broke into a trot telling himself it was to warm up, and for no other reason.

When Rod reached the jetty, it became apparent that there were on the launch others in addition to Chin Sung and the crewmen. He could not think where they had come from without his seeing them, but he fervently hoped that they would explain what was going on here. He climbed aboard, and went to the cabin attached to the small dispensary, which had been fitted out as a treatment room. When he entered, all thought was suspended. The three Chinese were huddled against a bulkhead behind two men in rough, crumpled khaki uniforms who faced Rod with rifles pointing at his stomach.

'What's going on here?' he demanded instinctively, knowing the quantity of drugs aboard were his responsibility.

Neither man replied, but one gestured a command to sit on the treatment table while the other dragged a crewman outside to cast off. Although physically Rod could have made mincemeat of the pair he respected the rifle held by an expressionless youngster who would probably not hesitate to use it. As the launch got under way, Rod turned to Chin Sung who was looking shattered.

'Who are these blokes? Trigger-happy Communists?'

The soldier took two paces, swung his rifle and slammed the butt against Rod's right temple. He slumped sideways, temporarily stunned by the blow, the throbbing of the engine merging with the acceleration of his pulse as he lay against the leather-covered bench, fighting pain.

It was not long before the engine was cut, and the boat glided silently to a halt. The soldier left the cabin, and Rod pushed himself upright with a handkerchief pressed to the bleeding cut. From his window he saw something he could never have imagined. Several grey motor-launches were standing offshore, and a large inflatable dinghy had been beached. A number of armed soldiers stood around on the narrow shore. At their feet lay a row of dead pigs and poultry. The villagers clustered together, watching their boats being holed by several of their number under duress from soldiers who used boots and rifle-butts freely. Beside the boats already broken sprawled the bodies of two male villagers, killed either because they rebelled or as an example to the others.

Aware that Chin Sung had come alongside, Rod turned to him. 'What the hell's happening here? Are they Communists or Nationalists?'

'They are Japanese, Doctor,' came the despairing reply. 'Hong Kong is about to be attacked, and we can do nothing. They say we are prisoners of war.'

Chapter Eight

Alex was enjoying his usual Sunday breakfast despite the difficult evening he had spent with the Jays, who viewed his resignation and imminent departure from Hong Kong as an act of unforgivable ingratitude. Reginald Jay had expounded on the selfishness of the younger generation, who believed the sun would never go down on their carefree, indulgent world. Words like integrity, loyalty, duty and application had been flung at him in tones loud enough to bounce back from the walls of that mid-levels mansion. Alex was sorry he had taken his news in such melodramatic manner. Once he calmed down he would surely see good fortune in losing an 'appendage' who had scarcely deserved the effort expended on him.

The Jays had not asked about Alex's plans. These had changed direction during the past few days and he was still coming to terms with them himself. Booking a cabin to South Africa for Sarah had awoken Alex to a startling notion. He did not want to say goodbye to her. For once, a girl had penetrated his defensive shell to touch him in unexpected manner – a girl deeply involved with another man. How deeply Alex was not certain, but the fact bothered him a great deal. It was completely irrational. He was no knight in shining armour, yet he could not forget the sadness and desperation in her eyes as she had asked for his help in leaving Hong Kong. He knew what it was to run from an unacceptable truth; how it felt to face guilt alone. He longed to console Sarah; wanted to provide a strength he had never before offered a woman. He believed he must be halfway in love with her.

Two months ago he would have derided such a possibility. It now dominated everything he did. He had no plans beyond the voyage to England. Time enough for that when they both set foot in their homeland after weeks, possibly months, in each other's company.

Leaving the table, Alex strolled to the balcony overlooking that part of the harbour occupied by neutral merchant companies still operating a worldwide service. Now he was leaving the place he could view it with a less jaundiced eye. There was a wintry nip in the air which made him glad of the cashmere sweater he had pulled on over his tennis clothes. He had agreed to put in a final appearance at the courts at Giles's request, but his friend was unaware that it would be Alex's last. He supposed he must inform his cronies of his imminent departure; resign from various clubs and from the Volunteers. He did not believe he would be badly missed.

His lazy scrutiny of the morning panorama suddenly focused with clarity on a sight that brought him from reverie to alertness. 'What the . . .?' he murmured, frowning.

A minute later, he was inside the apartment to fetch binoculars. Back on the balcony, he focused them on the narrow Leimun channel left unmined but protected by a boom. Leaping up in magnified relief came confirmation of something unbelievable. The only safe route from Hong Kong was filled with ships steaming away from the colony at maximum possible speed. One of them was the *San Maritino*, on which he and Sarah were booked to sail the coming week.

Foreboding washed over Alex as he watched the departure of a virtual merchant fleet, and realized the boom had been raised to allow them through to the open sea and beyond. Visions of those fast Japanese launches he had overflown returned to reinforce the conclusion reached by his stunned mind, while the only means of escape grew ever more distant through the lenses. Why had they been allowed to go without taking on as many civilians as could be crammed into the available space? Women and children had been abandoned here; old people and the sick. His expensive pullover no longer staved off the chill as coldness crept through his veins. Someone had heard of imminent danger, someone had tipped off the captains of those neutral ships. Was everyone else in Hong Kong to be kept in the dark?

Binoculars in hand, Alex turned into the airy bachelor apartment furnished in art deco style and made for the telephone. It rang before he reached it. He snatched up the receiver after three hasty strides across black rugs.

'Yes, who's this?' he snapped.

'Charles Martin. We're to report for duty, pronto,' said the voice of an architect who captained Alex's company of Volunteers.

'What the hell's going on?' Alex demanded.

'Search me, old boy. Orders came from above. It's just another bloody scare, in my opinion. Some army wallah read signs of aggression in a group of Japs playing one of their incomprehensible games over the border at Fanling. It's happened before and it invariably ruins one's Sunday arrangements. It's all right for you, but my wife's livid. She's arranged a rather special luncheon party at Repulse Bay for our fifteenth wedding anniversary, and it's damned likely to be our last if I miss it.'

'Charles, all the merchant ships have gone!' Alex said with impatience. 'This is no scare, it's the real thing – and your wife will oversee a hen party because all of us will be standing-to until we know the facts. How could Sir Mark have let those ships steam away without sending the women and children to safety?'

'Not you, too,' came the disgusted comment. 'You're like panicky old maids who believe any male who looks their way is about to rape them. The Japs'll never attack. They'd be taking on the whole British nation *and* the Commonwealth. They've enough to do trying to conquer China without joining our war. No, this is a case of yet another crackpot old military buffer crying "wolf". When I discover who it is, I'll slay him!'

'You'll be too busy slaying Japanese – unless you still believe it's all a game when they come for you with bayonets.'

Alex slammed the receiver on to the cradle and headed

for his bedroom, shouting for the elderly servant engaged by
Frances Jay on his arrival at the colony. Alex had never
formed a bond with the sober old man, preferring to keep
the relationship on an impersonal footing to avoid the
pitfalls some Europeans encountered when employees trusted
too well took advantage of them. Fung Ho had appeared to
welcome the arrangements and harmony reigned. He had
run Alex's bath this morning, set out tennis clothes and
served breakfast, after returning from a Saturday night
spent with his family as usual. He did not come in answer to
his master's call, however, and Alex cursed under his breath
as he searched through the two deep wardrobes for his
uniform.

'Fung Ho,' he called again. 'Come here, chop chop!'

Finding the khaki between two dinner jackets, he changed
into it whilst considering the consequences of Charles
Martin's call and the departing ships. He knew in his heart
the unexpected had happened. Why, after all these months,
the Japanese should decide to attempt to take the colony he
could not imagine, but the scornful bravado he had heard
from military and trade giants was overshadowed by a
sudden conviction that Hong Kong was about to be invested.
His heart raced as he buttoned the tunic he had always
looked upon as ridiculous fancy dress. Donning it now
turned him into a warrior liable to be attacked by an invading enemy. The notion was incredible, yet it must be
faced.

'Fung Ho!' he yelled at the top of his voice, scanning racks
for a pair of boots among so many polished shoes.

Highly charged with differing emotions vying for dominance, Alex strode the long corridor to the rear quarters of
his apartment and flung open a door at the end.

'Didn't you hear me calling?' he asked of an empty room.
'Fung Ho? Where the devil are you?' Certainly not where he
was normally to be found.

To Alex's astonishment, evidence suggested that the
ageing servant had gone, with no intention of returning.
The small rattan hamper containing Fung Ho's few possessions was missing from its place on a three-legged stool,
which had also been taken. The cheap eating-bowls and

201

chopsticks normally placed on a shelf above the stool were no longer there. Nor were the abacus and folding bag used for shopping at the market. The floor was bare of sleeping-mat, wooden neck-rest and woven cover favoured by a man steeped in the old ways of his motherland. Fung Ho had apparently returned from his night off only to collect his belongings. Years in service had led him to perform his usual morning tasks for a master to whom he no longer felt any obligation, before picking up the essentials of life and departing.

When Alex walked through to the kitchen he found that also deserted. After preparing breakfast, the cook-boy had washed up china and utensils, made everything tidy, then left without a word. It was clear the Chinese backstreet gossips were aware of what was afoot, and word had spread. Determined to find out what they apparently knew, Alex returned to his bedroom and put on the stoutest shoes he could find in place of the missing boots. He prayed a spare pair would be made available to him, or that, however serious the situation, there would be an opportunity to come back to his home for a wash, a rest and a fresh search for footwear essential when tramping overgrown hillsides for hours on end.

A telephone call to his usual taxi hire firm went unanswered, as did two others to rival companies. He cursed and slammed down the receiver. The male population of Hong Kong was commandeering every available vehicle this morning. When he opened the front door he found Jakob Myburgh outside about to knock on it. The elderly Dutchman's anxious expression increased at the sight of Alex's khaki.

'What is happening, my friend? Why are the ships leaving all together, line astern? Is it just an exercise?'

It was pointless to lie. 'I don't think so. The Volunteers are being called in, and mercantile neutrals would never take part in a military exercise. I imagine they've been told to get away while they can. There's something deeply disturbing about it, and about the sudden desertion of my servants. Have yours gone too?'

'Asham has nowhere to go. Like me, he left his native land some years ago. We shall never desert each other.'

'You're very fortunate.' Alex made to pass, but was halted by the man's next words.

'Not so our dear friend, Miss Channing. She should never have come here, and now cannot leave. Such talent, such sensitivity! The wisdom of the Almighty is often difficult to understand.'

A further implication of what he had witnessed this morning came home to Alex. Sarah was trapped in Hong Kong like everyone else. Had she taken up that earlier booking she would now be safely in Singapore. He questioned Fate, not the Almighty whose existence he had always doubted. What lay in store for Sarah here? Escape from Durman and the consequences of her involvement with him was now impossible. Came the chilling thought that the coming days could bring trials far greater than she might presently be facing.

This dread remained as Alex made his way to the front entrance. The place at the corner of the street where rickshaws were invariably parked while men squatted beneath the shade of trees was deserted. He cursed again and began walking briskly towards the main road, where he hoped for better luck. Some minutes passed before he spotted an empty rickshaw in streets more than usually busy on a Sunday, and reached Blake Pier, where the Kowloon ferries arrived and departed. Aboard a crowded vessel he spotted Giles Courtney and Bunny Forbes, his two closest and most reckless cronies, with whom he was to have played tennis this morning. Pushing his way through the mass of first-class passengers, half of whom were in uniform and the other half the usual crowd flocking to the Peninsula Hotel for lunch, he greeted them with the obvious question.

'Have you heard anything definite?'

'The Japs have massed along the border,' said Giles languidly. 'Taken them long enough to crack up the courage to take us on. Wonder what's prompted this move?'

'I'll *tell* you what,' said Bunny with authority. 'They've lost face over their inability to defeat Chiang Kai-shek's army, so they've turned against our little colony to boost their morale. *Doomed* to disappointment, they are, silly bastards.'

Leaning against the rail in their smart uniforms, their faces whipped into a semblance of youthful vigour by the chill breeze, they looked ridiculously heroic, Alex thought. How deceptive were appearances. This pair were two of the colony's most dissolute wastrels. How would they stand up against troops known to be merciless? How would he?

He leaned on the rail beside them. 'Why the hell did they have to choose today and ruin our tennis?'

Immediately the words were out he regretted them. These so-called friends expected from him the kind of silly-ass nonsense they normally exchanged, and he had done what they expected even though he knew this development was extremely grave. It was time he stopped living up to society's image of Alex Tennant.

Straightening, he said, 'All right, we've had our little joke. Now let's get down to brass tacks. I warned the garrison of this probability after seeing those motor-launches from the air. I was told not to interfere. If, as you say, they're massing on the border, it's a cert they're going to launch an attack on the outlying islands at the same time. I'll wager this is no mere morale booster.'

The two men gazed at him fascinated. 'You sound so bloody serious,' marvelled Bunny. 'You *can't* believe any-thing'll come of this.'

'Of course it will!' He practically shouted his words to be heard above the chatter and laughter of the crowd. 'We'll be doing battle with them before Christmas.'

Giles shook his dark head as he continued to prop himself up with the handrail. 'The minute they attempted to cross the border, our boys would be up and at 'em. From all we've been told, they're poorly armed, poorly trained and poorly fed. A band of Oriental coolies, no less. They'd not last long against crack troops.'

Alex was driven to point out that although the regiments of Hong Kong's regular garrison were among the best, they had been languishing on a tiny island for too long with nothing but parades, tattoos and half-hearted exercises as regimental duties. 'Even crack troops need to be kept on their toes, and the pleasant sunwashed life led by our garrison must have softened them considerably,' he said. 'In any case, if the enemy is present in overwhelming numbers, even Oriental coolies can overrun an undermanned bastion. This isn't going to be a lark, by any means. I suggest you ponder on that when we're told to take up our posts.'

His friends decided that the only way to deal with such uncharacteristic behaviour was to ignore it, so they began a conversation on the success of the Chinese charity ball held in Kowloon the previous evening. Alex turned to watch the coast as they neared it, wishing *Dragonfly* were still there riding at anchor. But all he saw were three RAF marine aircraft which could not be flown beyond Hong Kong territory for fear of appearing aggressive. What price that caution now?

When they reached their appointed emergency post there was much excited speculation between the Volunteers, who had gathered from all points of the colony. Chinese, Indians, British, French, Australians, New Zealanders and a few Dutchmen had all come together, uncertain what was really happening. From company directors down to laundrymen, they had been given an obligation to defend Hong Kong with their lives, if necessary. Some readily accepted the responsibility; others resented being called upon to act as professional soldiers.

Messages came and went. Rumours flew, but no one knew their source. The waiting, the inactivity, quickly categorized the men into the braggarts, the nervous, the sensible or the impatient. Plans devised in 1939 and changed many times had allowed for mobile canteens to serve every military post. But it was Sunday, no one knew for certain whether or not this was a real emergency, and who was in charge of victualling, anyway? By six p.m. they were all weary, cross and hungry. The European officers went *en masse* to the Peninsula Hotel for dinner, but it was a favourite Sunday-night haunt and all the tables were booked. Some sought lesser restaurants, some prevailed upon friends living in Kowloon, a few even took the ferry back to the Island and dined at home. Alex was among them, his main object being to look for his boots.

As the ferry crossed the water, his sense of foreboding increased. The Peak, normally rising like a twinkling

Christmas tree with ribbons of tinsel at its foot, was dark and barely discernible against the night sky. Hong Kong was blacked out! Curiously, it made Alex's blood run cold. Sarah had spoken to him of a homeland without lights, but he had been unable to imagine such total darkness. It was as if Hong Kong had died. He shivered in the cold wind, but felt compelled to remain on deck to witness every aspect of this strange night. It seemed to herald a new sombreness in a colony with a colourful history. Despite poverty and over-crowding, there were always festivals with lanterns, silken dragons and bright banners, and a noisy bustle to offset the despair. There were balls and parades, parties, tattoos and games. Tonight, all those things had been symbolically banished with the turning off of the lights.

Paradoxically, the streets of the Island were busy. The residents appeared to be in a frenzy to get things done before it was too late. Alex's mood remained as his rickshaw bowled along in the dimness containing half a colony on the move. At the entrance to his apartment block, he paid the rickshaw boy and mounted the few steps to the glass doors which swung open as he reached them, almost hitting him. A woman hurried past to where a car was waiting in the street. She was followed by two of the block's Chinese attendants carrying a large trunk, piled on to which were a number of suitcases. Alex stopped to watch in surprise. Olivia Lord was clearly leaving her apartment with a large proportion of her belongings. Was she finally moving in with her partner in crime, Sir Peter Channing, at a time when society had more on its mind than gossip? Too late he recognized the chance to send a message to Sarah. The car drove away as soon as the luggage was loaded, but it headed for the docks not the road leading to the mid-levels. Alex turned into the vestibule reflecting that she was doomed to disappointment. All the ships had left this morning, abandoning the Island to its fate. In the lift, he had the further thought that maybe the partners in crime had fallen out. Why else would a woman who lived an enviable life, with the advantages but none of the ties of marriage to a prominent knight, be heading for the docks, fully laden, on an evening of such significance?

He forgot Olivia Lord during a vain search for his boots, and came to the conclusion that his cook had found them an irresistible perk on leaving for the last time. He would have to ask for a replacement pair from stores. Gathering up razor, toilet things and a change of shirt and underwear which he put into a bag, Alex then hesitated by the telephone before heading for a nearby restaurant in the hope of some dinner. Impulse led him to get through to Echoes and ask to speak to Miss Channing. He was not sure she would deign to come to the telephone when told the name of the caller, but he felt the need to make contact, however coolly she might respond.

'Mr Tennant, how good of you to call,' the familiar voice said against his ear. 'If it's about the *San Maritino*, I already know it sailed this morning.'

She was disappointingly formal. He tried to coax more warmth. 'I can guess how upset you must be. If there was any alternative, I'd do my utmost to ensure that it was made available to you.'

'Gracious, why should you? We're all in the same predicament and there must be others with greater claim to priority.'

'Not so far as I'm concerned.'

After a brief silence, she apologized. 'I was being ungracious again. Forgive me.' Another pause, then, 'Father says all Volunteers were alerted this morning.'

'Yes. I'm based in Kowloon. Everything's very confused; messages often contradict each other. Sir Peter must have more information on the situation than a humble part-time subaltern.'

There was something in her tone that encouraged him, despite her words. 'Modesty isn't your forte, Mr Tennant, so you really must be worried. All Father has heard is that a large force of Japanese has assembled along the border and looks set to cross it tomorrow or the day after. Shall we be able to repel them?'

'Probably not,' he said frankly, 'and I wish you'd call me Alex.'

'It's a little late for that, isn't it?'

'It's never too late for friendship . . . particularly at a time like this.'

She hesitated before saying, 'I'm not in need of moral support. I'm used to wartime conditions.'

'I wasn't referring to *this* emergency,' he said carefully. 'You had a pressing reason for leaving Hong Kong which has been flouted. You might need support in that respect.'

He feared he had driven her away, she was quiet for so long, but she eventually said, 'You're being awfully nice to someone who has often misunderstood you, but I really don't need a shoulder to cry on.'

'I do,' he told her swiftly, and could practically hear her smile as she told him he now sounded much more like the man she knew. 'You *don't* know me. I keep reminding you of that.'

The smile had definitely vanished with her next words. 'It seems I don't really know anyone. Thank you for calling. I appreciate your taking the time to do so when you must have so much else on your hands. Goodbye . . . and good luck.'

Replacing the receiver, he took a long look at his modern apartment which symbolized four wasted years and hoped to God they would not be his last. He ought to have something to show for his life when it came to an end.

The night hours dragged past without any reliable information on what was happening at the border. Sleep was elusive. There was an atmosphere of expectancy, of apprehension, which had never been present during exercises or annual summer camps. Quite a number lay wide-eyed in those huts near Kai Tak airfield. Alex welcomed his two-hour watch soon after midnight. It was a ridiculous time to review his life and find so much to regret, but he did, gazing across at the dark island to which he had run when he could take no more. What if he had been cut off on that homeland island and forced to face the consequences of his mistakes, as Sarah now was?

He was back between rough blankets with that supposition still troubling him when Charles Martin, whose wedding-anniversary party had been ruined the previous day, appeared with a torch and began alerting the officers. They got to their feet and gathered outside, half asleep and shivering in the pre-dawn temperature. Alex found himself

208

beside Bunny and Giles, both unusually subdued. Even Charles Martin's habitual heartiness had vanished as he stood, a shadowy figure against the night sky, to break his news.

'A radio message from Japanese sources has been intercepted by our HQ. It's extraordinary, unbelievable ... but an officer fluent in Japanese swears it's genuine. They're about to go to war with us *and* the Americans.'

Into the silence, a voice said, 'They *wouldn't!* They'd never bring the Yanks in. It's just propaganda.'

The Volunteer captain continued in trance-like tones. 'Our troops along the border are standing by to blow bridges, the railway tunnel and all demolition sites set up to prevent an advance on Kowloon. This is no storm in a teacup. They mean it.'

The hairs on the back of Alex's neck began to rise. Despite the attack on *Dragonfly*, despite his inner conviction that an assault was about to be made, despite his certainty that last night was the overture to an armed bid to take the colony, he had never imagined such a wide-reaching move. If they meant to take on the American nation, with its awesome manpower and resources, the Japanese must be very strong indeed – or in the grip of imperialistic madness. The latter could ensure victory as certainly as the first. History had been made by conquering madmen. One was presently on the loose in Europe. Was the East about to be beset by an entire army of them? He grew certain, there and then, that Hong Kong was all but lost.

Chinese civilians cooked breakfast from supplies finally unearthed, and the men ate in a mood of mixed relief and tension. They knew the score, at last, but were awed by it. Even the most notoriously optimistic warriors were silent. A token attempt by local Japanese to cross a border was one thing; all-out war against a rich, powerful neutral nation was another. The doubters also fell silent on receipt of the shattering news that the Japanese had successfully landed along the Malayan coast and were sweeping downwards to Singapore. Alex barely had time to reflect that Sarah might have been waiting there for a ship to take her further on her journey, if she had taken up that first booking, when further devastating evidence of global war was relayed to them. The American Pacific Fleet had been almost totally destroyed by a series of dawn raids on Pearl Harbor.

Alex stood-to with his platoon as the sun rose above Hong Kong, telling himself he would either be dead or a prisoner of war by Christmas. There was no one to care much, either way. He felt sorry for married men with the responsibility of wives and children still in Hong Kong. Their fate would be grim in the coming days. And what of the girl with a passion for music? She had come here against her will because her father wished her to escape danger. England had not fallen. She should have remained in her beloved homeland. All Hong Kong had offered her was heartbreak and disillusion. If she really was carrying Durman's child, she had even worse to face when the Japanese took over.

Alex's morbid thoughts were interrupted by a distant roar, fast increasing. Before he could identify the sound, he jumped violently. Heavy guns had opened fire from coastal emplacements. Next minute, the sky was full of aircraft diving towards Kowloon with screaming engines, guns chattering non-stop. He was momentarily paralysed as his brain tried to comprehend what his eyes could not accept. The formation levelled out over Kai Tak and flew low over his head with a deafening thunder of sound. But that was as nothing against the ear-shattering explosions when bombs hit the airfield all around them, sending up great showers of debris, setting fuel-dumps alight and destroying the RAF's few aircraft on the ground. Wave followed wave. There seemed no end to them as Alex watched, head tipped back, heart thudding. The three amphibious aircraft were sunk at their moorings, where *Dragonfly* would have been, and the great white Pan American Clipper due to leave for Manila at any minute disintegrated and began to burn as it rode the blue waters.

Just when he began firing his rifle and shouting at those around him to do so, Alex could not tell. It was futile action against solid aircraft, but it was the only way he could hit back as they continued to drop their bombs unhindered. Hong Kong's entire air defence had been destroyed in a matter of minutes. There was nothing to stop the Japanese from bombing the colony into swift submission. When their aircraft veered towards nearby Shamshuipo and began bombing and machine-gunning the main barracks and additional huts built to accommodate the recently arrived Canadians, that belief was confirmed in Alex's mind.

The air was full of flying dust and the smell of burning. Thick, dark smoke drifted over the whole coastal area of Kowloon. British guns were still firing, but the bombing continued unhampered. Through the general tumult came the faint ringing of ambulance bells as Hong Kong woke up to the reality of war. As Alex stared at the devastation around him, the only thought to penetrate his stunned senses was the realization of why Sarah Channing had had no time for young men like himself, after living on an island where this had been going on for two years.

Sarah had just finished breakfast when her father came down for his. She was astonished to see him dressed in golfing tweeds rather than a formal suit. The links were closed like all other sporting facilities, so it was unlikely he was shunning the bank for a morning's relaxation with his clubs. They exchanged a brief greeting while she got to her feet, picking up her shoulder bag, but he made no effort to sit and start his meal.

'Tan will drive you to the Halburton. He's not happy about it, but I feel certain I can trust him to do as I ask.' He gave a grim smile. 'Note that I *ask* these days. So many Chinese have turned their backs on us, only the fortunate still have employees loyal to them. We might have held the mainland longer if Chinese drivers and storemen hadn't vanished and left us stranded.'

'I suppose it's natural,' Sarah said, pausing beside him. 'They're not soldiers.'

'But it's their island we're giving lives to save.'

'No, Father, it's our valuable Far-Eastern outpost we're fighting to save.'

He sighed. 'There speaks the voice of someone who has made no attempt to understand Hong Kong. You were prejudiced against the place and its inhabitants when you arrived, and to that prejudice you have added, of late, cynicism. Nothing is ever black and white, Sarah. There are always shades of grey in between. Heroes have their flaws; villains their redeeming features.' He put heavy emphasis on that last phrase. 'I hope you now regret your conviction that your countrymen here care only for good living. Too many have died over the past ten days.'

'I know,' she said quietly, thinking how careworn he looked in the harsh morning light. 'I'll admit my judgements have been wrong in a number of cases, and I certainly *didn't* understand the people here. I only wish you had found the time to enlighten me.'

'I left that to Olivia ... but I'll accept I should have perceived that your personalities would never happily merge.'

'As yours did?'

'Yes ... yes, we suited each other well enough, on the terms we both agreed. Perhaps she was wise to go to her Portuguese friends in Macau. She could never have withstood privation and danger. Parties, restaurants, beauty parlours, *haute couture* made up the core of her life. Without them she'd be lost.'

'As will a number of women trapped here,' Sarah pointed out rather sharply, 'but they're doing what they can to help. Where Olivia is concerned, I think my judgement was accurate.'

They both stood in awkward silence for a moment or two, their conversation having gone deeper than they intended. How curious, Sarah thought, that they should find some common ground at this late stage.

'I must be on my way.' She gave a faint smile. 'I little thought when I offered my services to the Halburton that I'd be applying dressings, washing blood from wounds and calming the terrified. I could have stayed in England and done that.'

'Sarah, I ...' He put out a hand in a useless gesture, then let it drop to his side again. 'Had I ever believed this could happen, I would not have obliged you to uproot and come here. I'm deeply sorry.'

It seemed impossible that she could pity him, but she

did – and had no idea how to handle it. Any urge to offer warmth to another person was instantly quashed these days. She had learned too painful a lesson.

'Nobody believed it could happen, Father. Mr Chamberlain didn't believe it could happen in Europe. You're not alone.' She walked past him to the door, adding, 'I'm not sure when I'll be home. Someone'll give me a lift, I expect.'

'I won't be here for a while. I thought you should know that.'

She turned. 'Here at Echoes? Where will you be?'

'Up on the Wong Nei Chong Gap. They'll need every gun they can get, and I was pretty handy with one in the last scrap.'

'You're going to *fight*?'

'Defend! Not only is Hong Kong our valuable Far-Eastern outpost, as you pointed out, it's my home. I've made my life here, Sarah, so I feel as you would if the Cotswolds were under attack.'

Totally disarmed, she asked, 'What about the bank?'

'It will be maintaining an emergency service only. My Chinese head clerk can oversee that.' He gave a long sigh. 'Our reign here is almost over, you know, but we'll go out giving this colony we created our very best effort.'

'I'm sure you will,' Sarah said through a throat thickened by unwanted emotion. 'Good luck, Father.'

The drive through Victoria with a dismal chauffeur at the wheel banished sentimentality. Each day brought further devastation. Sarah did not share the distress of long-term residents over the destruction of favourite haunts, but she was moved by the sight of rice queues, people picking over ruins for treasured possessions, children wailing with fear and incomprehension, shops gutted, looters fighting over their spoils, too many funeral processions. Palm-lined avenues were now pitted and scattered with rubble; elegant colonial buildings blackened by fire. Narrow back streets were frequently blocked by collapsed buildings, so bodies lay stiffly awaiting collection by overworked drivers who could not reach them. The smell of death mingled with those of smoking debris and blocked sewers. Soldiers and military vehicles were everywhere. Above it all, Japanese aircraft suddenly appeared each day for a further onslaught. When they vanished once more, the scene had changed like the turn of a gruesome kaleidoscope. Apart from those Chinese serving with the Volunteers, they had fallen into three definite categories: the apathetic, the loyal and the enemy sympathizers. Some appalling truths had come to light. Japanese residents had been working undercover to learn British defence plans and relay them to their own military. Maps of every gun-site, fuel-dump, fortification and armed post had been drawn by these people who had been accepted and befriended by British and Chinese alike for some years. In addition, many Chinese in positions with access to valuable information, be it documents or drawing-room conversation within earshot of trusted servants, were in the pay of Japanese. Having betrayed their own countrymen and their administrators, they now spread false rumours, created panic, forced others to join them through threats, incited riots and killed the colony's defenders whenever they could do so without being detected. Stories were rife of fifth columnists flashing lights to guide Japanese night bombers to their targets in the hills. They were so accurate no one doubted the truth of this.

The mainland defence troops had been forced to withdraw sooner than expected. Panic-stricken Chinese had rushed the ferries in a bid to reach the Island, but they had been driven back to prevent boats from capsizing and further troops being lost by drowning. Marion's husband, Bill, had related heartrending tales of scenes viewed from the deck of his ship assisting the hurried withdrawal. Europeans had also been left in Kowloon to fall into enemy hands, because Japanese guns had drawn near enough to shell the narrow waterway so comprehensively it became impossible for vessels to repel a seaborne attack, which must soon come. No one any longer believed Hong Kong could be saved. It was merely a question of holding out as long as humanly possible.

Sarah was as afraid as everyone else of what would follow defeat, but her inner misery was so great it overrode that fear. Through one of the nurses at the Halburton she learned that Rod had not returned with the floating clinic,

214

so it was assumed that he had been killed or captured on one of the islands. The news made her aware that her love for him had been merely dented, not destroyed. Her sense of loss was even more acute than when they had parted on Stanley Beach. Quite irrationally, she felt deeper than ever jealousy of his wife, who now had the right to grieve over him and receive comfort from friends while she, Sarah, must bear her pain in isolation.

They reached the clinic safely through a roundabout route. Tan remained wooden-faced as she thanked him, so that she wondered what his true feelings were for someone doing her best to help those of his people brought to Stanley by makeshift ambulances. The first of the two white buildings housed offices and a couple of wards. A covered walkway linked it to the other containing the remaining wards. Sarah went first to the tiny cloakroom, where she put on a white overall. There was no longer any typing to do. European doctors, including Rod, who had made meticulous notes and reports on cases, could not serve the clinic on a voluntary basis because they were needed in their own overcrowded hospitals. Two Chinese doctors and four nurses struggled to cope with three times more patients than the wards were designed to hold. They had no time for detailed reports. Their very brief notes were in Chinese characters, save for medical terms which had no Cantonese equivalent. These were jumbled into boxes to be dealt with when time permitted.

Sarah and Marion, along with other volunteer typists, came each day to deal with all manner of unskilled jobs which freed the qualified nurses for tasks needing medical knowledge. Two of the team gave up after the second day, finding the work too distressing. A third, who was pregnant, fainted twice and was advised not to come any more. Five others remained: an American lawyer's wife, the daughter of an official at the criminal courts, a Eurasion widow, and two wives of Indian policemen. Sarah had initially found it difficult. Bleeding wounds had taken some getting used to, and she worried about her hands. Only when it became clear that Hong Kong must fall did she realize music would be absent from her life in the days to come. Her hands would have other things to do.

Marion had taken to nursing as if born to it, but she confessed to Sarah that her mind was so occupied with fears for her husband all she did was automatic. 'I know it's terrible, Sarah, but my love and concern is so totally concentrated on Bill, I feel absolutely nothing for these people,' she said, as they disrobed one day. 'I slap on a dressing with no more compassion than when I type a report. They are in distress, but mine is so great I can't encompass theirs. I don't suppose you understand that.'

'I do,' she had replied. 'Yes, I do.'

Today, Marion looked particularly drawn, with red-rimmed eyes, and Sarah immediately feared that some disaster had befallen the adored Bill. She walked to where her friend was tearing open boxes of dressings and setting out dishes for swabs. 'Is something wrong?'

Marion shook her head. 'Not the way you think. He's safe.' She continued with her tasks for a moment or two, then looked up at Sarah with tears on her lashes. 'I'm going to have a baby. I rushed home to tell Bill, and all he said was, "*Oh hell, what a bloody time to choose!*" What should have been one of the highlights of our marriage became instead our very first quarrel. Now I feel the child is doomed. Poor little brat!'

As a friend, Sarah failed. The comfort she should have offered was pushed away by thoughts of another untimely child, possibly a fatherless one now. Curiously, her silence stopped the other's tears as comfort possibly would not have done.

Marion forced a smile. 'Fine mother I'll be. Crying over the bandages when there's work to be done!'

They were busy all the morning and had no time to speak privately until a Chinese woman brought tea, and sandwiches filled with strong-tasting paste.

'Geez, not this goddamned poisonous fish again!' exclaimed the American, who unfailingly attended resplendent in pearls and gold bangles. Outspoken, brittle, with an acid wit, she invoked admiration in Sarah, who saw in her a woman of Olivia's type who had nevertheless taken on very unpleasant voluntary work in this crisis.

'I hope I don't form a passion for it later on,' Marion said with a giggle. 'Expectant mothers are said to have cravings for the most unlikely food.'

The delight and congratulations Bill had failed to express were forthcoming immediately, as the women asked Marion all the right questions. Sarah remained silent, wondering how Celeste Durman had broken the news to a husband who claimed to have lived a separate life for several years. Had he exclaimed, 'What a bloody time to choose!' or had he been delighted? *His* child was certainly doomed. If Rod were still alive on some offshore island he must be in torment watching Hong Kong being systematically bombed.

They were joined by two nurses, who made short work of the sandwiches spurned by the other women. There was news to impart as they munched. They had been told by an ambulance driver, who had heard from another, that a launch flying a white flag had crossed from Kowloon bearing Japanese officers with another surrender proposal. Sir Mark Young had rejected this as firmly as the first.

'Quite rightly,' said the court official's daughter. 'Daddy says Mr Churchill has asked us to hold out to the last, so that's what we shall do.'

'Your Mr Churchill is not here to see how our people are suffering,' one of the nurses put in. 'I think we should agree to their terms and stop further attacks.'

'Of *course* we shouldn't!' Marion was indignant. 'Mr Churchill has seen his own people suffering for two years, but he knows there's always hope. England could have surrendered last year under pressure from saturation bombing. She didn't, and Hitler gave up at the eleventh hour. The same might happen here.'

'I don't think so, honey,' said the American sorrowfully. 'Destroying our fleet at Pearl Harbor has left them jubilant and in a winning position. I agree with So Ping. Aggravating them with foolish bravado will make things worse for us when we finally surrender. Let's shorten the agony and preserve lives.'

Sarah was angry. 'Give in without a fight?'

'Girl, we've *had* a fight. What more do you want?'

'I want the Japanese to realize the strength of our will, be aware of our courage. We British have a reputation for

217

fighting the fiercest with our backs to the wall, and for pulling victory from certain defeat. I think that's unlikely here, but the people at home, who've been bombed, shelled and set on fire, who've had clothing, water and fuel rationed, who've been living in blacked-out towns and villages for more than two years, *and* who've given thousands of lives in the fight for freedom, are entitled to expect us to refuse to surrender after only *ten days*!'

'My God!' exclaimed the woman, taking out a cigarette. 'You don't usually have much to say for yourself, but that was quite a mouthful. You British always get so damned steamed up in defence of that little island of yours.'

'If you had lived there at any time over the past couple of years you'd do the same,' Sarah told her, still angry. 'I know every additional day means further loss of life, but that includes Japanese. After what they did to your naval men in Pearl Harbor, you should want maximum revenge.'

'It won't bring back those poor bastards killed without warning,' came the bitter comment.

'But it'll mean less of them to do the same to other Americans.'

The nurse, So Ping, rejoined the argument. 'It is easy for you, Miss Channing. You have no husband facing danger.'

'*I* have,' said Marion at once, 'and I agree with every word she said. I think we should keep them at it for as long ... as ... we ... can,' she finished slowly, eyes turned to the ceiling as aircraft suddenly roared overhead.

Next minute, they all dropped to the floor willy-nilly as a tremendous explosion very close by blew out the windows and brought down an entire corner of the room in which they had gathered. Plaster showered from the ceiling to settle amongst the fine particles of masonry and splinters of glass coating the cowering women, but screams from within the adjacent ward suggested worse damage there. They all began coughing as thick choking dust penetrated nostrils and throat.

'Is everyone all right?' asked the court official's daughter between spasms. 'Anybody hurt?'

'I have a cut on my arm,' said the other nurse, who had been silent during their argument. 'It is nothing. So Ping will apply a dressing. We must go to our patients if we are all able to.'

Sarah got to her feet cautiously. Something had given her a blow on the left temple, but she could not feel blood oozing from the spot so little harm could have been done. A bad headache would probably develop later. Marion was still on the floor, so she bent in swift alarm. 'Are you all right?'

Her friend turned up a dust-coated face. 'I think so . . . but I feel dreadfully sick.'

'Perhaps you should lie down for a while.'

Marion grinned. 'How could I? We've just been advocating the policy of carrying on against all odds.'

Sarah smiled back, guessing she looked equally filthy. 'We'd better be as good as our words, then. I'll have a bowl handy for you, just in case.'

She helped Marion to her feet, and they brushed themselves down as best they could before joining the others queuing to wash hands before returning to their work. The ward was full of dust which hung in the air and lay thickly over everything, including the patients. A number had suffered lacerations from shattered windows above their beds. Blood was everywhere, congealing in the debris on white counterpanes. It looked like a massacre.

'Oh, Lord, where's that bowl,' moaned Marion at Sarah's side, and was promptly sick on the floor.

More than an hour passed before the cuts had all been dressed and the sufferers calmed. Fresh counterpanes were put on leaving the store empty. Until the laundry returned yesterday's batch, no further changes could be made, but as the place had been bombed last night it was likely that the bedding was lost. Sarah longed to wash and change her clothes but there was no time. Throughout the day waves of aircraft droned over Stanley Peninsula to bomb defences and other vital targets. Columns of black smoke rose all along the waterfront as oil tanks burned alongside godowns and factories. Victoria itself seemed to be afire length and breadth from the pall that hung high above it. In addition to the bombing attacks, there was continuous bombardment from Japanese guns on the mainland. This fire was returned

219

by the Island's heavy artillery until it grew dark. The thunder of sound grew nerve-racking as hour succeeded hour.

A steady flow of wounded came in during the day. These unfortunates had to be settled on mattresses on the floor, thus making it difficult for the staff to move about. Sarah had developed a sickening headache. Every deafening round of fire, each earth-shuddering clutch of bombs added to her distress, but she would not give in to the longing to take a rest for fear of being reminded of her words by her fellows. A glance in the mirror revealed a formidable bruise appearing on her temple, but she was lucky to have escaped with nothing worse.

When darkness fell she suddenly grew aware that no new victims had arrived for some while. It should be possible to go home for a meal, some sleep and a welcome bath. If she looked as weary as the other former typists, the sooner the better. But there was no hope of that. So Ping came through the ward, her wistful oval face pale in the light of lamps used since power was cut off.

'Miss Channing, Mrs Bennett, I regret you will have to remain here tonight. The coast road is blocked, and soldiers will allow no one to leave the Peninsula. They are very nervous. Already some Chinese have been mistaken for Japanese, and shot. It is not safe to leave the clinic. They will kill us on sight. We should have surrendered.'

Marion was upset. She hoped Bill might get home for the night to repair their quarrel. Sarah pointed out that he would almost certainly be on duty continuously with the attack intensifying, so it was better that she was with friends while it raged.

'We'll be relatively safe here,' she added. 'The red cross on the roof will tell them this is a hospital.'

'Oh yes?' Marion sniffed. 'What about this morning?'

'That was bad luck. They were after the gun emplacement and the fort.'

'It's a mistake they could make again ... if it *was* a mistake. Word is they're pretty ruthless.'

Sarah said nothing. It was better for peace of mind not to discuss such things. They were given a meal of fish soup and rice with fried vegetables, counting themselves fortunate to have it when food was so strictly rationed. The medical staff set shifts as they had done each night for a week. Those women who had given their time on a voluntary basis were offered a palliasse and a thin blanket to settle for the night in the empty bedding store. They had to sleep in their clothes because a single blanket was little comfort against the December cold. In a week's time it would be Christmas Day. Would they still be free? The question was in each woman's mind as they lay staring into darkness.

Long after the rest were sleeping, Sarah was still awake. She thought of her father up in the Wong Nei Chong Gap in his golfing tweeds, ready to defend Hong Kong with the ultimate sacrifice, if necessary, and recalled his words. *Heroes have their flaws; villains their redeeming features*. Perhaps he was right and she had never tried really to understand this colony and its residents. In the coming dark days there would be more than enough time to do so. She thought of Ellie and wondered if she would ever again see that beloved face, when Hong Kong was freed. Time was marching on her grandmother. This tragedy, with its attendant anguish of the unknown, would burden Ellie further. Then she thought of Rod.

Unable to lie still, she stepped carefully between her slumbering colleagues to gaze from the window at the panorama of Stanley Bay. A hazy moon appeared spasmodically between clouds, flashing pale light momentarily to break the darkness. Her romantic senses ached with the poignancy of the situation. Those moments when the sea became a pewter expanse, shifting and dully shimmering as it broke upon silvered sands, represented the glorious certainty of her love for Rod. When clouds covered the moon, hiding the beauty, suggesting that *anything* might be there in that void, she recalled the confusion and pain of those moments out there when he had crushed that love. It was too late to believe she should not have walked away, but instead waited for an explanation. These critical times had regenerated the conviction that he had been as shattered as she that day, yet she had flung abuse at him and turned away. Regret had come too late. Perhaps he was dead. Perhaps she soon would be.

For the first time she compared her life with a concerto. For twenty years she had been a solo instrument well able to produce music. Rod had provided the full orchestra to turn her music into a soaring melody that stunned the senses and made the soul ache with the immensity of its impact. Standing at that window, Sarah began mentally to play the Rachmaninov Second so significant to them both. As the music swam through her head she grew infinitely close to the man who would be for ever linked to that concerto. As one movement followed another, she relived every meeting; remembered every expression of his, every word they had exchanged. When the dramatic, unbearably intense main theme filled her senses to the exclusion of all else, tears trembled on her cheeks. It was then she knew she could never play that work again.

When morning came it revealed that the night which had been so emotive to Sarah had hidden small boats carrying the enemy across from Kowloon. The Japanese had landed and were pushing towards the Wong Nei Chong Gap with dismaying speed.

Chapter Nine

There was no moon; nothing to relieve total darkness. They were very nervous. Every rustle, each crack of a twig, any stirring in the undergrowth had them tightening fingers around triggers. Military exercises had not prepared them for this. They had had nothing to eat for twenty-eight hours; water was rationed. The reservoirs were in Japanese hands. Bombs had ruptured the mains leaving the Island without running water. The Wong Nei Chong Gap, that strategically important area of high ground, had been captured with ease by an enemy force far larger and more efficient than they had ever been led to expect. The supporting attack from the mainland by Chiang Kai-shek's troops, promised in the event of a Japanese assault on Hong Kong, had not materialized. They were on their own.

Alex stared into the night, seeing phantom figures approaching every few minutes. He could hardly remember when he had last slept; had lost count of the number of men he had seen die. There no longer seemed to be anything remotely ludicrous about the uniform he wore. It was blood-stained, torn and filthy. Maggots crawled all over the bloody patches. There were tiny insects in his hair. Bunny had been machine-gunned during the evacuation of Kowloon; Giles had advanced with his platoon in a bid to recapture a position along the Wong Nei Chong Road, and no man of them had been seen again. The defence plan was proving to be a disaster.

Four days before Christmas, and further resistance was pointless. Churchill had apparently signalled his encourage-

223

ment to hold out as long as humanly possible, day by day, hour by hour. Alex could not see how dying to the last man on this small isolated island would affect the outcome of what had now become a world war. Too many had died already. He could not forget the sound of Bunny's screams as he was peppered with bullets from a diving aircraft. Only twenty-six, his friend was an expert at the foxtrot, clever at cards, a clown on the tennis court and had worked in a bank until December 8. It was unforgivable that he should have been murdered by strangers who had believed him to be an enemy because he wore a khaki suit. What had befallen Giles, the stockbroker who had a canny gift of choosing winners at Happy Valley, and who could play a banjo rather well? The Japanese were averse to taking prisoners. British, Canadian and Indian troops' bodies had been found either decapitated, shot in the back of the head or bayoneted to death with their hands tied behind their backs. Alex did not know if Giles had been thus murdered. It did not bear thinking about. Even more appalling was the prospect of falling into enemy hands himself. The fear haunted him constantly. Life had become a nightmare, turning him into a stranger.

Alex had been given orders to recapture a pillbox lost two days ago. It commanded an excellent view of a bend in the uphill road. Whilst in enemy hands it was impossible for the company of men he was now with to force the Japanese from their strategic position on the crest. He had been wondering for the past hour why, if the pillbox was so well situated as to prevent troops from using the road, it had ever been overrun by Japanese. And how had the strategic position on the crest been lost in the first place? Waiting for the first glimpse of dawn, uncertainties, terrors and inner voices whispering of treachery assailed a man. He was no longer with people he knew. As each defensive position had been surrendered, each small battle lost, the survivors had sought refuge with other groups still offering resistance. In Alex's hotch-potch platoon was one face he knew and liked. Jim Maiden, along with other RAF men, had attached himself to the military force in Kowloon after the airport and their few machines had been destroyed. The air force personnel had gone various ways on leaving the mainland; Jim had elected to stay with Alex. They had both survived somehow, the curious friendship based on love of a lost seaplane helping them through the grim days. It was to Jim Alex turned as an almost imperceptible lifting of night occurred.

'If we're going, it'll have to be now,' he whispered. 'Leave it any longer and we'll be too visible.'

Jim's expression could not be seen, but his voice said it all. 'I don't like this one bit. Of all the things I've done, this is the most pointless. Even if we take the pillbox, which we can't against the odds, it's impossible to recapture a whole hill in broad daylight. They done it at night, creeping through the undergrowth, not marching up a road in full view.'

'What d'you suggest instead – holding up our hands and calling it a day?'

'Finding a boat and getting away, that's what.'

It was the best proposal Alex had heard for a long while. He felt almost lightheaded with relief. 'You're on! Let's get this over then make our way to the coast.'

They got there the hard way. After advancing no more than ten yards, the silence was split by machine-gunfire. An excruciating pain in his thigh caused Alex to stumble over a small mound, which probably saved his life. The man directly behind him was killed by vicious fire that raked his chest from side to side. Screams and cries arose from the scrub all around, and the advance became a faltering retreat. His voice was hoarse as Alex shouted orders to collect all wounded before retiring to the shelter of an overhang. He looked for Jim in the greyness of dawn. Jim was looking for him.

'All right?' asked Alex.

'Yes. You?'

'My leg. Can you help me along?'

'My head hurts. I think I've lost an ear.'

'Oh God, what a bloody stupid thing to ask us to do.'

Aiding each other as best they could, the pair made for safety over uneven ground covered thickly with vegetation. Others were doing the same; ghost figures limping, dragging or stumbling through another death-filled morning. The firing had ceased. Well over half the platoon must be lost, for the numbers retreating were few. Alex felt no sense of failure. Potential heroes might have pressed on for King and Country until they and their men had all died in a valiant bid to obey orders. Alex was no patriotic daredevil. The capture of that pillbox would have made no difference to the certainty of Hong Kong falling. He preferred to give others a chance of life, along with himself.

Once under the protection of the overhang, Alex sat panting with pain while he took stock of the situation. As a fighting unit they were useless. Only two men were unscathed: a Chinese sergeant and a regular soldier from a Highland regiment who had no idea where his comrades now were. Three Volunteers were so badly wounded he guessed they would not survive being carried to the bottom of the hill. The rest looked in very poor shape. Jim had, indeed, lost most of an ear and was bleeding profusely. Alex's leg wound, although agonizing when he moved, appeared to be through flesh and muscle rather than through bone. It needed medical attention as much as any other, however.

He sent the Chinese sergeant to inform those below waiting to storm the hill once the pillbox was recaptured. Many of them would surely be relieved that their action must be called off. Apart from the moans of those who could not bear their pain, the group was silent, lost in thoughts best unrevealed. Alex leaned against a scratchy bush, longing for a de Reske. It seemed even more desirable than food. In hospital they would finally be given a meal and a drink. They would sleep in a bed. However hard, it would be luxury compared with freezing nights on verminous hillsides. After a rest and something to eat, he and Jim would work out how best to seize a boat. A gammy leg and a missing ear would not hamper their rowing capabilities. He was too weary to think about a possible destination. The priority was to get away from Hong Kong.

They all lay on that hillside until late afternoon. The three most badly wounded died within the first hour. The condition of some of the others worsened dramatically because of the cold and lack of water. They all suffered from that, and from dread of the Japanese discovering them. By four-thirty they all believed they had been abandoned to their fate. Alex's leg had grown numb enough for him to consider a further bid for help, but standing brought a rush of blood and fresh pain. Then men were suddenly climbing towards them with stretchers. Abuse died on the lips of those who had been waiting ten hours, for they were given news that Repulse Bay was surrounded and British families who had sought refuge in the renowned hotel were certain to be captive within twenty-four hours.

'So it's all over,' exclaimed a Cockney clerk employed by Lane Crawford until December 8.

'Not likely,' his stretcher-bearer retorted grimly. 'We're making a last stand here at Stanley. The Brig told us we're Hong Kong's final hope and he has every confidence in our ability to hold off the Japs until New Year at least. We all think he's barmy. But what can we do?'

'Shoot him!' shouted a corporal in great pain. 'Shoot him in the guts, like me. He won't want no bleedin' last stand then, matey.'

They were all taken down to ambulances that had been so frequently used over the past fourteen days they stank of blood and vomit. Not a man complained. Nor did they during a bumpy, grinding journey that exacerbated their suffering. Alex lay thinking about the boat and escape. If some crazy brigadier wanted to fight to the death, he was welcome to, but he had no right to order others to do so. The regular troops were trained to obey without question, but *he* was an unwilling volunteer with no such obligation. He believed he was entitled to choose his own action now the end was in sight.

The wounded had been categorized by the senior medical orderly and loaded into ambulances according to the seriousness of their condition. The extreme cases were to be driven to the hospital in Stanley Prison, the rest were taken to St Stephen's College, which had been turned into a hospital very hurriedly. On a slight rise, it was a prominent two-storey building comprising two wings with a third floor joining them. Despite Red Cross flags flying in full view, it had been shelled several times. The damage, combined with absence of electrical power and water, made treatment difficult.

Already packed with wounded, the old college somehow accommodated a few more. Alex's fear that he would be put in an officers' ward separated from Jim was groundless. There was no longer space or time for niceties of rank. The new arrivals were carried to a small room on the first floor, where they were seen by an RAMC doctor then treated by nursing sisters close to exhaustion. All that was possible to offer by way of sustenance was hot soup made from vegetables that had been boiled more than twice. The supply of fresh water had ceased some days ago, and facilities for laundering were now non-existent. The odour of sickness and its attendant afflictions was almost overwhelming.

As Alex lay in darkness that night, his leg throbbing from the makeshift treatment it had been given, he wondered if he might not have been better off on that hillside. The air was purer there, and the stars would make a better ceiling to stare at than one with chunks of plaster missing and the rest likely to fall at any time. A night-long bombardment kept all but the unconscious awake. One of the nurses came at hourly intervals with a lamp to check that all was well. What would happen if an emergency arose between visits Alex could not guess. There were no means of summoning aid, and shouting would be covered by the noise of battle. Too far from Jim to discuss plans, Alex made up his mind to go as soon as they gained the opportunity. He would hobble to the beach somehow.

By dawn they were all suffering from food poisoning. Their situation worsened immediately because of the total lack of facilities. Alex felt so ill he was unable even to lift his head, much less walk to the beach. The medical staff did what they could, but lacked the means to relieve their patients' misery. During the next two days only the strong survived, and the college was shelled yet again during the savage battle for Stanley. Alex was left exhausted by sickness, and felt no sense of shame for welcoming the added space provided by the deaths of four men. They had been in constant pain and their moans had been unbearable. It was a relief that it had come to an end.

He was approached by Jim, who seemed in better shape than himself. 'I've been thinking about that boat, Mr Tennant,' he began in a low voice, sitting on the floor near Alex's head.

'So've I, Jim.'

'You see, it's a bit awkward for me, being a reg'lar and all. Don't really see how I can go while we're still fighting. Could be had for "desertion in the face of the enemy". On the other hand, it's not as if I'm a soldier. So far as the RAF's concerned, we're out of this war – have been since they destroyed our base and aircraft that first day. What do *you* think?'

Alex looked at the man's grimy face which had aged alarmingly, and he thought of the family awaiting him in England. 'I think you have every right to get away by any possible means.'

Jim's brow puckered. 'You do?'

'Look at it this way. If you escape, you'll be sent elsewhere to fight. You don't intend hiding away until the war's over, do you? *That's* desertion in the face of the enemy. You'll be more use to the RAF as a free man than you will be as a prisoner here, or in Stanley cemetery.'

'Well, I kind of thought that myself. If you think it's all right, then I'll say no more. I've been thinking about what we'd do if you agreed I could go, and I've come up with an idea I'd like you to consider.'

'It had better be a good one, Jim. It's a long row to England.'

Jim let that pass. He was too eager to expound on his theme. 'In a cave along Stanley Beach there's bits of *Dragonfly*, ain't there? One of her floats is damaged, but there's enough of it to be useful. What say we get down there and lash some spars to the floats to form a raft? You see, Mr Tennant, it seems to me the Japs'll be keeping an eye out for boats with people like us in them. If we took off our uniforms and draped seaweed and stuff over the floats, we could be mistaken for Chinese on a crude sort of raft. Some of their fishing-boats are little better than that. If we went night-time, I reckon we could fool them into taking us for poor locals.' He studied Alex for a moment or two. 'When d'you reckon you'll be well enough to make a dash for it?'

It was such a good idea Alex was momentarily silenced. How had he failed to remember that they had piled what they could salvage of his seaplane into a rough cavern on the shore where he had crashed?

'Give me until dawn tomorrow, then I'll be strong enough to walk to the beach *and* help to build the raft.' He lowered his voice, suddenly remembering the need for secrecy. 'Let's outline what we left in that cave.'

'If it's still there,' said Jim heavily.

'It'll be there. We put it far enough in, and disguised it with flotsam. How will we construct this raft?'

They forgot the stench, the battle raging outside and the one raging within their empty stomachs as they sat on the floor in that upstairs room planning a floating platform to start them on a journey to the opposite side of the world. The notion did not seem in the least ridiculous to two men facing an unthinkable alternative.

When darkness fell they had said all they could on the subject. Doubts began to set in as Alex lay once again staring at the broken ceiling listening to the bombardment outside. How would they reach the cave without being spotted by Japanese machine-gunners? Or by their own troops, who would take drastic measures against men leaving them to battle on? Seen from their point of view, it did seem remarkably like desertion in the face of the enemy. All at once, the plan on which he had been so determined made him feel uncomfortable – almost guilty. Yet the continued presence of an RAF corporal mechanic, and Maurice Tennant's playboy son, could make no difference to the last agony of Hong Kong. An inner voice reiterated what he had said to Jim. If they got clean away, they would continue the fight elsewhere. Better than rotting in a prison camp. *Or dying slowly in one.*

Alex was not sure quite when during that night he knew he would join the RAF if he ever reached safety. All he was certain of was that it had been pre-destined from the moment he met Sarah Channing. Thinking of her now made his proposed escape appear almost cowardly. He knew in his heart *she* would see it in that light. Rod Durman, of course, would be here at the end, nobly tending the sick and wounded. Any woman would be impressed by that. He had been a fool to hope he could ever have a future with someone whose ideals were beyond him. What would become of Sarah now?

Haunted by his thoughts and fantasies, Alex watched two British nurses tending, by the light of a lamp, a Canadian in extreme pain from a chest wound. The sight of these women going calmly about their work when shells were falling nearby, and an enemy known to be merciless was no more than a mile or two away, gave him fresh cause for guilt. What if *they* believed escaping to fight elsewhere was the better thing to do? What if they walked out of this makeshift hospital and left their patients to their fate? How would he feel about their action? He began to toss and turn. It would soon be morning. Jim could not build a raft without help, and could not cross to the mainland on his own. The man had a wife and children in England he was anxious to reach. Could he tell Jim to forget the plan, condemn him to years of imprisonment simply because he now had a conscience?

When daylight was not far off, Alex had grown almost feverish. One silent voice was urging him to run; another commanding him to stay. Behind visions of Jim and Sarah was the shadowy figure of Rod Durman with a band of dedicated nurses.

Someone shook him and he awoke from the tormenting dream to find Jim crouching beside him. In the pale light the man looked drawn and desperate. 'How do you feel?' Jim rasped. 'Will you make it all right?'

'Do you reckon it's time to go?' Alex asked, still affected by the dream.

Jim nodded. 'There's no one here now. The nurses left about half an hour ago, so we can get away without them stopping us. It'll be light soon. If we can get to the beach before then, we'll be safe enough. No one'll see us in that cave. Make the raft and hide up during the day, then get into the water just as it's growing dark. That's what we planned, isn't it?'

Alex began to move. He was weak from food poisoning, and he had lost blood from his wound. Getting to his feet was an effort. He almost collapsed once he was upright. Several men lying awake watched them with dull eyes and little curiosity. Jim led the way between sleeping wounded to where a door opened to stairs that would take them down to a yard. From there, they would reach open country. As they were about to pass through the doorway, a faint voice from within the room said, 'Merry Christmas, lads!'

Alex hesitated on the threshold. He had forgotten it was Christmas Day. Running out on these men seemed even worse on a festival renowned for close ties between family and friends.

'Come on! Coast's clear,' whispered Jim from the top of the stairs.

Alex closed the door on those lying helpless in the room with a broken ceiling. He felt dreadfully unsteady as he crept down the stairs behind Jim, and his heart was pounding. Yet it was guilt rather than fear causing the sensation. Reaching the yard without encountering a soul, it was then possible to look into the long rooms being used as general wards for the most serious cases. Two of the doctors and some nurses were gathered there in the lamplight, apparently in urgent discussion. They were beginning another day of non-stop work, gunfire and exhaustion.

Alex turned to Jim, knowing he must leave the man to try his escape alone. 'I'm sorry, but I really can't –'

'Christ!' swore Jim in tones of shock, staring at the long room to their right.

The chilling sounds had already begun before Alex turned back to follow his companion's gaze. He froze. His scalp crawled with horror. Japanese soldiers had entered from a door standing open at the far end of the ward, and they were bayoneting the men in those beds nearest them. The helpless patients screamed as their enemies thrust at them time and again, until the bedclothes were running with blood. Both doctors rushed towards the scene, but were shot before they were halfway there. The Japanese then stabbed at their bodies repeatedly, as they lay on the floor beyond Alex's sight.

232

Dawn became a massacre. The early morning calm was shattered by shrieks, savage staccato voices and rifle shots. Alex and Jim automatically shrank back into the shadows as they watched an obscenity for which nothing had prepared them. The nurses were dragged from the room at gunpoint. Terrified of betraying their own whereabouts, the two men were then forced to witness further bestiality no more than yards away. The women were thrown to the hard floor of the yard to be repeatedly raped under the bayonets of those watching impassively. The desecration seemed to go on for ever, for other soldiers appeared from the building to take their turn. The women's cries mingled with the screams of wounded men being slaughtered in an orgy of hatred.

An eternity could have passed during those minutes. Alex pressed further and further against the wall until he almost became one with the stone. His head rang with the sounds of hell; his eyes could watch no longer. Hardly breathing, eyes fast shut, heart pumping blood so fast he felt giddy, he waited for his inevitable, agonizing end.

The screaming gradually died; no more shots were fired. A few harsh commands, the clatter of boots on stone. Then silence. It continued for some time. Breathing grew normal. His lids opened. Dawn had advanced enough to show that the nurses were dead, piled up in a corner beneath a bush. Nothing could be seen through the windows of the long room; no movement. Either the occupants were also all dead, or they were too terrified to do anything. It suggested that the Japanese had left the building. Alex slowly turned to Jim. The little corporal looked yellow in the faint light, his eyes reflecting all he had just seen. By unspoken consent they eased themselves away from the wall and moved off, walking like men in a trance, silently, their sights on some far-off goal. It was as if they no longer controlled their own actions.

Christmas Day held such significance for the Christians at the Halburton that they gathered in the ruins of the office block to sing beloved carols. None thought of it as an act of defiance, yet it was. They knew freedom was within days, perhaps hours, of being taken from them, so they celebrated the festival that had been an integral part of life since childhood. It made them feel close to home and loved ones, and enabled them to hold their fears at bay.

Sarah was close to tears as she sang. Memories of services in the village church decorated with holly flooded back to add further poignancy to the moment. In those past years – even during wartime ones – she had never dreamed a Christmas such as this would come. Nothing was further from those Cotswold festivities, sometimes with Ellie's friends, sometimes just she and her grandmother. The walk to church and back with frost nipping their faces, fir trees decked with ribbons and candles, the aroma of roast goose and hot punch, dogs stretching before a log fire and herself playing carols and Christmas music on her piano in the low-ceilinged parlour.

Now she stood amidst the rubble of offices where she and Marion used to type, and where Rod compiled his reports, singing those same melodies that spoke of yesterday. She and her companions were no choristers. Voices grew cracked or muffled by emotion, some were off-key. In their own ears, however, the sound was sweet and true and uplifting. For a while it made the din of war fade to the background. But it could not be totally drowned. This was the eighteenth day that it had been constantly in their ears, reaching full power over the past few.

Stanley was the last area of Hong Kong flying the British flag. It would do so until it was overrun. No one doubted that it would be. If the main forces on the Island could not retain strategic strongholds, a tiny peninsula at its extremity would not. They had heard of the capture of the Repulse Bay Hotel along with many women and children hiding there. They had been marched away by an armed escort; their husbands and other men who had tried to defend them met with various fates. One Chinese who had brought food for a relative in the Halburton had spoken of army prisoners being forced to sit on the edge of a cliff, so that their bodies fell to the beach when they were shot. There were also tales of beheadings and other atrocities. In contradiction, some Chinese spoke of Japanese troops offering prisoners water and cigarettes.

Those under seige at the Halburton Clinic did not know

what to believe of the enemy, although tales of harshness outnumbered those of them as reasonable, humane captors. The staff were all dirty and unkempt. There had been no water supply for days. The tank holding a small reserve had emptied yesterday. A procession of volunteer water carriers had brought full buckets up from the sea for washing, but thirst had now become a major problem. The supply of soap had run out at the weekend; medicines a day later. All that was possible to do for those crammed into the remaining undamaged building was wash them in sea water, feed them fish stew and make them as comfortable as conditions allowed. Only Chinese staff were able to communicate freely with patients. The European volunteers trapped at Stanley applied themselves to all manner of tasks to compensate for their lack of linguistic ability.

This bothered Sarah a great deal, especially when she saw someone in pain or a child in tears. At first, she had tried to give comfort with smiles and hand-holding, but the distrust of centuries lingered in those whose lives never crossed the ethnic barrier. Only if the patient had been employed by Europeans was there a hope of some rapport. However, one man who spoke a little English revealed that many of his compatriots had lost all respect for their administrators since they had shown such weakness in defending Hong Kong. To live under the rule of masters it was necessary to look up to them in admiration, he added. The Japanese had shown their strength. Might they not prove better administrators in days to come?

In her weary, depressed state Sarah found the man's philosophy disturbing. Having had little time for her countrymen here, she now inwardly rose to their defence. Hong Kong had been left to its fate by the greater demands of the war in the West. The defenders had not really stood a chance once the Japanese decided to conquer the East. Isolated off a barbarous mainland, it was not considered strategically important enough to pack with troops and equipment needed more desperately elsewhere. In China itself, General Chiang Kai-shek had failed to prevent the Japanese from taking control of the coastal belt. Surely he should be condemned for weakness in defence, when he had the entire Chinese army available for that purpose. Had their own people any greater right to be admired at present?

Standing in a soiled gown in a building now open to the sky on Christmas Day 1941, Sarah finally realized what Ellie had meant about discovering that there were people in the world. The last days and nights at the clinic had taught them all a great deal about each other, but none had learned as much as the girl who had only ever before come alive when immersed in music. In adversity, all barriers had fallen. Sarah now knew that the American, named Roma, wore her jewellery as an outward sign of confidence because she had lost the love of her husband; that the court official's daughter, Chloë, had been denied the opportunity to train as an actress because her parents disapproved of the profession; and that Marion had stolen her Bill from a friend on the verge of marrying him. None of the women learned anything of Sarah apart from her musical aspirations, yet she felt closer to them than she had ever been to her schoolfellows.

Each of them was concerned about the fate of relatives elsewhere on the Island. The American and, more desperately, Marion were fearful for their husbands' safety. Sarah was equally fearful for the safety of another woman's husband. *She* could not seek comfort from her companions on that score. Instead, Sarah supported Marion by saying all the words she herself wanted to hear. So the days had passed in giving what help they could to Chinese strangers who had been injured by bombs and shells, and doing the same for each other's emotional wounds. Not once did any of them speak of what would happen when Hong Kong fell into enemy hands. That terrible moment seemed very near. Singing carols through dry throats amidst broken masonry, twisted iron spars and shattered glass was their means of keeping it distant. They were on the first bars of 'Hark! the Herald Angels Sing' when two men appeared, to stare at them through a gaping hole in the seaward wall. Sarah's heart lurched with fright. The singing petered out as the women waited in petrified silence. Yet the men's faces were not Oriental.

For a long moment nobody spoke or moved, then a

236

cultured English voice croaked, 'What the hell are you all doing? The Japs are overrunning the Peninsula.'

Sarah recognized the voice, but moved forward in some confusion, because surely this could not be Alex Tennant. He wore a stained, torn uniform; his eyes were bloodshot and wild like a madman's; his face, covered in thick stubble, was gaunt; his blond hair was matted and filthy. Yet, although the caressing lightness of tone was absent, Sarah knew that voice well enough to believe he *must* be the man she had so misjudged.

'Alex?'

'My God – *Sarah!*' He grew agitated to the point of desperation. 'They're raping nurses – killing everyone in sight. You've got to get away.' He scrambled through the rough gap in the wall, stumbled on rubble, then collapsed almost at her feet and began to sob.

As she crouched beside him, Sarah was vaguely aware that Alex's companion was being coaxed into the roofless room by Marion and Roma. He appeared unable to reply to their anxious questions. Sarah concentrated on Alex, filled with horror at the change wrought in him by some unimaginable experience. He clung to her, speaking wildly about bestiality towards women and a bloody massacre of helpless men. 'You must leave – dear God, *all* of you must leave. They'll do it here when they come. They'll do the same again.'

Cradling him in her arms, she asked through a throat now dry with fear, 'Where have you come from, Alex? Tell me where this happened.'

The convulsive sobbing ceased, but he was shaking like a man in the grip of excessive coldness. 'The College. They b-bayoneted them as they lay in b-bed. They sh-shot the doctors in c-cold blood, then took the nurses out-outside.' He gripped her arm until it hurt. 'We couldn't do any-anything to s-stop it. We couldn't do a thing to – to help them.' He grew wild again. 'You've got to leave. All of you!'

Across the room, the other women were trying to coax some life into the small man with the bandaged head, who might as well have been unaware of their presence for all the response he made.

'They're suffering from shock,' declared Chloë. 'He's rambling. We'd better take them to one of the doctors.'

'Do you know him?' asked Marion of Sarah.

She looked up in distress. 'Yes, and I believe what he says. We should tell Dr Koh immediately.'

Marion was deeply shocked. 'The College is only a short distance from here.'

Alex struggled to his feet, Sarah beside him. 'Just go!' he cried, throwing out an arm. 'Get down to the beach. We'll hide in the cave until the raft is ready. Then we'll all leave.'

'He's crazy,' declared Chloë.

'I guess this one's deaf,' put in Roma. 'Looks like he's lost an ear.'

Marion moved off. 'I'm going for Dr Koh.'

Alex turned back to Sarah, his face working. 'Get down to that beach, for God's sake! Tell these others to do the same. I can't protect you here.'

'It's all right, Alex,' Sarah murmured, still shaken by the change in him. 'Someone's gone for the senior doctor. He'll know what best to do.'

'There's no time. *Oh God, don't you hear what I'm saying?*' He seized her arm again, attempting to drag her forward to the gap in the wall. 'Come *on*.'

Totally thrown by what was happening, Sarah allowed him his fevered dominance while her companions watched in a state of confusion.

'Don't go with him, Sarah. He needs help.'

'He's crazy!'

'They wouldn't kill helpless patients, surely. It's against all the rules of war.'

'How *could* we get away?'

'What's he mean about a cave?'

'They wouldn't lay a hand on *us*. We're not soldiers. We're not even real nurses.'

The silent man in a dirty uniform with wings on the shoulder retained enough awareness to see that Alex was leaving. He moved towards the hole in the wall, reaching it first. With all thought suspended, Sarah was halted by the sound of Marion calling her name. Turning, she saw her friend beside Dr Koh. His thin face, frequently impassive, now wore an expression of anger she had never before seen on it.

'They must go!' he said, pointing to the men. 'Go now!'

'But they need aid. They're suffering from shock and probably exposure,' protested Roma. 'You can't send them away. This is a hospital.'

'They are soldiers! They must go. If Japanese come and find soldiers they will be angry. Kill us all. This is not a military hospital. This is for Chinese only. We quite safe. No one fighting Japanese here.' He advanced across the rubble waving his arms in a shooing movement at Alex and his companion. 'Go, go! Hong Kong no longer yours. We not want you. *Go!*'

'Well, I'll be . . . After we've worked our goddamned fingers to the bone for your people you won't lift one of yours to help ours.'

Dr Koh was unabashed. 'Japanese now our masters. *You* their enemies, not us. Everything now changed. I say you go.' He pointed. '*They* go.' To add pressure to his words he came up to Alex and began to push him through the gap. 'Go, go!'

'You two-faced bastard!' cried Roma explosively.

'Leave him alone,' said Marion, almost in tears. 'Call yourself a doctor!'

'God help you when we take Hong Kong back,' put in Chloë icily. 'We have long memories, you know.'

Sarah had experienced several deeply painful revelations of character changes in Hong Kong, so spent no time protesting over another. She went with Alex through the gap. Although he gripped her arm with determination, it was she who actually led him towards the steps down which she had gone to meet Rod for the last time. This entire morning had been so bizarre, she derived surprising comfort from the presence of a man she had repeatedly insulted as she went with him across the beach. When she grew aware that they headed a small procession she knew further comfort. These were her friends, her countrymen and women who had shown her their true colours during these past days. They compensated for disillusionment from other sources.

239

Once on the beach, Alex appeared to know which direction to take and increased his limping pace. His RAF companion stumped along showing no interest in the women scrambling through the soft, shifting sand behind him. Sounds of distant rifle-fire were suddenly augmented by the heavier roar of artillery as the last desperate battle for Stanley began. Stumbling through the growing morning as the fear of being spotted and shot at seized them all, the little group automatically ducked as shells screamed over their heads. The sea was pewter, whipped up by a cold wind into high waves that broke upon the shoreline with a thunder all their own.

Even in that moment of danger Sarah felt the pain as she crossed the spot where she had walked away from Rod. If he was alive did he feel that pain also? Did he suffer the agony of not knowing *her* fate?

'In here, quickly,' Alex panted, bringing her from retrospection as he dragged her across a spread of seaweed to where a jutting sandstone ridge practically concealed a narrow cleft. Another shell whistled across so low it banished any reluctance to enter the dark, odorous split in the bank a hundred and fifty yards from the clinic. An explosion shook the area bringing down upon them a shower of sand and fine shingle. The trailing women rushed in to collide with Sarah and Alex.

'That sure as hell hit the Halburton,' said Roma breathlessly.

'Old Koh is certain to blame it on the arrival of these two,' Chloë grunted. 'But he won't view the Japs in such a favourable light now.'

Marion sounded on the verge of tears. 'What are we supposed to be doing in here? We'll be buried alive if a shell hits much nearer.'

Alex, still gripping Sarah's arm, was apparently more in control of himself now. 'In this cave are the means of escape. We intend to build a raft, make ourselves look as Chinese as possible, then set out for the mainland at dusk. The light will be fading enough to aid our disguise.'

'A *raft!*' exclaimed Roma, in disgusted tones made more explosive through fear. 'Chloë's right, you *are* crazy.'

'The mainland's occupied by the Japs, have you forgotten?' Chloë said heavily. 'And who's going to propel it – you two? No, thanks.'

'What's the alternative?' asked Sarah, wondering how Alex meant to build a raft in such a place. She could scarcely make out her companions in the dimness. Silence followed her question.

Another explosion shook the cavern, producing a second shower of debris upon their heads. Marion gave a soft cry. 'I'm not stopping here. It's not safe.'

Alex became forceful. 'I can't allow you to leave. We must go further in, away from the beach. They'll search it when they take the Peninsula. I can protect you if we go right to the back. That's where the floats of *Dragonfly* are.'

'What the hell's he talking about,' demanded Chloë, betraying her anxiety. 'You say you know him, Sarah. Is he normally as loopy as this?'

What could she say? She had never before stood in a dark cave with him during bombardment designed to force their capitulation to a cruel enemy. Yet Sarah had surprising faith in him in that moment. 'He's been fighting this war from the first day. We've only been passively helping those victims of it. I think we should trust him and go further in. I just wish we had some light.'

'What a goddamned fool! I'm not thinking,' came Roma's voice from Sarah's right. 'When my lighter ran out I bought some matches from that old coolie who came round with joss sticks and good-luck tokens.' Accompanying the rattle of matches in a box came a flare of light as the American struck one. 'They won't last long so we'll have to make a torch from something.' She forced a smile in the eerie yellow light. 'You all look sick to the teeth.'

The match died as Alex said, 'This is no time for jokes. Give me the matches and I'll lead the way. We can light a fire back there.'

There was an authority in his voice which must have impressed Roma, for she offered a quiet 'sorry' against the sound of the box being transferred from hand to hand.

'Be ready to move when I strike each one,' Alex continued, 'and move fast. I don't want to use any more than necessary.'

During the brief periods of illumination, they all made their uncertain way through a twisting cleft which narrowed for some yards before opening to an area practically circular. Sarah gazed in astonishment at a collection of items resembling a car that had been taken apart. With them were two long cylindrical objects painted red. The floats of *Dragonfly*? Of course! He had boasted enough of his scarlet seaplane which had crashed off the coast of Stanley. He might well have drowned if Rod had not changed duties to avoid meeting her at the clinic, and so been on hand to swim out in a rescue bid. Her eyes filled with tears as the anguish of regret swamped her once more. These tangible reminders of an incident brought about by Fate made Rod seem so close. Like Wang Chua, Alex should owe a lifetime debt to the man who saved his life.

Her female companions asked endless unanswered questions of the two men as they pulled sections of the wrecked aircraft together to one side of the cavern by the light of half a dozen precious matches. Sarah watched in silence, knowing Alex Tennant had become a different man since December 8. They had all become different people.

The men considered the height of their pile, conferred in low voices, then walked to where one of the floats lay, apparently intact, upon the sand. Alex unscrewed something, put his cap upside down alongside it, then helped his companion to roll the float forward until fluid poured from it into the khaki cap. There was a strong aroma of fuel to combat the darkness, and Sarah knew that Alex was not talking wildly of his intention to escape. He and the corporal knew *exactly* what they were doing. His capful of aviation fuel was poured over the makings of the fire, which soon burst into life, cheering them all with its bright glow and warming flames.

Such was the emotion of the moment, the women hugged each other, then Chloë walked up to Alex. 'Loopy or not, you're a marvel.' She threw her arms around him and planted a kiss on his grimy cheek.

His response was to say over her shoulder to Roma, 'If you had matches, you must have cigarettes. I'd like one, even if it's your last.'

'Honey, we'll share the packet between us. How about the little guy?'

'I wouldn't say no, thanks. But don't get smoking anywhere near this float. It's a fuel tank, see.'

Roma threw the packet of cigarettes to him. 'Your deafness has worn off. That's a relief.'

'I got other things on my mind, that's why.' He took out two cigarettes, threw the packet back, then lit them both and handed one to Alex.

The three smokers sank to the gritty floor to enjoy their nicotine. Sarah, Marion and Chloë also sat near the warmth, silent now the excitement at the fire's creation was over.

For a while each was lost in thought, then Sarah turned to Alex. 'How is it this hasn't all been taken by the local people? They must have seen you bring it in.'

'There's bad *fung shui* here. No Chinese will come near, much less inside this cave.' He drew on the cigarette hungrily. 'Some devils were reputedly seen snatching the spirits of fishermen drowned just off the coast and carrying them in here. Soon afterwards terrible screams were heard. Locals believe devils are still here waiting for fresh victims.'

'It's all nonsense, in my view,' said Roma, puffing just as hungrily as Alex. 'But *fung shui* comes in mighty useful at times.'

'Do Japanese believe in it?' asked Marion, in faint tones. 'If they do we could stay here until Hong Kong is freed again.'

'You're coming on the raft,' Alex told her. 'We'll make it large enough for you all.' He turned to his companion as he got to his feet. 'We'd better make a start, Jim.'

'Can we help?' asked Sarah. She had not the first idea how to build anything, but the day had been so unreal there seemed nothing odd about her offer.

'Just keep that fire going and don't block what little light it gives. Keep your voices low. The Japs might not give a damn about *fung shui*.'

Sarah watched for a while with the others as the men selected from the wreckage any piece they believed might be useful, then began to lay it out on the floor ready for assembly. She wondered about this obviously close relationship between a wealthy playboy shipper and an RAF corporal, which could surely not have sprung up over the last eighteen days. Yet hazardous situations hatched curious friendships, as she had discovered. Each time a shell landed in the vicinity, the roof of the cavern shook and scattered them all with fine dust. Marion was clearly suffering from claustrophobia. She sat biting her lip, frequently dabbing her face and neck with a handkerchief, but she kept her fear to herself. Roma smoked her share of the cigarettes one after the other. Chloë watched Alex's every movement. By the yellow glow of the fire, they presented a sorry picture with strained expressions, soiled white overalls and bedraggled hair. Sarah supposed she must look the same as they.

It soon became clear that the men were finding the exertion too much for them. They began dropping things; made several attempts at lifting heavy spars. Chloë stood up decisively.

'Take a break. You're both exhausted. Daddy has a boat so I know how to splice securely. Show me what you want done and we'll do it in half the time you'll take.'

'Surely we will,' agreed Roma, lighting another cigarette from the butt of the last. 'But not Marion. She needs to take care of herself.'

'Of course I'll help,' insisted the pregnant girl. 'This is no time for pampering, and it'll be better than sitting still listening to the last few miles of Hong Kong being blasted into surrender.'

While Alex and Jim rested, the four women continued working on the makeshift raft, cutting lengths of fabric from the broken fuselage with bayonets to fasten ill-assorted spars across the floats, one of which was a great deal shorter than the other. Sarah was certain her companions shared her scepticism, but none voiced it. She could not believe this would stay afloat for long, and it certainly would be unlikely to bear six people. As a person who believed in fighting circumstances, however, she backed the men in their determination to do anything positive rather than sit awaiting capture. They had witnessed the fate of many and it had taken its toll of them. She admired their efforts here, however futile.

The women tired sooner than they expected. Only then did they all realize the fire was reducing the oxygen available, which was not being replaced because they were too far from the beach. As the fire was essential to light their working area, they decided to go in pairs for ten minutes at a stretch to the entrance where they kept a lookout for Japanese troops.

Thus the day wore past. By late afternoon they were all hungry, but thirst was the greater enemy. The foul air in the cave made this worse. Anything inflammable had been doused with fuel drained from the float and flung on to the fire, so a layer of fine smoke added to their breathing problems. The men were now minus shirts and vests; blood had begun to ooze through the dressing on Alex's thigh. Sarah made him stop work while she bound a strip from her overall around it.

'You should have rested more,' she chided as she fastened the crude bandage.

'I will, when we're away from here. It'll be dark within a couple of hours.'

'But the raft is practically finished, isn't it?' She thought it best to go along with the notion of escaping. He looked so drawn and ill and filthy, vastly different from the debonair, good-looking man with a reputation for womanizing. Yet, in the smoky, smelly cave by the flickering light from a fire of rags and scraps, she understood *this* Alex Tennant where she had not the other.

'I wish we could make it stronger,' he said, leaning wearily against the rough wall and drawing in laboured breaths. 'And I wish the sea was calmer than when I saw it the last time I went to the entrance.'

She sat beside him, resting back against the wall close to his bare shoulder. 'You've done wonders. I always said you could if you wanted to.'

His unshaven, sweat-sheened face turned towards her. 'You're the only person who has ever believed that.'

'You worked very hard to prevent such belief.'

He looked away again. 'Perhaps.'

The rest were busily trying to weave Jim's battledress jacket through the struts before starting on Alex's, so Sarah asked the question only he might be able to answer.

'On my last morning at Echoes, Father told me he was going to the Wong Nei Chong Gap to do what he could in its defence. Did you hear any news of him, and of those who were up there trying to hold it?'

Alex turned back to her. 'Sir Peter was too old for the Volunteers, wasn't he? Did he go on his own initiative?' At her nod, he said, 'Good for him. No one knows much about any of the defence groups, I'm afraid. It was a shock to be met with numbers far greater than expected, and an attack of such organized ferocity. Our plan fell apart almost immediately. Battalions were cut off from each other, communication lines were severed, orders were misconstrued or never arrived. Many Chinese civilians deserted us, some even sabotaging vehicles or destroying supplies as they left. Their countrymen in uniform, on the other hand, have been magnificent.' He ran a hand over his wet face and sighed. 'You have no idea what has been happening to this little island over the past two weeks.' After a moment's silence, he added, 'I thought of you often. I could hardly believe it when I saw you singing carols in that wrecked building. Thank God I did. You can leave this terrible place.'

She strove for lightness and nodded towards the raft. 'This is hardly the *San Maritino*, is it?'

'I booked a cabin for myself on that ship.'

The statement surprised her. 'You were going home?'

He nodded. 'Hong Kong had lost its appeal.'

Before she could pursue the subject further, Chloë called to them. 'Hey, you two, come and look at the finished craft.'

After struggling to their feet, they joined the others gazing at the fruits of their labours. Shaped like a trapezium because one float was broken, the raft's only virtue was its ingenuity. Basically, it looked frailer and less seaworthy than the poorest of sampans. No one said a word. Sarah glanced at the men's faces and saw resignation written there. Chloë and Roma were expressionless. Tears rolled down Marion's cheeks.

Sarah felt compelled to break the silence. 'How do you intend to propel it, Alex?'

He returned from his thoughts at the sound of her voice, nodding at what little remained of *Dragonfly*. 'We'll use the docking pole Chinese fashion - attach a paddle on the end of it and make a fabric rowlock. It'll add authenticity to our disguise.' He glanced at his watch. 'Not long to wait. We must all rest until it's time to leave. It'll take quite an effort to carry this down to the water, so I propose that we move nearer the entrance for fresh air. Jim and I will watch alternately while you get some sleep. You'll need all the energy you can muster when the moment comes.'

It was certainly fresher just a few feet from the beach, but the sounds of battle were louder and more intimidating. The women all lay on the gritty sand as instructed, but Sarah doubted that any one of them slept. Building the raft had kept fears at bay. Now activity had ceased, they rushed back. The scheme was little short of madness. The confidence she had felt in Alex's presence evaporated. It was a choice between the devil and the deep blue sea, except that this sea was *grey* and deep. Did these two truly intend to attempt an escape, or were they simply fending off the dread of capture with wild pretence? Were they now facing the moment of truth? She studied Alex as he lay a few feet away while Jim stood guard. Had he faith enough in himself and that raft to do as he proposed? They had no food or water. Even if they should reach the mainland, it was held by the same enemy. How could they possibly survive and cross hundreds of miles to reach that part of China still under the control of their ally, Chiang Kai-shek? The whole plan was doomed.

Guilt suddenly angled across these thoughts. She had preached to others, including Rod, the virtue of never tamely giving in without a fight, yet she was considering doing just that. Alex and his friend were prepared to continue fighting circumstance by the only means open to them. She must back their courage with her own. Even so, when Alex said quietly that they should get ready, her heart raced. She was a poor swimmer and the evening was cold.

They returned to where the fire had died to a glow, making the raft appear more ramshackle than before. Alex faced them, his face almost sinister in the red light. 'The Japanese might be fooled into thinking this construction typical of some local craft, but we are all too obviously *not* poor Chinese fishermen. We have to make our clothes dirty;

247

darken our skins. Those of us who are blond must disguise our hair in some fashion. I'll leave you all to do that as best you can but, although no longer actually white, those overalls cannot be worn as such. I suggest you tie them by the sleeves around your waists, after rubbing them with ash, then draping those scraps of aircraft fabric over your shoulders. When we reach open sea, remember to sit hunched as you've seen Chinese do on their boats. I just pray the light will be too poor for anyone on shore to see us clearly.' He began turning away. 'Let's get started.'

'Alex,' said Marion quietly, 'I'm very grateful for your invitation, but I can't leave without Bill.'

'Nor I without Arnold,' said Roma.

'My parents are probably prisoners somewhere on the Island,' put in Chloë. 'I have to stay with them.'

'But you've helped build this thing,' cried Jim, clearly distressed at the thought of their remaining to face horrors such as he had earlier witnessed.

'It was an unforgettable experience and it kept us all going for a while, but this is where we part. I hope with all my heart that you both make it to safety.' She turned to Sarah. 'You'll be staying with your father, of course.'

Came the moment from which Sarah had shied all day. Chloë had spoken the truth. Building the raft had been something to occupy time and create false confidence. She now faced a choice between embarking on this impossible voyage offering danger and probable death by drowning, or risking rape and possible death at the hands of the enemy. She had no love for her father; he might have already been killed along the Wong Nei Chong Gap. If he was captive he would derive little comfort from the presence of a daughter about whom he knew little and understood less.

As she stood beset by inner conflict, Alex laid a hand on her arm. 'Sarah is coming with us. She had a cabin booked on the *San Maritino* due to sail a fortnight ago. Sir Peter wished her to go home to deal with a family emergency. He'll be thankful that she got away safely.' He appealed to the others. 'Don't you think your loved ones would feel the same? They'd want you to seize this chance. There's no guarantee that you'll ever see them again ... and no guarantee that you'll be treated humanely. I *beg* you to come.'

Chloë approached and kissed him, saying, 'You're a splendid person, and I envy Sarah no end, but I can't walk out on two people who've built their lives around me. Roma might find reconciliation with her husband in shared danger and, if you'd ever heard Marion rave on about her Bill, you'd know *nothing* would make her part from him.'

'But what are you going to do?' asked Jim, still upset by their decision. 'We can't leave you here at their mercy.'

Roma answered. 'We'll wait here until the fighting ends, then give ourselves up. There shouldn't be any problem with them then.'

'We won't say a word about you three,' said Marion. 'Please get started or you'll miss the dusk. Come on, we'll help you.'

Overwhelmed by the way Alex had relieved her of a painful decision, Sarah took off her overall, dragged it through the hot ashes, then ground it into the floor with her feet. It was thoroughly dirty when she tied the sleeves around her so that it hung like a sarong. Next, she and Marion rubbed cold ash over her arms and the bodice of her silk petticoat until all was suitably darkened. The problem of her hair remained. How could they make it resemble the black tresses of a Chinese woman?

'I don't suppose I'll need this where I'm going,' joked Chloë, forcing a laugh as she unbuttoned her overall to reveal black chemise and panties. Without hesitation she peeled off the top and handed it over. As Sarah tied it around her head so that it hid her golden hair, Chloë added, 'I've worn it night and day since the eighteenth, so it's suitably odorous. I'm sorry.'

She found it impossible to reply. Now the moment of parting was near she saw how difficult it would be to say goodbye to the first real friends she had found. Beneath their assumed confidence they must be as sick with fear as she, yet they refused to leave their loved ones. Sarah knew in her heart she would do the same if an unborn child had not made a future with Rod impossible.

They were ready. Alex had sliced the rim from his service

249

cap with his bayonet, now thrust in his belt, and jammed the fuel-soaked crown over his matted fair hair. Jim was dark and needed no such disguise. Both men had darkened their torsos with paste made from ash and fuel, and had ripped the legs of their uniform trousers so that they more nearly resembled those of local fishermen. The trio of pseudo-Chinese faced the three they were leaving behind, but words would not come.

After gazing at each other in silence for a moment or two, Sarah, Alex and Jim turned to lift the raft, swing it to a vertical position, then start off through the narrow cleft. Their burden was heavier than Sarah had expected. The exhausted men also found the effort too great for them. Roma, Marion and Chloë saw this and helped move the clumsy construction as far as the entrance and beach. There, they lowered it on to the floats and straightened. Alex then spoke for them all in a voice grown husky.

'Christmas Day will never pass without my raising a glass in memory of this one. God go with us.'

He and Jim then bent to begin pushing the raft across the sand. Sarah was too choked to do more than gaze one last time at three faces she would never forget, before adding her strength to the task of getting to the water's edge. Bitter wind swept the beach hinting of a cold night to come. The tide was low, increasing the distance they must cross in full view of any watching eyes. Sarah was haunted more by the fact that she was a poor swimmer than by fear of being shot at. It was almost dark. They all looked so frail and ragged, surely no one would take them for British escapees.

Intermittent flashes lit the sky to tell her Stanley's last stand continued despite fires raging across the peninsula. While they had a short rest, Sarah took a quick glance at the white building behind her. The clinic had again been badly hit by shells. How terrible for those lying there helpless! The beach was empty. The entrance to the cave was now impossible to make out. She could no longer identify the spot where she had walked away from Rod.

'Don't look back,' said Alex softly. 'One more push and we'll reach the sea. Come on, bend to it.'

They had now to cross wet sand where jellyfish lay

stranded and crabs scuttled away from their approach. The floats no longer glided easily, so the effort was greater. So that they would not tilt and stick in the sand they had to push almost from a crouching position, which made their every limb ache. It seemed an eternity before Sarah felt the iciness of water over her toes and knew she was reaching the point of no return. With her feet still on the beach she could run back to the cave and her friends; once on that raft her farewell to Hong Kong would be irrevocable. Glancing around once more she found the upper stretches of beach, the cave, the low cliff and the Halburton Clinic hidden from view by darkness. Hong Kong had said farewell to her.

It immediately became apparent that steering the raft was difficult, if not impossible. The long pole method applied with such skill by the Chinese was not easily mastered by men used to rowing with two oars from a sitting position. They were carried shoreward by every wave until Alex and Jim began to wield the pole together. Even their combined strength barely prevented an incoming tide from frustrating their purpose.

Sarah sat on the frail structure gazing at the ravaged peninsula visible only during flashes of gunfire. Already, she sensed the raft was waterlogged. She was growing wetter and colder by the minute. The men, having waded through waves to launch the homemade platform, were soaked to the skin and had lost the coating of ash paste smeared over their bodies. They could not long withstand the punishment they were taking, and surely no one would now take them for Chinese fisherfolk.

At that point, it occurred to her that no coolie woman would sit like a lady expecting two gentlemen to work themselves to death on her behalf. Struggling to her feet, she wobbled uncertainly across the heaving platform to where Alex and Jim were fighting a losing battle with the pole.

'Take a short rest,' she yelled at Jim. 'I'll help Alex.'

Jim's face, covered with dark stubble, was hardly discernible now night had descended, yet she sensed his rejection and spoke before he voiced it.

'We've a long way to go. Please do as I say.'

The raft was tilting ominously because they were standing together, so Jim sank on all fours and crawled to where Sarah had been sitting. She grasped the pole just below Alex's hands and began the swaying rhythm necessary to give paddle power against the sea. They were soon moving together, bodies touching, and she gained amazing comfort from the contact. Confidence began to flow to her from this person who claimed she did not really know him. It was absurd to feel attraction to a man while standing on a slowly sinking raft on a night when her world was about to end, yet Alex somehow represented the youth she had never quite discovered. If she had to lose it again shortly, it was natural to relish it. When he cradled her with his arms as they battled on, she forgot the bitter wind and miles of dark sea surrounding them. This man cared enough for her to bring her away from an island where she had encountered only heartache and disillusion in those closest to her. What happened to her now was in the lap of the gods. She was surprisingly content with that thought.

Two minutes later, the silence broken only by the whoosh of the wind was shattered by a loud roar as a huge grey shape burst from the darkness. It flashed past so close it pushed up a wave that rose like a wall ahead of them. There was no time to think; nothing they could do. Sarah was knocked off her feet and swept away in a black suffocating tide against which she was helpless. Her heartbeat thundered in her ears. Terror possessed her as the blackness pressed in, preventing her from breathing.

She broke through to the surface, gasping and flailing her arms and legs in desperation to stay afloat. Panic-stricken, she wasted precious energy in a feverish breaststroke useless against a choppy sea that soon covered her once more. When she surfaced for the second time turbulence had calmed to a steady swell, yet terror still ruled her. She was alone in a hostile sea. The gods had made a swift decision!

Although commonsense told her to float and conserve her energy, the compulsion to find Alex was too strong. If this was to be the end of her life, she wanted to go out with him alongside her. Striking out in a direction that left gunfire flashes behind her, she fought the swell until her arms were too weary to move. Floating was then her only option apart from letting herself sink for ever below the surface. The clawing fear had subsided enough to allow a partial return of her belief in fighting back, so she rolled over to lie as flat as possible on the shifting water. She had abandoned the overall around her waist to aid swimming, so now wore only her underclothes. When the tide deposited her on Stanley Beach the Japanese would know no coolie would wear silk, so it was pointless keeping Chloë's black chemise over her hair. The garment floated away as one with the black swell.

Sarah's life did not flash before her eyes, as myth said of those about to drown. She had lost Alex on the point of finding him, so he must be forgotten. She did not even think about Ellie and Rod, the only two people she had loved in her short life. Instead, she remembered something Jakob Myburgh had said to her: *My ears are my greatest possession. When the rest of Jakob Myburgh is worn out, these will continue to hear Brahms, Beethoven, Wagner, Tchaikovsky and Mahler. And if they ever wear out, those glorious melodies are in my head where I shall still hear them.*

Closing her eyes she went through the great classics in her mind, hearing them as if in a concert hall with the orchestra. A discordant note gradually marred the beauty of the melodies. There was loud drumming, voices shouting. Both grew louder until music fled on the wind, leaving her inexplicably sad.

"Old on, luv, we gotcha. Jest relax and let us 'aul yer aboard.'

The first thing Sarah saw was Alex leaning over the side of a grey ship. Arms reached out to her. She was borne up by strong hands then seized by others which lifted her to where he stood wrapped by a blanket. A few feet away, Jim was being pulled, dripping, from the sea to be similarly wrapped. Then the scratchy warmth was around her, too. A tin mug containing rum was put to her lips by a man in British naval uniform. Sarah hated the taste, but it warmed her. Yet the comfort she most wanted could only be given to her by Alex. She said his name and he moved to hold her close in thankfulness. They were standing thus when a young officer came to them.

'You gave us the deuce of a fright,' he began in typical drawl. 'We were on you before we suspected anything was in the area. Sorry about that.'

There seemed no suitable reply to his careless apology for having almost killed them.

'Thought you were Chinese, but clearly you're not. Just who the devil are you?'

Alex's voice rumbled against Sarah's ear as she lay against his chest. 'Lieutenant A.D.R. Tennant, Hong Kong Volunteer Defence Force, Corporal J.P. Maiden, Royal Air Force, and Miss Sarah Channing, daughter of the President of Channing Mercantile Bank.'

'Good God!' A pause, then, 'Where were you hoping to get to on that . . . er . . . construction?'

'It was more a case of leaving than arriving. We would have worked out a destination, in time.'

'Really? Well, all I can say is that it's a damned good thing we came along. It's obvious none of you is familiar with even the basics of seafaring.' His voice gained authority. 'Jackson, take our guests below and make them comfortable. We've a long night ahead.'

'You going into action, sir?' asked Jim heavily.

''Fraid not. It's all over. The Governor's surrendered the colony. Captains of any ships in this flotilla still afloat have been ordered to scuttle ships and make their way to Chiang Kai-shek's troops on the mainland. I'm heading for Mirs Bay right now. It's the deuce of a way from Chungking overland, but you military chaps can take over then. One good turn deserves another, eh?'

Sarah heard all this through a daze as she stood in Alex's embrace. Only later did it dawn on her that these men were planning a journey of more than a thousand miles over wild territory roamed by Japanese troops, and she would some-how have to survive it with them.

Chapter Ten

The Japanese drove his truck slowly through streets Rod scarcely recognized. Almost every building bore some damage. Broken rickshaws, burnt-out cars and lorries, masonry and corpses littered the Island overhung with the combined stench of death and broken sewers. Many Chinese picking their way through the devastation wore European clothes looted from houses or shops. Black marketeers moving from street to street offered French perfume, champagne, cashmere sweaters and tins of Australian fruit, probably still bearing the labels of shops from which they had been stolen. Road signs had Japanese names. The Rising Sun flew over banks and offices. Hong Kong had rapidly changed hands.

Rod had been separated from his assistant pharmacist on landing this morning. Chin Sung was now a free man after two months as a virtual prisoner tending Japanese wounded with medicines from the floating clinic. A surgeon from Nagasaki had dealt with operative cases brought from the mainland, and Rod had been ordered to treat those suffering from fevers, dysentery, flesh wounds and venereal disease. He had tried to concentrate on the humanity of his profession and not think of Hong Kong being bombed and burned into surrender.

Those weeks had brought personal anguish. Haunted by fears for Sarah and unable to forget his wife, pregnant and in an acutely unstable frame of mind, Rod had mentally and emotionally kicked against imprisonment on those offshore islands. He and Chin Sung had been reasonably well treated, and given the same rations as their military patients. The Chinese had accepted rice meals without a grumble; Rod had found them vastly inadequate and unappetizing.

On this first day of February his usefulness had come to an end, so his captors had brought him to the Island with a number of troops he had restored to fitness. Due to his good work with enemy wounded he was given the courtesy of riding to Stanley Internment Camp in an army vehicle instead of walking there, as many of the civilian captives had been forced to do when rounded up from various hiding places. The young Japanese officer commanding the offshore islands' defensive troops had many times watched Rod at work, at first suspicious that he would take the opportunity to kill his patients. Suspicion had turned to admiration. When he offered friendship, Rod told him, with some force, that professional ethics obliged him to treat anyone in need of medical aid but they did not extend to making friends with enemies. Lieutenant Ogata could not understand this fine distinction and never tired of making overtures to a man he held in esteem. His upbringing insisted that he should do this, but each successive rebuff by Rod was a blow to his personal honour. Giving this incomprehensible Australian a seat beside him in a truck was one gesture of generosity that could not be refused, and honour was partially soothed.

Rod was shocked and silent during the journey. The commercial centre was full of blackened and battered buildings. Banks, including Channing Mercantile, had sustained structural damage and lost windows. The Rising Sun flew above them and business appeared to be continuing under new masters. Leaving Victoria, the truck followed the road leading past the apartment block where Rod had lived so unhappily with Celeste. A greater shock awaited him as they turned a corner, for no more than the ground floor remained intact. The rest of the building was rubble piled around it. Bodies still lay there while Chinese who had escaped the odorous, pestilential streets passed in and out of the unsafe rooms they had claimed as homes. Rod must have given an involuntary cry, for Lieutenant Ogata asked what was wrong.

'My wife was living there,' he murmured, still deeply shaken.

An order was snapped at the driver, who halted, reversed to the bomb site, and stopped. Rod was invited to accompany the officer on an inspection of the bodies. Time and the elements had made them almost unrecognizable but none was that of Celeste. Ogata, who could speak Cantonese, addressed two women searching the rubble for anything of use. Their reactions were twin expressions of incomprehension which remained while he twice repeated his questions. Angered, he struck then both across the face with such force they broke into rapid speech. When he pointed at Rod, they shook their heads vigorously. Then, before Rod realized what was about to happen, Ogata drew his revolver and shot them. Turning, he gripped Rod's arm to escort him back to the truck.

'They know nothing of your wife, Doctor, but I shall be honoured to discover for you where she is. It will be my first duty.'

Rod threw off the man's grip, his raw temper exploding. 'You bastard! Are you also honoured by murdering people because they can't answer your questions? If the officer class is barbaric, your rank and file will never be better than the lowest form of life.'

The man was unperturbed. His smooth face betrayed no sense of guilt. 'They were stealing from their new masters, their liberators from the Western yoke. Hong Kong is now part of Japan. Everything here belongs to our government. They were thieves.' He bowed and held out a hand as an invitation to climb back into the truck. 'We must continue our journey.' Sitting beside Rod, he added calmly, 'You will see we are not barbaric when I find your wife and bring her to you with the greatest courtesy.'

Stanley Internment Camp was merely a large area of the peninsula which had been enclosed by barbed wire. Within its bounds were St Stephen's College, the grounds of Stanley Prison and many accommodation blocks formerly used by prison guards. Above the beach stood what remained of the Halburton Clinic. In a ludicrous ceremony, Rod was bowed into his captive life by his commissioned guard as if he were entering some grand palace. Then the Japanese departed, after consulting the list of prisoners from which Celeste's name was absent, vowing to trace the honourable Madam Durman without delay.

Rod was left standing beside a sullen, slovenly guard who took no interest in him whatsoever. Despite shell craters and intermittent piles of rubble the internees appeared to have settled wherever they could. Washing was fluttering from lines strung between any two convenient uprights, and children were playing hop-scotch outside the college building as they would in a school playground. Rod remained where he was for a minute or two. After eight weeks in the company of Orientals, he relished the sight of those whose ways of life and reasoning were like his own. He had had enough of men with what he considered upside-down values. He also hesitated because he was afraid. Celeste *must* have been killed when the apartments were bombed or she would be here. If he now did not find Sarah somewhere in this camp, then she must also be dead.

The cold eventually spurred him into action. His only possessions were a few Hong Kong dollars and the clothes he had been wearing when captured. His watch, signet ring and wallet had initially been taken by a yellow-toothed NCO but Ogata had returned them on making his offer of friendship. Rod had been allowed to wash socks and under-clothes once a week, but it had been too cold to go without his shirt, which was now filthy. Those items, plus shoes, trousers and a thick sweater were all he had in the world at this moment, and the February wind was whistling in from the sea.

Instinct drew him towards the Halburton, where several men were attempting to fill gaps in the walls with chunks of masonry lying nearby. It was like attempting an oversized jigsaw, for they had no cement to bind the pieces together. Rod hoped there might be room for him inside this place with which he was familiar.

Halfway to his destination Rod saw a man come out of a stone bungalow and recognized Bill Charlton, the gynaecologist who had been monitoring Celeste. He called out Bill's name, but it was plain the man did not recognize him.

Rod approached, hand outstretched. 'Rod Durman.'

'Good God, is it really you behind that swashbuckling black beard? We all assumed you had departed this life.'

'Not likely.'

Bill had grown gaunt and his bald patch was surrounded by hair that looked to have gone greyer, but there was warmth in his smile and his grip on Rod's hand was strong.

'It's good to see you. Where've you been?'

Rod related how the floating clinic had been seized and used for Japanese wounded. 'Wang Chua never expected it would be put to such purpose,' he ended bitterly.

'Word is that the old boy and his family have vanished, taking their wealth with them. The House of Wang contained only a fraction of its expensive merchandise when looters smashed their way into the premises. The storerooms were empty; godowns much the same. They must have had wind of the invasion in advance and cleared everything over the weekend, crafty blighters.'

'Bloody good luck to them,' said Rod with vehemence. 'The family was twice bled by Triads because the old fella made a stand against them. I hope he ends his days in peace and prosperity.'

Bill gave him a shrewd glance. 'Considering you were so pally with him he didn't do much to further your status in Hong Kong, did he?'

'It wasn't that kind of friendship.'

There was a brief silence before Bill asked, 'Have you found out what happened to Celeste?'

Rod slowly shook his head. 'They didn't know. You'd better tell me, Bill.'

'*I* don't know, old chap. No one in the camp seems to have seen her since the day of the first attack.' He sighed. 'I'm very sorry. Your apartments received a direct hit.'

'I know. My escort here, a smooth-faced little bugger with drawing-room manners and a tendency to shoot people who don't know the answers to his questions, allowed me to inspect the bodies still lying about the rubble. He's undertaken to trace Celeste as a favour to me, someone he's squirming to honour with kinky Jap admiration for treating their wounded without prejudice.'

'Well, I hope he gets an answer for you, one way or the other. It's tough not knowing whether or not she's alive – especially with a child finally on the way.'

Rod changed the subject. 'This is a bloody ramshackle prison camp. The guard at the gate was more interested in scratching his arse than in me, and didn't give a damn when I walked away.'

'Are you to be a permanent resident?'

'I guess so.'

'You'll need to find quarters, but they're all pretty well full.' He nodded towards St Stephen's College. 'We used that as a temporary hospital before Christmas. They burst in, bayoneted patients and raped the nurses. None of us wanted to live there when we first arrived, but one's attitudes mellow in these circumstances. You'll find out.' Bill shivered in spite of the thick overcoat he wore. 'Let's go inside. You must be frozen in that pullover. Is it the best you can produce against the cold?'

'I had to make do with it for eight weeks. Guess I'm hardened to it.' Rod fell in beside the other man, who headed for a nearby stone building. 'What about the Queen Mary?'

'The Japs have taken it over but, like other hospitals, have kept some of the staff on. Their military chaps have little knowledge of general medicine.' He looked over his shoulder and made a face. 'Those of us not much in demand have been put here to rot. We're holding a meeting to discuss how best to pass the time without losing our touch.'

Rod appreciated the warmth from a small fire smoking in the hearth, but whatever had been used for fuel fouled the air breathed by around twenty men gathered there. As they were all doctors, some minutes were spent greeting the Australian they had all believed dead. They then drew Rod into a discussion concerning the setting up of a hospital within the camp. A suitable building had been chosen and the Japanese were willing to provide some basic supplies.

'We've considered asking everyone to cough up cash for extra medicines,' said a haematologist, 'but they want to hang on to all they have to buy food from the guards. Can't blame them. Many have children, who must come first.'

260

Rod was immediately appalled. 'You mean you have to *buy* your food?'

'Unless you can exist on a bowl of weevily rice morning and evening, with stewed weeds and the water they were cooked in,' another doctor told him. 'You've no idea what's been happening here while you've been away. They rounded up all non-Chinese civilians because they felt they must, but they really have no idea what to do with us. We spent three weeks holed up in waterfront hotels used as brothels, until they marched us all here. I think they chose Stanley because there was ready-built accommodation. Apart from being fenced in, and fed garbage twice daily, we've been left to our own devices. We elected a housing committee, another to deal with the fair distribution of food, and another to monitor health during captivity. An outbreak of cholera or typhoid would be disastrous. Even the Japs are frightened of that.'

'But they won't give us enough vaccine to deal with it,' the haematologist reminded him.

'Some of our chaps still working in the hospitals have hinted that they'll send stuff to us when they get a chance, but we can't see how they'll manage it,' Bill said. 'They're pretty well prisoners within the hospitals and have to toe the line if they want to continue working. We can't blame them if they do. Until Hong Kong is freed, several of us have decided to study a specialized subject while we have time to do it. Otherwise we'll get rusty. Grenville's boy, Chan Lo, has been here twice to bring food and a woollen jacket for the baby. He's a tremendous lad. Promised to get hold of the list of books we want, if he can. A lot of former servants have taken risks coming here with food or blankets. Does the heart good to know some Chinese still have a fondness for us. Came as a rude shock during the fighting to see people you trusted turn their backs rather than help you.'

'There were those who did worse than refuse to help,' put in a young medic squatting in the corner. 'Countless numbers changed sides even before the surrender. Hong Kong'll never be the same when this occupation ends. I won't stay here.'

Rod was finding the atmosphere too stuffy and the news depressing. He had eaten nothing since six a.m. and hopes of a hot meal had faded early in their conversation. He had very little money to buy anything from the guards, so prospects looked dark indeed.

'What do I do about finding somewhere to live?' he asked.

They had all been so wrapped up in their reminiscences they had forgotten he was a new arrival, and he sensed that they resented his concern for his own welfare in the midst of their general discussion.

'I didn't have the chance to collect any of my stuff before capture,' he said, with some force. 'I was smacked around the head with a rifle-butt and told I was a prisoner of war. All I have is my watch, twenty-five dollars and what I'm wearing. My apartment no longer exists and no one knows where my wife is. I'm hungry, homeless and flaming frozen. Could one of you spare the time to tell me what I do about settling in here?'

Bill looked abashed. 'We tend to yarn non-stop here. There's little else to do. You'll be the same within a week.' He stood up. 'I'll take you over to the chap who organizes accommodation. You won't get anything to eat until this evening's rice allocation, but the food committee might be able to rustle up something for you before then. Clothes will be more difficult, and twenty-five dollars won't buy much. If you've money in the bank, it's possible someone might accept a cheque to sell you yen. It's been done in a couple of cases. You'll have to put out a few feelers and see if anyone makes you an offer.'

As Rod returned to the cold wind, he reflected that he had spent most of the money sent him by his father on two air tickets to Australia. There was very little left in his bank account. If he bought a coat from someone he would have to use it as a blanket as well. He was physically strong and in excellent health, but he had lost weight since captivity and would need all the money he could get for additional food, if he was to survive in the coming months. He and his brothers had frequently slept rough out on the station. The ground was a familiar bed, the elements familiar enemies. He could cope with that side of captivity, but semi-starvation would defeat him swifter than anything.

A member of the housing committee welcomed Rod to

their 'little community', but regretted an addition to the problem of living space. After some minutes' study of the man's sheaf of papers, Rod grew impatient.

'I'd like to shack up in what remains of the Halburton, if there's room.'

The man looked up quickly. 'Oh, no, you can't go there. It's unsafe. The only section at all weatherproof is a very small room once used as an office. Two ladies occupy that, one of them an expectant mother. *You* couldn't possibly move in.'

His fussy tone and manner made Rod bristle. 'It sounds just right to me. Two women on their own in an isolated building should have a bloke on hand, especially the pregnant one. I could soon build up some kind of shanty for myself alongside their room, and help in any way I can.'

'No, no, I couldn't allow that!'

Rod squared his shoulders. 'I don't see how you're going to stop me. Every other place is overcrowded, so I'll solve the problem by organizing my own quarters.' As the man made to speak, Rod added, 'I'm not one of your idle rich, you know. Where I was reared a bloke had to look out for himself in harsh country, or he was a goner.' About to leave, he asked, 'Why are these two women there alone? Have they been ostracized for some reason? The pregnant one unmarried?'

'Good gracious, no!' The man was deeply affronted. 'The lady is married to a naval officer. Sadly, crews of ships still afloat on surrender were ordered to make for the mainland, destroy their vessels and endeavour to link up with Nationalist troops under Chiang Kai-shek. She has no idea where her husband is, or even if he is alive. Her companion is single. She elected to live with her friend because they had both worked at the clinic during the last days of fighting. An American lady was anxious to remain with them, but her husband could hardly stay there. In any case, the Americans have congregated together and remain independent, like the Dutch.' He shrugged in finicky manner. 'It seems rather ridiculous to live in separate groups when we're all behind the same wire fence, but there you are.'

Rod's every sense had become alert, his heart pumped

with excitement. 'These two women worked at the clinic? I probably know them. Who are they?'

'Mrs Bennett and Miss Reynolds.'

'Oh . . . yes, I remember,' he said, deeply disappointed, but driven to add, 'There was also a Miss Channing – daughter of the banker.'

The man's long face grew longer. 'Very sad. Very sad indeed! She was persuaded to attempt escape on a flimsy raft made from the wreckage of a seaplane. Mrs Bennett and Miss Reynolds assisted with the building, but declined to put to sea on it. A most wise decision, but one made in the belief that their loved ones would be in Hong Kong. As it turned out, Mrs Bennett's husband had left, and Miss Reynolds's parents were killed in an air raid.'

Swamped by mixed emotions, Rod had to confirm his suspicions. 'Miss Channing was *persuaded* to leave on this raft. Who by?'

'A chap in the Volunteers. It was his seaplane. Well, it *was* before he smashed it up just off this beach. An RAF corporal went too, I heard. A mad scheme doomed to failure. Rather cowardly in my opinion. The raft – or what remained of it – was washed up on the beach several days later. You can see it from the Halburton. The bodies must have come up further along the Peninsula. The Japs won't do anything about them. They've left corpses all over the beaches and hillsides, refusing to allow our churchmen to identify or bury them. They're inhuman.'

It was more than Rod could accept. To know Sarah was dead was bad enough. To think of her body rotting on a nearby beach broke his mind, when facing the thought that he was responsible for her decision to go with Alex Tennant and end her sweet life.

Two days after he settled into makeshift quarters adjacent to the former office inhabited by Marion and Chloë, Rod was in the midst of constructing a more satisfactory roof over the area he had made his own when he was accosted by a voice he loathed. Beyond the broken wall stood Lieutenant Ogata. Beside him stood Lim, tears rolling down his smooth cheeks.

'I have honoured my promise to you, Doctor,' said the

Japanese. 'I am now your friend. You see we are *not* barbaric.' With a bow, he spun on his heel and marched away with great military pomp.

Rod stepped over the rubble to seize Lim by the shoulders. 'How are you, old friend? You escaped the bombing!'

The young Chinese was too upset to speak and hung his head as if in shame. Rod swiftly put two and two together. His hopeful Japanese friend had traced Lim, who probably knew what happened to Celeste, and Lim felt he was losing face by being forced to confront his former employer living in such humiliating circumstances.

He tightened his grip on Lim's shoulders. 'This is not your fault, old son. There's no reason for you to take it this way. I'm very glad to see you.' When Lim continued his hangdog attitude, Rod asked quietly, 'Do you know what happened to my wife?'

The round, tear-stained face came up then. It was obvious the poor man was deeply burdened by wretchedness. 'Day before airplane come makee bombing, man come see Missy. Him from House of Wang. Say old man wanchee you, Missy, go away Hong Kong, chop chop. Japanee come soon; you go on junk. Old man house, dollar, rice yours. You wanchee, he give you.'

'Wang Chua?' asked Rod, mystified.

Lim nodded. 'He say wanchee you go with Wang family before Japanee come. You no come back islands and Missy aflaid. She say she go, but send man away. Say come taxi later. She take big box. Fill clothe, shoe, many thing. Taxi no come. Too many wanchee taxi go Kowloon-side, go Wong Nei Chong, go Lepulse Bay. Come dark, Missy cly but no go without box. Morning, man come again. Say go now. Take Missy, box. I go watch Missy, look for you come soon.' He almost broke down again as he recounted the next part of his story. 'Missy give me muchee dollar, say good luck. She go in small boat. Junk ready go.' Hanging his head, he said, in abject misery, 'Airplane come. Muchee noise; gun. Boat go under sea. Box go.' A pause as he struggled to speak. 'Missy go. Lim unworthy servant. No look after Missy you not here.'

Rod was so shaken he turned and walked a few paces to

stare across a sea that had claimed both his wife and the girl he had loved. If Celeste had not insisted on taking all her fancy clothes, she might have got away safely on the day *before* that first early morning attack. He would now never know if the child had been his, or that of some man taking part in a drunken party game. He lost all count of time as he thought of the old man with a house on a hill, who had tried to honour his debt in the most unforeseen manner. When he came from his sombre musing and turned back, Lim had gone. On the ground where he had stood was a neat pile of dollars.

That money came in handy during the following weeks. A canteen selling additional food was soon opened and Rod took full advantage of it. Reasoning that when spring and summer came he would have no use for a coat, he decided to buy instead a tartan rug to roll into at night, and which he could wrap around his shoulders during the daytime. Within several days of the decision, a parcel was delivered to him. It contained a Chinese padded coat, some cheap shoes and a cut-throat razor with shaving soap. These things were a welcome addition to his simple life. A parcel came each week. Sometimes it contained clothing, sometimes food; often such things as soap, toothpaste, ink and paper, or a book.

Believing these to have been sent by the persistent Ogata, Rod only accepted them because survival was more vital than pride. He gave away much of their contents to those internees most in need but, as time went by and sickness, dysentery and malnutrition increased, he realized he had the means to acquire badly needed medicines. The parcels arrived on Tuesdays, so he made a point of lingering near the main gate when the next was due, intending to waylay his determined benefactor and ask for supplies of kaolin, quinine, glucose and powdered milk. He missed the eleven o'clock issue of mouldy rice in his determination to be on hand when the Japanese arrived, but it was not until two p.m. that a figure trudged across the rough grass with a box under his arm. Rod went to the wire with no hindrance from the guard.

'Lim! Have you been sending all that stuff in for me?'

The young Chinese seemed unhappy at being caught. 'Man come early morning. Give me, take you.'

'What man?' asked Rod, still thinking of the enemy officer. 'That same one who brought you here first?'

Lim shook his head. 'Chinee man. Say muchee flend. Doctor makee son better long time go by. Chinee no forget.'

'Wang Tan Ho, whose son was knocked down by a tram? I thought the entire family had escaped in a junk,' said Rod, finding the whole business bizarre.

Lim clearly knew none of the details, so Rod could only conclude that it was to the advantage of the Wangs for one, or maybe more, of the clan to retain a presence in Hong Kong. When war ended and trade resumed, a race would be on to seize prominence before impoverished Europeans could re-establish dominance in all areas. The wily old man who headed the family still had an eye to its fortune.

Drawing nearer the wire, Rod said, 'It's good of you to act as delivery boy, Lim. I appreciate your friendship.'

The guileless face crumpled in distress. 'Lim no likee Doctor, flends' – he waved his hand at the barricaded area – 'all these live in cage. Velly bad. Japanee bad people do this. Chinee lose face see flends, Master, Missy, baby all live here. But Japanee do bad thing Chinee no work. I come here allight. Japanee man come take me here, say allight. So I come.'

Buffeted by a strong wind that whipped across the peninsula, Rod explained to his former servant that they needed medicine very urgently. He asked Lim to give the list of requirements he had written to Wang Chua's son the next time he came. They began to walk on opposite sides of the wire, to where a guard was watching them with bored indifference. His mien did not change when they reached the gate. He allowed them to exchange an envelope for a large cardboard box without attempting to interfere, so Rod took the opportunity to reach out and shake Lim's hand. 'Thanks for everything.'

Such a gesture from a man he had served with dedication and respect threw Lim into confusion, but he appreciated Rod's next words much more.

'You're not to blame for what happened to my wife, Lim,

not in any way. You did all you could for her. I know that, and I'm grateful. No people could have had a better boy than you. Don't take any risks on my behalf. These devils are totally ruthless. You must put your family before loyalty to me, at all times.' He backed as the guard grew impatient and began closing the gate. 'I'll come to the wire next Tuesday, now I know it's you. Tell me what's happening on the Island. We feel so cut off here, and they print so many lies in their daily news-sheet, we don't know what to believe.'

One piece of news the internees *did* believe was that Singapore had fallen. Knowing the truth concerning the fighting powers of the Japanese army, they could well understand that yet another small garrison isolated from allies could be overwhelmed by troops used to tropical terrain. Rumours abounded concerning their advance on *bicycles* through the Malayan jungle, while British and Australian troops mounted guard over the few roads. This news depressed everyone terribly, bringing additional malaise. The tiny hospital could not cope with the maintenance of health, and morale plunged further.

Within ten days, parcels of medicines began to arrive in response to Rod's list. He was ridiculously touched by evidence that these had come from two or three Chinese healers he had associated with, owing to his interests in their methods. The substances were not necessarily what he had asked for, rather the equivalent curative favoured by Eastern dispensers. His colleagues were initially adamant against using them. Only when he treated them to a few choice words on the subject did they unbend.

'We'd never prescribe as a diet what we're served with twice daily, but that's all we have and everyone eats it. You don't stop them from eating it – there'd be a riot if you tried – so, by the same yardstick, you must use this. If it works on Chinese, why should you imagine it'll kill off British patients? *I'm* going to use it for those who come to me for help, and woe betide any of you who tries to stop me.'

Work was Rod's salvation. He was possessed by the spectre of Sarah's body rotting on a beach so near him; he could not help dwelling on memories of Celeste in the early days of their marriage. So lovely, so full of fun and vivacity. How he had wanted her! What a way for her life to end. Pregnant with a child whose father she could not name, addicted to gin, desperate and frightened: death in the early morning beneath a foreign sea. In addition to those nightmarish thoughts, he found confinement difficult to accept. He had never been a social man – life on an isolated sheep station had made him shy of crowds – so living in a small concentrated community bothered him a great deal.

Comments had initially been passed on his choice of accommodation, but he silenced them with a flash of his irrepressible temper. The arrangement worked admirably. The two women did his washing and prepared any extra food he got for them; he worked hard on making their abode weather- and draught-proof. He also did any heavy lifting for them, and ensured that Marion's pregnancy was trouble-free. She and Chloë were glad of his presence alongside their quarters, because they felt safe from any intruder. From them Rod learned full details of Christmas Day, and the subsequent building of the raft from Alex Tennant's seaplane. Unbelievably, they suggested there was some kind of bond between him and Sarah; that she was swayed by his decisions, and that he had acted in a firm, decisive manner over the escape.

Plagued for some days by this description of a man Rod had intensely disliked, he then realized it was of no importance. Both Alex and Sarah were dead. The episode was over. All that was left to him was his profession, and the hope of one day returning to the vastness of a country where he could use it to help those living in isolation. As days and weeks passed, he longed for it more and more. Only then would he be free of all that had happened in this lost colony.

Summer came. They were allowed down the steps to a small cove beyond the prison for swimming. It was a delightful concession which lifted morale somewhat. Internees flocked there in almost holiday mood, yet Rod could not bring himself to join them in the sea. But even that psychological phobia passed as days grew ever hotter, and the sparkling water beckoned. A powerful swimmer, he went so far from shore one day the guard began firing at him. He was momentarily tempted to continue, then sanity returned and he turned back.

Quite unexpectedly, the Americans in the camp were told they were to be repatriated in exchange for Japanese interned in the United States. Morale rose in the expectation of British and Dutch civilians receiving similar news, then plunged again as the departure date for the Americans changed time and time again. Finally, at the end of June, a Japanese ship arrived offshore to take them as far as Africa, where they would be transferred to an American vessel bringing the Japanese. Those left behind as the ship sailed into the distance wept, even the men.

In July, two events demonstrated the facts of life under enemy rule. Sir Kingston Dailey, who was one of the staff allowed to remain at the Queen Mary Hospital, fell foul of a high-ranking Japanese general who had him thrown into the local prison cells along with the most villainous criminals. His crime: allowing the general's nephew to die from serious wounds to his stomach inflicted during a brothel skirmish. Any Chinese who had frequented the place on that night was executed without delay; the prostitutes forced to gratify their Japanese clients without payment from then on. An unsuspected heart problem was exacerbated by the appalling conditions in prison and Sir Kingston was to die of a seizure less than a month after his incarceration.

To offset that tragedy, Rod was delighted to assist at the birth of Marion's child, a surprisingly healthy girl with hair as red as her mother's who was instantly named Sarah. Everyone rallied round to produce some kind of gift for the babe of captivity, and food kept for special occasions was generously produced when a party was arranged to celebrate the advent of Sarah Elizabeth Bennett. For an hour or so, the internees pretended that the wire around them did not exist, but when Rod and Chloë were left alone with mother and child sadness intruded once more.

Glancing up from the child in her arms, Marion said, 'I wish she looked like Bill. I'd then remember his face. I can't, you know.' She turned back to her baby. 'I don't suppose it matters. When we win the war, Hong Kong will be the last place they'll free. By then, we'll be total strangers and won't give a damn about each other.'

'You'll have Sarah to draw you close again,' Rod pointed out.

Marion waggled the little hand clutching her finger. 'No. She'll be dead before long. You can't rear a baby on rice and stewed weeds.'

'I'll ensure that she gets all she needs,' Rod assured her. 'I've got stakes in that girl's life. She won't go without all the time I'm around.'

He was around for only one more week. Summoned to the camp commandant's quarters one morning, he found Ogata, with an escort of four soldiers, waiting for him outside the building. 'You are being transferred, Doctor. There is a shortage of medical staff at Shamshuipo Camp on the mainland. Collect your things and go with these men.'

Rod made an immediate protest. 'You can't class me as a prisoner of war. I'm a civilian. I've never fought you people. Good God, I treated your wounded to the best of my ability over on that island.'

'That is why you have been chosen. I recommended you, because of your excellent work with soldiers. You must come now.'

There was a subtle difference in the man today. He still bowed a lot and spoke in a polite manner, but Rod sensed a chilling animosity beneath it all. A friend he was no longer.

'I'm not going anywhere,' said Rod, digging in his heels. 'If I have to be behind wire, it's going to be here.'

'You go!' the officer insisted. 'I have orders.'

'Then you'd better show them to the British camp committee. There are rules, you know, and one of them is that civilians are entitled to be kept in a place apart from captured troops.'

What happened next was so sudden, Rod could do nothing. The four soldiers lolling nearby were galvanized into action by a click of their officer's fingers. They rushed at Rod and, with two gripping his arms and two prodding his back with bayonets, he was forced to climb into the truck with his guards. The vehicle moved off immediately, leaving Ogata impassively watching the abduction.

271

Knowing only too well what these men were capable of, Rod had to bow to the inevitable during the drive to North Point where a small boat took them along the Kowloon waterfront to Shamshuipo. He was determined to speak to the senior British officer in camp on arrival, to register his protest and get himself sent back immediately. He had never been with the Volunteers; was not even British.

The difference was immediately apparent when they entered the camp. Armed guards were everywhere. Accommodation was basic and crawling with flies, rats scampered underfoot, there was an overpowering stench of human excrement and the prisoners looked gaunt, dirty and ill. Rod was appalled. What of the Geneva Convention; where were the Red Cross representatives? Then he recalled stories of atrocities by their Oriental enemies and knew fanatics never observed rules. His heart sank. Hopes of a hearing were dim. It seemed more than likely he was in this hell-hole to stay. By comparison, Stanley, with its open spaces, lack of discipline and little bathing beach, was almost pleasant.

The senior spokesman looked ill and under stress. He promised to send a lieutenant who spoke Japanese to the camp commandant on Rod's behalf, although he did not believe it would serve any purpose. It would probably be a day or two before an interview was granted, so Rod was advised to find a corner as far from the latrines as possible to settle in and wait. This was not easy. He was refused a space in the first dozen places he tried, but was hardly sorry. Conditions were appalling and a large number of prisoners were suffering from dysentery, which added to the trials of everyone living there.

Finally, on joining the long queue for rice, Rod encountered a former chemist in the uniform of the Volunteers, who had been in the water-polo team. Sam Batchelor was pleased to see him, and immediately offered him a home with a small group of businessmen who had fought for their adopted country and lost. They were not best pleased with Sam's generosity, but grudgingly admitted Rod to their cramped quarters when they learned his profession. Doctors were usually better tolerated by guards whose strict Oriental beliefs led them to despise men who allowed themselves to be captured, rather than die honourably at the hands of their enemy. Rod would also be available to offer swift treatment for their ills, and secure for them some of the scarce medication locked in the hospital. A reasonable bargain.

The men in Shamshuipo had not received visits from Red Cross representatives, nor been allowed parcels from the organization. News of loved ones or friends on the Island had been denied them: exchange of letters with relatives at home was forbidden. They had no assurance that notification of their capture had been forwarded to next of kin. For all they knew, everyone believed them dead. Rod was able to help these dispirited prisoners by giving them news of relatives who had been at Stanley with him, in addition to treating them in the hospital.

After three days, the officer who acted as interpreter came to Rod with information garnered from his meeting with the camp commandant. The Japanese had discovered that he had been receiving weekly parcels from Chinese who were showing friendship to Japan's enemies, and thereby insulting their liberators from the Western yoke. These people had been dealt with as they deserved, but Lieutenant Ogata had interceded on Dr Durman's behalf so he had merely been moved to a secret destination his disloyal friends would not know. He was expected to show his gratitude for this consideration by behaving with the greatest respect towards all Japanese, and by informing the guards of any prisoners receiving items or communications from Chinese people.

There followed a period during which Rod realized Ogata's intercession had been based on a desire to punish him. The Japanese had very obviously felt humiliated by his Australian 'friend's' betrayal of trust over the parcels, and was exacting appropriate revenge. Rod's clear lack of gratitude for his captor's 'generosity' in sending him to Shamshuipo brought savage reprisals. He was dragged from the rice queue one day, confronted with another prisoner clutching a bag of flour supposedly sent in by a Chinese, and accused of not informing the guards of this treachery. Two sadistic guards pinioned him against a wall, while another beat him with his rifle until he slid semi-conscious to the ground. He was left to lie in the noonday heat while would-be helpers were kept at bay for more than an hour. Although he was concussed and every step was agony, Rod queued for his rice that evening with the help of his friends and the anger burning within him.

Two weeks later he was summoned to the office used by one of the officers, who threw at his feet an envelope containing a letter and a wad of notes apparently intended for a Canadian captain. The Japanese claimed it had been smuggled in by a Chinese sweeper. He demanded to know why Dr Durman had not reported this transgression of the rules, and was infuriated when treated to silence. Rod was locked in a windowless room without food or water for twenty-four hours. He emerged knowing the persecution would continue until they broke him.

As July ran into August, then August into September he wondered how long he could stay sane. Days would pass without incident, then he would be faced with another trumped-up charge. Punishments varied from humiliation to acute pain, from semi-torture to the confiscating of his soap and razor. Protests from the camp committee were pointless. The prisoners had learned that these only brought increased vindictiveness.

Over these terrible weeks Rod lost weight dramatically, his muscular physique growing weak and vulnerable. Deprived of soap and the means to shave, he became dirty and unkempt. No one dared lend him these things, for wrath would then descend on them both. His black beard provided a haven for lice, his hair grew long and matted.

What worried him more was his mental state. His notorious temper had to be suppressed; his natural compassion for others denied in order to stay alive. Changing his basic personality added to the stress of the emotional shocks he had suffered over the past year. He recognized the signs: depression, lack of confidence in his decisions, a sense of total failure. He had lost Sarah's love through sexual weakness, his wife had been impregnated by a man whose procreative powers were far stronger than his own, and he was powerless to put an end to the bestiality of people who enjoyed watching him suffer. Voices were whispering of the peace to be found in death. It would be very easy for him to swallow a lethal mixture of medicines; a sudden rush for the wire when guards were watching would bring a hail of bullets. Would the world be any worse off without Roderick James Durman?

He was at his lowest ebb at the start of September, when he was waylaid by one of the Formosan guards, worse clothed and fed than their Japanese counterparts, and forced to march to the extremity of the camp. Wondering whether this might be the moment to rush for the wire, Rod was astonished when the man reached behind a bush and produced a flat parcel, indicating that his prisoner should take it.

Rod began to laugh with a touch of hysteria. 'Oh no, mate, I'm not a bloody fool. If this is the best you can invent, it's time you devils gave up. I'd no sooner take that from you than your pals would come out of the bushes, catch me red-handed and string me up again. Bugger off, old sport. I'm not playing your kinky Oriental games.'

As he made to turn away, the man thrust a piece of paper at him, gesturing that he should read it. The message was printed in perfect English.

THE GUARD IS A FRIEND AND HAS BEEN WELL PAID. HE WILL NOT BETRAY YOU. MY VENERABLE GRAND-FATHER WISHES ME TO CONTINUE WHAT MY HON-OURED FATHER NOW CANNOT. THE HOUSE OF WANG DOES NOT FORGET.

After reading the words through twice, Rod sank to the ground and began to sob.

Chapter Eleven

Parcels arrived by the same method the following two weeks. They contained sugar, milk powder, tinned meat and fruit, and small bottles of Chinese medicines. Rod took it all to the little hospital. No one asked where he had obtained such things, but they all knew the risk he was taking in accepting them. It was that risk, that feeling of somehow hitting back, that gave Rod the boost he needed. He regained confidence and control of himself.

It was during the third week of September that a man suffering from beri-beri was brought to the overcrowded, airless ward. Rod was astonished to learn that the wasted, white-haired patient was Sir Peter Channing. Staring down at the sunken eyes and parchment-like skin stretched taut over the bones of the once-suave face of Sarah's father, he could hardly believe this man had once tried to ruin him. Of what use to Sir Peter and his clients would that elusive introduction to Wang Chua be today? Of what use to himself the post in Tropical Diseases? Now the only thing that mattered to anyone here was staying alive.

'How long has he been at Shamshuipo?' Rod asked of another doctor. 'When I didn't come across him at Stanley I assumed that, along with other bankers, he was being forced to run business as usual. He should no more be here than I.'

The army man sighed. 'The old boy was captured up on Wong Nei Chong with a rifle in his hand, alongside some of his high-ranking chums in the Volunteers. It was pointless trying to persuade the Japs he was an innocent civilian, so he came here with those who survived the battle for the Gap. He was all right, until spotted by a Chinese who had joined forces with fifth columnists. This devil told his new masters Sir Peter had oppressed his servants, and regarded Orientals as inferior beings. The Japs love any excuse to vent their spite on Westerners, as you know, so Channing was forced to perform the most menial, filthy chores for them whilst suffering the greatest humiliations they could devise. Only because he's too ill to gratify their vindictiveness has he been thrown back among us.' The doctor sighed again. 'One of Hong Kong's most respected and influential citizens is now a broken bag of bones, driving himself crazy over the thought of what they must also be doing to his daughter somewhere on the Island. The Chinese who accused him once worked as his chauffeur, until dismissed over some misunderstanding to do with the girl. Wonderful pianist – I heard her play on several occasions – but a rather prickly personality, I believe.'

'Ming,' said Rod, immediately back beside the Peak tram where Sarah had told him of the man's instant dismissal on the day they had visited Wang Chua. 'A case of badly lost "face", without a doubt.'

Surprised, the other asked, 'You know about the affair?'

'Vaguely.' He lowered his voice. 'Sarah Channing drowned, attempting to escape from Stanley on a raft the day we surrendered. Will you tell him, or shall I?'

'As you appear to know the family, you can try. But I should wait until he's more *compos mentis*, or your words won't sink in.'

Two days passed before Sir Peter was well enough to heed anything said to him, but he remained confused and uncertain of where he was. Rod made no attempt to identify himself. Sir Peter was unlikely to recognize an unshaven, unkempt man half his previous weight and build. He carefully told a father who had never cared about his daughter of her fate, and should not have been surprised at the response. Pale blue eyes gazed into some unidentifiable distance; the cracked lips moved with an effort.

'So that's that! Now I *have* to stay alive. There's no one to carry on.'

After several days, those words began to inspire Rod in a curious fashion. On Sir Peter's tongue they had been dismissive, but they had the opposite effect on the man who had loved Sarah. The father felt he must stay alive because his daughter – the next generation – had gone. Rod knew the same determination, because she would *never* be gone all the time he held her in his memory. Depression was firmly suppressed; hopelessness was replaced by the will to endure whatever came and survive until Hong Kong was freed. He little knew that his greatest test of courage and stamina was almost upon him.

On September 25, guards came through the camp telling men from a list of names to assemble on the parade ground. Rod was literally dragged from the hospital where he was replacing dressings on several patients, and marched with others being prodded with bayonets to hurry them along. He was surprised by the vast number already gathered where they assembled for roll-call. His apprehension increased. What was this all about? Summary executions of prisoners on charges of spying or treachery, or for trying to escape, were frequent, but surely they would not slaughter on such a large scale as this. Yet, why else would they have been summoned, if not for some kind of punishment?

The murmuring and shuffling ceased when a Japanese junior officer appeared to announce, through an interpreter, that they were to leave Hong Kong for a beautiful country where they would be well treated. He and twenty guards would accompany them and be responsible for their treatment on board. They were each to have a medical examination to confirm their fitness, so they should present a clean and tidy appearance for the doctors.

They were left to return without supervision, but many lingered to discuss the meaning of what had been said. None doubted that the 'beautiful country' was Japan, but most were sceptical about the promises of good treatment. Rod wandered back through the camp with Sam Batchelor who voiced his regrets.

'I'm certain we're destined for Japan, and God knows when we'll be freed. I wish I'd made a break from here. I've friends in Hong Kong with relatives on the mainland, who would have helped me. Once we're in Japan, everyone'll be an enemy.'

Rod was trying to come to terms with the implications of this move. 'If you'd tried an escape, you'd now be dead and never see what kind of country breeds men like these,' he murmured thoughtfully. 'It's my guess we're being shipped there to work. In the past, you British have taken thousands of Orientals as cheap labour on railways and other engineering projects. I suspect we're going to be used the same way. The only consolation is that it'll be in their interests to see we keep fit enough. They'll have to feed us better than this, for a start.'

'Don't count on it,' said Sam heavily. 'Cheap labour means just that. When they drop dead, chuck them out of the way and get more.'

Rod walked on lost in thought, fearing Sam was right. Huge numbers had been caught in Singapore and the Philippines; Java and Sumatra had fallen in the Japanese sweep through the Far East. Prisoners of war were two a penny. None would be fit enough for heavy manual work at which they would be literally worked to death. Could he allow that to happen, making no protest or effort to help them? He had learned the hard way the cost of self-assertion, yet he was dedicated to helping the suffering whoever they were. It was almost certain he had not been selected as a doctor, but as a human working machine, so the coming months might be worse than any he had yet experienced.

The medical examination of each chosen man was a farce. They were all passed fit even though a large proportion were in the early stages of dysentery, and a handful had diphtheria. Protests from imprisoned doctors were met with the comment that sea air would put them all back on their feet. So, two days later, almost two thousand officers, men and uniformed civilians were loaded into a fleet of lighters which took them out to a freighter named *Lisbon Maru*, with three empty holds awaiting them.

Rod felt curiously emotionless as he drew alongside the rearing side of a ship that would take him from Hong Kong, and even further from his home country. This place exercised no pull on him as it did on those who had made their home here, or on men who remembered good times in the colony, and what lay ahead was an unknown quantity. Even so, Rod was daunted when ordered into a hold where men were already jostling each other and complaining that there was no more room. Sitting on the floor with no space between them, perched on small platforms layered up the sides like sardines packed in a tin, they were forced to accommodate the entire complement of another lighter. Latent claustrophobia, plus his dislike of communal living, overcame Rod with a vengeance. He hesitated momentarily on the brink of the huge gaping hold. One of the guards pushed him in the small of his back, so that he would have pitched headlong if there had not been a handrope alongside to grab.

It was fusty and pungent within the dim cavity; odours of past cargoes now mixed with the smell of sweat and unwashed bodies. Rod found a place on one of the platforms halfway down, and wedged himself between Sam Batchelor and a thick metal bulwark, his senses recoiling at the thought of spending days and nights in such cramped conditions. When darkness came it might not be too bad to lie looking up at the stars, but with sun beating down on them during a long day it could grow wellnigh unbearable.

The ship sailed when all were aboard. There appeared to be travelling with them a very large contingent of Japanese troops, surplus to the two dozen guards under command of the officer who had addressed the prisoners at Shamshuipo.

Contrary to expectations, life aboard the *Lisbon Maru* was in some ways better than before. A slice or two of meat and a spoonful of vegetables augmented the evening ration of rice, and the prisoners were allowed on deck in small parties for exercise. Those suffering from diphtheria remained up there all the time, a generous gesture from men not renowned for their compassion.

Rod looked forward to those brief periods in warm sunshine, watching the marine life as the freighter cut through sparkling water. He longed to dive over the rail into it; they were given no water to wash themselves. He welcomed the fresh air after hours below in an atmosphere further fouled by men who were suffering from seasickness or dysentery.

He and Sam paced silently together revelling in the short spells of semi-freedom. Both powerful swimmers, they gazed longingly at the Chinese mainland sometimes visible from the port side. So near and yet so far!

On the fifth morning at sea, Rod was permitted on deck before early morning roll-call to look at the sick men. It was while squatting beside the last of them, more seriously ill than the rest, that a loud explosion below decks sent a shock wave throughout the entire vessel. He stood up in alarm and saw members of the crew running to man the guns. Japanese on the lower decks began to shout in mass panic when the engines stopped, plunging the interior into darkness as it swung sharply to port before shuddering to a halt.

'Blimey, Doc, what was that?' asked one of the patients.

'I reckon we just hit a mine,' he replied, troubled by thoughts of the shortage of lifeboats and who would be first into them. 'Don't worry, we're not in serious trouble.'

The reassuring words were hardly out before the guards were rushing forward with bayonets at the ready, to drive those few prisoners on deck back into the holds. Rod's protest was drowned when the guns opened fire, and he was prodded away from the sick man by a guard who looked remarkably scared despite his armed superiority. Down in the hold men were agitated and noisy, ignoring their officers' orders to keep quiet so that one of their number who understood Japanese could overhear what was happening. Rod shouted to Sam above the din that he believed they had sailed into a minefield, and the crew were attempting to clear a way through by shooting at them.

'We've been hit by something, that's for sure. I hope to God it's not serious because those lifeboats won't hold half the number on board.'

'There are other Jap ships around. We've seen their smoke on the horizon, and they'd get here soon enough in an emergency,' Rod reasoned. 'They'd never let their own troops drown. There must be near on a thousand of them.'

'It's not *them* I'm worried about,' said Sam, with feeling.

'They wouldn't let us drown, either. We're too valuable as slaves.'

281

Order was slowly restored, and an attempt was made to discover from shouts and commands above them what had happened. This was hampered by the handing down of the sick men, with the abrupt comment that they should be isolated to prevent risk of infection. Not only was this impossible, due to lack of spare inches, no one wanted the patients nearby. But they had to be given room, to the accompaniment of very audible grumbles. Those were immediately silenced when a further series of compacted explosions shook the hull of the *Lisbon Maru*, and the roar of guns overhead turned the morning into one of mounting fear of the wall of water against which they would all be powerless.

Then, during a brief lull, the linguist managed to deduce what had happened. They had been torpedoed by an American submarine. Uproar resumed.

'The bastards! They're going to kill us all, just to bump off a few Japs.'

'They don't know we're aboard, man.'

'Then bloody let them know.'

'And p.d.q.!'

'Get them to let us up on deck, sir. We can wave and stop the Yanks attacking.'

'They're in a *submarine*, Corporal Mead. How could they see the decks?'

'Through the mugging periscope, that's how.'

'All right, that's quite enough! Panic will get us nowhere.'

'We're going to the bottom. Oh my gawd, what a terrible way to die!'

So the chorus continued until separate remarks were drowned in a general outcry of injustice. Officers tried unsuccessfully to parley with their captors and, soon afterwards, the hatches were practically closed, leaving only a small opening to allow some air to reach those crammed below. This doubled the strength of the protests from men whose nerves were reaching breaking point, after nine months of hardship, near starvation, and lack of contact with loved ones. However vociferous a complaint, however desperate the person voicing it, time eventually silences him, and so it was that morning. Resignation set in, and soon it became obvious the attack was over. Gunfire ceased; no more explosions were heard. There was no relief for the suffering prisoners, however. No tea or breakfast rice were brought; all requests for it were ignored. Pleas for drinking water fell on deaf ears, and the hatch covers remained as they were.

There was a great deal of activity on deck, and overheard remarks suggested that the Japanese troops were being transferred to another ship, thereby angering the few left to guard so many prisoners. They were afraid of being overwhelmed and killed. The men in the hold then knew the score. They were to be kept down there until a rescue vessel arrived to take them aboard. Nothing could be done, meanwhile. Any attempt to squeeze through the small opening in the hatch cover would bring instant death from nervous guards.

Throughout the long sweltering day Rod fought his claustrophobia as best he could. Regular checks on the sick kept his mind occupied, and he joined with officers in making repeated requests for food and water while the sun beat down on the motionless *Lisbon Maru*. None was supplied and the situation for many men was growing serious. Conditions in the hold were worsening hourly. The air was dangerously foul after more than twenty-four hours below decks, and Rod knew some were certain to die unless they were soon given some relief.

Evening brought alarming signs that the ship was listing. The officer who acted as their interpreter called out repeatedly for permission to go on deck in small groups to visit the latrines and get some fresh air. Others requested water for men who were dying of thirst. If it had not been for the fact that guards could be heard talking to each other, the prisoners might have believed they were alone on the damaged ship. The presence of those callous guards provided a small crumb of comfort, for they would not still be aboard if the ship were sinking.

At around nine p.m. there was a flurry of activity. Faces peeped through the opening in the hatch cover, although they would have seen little with no lights to brighten the depths. Several prisoners raised a cheer; some shouted that it was about time they were let up. Hope turned to horror when, instead of the heavy baulks of timber being lifted away, the hatch was closed completely then covered with tarpaulin that shut out both air and the only faint light from the night sky.

It was the last straw for men already suffering extreme conditions. Shouting, banging the bulkheads in protest, served only to exhaust the desperate further, and several collapsed. With his own fear of confinement exacerbated by this move, Rod struggled to remain calm and persuade those around him to do the same. Panic nevertheless reigned until lack of oxygen so wearied the agitated, they fell silent. Into the silence, the senior officer pointed out that even the Japanese would not leave men battened down in a sinking ship. At that time, everyone believed him.

The dark, terrible night dragged past. Those who lost consciousness were so tightly wedged between others, no one noticed their plight. For everyone, breathing became a labour as the hours wore by. Some became so distressed by claustrophobia they struggled free from their physical confinement, missed their footing, and plunged to the bottom of the hold where they lay inert. No one could tell why. Amid their own suffering, no one cared. Despite his own sense of panic, Rod was able to think fairly clearly, and he knew some men would die before long unless air was allowed in. Contact with those imprisoned in the holds on each side, by tapping on the bulkheads, revealed that two naval men had already died of diphtheria in one, and that water was now entering the other and rising hourly. Some had already drowned. This news was so dire, morale plunged to new depths.

Rod inched his way along the platform until he could speak to the senior officer and his subordinates on the next level up. The movement had taken so much effort, he had to fight for breath before giving his opinion that they were all in danger of suffocation within the hour, unless the hatch was opened. He was told that several officers had attempted to cut the tarpaulin through cracks between timbers, but had collapsed from exhaustion. Perhaps Dr Durman would care to take over until they recovered.

At that moment, the ship gave a violent lurch, tilting so steeply Rod was thrown off balance and fell backwards to the depths of the hold, where conditions were the most poisonous. He landed on men beyond knowing or caring what was happening, and was so winded he could not move for a moment or two. Cries of alarm rose on all sides, as no one any longer believed their officers' statement that even Japanese would not leave men battened down in a sinking ship. They had done just that!

Next moment, a narrow shaft of light penetrated the hatch, making it possible for Rod to see several figures hacking at the tarpaulin stretched tightly across the timbers. Then welcome daylight flooded through; fresh air was blown in by the stiff sea breeze. Escape was possible. But was it? Two or three men scrambled through to the deck only to be met with rifle-fire. They returned hastily, one clearly wounded, and a discussion appeared to be taking place. All around Rod men were dragging themselves to their feet, swaying uncertainly, then staggering towards wooden steps leading up the sides of the hold, careless of comrades heaped on the floor. Better to risk being shot at than face death trapped in a slowly sinking ship.

Their desperation set Rod scrambling up, only to be flung backward again as the vessel lurched once more, shuddered throughout her length, then settled at a sharp angle bows upward. Flattened against a bulkhead, Rod saw his fears confirmed as water entered the hole in the hatch to cascade into the hold. The *Lisbon Maru* was fast sinking. Sea water swept men from their places on platforms or steps to drown in the depths with some unfortunates too weak to move from the few feet they had occupied for the past five days. The thunder of this threatening waterfall almost deafened the shouts and cries as men fought, clawed and dragged themselves towards freedom glimpsed through a second gap being forced in the hatch covers by those already on deck.

Galvanized into action, Rod struggled across the angled floor to where those too weak to help themselves were in imminent danger of drowning. The water level was rising frighteningly fast. Ruled by instinct, he began to pull men from the filth of human excrement and sickness before the sea claimed them. If they had to die, let them do so in the clean, fresh air with some dignity, not like penned cattle at the mercy of a sadistic inhuman enemy. Anger greater by far than any before experienced gave him the strength to lift men as if they were featherweights and carry them to the steps, where he bullied others into helping them towards freedom. Time and again, he slipped on the ordure to slide down the sloping floor into the water, finding it increasingly difficult to mount the slope again. The echoing thunder of water, the awesome chorus of men screaming their fear, the distant clamour on deck all became part of his rage as he defied physical frailty until the rising water made his efforts futile. As he swam around in the greyness, bodies bobbed on the surface. None moved. They had died seeing freedom a short climb away. He joined the living on their way up to it.

Daylight blinded him. He stood with a heaving chest in warm sunshine, relishing the pure, clean air, vaguely aware that the deck was remarkably steady beneath his bare feet. Sunblindness slowly faded to show Rod that the bows were still angled clear of the sea. Prisoners were leaping into it with all manner of spars, boxes or oddments to use as buoys. A thousand or more heads bobbed in the sea; lifeless bodies floated in areas of reddened water. Several destroyers stood some distance off, their decks crowded with observers. There was no sign of the guards or the crew of the *Lisbon Maru*. The rats had left the sinking ship.

Rod took stock of the situation while inhaling deeply to prepare his lungs for further severe effort. Some men had already swum as far as several tugs supporting the destroyers, but they were pushed back into the sea as they attempted to climb aboard. Many had no lifebelt. They were all shot at as they floundered helplessly in the swell, and some sank beneath the surface. Rod noticed that those who survived appeared to be caught in a powerful tidal flow, that carried them past the boats and beyond firing range. Narrowing his eyes, he spotted a group of small islands on the horizon. Although some distance away, he reckoned they offered the best chance of survival no matter who inhabited them, and he could use that tide to advantage.

A small group had gathered in the bows showing no signs of haste to leave. Some were even smoking cigarettes they had discovered. All were drinking thirstily from the water containers. Rod swallowed only enough to sustain him for several hours. Too much would bloat his stomach, thus hampering his progress in the sea. It was a very long way to the islands, as much as five or six miles. A man would need all the stamina he could muster to reach them. He offered a brief word of advice to the soldiers relaxing on a ship slowly slipping beneath a very treacherous sea, but they were living for the moment and gave the impression of caring very little what happened next. He could do nothing but wish them luck. Their lives were not in his hands but their own.

Stripping off his filthy clothes, Rod dived into the cold freshness of salt water. His body quickly responded to the reviving qualities of this element in which he felt so confident, and he embarked on a leisurely crawl aided by the strong pull of a current sweeping towards his goal. No more than ten minutes later, he heard a muffled explosion and, rolling over, he saw the *Lisbon Maru* slide beneath waves that foamed and bubbled as they closed over the floating prison. Had those last few troops gone down with it and their comrades who had not lived to face the choice?

All around Rod others were borne on the tremendous tidal flow. The inexperienced wasted their feeble energy on fruitless attempts to reach the tugs, where survivors were now being hauled aboard. Those fortunate enough to have a lifebelt just drifted lazily so that it was impossible to tell whether they were exhausted, asleep or dead. Bodies floated between the swimmers, their destination unimportant. Rod was determined on his. He reasoned that the islands must lie off the Chinese mainland. He could hide there and take his chances of survival. They were certain to be better than those he would have as a forced labourer in Japan.

He measured time by the sun, like he and his brothers had done as boys when riding the boundary at Dalgara. Noon came and went as he alternately swam and floated with the help of the sea's irresistible force. At one point he came upon a young lad in difficulties, and took him in the lifesaving hold to tow him while he rested. Already beginning to tire himself, Rod found the additional effort hastening his own exhaustion. The sun blazing down on his upturned face forced him to close his eyes so that he was swimming blind for some while. Afraid of being swept wide of the islands, he told the lad to float for a moment or two while he assessed their position. Rolling over, he rose on the swell to come face to face with a body whose staring eyes were inches from his own as it drifted past. Sam Batchelor had a bullet hole in his forehead. The shock took all other thoughts from Rod's mind, and he watched the man who had offered him a place in the filth of Shamshuipo float away on the same sea that had claimed Celeste and Sarah to rest, as they did, without any sign of passing. When he came from those dark recollections and looked for his young companion, the boy had vanished.

The sun was dipping below the horizon, turning the sea blood red, when Rod drew close to a large island. Dangerously tired and chilled, swept inexorably towards it on the increased power of the tide, he saw with a sinking heart that the coast was very rocky, waves crashing over and between them before retreating in a mass of white foam. He could just make out the sight of others ahead of him being dashed helplessly against these rocks, before being sucked back by the undertow. Some were then carried further out and swept away from salvation, unable to combat the power of the tide. To reach safety and be snatched from it seemed so cruel a trick of Fate, Rod's anger lent him renewed strength. Fate had dealt him many blows in the past year, but in this one instance he could take control and triumph.

As he was carried closer to the rocks around which water foamed and churned, Rod attempted to use the sea's impetus to his own advantage. Then, fifty yards from the island, he was lifted on a high tidal wave that raced shorewards with such speed Rod knew Fate had won. He was powerless as he was tumbled headlong in a roaring, echoing surge of water before being slammed against a solid surface that knocked all breath from his chest, and brought acute pain in his left arm. Instinct had him gripping that rock and hanging for dear life while the sea attempted to suck him free. He was soon hurtled forward once more at the mercy of a force greater than any human strength.

Hands fastened over his wrists bringing an agonizing tug of war with the receding waves. He was dragged over an abrasive surface that tore at his bare flesh until he came to rest on dry shingle, where the wind bit into his icy-cold body. The sea was no more than a thunderous roar in his ears as he lay face down, gasping and exhausted. He was turned on to his back. Against the dusk sky he saw men in drenched cotton trousers looking down with nods and smiles. He was deathly tired, chilled to the bone, and his left arm was ripped open from elbow to wrist, but he had never felt this wonderful in all his thirty-one years. He was with friends. He could rest.

When awareness next returned, Rod found himself wrapped in a padded gown in a simple hut much like the ones on Hong Kong's offshore islands. A young girl with an amazingly beautiful, calm face brought him hot fish stew and a curious scented drink. When he had finished the meal, she brought a balm he knew well and spread it over the wound in his arm that had been wrapped in leaves to stanch the blood. He knew the ancient Chinese remedy would heal and cleanse in a very short time, so smiled his gratitude. Through the doorway he glimpsed a constant lamp-lit procession of Chinese carrying or assisting the British prisoners to huts along the shore. Two other men were brought to lie near Rod, but he was practically asleep by then and merely reflected that Providence had smiled on a good many today.

He was shaken awake by the girl who pointed through the doorway. A flotilla of Japanese launches rode the sunlit sea, while troops who had been rescued from the *Lisbon Maru* came ashore to round up those who had reached safety. The soldiers stormed into huts and dragged out the men they had left to drown. They knocked aside Chinese who tried to prevent them from entering their homes, and struck the captives with rifle-butts if they walked too slowly. Slipping out of the padded gown, Rod made his way from the rear of the hut, running from one group of rocks to another, to where the sea was racing in with green, white-capped fury to cover them. It was a dangerous place to hide, even for a powerful swimmer, but the only possible one. He would sooner take his chances in the deep than be taken prisoner once more.

Chapter Twelve

They were driven to Noon Cottage from the RAF station by a perky girl in WAAF uniform, whose eyes were more often regarding Alex in the rear-view mirror than watching the road. Sarah was not surprised. He had regained weight in India, where lazy days in the sun had turned his skin golden brown and bleached his hair even fairer than before. His natural good looks were now heightened by an air of toughness that made him appear older than his twenty-eight years. There was hardly a trace of the Hong Kong playboy in this assured man who had become her lover on a haunting, moonlit night in Calcutta.

Sarah turned from watching the driver's avid study of a man who must have been represented to her by Wing-Commander Staines as something of a hero, and studied the passing scene. England seemed so small. But remarkably beautiful. The tiny patchwork fields were a rich green; the trees a glory of gold, russet and red in pale sunshine. No deep, fierce blue overhead; just a gentle friendly sky the colour of forget-me-nots. The country was experiencing what the English called an Indian summer and, despite most traffic being military, it looked wonderfully peaceful and welcoming.

'It's like another world, isn't it?' said Alex quietly.

'Mmm. A miniature one. Little winding lanes, villages you leave behind almost before you know you've arrived, squat cottages, low-ceilinged pubs and handkerchief-sized gardens filled with asters, dahlias and Michaelmas daisies. I'd forgotten all that.'

'Do you know what I like best about it?'

She turned back to him. 'It's home.'

He shook his head and smiled. 'Everyone understands what I say to them.'

Sarah gave a return smile. 'In China you vowed to become a linguist.'

'No need for that now. I've always been a lazy tyke.' He took her hand. 'Happy, darling?'

'No, nervous. It'll all be the same, yet I'm so different.'

'She'll be expecting that.' His hand squeezed hers reassuringly. 'If there's an initial problem, I'll be ready to step in and charm her.'

'You've done quite enough charming today,' she said drily, nodding towards their driver.

'She's cute, isn't she? Do you think I'll find a lot like her when I'm sent to an RAF station?'

'Quite enough to keep you in practice.' She turned away to watch the scenery once more.

After a pause, he said, 'I wish I could detect even a *faint* hint of jealousy in your voice.'

They were very near Kingsmill now. All Sarah's attention was taken by the sights that were familiar to yet somehow detached from her. There was the platform bearing milk churns at the bottom of a lane leading to Prosser's Farm; now, the agricultural workshop which had switched to making gun carriages. Across the field was the sixteenth-century church where her mother had married the widowed Captain Channing during his brief leave from Flanders. There, too, Ellie had married the grandfather Sarah had never known. On the right lay the gamekeeper's cottage on the boundary of Lord Frampton's estate. Did Robert still take Ellie to see badgers or fox cubs at play? Was she still illustrating books? Around this next bend was the school serving three villages. Heavens, it was no larger than a country house! Had it always been that size? Ah, here was the fork in the road. To the left lay Mills Cross; to the right, Kingsmill.

The WAAF driver went carefully through the narrow lane overhung by golden beeches and bordered by autumn-tinted hedgerows. The many bends hid from view any traffic approaching and, as this was almost certain to be wide farm vehicles, caution was vital. The car went unhindered past the shop and sub-post office, the village hall, the row of tied cottages, the Dog and Duck Inn, the smithy and the mill which no longer operated because the course of the river had been artificially changed in 1812 by a squire who had had a fancy for water running through his estate. Out of the village centre now, the lane ran past the rambling houses of Dr Barnes, the local vet, retired bank managers, solicitors and other professional men who bought country homes with the fruits of their success and enjoyed rural solitude. There were others who saw these lovely old stone houses as investments, swooping down from big cities in their Daimlers for weekend entertaining, then returning to the bright lights. That section of Kingsmill's population had rarely been seen since the outbreak of war. There was no petrol for their cars, no food for lavish entertaining. Their sons and daughters were all in the forces. The houses were neglected; furniture all covered by dust sheets.

Sarah then realized that Noon Cottage was around the next bend. Her heartbeat quickened with apprehension. Would she be disappointed? Would it mean nothing to her? If this was no longer home, where would she find it?

'The next gate, please,' she called to the girl in uniform.

'Yes, ma'am.'

The driver slowed, then turned through a wide entrance where the gate stood open in welcome. Sarah held her breath. The old mellow stone house with neat thatched roof was bathed in late afternoon sunshine, the warm yellow wood of its front door gleaming. The holly hedge was as shiny green as if it had been polished. The twin cedars had surely grown taller! Brass on the antique coach lamp in the porch dazzled in the sun's rays; the pyracantha was yellow with berries. An air of timeless peace hung over the house to which she had been sent at the age of four by the father who did not want her.

The front door opened as Sarah stepped from the car. How frail Ellie had grown! She wore one of her good tweed costumes with an amber blouse. The grey curls had been replaced by a bun, but the country glow was still in her cheeks and her blue eyes were as bright as ever. Sarah crossed to her grandmother. They gripped hands, gazing at each other wordlessly. The emotional moment continued for a painfully long time until, from the square hall, two borzois rushed forward in a frenzy of greeting to engulf Sarah with canine ecstasy. She knelt to hug them both, murmuring their names, overcome with tears because they immediately knew her. Then she was hugging the dogs and Ellie alternately as they all went inside. Yes, this *was* home.

In turn, Sarah exclaimed over the ancient grandfather clock whose chimes were at odds with the time shown on the face, the sampler her mother had sewn as a child, the blue gold-inlaid dish handed down by Great-aunt Hetty who had been a suffragette, the rag rug made by Mrs Perkins in aid of the orphans of London's Blitz, and the silver-framed photograph of herself at her last school concert.

'It's all the same,' she cried. 'It's as if time had stood still.'

'But it didn't, my dear,' Ellie said quietly. 'I can see that. If I had had any notion of what was to come, I never would have persuaded you to go out there.'

Some of the joy of reunion faded. 'Father said that, too.'

'Have you heard any news of him yet?'

Sarah shook her head. 'They tried once more just before we left Calcutta, but the Red Cross in Hong Kong still can't get names or details from the Japs even now. It must be terrible for those left behind.'

That other world had intruded and brought curious constraint between them. Sarah could no longer rejoice in the familiar objects of her childhood; it had gone beyond recall taking innocent happiness with it. As they stood trying to find words, a knock on the open door heralded Alex, who asked if he might come in. Sarah had momentarily forgotten him. He had either tactfully left them to their private greeting, or he had been enjoying the admiration of the little brunette driver.

Glad of the interruption, Sarah said, 'This is Alex Tennant, darling. I told you all about him in my letters from India. Did you receive them? I've invited him to stay for a few days while he arranges to join the RAF.'

Ellie smiled warmly. 'Do come in, Mr Tennant. You look

so uncomfortable bent almost double in that low doorway. You are welcome to stay for as long as you wish, but I'm unused to male guests. You'll have to put up with sugar and spice and all things nice, I'm afraid.'

Alex advanced and kissed her firmly on the cheek. 'There's nothing I like better than being surrounded by ladies, as Sarah must have told you. Please call me Alex, because I fully intend to call you Ellie. Over the past nine months I've heard so much about you I feel I know you enough for first names, and we're going to be seeing a lot of each other.'

'Sarah was right about your charm, young man,' came the amused response. 'No doubt your appetite is as keen as your eye for a pretty girl, so come along and have some tea.'

As Ellie led the way through the house to where a round polished table was set with sandwiches, scones and a large cream-filled cake, Sarah remembered the WAAF driver. She turned. 'We should offer that girl some tea.'

Alex slid his arm around her waist to coax her forward. 'She was reluctant to come in when I told her you were a banking heiress.'

'Alex, you *didn't!*' she cried, halting him.

'So you are,' he declared, drawing her into his arms in the centre of the room. 'I also told her we were engaged. She looked very disappointed, so I gave her a quid to get something in a café in Cheltenham.'

'You're incorrigible,' Sarah told him with a laugh, glad of his lightheartedness. She took his hand and pulled him to the table in a window bay looking out on the extensive garden. 'Come and look at this tea. Now I *know* I'm back in England.'

They all sat after Ellie brought in a silver teapot and covered it with a padded cosy to keep it hot. Conversation was light and mainly concerned what they were eating.

'Mr Hapgood saved this tin of salmon for me as soon as he knew you were safe in India. It's only pink, I'm afraid. You can't get red any more. London hotels take the little available, I expect.'

'Did Mrs Mullinger make the cake?'

'Of course. No one can bake a sponge quite as well as she. I sent along the blackcurrants for the filling. She stopped coming here last year. Malcolm lost both legs in North Africa, so she looks after the baby while Mary visits him. He's had artificial ones fitted, but finds it agony to stand on them. Poor boy!'

'Poor Mary, having to see her husband suffer. So who looks after you now?'

'I do. It's quite fun really. Do have another scone, Alex, and some more of my plum jam. I'm quite pleased with my efforts.'

'So you should be. Both are delicious. Do you still manage to do book illustrations?' he asked.

'Of course. More than ever children need magic in their lives. Our sales have trebled in the last year, Sarah. The publishers say parents are reading to their children in air-raid shelters to allay their fears. Do stop feeding Sasha and Vlad with cake, girl! They'll want it every day.'

'Then I shall give them cake. I haven't seen them for two years. Allow me to spoil them just a little.'

After tea Sarah helped her grandmother prepare a room for Alex, and they laughed together over rose-patterned sheets, frilled pillow cases and pink towels.

'Had I known you would bring him here I could have borrowed more suitable linen from Mrs Hemmingway. It's impossible to buy new without coupons, dear, and I used all I had to get things for you. I do hope he won't object to feminine fripperies.'

Sarah looked up from soothing the pink coverlet. 'Alex is grateful these days for a bed, soap and towels; all the ordinary things of life. He doesn't care what colour they are.'

Ellie laid a hand on Sarah's arm as she straightened. 'Are you engaged to be married?'

'No, darling. He said that to deter the girl who drove us here. She was very taken with him.'

'And no wonder. He's very handsome. He's also in love with you.'

'He thinks he is. It's merely a total dependence which isn't easy to shake off after nine months. I'm the same. I feel insecure and lost if he isn't near me. That isn't love.'

'I see,' said Ellie thoughtfully.

Sarah put her arm around her grandmother. 'Show him the garden before it grows dark, while I change.'

She wanted to go alone into her room. It was something she had so often yearned to do, yet it proved an anticlimax. The pansy-patterned wallpaper had lost its charm. The bed in which she had lain with dreams of successful studies in Vienna or Paris, her concert début at the Albert Hall, the accolades heaped upon her after a sell-out tour of Europe, seemed almost to mock her. She pulled open the drawer of her desk and found the pile of books she had filled with notes on fingering and technique taken down during tutorials. The words blurred. Where was Jakob Myburgh now? The books slid from her fingers as she gazed at framed certificates lining the walls. A record of dedication to something which had meant all in life to her. A record of growing aptitude and application. A record of future brilliance. Was it lost for ever? Did she care? The girl of this room no longer existed. The woman she had become did not belong here. She had been mistaken, after all, to believe this was home.

The wardrobe smelled of mothballs. It contained a pair of jodhpurs, a green wool skirt, two patterned blouses, a cream cashmere sweater and a black dinner dress, all new. Ellie's precious coupons had been surrendered for these. Sarah sat on the bed gazing at the things her grandmother had bought to greet her return, and realized what had happened during the two years she had been away. Ellie had nurtured memories of the girl she had reared, and believed she had her back; that life would continue as before. Only now was Sarah aware of how much it had cost her grandmother to lose the child of her own lost daughter. Because of that she would have to stay at Noon Cottage for a while, before deciding what to do with the life she had fought to hold on to for those terrible months.

After dinner they sat with glasses of wine before a log and fir-cone fire with the dogs at their feet, and talked of pre-war days and how things had changed in the village. As the evening passed, Sarah relaxed. She had forgotten the pleasure of lazy evenings gossiping around a fire. Ellie brought out her latest illustrations and copies of six books Sarah had not seen. Alex found them enchanting and asked if he could take them to read in bed. They all laughed a lot and indulged in lighthearted teasing. Nothing was said to spoil the tranquillity of that first evening in England.

Clutching the children's story-books, Alex got to his feet at ten declaring that he would have to turn in or fall asleep in the chair. He took Ellie's hand and kissed it in a gesture that seemed perfectly natural. 'Thank you for the kind of evening I have never been lucky enough to spend before. This is all quite as wonderful as Sarah said.'

Ellie smiled warmly. 'Goodnight, Alex. I'm glad she asked you to stay. Would you like a bedtime drink?'

'Oh . . . no, thanks,' he said hastily.

She chuckled. 'I do believe you think I'm going to send you upstairs with Ovaltine. You'll find a bottle of whisky in the cupboard beneath the stairs. I keep it there out of the vicar's sight, because he's shameless in asking for refills when parishioners offer him a tot. He thinks I have none in the house.' She waved a hand at the door. 'Go on, take it up with you.'

Alex sighed. 'What a wonderful woman you are. If it weren't for Sarah, I'd ask you to marry me.' He went out touching Sarah's hair in a farewell caress as he went.

Silence reigned for a while after his departure. Sarah lay back in her chair watching the light of flames playing on the borzois' fur and listening to the sound of Alex moving about the room overhead. It was comforting to know he was there.

Ellie broke into her reverie. 'I know you'll tell me about your experiences when you're ready, my dear, but do give me an explanation of why that young man has never spent this kind of evening.'

Sarah smiled. 'I should like some Ovaltine. When I've made us both some, I'll tell you anything you want to know about him. He's wound you round his little finger. As it happens, this time he's quite sincere. Your charm is a match for his.'

Over beakers of Ovaltine Sarah told her grandmother all she had learned of Alex's past during the months they had spent together, including the wager that had resulted in the death of his friend.

'I disliked him intensely for a long time. Had I known why he behaved as he did I might have understood,' she confessed softly. 'You were right to send me to Hong Kong. I really knew nothing about people and what makes them the way they are.'

'And now you do?'

She glanced across at the beloved face softened by age. 'Father told me heroes have their flaws and villains their redeeming features, but it's more complex than that. I've seen brave men cry and women kill. The most basic savage creatures offered amazing kindness; civilized high-ranking officials could be barbaric. Humanity can overcome language and ethnic barriers, yet these same things often create blind hatred. The overriding fact I have learned about those around me is that it's impossible to judge them, because one can never see fully into their hearts and minds. You said I must discover that there are people in the world. I've certainly done that.'

There was silence for a while as the fire crackled and flared to cast a warm glow over the familiar room. Sarah was lost in the world she had left behind when Ellie spoke.

'Is it your father who hurt you so much you feel unable entirely to trust anyone?' When Sarah looked up swiftly her grandmother added, 'I received your last brief letter from Hong Kong telling me you were returning home because the experiment had failed. Was the fault his?'

Sarah had forgotten that letter announcing her proposed departure on the *San Maritino*. The reasons for it now seemed unreal and self-indulgent.

'I don't think I can answer that. War changed everything. I was so very inexperienced and we had been apart too long. If we meet again I shall be more tolerant, he less aloof. But our basic differences will always be there. He wants a suitable son-in-law to provide a suitable grandson to take over the bank. A daughter who wishes to be a "piano-player" doesn't fit in with his plan.'

There was another pause before Ellie commented, 'You haven't yet been in the music room to look at your piano.'

Sarah sighed. 'I haven't played a note for almost a year. After I left the hospital in India I stayed with the

299

Crankshaws, who owned a handsome Steinway they were always begging me to use.' She cast her grandmother a bewildered look. 'I think I may have lost my talent. I can't go near a keyboard. There's no longer a flame within me burning to escape into the fire of passionate melody. My talent was lost with a colony.'

Silence again for some minutes, then Ellie said briskly, 'Well, I'm sure Alex will make the suitable son-in-law your father wants. A merger between Tennant's Steel and Channing Mercantile could hardly be bettered. Both parents should be highly satisfied. Do bring your boys on a visit now and again, dear. I'll be able to take them to see badgers, foxes and otters. How delightful that will be.'

Sarah stared at her grandmother, the bedtime drink forgotten, until Ellie began to chuckle. 'If you could see your expression! I'm not the poor old dear you clearly believe I have become during your absence, my girl. Talent such as yours is never lost. It sometimes goes astray during periods of emotional upheaval, but it's always there waiting to emerge at the right moment. Relax, enjoy that young man's company, and rediscover the pleasure of your roots. The flame will burn again, believe me.'

Sarah went across to put her arms around the only mother she had known. 'Forgive me. I'd forgotten there was someone whose love is unconditional, who knows me probably better than I know myself.'

'No, Sarah, you're the only person who knows the real you. The horror you've been through has left you confused and uncertain, that's all.' She smiled, her eyes glowing with love. 'Thank God you're home! Now I can live again.'

By the soft light of her bedside lamp the bedroom seemed more familiar than before dinner. It was still full of the spirit of a girl who no longer existed, yet this present Sarah now felt at ease with her. She lay wide-eyed in the moonlight feeling no inclination to sleep, despite the overnight flight from Alexandria. When Alex came silently to her bed and sat on the edge of it she knew he also could not sleep, and was not surprised.

'It's so quiet,' he said softly.

'I suppose we'll get used to it,' she replied from her pillow.

He took her hand in his, stroking her fingers with his thumbs. 'I think I'll leave it a week or two before I contact the RAF. Is that all right with you?'

'Of course. Ellie'll love it.'

'She's one in a million.'

'I know.'

'Is there anywhere we can get hold of horses?'

'Yes, I'm sure Lord Frampton's stables can let us have a couple.'

'I thought we'd go riding. I'd like to see something of the place while I'm here.'

'Good idea.'

'And we must go across and see Jim one day. It's not far from here to his station.'

'Not on the horses,' she teased softly.

'No, not on the horses.'

He reached out and drew her into his arms. His kiss began gently, but soon became demanding as his hands moved over her body. She gripped his arms to still them, and drew back from his searching mouth.

'Not tonight, Alex. Not here.'

'She must know we're lovers,' he protested, reluctant to stop.

'No, she's of another generation.'

'She's no fool.'

'Her code of conduct dates back to the turn of the century. What we're doing breaks it. Please understand that,' she whispered urgently.

'If you'd only agree to be married we could make love wherever we were.'

'That's lust talking. We decided before leaving India to keep things as they are until we have been home six months.' She put her hand on his cheek and kissed him very lightly. 'Please go back to your bedtime reading before things become too difficult.'

He stood up reluctantly. 'I'll probably drink the entire bottle of whisky instead.'

She smiled up at him with great affection. 'Better that Ellie should believe you're a drunkard than a cad. Good-night, Alex.'

The minute he had left, Sarah regretted the need to send him away. Would Ellie's upbringing allow her to accept unmarried passion under her roof? She thought not. A year ago she, herself, had condemned those who indulged in it. A year ago, she had not been put to the test. She lay tense in every limb until a soft knocking on the connecting walls allowed her to relax. It was Alex sending his usual message, in morse. *Goodnight, and may your morning rice bowl be full.* She sent back: *Sleep well until the moon is covered by the sun.* Would they ever forget? The pansy-covered wallpaper faded until moonlight illuminated only those things she believed would never be driven from her memory.

It was not until they sat before the fire after dinner the following evening that Alex took things into his own hands. 'You've been remarkably patient and understanding, Ellie, but you deserve to hear what Sarah has been through since you said goodbye to her two years ago.'

Sarah made no protest. The story had to be told, so perhaps it was best to speak of it now and then never mention it again.

Ellie regarded him thoughtfully across the cosy, flickering firelight. 'Is this a combined decision?'

'No, it's mine,' he said firmly. 'Your granddaughter will never give you the complete facts, so I'm going to speak for her. She still has nightmares over it, and I believe relating it all to you here in this wonderfully normal atmosphere might lay them to rest.'

'Perhaps you would pour us another glass of wine before you begin.'

As he moved away to do so, Ellie looked questioningly at Sarah. She nodded assurance that she had no objection to Alex's decision, guessing from her grandmother's expression that two and two had been put together to make a satisfying sum. Perhaps Ellie was right. It was too soon to tell.

With glasses recharged they settled in the gold velvet chairs, at ease with each other, the dogs sleeping peacefully on the old rug as they had done for years. Sarah knew a sense of inevitability. Alex was right. Perhaps the nightmares would cease once they had been challenged. He began with their meeting at the Halburton, and the subsequent building of the raft. Sarah's thoughts flew to the three they had left behind. She and Alex had asked for news of them as well as her father, but the situation in Hong Kong was impenetrable. Marion's baby would be three months old now, if it had ever been born. Had she been reunited with her adored Bill? What of Chloë and Roma? They had heard of the repatriation of American civilians, so Roma was most probably free and at home by now ... if she had not been raped and murdered.

'Sarah had on only her underwear when they pulled her from the sea,' Alex was saying. 'They gave her a spare pair of seaman's trousers, a thick pullover of the ship's captain's, and laced boots. She wore those for four months.' He cast Sarah a glance so warm it steadied her. 'We cut her hair and made her wear a cap so she would look like one of the crew when we were in the midst of them.' He turned back to Ellie. 'I had seen what Japanese did to nurses. I wouldn't let that happen to Sarah, so I'm afraid I was rather brutal in my insistence that she should act the man from then on.'

'I can't imagine you ever being brutal, Alex.'

'War changes us all. The captain of our MTB was a very cocksure type derisive of a civilian soldier who had set out on a homemade raft to cross a particularly treacherous stretch of water, but he was choked with tears while he watched his ship go down by his own hand. I admit it's an awesome sight, even for those with no sentiment for the vessel. The entire crew wept, but they were safely away from Hong Kong.'

'Still in danger, surely,' commented Ellie, throwing another log on the fire.

'We had a compass, an old map of the coastal area, three kitbags of supplies, and a bottle of drinking water each when we set out for Chungking, where the Chinese are still in power and we have our embassy. Japanese patrolled the area between Mirs Bay, where we landed, and some hundreds of miles inland. We were unsure of the loyalty of rural Chinese, and we knew guerrilla bands roamed the wild countryside. We had to take our chances with them all. The naval men were all armed and very fit. We three were lame ducks, so far as they were concerned. Sarah wrote of Jim Maiden in her letters, didn't she?'

Ellie nodded. 'A brave little man who lost an ear.'

'A half-deaf RAF mechanic, a part-time soldier with a gammy leg, and a wealthy banker's daughter. Not the ideal trio to have along on a thousand-mile trek across unknown country, I suppose.'

'Quite a liability,' agreed Ellie.

'So we proved,' he said. 'Sarah was splendid, marching with teeth gritted in her determination to keep up with us all. Jim gamely took his turns with the heavy kitbags. I was the one who let us down.'

'Not deliberately,' put in Sarah swiftly. 'How you walked on that leg for so long none of us knew.' She turned to her grandmother. 'The wound had never received proper treatment, so the constant walking split it open. Alex had been stuffing leaves beneath the bandage they'd given him on the ship so that none of us would realize he was losing so much blood. Poison seeped into it from the sap, and his leg swelled to about three times normal size. He finally collapsed in high fever a week after we had set off.'

'By that time we had reached a hamlet at the foot of some hills. The Chinese there were simple souls who had possibly never seen Europeans before. They had no idea who we were and we had no means of communicating with them, but they saw that I was ill and took us in.'

'We had split into three small groups,' Sarah explained. 'We all thought it was wise, so that if Japanese were patrolling we wouldn't all fall into their hands *en masse*. We were bringing up the rear and there was no way we could let the others know what had happened. There were two sailors with us.'

'They were pretty good about it on the whole,' put in Alex, 'although I'm sure they weren't happy about being separated from their shipmates.'

'And grouped with the liabilities,' put in Ellie drily.

Alex smiled. 'Apart from that, they were under direct Admiralty orders to get themselves to Chungking as soon as possible.'

'We understood their dilemma,' said Sarah, seeing quite clearly the faces of those two sailors as they reluctantly explained why they could not stay.

'They begged Sarah to go with them, apparently. So did Jim. They were armed, they had food supplies, and they were fit. I was delirious and dangerously ill, and Jim could provide little defence if we should be attacked. Yet she refused to leave us.' Alex gave Sarah a long, loving glance. 'I would never have survived if she hadn't stayed.'

'That's nonsense,' she declared.

'It isn't, and you know it. Ellie, the Chinese gave her some hot concoction to pour down my throat every morning and evening, and she took it on trust because she knew of a doctor who believed in Oriental cures. But only due to her constant care of me for five days and nights, dousing me with water from the nearby stream and helping Jim hold me down so that I wouldn't toss around and deepen the wound, did I eventually pull through.'

Sarah hardly heard his last words. Mention of Rod brought him so vividly to life in her memory. If his wife survived, his child would now be several months old. Was it like him? Did it have those same dark compelling eyes? Was he alive to see it? Were he and Celeste in some camp, reunited by war and the product of their passion? Sarah now understood – oh, how well she understood – the passion born of desperation. It bound her to Alex; it was not in the least like the irresistible, overwhelming yearning she had known during those brief few months last year before she walked away from Rod on the sands of Stanley Bay.

'Where are you, darling?'

Alex's gentle question brought her from Hong Kong to face him. His was the fault for mentioning Rod. Pointless to look at her in faint accusation. 'I think you know very well where I am,' she said. 'It was your decision to speak of it this evening. You must accept the consequences.'

'Would you rather talk of other things, dear?' asked Ellie in soft concern.

She ruffled Sasha's fur with the toe of her slipper, enjoying the way he wriggled with pleasure even in sleep. 'We didn't leave the village for a further week, which put us way behind the others. We later learned that they had reached Chungking in record time. Very determined, aggressive men, they were. They're back on active service in the Med. Watch out, Hitler!'

'Are you *really* happy to continue?' asked Ellie anxiously.

Sarah looked up. 'Of course. It's got to be said. Let's have some more wine and say it.' She held out her glass to Alex. 'Will you continue, or shall I?'

He got to his feet. 'You. Another helping of this stuff and you'll be beyond speech.'

'By the time we had moved on we had eaten our share of the food left by the two sailors. The compass and map was with the leading group, but we knew the names of places to aim for along the route. At the first of these, the locals were hostile. None offered rice or fruit, and they practically ran us out of town. We soon discovered why, didn't we, Alex?'

He handed both women full glasses, then fetched his own before going to lean on the mantelpiece. 'We were sleeping in a ditch beside a field when armed Chinese pounced on us and tied our ankles and wrists. One spoke a form of pidgin English. He told us they could sell us to the Japs for a great deal of money, especially the woman. They were army deserters, existing by robbing villages and constantly moving from place to place to evade their former comrades. We were outnumbered four to one, and they had knives and rather nasty-looking whips, so we were at their mercy. For an entire week they kept our hands tied as we walked miles in search of Japanese. We were given little to eat or drink, and the threat of being handed over to enemy troops haunted us the whole time. Jim and I worked out a plan that would enable Sarah to escape and hide when we were about to be handed over, so she had the additional dread of being left alone miles from Chungking. She was afraid that we would be tortured to reveal her whereabouts, but we insisted she do as we said. We believed that Jap troops would not bother to hunt the countryside for her when there were women in the villages to satisfy them.'

Alex appeared to be lost in that other time, too, as he stood silently gazing at the golden wine in his glass. Sarah continued the story.

'We eventually met up with a large company of troops. Well, not exactly. They ambushed us at night, so there was not a thing we could do about it. You can imagine our feelings, Ellie dear, when we discovered they were Chinese

Communists, not Japanese. Their commander had been educated in San Francisco and spoke to us in very comical American-style English. He promptly press-ganged our captors into his company, and gave us what amounted to a splendid meal compared with what we'd been having. We stayed with them for three days. One confiscated bicycles from Waichow, a nearby town, and presented them to us. Afraid of offending them, Alex said nothing about his leg and pedalled for five miles in absolute agony until we reached the river. There, Captain Hong arranged for us to travel on a boat owned by a distant relative. Can you believe that it was bliss to lie on a cargo of hemp on a slow-moving boat for two weeks, even in the rain, with rice and vegetables for every meal? We were finally able to wash our underclothes, in the river. I even made an attempt to clean the lice from my cropped hair. I didn't entirely succeed.'

'None of us did,' said Alex, back from his thoughts. 'But those eleven days, plus regular applications of ointment offered by our host, did my leg a power of good. When he reached his destination and said goodbye to us, he gave Sarah the pot of ointment. He spoke no English, but it was very clear he wished us well. He drew a map in the dust with a stick so that we should know where to go next.'

'We set off on our bicycles once more over a terrible track of earth and large stepping stones. Quite unsuitable for anything save mules, I imagine,' Sarah explained. 'It turned bitterly cold and we had to stop frequently to rest. How we longed to be back on the boat!'

'It was then Sarah's turn to succumb,' said Alex. 'Although we did our best to find shelter for the night, we often ended up sleeping in ditches. There was a severe frost on one of those nights. We all felt like death in the morning, but it was soon clear Sarah was very ill. Lady Luck must have been travelling with us, because a mile or so ahead we came across a French Catholic Mission.' Alex made a wry face. 'I'd always thought missionaries religious crackpots. I've changed my opinion. The nuns were wonderful. We were given beds, hot meals, and that most precious commodity, *soap*.'

'I remember very little about the first few days, Ellie. I was

307

so cold it affected my brain. Alex said neither he nor Jim could get any sense into or from me.'

'I knew enough French to converse in basic terms with the nuns. They reckoned Sarah's blood temperature had dropped so drastically she might never regain her full senses. That cheered Jim and me a lot, as you may imagine, but their constant care, plus medicines from their tiny dispensary, brought recovery within the week.' He smiled at Sarah. 'I was so thankful I almost promised to become a monk.'

'No monastery would have you,' she murmured affectionately.

Alex looked back at the elderly woman sitting listening to their adventure without turning a hair. 'The nuns offered us some clothes they had collected for the poor. Warm clothes. When we left the mission they gave us money to buy food in the villages we passed . . .'

'. . . and they sent a lovely little Chinese man to escort us back to the river where the towpath made cycling easy,' finished Sarah. 'It was from him we learned the meaning of the two phrases the boatman had repeatedly quoted when we settled for the night. We grew to know and repeat them, without understanding the Chinese words. We've adopted them as our own, haven't we, Alex?'

He nodded. 'I lived in Hong Kong for four years, Ellie, and learned nothing about the people, their language or their customs. I was supremely self-indulgent and blind. Sarah repeatedly told me so. In the four months from Christmas, I discovered more of Chinese life and personalities than I ever expected to know.'

'You're not alone,' said Sarah swiftly. 'I was a pot calling a kettle black.'

'You worked at the Halburton and gave piano lessons to Chinese children,' he pointed out.

'Only because I chose not to live the way Olivia planned. The piano lessons satisfied my obsession with music; the job at the Halburton was taken on as an act of conscience.'

'And continued for another reason.'

There was that evidence of undeniable jealousy he voiced every so often. Did he still believe she and Rod had been lovers?

'It continued because I truly felt I was being of some use to the community,' she said firmly. 'But I knew little about the real Hong Kong. I suppose I never will.'

'Neither one of you plans to go back, despite your new understanding of the Chinese?'

Ellie's question threw them both. They had forgotten her presence. Sarah answered before Alex.

'There's nothing for me in Hong Kong.'

Alex took his time, before saying thoughtfully, 'If I make it through the war, I'll have a crack at commercial flying. If it comes off, I may find myself touching down in Kai Tak one day. I'll be interested to see how the colony has changed – which it must – but glad to leave. I probably treated Hong Kong as badly as it treated me.'

A smile broke on Ellie's face as she looked from one to the other. 'It seems to me that your dreadful experiences produced an element of benefit to you both ... or perhaps this soul-baring is a result of the wine and the firelight.' She got to her feet. 'I'm rather tired. Forgive me if I leave you to lock up and settle the dogs for the night. Perhaps you'll tell me the rest of your story in the morning. I think you've relived enough for one evening. God bless you both.'

She kissed each on the cheek, then went out closing the door with its velvet draught curtain. Alex threw another log and a handful of fir cones on the fire, before going to sit on the floor by Sarah's feet.

'She was just being tactful,' she murmured, dropping a hand on his shoulder.

'I thought as much.' He angled his head to smile up at her. 'Her turn-of-the-century code allows two people in love to stay downstairs fully dressed while she sleeps. Are we on our honour not to remove our clothes?'

She made no answer. Were they in love, or merely bound by shared experiences? The rest of the story was relatively uneventful until they reached India. Dressed more warmly and with money enough to buy fruit to sustain them between humble meals in villages, they had covered the remaining distance to Chungking without spotting a single Japanese. The three bicycles had eventually been exchanged for a ticket on a train heading north. At the terminus, they had presented themselves as allies at a Nationalist Army camp only to languish for almost a week, because the senior officer had gone on leave and no one would take on the responsibility of three Britons dressed as Chinese. On the point of striking out on their own, the man had returned and immediately arranged for them to be driven to the next large town, armed with a pass which would allow them to join a convoy of recruits going to Chungking.

They had arrived at the British Embassy four months to the day after setting out on the raft. The Ambassador and his staff had welcomed them warmly and offered food, hot baths and bedrooms for the night. Alone in a room hung with brocade and lit with elegant crystal, panic had overtaken Sarah. She could not possibly stay in such a place. Seeking Alex, she had found Jim already with him. They had all slept on the floor wrapped in blankets. The following morning had brought an interview with the Military Attaché, who questioned them for most of the day about the eighteen-day battle for Hong Kong. He then arranged seats on an aircraft flying to Calcutta the following afternoon.

On arrival in India, they had all been admitted to a military hospital. The two men had had their wounds treated by doctors with enough drugs and expertise to counteract the damage inflicted by the last four months. Sarah had been installed in a room on the other side of the hospital, cut off from the men. That night she had had a breakdown. The return to normal life proved too much to face. Without Alex she was lost.

During the journey to Chungking, the first section of which had also been shared with two sailors, she had lost all semblance of modesty and feminine grace. She had grown dirty and odorous, like her companions. Her cropped hair had been alive with lice which also invaded her body. Privacy had been unattainable. The Chinese countryside had been their toilet. On the hemp boat it had been the river. The humiliation of trying to cope each month in such conditions with the most private event had swept away the last of her pride. She had become a basic creature struggling to survive; a creature dependent on the others. Take them away, and she was nothing.

Jim was quickly flown home to his wife and children on extended sick leave, but nurses brought Alex to Sarah each morning and evening. All she did was weep and cling to him. It was the only comfort she could gain during those terrible weeks. Alex was discharged, but came every day to see her. Eventually, the psychiatrist realized he would get nowhere unless the companion of her ordeal were present during his sessions. Although the doctor sensed there was some deeper trauma, he nevertheless gradually restored Sarah's self-respect and female identity with the help of a man who clearly loved her.

A nurse took her shopping for some pretty clothes, then to a hairdresser who shaped her short blonde hair into a gamine style immensely attractive around her fine features. She and Alex were invited to a hospital party that evening. Although quiet, she had retained her composure well enough to be told she could be discharged the next day.

They were invited to stay with the family of an Indian Army colonel presently in Burma. Sarah withstood the test well. The wife and daughters clearly knew her history, but were very sweet and understanding. The elder girl fell for Alex in a hearty adolescent fashion. Her persistent demands of Sarah to recount details of their adventure, in which Alex figured as some kind of hero, helped exorcise the remaining echoes of degradation.

Each night Alex tapped on their connecting wall the message he had taught her in morse in hospital: *Goodnight, and may your morning rice bowl be full.* She would tap back: *Sleep well until the moon is covered by the sun.* That contact had comforted her until the fourth evening. Their hosts were attending a military ball, so they were alone in the house. They had dined early for the family's convenience and the evening stretched before Alex and Sarah.

What an evening it was! The moon was huge and breathtakingly translucent. The air was heavy and still, as it had often been in Hong Kong. As they had sat together on the veranda running around the first floor, the sound of monsoon water rushing through a nearby nullah provided the final element to transport Sarah, in spirit, to Echoes. She was suddenly full of the aching unhappiness she had known in that house, on that island. Why had she walked away that day on Stanley Beach? Was he dead or alive? Was he in a prison camp? Would she ever stop caring?

Tears had rolled down her cheeks, and Alex had been there beside her. The comforting embrace had heralded a long kiss which somehow answered the cry within her. A spark flared. Fanned by Alex's gentle expertise, it had become a flame. Giving herself to Alex continued her cure. His tenderness had gradually enabled Sarah to regain her natural assurance. Alex had seen her throughout those animal months; he now saw someone entirely different. He therefore became the most important person in her life from that night onward.

That situation might well have remained, but for the day that he confessed that he had believed her wish to leave Hong Kong on the *San Maritino* had been due to the discovery that she was pregnant by Rod Durman. Only then had she realized that her nights with Alex were prompted by desperation. Had Rod turned to his wife for the same reason one night, with fatal result? Passion was relative. It was not necessarily ruled by love. She had continued to sleep with Alex whenever she needed to, but their relationship changed once more. As she slowly withdrew, he followed. He had asked her to marry him as soon as they got to England. Almost certain his feeling for her was based on mutual dependence, like hers for him, she had said he must wait six months before pursuing the subject. Anything could happen in six months. They both knew that only too well.

Sarah came from her reverie to find a pillow beneath her head and the eiderdown from Alex's bed tucked around her. The fire was little more than ash. Sasha and Vlad had gone, and Alex was sound asleep rolled in a blanket on the floor. She must have succumbed to the power of the wine and drifted into sleep. For a long moment she fought the impulse to lie alongside Alex, wrapped in the eiderdown. All that was behind them. A new phase of their lives had begun. Getting to her feet, she covered him with the eiderdown then crept upstairs to the room with pansy-patterned wallpaper. Once in bed, however, she wished she had given in to impulse. It bothered her that he was alone down there. He would be joining up soon. How would she bear his absence? He was the only person who knew about that other life. The new, unknown one filled her with apprehension.

December 8. A year ago Japanese aircraft had swooped on Kowloon in a bloody declaration of war. At Kingsmill, the day began as peacefully as every other. As soon as it grew light, Sarah took the dogs for a walk across fields stiff with frost and bordered by bare trees standing like sentinels. It *smelled* cold. Her nostrils stuck together when she inhaled; the chill vaporized her breath as she breathed out. It could be like that in China. A silvery-grey haze over bare land where nobody moved, even in the far distance. She was clad in woollen skirt and jumper, a thick red overcoat with its own hood, and high boots. Very different from a rough, mud-covered seaman's uniform and lace-up boots that rubbed feet until they bled because they were too large.

Smoke was curling from chimneys down by the village. Sarah kept well clear of that area. Nobody had said anything to her face, but their expressions and sudden silences when she appeared told her what they thought. It was well known – probably in much exaggerated form – that she had escaped by trekking across China, but people were performing all manner of amazing feats all over the wartorn world and she *had* been at Noon Cottage for over two months now. Was it not time that the Channing girl pulled her weight for the war effort? After all, she only went to Hong Kong to avoid being called up and had a year or so of easy living out there before it fell. Mooning around the countryside and being fussed over by her doting grandmother helped no one. Let her join the ATS or work in a factory. Better still, help out on one of the farms. With the Min. of Ag. urging greater productivity from the land, every pair of hands was welcome.

Sarah felt guilty. They were right, and she had given her opinion freely and often in Hong Kong of those who self-indulgently frittered the time away. She had come to eat many of her words. It was not that she was shirking her plain duty. Without Alex she was disorientated. Decisions evaded her. The war ministry had not yet caught up with

313

the fact that she was back in England. Despite the issue of a ration book and clothing coupons, no registration papers had been sent. She truly wanted to volunteer her services before that happened, but the days slipped past while she remained undecided. After Christmas she would act. The festival was looming darkly with its strange, tragic memories. Once she had got through that, her resolution would be stronger.

Ellie was busy with illustrations for a new book, so Sarah was cooking their meals and helping to clean the house. She was not very good at either yet, and did not enjoy any of it. Her piano stood untouched. The practice recordings and sheet music were irretrievably lost. Echoes had probably been overrun by Japanese troops, or Chinese looters. All her clothes and most precious possessions had been left behind. Sarah Channing, winner of competitions and scholarships, girl with a brilliant concert career ahead, no longer existed. Only because she had cared about little else but her music had she succeeded. Now, her emotions were tangled around so many people and incidents, the passion which had been so concentrated was diffused. Never again could she pour pain, ecstasy, fire and sensitivity into melody after experiencing them in reality. Jakob Myburgh had told her that only by making music the single love in her life would she be a true mistress of her art. At the moment she cared more about the old maestro's fate than his advice.

On this anniversary of the first raid on Hong Kong, Sarah returned to Noon Cottage with the two borzois, her thoughts on that colony. At the gate she met Ned Parsons, out of breath after cycling up the hill to deliver the post. He had been doing the job for fifty years. At seventy-two, his 'puff' was not what it used to be, he told her. He had known Sarah since she used to come to the gate as a child and tell him that she had had an amah and 'hundreds of servants' in Hong Kong. Later, she would shyly confess her successes in piano competitions in answer to his queries about her trips to London. He had never visited London – had no wish to – but was eager to know what it was like there. Ned was one person whose manner towards Sarah had not changed. All human drama could be observed in village life. Ned was wiser than most.

'Quite a lot for Noon Cottage today, Miss Channing,' he said between pants. 'There's one from Mrs Fairlie's publisher, several from book stores and a big thick envelope come from America. Looks a bit knocked about, that one does.' He paused to steady his breathing, then took several more letters from the bag over his shoulder. 'This un's from London. Official. Addressed to you, miss. One from just outside Gloucester. That'd be from the corporal what escaped across China with you.' He leaned on the handlebars with the letters in his hand. 'Now, there's a country I've never had an urge to visit. All them chopsticks and temples. As for what they call music! Turn me stomach, it would.'

'Care to come in for a cup of tea?' asked Sarah, knowing he would stand talking until he was offered one.

'Well, I'll be going back soon for me breakfast, but a cuppa would go down nicely after that hill, miss. I'm not as young as I was.'

Not until three-quarters of an hour later did Sarah and Ellie sit to eat their breakfast and read the mail Ned had eventually handed over. Sarah opened first the one from Jim. He was now a sergeant and had received a commendation for his successful escape with valuable information concerning the failed defence of Hong Kong. His wife was expecting, and he had found her and the children a small cottage near the airfield away from the bombs in London. He hoped she would visit them soon with Mr Tennant. Curious how, throughout their levelling experiences, he had maintained formality with herself and Alex although they both addressed him by his first name.

'Pass the honey, dear,' said Ellie, busy with her own letters. 'Gracious, how absurd! Jason Winters feels that to have Bertram Badger holding a party for his birthday, with some cream cakes, jellies and sausages and lots and lots of jam sandwiches, is setting a bad example to children in these days of rationing and cutting down. Could we alter that chapter and have, instead, Bertram and his chums collecting salvage from the residents of Woody Rise? What balderdash! Children need to escape reality as much as we. Might as well say fairies will have to be replaced by Spitfires. I shall phone Violet after breakfast. She'll have received a copy of this and be as incensed as I. A bad example, indeed! I've not yet come across a child who doesn't revel in the idea of a party with lots and lots of jam sandwiches. We shall make a stand. Yes, indeed we shall!'

'Good for you,' laughed Sarah. 'Jason Winters sounds, from all you've told me of him, very much like a stuffed shirt. Wasn't he ever a child?'

'I doubt it,' said Ellie tartly. 'That man was born an adult. Pass the honey, dear.'

'Sorry.' She did so. 'I was trying to decide whether to read this one in the brown envelope next or leave it until last. I suspect it's a command to report for assessment for war work.'

'Then open it. No point in putting off the inevitable,' said Ellie firmly. 'You complain of being unable to make a decision. Rejoice! They've made it for you.'

Sarah gave her a rueful glance. 'I wish I possessed your philosophy.'

'You're a romantic, my dear. An artist. No, don't look like that. You will lose your insecurity and rediscover your muse.'

'You're also an artist,' Sarah pointed out.

'Only by design ... and the need to earn a living. You were born with a gift that will remain for life. Read your letter! If they want to send you down a coal mine, you'll soon remember why you must protect your hands.'

Her grandmother opened her next letter to read while spreading honey on brown bread and butter, and Sarah watched in dismay. Ellie had lost patience with her! The sense of guilt doubled. She was not only dodging her plain duty, she was letting down someone who had taught her to be resolute. Jim was back on duty – had been for several months – and Alex had fulfilled his vow to join the RAF. She was letting them down, too.

The brown envelope tore beneath the force of her hands, the pages inside suffering similarly. This was no official form but a letter written by hand. Before she could begin to read it, the telephone rang.

'That'll be Violet calling about the publisher's letter. Tell her I'm in the middle of breakfast and will ring back when

316

I'm finished,' Ellie told Sarah as she left the table. 'She's a charming woman, but she *insists* on telephoning at meal-times and talking until everything on the table has grown cold.'

It was Alex. 'Hallo, darling. Haven't dragged you out of bed, have I?'

'It's more often the reverse,' she teased, so glad to hear his voice. The sun seemed to have come out. 'It's rather early to ring, isn't it? I thought you had lectures and so on pretty well non-stop all day.'

'So we do. I'm playing truant. It's December 8 and I wanted to know how you are.'

'Bless you, Alex!' She told him how she had taken the dogs for a walk and thought the scene was very like China. 'I can hardly believe a year has passed from that day I watched aircraft dropping bombs on Kowloon. It was such a shock.'

'Even more so from where I stood. Listen, sweetheart, I rang for another reason, too. After Ellie ticked me off for not writing to my mama, I put pen to paper . . . with reluctance, I'm afraid. I had a reply this morning. Made me feel a bit rotten. I suppose it didn't occur to me that she'd be sending letters to Calcutta thinking I was still there. She was upset because I hadn't been to see her.'

'It's natural, Alex.'

'She bally well knows why. I was told never to darken the door again.'

'You could have arranged to meet in a hotel.'

'So I did . . . in my letter. The reply was from my father, couched in suspiciously conciliatory terms, suggesting the return of the prodigal. I'm invited to spend Christmas at home. I've never thought of it as *home* in my life! Here's the most curious part of all. He wants me to bring you and Ellie.' His sigh was audible through the receiver. 'There was a lot of balderdash about thanking the people who had thrown open their doors to me at what must have been a difficult time, considering the memories this country contains.' He sighed again. 'Oh Lord, darling, I was counting on being with you at Noon Cottage for Christmas, but I can't decline his invitation on the grounds that we want to be together, can I?'

Sarah was disappointed. 'I'd say he's left you no leg to stand on. You'll have to accept his olive branch.'

'It's no olive branch.' He sounded bitter. 'There's an ulterior motive behind this. Although I wrote to my mother, *he* replied. Seems to me their marriage is no better than when I left the house. She's a doormat – a very sweet one, but a doormat nevertheless.'

'Write and say you can't get Christmas leave,' she suggested.

'No use. Mother already knows I can.'

'Write that it's been cancelled.'

A third heavy sigh. 'He won't give up. I know Maurice Tennant. Could you and Ellie possibly *bear* to come to Sheffield with me for a couple of days, then we could all return to Noon Cottage for New Year before I join my squadron? I've bought a car – rather a zippy machine. If you could get to Birmingham by train, I'd pick you up and drive you the rest of the way. What d'you say, Sarah?' To aid her decision, he added softly, 'My people don't have turn-of-the-century attitudes like Ellie.'

She smiled. 'That won't make any difference if you persist in sleeping on the floor rolled in blankets.'

'I've lost that habit,' he said. 'Doing this training course has driven many of those inhibitions away, thank God. Darling, help me out over this Christmas business.'

'We'll come to Sheffield.'

'You're an angel.'

'How many others have you said that to?'

There was a slight pause. 'I was hoping to sort things out between us at Christmas.'

'The six months aren't up until March, Alex. Let's wait. How well are you doing on the course?'

He accepted her change of subject, and they chatted for a further ten minutes about the training programme he was following in order to be commissioned as a pilot on December 22. Alex eventually noticed the time and said he must change into flying-gear in readiness for a practice flight at nine-thirty.

'Can't miss *that*, darling. Must dash. Love you. Goodbye. May your morning rice bowl be full.'

'Goodbye, Alex. May you sleep well until the sun covers the moon.'

'Fat chance of that on a day like today. Cheers! Love to Ellie.'

Sarah returned to the breakfast table lighter hearted, but full of speculation on the visit to Alex's family in Sheffield. It was unlikely to be enjoyable, but he would be out of an awkward situation. She thought lions had the best arrangement. After doing their part in the creative process, the males went off having nothing further to do with their offspring. Fathers were best kept at a distance.

Ellie looked up from a multi-paged letter, her breakfast forgotten. 'How very extraordinary this is! I can scarcely take it in.'

'What, darling?'

'A woman has written to me from America. The letter has come via our embassy in Washington and goodness knows how many official departments. She sends me her condolences on your death by drowning at Stanley last Christmas Day.'

Sarah sat down quickly, her skin rising in lumps. *My death by drowning?* Who is this woman?'

Ellie glanced again at the letter. 'Mrs Roma Dillburger.'

'Oh ... *Roma!* She did get away with the Americans!' Sarah could hardly speak. 'What does she say? How long has she been free? Is her husband with her?'

Ellie passed her the letter. 'Read for yourself. Perhaps you'll then explain it all to me.'

Sarah read the first paragraph in which Roma wrote that she had done her darnedest to trace the grandmother Sarah had once mentioned, having as her only clues the fact that she wrote books for children under the name Eleanor Fairlie, and that she lived in a house called The Cotswolds. Her husband finally asked a senator friend to contact the British Embassy. Someone there promised to forward a letter by diplomatic bag to London because of the valuable information it contained regarding someone caught in Hong Kong. She hoped it would reach Mrs Fairlie eventually.

Roma then wrote of how she and her husband, along with other Americans exchanged for Japanese internees,

319

had been able to supply many names of fellow prisoners thus providing the British with information the Hong Kong Red Cross could not obtain. She told, in vivid prose, of those final days at the Halburton and the making of the raft.

> A young lieutenant named Alex, whom your grand-daughter knew well, persuaded her to go with him and a little air force corporal on this frail affair [she wrote]. But don't think Sarah was in any way forced. She seemed happy to stay with him. We were all so upset when the wreckage was washed up several days later. Please accept my condolences on your loss, dear lady. Sarah was a very special person. You can be proud of her courage in those dark, terrible days. Your only consolation is that she is not suffering deprivation and near-starvation in Stanley Camp, as her friends must until Hong Kong is freed. By then, it will be too late for many of them. If you'd care to write to me about Sarah, if that will help, then please do so. Meanwhile, I have sent off a food parcel for you. I hope this won't cause offence, but we have so much over here and you have so little. Having known hunger, this is the least I can do for someone Sarah loved very much.

Lowering the letter to her lap, Sarah sat overwhelmed by emotional memories. That it should come on a day so significant seemed to make this message all the more moving. If Roma, Chloë and Marion believed her dead, then so must others in Hong Kong. Unnerving though it was to read condolences on her death, she felt choked with warmth for the generous gesture of a woman she had known for only eighteen days. Here was an address, a means of contact, a way of learning news of what happened after they had all parted at the mouth of that cave. Here, in her hand, was the other life reaching out to claim her back just as she was struggling to start anew.

'What does it all mean, dear?'

Sarah glanced up, still seeing the strained expressions of those three women remaining to face an uncertain fate. 'It means the sort of friendship I've never dreamed possible. Ellie, you've no idea what it was like during those last days; how people showed the most surprising resources. She –

Roma – was outspoken, worldly and always decked in osten-
tatious jewellery. You'd . . . you'd never imagine she would
do something like this, would you?'

Ellie regarded her with shrewd fondness. 'I might, dear,
from my greater experience of life. You are still getting there
where judgement of human nature is concerned.'

Sarah got up and walked across to the window to gaze at
the garden silvered by frost. Her grandmother's words had
touched that still sensitive Achilles heel to bring the tears
that had been threatening since first waking. The rimed
shrubs and lawn shimmered before her eyes as she fought
surrender to emotion. It was quiet save the ticking of the
clock in that room of polished walnut and chintz, and Sarah
was twelve thousand miles away on a sandy beach.

She returned abruptly when a cold, wet nose pushed into
her hand, and a warm tongue ran over her palm in canine
consolation. She caressed Vlad's ears in appreciation of the
dog's instinctive desire to make amends for an imagined
misdemeanour, brushing the tears from her lashes with the
other hand.

'I think we could do with a fresh pot of tea,' said Ellie
from the table. 'I'll make it while you finally read that letter
calling you to work in the coal mines. Come, Sasha! Stop
drooling all over the carpet. There's no more bread and
butter for you this morning.'

Sarah returned to her chair and picked up the page she
had been prevented from reading by Alex's phone call. It
had nothing to do with war work.

Dear Miss Channing,
    I am very pleased to be able, at last, to give you
some news concerning your father, which has been
sent to us from Chungking. On September 27, Sir Peter
was alive and recovering from beri-beri in the hospital
of Shamshuipo prisoner-of-war camp. It appears that
he was captured during the battle for Wong Nei Chong
Gap, and classed as a combatant. Hence his placement
in a military camp rather than with civilian internees.
    This information was given to the embassy in
Chungking by a doctor who treated Sir Peter there,
just before being transported with several thousand

prisoners for forced labour in Japan. His ship, the *Lisbon Maru*, was sunk with considerable loss of life off the China Coast. Four men evaded ture to make their way to safety with much valuable information regarding those still in Hong Kong.

Our informant, Dr Roderick James Durman, was deeply shaken by the news of your earlier passage through Chungking. It is generally believed that you drowned whilst attempting to escape, and he conveyed this to Sir Peter. We shall attempt to acquaint your father with the truth as soon as we are able.

As Dr Durman is a family friend, you will doubtless be pleased to know that he was flown to a hospital in Perth unscathed and in reasonably good spirits after his ordeal.

Sarah could not read the signature because the letter was shaking in her hands. Uncontrollable sobbing overcame her until she slowly slid from the chair to double up on the floor, rocking back and forth with the force of her emotion.

Chapter Thirteen

Alex parked his car in the forecourt of the inn, giving its yellow chassis a pat of pride as he got out, threw his greatcoat on the back seat and headed for the ivy-covered entrance. Ellie had declined the invitation to Sheffield, making the dogs her excuse. Alex guessed she felt the two-day visit would be better made by just himself and Sarah. They planned to drive down to Kingsmill on the twenty-seventh anyway, so he would see the woman of whom he had become so fond she might almost be his own grand-mother. He had arranged to pick Sarah up on the outskirts of Worcester, where the bus terminated its route at a famous 200-year-old inn.

As he crossed the forecourt he glanced down at the wings recently added to his jacket. He was proud of them, although the type of flying he had been doing was nothing like the unbridled, rather risky sessions in *Dragonfly*. Nor was the RAF reminiscent of the Volunteers. He was now bound by service law made even stricter by the rules of war. His companions were not civilians who donned a uniform twice weekly; men who could not take rank seriously because they were business friends. Each one on the course with him was fully committed to flying, each did as he was asked without question and was aware that discipline was the backbone of efficiency. It had taken Alex a while to adapt, but he had been aided in this by the fact that everyone accepted him as a man of worth and experience. The playboy tag had finally been lost.

Elation at gaining his wings, and at the thought of seeing

Sarah, vied with dread of meeting his father after nine years. How daunting to acknowledge that, in this year of 1942, after all he had suffered, he could still be so strangely affected by memories of those boyhood beatings and humiliations. Surely he should have greater strength of character. He could not possibly confess his fears to Sarah, but he never would have agreed to the visit if she had refused to accompany him.

His thoughts were all on her as he walked into the faded foyer panelled in dark oak, adorned with mounted heads of game bagged by a long-ago royal patron. Alex looked away swiftly. Severed heads had horrific connotations after those eighteen days in Hong Kong. It would be easy to see not horned animals, but men he had known nailed up around those walls. Sarah was waiting in an inglenook beside a log fire, and horror fled as she looked across and smiled.

Drawing her to her feet and into his arms, he kissed her with more than usual passion in public. Couples met and parted so much these days, open displays of emotion had become acceptable. 'God, how I've missed you,' he said, gazing deeply into those clear green eyes. 'Let's book a room here and spend Christmas making up for the weeks we've been apart.'

She ignored his words, but he was more than halfway serious about the proposal. 'How splendid your wings look, Alex. Many congrats on doing so well on the course.'

'You've finally had your way and got me in the RAF to fly in defence of my country.'

His lighthearted comment upset her. 'Don't throw that in my face. I must have been an awful prig in those days.'

He squeezed her, enjoying the warmth of her body against him. 'We were all a bit precious, sweetheart. We believed the world was ours for the taking, never guessing the Japs had the same idea. Let's not talk about Hong Kong.' He led her towards the bar. 'We'll have a drink while we order lunch, then you can bring me up to date with all the news of Kingsmill. How's my adorable Ellie?'

'Looking forward to your visit. She dotes on you.'

'But not her granddaughter?'

'I'm sure you have enough pretty WAAFs goggling at you to satisfy your terrible vanity, without my adoration.'

It was said lightly but he was disturbed. There was a subtle difference in her that he could not identify. While she told him of the small day-to-day events in and around her home as they drank gins and tonic, he studied her, trying to calm the sensation of faint alarm she was instilling.

Her classic beauty, so out of fashion, was even more pronounced in a pale-blue sweater of soft angora and a slim skirt in the same shade. The short gamine hairstyle cut by an enthusiastic Frenchman in Calcutta could not be copied by the middle-aged woman in Cheltenham so Sarah's fine hair had been allowed to grow freely. Not yet back to shoulder length, the straight golden fall was held from her face by a band of blue ribbon. Having left her few pieces of good jewellery at Echoes – they were possibly adorning a Chinese courtesan by now – she wore a fine silver chain, and the filigree bracelet he had given her in Calcutta on her twenty-first birthday. Across the neighbouring bar stool lay a smart black coat with a broad fur collar, and a black leather shoulder bag. On the floor beside them stood an expensive suitcase with the initials S.R.C. engraved in gold.

For a moment Alex wished for the spike-haired girl in a seaman's torn and grubby uniform, then changed the image to that of someone with a short crop of hair who had needed him so much one night she proved, beyond doubt, that no man before him had been her lover. It was then he recognized the difference in her. Dependence on him was no longer as strong: Sarah had retreated a little.

He asked impulsively, 'Was your morning rice bowl full?'

Her smile was so intimate it should have dispelled his apprehension. 'Very full. How about yours?'

'Not full enough. I'm ready for lunch. Let's go and find our table.'

Taking her suitcase and coat to the cloakroom, he tipped the elderly attendant and left his cap and gloves there, too. Then he took Sarah's arm to walk to the dining room already half full. With Christmas two days away, some people were eating out to save using precious food supplies ready for the festival. Others were meeting up with friends and relatives, but most of the diners were servicemen and women en route for their Christmas leave destinations. Eyes were drawn in their direction as they walked to a table by the window. He knew they were a striking couple, but was more interested in the appreciation of Sarah by the other men than the girls who eyed him. It pleased him to know that he was envied by his fellows. He was surprised to discover that Sarah had been adversely affected by the attention.

'I know how they feel. I still haven't had an official demand to register for war work, but I do mean to take the initiative when your leave ends, Alex,' she said earnestly. 'I'm riddled with guilt.'

'You shouldn't be. You went through more at the Halburton than they've ever suffered. I'll never forget how terrible you looked when we met last Christmas. I hardly believed it was you.'

Sarah took from her handbag a letter to hand him. 'Ellie received this last week. I'm sure you'll be as delighted as I was when you read who sent it.'

He took the envelope and read the contents in amazement, seeing the American woman who had shared her cigarettes with himself and Jim in that cave. He looked up to find Sarah with a faraway look on her face and assumed that she was sharing his vision.

'What a nice gesture! So they believe we drowned. Well, I suppose we would have if we hadn't been in collision with the MTB. Will you write and tell her the good news?'

'I've already done so, and asked about Marion and Chloë.'

'Good. Let me know when you hear. Ah, here's the waiter, at last. I think I'll have the potato soup, rabbit pie and plums and custard. What about you?'

They chose their meal, then Alex told her about the car he had bought with another man on the course. 'Neither of us could afford a jalopy of our own, so she's owned by both of us. It was fine over these past weeks, but we're pretty certain to be posted to different squadrons at the end of our leave and there lies the rub. Whoever first saves enough to buy the other half keeps her.'

Sarah looked surprised. 'I thought your mother's family has been financing you rather well since you wrote to her from Calcutta.'

He concentrated on the arrival of his soup. 'I've decided to survive on what the RAF pays me from now on.'

'I see.'

'Hope you're not expecting a mink coat for Christmas.'

'I'm not the mink coat type.'

'I'd manage a decent ring,' he said persuasively. 'No family heirlooms, I'm afraid, but I've put enough aside for a diamond or two.'

'This soup is quite tasty, despite its depressing colour,' Sarah said with deliberation.

'All right,' he sighed. 'Just thought the excitement of seeing me in a dashing uniform might have done the trick.'

She put the spoon in the bowl and faced him frankly. 'Alex, December has proved a difficult month, one way and another, and Christmas is the wrong time for romance. I can't forget what happened last year.'

'No more can I, darling, but we have to make the most of our freedom. The future is so uncertain, we should live to the full. Why wait until March just to fulfil some silly time limit imposed months ago? We love each other. That's the only important factor.'

To his consternation she seemed almost on the verge of tears as she asked quietly, 'Do we? Isn't it just that we each feel lost without the other?'

Sensing that he had chosen the wrong moment, endangering the harmony between them which he hoped would counterbalance the stress of this visit, he gave a reassuring smile to accompany his lighter approach. 'I've ten days' leave. No fear of feeling lost until January 3. Let's enjoy each other until then.'

They had started the main course of their meal, when Alex said, 'Don't mention my half-share of the car to my people. Father will immediately buy the other half for me. Or, worse still, tell me to give Ermintrude to my friend, then buy me some sleek limousine worthy of Maurice Tennant's son.'

Sarah had regained her composure, he was glad to see. 'You haven't told me much about your parents. Whenever I've brought up the subject, you've switched off. You'd better brief me.' She smiled. 'Isn't that what you dashing RAF types do before an operation?'

He restrained the urge to reach across and kiss her, but it remained as he gazed at the most striking girl in the room listening to his description of two people he would like never to see again.

'Mother is pale and fragile with absolutely no will of her own – quite your opposite, darling. She thrives on luxury. The de Bouchers have French blood from way back. Before the war one branch was living in a château owned by the family since before the Revolution, and restored to them when hatred of the aristos lessened somewhat. There's always been wealth and breeding on Mother's side. On Father's there's neither. Brought up in an orphanage, he has enough willpower for Mother and anyone else weak enough to be trodden on by his handsewn leather boots. One would be forced to admire his drive and ability if he were not so much of a bastard.'

'*Alex!*'

'I don't use the word lightly,' he told her with bitterness. 'In that one man is combined all the worst human traits. Greed, disloyalty, cruelty, swagger, selfishness . . .'

'Alex, stop!' she begged. 'I know you quarrelled years ago and he threw you out, but I had no idea you nursed such hatred for him. You make him out a monster.'

'So he is,' Alex vowed, remembering those boyhood thrashings.

'Perhaps he's mellowed over the years, or maybe you saw him through resentful eyes.'

'No, Sarah. Ask any one of a number of people who have encountered Maurice Tennant, and they'll say the same. He's made his fortune by ruining others.' He threw down his knife and fork. 'Oh hell, let's go off to a cosy little place in the country for Christmas instead. I'd no right to ask you to accept the invitation of a man like him.'

The waiter took Alex's gesture to mean that he had had enough of the rabbit pie, and brought stewed plums floating in canary-coloured custard.

When he departed, Sarah put her hand over Alex's. 'I've told no one this, even Ellie, but I think you deserve to know. Some years ago *my* father was involved in a conspiracy to raise the value of shares in a company doomed to collapse. He had –'

'Bolton Rochas,' said Alex quietly.

She was astounded. 'You know about it?'

He nodded. 'I discovered a lead quite by accident, then followed it up out of pure malice.'

'Whyever didn't you make it public?'

'Search me. Perhaps I hesitated to make anyone suffer as I had when my father was reviled . . . and perhaps I was a little in love with you even then. In any case, it was merely one scandal amongst many out there. Fortunes are rarely honestly made, sweetheart. Big business is a cut-throat affair. Those who indulge in it have to be pretty cold and ruthless. Sir Peter struck me as very much that type. Poor little Sarah!'

'He's alive,' she said, as if on impulse. 'I heard last week.'

'Good God! You've been a long time telling me.'

'I . . . we were speaking of other things.'

Alex had the impression she was evading the truth in some way and waited for her to continue. When she did not, he said, 'I'm glad you know, one way or the other. Have they finally had lists from the Japs?'

'No.'

'So how did they find out?'

She looked almost desperate as she faced him across their untouched plums and custard. 'Rod arrived in Chungking as one of four survivors from a prisoner-of-war ship sunk off the coast. He had treated father in Shamshuipo camp at the end of September, so the authorities assume he is still alive.'

'And Durman?' asked Alex, fighting a jealousy that put the final nail in the coffin of this Christmas trip.

'Flown to hospital in Perth.'

'What about his tart of a wife?'

Colour drained from her cheeks. 'Need you be so beastly?'

'Yes, I think so,' he snapped. 'Everything was all right until *he* came back on the scene.'

'He's *not* back on the scene,' she cried. 'He's on the other side of the world . . . and I've no idea where his wife is now. She may be suffering all manner of deprivations, so he's probably out of his mind with worry. She was pregnant.'

Wanting to lash out, Alex pushed away the congealing pudding, saying, 'It's only a five-to-one chance it's his. Giles was at a party where they all embarked on a sexual merry-go-round. Celeste was as free with her body as her husband is.'

Sarah got to her feet so suddenly, the chair tipped backwards. 'Goodbye, Alex.'

She was halfway from the room by the time he leapt up, threw a handful of notes on the tablecloth, and went after her, dismayed by his own stupidity. He had to remain silent while she asked the cloakroom attendant what time the bus returned to Cheltenham, then he helped her into her coat before grabbing the suitcase when she made to pick it up. She would hardly leave without it, he reasoned. The coldness hit them as they left the hotel. He took her arm to halt her.

'You can't stand out here for half an hour, Sarah.'

'Shouldn't you be setting out for Sheffield? Your ghastly parents are expecting you in time for dinner,' she said tonelessly.

Curiously, her attack raised a faint smile. 'My ghastly parents are expecting us *both*,' he pointed out gently. 'Forgive me, darling.'

Her eyes were stony as she looked fully at him. 'What you said was *un*forgivable.'

'Not about her. Giles wouldn't lie about something like that.' Without waiting for a further comment, he added persuasively, 'Come and sit in Ermintrude while we thrash this out. If you still want to go back, I'll drive you to Kingsmill and book a room for myself at the Dog and Duck. I can't face Christmas up there on my own.'

She allowed him to lead her to the yellow car and settle her in the front passenger seat, but she was still visibly upset. Damn Durman! He *would* have to surface now, when last Christmas haunted them and he, himself, was on edge over this one. The last piece of the puzzle had finally been provided. It was the wife's pregnancy, not Sarah's, that had brought the affair to an end. Or had it? Her behaviour suggested otherwise. That man still had the power to affect her deeply. Was he going to come between them from the other side of the world?

After slipping on his greatcoat, Alex squeezed into the driving seat and turned to the girl who sat in unapproachable immobility. 'I'm jealous,' he admitted, deciding to tackle the subject head on. 'Where he's concerned I think I always have been. I first saw him as a fortune-hunter, then, when he turned up with the flashy wife, I decided they must be two of a kind. Doctors are often idolized by female patients, and you had certainly cast him as some kind of hero, you can't deny.'

He waited for her to speak, but she remained silent and stony-faced. He sighed. 'Darling, you maintained that he played the gentleman at all times, that he was not the philandering type. I'm entitled to my own opinion of him as someone better able to judge men than you. However, I accept that I'm not entitled to air that opinion, particularly when the chap can't defend himself. But now you've revealed that his wife was pregnant, I'm afraid I condemn him further for playing on your feelings. The unborn child was the cause of the break between you, then?'

She nodded.

'Poor little Sarah.'

There was silence for a moment or two, then she asked, 'Why didn't you mention that abominable party before this?'

'Would it have made any difference?'

'Oh, yes. A great deal.'

He had to ask. 'Are you still beneath his spell?'

'It wasn't like that, Alex,' she said, gazing straight ahead. 'You wouldn't understand.'

'Oh, God. Don't give me that old line again!' He was angry immediately. 'Haven't we grown close enough by now for you to know I *would*? Haven't we been through too much together not to understand each other probably better than anyone else? If you're going to walk out on me because of him, don't you think I'm entitled to know just what went on in Hong Kong?'

She waited a while before saying, still without facing him, 'Throughout an entire career a pianist will possibly give just one superb performance. There will be just one evening when the artist's perception of sensitivity will find perfect rapport with a composer's genius. The audience will be stunned by the brilliance of it, and they'll know they have never heard the piece so entirely before. Although the pianist will continue to perform the same concerto or prelude to thrill audiences, there will never be perfection again. I don't expect you to understand – I hardly do myself – but that's how it was wherever we met.'

Alex's heart sank. She was telling him he would always be second best. How could a sensitive, lovely creature with Sarah's background have found perfect rapport with a heavy-weight Australian doctor from the Outback, whose taste in women was evident by his choice of wife? He switched on the ignition. 'I'd better get you back to Noon Cottage before you freeze to death.'

'No . . . head for Sheffield,' Sarah said, putting a hand on his arm. 'We promised Marion, Roma and Chloë we'd raise a glass to them every Christmas. Let's do it together, Alex.' When he hesitated, she added, 'You claimed you *would* understand.'

He set off without comment, knowing he did not.

It was dark long before they reached the street in which stood the great solid house that had been Alex's childhood home. He remembered it as formidable, but it loomed like a dark fortress with every window covered by blackout shut-ters to deny any hint of welcoming light. They had made the journey with a certain amount of restraint between them, stopping for tea and toasted buns in a place called The Copper Warming-pan. The fire had eased their chilled limbs, but not the mood that had settled on them. One look at the redbrick mansion named Deedes House had Alex vowing to leave it early on Boxing Day. Forty-eight hours here would be as much as he could take.

'The abode of my ghastly parents,' he announced with as much cheerfulness as he could muster, hoping to lighten the atmosphere before they entered.

'I shouldn't have called them that,' she responded, pulling her collar higher around her throat. 'My father and Olivia could challenge anyone for that epithet.'

He tried his luck. 'Am I allowed a kiss to give me Dutch courage?'

'I thought drink provided that.'

'Your kisses are intoxicating enough to turn me into a Hercules or a Jason.'

Her eyes shone in the darkness of the car. 'You have a very smooth tongue, Alex.'

'You should know,' he murmured, sensing success. 'It's been all over you at one time or another.'

He won his kiss, but success was not total. She drew away sooner than he wished, and he had to be content with a partial breaking of the ice before helping her from the car and up the four stone steps. Frost was already settling on them, making the going slippery, so he circled her with his arm and kept it there as he pulled the metal handle to set the bell clanging in the servants' quarters.

'Oh Lord, I wish we hadn't come,' he said, with the heaviness of inevitability.

Sarah smiled up at him, shivering in the bitter temperature. 'Hercules or Jason, did you say?'

'Right now I feel more like the boy who never reached expected standards.'

'Poor little Alex,' she whispered, using his words.

The door was opened by a man in tails and starched shirtfront, a dim figure before the blackout screen that prevented light from flooding out. Alex did not know him.

'Where's Roberts?' he asked to cover his nervousness.

'Mr Roberts is the Butler, sir. He never answers the doorbell.'

Annoyed by his superior tone, Alex drew Sarah with him into the entrance hall. 'Things have changed since I was last at home. Roberts did everything in those days.'

'Mr Tennant?' The man's attitude changed. 'I beg your pardon, sir. You were expected, of course, but I failed to notice a car in the drive.'

'It's there,' he said tartly, 'but you have to look closely to find it.'

'Mr and Mrs Tennant are in the Green Room, sir. I'll conduct you and Madam there immediately.'

Stepping around the screen, Alex was dazzled by the light from several crystal chandeliers that sparkled as if newly washed. The black and white tiles were now covered by amber carpet so thick that he almost sank into the pile as he walked, and the circular walls bore a number of paintings he recognized as of the Impressionist school. A far cry from the bare vaulted hall where his timorous footsteps had echoed to betray his presence to the harsh parent listening for his arrival.

'May I take your coat, madam? And yours, sir?'

Alex turned to find a youngish man who surely should be in the forces, dressed up like a relic from the Edwardian era. He even wore white gloves. It was ludicrous. Alex grinned at Sarah, saying, 'What was that word you used. Ghastly?'

She turned slightly pink, but her lips twitched with amusement as she walked beside him behind the effigy from another age. When the servant opened elegant double doors – another new addition – a burst of animated conversation escaped into the silent hall. To Alex's dismay the entire population of Sheffield appeared to be congregated inside a room decorated more like a salon in a stately home than the parlour of a factory-owner's house. People were sitting on green velvet chairs and banquettes, standing beside emerald brocade tasselled curtains, leaning against *eau-de-Nil* walls, fidgeting on a cream carpet splashed with pale-green chrysanthemums, or conversing beside the olive marble fireplace. An abundance of gilt embellishments completed the 'Versailles' look. Alex could only remain in the doorway longing for the tasteful comforts of Noon Cottage.

'This is far worse than my deepest fears,' he murmured to Sarah. 'How could I have inflicted this on you?'

Her hand slid into his. 'It'll be warmer and more comfortable than a ditch outside Waichow. Think of it that way.'

'I'll take the ditch,' he said casting her a swift glance. 'We should never have come.'

The Edwardian servant had threaded his way through the guests to find his employer. That he had succeeded was marked by a roar that rose above the din. 'Splendid. Here at last!'

Alex cringed at the sound of that booming voice. He could almost hear it saying, *You haven't the pluck of a toad, lad. A toad. Stop snivelling and take your punishment like a man. By gum, if I'd a pound for every beating I got in the orphanage, I'd be a millionaire. I never snivelled. None of us did. We knew it was justly deserved, and learned how to avoid it. We were better for it. But you! Your ma spoils you, encourages namby-pamby ways. You'll never make your way in the world unless you're smarter and tougher than all the others and, by gum, I'll thrash some pluck into you.*

Maurice Tennant was walking towards them from the chattering crowd, and Alex knew hatred of his father had not died over the nine-year absence. Heavy-set, fleshy-faced, with thick hair greying at the temples, and dressed in an expensive dinner jacket, the man exuded an air of prosperity and smug satisfaction as he advanced in so flamboyant a style his guests began to fall silent and turn to face the doorway.

'So you're here, my boy!' he boomed. 'By God, you'll have found a trip to Sheffield, even in the blackout, a damned sight easier than crossing China, eh? Don't hang about in the doorway, lad. Where are your manners? Bring Miss Channing in to the fire. Poor lass looks chilled to the bone.'

Circling them, he threw an arm around each and propelled them forward to the blazing fire revealed as guests parted to let them through. Concentrating on Sarah, Maurice maintained a hearty one-sided conversation full of his pride in the son who had conducted her to safety across wild country patrolled by the enemy.

'Always knew he was made of the right stuff. A bit wild when he was younger, but lads will be lads, eh?' he said on a laugh. 'A chip off the old block, is Alexander. Look at him now! Goes off under a bit of a cloud, but comes back a hero. Here, now, get yourself warm by the fire, lass. A fine piece of marble this. Italian, you know. Picked it up for a song last year. Sam Mucklethorpe was after it, too, but I had the edge on him.' He laughed again. 'Friends in the right places, a bit of "I'll scratch your back if you'll scratch mine." You know how it is. Your father will, if you don't. Have you had any news of him yet? Terrible business. Terrible. Ah, here's my good lady. One of the de Boucher family, you know. She's anxious to meet you. Dotes on Alexander, so it's natural she's been on hot coals since he wrote to tell her of his escape with Sir Peter Channing's daughter. Mothers are all the same, eh? Never believe any girl is good enough for their sons. Don't fret! She's already halfway to accepting it.'

Miriam Tennant had aged very gracefully indeed. Alex

saw hardly any change in his mother. Frail and willowy, her blonde hair touched up to hide any hint of grey, she was dressed in a youthful pink chiffon dinner gown that had a wide stole to cover her bare shoulders. She looked gentle, quietly beautiful and a cut above most women in the room, but Alex felt nothing for her as she breathed his name and went on tiptoe to kiss him.

'How handsome you look! You were always such a lovely boy, but that uniform looks so well on you.' Her pale-blue eyes grew misty. 'You will be careful, darling. I thank heaven I knew nothing of that dreadful journey across China until you were safely in India. I would have *died* with worry.' She turned to Sarah. 'How pretty you look in blue, Miss Channing.'

'Now, now, Miriam, none of that,' said Maurice, intervening with forcefulness. 'It'll be Sarah right from the start. Your son won't be best pleased with you calling his young lady Miss Channing. Best get used to the facts, woman. It'll be Sarah, Maurice and Miriam. Start as we'll go on. Saves unnecessary flim-flam.' He clapped Alex on the shoulder. 'How about a drink, lad? You'll be all right in that uniform around the dinner table, but Sarah will want to change. She'll know what's what when it comes to etiquette. Miriam, pull that bell-rope!' He tucked his hand beneath Sarah's arm and bent confidingly to say, 'I've hired a personal maid for you. French, of course. No, no, don't protest. I know what you'll be used to, lass. Only the best for my son's young lady. I'm not short of a brass farthing, you know. Gained by the sweat of my own toil, but it's none the less for that. You run along now and dress. I'll hold dinner until you're ready, but I don't like eating later than eight o'clock, I warn you. Gives me flatulance at bedtime, then I can't sleep.' He laughed. 'Tend to bark at everyone in the morning when I've missed my shuteye.' Looking up, he said, 'Ah, here's Blenkinsop ready to take you up to your room. Used to be in the Works, you know, but I've trained him myself and I take pride in how he's turned out. Off you go, lass. After we've eaten, I'll introduce you to all these people. The cream of Sheffield, I promise, come especially to meet you. When I told them my lad had picked a Channing, they were

336

very impressed. Now they've seen what a pretty little thing you are, they'll be doubly so.'

Alex was transfixed by the absolute awfulness of what was happening and did no more than cast Sarah a desperate glance as she went off with the caricature, Blenkinsop. In nine years, most of which he had spent in company of people of some taste and education, he had forgotten how excruciatingly embarrassing his father could be. There was nothing wrong with self-made men – all credit to them – or with those who remained true to their local background, but Maurice Tennant was a tasteless braggart who advertised his roots blatantly while betraying them with a ridiculous pose that grated on everyone and fooled no one but himself. Alex longed to collect Sarah and leave. How would he ever apologize for his parents' acceptance that they were practically married? Surely she would not believe that he had given that impression in his letters; that he had suggested an engagement at Christmas. It was what he had hoped, but would not have mentioned to anyone, even Ellie. Now Rod Durman had touched Sarah's life once more, everything had changed. Christmas looked set to be a disaster for a second time.

The evening went from bad to worse. Alex was not allowed a single moment with Sarah, who looked every inch a Channing in a slim dress of moiré taffeta in rich ruby-red. It was some consolation when she smiled at him across the dinner table, but Maurice monopolized the girl he saw as his future daughter-in-law, ensuring that each of his guests was introduced and acquainted with details of the Channing banking chain. Sarah appeared to stand up to the demands of the evening well enough. Although rather pale, she carried off an almost insulting situation with a poise Alex recognized as learned from Ellie. At that thought, he thanked Sasha and Vlad for keeping her at home. It would have been even worse with Ellie here ... and yet, maybe she would have been a match for Maurice.

The Tennants thankfully kept early hours. The guests were practically shooed from the house by eleven. Alex's parents bade him goodnight and practically shooed him and Sarah up the stairs before them as servants began dousing lights. Once inside his former room, now decorated in plum and ivory with gilt wherever it could be added, Alex undressed with resignation. The misery of his boyhood seemed encapsulated by these walls, and it descended on him like a great weight. He did not go to Sarah. In his present mood lovemaking was unlikely to be successful, and with that damned Australian doctor back on the scene he was not going to risk rejection from her.

Half an hour later, a tap on his door heralded Sarah wrapped in a fluffy blue dressing-gown. 'I tired of waiting for you to come to me, so I thought I'd better cheer you up. Can we talk over here by the fire? This house is terribly draughty. I'm frozen.'

She sounded so normal, so friendly, his spirits rose instantly. Grabbing his dressing-gown, he went across to where she sat on a striped chair and settled himself on the floor beside it. He made no attempt to kiss her, but her hand moved to his shoulder and that contact was enough.

'Thank goodness there are fires everywhere,' she said then, 'but there *are* an awful lot. What about coal rationing?'

'Father would know how to get around that.'

'The same would appear to apply to food and alcohol. I've not seen so much since my first days in Hong Kong.'

'I'm ashamed of having brought you here,' he confessed, gazing at the fire.

'I know. Don't be. Now I've met them, I understand so much more about you.'

'They *are* ghastly, aren't they?'

'*He* is. How soon can we leave?'

He tilted his head to look up at her. 'In the morning, if you like.'

'Perhaps I could ring Ellie, then pretend she's been laid low with flu. Might be easier that way.'

'Just as you like. Sarah?'

'Mmm?'

'I've never suggested to Mother that we're planning to get married.'

'I didn't believe you had, silly. They've simply jumped to the wrong conclusion. Don't worry about it.'

He looked back at the fire. Her reply gave him relief that she did not hold him responsible, but dismay over her dismissal of the notion.

She began to giggle. 'That pseudo-footman was bad enough, but when your father called him *Blenkinsop* I almost choked. Oh, and what did you make of that woman in vibrant orange who claimed to be an opera singer?'

'More like the opening act with the local music hall,' he said. 'You should have asked her about Mozart or Puccini.'

'I *did*. She brazened it out very well, but it was clear she was all at sea.'

'They were all putting on an act.'

'No, Alex, one or two were very nice. They didn't compensate for the rest, unfortunately.'

'I'm so sorry.'

After a pause, Sarah said, 'Doesn't it strike you that this evening was very similar to many spent in Hong Kong? When people gather socially, they change. They either brag or laugh too much. Or talk too much.'

'Or drink too much,' he added.

'I suppose it's a form of insecurity. You were like that when I first met you.'

'And you were gauche and tongue-tied.'

'You're much nicer now.'

'You were splendid this evening.' He waited a moment before adding, 'I love you, Sarah.'

Her hand moved on his shoulder. 'Perhaps.' After a while she said, 'This is nice, just sitting together in the firelight. I suppose Jim is with Ellen and the children.'

They spoke of their friend and his family, then of others not as lucky as they three. They remembered the Chinese officer who had got bicycles for them, and the boatman who took them up the river. They wondered about the crew of the MTB, especially the two seamen who had been with them for a while. The fire burned low and still they talked. Morning found them asleep side by side, rolled in blankets on the floor.

The telephone call to Ellie changed their plan. She told Sarah she had no intention of pretending to have flu, and that they must stick it out until the visit was over. They made long faces at each other, then laughed and agreed that she was right. Maurice had gone to the Works at seven, as usual, and Miriam always breakfasted in bed, so they ate porridge, eggs and bacon, toast and marmalade feeling slightly guilty over such quantities of food being on offer. Was it another case of 'I'll scratch your back if you'll scratch mine'?

They went shopping in Sheffield, had lunch in its principal hotel, then Alex drove Sarah out past Tennant's Steel Works to a local beauty spot where he persuaded a woman in the nearest village to give them tea, toast and home-made cake for half a crown a head. The woman's dog had had puppies, and Alex wanted to buy one for Sarah.

'I couldn't take him to Noon Cottage, Alex. Sasha and Vlad are quite enough,' she told him, cuddling the little black body to her face. 'But he's so adorable.'

'I'll look after him for you,' Alex declared. 'Life on an RAF station is paradise for dogs. There's always someone there willing to take them for walks, or have a rough and tumble with them. The chaps in the cookhouse slip them all the leftovers and, if their owners don't come back one day, someone else takes them on. In that case, he'd be sent to you.'

She looked up swiftly. 'Don't, Alex.'

'It's a possibility, darling. That's why I want us to be married,' he told her. 'It might not last long, but we'd make the most of it.'

'We do now,' she said, then turned to put the tiny dog with the others. 'Let's go. It'll be getting dark soon.'

They arrived back as it was starting to snow. Deedes House seemed almost welcoming after the bleakness outside. Miriam greeted them with the news that her cousins, Hélène and Diana, plus their husbands, and their mother, Florentine, had come to stay over the Christmas holiday.

'Your father normally refuses to have them in the house, darling,' she told Alex nervously, 'but as Aunt Flora was so generous when you were in trouble, he thought you'd like to thank her and introduce Sarah to them all. I do hope it's going to work out all right.'

'They're a reasonable lot,' he confided to Sarah, as they went to their rooms to change. 'Should be a better evening than yesterday.'

So it proved. The intimate group made conversation more manageable, Miriam's family preventing Maurice from monopolizing every subject raised at the table. He was still able to dominate to a certain extent, and it was not until they gathered after the meal and he embarked on a huge cigar that his voice no longer overrode the others. Hélène and Diana were twins who must have been a sensation in their heyday. They possessed humour, intelligence and deep knowledge of their father's country, which they spoke of with sadness over its present split situation. Their mother was a sprightly widow very fond of ragtime music. Her merry laugh matched Maurice's voice in decibels, but she mostly ignored him to concentrate on Alex, for whom she had always felt sympathy. Sarah appeared to take to Great-aunt Flora, which pleased Alex and instilled relief that the girl he loved had found some congenial company in his old home.

But Sarah was to find company even more congenial in Charles Spencer, Diana's husband. Alex had completely forgotten that this quiet, dignified man had once been something of an impresario, so it was not until Diana referred to an acquaintance 'who used to play in Charlie's orchestra' that he pursued the subject eagerly.

'Weren't you connected with a symphony orchestra in some way?' he asked. 'I seem to remember Mother once mentioning that you were in Sheffield for a concert, but music didn't interest me then so I took little notice.'

Charles took his pipe from his mouth, nodding. 'Music interests you now?'

'Cole Porter ... that kind of thing. But Sarah plays Tchaikovsky, Chopin, all the great masters. She means to be a concert performer ... or she did, until the war put paid to her chances.'

'How interesting.' Charles turned politely. 'Perhaps you'll play for us.'

'No.' It was said so abruptly, it was almost rude. 'I haven't tackled a piano for over a year.'

'Pity to let it slide,' Charles commented, still in polite manner. 'It can be such a pleasant form of relaxation.'

Seeing Sarah's expression, Alex said quickly, 'She didn't play for relaxation. She spent *hours* in practice each day, and performed at concerts in Hong Kong to great acclaim. I introduced her to a Dutchman who was a neighbour of mine. He was immensely impressed by her talent, and he should know. He'd once been a concert pianist of world class.'

'Really?' The tone had changed to one of some interest. 'Who might that have been, Alexander?'

'Jakob Myburgh.'

Hélène gave a little shriek. 'I once owned a recording of his ... until Diana trod on it. Do you remember, Di? You tried to get me another, but they were out of print.' She turned to Sarah. 'You must be very good indeed. *Mon dieu*, I thought Jakob Myburgh had been killed in an auto crash *years* ago. He must be in his eighties. And he's *still* able to judge a person's talent?'

'*I* am in my eighties, Hélène,' her mother told her tartly, 'and well able to judge anything.'

'*Pardon*, Mama,' laughed her lively daughter, who was fond of interspersing French exclamations in her conversation.

'You were a pupil of Myburgh's?' asked Charles, leaning forward in his chair.

'Briefly,' Sarah admitted, clearly reluctant to speak about the passion she had forsaken.

'You studied in England before that?'

She nodded.

'May I ask with whom?'

The normally reticent Charles grew animated when Sarah gave him several names that meant nothing to Alex. He had begun to enjoy the evening. All attention was centred on Sarah; even Maurice seemed content to stay in the background. She looked particularly striking tonight in black, with the silver chain and his filigree bracelet. Every inch a Channing. Unbidden came the question of how she could find perfect rapport with a man like Durman, as she claimed.

Charles left his chair and crossed to sit beside Sarah, wedging himself between her and Alex on the long silver-brocaded settee.

'I wish you would consent to play,' he said persuasively. 'For my ears alone, perhaps? You must be extremely talented to study with several of our most prominent maestri.' Sarah remained silent. 'I have a specific reason for pursuing this request, my dear. I would not press you otherwise. May I tell you about a project I have undertaken?'

Accepting her unspoken consent, Charles told her of his career as manager of the international Clemens Orchestra, created by Sir Hugo Arnheim-Clemens during Queen Victoria's diamond jubilee. 'We travelled Europe giving concerts with some of the world's greatest soloists,' he revealed with a hint of nostalgia. 'Twice we crossed to America, but went no further than New York. Cities are so far apart over there, and transporting an orchestra with all the instruments is highly expensive.' He sighed. 'The poor old Clemens ran into financial trouble when the last of Sir Hugo's family died, ending the backing upon which we had heavily relied. We struggled on for a few years with the generous help of a few philanthropists, but when the war came we disbanded – a group of musicians who had served music as well as audiences with distinction for over forty years.'

'I remember feeling very sad when I read the news,' said Sarah, warming to Charles now the focus was on him, not her. 'It must have been a great blow to you.'

'To us all, but there were far more disasters all around us and many of the musicians were called up. The emphasis was on defence of Britain, not entertainment. Concerts were a thing of the past. But you'd know that only too well, Sarah. You were here during those first years of war. Things came to a standstill for a while.'

Sarah coloured slightly. 'I felt guilty about going to Hong Kong, but my grandmother insisted that one gifted pianist for the future was a better offer for my country than two more hands packing shells.'

'She was right ... but you're not using that gift, apparently.'

It was said quietly, but his words deepened Sarah's colour and she looked away at the blazing logs. Alex spoke in her defence. 'After all she's been through this year, it's not surprising. Sarah's an artist. You should be more understanding than most of how bombing, death, fear and malnutrition would affect her. She's made it more than clear that she doesn't want to play for you . . . for *anyone*.'

'Now, now, no need for that,' boomed Maurice, getting to his feet and crossing to them. 'You said nothing of this in your letters, Alexander. Your young lady a famous pianist!'

Sarah rose in surprising anger. 'I'm not . . . nor am I your son's young lady. There's been a great deal of misapprehension over that. Alex and I . . .' she faltered. 'Please don't jump to conclusions and make them fact, Mr Tennant.'

Maurice was unabashed. 'There's no call to fly at me, lass, just because Charlie here has hit a raw spot. I think we should all have another drink and straighten our ruffled feathers.'

Alex stood up, upset by Sarah's denial of being his girl but furious with his family for precipitating it. The early harmony was deteriorating fast. 'If feathers are ruffled, you're the one behind it all,' he said to his father. 'Sarah was paraded before half Sheffield last night like your latest acquisition. You wrote that Mother wished desperately to see me after so long an absence, and I thought it my duty to come. I also misguidedly imagined you were offering some kind of olive branch. I'm not sure what's behind your invitation. You'll probably get around to it sooner or later, but I won't have Sarah treated to your brand of dominance.'

'Please, Alex,' begged Sarah, touching his arm in her distress. 'I'm rather tired, I think I'll go to my room.' Traces of her inbred dignity remained as she said to Charles, 'Forgive me, Mr Spencer. Perhaps we could talk about the Clemens and your work with the orchestra tomorrow. I'd like that very much. Goodnight, Mrs Tennant . . . everyone.'

Alex watched her leave, his anger growing. As soon as the door closed he turned back to his father. 'This is no Christmas homecoming, it's a solo performance by someone who needs to compensate for an insecure childhood by shouting louder than anyone around him.' As Maurice

344

made to speak, Alex continued quickly. 'During the battle for Hong Kong, the quiet men were heroes. Those who blustered and bragged were the first to turn and run. You're still insecure, Father, and you're still shouting to cover the fact. I'm taking Sarah home in the morning.' He turned to the others watching with interested approval. 'I'm sorry my father has ruined what started out as an enjoyable evening. Goodnight, Mother.'

Maurice followed Alex out like an attacking bulldog, grabbing his arm to pull him to a halt. 'By God, your spine has stiffened a bit since I knocked you down and ordered you from the house. Ay, and your tongue's got a bit too acid. You'll come down in the morning and apologize,' he said harshly. 'You'll also announce your engagement to that girl. Are you a man or not? I left your mother no chance to speak. They like it that way. Know where they are.'

Alex made to turn, but he was seized and spun back to face a man bristling with purpose. 'Now look here, you'll never make a better deal than this. She's got class, that certain kind of look good breeding produces, and the right kind of connections.' His eyes narrowed. 'When I read your letters from India I made some enquiries about Channing Mercantile. They're worth, collectively, almost as much as Rockefeller. That girl's heiress to the Far-Eastern branch, and might inherit sooner than you think. If the Japs finish for Sir Peter, she'll step in nicely – when the war ends and things get back to normal.'

Still gripping Alex's arm, Maurice walked him across the amber carpet towards the stairs, a steely note entering his voice. 'I've not been wasting my time since this war began. There've been some very lucrative contracts flying around, and I've made certain they came to Tennant's. I went out of my way to meet the right people and do them a favour now and then – the kind of favour they'd not want made public, if you follow me. Every man has his weakness. They had no difficulty accepting my tenders when I reminded them how much I'd done for them. Tennant's has quadrupled its profit over the last three years. Deedes House is testament to that. Now, a merger with a major commercial banking house would make our Works so powerful we could virtually close every other steel manufacturer in the country. A *monopoly*, boy! Think of it!' He tugged Alex to a halt and smiled. 'If you're worried about her father being Sir Peter, I can tell you on the quiet I'm in line for a knighthood in the very near future. *Sir* Maurice Tennant. No, I'm not honoured. I've worked bloody hard for it. But she'll have no call to look down her nose at you when I'm on a par with her father.' He released Alex's arm as his smile faded. 'Now get up there to her room and tell her what's what! I want an announcement in the morning, boy. Assert yourself, for God's sake. Don't tell me you two crossed China in primitive conditions without getting more than cosy. Do the necessary, then tell her it's time you made an honest woman of her.'

A wave of revulsion washed over Alex as he stared at the full face, the grating, overbearing voice echoing in his ears. Added to his anger, and the hurt of Sarah's public denial of him, it provoked an uncharacteristic urge to lash out. He hit Maurice squarely on the chin with such force his father lost his balance and staggered backwards several feet before landing in a sitting position on the thick carpet his 'favours' had paid for.

'I should have done that nine years ago,' Alex told him. 'If it weren't for the snow, I'd take Sarah away tonight. Damn your merger, damn your knighthood! You're nothing but a loud-mouthed, ill-bred bastard.'

Maurice recovered from his astonishment and began to laugh. The sound of his amusement floated up the stairs behind Alex. 'By gum, you're a man, at last. A son in my own image. Get that merger and I'll leave everything to you in my will. Go to it, lad.'

'Go to hell!' Alex cried.

'You'll not get a penny otherwise.'

At the top of the stairs, Alex leaned against the wall breathing heavily. He had never before punched a man on the jaw; had never been driven to. The skin on his knuckles was broken. He dabbed with his handkerchief at the blood oozing through. His heartbeat was fast and painful. It had been like that since Sarah dashed his hopes in the unkindest manner. She had been made angry, he knew, but her announcement had left him looking a fool. It was not like her to be cruel, so he could not leave things as they were. Looking behind a blackout curtain over a nearby window, he wondered if they *could* leave tonight. Snow was falling fast. Driving would be hazadous, and Ermintrude had little protection against the cold. It was out of the question to ask Sarah to go in this.

She was in her dressing-gown beside the fire, and the French maid unnecessarily hired by Maurice was hanging the black dress in the corner wardrobe. Sarah looked tense, but calm. She dismissed the woman, causing her to smile knowingly as she wished them both goodnight and left.

'I'm sorry, Alex,' Sarah said, studying the fire. 'I couldn't stand any more. Despite your description of your father, I wasn't prepared for him to be so ... so *overbearing*. He sweeps everyone along in his determination that things will be as he dictates.'

He crossed the floral carpet to her. 'You made it pretty plain that they weren't, in front of the entire family.'

'No,' she cried, looking at him in distress. 'It was his ...' She broke off and changed direction. 'What we mean to each other is a relationship others wouldn't easily understand.'

'I'm not certain I do,' he said deliberately. 'We're lovers, we're only truly happy when we're together, we keep talking about marriage. Doesn't that make you my "young lady"?'

'Not in the sense they mean – *he* means! Alex, we didn't meet at a dance, start going out on dates, then decide to meet each other's parents. *We went through hell together*,' she added vehemently. 'We're not sweethearts, we're bound by all we endured. What we share is far, far deeper than your obnoxious father could possibly imagine.'

'But not deep enough for marriage.'

His thrust went home. She looked almost afraid as she said, 'We agreed to wait for six months.'

'Nothing's going to happen between tonight and March to change the way we feel ... unless I get killed.'

'Don't, Alex.'

He drew her into his arms, murmuring against her ear.

347

'We have to face the fact that it *could* happen when I'm on active service. Let's get married before it's too late, darling. I want you so badly.'

His kiss was powered by the emotion this evening had generated and was unlike his normal gentle caress. Even so, he was unprepared for her instant withdrawal from his embrace to retreat to the other end of the hearthrug.

'We're in the wrong mood for that, Alex.'

'I'm not. It's Christmas Eve. A year ago I was lying in a filthy, makeshift hospital, half-starved and covered in lice, wondering if I'd escape before I was captured and beheaded. I'm free, clean, well-fed, and very much in love with you tonight. I want to celebrate my good fortune in the most satisfying manner possible.'

She evaded his embrace, moving slowly away from the fireplace towards the adjoining bathroom. 'I'm afraid the memory of last Christmas affects me differently, and that contretemps downstairs has made me more depressed. I'll take some aspirin and try to sleep.' Pausing at the bathroom door, she said apologetically, 'I hadn't expected to feel so close to those three after a year's absence. I can't think of anything but that cave, the beach, and their faces as we left.'

Intuition came in a flash, as he flung words at her. 'It's not them but *him*, isn't it!' She said nothing, which made things worse. 'Since that damned letter arrived you've changed. It's been him all along. I was a convenient substitute for your frustrated passion. Now you know he's alive, I can go fly a kite – or a Spitfire. It's immaterial to you so long as I leave you to your memories of those illicit days in Hong Kong while his wife entertained all and sundry.'

'Stop it, Alex!' she cried, putting her hands over her ears.

He strode across and pulled them down, so that she had to hear his condemnation. 'You fool! He's on the other side of the world . . . and he still belongs to another woman. Do you think he gives a damn about *you*? Do you?'

'You're hurting my wrists,' she told him heatedly.

'All that artistic nonsense about perfect rapport between the pianist and a concerto only happening once,' he raged, releasing her hands with a throwaway movement. 'Is that why you'll no longer play, why you've abandoned something that once meant the world to you? Did you see him as a concerto?' He gave a harsh laugh. 'Grow up, Sarah! Whatever there was between you two was as basic as the need that drove you to surrender to me. It happens to people all the time, and there's nothing in the least musical about it.' She turned away, but he reached for her and held her steady. 'Now I've hurt you, the way you hurt me downstairs. I didn't come here to do that. I'm sorry.' He tried to draw her back against his chest, but she resisted. 'Don't ruin your life over him, darling. Does a pianist give up because she once gave an unrepeatable performance? By your own words, she continues to thrill audiences with the same compositions, even if perfection is never again achieved.'

'Please go,' she begged. 'I can't take much more.'

To stay would merely bring further distress to them both. He released her and went to his room, knowing their relationship had changed from one of intense interdependence to the normal kind ruled by familiarity, sexual desire and self-preservation. Perhaps it had changed for him some time ago. Could he hold on to her now Rod Durman had reached out across the miles?

Making no attempt to undress, he moved about the room smoking one cigarette after another, trying to decide what best to do. He could not remain here now his father had brought into the open his reason for pretending all was forgiven. Alex's lip curled. What if he told Maurice his planned merger had been rendered impossible by an Australian medic with origins as lowly as his own? Jealousy burned Alex up as the minutes passed and he heard the rest of the family go to their rooms. He told himself there were girls enough to console him. Why feel so cut up over this one? The one he could not have, she had once called herself. Was that the basis of his desire? Yet he did have her. *Had* had her! Not only physically, but bound so closely to him in spirit she was lost when he was away. Was Durman's power over her so much stronger, she could abandon those ties at the mere mention of his name in an official letter concerning her father? He had to test that theory before he could hope to sleep.

Making no attempt to enter he tapped the familiar message on her door, certain she was lying awake. On the point of returning to his room heavy hearted, he heard her response on the inner surface of the door. *Sleep well until the moon is covered by the sun.* It was enough to enable him to undress and relax in bed, the horrors of last Christmas Eve pushed to the back of his mind.

Christmas morning was clear and sunny, with a white layer untrodden and glistening as if scattered with diamanté. Alex dressed and went outside to test the depth and condition of the snow. Slightly worried, he went indoors to telephone Noon Cottage and explain the situation to Ellie.

'Developments have made it impossible for us to stay,' he said. 'I'm going to have a shot at bringing Sarah home, but conditions aren't ideal. If I run into worse *en route*, we'll book into an hotel and try again tomorrow. Don't be anxious. I won't take risks. How thick is the snow down there?'

'It appears to have drifted,' she told him. 'There was a fierce wind last night. I've no idea what the roads are like. I've not been out. The dogs had to make do with a roam around the garden.' A pause, then, 'Alex, take care of yourselves.'

'It's a promise. With luck, I'll be there tonight to finish off the bottle of whisky you've hidden from the vicar.'

He rang off, then scribbled a note which he pushed beneath Sarah's door to tell her to pack ready to leave after breakfast. Knowing his mother always breakfasted in bed, Alex wrote a note of farewell explaining that it was impossible for him to remain in the same house with a man who had learned nothing about human nature in the intervening years. He promised to keep in touch with her, and wished her a merry Christmas. With that letter in his pocket to hand over to Roberts at breakfast, Alex packed his bag in the knowledge that Miriam Tennant had grown so self-indulgent her son's sudden departure would cause little upset to her.

Going downstairs with his holdall and the gifts he had purchased in Sheffield, he placed the packages beneath the huge decorated tree, before going out to bring Ermintrude round to the front entrance. For one daunting moment he believed the engine was not going to start. The air smelt sweet and invigorating; the snow crunched beneath his shoes. He longed to get going, longed for Noon Cottage and the sense of belonging he found there. Deedes House towered grimly behind him. He would soon turn his back on it for the last time.

Sarah came downstairs in her blue sweater and skirt, carrying the initialled suitcase and some gift-wrapped packages. 'What should I do about these?' she asked.

He made no attempt to kiss her, just took the suitcase from her to place near the door. 'Leave them beneath the tree, as I have. What else can we do with them?'

They ate breakfast in silence after Alex related the gist of his telephone call to Ellie. Sarah appeared heavy-eyed but calm. He was dreading the sound of his father's heavy tread on the stairs. They ate as fast as they could enough to sustain them during their chilly journey, so conversation was not really possible. Alex handed the butler the note addressed to Miriam, then led Sarah out to the cloakroom. While he was helping her into the black, fur-collared coat, Charles Spencer came down the stairs and crossed to them.

'I was so afraid I'd find you had already left. Such a pity, but Maurice is really impossible and will never see it, I fear.'

Alex shrugged on his overcoat. 'Please say goodbye to the aunts and dear Great-aunt Flo. Tell them I'll write.'

Charles took a business card from his pocket and offered it to Sarah. 'This is where you can reach me. I've been given the delightful task of arranging concerts nationwide in towns and cities subjected to air raids. Places which are sometimes as much as fifty per cent rubble. The fighting men and women have ENSA, but passive victims of war also need cheering, so I was asked to organize some form of entertainment for the residents of our worst-hit areas. The venues will, of necessity, be any suitable large building still standing – no pukka concert halls, you understand – and no fee will be offered to the performers. Travelling and overnight accommodation expenses will be met, of course, and every effort will be made to provide sufficient heating for the concerts. Apart from that, I can offer nothing but the satisfaction of taking to those who are weary, frightened and despairing the pleasure of brief escape into that world they fear is lost. Please consider joining my list of artists willing to perform at one or more of my concerts.'

Sarah seemed at a loss for words as she studied the oblong of printed card. Then she looked at Charles to say, 'I'm sorry. I haven't touched a piano since I was cut off on Stanley Peninsula last December. My hands ... I ... *we* lived rough for four months in China. It's very good of you to ask me, but I'm afraid –'

'I'm not being good in asking you,' he interrupted. 'I'm being selfish. I want to make a success of this project. I've felt so useless since the Clemens was disbanded. I need something to get my teeth into ... and the people in bombed cities need artists like you.'

'I'm no artist,' she protested.

Alex stepped in swiftly. 'You won't be if you keep fooling yourself you'll never again play the way you played in Hong Kong.' He opened the front door, her suitcase in his hand. 'Of course she'll join your group, Uncle Charles. Give her a few weeks to get back into form, then she'll give you a call. That's a promise.'

With his hand beneath her elbow, Alex led Sarah outside and down the steps to his car. He settled her in the seat, squeezed behind the wheel, gave Charles Spencer a jaunty wave, then drove away from his home knowing nothing would persuade him to return.

They were cruising along the crisp surface of the main road through Sheffield when Sarah said coldly, 'Who gave you permission to speak on my behalf?'

'I don't need permission.' Then, because it seemed to be the season for speaking his mind, he added, 'You were looking salvation in the face, you idiot. Charles has a great deal of influence in the concert world. I'll wager his list of artists includes some names to make you gasp with surprise.'

'All the more reason why mine has no right to be among them.'

He took a quick glance at her set expression. 'Rubbish! Old Myburgh knew what he was talking about when he told me you had a rare gift, and a year or so ago you'd have given your eye teeth for an offer like this.'

'A lot has happened since then.'

'That's why you should make up for lost time,' he insisted. 'My dear girl, you've been riddled with guilt because you're not doing your bit, imagining village vilification because you're idling the days away at Noon Cottage. Charles can solve your dilemma. Joining his organization would make you exempt from other war work.'

'I don't want that,' she protested immediately. 'I haven't been shirking my duty. It was simply that I . . . that I . . .'

'That you couldn't forget Hong Kong and all that happened afterwards? Well, it's time you did,' he said ruthlessly. 'Jim and I went through eighteen days of bloody hand-to-hand fighting before *we* embarked on those four months in China. He returned to his squadron three months ago. I picked up the pieces and joined the RAF eight weeks ago. Isn't it time you pulled yourself together and started living again? Those we left behind can't. Don't we owe it to them to make the most of our freedom?'

She remained silent as he crossed the city and took the road south. When they reached open country, where fields lay beneath snow dancing with diamond lights, Alex told her what had transpired between himself and his father.

'I told him a merger between Tennant's Steel and Channing Mercantile is not on the cards, even if he becomes *Sir Maurice*.' He slowed and stopped on a long, white, sun-washed ribbon of road edged by the dark skeletons of trees. Taking her hand, he said gently, 'Any girl can plough a field, pack a parachute or turn a lathe. Very few can hold hundreds enthralled with a sonata or étude. If you won't agree to fry my breakfast eggs and darn my socks, for heaven's sake join Charles Spencer's group and do what you're destined to do.'

Chapter Fourteen

They reached Noon Cottage in time to drink a toast to
Marion, Roma and Chloë on Christmas night. It was a relief
to be home again. Even Alex thought of it as home, so they
all settled to enjoy the rest of the festive season at ease with
each other. After the débâcle of the visit to Deedes House,
Sarah had much to think about. Alex had revealed that he
knew about the Bolton Rochas affair and had said nothing
because he had not wanted her to suffer the humiliations of
a father's disgrace, as he had done. It had been the decision
of a man she had at that time condemned as shallow and a
wastrel, which again highlighted her inability to judge character with any soundness. That led to Alex's revelation
regarding Celeste Durman's participation in some kind of
orgy. Remorse over her response to Rod's announcement of
the pregnancy had trebled since that lunch *en route* to
Sheffield. Had Rod been ruled by compassion; by a sense of
honour – they had discussed the old-fashioned virtue – that
had compelled him to stand by his wife and claim the child
as his?

Overriding all other uncertainties was the question of
whether Alex was right to suggest that she had involuntarily
lost the will to resume her musical career because her love
for Rod was inseparable from her love of music. If that was
so, she would never play again. Yet, knowing that he was
alive and safe in Australia as well as believing in extenuating
circumstances surrounding Celeste's pregnancy, could she
not now find consolation in music? Was it even possible to
maintain that love through her other passion?

Alex left Noon Cottage at the start of January to join his squadron. He was bitterly disappointed to learn that he would be flying large, heavy bombers rather than the swift Spitfires or Hurricanes he had set his heart on. Ellie and Sarah commiserated as best they knew how, neither having any real notion why he should be so concerned with the distinction. Flying was flying, to their minds, and his life at risk whichever machine it was.

Three days after his departure, Sarah lifted the lid of her piano and stood looking at the keys. Ellie was working on illustrations for the latest book, and had gone out in boots and overcoat with Robert to see some stoats he had trapped for her. The house was silent save for the spluttering of the fire; the dogs were asleep in their favourite places.

In that English room bathed in winter sunlight, with plates on a narrow shelf running around the room, and cherrywood furniture that smelled of lavender polish, the miles between Sarah and a man who had taken her by storm suddenly dropped away. She felt very close to him. She had told Alex there would never be another love like that; never another perfect performance. He had suggested there could still be affection in her life, and a flood of melody. Rod would not want her to sacrifice music when opportunity offered. Should she not seize this chance for his sake?

Her fingers began to wander over the piano keys in abstract fashion as she sat before them. Not as inflexible as she feared, they nevertheless lacked strength. When she tried several chords, full resonance was missing. She repeated them several times, muttering admonitions as usual when dissatisfied with her performance. The scales were abysmal. Pushing her hair behind her ears, she flexed both hands and concentrated on basics. After half an hour, the joints in her fingers ached so badly she was forced to stop, yet she knew a sense of fulfilment missing since that afternoon on Stanley Beach when she had run to meet Rod, then walked away devastated.

It was not until evening, when curtains were drawn, and a fire blazed cheerfully in the hearth that Sarah said casually, 'While you were out with Robert I tried a few scales and chords. The piano is in remarkably good shape.'

'I had Claude Radford here to tune it the day before you came home,' Ellie replied equally casually. 'Did you know, my dear, stoats can look almost endearing in their winter fur. How curious it is that we associate white with heroes and black with villains. In summer, stoats are nasty, vicious creatures who slink around close to the ground grabbing victims with their razor teeth. Today, they looked smart and spanking clean as they frolicked in the snow. Eyes that look vicious against nondescript brown seemed brightly inquisitive this afternoon. I found the little demons fascinating. So much so, I think I'll suggest to Violet that she should create her next story around a lovable stoat. After all, even the most objectionable creatures have virtues. None of us is all good, or irredeemably bad.' She gave a wicked smile. 'If the publishers protest that stoats are not sweet cuddly animals beloved by children, I'll tell them that we've done it to persuade our readers that not all Germans are evil, as government propaganda suggests. They're always harping on about moral issues in our woodland tales, so I'll confound them with one.'

Sarah laughed. 'You lead poor Jason Winters a dreadful dance!'

'Well, he's pompous. A bit like Toad of Toad Hall. Pompous with a rather lovable personality trying to struggle to the surface. He needs a woman to humanize him. You wouldn't care to take him on, I suppose?'

'No, thanks.'

'How about Alex?'

Sobering, Sarah said, 'He's not pompous, and his lovable personality surfaced some time ago.'

Ellie regarded her shrewdly. 'He told me he wants to marry you.'

'He told *me* that.'

'And you said no?'

'I said wait.'

'For what?'

Sarah hesitated, then told her grandmother about Charles Spencer's project.

'I see. So Alex has been asked to wait until you have decided whether or not to accept Mr Spencer's invitation?'

'Not exactly.'

'Because the decision has already been made? Hence your experiment with the piano today?'

Sarah was driven to say, 'How very stoat-like of you to slink up and grab me when I'm least expecting it.'

Ellie smiled. 'I'm one of the endearing stoats – not all bad. You *have* decided to join this organization, haven't you?'

'I wasn't aware that I had until now,' Sarah confessed. 'It will be months before I'm ready, of course. By then I'll be boxing shells in a factory.'

She might have been, except that the authorities apparently still failed to realize that she was eligible for war work. No longer imagining condemnation by the villagers, and boosted by the knowledge that she had done all she could for those at the Halburton Clinic under shot and shell, Sarah put all else aside in the effort to recapture her skill. Noon Cottage was filled for hours on end with the sound of scales, études and themes with variations. Alex spent a forty-eight-hour leave there and entertained Ellie for most of that time. Sarah was now so tired each night, she failed to hear his knock on the connecting bedroom wall telling her he hoped her morning rice bowl would be full. He received no answer.

Now in regular correspondence with Roma, Sarah was able to tell of her escape across China without resulting nightmares. She had once considered writing to Rod via the embassy in Chungking, but only once. He was aware that she had escaped safely from Hong Kong; she knew he had. That was how things should be left.

On an afternoon in spring, when lamb's-tails hung from trees in yellow clusters, flowering cherries were smothered in pink and white blossom and bluebells grew through the grass along railway embankments, Sarah took the train to Arundel where Charles and Diana Spencer lived. An air raid on London kept all trains standing for almost two hours on lines outside the capital's main stations. Watching the distant bombing reminded Sarah of those eighteen days in Hong Kong, and her heart ached for those suffering pain and loss while she could do nothing. Yet Alex's Uncle Charles believed she could help tremendously by providing an escape into music for people in stricken cities. So must she, or she would not be on her way to play for the man who wanted her to join his group.

A taxi took her several miles beyond the estate surrounding Arundel's ancient castle to a house with a large vaulted extension with walls mainly of glass. A music room, without doubt. Sarah's interest grew. She had had no opportunity, in Sheffield, for a long conversation with Charles before their abrupt departure. It would be a delight to discuss music with someone so knowledgeable, even if he changed his mind about adding her to his list of performers after he had heard her play. In her heart she knew he would not.

Both Spencers came to the door as her taxi drew up. Charles walked across to pay the driver and take her suitcase, greeting her warmly and inviting her to go inside out of the evening chill.

'I'm sorry I'm so late,' she told her hostess at the doorway. 'There was a raid.'

To Sarah's surprise, Diana Spencer kissed her by way of a greeting. 'Charles telephoned the station. They told us *everything* was running late. When isn't it?' she asked on a laugh. 'You must be famished, my dear.' Leading her into an oak-panelled hall, she said, 'I'll show you your room so that you can change for dinner straight away. Sorry to hurry you, but the gem of a woman who cooks for us has to leave just before nine to catch the last bus to her cottage. Charles applied for petrol coupons so that he could use the car for all the running about he has to do now his scheme is under way, but he had no joy. The Powers That Be ruled that his is not a vital occupation.' They ascended a wide staircase carpeted in powder blue. 'So Mrs Pusey, our cook and bottle-washer, can't be taken home by car if she misses the bus.' She flung open the door to a pretty low-ceilinged room decorated in lavender and cream. 'There you are! If there's anything I've forgotton, pull that little tassel over by the window and I'll pop back.' She waited in the open doorway until her husband arrived with Sarah's black suitcase. 'We're not as grand as the Tennants I'm afraid. I'm the chambermaid and Charlie's the footman.' She laughed again. 'Wait until you see Mrs P. She's not a patch on the haughty Blenkinsop. Serves dinner in a wrapover skirt and an old cardy ... but she cooks like an angel. Don't rush, dear, but do remember her nine o'clock bus.'

The evening passed very pleasantly. Sarah enjoyed the company of two people she had had no opportunity to speak to at length when Maurice Tennant had monopolized the company. She found them both amusing, with a wealth of anecdotes concerning Diana's second home, France, and the orchestra with which Charles had been so occupied. Alex telephoned soon after Mrs Pusey left to catch her bus. He was deeply disappointed because he had applied for a forty-eight-hour pass and been turned down because of what he described as 'a dreary mission to drop messages in the land of stop me and buy one', which Sarah took to mean a place of ice and snow. Norway, Russia? She begged him to take care; he wished her luck with her audition. They exchanged loving messages, then rang off.

'I always knew he'd make good,' Diana commented, as Sarah sat beside her again. 'A childhood like his produces either a rebel who goes through life expecting the world to compensate him, or a lad determined to shake his parents off and go it alone. I think *you* had a lot to do with this one's redemption, Sarah.'

'No. You have the Japanese to thank for that,' she said immediately.

Charles chuckled. 'Both Diana and her twin, Hélène, believe that behind every good man is a splendid woman. Although I'm inclined to agree with them, in Alexander's case, I'm far more interested in your musical skill, Sarah. Unlike this splendid woman of *mine*, who would keep you up half the night chatting, I know a little more about musicians and their need for sleep before a performance.' He nodded. 'Oh yes, I'm sure that's how you regard our session together in the morning. What's more, you've had a tiring journey.' He stood up. 'We cook our own breakfast whenever we're ready. As we've a lot to get through tomorrow, shall we say coffee and toast at eight and down to work at nine?'

Despite the luxurious room Sarah slept badly, dreaming of Japanese, Alex crashing on an iceberg and herself at Echoes trying to play a piano with no keys while water thundered through the ravine. Charles was totally business-like in the morning, leading her at nine o'clock to the music room and firmly shutting the door on his vivacious wife. It was a wonderful place, full of light and acoustically balanced to produce excellent tone.

'While you settle down, I'll play some scales and chords to enable you to judge the instrument,' Charles told her. 'Just wander about or do whatever you prefer until you feel ready to begin.'

Sarah realized that her host was an accomplished pianist himself and thrilled to the tone of the piano as he ran through familiar practice routines with great ease. She stood quietly by the spread of glass watching a green woodpecker hammer at a tree-trunk in the garden. Jakob Myburgh had said music must be her only love. Rod was out of her life; Alex had apparently accepted their present relationship. Here was a chance that elderly Dutchman would say she must seize.

It was he who inspired her when she concluded her warm-up and began her programme of one of Mendelssohn's Songs without Words, two Liszt Hungarian Rhapsodies, Beethoven's Sonata in E Flat Major, Chopin's Study in C Minor and, finally, Rachmaninov's moving Prelude in G Minor. Sarah forgot the man standing in the far corner watching and listening. Only when her final chord stopped echoing in that high-ceilinged room did Charles come forward to remind her of his presence. His eyes were glassy.

'It's not often that I'm moved to tears, these days,' he confessed. 'After a lifetime associated with music I've grown used to the wonder of man's ability to create perfection with blobs on paper, and the skill of artists to translate them into a paradise of sound, but it has been a long time since I heard familiar compositions as if for the first time. You are remarkably gifted, Sarah. I thank Providence for the curious circumstances that brought us together at Deedes House.'

Diana brought coffee and biscuits, and left them to their happy accord. For pure pleasure they played several pieces for four hands. Then Charles suggested a final treat.

'How about a concerto? The Rachmaninov Second is always a favourite with concert audiences. I have an orchestral recording here.'

Happiness drained from Sarah with dismaying speed. 'No, not Rachmaninov! Beethoven, perhaps. Or Tchaikovsky.'

He glanced at her keenly, but said only that she should make her own choice, of course. The sombre mood of Beethoven suited the bleakness that had crept into her soul, and she knew Charles would not be moved by a performance that lacked the inspiration of her earlier work. He was nevertheless impressed, and led her over to some chairs beside a small table. From it he took a sheaf of papers.

'Here are the details of my organization, which have just been finalized. In order to gain financial aid, permission to use for our concerts churches or buildings commandeered by the Government, and to be allocated transport for the instruments, I have been told that we must become members of ENSA. A reasonable enough demand, I suppose. The events are to be billed as Charles Spencer Celebrity Concerts, which takes them out of the music-hall category often associated with ENSA concerts for the troops.' He smiled. 'That sounds rather toffee-nosed, I know, but I have gathered together a distinguished group of artists and I'm determined to present performances of an extremely high calibre.'

'It all sounds very exciting,' Sarah said.

'Ah, you haven't heard the down side yet, my dear. They insisted on the two who are of call-up age being employed as my organizational staff. John Pine, the sensational young violinist, had enlistment deferred for six months due to injuries sustained during an air raid on his school. By working for me as a concert co-ordinator he will remain exempt. The same will apply to you. Working from here would be inconvenient and nowhere near central enough, so I've won from them a small office in Cheltenham.' He leaned back with a pleased expression. 'It would give me the utmost gratification to present you to concert audiences nationwide, and to further your career in any way open to me. You would be employed in my office three days a week, leaving plenty of time to practise. There'll be rehearsal sessions prior to each concert, and time off for travelling. As the office is near Kingsmill, you could continue to live with your grandmother.'

Sarah sat for a moment or two assimilating the facts he had presented, then said, 'You're offering me a wonderful opportunity to gain performing experience and to learn from long-standing artists. I'm extremely grateful. Your thoughtfulness in choosing an office near my home means that I can work at my music as well as working for you. But what about the others?'

'There's only John Pine – the rest will continue as they always have. He lives with his mother in Bishop's Stortford, where he'll go at weekends. I've said he can sleep on a camp bed in the office and eat at the nearest café or British Restaurant. I'll stay at the Crown on those three days a week. He's a moody sort of fellow; very set in his ways. Likes to practise into the early hours. No boarding-house would put up with him. Ah, but when he puts bow to strings, he creates magic.'

'What will he create in an office?' she asked caustically.

'Havoc, without a doubt. Can you bear it?'

She thought of a stifling afternoon when a man in a white coat had stormed into an office to throw at her a report and a string of heartfelt abuse. 'Yes, of course,' she told Charles absently. 'I worked in an office in Hong Kong for a while. I can type reasonably well.'

'Splendid! You accept?' he asked eagerly.

'Of course. I'll try to live up to your confidence in me.'

They spent some time discussing details of the work surrounding a concert tour, then Charles told Sarah, 'These are the dates of six concerts I've already arranged. I'd like you to participate in them all. The first is at the end of next month. Can you be ready?'

She nodded, full of confidence.

Charles laid the papers on the table, saying as he did so, 'You *are* aware that the object behind my organization is to provide musical entertainment for the weary residents of cities suffering regular bombardment? There is an element of personal risk involved in taking part in these concerts. Are you prepared for that?'

She thought of the slow death of Hong Kong and the wreck of the Halburton Clinic. 'Yes, quite prepared.'

*

Christmas 1941 had been spent in the ruins of St Stephen's College. Last year, as a newly commissioned RAF officer, Alex had bid his final farewell to boyhood at Deedes House. Three days before Christmas 1943 found him lying on his bed on a cold, bright afternoon trying to get some sleep before the night's operation. Dropping bombs on people he could not see, plus the fact that he did not actually pull the lever releasing them, somehow made it acceptable. He had initially paid for what he was doing with regular nightmares. Now, flying across darkened Germany to destroy factories, docks and essential installations had become a normal part of his life. He had ceased to consider the people manning those objects. The Germans did it without qualms. Why should he have them?

This would be his thirtieth operation as captain of a Halifax bomber. He was due for three months on the ground when he got back from Christmas leave. It would be a relief. Sarah had no idea what her exhortation to fly in defence of his country entailed. He had not enlightened her. Time had eased his disappointment over being sent to Bomber Command. Halifaxes were heavy lumbering aircraft, unsuited for his love of speed. They were the complete opposite of the elegant *Dragonfly*. Flying, as he enjoyed it, entailed a brief exhilarating zoom through the heavens in something small and fast which he alone occupied. His present duty meant spending almost the entire night in a freezing cumbersome machine shared by a large crew for whose lives he was entirely responsible. When he had joined the service, the Battle of Britain was over and emphasis was on hitting the enemy on *their* home ground. Bombers were being lost at a disastrous rate, along with their pilots. Now twenty-nine, Alex was an old man by comparison with boys from school who had trained with him – older, experienced, with understanding of the basics of aeronautics and the stress of warfare, and therefore ideal for the tedious, demanding business of captaining a bomber. He would be a steadying influence for the youthful, headstrong lads who manned most squadrons until their luck ran out. Alex's had held for almost a year. He prayed it would continue tonight, wherever he was headed.

Worry about that had prevented him from sleeping this afternoon. His co-pilot, Peter Mason, was not yet twenty-two. Getting married six months ago had matured him, which had accentuated his reliability in tight corners. Last month, his effervescent young bride had been told that she was expecting twins, and Peter had started worrying about being killed. On their last two raids he had been jumpy; his concentration had wandered. They all worried about dying, of course, but swamped it by drinking, raving it up with the girls, pursuing a passion for golf, fast cars, gambling or cheap thrillers. Young Mason no longer hid his fear and had become a potential danger to C for Charlie's crew. There was wisdom in remaining single at times like this, Alex acknowledged. Then he owned up to himself. There was no wisdom attached to it. The girl he loved still refused to marry him.

He had seen little of Sarah since March. There had been a forty-eight spent at Noon Cottage in July. They had gone riding before breakfast each morning and walking each evening. The time between she had spent at her piano, while he lazed in the garden with Ellie and the dogs. Sarah still would not share a bed with him beneath her grandmother's roof, so the brief leave had been frustrating in that respect. He thought of Noon Cottage as home, and was looking forward to another Christmas there. Get this raid over, then he would set out happily in Ermintrude. He had inherited the other half of his car from his friend, who had had less luck than himself. He had acquired a shaggy dog called Ben by the same means. He spent most of his free time tinkering with one and walking the other along the cliffs and valleys of Dorset.

In October, and at the start of this month, Sarah had had concert engagements in Portsmouth and Southampton. Both cities were near enough to his station to enable them to meet. Fate had ensured that those two days were between operations, so Alex had booked a room in local inns and they had shared afternoon love. Even that had left him unsatisfied. Sarah had changed since joining his uncle's organization. Slim and attractive in uniform, with her hair fashioned once again into the gamine style she had worn in

India, she had become an assured woman dedicated to her career. The last remnant of dependence on him had vanished; her response to his lovemaking had been one of relaxed enjoyment rather than desperation. The stress of continual night raids, the aggression that filled his day-to-day life demanded gentleness, submission and full-blooded feminine allure as compensation. He occasionally sought these from women with pouting scarlet mouths, generous curves splashed with perfume, and satin underwear, then discovered it was not what he wanted after all. In truth, he wanted the girl he had brought out of Hong Kong. She had been replaced by someone growing more and more out of reach.

Sarah Channing was becoming a celebrity. She had been broadcasting regularly with the BBC since the start of November. Although Alex knew their relationship had all the wrong qualities for a happy-ever-after ending, no other woman affected him the way Sarah did. She had made no mention of Rod Durman since last Christmas. Music had now become Alex's rival. He had been fool enough to bully her into returning to it.

News had begun to filter through from Hong Kong regarding prisoners. The Red Cross had finally been allowed limited access, and letters, describing pleasant conditions but clearly written under duress, were being received by relatives at home. They might be full of lies, but the familiar handwriting proved the survival of loved ones. A letter from the Jays to Miriam Tennant had commiserated on the death of her son whilst attempting to escape on a raft. His mother wrote to Alex of the distress the letter had caused, at the same time gleefully rejoicing in the benefits that being *Lady* Tennant had brought her. Alex had not replied. He had no wish to, although he was glad the Jays were still alive. They had been good to him.

One happy development this autumn had been Jim Maiden's transfer to Alex's squadron. Although officers were not supposed to conduct close friendships with sergeants, a tolerant eye was turned on them because of the Hong Kong connection. Alex often visited the Maidens for tea, and played boisterously with their children, afterwards returning to his lonely room determined to have another shot at persuading Sarah to marry him. Sanity invariably prevailed to remind him that it would not bring him a cottage with roses at the door, home cooking and pink-cheeked children. Those things seemed immensely desirable at present. The satin-clad perfumed temptresses he visited would not provide them either. Small wonder he was finding it hard to sleep to order this afternoon. As in Hong Kong, he had no plan for his future. If his luck ran out that night it would be over within the next twelve hours, he reasoned, so why worry about it?

C for Charlie took off at ten-thirty on a clear, frosty night leaving behind a bevy of off-duty men and WAAFs decorating with holly and tinsel the gymnasium used for station dances. If it were not for the danger it represented, Alex would revel in the beauty of an immense sky filled with stars so bright they practically dazzled. When he had lain wounded two years ago on a hillside, gazing at the sky, he had little dreamt he would one day be up there seemingly so close to the stars he could reach from the cockpit to touch them.

After half an hour, Alex locked the controls on to automatic, having set the course that would take them up over the North Sea to dodge German fighter range. Then they would make a turn to send them towards Bremen, their target for tonight. They had been there before and knew the city well from studying aerial photographs, but they had had a close shave over Bremen and felt unhappy about the place. Gremlins, those tormentors of airmen, seemed to haunt that area. As Alex made his way through his aircraft, checking that everything was under control, he hid his depression from crewmen also hiding theirs. Part of the pilot's job was to keep morale high and exude confidence. Alex worked hard at it. Peter Mason remained silent and restless, however. His unborn twins were heartily cursed by the man who would have to rely on Peter to take over if anything put him out of action during the raid.

When they crossed the English coast, Alex gave the order for guns to be tested, and was glad to hear the familiar stutter from front and rear. Although they were surrounded by other bombers, each aircraft had its set height and, providing they all maintained it until reaching the target, they were in no danger from each other. Tonight, aircraft from other squadrons were to rendezvous with them for a saturation raid. No merry Christmas for the citizens of Bremen!

By midnight, Alex was already desperately cold, despite his flying-suit and fleecy lined boots. The gunners in their perspex capsules would be colder still. What he would give for a hot toddy! He thought of a blazing fire with borzois sleeping before it, chairs that cocooned one's body with softness, a glass of clear pale wine, a sparky grey-haired woman who had grown close to him, and a girl with a silken cap of hair and large green eyes who was dearer than any other person in the world. All these would be his within two days. He let his thoughts dwell on that as they droned on through the night, with other dark, deadly shadows above, below and on each side.

He came out of his pleasant dreams just as Peter Mason said harshly, 'There it is! Oh God, another bloody inferno!'

In the far distance could be seen the glow of fires from incendiaries dropped to guide them in on the target. With the dark night all around them, the slightest brightness seemed remarkably clear. Above the burning city searchlights were ranging the sky to fasten on aircraft unable to escape the trap. Shells were bursting all around the area like a pyrotechnic display.

'We'll never survive that,' claimed young Mason heavily. 'They must've increased their artillery since our last op. It wasn't as bad as this.'

'Yes, it was,' Alex told him firmly. 'It always is . . . and we always survive. Get an estimate on the range of these guns. We'll try to go above or below them.'

He was now totally at one with the job. He was flying a heavy machine laden with bombs and it was essential to weave from side to side to make things difficult for the German gunners. The manoeuvre took skill and concentration. It would be too easy to wander off course or change altitude, unless he kept his eyes on the instruments. The bomb-aimer relied on him to get the aircraft on the best line of approach over the target. The entire crew relied on him to get them home again. He had done so twenty-nine times and meant to make it thirty tonight, despite Peter Mason's gloom. He wanted his Christmas at Noon Cottage.

The entire crew prepared for the most dangerous part of the night. The eyes of the gunners ached as they swivelled continuously to scan the darkness around them for fighters looming out of the night. The bomb-aimer went on his knees preparing the sight in readiness for the run over the target. Alex aimed at doing only one on each operation. Mostly, he succeeded. Tense comments passed between him and his crew over the intercom as they drew nearer and nearer to Bremen, a good, successful team. They saw others of their squadron ahead. There would be more behind as they formed up to go in whenever they felt ready.

They were soon near enough to make out streets and buildings thrown into relief by the yellow glare of fires. The river resembled a stream of molten gold. Alex's concentration intensified as he scrutinized the flaming scene for the set of the buildings they must attempt to destroy, and also kept an eye on the aircraft nearest them. Although he was eager to off-load his bombs and turn for home, haste could breed carelessness, and that could cost them their lives. Hot on that thought came white light that blinded him and set his heart thudding. A searchlight had caught and held them; selected them from a skyful of bombers. Several others swung across to form a cone of brilliance they could not escape. Alex swore beneath his breath. The co-pilot swore aloud.

Having identified his target, Alex had to stay on course perfectly illuminated for the guns below to take aim. Shells began exploding all around them, their brightness swallowed by the glare of searchlights, their roar minimized by that of the Halifax's engines. The harsh light had turned Peter's face deathly white. Alex guessed his was the same as he strained to read the instruments through the glare. His heart was now thudding so loudly it seemed to reduce all other sound to mere background noise. He continued to exchange clipped words with his bomb-aimer while homing in on the factories, already burning well. 'How much longer?' he demanded, licking his lips nervously as another shell exploded too close for comfort.

'Half a minute. Hold her steady as she is! Steady. Steady. A little to the left!'

Alex obeyed each instruction, sweating where he had been cold before as he coaxed dainty manoeuvres from a giant machine.

Bombs away!

The sweetest words in the world right then. They could go home! Alex hauled on the wheel to climb away now they were so much lighter, then threw all his weight against it to send them into a tight bank as the rear-gunner yelled that another of their squadron was out of control and about to collide with their port wing. The engines laboured; Alex felt sick. A great black shadow passed so closely over the cockpit he feared it must hit their tail, and waited for the bang that would tell him they would not get home tonight. It did not come. Instead, over the intercom came a flood of invective from his rear-gunner as the doomed bomber plunged earthwards out of control. Alex pulled out of the manoeuvre forced by the other aircraft, eyes narrowed against the glaring white light still holding them. Next minute a violent explosion right beside Charlie set them bucking and swaying so violently Alex almost lost his hold on the wheel.

'Christ, we've bought it!' cried Peter Mason in tones of near hysteria.

Alex was fighting to control a machine being subjected to too many demands at once; he was too occupied to panic, even when his rear-gunner announced in faint tones that he believed the gun was useless and *he* definitely was. With aching arms, Alex finally held Charlie steady enough to demand from the navigator a course for the coast. It was suddenly dark. The searchlights sought a new victim, leaving Alex unable to see his compass until his eyes adjusted to the usual dimness inside the cockpit. Only when he had set the course did he send Peter aft to ascertain the damage sustained, knowing it must be considerable from the way he had to fight to keep Charlie level. Questioning each of his team in turn, Alex then learned that two had been wounded – one in the hand, the other in the shoulder – and the

369

rear-gunner, who had caught the worst of of the shell-blast, had serious stomach and leg wounds. His greater concern, at that moment, was the damage to the aircraft. If it was too bad, they might all die and the wounds would be immaterial.

It was bad enough. Several gaping holes in the rear fuselage, a gun hanging from its mounting and bomb doors fixed in the open position. The engines were all right; so were the fuel tanks, the wings and the instruments. So was the pilot. The essentials for successful flight. They would make it home; late and limping, perhaps, but they would all celebrate Christmas this year.

Peter Mason organized the limited medical aid for wounded crew members, and reallocated tasks to the rest. They were not yet out of the woods. There was always the dread of night fighters chasing them now they were away from Bremen. They would be easier prey with no rear gun and slowed by damage.

They reached the coast safely having evaded further gunfire from defences on the lookout for returning bombers, and then ran the gauntlet of coastal batteries to reach the comparative safety of the sea. Alex was very cold and deathly tired. Holes in the fuselage allowed icy air to flow through the aircraft, freezing them all, but the effort of flying a badly unbalanced machine had taken all his concentration and strength. Once safely over the sea, he gave the controls to Peter and went off to cheer his crew and size up the damage ready for a difficult landing. He cursed the fact that the near collision over Bremen had demanded action that prevented his closing the bomb doors immediately. The shell had torn one in half, thus preventing them from folding up. Through the large opening he could see the dark, heavy waters of the North Sea and offered a prayer for any poor devils forced down in it tonight.

With an estimated two hours to go before they were home, they were told to watch out for fighter activity due to a heavy raid on Liverpool. German fighters would almost certainly rendezvous with their returning bombers to defend them from home fighters. The sky between Britain and the mainland of Europe would be full of aircraft before dawn. No merry Christmas for the people of Liverpool either.

Alex returned to the cockpit after reassuring the wounded men and telling the rest to keep their eyes skinned for Messerschmitts. He left Peter at the controls knowing he would have to take over for landing ... or if there was an attack before then. Peter seemed calm and competent now the disaster he feared had happened, so Alex tried to relax and not think about landing. Through the open bomb doors he could still see white-capped waves below. He was reminded of the time he had tried to land *Dragonfly* on such a surface. Rod Durman had saved him from drowning that day. He was no longer jealous of the man. Good luck to the blighter ... so long as he stayed in Australia. His thoughts dwelt on Hong Kong. What a waste of four years of his life! He recalled Giles and Bunny leaning on the rail of the Kowloon ferry, looking absurdly heroic in uniform. They had been given no chance to compensate for *their* lost years. Yet, in their decadent way, they had given something good to the world: merriment. They had not continued living to kill and maim as he did on nights like these. Was he really compensating for wasted years, or wasting more in this round of death?

He switched from that line of thought and tried to picture Noon Cottage, but all he could see was Bunny being riddled with bullets on the ferry leaving Kowloon in retreat. It was proof of how tired he was that his mind doggedly dwelt on death and destruction. Concentrate on his dog, Ben, who had to be left on the station over Christmas. They had been eating dogs in Hong Kong during those final days!

He got to his feet and went to look at the navigator's charts, asking for a fix. It was pointless trying to relax. He had to keep his mind occupied with the job in hand. An hour to go, and they were too far south now for a chance encounter with the Germans on their way home. They all began to talk of cocoa, sandwiches and bed, before going off on leave. No one mentioned that they had to get on the ground first. They talked all around the subject while Alex surreptitiously registered the time passing on the face of his watch.

With twenty-five minutes to go Alex resumed his seat at the controls. The wireless-operator was set to signal their casualties and damage. They were well overdue, so the station must guess they had problems and be ready with ambulances and fire-engines. Not that the latter would be needed, Alex told himself. Landing would be a piece of cake.

He repeated that piece of bravado when he saw, in the distance, the runway jump into relief against the dark fields as the two lines of lights came on. He had never before landed a bomber with a colander for its rear. Charlie did not behave normally with holes all over the fuselage, so Alex started to sweat. He began dropping slowly towards those lights, finding the machine responding more swiftly than usual. His eyes ached; his arms felt like lead weights. The ground seemed to be coming up far too fast. He pulled gently on the wheel, then hauled with all his might when there was no response. The engines protested. He quietened them. Nothing could quieten the thumping of his heart. Yet his voice sounded normal and confident as he issued the usual commands. Thank God they would not know he was scared to death. All at once, they were over the runway and dropping like a stone. There was nothing he could do but try to keep control once they touched down. There was every chance of running amok or somersaulting.

Charlie hit the ground so hard the undercarriage buckled to leave Alex struggling to hold steady a machine racing forwards on its belly. The following moments were a nightmare as lights turned crazy circles before his eyes; the shadowy shapes of vehicles changed from left to right of him in bewildering fashion; and Charlie emitted groans, bangs and a high-pitched screaming which came from beneath his feet. His arms were certainly being yanked from their sockets, his back was breaking, he was choking on smoke and dust which arose around him to shut off all sight of the kaleidoscope outside the cockpit. There was a sudden tilt and a bang. He was dangling head downwards.

Tumult slowly subsided. Movement eased. The obscurity was thickening, but there was now only the sound of a bass drum banging. No, it was his heartbeat. Distant clanging bells grew louder. A deluge of cold water hit him, bringing him up from his position slumped over the wheel. People came at him in a swarm while the deluge continued. He was seized beneath the armpits and carried, retching, away from the gritty cloud filling the cockpit. Then he was lying on the ground. No, it was a stretcher about to be picked up by two orderlies.

'Hey, none of that,' he croaked almost inaudibly. 'I'm all right. There are two wounded men in there.'

'It's all right, sir. You're the last one out. Nothing to worry about. We're just going to get you to the hospital.'

'Oh no you don't,' he countered, rolling from the stretcher and struggling to his feet. 'I'm going off on leave in twelve hours from now.'

He took one step towards the truck containing those of his crew who were unhurt, then found the grass rising up to meet him.

He came to in a hospital bed to learn that his rear-gunner was in a serious but stable condition, and the rest of his crew were preparing to go on leave. He could not, because he had concussion, a broken ankle and severe back strain. The doctor ordered complete rest and no excitement for the best part of a week. The squadron regarded him as something of a hero. Charlie was finished, but could be dismantled and used to repair other aircraft. His crew would stand him a drink when he was allowed it.

Alex was deeply disappointed. He felt like death – every part of his body ached – and his vision was very definitely wonky, but he had built all his hopes on Christmas at Noon Cottage. Leave was only deferred, but it would not compensate for being deprived of something he wanted so badly. Peter Mason, his wireless-operator and his navigator all called in to wish him seasonal cheer and slip a bottle of whisky beneath his bedclothes, but he felt so bleak he could not respond to their camaraderie as he usually did.

The nurse who tended him was clearly persuadable, but not enough to agree to his suggestion that she should get a wheelchair and take him to the nearest telephone.

'Complete rest means exactly that, Mr Tennant,' she told him, her severity modified by a dimple in her cheek.

All he could do was get her to ring Noon Cottage on his behalf to tell Sarah why he would not be coming. Because he had somehow made the decision during that homeward flight, and because he was not altogether himself, he added a rider. 'Tell her I want us to get married during my leave, and I won't take no for an answer this time.'

He lay drifting in and out of full awareness elaborating on that theme. It was time the business was settled. Marriage would not interfere with her career, the RAF would see to that. They had been lovers for a long time, but he needed something more permanent. Within a few months he would be thirty. Peter Mason was married with twins on the way, and he was a mere boy. Making Sarah his wife would be a step towards acquiring that elusive future ... and if Fate decided to cut it short, he would at least have made her his own in the eyes of the world.

When the nurse next appeared it was halfway through the evening. She had a little radio hidden beneath her cloak.

'You've been asleep for hours,' she said quietly. 'I shouldn't do this – I'll get a rocket if anyone finds out – but I thought it might make up for spending Christmas in here.' She plugged in the radio. 'Keep the volume low, won't you. They're broadcasting a concert recorded by your fiancée.' She gave a winsome smile. 'After what you did last night, you're almost as great a celebrity as she is.' She adjusted the set so that the sound could just be heard. 'I'm going off duty now. Nurse Staines has promised to smuggle it out again at the end of the concert.'

'Did you get through to her?' he asked from his pillow.

The girl nodded. 'She was very concerned – asked all sorts of questions about what had happened – and said to tell you she'll come to see you after her concert in London on the twenty-eighth.' Turning away, she added, 'That's only five days to wait.' She stopped briefly in the doorway. 'I'm sure she'll say yes, this time.'

Alex lay listening to the faint sounds of Beethoven, feeling close to Sarah and remembering the girl who had put her trust in him by setting off on a raft that had no hope in hell of remaining long afloat. He must somehow recapture her.

Chapter Fifteen

Three days after Christmas. In Australia the beaches would be crowded; people would be eating on verandas or under the shade of wattle trees. On Dalgara they would be working; sweating in high temperatures, their eyes screwed up against the glare. There would be the smell of horsehide and leather, freshly chopped wood, bread baking in the large black oven. There would be the clatter of yard activity, drovers shouting to each other, the Aboriginal girls' high, excited laughter, the clang of the tucker bell. There would be dust, heat and a horizon that went on for ever beneath a cloudless cobalt sky.

Rod suddenly yearned for it as he sat at a small table covered with a grubby red-checked cloth and set with what the ageing waitress had called 'tea, skonz end fency cakes'. The tea was a pale lemon shade. The 'skonz' were rock hard; the cakes not a lot softer and daubed with lurid jam. Dalgara tea was almost black and as sweet as treacle. Ma's cakes and flapjacks melted in the mouth ... and the sun shone. Outside this fly-specked window decorated with black letters announcing 'THE COSY CORNER TEA ROOMS', rain fell from a grey sky on to grey streets, and people shuffled along with their faces muffled by thick scarves. Even the uniformed majority had greatcoat collars turned up against the bitter wind. Rod had only taken his off on entering this depressing place because it was uncomfortably wet, but the stark room with a small, smoking fire was so cold he considered putting it back on.

A glance at his watch showed that barely twenty minutes

had passed since he had entered, principally to escape the rain. He considered the food before him once more. Not so long ago he would have fallen on this ravenously; the watery tea would have tasted marvellous. How quickly the human body recovered from suffering and privation! The mind took longer, which was why he was here in London instead of with his family in Dalgara.

It would have been easy to follow his plan to join the Royal Flying Doctor Service. After all he had been through no one expected him to do more towards the war effort, but Shamshuipo haunted him. So did the *Lisbon Maru*. His body had quickly recovered from malnutrition and the effects of physical stress: the beatings amounting to semi-torture that had been inflicted as punishment for trumped-up charges. He was sturdy and muscular again, but his mind had not recovered. Humiliation, bodily filth, despair and human suffering wherever he looked *would* not be banished from his memory. His earlier desire to help those of his countrymen isolated in inhospitable areas vanished. They might be isolated, but they were free, well fed, masters of their own destiny and often very wealthy.

Three months on Dalgara after leaving hospital had put him back on his feet physically. He had taken up the old life of his home: riding with his father and Cliff to inspect the flocks, sleeping beneath the stars, swimming in the tank, yarning on the veranda at the end of the day. His brother had married a jolly, well-built girl ideal for station life. They had two children and were certain to have more. Cliff was a lusty six-footer, and there was not a lot else to do out there during the long hot nights. The procreative strain was strong enough in Cliff. Rod had made no mention of Celeste's pregnancy. His family had heard his brief account of her death and thereafter avoided the subject.

They had listened to his description of the journey across China to Chungking with polite interest, after which his father had said, 'My word, who'd have thought one of our boys would ever do something like that?' Then he had stretched and suggested another beer all round. That was when Rod knew he could stay no longer. He did not belong with these kindly, simple folk whose world was wrapped up in wool, stock prices, and good honest labour. He had taken the station wagon to Melbourne one morning and swallowed whisky until he passed out in the hotel bar. Next morning, he had had an almighty hangover, but knew what he should have done on first leaving hospital.

So great was the demand for troops now the tide of the war was turning quite dramatically, Rod had only to say that he had been reared on a sheep station for the authorities to accept that he knew how to handle a rifle and live rough. When he had mentioned his time in Hong Kong, they had welcomed him gladly as a man already experienced in war. Apart from giving him a khaki uniform with the rank of captain and making him attend several lectures on military law and procedures, Rod was given no basic training before being told to prepare for an overseas posting. His expectation of serving in the Pacific war was way off course. On a sweltering late November day he had boarded an aircraft with an entire military medical contingent, and arrived six days later at a small aerodrome on the south coast of England. He had felt cheated of his desire to help men fighting the Japanese.

After a month in England he still felt cheated, but his dislike of the situation was beginning to fade. The people here were vastly different from the British in Hong Kong. They were ridiculously polite, of course. Everyone said 'please' and 'thank you' – or '*ta*', which Rod thought comical. Women often called him 'luv' or 'ducky', which was even funnier. He was 'sir-ed' everywhere he went, and suffered interminable jokes suggesting that he should be standing on his head. The British thought that hilarious. He found Americans easier to understand, but far too bumptious. They *could* be silenced by revealing that Dalgara was a spread as large as any in the United States, but they bounced back when discussing skyscrapers, baseball or ice-cream parlours. No one, but no one, man, had anything to match *those*!

Moxworth Hospital was a converted country house standing on the banks of an estuary. Lawns ran down to the river, and the giant oaks housed wildlife Rod had never before seen. It was a convalescent home for men with serious wounds that would put an end to their fighting days. Those with amputated limbs, the blinded or those whose chests or stomachs were disastrously damaged received Rod's devoted care without qualification. The shell-shocked and battle-scarred were a problem. He empathized too closely with them; his approach became too personal. It was bad medical practice and he knew he must soon tackle Colonel Treems on the subject.

Moxworth was quiet and uniquely beautiful. A man could breathe there. He could be alone if he wished. There was in the nearby village an inn dating back to 1724. Rod marvelled at the age of this delightful place and, apart from the jokes about standing on his head, found The Exciseman and its patrons very much to his liking. Most of the doctors preferred the grander premises of the Moxworth Arms Hotel in which to pass their off-duty evenings. Some had wives lodging there, or in rented cottages. A few had girlfriends similarly handy. Quite a few were married to women also in uniform, so there was a great deal of toing and froing on both parts in order to snatch hours together. Rod had spoken of the loss of his own wife during the fall of Hong Kong. Perfunctory regrets were expressed and the subject dropped. Death was commonplace. No one dwelt on it.

The peace and contained charm of Moxworth, plus the unfussy cosiness of The Exciseman with its regulars, had sweetened the pill of being in England rather than on a Pacific island. It was good to work again with drugs, instruments, plasma, antiseptics and sterile dressings. It was good to have clean bedding, nourishing food and washing facilities for the patients. It was good to know he would not be suddenly dragged away, confronted with a counterfeit parcel or letter, then held against a wall and clubbed with rifle-butts until released to collapse at the feet of his laughing captors. Perhaps it was as well to be here rather than any place where such men could be encountered. The cold, green charm of England might be just what he needed.

He knew very well Moxworth was a temporary posting. The men he had flown over with had all been put in hospitals around the country, but the reason for their presence was all too obvious. Talk of Allied landings in France had begun some months ago. Rumours were legion about when and where these would take place. In The Exciseman one faction felt that Churchill should have struck by now. The Germans were on the run and they were all for giving them a prod where it most hurt. Another viewpoint was that Winston knew exactly what he was doing and would go when the time was right, not before. The argument crept into the conversation each time Rod was there, and would doubtless continue until supposition became fact. When it did, he knew he would be among those setting foot on French soil. The Germans might be on the run, but they would not easily surrender France. Heavy losses were inevitable, and medical services would be stretched to the limit. While winter lasted the waiting would continue, but an assault on the mainland of Europe *must* be launched when spring came. Rod did not relish the prospect. He determined to enjoy his comparative freedom at Moxworth while it lasted.

On a freezing, wet day in London he found it hard to enjoy anything. Some fellow doctors, knowing he would be alone over Christmas, had invited him to join them at a party. It was to be given by the staff of a London hospital, among whom two of his colleagues had girlfriends, and another, a wife. He had booked a hotel room for five nights, deciding to take a look at the capital's famous landmarks whilst there. The party had been a wild affair – the kind that Celeste had loved – with too many girls eager to make his Christmas memorable. Rod had left early, walked through the blacked-out streets to his hotel, then lain awake in a cold bed until the early hours brought the drone of aircraft returning from a bombing raid. He thought of the poor devils who had spent his own party hours being shot at over enemy territory, and felt so fortunate by comparison, he fell asleep.

He had passed Christmas Day walking beside the Thames, and inspecting Hyde Park. The former was slate-grey and choppy, the latter contained water tanks, barrage-balloon sites, a mass of mobile guns, and courting couples going as far as they dared in such bitter temperatures. There was no transport – buses and underground services apparently never ran on Christmas Day and the few taxis on the road were fulfilling advance bookings. Rod had eaten a curious meal comprising a brownish-grey leg of some bird described on the menu as a 'turkey', with mounds of vegetables: one green and one bright orange. The roast potatoes had been good, but not nearly enough. This had been followed by an abomination called plum pudding: a vicious solid mass which would lay on the consumer's chest and play havoc with his intestines.

The other guests had spent the evening playing parlour games or cards, or listening to a radio programme entitled ITMA, which they all appeared to find hilarious. Rod knew about this national craze through his friends at The Exciseman, but the patter was so fast it made little sense to him. He supposed one had to have listened from its inception to understand the humour. There was one reference to an Australian pilot who could not figure out why it was impossible to release his bombs, until the crew pointed out that he was flying upside down. Rod understood *that* joke.

He had now seen the Tower of London, Buckingham Palace and St Paul's Cathedral. As each was surrounded by sandbags the beauty of the architecture was marred. Every hotel bar was full of Americans and admiring girls; they occupied the tables in all the better restaurants and seemed to have a monopoly of taxis. The deluging rain was the final straw for Rod. He had had enough of London, with its sandbagged grandeur and vast areas of rubble which had once been houses, shops and factories. It was immensely depressing and reminded him of driving across Hong Kong Island after the surrender. It would have been more sensible to spend Christmas at Moxworth. The last four days had been very lonely, provoking an aching sense of futility in him. The Cosy Corner café in the pelting rain epitomized all those feelings. He decided to collect his bag from the hotel and get a train to Moxworth tonight.

The waitress brought his bill and cast him a haughty look on seeing how little of the fare he had eaten. It changed to a thin-lipped smile when he offered her a tip. She stood at the door as he left.

'Goodbey, sir. I hope you have a neyce evening.'

'Thanks.' He felt sorry for the woman. She was old enough to be a granny. It must be damned cold and tiring serving teas in a place like that, travelling back and forth in the pouring rain through a city half levelled by bombs. Perhaps she was as lonely as he. Rain was whipped against his face the minute he left the café. He turned up his collar and stepped out with resignation towards a distant bus stop. Taxis were swishing past full of Americans so it would have to be a bus – or several. With his head down to counter the stinging rain, he did not see a girl approaching. Because she was using her umbrella as a shield, she did not see him. They collided, the umbrella flew from her hands, and she fell against the wall.

Rod steadied her swiftly. 'Are you all right?'

She nodded and pointed to the umbrella careering down the pavement beneath the force of the wind. He set off after it at a run, cursing the delay to his hopes of getting back to Moxworth. He had no idea of train times, but he had a violent desire *not* to spend another night here. After dodging a bus and two bicycles when the umbrella crossed the road, he finally seized it as it slammed against a wall. Wisdom led him to close the thing before attempting to take it back to the girl. The umbrella was successfully collapsed, but he stayed where he was, staring at a poster on the wall before him, while the rain beat down on his peaked cap and thick overcoat, and slid relentlessly over a printed name that made him forget time, place, the whole world.

'You orlright, luv? Hey, you orlright?'

Rod heard the voice as if at the end of a long tunnel, remaining mesmerized by the large black letters on the poster half washed from the wall by the downpour.

The voice was then in his ear. 'Come 'ome with me, ducky, an' I'll give you more'n me brolly.'

He turned to see a face thick with make-up designed to make it look half its true age. Mascara was streaking her cheeks and her eyelashes were half an inch long. It was so hideously different from the face he saw in his mind, he returned to reality swiftly.

'Where is this place?' he demanded, pointing to the poster.

'Eh?'

He grabbed her arm urgently. 'Where's the Gospel Hall?'

The prostitute's face twisted. 'Blimey, trust me to pick 'em. C'mon, give me me gamp, padre. I'm orf.'

He tightened his hold on her arm. 'Just tell me how to get there.' Fumbling in his pocket, he drew out a note as persuasion.

The face brightened. 'Ten bob! That's me boy! If you wants to spend a bloomin' awful evenin' like this singin' 'ymns, you must be barmy,' she said, plucking the note from his fingers, 'but each to 'is own. Best get a cab, dearie. It's a long walk, an' you don't look too good ter me.'

'I'll get there,' he said impatiently, heedless of the fact that his uniform was drenched, his shoes sodden. 'Tell me which way to go.'

'OK, luv, keep yer 'air on,' she said, then gave so many instructions he lost them somewhere along the way.

'Thanks.' He set off along the road, hardly hearing her request to say a prayer for her.

Half an hour later he arrived at his destination after making further enquiries *en route*. It was not a prepossessing place, but it was very large. The paint-flaked doors stood open. Inside, two old men were slowly unfolding wooden chairs and placing them in rows with much meticulous measuring to get them absolutely straight. One had a most distressing cough which echoed through that bare hall with a raised platform at the far end. Rod entered and walked up to him. Before he could speak, however, voices in the region of the platform took the old man's attention.

'George, can you come and operate this boiler? If it goes out we'll never light it again, and you know how to humour the damn contraption.'

'Just coming, Mr Spencer, sir,' called the man named George, and hurried in the direction of the door at the side of the hall.

Lights came on above the stage to illuminate the way for several men to manhandle a grand piano from the back regions to the left of the raised platform. Rod's scalp turned icy; his throat grew uncomfortably tight. Within ninety minutes she would be here. If he had any sanity left he would walk away now. Those two at Stanley had been quite definite in their assumption that Sarah had been swayed by Tennant. At Chungking, the embassy staff had inferred that the two were extremely close. They were probably married by now. There was no point in staying here.

'Can I help you, sir?' The old man's smile was wide and friendly. 'If you've come for the concert, you're rather early. It won't start till six, you know.'

'Where can I buy a ticket?' Rod asked, certain they were all sold, which would decide the matter.

'Bless you, sir, there's no tickets for Mr Spencer's concerts. It's open house, you see. People pop in for half an hour on the way to work, or on the way home, and if they're on shifts they can't get here when it starts, or they have to leave before the end.' He gave a chuckle. 'Why, the ladies often pop in from the bus terminal next door while they have their tea and buns before taking the next one out. This is the sixth we've had here at the Gospel Hall, and tonight there's Sarah Channing – you know, the one on the wireless sometimes.' He put a hand on Rod's sodden sleeve. 'I see by your shoulder flash you're an Aussie, sir. As our weather isn't being very kind to you, I tell you what I'll do. There's a little café just around the corner where you could have a nice cup of tea and a sandwich to warm yourself up, and I'll make sure there's a seat kept for you down the front. How would that be?'

He thought of another concert, in another life, and knew he had to leave right now and catch the train to Moxworth. 'No, I have to report back to my hospital.'

'You a doctor, sir? Wish you could do something for George's cough. It's a real graveyard one. Oh, you off then?' The cheery voice floated after him as Rod went out into the rain again. 'Perhaps another time, sir.'

At six o'clock Rod was back at the Gospel Hall with no idea where he had been meanwhile. He would stay for ten minutes just to hear her play. The hall was practically full, which meant he could join a number of people, including some women in the uniform of bus drivers and conductresses, standing at the back ready to depart without disturbing those in the rows of seats. It was warm inside, and rain no longer thundered on the roof. A man appeared on the stage to introduce himself as Charles Spencer, and to explain the purpose of the concerts he arranged.

'The artists give their services free, and we have no admission charge for that reason,' he added. 'You are welcome to leave when duty calls, ladies and gentlemen, but I do ask you to do so as quietly and unobtrusively as possible for the sake of the performers and others in the audience. It is now my privilege to introduce The Royce Chamber Ensemble.'

After the string ensemble came a woman harpist who played Irish airs, then a well-known soprano. She was joined by an ageing tenor with amazing power in a youthful, heroic voice which belied his appearance. The harpist then reappeared with the strings for two rather mournful madrigals, before the tenor came on alone to sing a trio of Victorian ballads with such feeling quite a few of those listening had to brush away tears.

At seven o'clock three men in overalls came to move the piano to a central position. Rod grew icy-cold in that heated hall as a slender figure in a full-length black velvet dress walked out to take her seat at the keyboard. She waited for perhaps half a minute to prepare herself, then began to play a Chopin nocturne with great delicacy. Her programme built in power and brilliance to her final item, Beethoven's Sonata in A Flat major.

When the last notes from her flying fingers died away, she needed only a short while to emerge from her mood before getting to her feet to acknowledge the applause with a wide smile. No hesitant, bewildered girl overcome by an audience she had forgotten! Sarah Channing had become what she was destined to be.

The hall slowly emptied until Rod was the only one left in it. Coughing George and his partner came to start folding the chairs and stack them against the walls. The overalled men began taking the piano backstage, talking in loud, cheery voices. Rod walked down the side of the hall to the door through which George had gone to service the boiler. There was a great deal of activity. A large van stood outside an open pair of doors, through which the piano would be taken to a ramp; music stands were being packed into the vehicle. The soprano was leaving wrapped to the chin in an expensive fur, followed like a dog at her heels by her accompanist, then by the tenor. The Chamber Ensemble were arguing quite heatedly over some musical nuance as they came from a side room in heavy overcoats, instrument cases in their hands.

A door opened almost beside him. A young woman with a black, fur-collared coat over her long dress came out with Charles Spencer. She glanced up, caught sight of Rod, then stopped and grew incredibly still. He gazed back at her, knowing nothing had changed. After two years apart, months of degradation, pain and fear, after death and destruction and the loss of ideals, this one thing remained constant. They stood as they had in Wang Chua's garden, acknowledging an irrefutable bond. Time was suspended, until he saw tears rolling down her cheeks and realized she was shaking uncontrollably.

He started forward. 'I'll find a taxi.'

'I have one waiting.'

They went out side by side, not touching, to where a cab stood behind the van. During the short journey neither spoke, and her silent tears continued to fall. The foyer of her hotel was full of service personnel, mostly American. Rod was forced by others into the opposite corner from her in the lift. They fought their way out on the third floor and walked along a blue-carpeted corridor to Room 321. Warmth greeted them as they entered. When Rod turned from closing the door Sarah went into his arms with an anguished cry. Questions and answers were smothered by passion which had been denied too long. His own cheeks grew wet as they kissed feverishly, cherishing the reality of the other with fingers that trembled as they caressed each feature of a beloved face believed lost for ever.

A heavy raid began soon after midnight, but they remained in each other's arms while the earth reverberated and windows rattled. Danger meant nothing to them. If they should die, what better time to do so? The streets outside were filled with the sounds of whistles, ambulance bells, breaking glass and the metallic rain of shrapnel; all

Rod and Sarah heard were whispered endearments and the soft cries of shared desire.

Possessing Sarah was a revelation to a man used to Celeste's battleground brand of lovemaking. Her generous submission, although clearly learned through experience, went to his head. The night became an unbroken reciprocal act of surrender. Rod had not had a woman since that fatal morning with Celeste. Lying in firelit darkness with Sarah, making her his for all time, he wanted the night to go on for ever.

Daylight brought a different brand of hunger. They ate breakfast sitting in the crumpled bed, wrapped in blankets, continuing ravishment with their eyes. It became so unbearable, Rod pushed aside the tray and reached for her again. 'To hell with food,' he murmured against her throat, then jumped nervously as the telephone rang beside his right ear.

Sarah looked startled and took a few moments to come from the mood to identify the insistent ringing. Her hand reached for the receiver; she spoke her name almost dreamily. Then she sat up, clutching the blankets across her bare body.

'No, Charles, I'm perfectly all right . . . An old friend from Hong Kong. I had no idea he was in England . . . Yes, it *was* a shock . . . No, I'll make my own way back to Cheltenham. There's bound to be a suitable train . . . Please don't. I can't give you a time, so you'd be wasting a day you could spend at home . . . No, *truly* . . . Yes, of course. Give my love to Diana. Goodbye.'

Watching her, Rod knew why he had wanted to delay morning. Their private ecstatic world had been shattered by the demands of living. For a very brief moment he wished life *had* ended last night, as it had for others. Then she glanced back at him and he regretted the thought. She was so vital; so generous in passion. That promise of artistic brilliance had flowered, and the latent warmth of her personality had emerged to add power to the person she had become.

'That was Charles Spencer, the man who organizes all the concerts. He was worried about me.'

'Walking off with that Durman bloke again!' He waited a

386

moment before asking, 'Is anyone else likely to be worried about you?'

She took his hand up to her cheek, her eyes glowing with love. 'Let's spend today together as carefree lovers. Let's put the world to one side for a little longer before we say all that has to be said. Please, Rod, I need it so badly.'

London was a different city. The sun shone; empty taxis miraculously cruised past just when they needed one. The Thames was blue and dancing with sun flecks. They spent the day strolling beside the river, through parks and past the landmarks of ancient eras, lost in the joy of their love while Sarah showed him part of her homeland. They collected his things from the other hotel and took them to her room, where they ate dinner in their dressing-gowns in front of the fire following an interlude into which had crept an element of fever. When they finished eating, Rod drew her back against his chest and laid his cheek on her hair, knowing reality could be cheated no longer.

'I have to go back to Moxworth Hospital tomorrow.'

She turned swiftly, her face only inches from his. 'Don't go.'

He kissed her with lingering dominance. 'I have to. The poor devils there need my help.'

Twisting in his arms, she put her own around his neck and returned his kiss ten times over. 'You make me surprisingly selfish. All I want for evermore is this. I love you so much, and I've waited so long.'

They were soon back to how they had been before sending for dinner, the world nudged aside for an hour or two longer. When they lay quietly once more, Sarah's warm, smooth body across him, she said against his chest, 'I'll go to Moxworth with you. Is there a hotel?'

'It'll be full for New Year. A lot of medical staff and patients will have wives or girlfriends staying there. I go to a local pub often enough to persuade the landlord to give you a room for a while. It'll be nothing like this, of course.' He ran his hand caressingly over her shoulder and back. 'If the bed's full of bugs, we can always sleep on the floor. We've both done worse, I reckon.'

Sarah stiffened beneath his touch, then slowly sat up

wearing a stricken expression. 'How terrible! I've forgotten.' She scrambled from the bed, snatching up her dressing-gown. 'I must make a telephone call.'

Rod watched her from the bed, knowing their brief intense honeymoon was over. Her distress banished any lingering desire, so he took up his short robe and walked across to pour himself the remnants of coffee grown cold, while she asked the switchboard girl for a number she wanted. It was quite a while before she was connected, during which her agitation increased.

'This is Sarah Channing. Put me through to Ward Ten, please.' Her fingers tapped the table while she waited. 'Night Sister? . . . Oh, I hadn't realized it was gone midnight . . . Yes, I'm sorry, but it couldn't be avoided . . . No, I'm afraid not. I have to go away for a while. Would you please explain the situation in the morning? . . . Thank you . . . A message?' Sarah ran a hand through her hair in distracted fashion. 'Take care and get well soon, all the usual things.'

She stood beside the telephone lost in some other place until Rod said, 'This coffee's cold and tastes rather like boiled wood, but would you like some?'

She came across the room to him, and there were tears on her lashes as she gazed up with such emotion he was shaken to the core. 'This isn't something I can control. It began on the day you threw my report back at me, and has magnified until it dominates me.' She slid her hands into his. 'I've regretted walking away from you at Stanley every minute of my life since then.' The tears now stood on her cheeks. 'I want you, I want *this*, at any price. Is that wrong? Is it terrible to love someone so much you would abandon everything else in the world to hold on to him?'

Rod was deeply disturbed by her words, and the mysterious incident which had prompted them. 'What's this all about, Sarah?' he asked gently. 'Who is in Ward Ten?' When she looked away, he added, 'This is what happens when you put the world to one side for a while. It has a habit of bowling up and knocking you for six.' He circled her with his arm and led her to the settee beside the fire. 'It's now time to say all that has to be said, don't you reckon?'

As she was still silently weeping, Rod began by telling how he had arrived at Stanley Camp to hear from Marion and Chloë that she had drowned whilst attempting to escape.

'I'm afraid I passed that news to your father. Did they contact you from Chungking? They said they would.' Sarah nodded, so he continued. 'He took the news philosophically. I reckon it gave him determination to stay alive, so it might not have been a bad mistake.' She was still silent. 'Marion gave birth to a girl. She named her Sarah, after you. I delivered her, and felt as delighted as if she had been mine.'

'Where *is* yours?'

The question was so quiet he scarcely heard it, but took a moment or two to decide on an answer. 'It never existed. I was captive on one of the islands for several months. Wang Chua sent his son to offer escape on one of the family's junks. Celeste died during the short journey out to it. A machine-gun attack. The Wangs were tremendous in sending parcels of food and medicines to me in prison. The old boy honoured his debt to the last.'

Sarah turned to him, her wet cheeks glistening in the firelight. 'Do you really want to talk about those things?'

'No, but we've got to clear the air, haven't we? We're not the people we were in Hong Kong. I had integrity then. Last night I took from you all I wanted, not caring whether promises, loyalties or social rules were being violated. You came to me in the same way. War has changed everything, Sarah. Love's no longer a happy-ever-after affair, it's something you snatch whenever the opportunity arises and don't give a damn who's being hurt. Have it today, because tomorrow you may be only half a man, or you may be dead. Or you may be a filthy, starving, demoralized animal in a prison camp.' He traced the path of a tear down her cheek with a finger. 'Don't talk of abandoning everything in the world for love. It's too late for that.'

'Then let me snatch it while I can,' she cried. 'Before your tomorrow comes.'

The room at The Exciseman was old and draughty, but they hardly noticed the discomfort with a good fire and a huge feather-filled counterpane over the bed. Rod was on duty during the day. He had no notion how Sarah had filled those hours. When he asked, she merely replied, 'Waiting for you.'

During that rapturous night they sometimes spoke of their homes or of the beauty of Moxworth's surroundings; never of anything else. There were many things Rod wanted to know, but could not bring himself to mar her shining happiness. So much remained to be told, yet he sensed that she was still setting the world aside. She wore no rings, so he assumed he was taking no man's wife behind his back. That someone close to Sarah was in Ward Ten of a hospital he did not doubt. The truth would have to emerge sooner or later, but he was prepared to wait until she was ready to accept it.

Nineteen forty-four was heralded with a party thrown by Moxworth's staff for the patients. Villagers had offered all manner of things ranging from food and home-made wine to balloons, party-hats, streamers and fancy-dress items brought down from attics. Moxworth's New Year arrived at nine-thirty to suit 'lights out' at ten, as usual, so the party began as soon as supper had been eaten. Wives and girl-friends flocked to the main hall where patients were assembled in wheelchairs or beds to watch members of staff perform acts they had been rehearsing for weeks. It was a little like pupils taking delight in watching teachers make fools of themselves in the end-of-year play, and men who had suffered painful or degrading treatment relished the self-inflicted humanization of their tormentors.

Rod collected Sarah from The Exciseman, and they walked close together through the drizzle along the narrow street to the hospital.

'It's not the ideal way to celebrate New Year,' Rod told her apologetically, 'but we've both experienced worse, haven't we?'

She glanced up at him, her face pale in the darkness around them. 'I don't care what day, or month or year it is. All that matters is that we're together.' She held his arm tighter. 'Rod, the war can't last much longer. We'll have to make landings in France soon, and the whole German army will collapse. Everyone says it will. When it does, we can be together all the time. Within this year.'

He slowed his steps and came to a halt by the tall gates of Moxworth Hospital. 'When landings on French soil are made, I shall be taking part in them. I thought you realized that.' Seeing her expression, he said, 'This is a non-combatant posting which can be filled by older men. I'm only marking time here until the big push starts. A whole contingent of us were brought over from Australia for that reason.'

'They can't send you!' she protested. 'You're a doctor.'

'A military one.' He took her shoulders in his hands as he tried to explain what she did not want to know. 'When I was at Dalgara I told myself I'd suffered enough and was entitled to start a new life out there. But I couldn't forget those men at Shamshuipo and on the *Lisbon Maru*. I reckon I'll never forget. I'd dream I was back there, and they'd all be looking at me in accusation – the one who got away and sat like a fat well-fed cat licking the cream in safety. We've stayed well clear of any talk of Hong Kong and after, because you wanted nothing to spoil these days together, but what happened is still in our memories, whether we like it or not. I became an army doctor because I wanted to help those still hitting the Japs – a sort of compensation for cheating Fate. I was sent here, instead. If I ever had the notion of trying to dodge what's coming, these poor bastards would give my conscience hell.' He pulled her close and kissed her very hard. 'You're all I ever wanted but you've come at the wrong time – the wrong time for us both. I warned you there was no happy ever after these days. Don't plan our future, Sarah. That's a dangerous thing to do.'

They were moved by the arrival of a boisterous crowd from the Moxworth Arms, which practically swept them to the hospital entrance. They occupied seats near the back, behind the patients, where the noisy reception of the various concert turns prevented them from hearing some of the sketches. It was a good evening, for all that. Rod collected refreshments for Sarah during the interval, before going to join other members of staff taking plates to the men restricted to beds. There was a great deal of chaffing and back-chat between patients, nurses and doctors in which Rod joined. When the second half began he returned to his chair to discover that Sarah had gone.

He sat through the rest of the amateur turns feeling uneasy. Sarah was expecting so much of a relationship built on the shifting sands of war. Her love was so complete and intense it almost frightened him. On his own part, she was everything he would ever want. He was alternately charmed, excited and moved by her, but the time was wrong for love like theirs. When he went into action, as he knew he soon would, he did not believe that Fate would continue to smile on him. Beatings and torture at Shamshuipo had not killed him, as they had many other poor devils; only four had escaped from the *Lisbon Maru*. His payment for survival against such heavy odds would surely come. He had held that thought throughout these past three days with Sarah. She had put aside everything. A sensitive artist viewed life more emotionally than others. She knew depths of passion beyond the experience of most people. Sarah had been shattered by their first parting; how would she survive a second?

As soon as he had joined with staff, patients and their loved ones in the nostalgic ritual of 'Auld Lang Syne', then shaken hands with the men he treated day by day, wishing them a new year of peace and freedom, Rod shrugged on his overcoat and left for The Exciseman. Sarah was not in her room. Her suitcase was missing. There was a letter for him on the lace-covered washstand. He opened it knowing a tremendous sense of loss. *He* was taking their second parting badly.

Darling,
I don't think I'm brave enough to say all this to you, and then walk away. What I feel for you is so strong it dominates me; it makes me utterly selfish and drives away commonsense. That's why I must leave before you melt my resolution. I'm not going because you said our love has come at the wrong time and I must not plan our future—I don't agree. If we had both believed in your defeatist philosophy we would never have reached Chungking. There has to be a future, or there'd be no sense in loving anyone or continuing living.

Something else you said, plus the image of those men in Moxworth without limbs or sight, brought me to my senses. The patient in Ward Ten is Flight-Lieutenant Alex Tennant. He crash-landed his bomber just before Christmas, and I promised to visit him after my concert at the Gospel Hall. You know why I didn't. He saved my life and my sanity. Seeing the men in Moxworth made me think of him. You spoke of your guilt over being a 'fat well-fed cat licking the cream in safety', and your determination to help those you left behind barbed wire. Those words touched my own chord of guilt. Over the past days, I've abandoned a very dear friend who, but for the grace of God, might have been killed in that bomber; I've left Ellie with no means to contact me to ease her certain worry over my safety; and I've disregarded the fact that I'm one of the fat, well-fed cats licking the cream in safety. I've also cheated Fate, darling, and left others behind barbed wire. My compensation for that is nowhere near as self-sacrificial as yours. I give concerts for those suffering destruction from the air. These have set my career on a glittering pathway. I'm gaining personal glory and satisfaction, without the dark cloud of battle looming over me. Some compensation!

You're still no 'ordinary bloke'. Your psychoanalysis is just as potent. Forgive my temporary madness. You should never have appeared without warning when I was at my most vulnerable – but you make a habit of that! I'm returning to the above address. I have four concerts to fulfil this month – all in industrial cities or dockland towns. I've been unable to play the Rachmaninov Second since we parted in Hong Kong. I intend to include it in one which is to be broadcast on January 15. Listen if you can. It will be my way of telling you what the past three days have meant to me, because words are inadequate.

For ever,
Sarah

Rod sat in a chair rereading her letter and telling himself he was still a fool with integrity. Any sane man would have taken all she offered for as long as he could coax it from her. Nineteen forty-four crept in while he sat in his quarters in the hospital, alone with memories and ghosts. The world had bowled up and knocked him for six.

Sarah spent half the night in Waterloo Station waiting room. There was no train to Cheltenham until five-thirty. The slow meandering one from Moxworth had missed the last connection by ten minutes. She was in merry company, mostly service personnel who had been to New Year's Eve parties and stayed longer than they should. Although certain to face punishment, they had had a good time and were past caring. The singing, jokes and rather abandoned kissing gradually subsided until slumber reigned.

Sarah could not sleep. Despite what she had put in her letter to Rod, the madness was still upon her. She wanted him desperately, longed to be back in that draughty room lying in his arms. It was, even now, difficult to believe he was here; that those nights had happened. The impact of his sudden appearance at the end of the concert continued to affect her. She believed he did not fully understand that. What *she* did not fully understand was attraction so powerful it could make her forget all else. Away from him she might recover her senses.

On reaching Waterloo she had gone immediately to a telephone, then stood fighting an inner battle. If she heard his voice she would go back to Moxworth on the first train, yet she longed for that distant contact. Three people had used the kiosk while she remained irresolute. Left with the decision to make, she had instead dialled Ellie's number. Her grandmother maintained her characteristic aplomb, saying that Charles had explained about the friend from Hong Kong, so she had not been unduly worried by her silence and looked forward to hearing about the reunion when she arrived in the morning. Sarah had then dialled the number of the RAF hospital, speaking to the same night sister who must think she made a habit of midnight calls. The message for Alex was that she was returning to Noon Cottage and would write to him from there.

The bus from Cheltenham took Sarah to the far end of Kingsmill, so she began walking, with her suitcase, along the narrow road bordered by trees decked with mist-spangled cobwebs. She had not walked far when Dr Barnes's car drew up beside her, and he leaned from the window to offer her a lift. 'Can't have our village celebrity walking two miles with a heavy suitcase,' he said heartily as she got in beside him. 'They should allow you a car.'

She shook her head. 'I'm not doing vital war work.'

'Yes, you are, my dear. The soul needs as much tending as the body, and you soothe a great many souls with your music. Irene and I heard your broadcast just before Christmas. When it ended, she said to me, "Thank God that girl got away from Hong Kong." I echoed that sentiment.' He slowed and waited while a Land Army girl guided a herd of black and white cows into a fresh field. 'Eleanor said you've been away giving another concert in London. Stayed for New Year celebrations, I guess. Mean a lot when you're young. Irene and I are too long in the tooth for tomfoolery. Last night we simply raised a glass to the year which will surely bring peace, and to all who will have to pay the price of obtaining it for us. Age brings reflection as well as stiff joints. Ah, here's Noon Cottage.'

Sarah thanked him for the lift, wondering if gossips would imagine the friendly balding man had lecherous designs on *her* now. He leaned across to say through the open passenger door, 'Keep an eye on your grandmother. She had a bit of a scare four days ago. Been overdoing things. Too much tramping around in the bitter winds with Robert! Out in all weathers to watch *stoats*. I ticked him off, but he says Eleanor is a law unto herself. Well, we know that, but her heart's not as young as it was and she needs to pander to its demands. Try to talk some sense into her, will you?'

'What happened four days ago?' Sarah asked in sudden alarm.

'Collapsed in the garden while feeding squirrels. Refused to go to the Cottage Hospital for a few days, but I didn't mince words when I reminded her that she is now an old woman.' He grinned. 'Didn't like that tag one bit, and told me so very acidly. She's all right, but get her to do a book about house mice, cats, budgerigars or anything she can study indoors during winter. We don't want to lose her yet.' He revved up and prepared to leave. 'Keep up the soul therapy, my dear. We're going to need it more than ever in the months to come.'

The dogs rushed to greet her as she let herself in, and the antique clock chimed eighteen minutes before the hour, as usual. Sarah felt tears threatening. This house, the elderly grandmother who owned it, meant so much to her, and yet she had wiped them from her life for three days. Had it been so wrong to want happiness at all costs? If Rod telephoned now and asked her to go back, would it be so terrible to go, as she knew she would?

Ellie appeared, clad in a floral overall, to kiss her warmly. 'Your cheeks are so cold,' she exclaimed. 'Go in by the fire. We'll have some coffee and one of the scones I've just made. I'm rather pleased with the way they've turned out.'

'No, darling, *you* go in by the fire and I'll get the coffee.' Sarah said. 'If you've cooked today, it's my turn to be bottle-washer.'

'We'll get it together,' Ellie decided firmly, 'and you can tell me about your friend from Hong Kong.' They went into the kitchen, the dogs still circling Sarah's legs in their delight. 'Charles was concerned when he telephoned. He seemed to think you'd had rather a shock and went off in that state without introducing him or saying goodnight.' She cut scones and spread them with a mixture of margarine and butter. 'He's a complete gentleman and so considerate, but has no notion about anything other than music. It wouldn't occur to him that meeting up with someone who'd revive memories of your experiences would naturally come as a shock. Charles said this person just appeared from the blue, and took you off from beneath his nose.' She walked through to the parlour with the plate of scones. 'Absurd man!'

Sarah followed with two cups of coffee. They settled on each side of the fire, the dogs lying across their feet in order to squeeze on to the rug where it was warmest. Ellie bit into a scone and chewed experimentally. 'Not as good as Mrs Mullinger's, but an improvement on my best so far. Do try yours, my dear.'

Sarah sat with coffee and scone untouched. 'Dr Barnes

gave me a lift. He said you've been overdoing things and need to rest.'

'Absurd man!'

'That's two absurd men in as many minutes,' she said gently. 'Charles told you the truth and so did Reginald Barnes, Ellie. I think we must have a heart-to-heart.'

Ellie put aside her plate, but said, 'Let's drink the coffee before it grows cold. You look as if you need it more than I do.' She watched Sarah take several sips. 'Reggie told me my heart's not as strong as it was. I've known that for some weeks. When one grows old, a decision has to be made: to live as fully as possible and go out early; or become a crotchety invalid putting demands on all and sundry in order to reach ninety and cause enormous relief all round when finally saying goodbye.' She stirred her coffee unnecessarily before putting it, untouched, on the arm of her chair. 'Your grandfather died young. It was a shock which was quickly followed by another, when Frances succumbed to malaria. Husband and daughter gone within a few months! I went to pieces until Peter cabled that he was sending you to me. It was an appalling prospect. A child I had never seen was to be given to me to educate and care for. I loved you from the start – you were so like Frances – but the responsibility for a four-year-old weighed heavily on me for several years. It gradually eased, and I discovered that my grandchild gave to me as much as I offered her. Oh yes, my dear, you have.'

Sarah put down her cup, wondering how she could have neglected this beloved person for three entire days.

'I knew the time would come when the love you gave me was overshadowed by love for someone else. I challenged that moment by encouraging you to join your father in Hong Kong. I was a fool. The break was too abrupt. I suffered even more when I believed you dead or a prisoner.' She sighed. 'When you returned there was a subtle difference. You had left here a girl and returned as a woman. Alex has helped my transition from guardian to loving friend. Seeing you with him reassures me.' A smile broke through. 'Dearest girl, you are keeper of your own life now, leaving me free to be keeper of mine. I have no intention of becoming an invalid wrapped in shawls, driving visitors mad with recitals of my ill health and sinking into despondency for years to come. I mean to carry on as I always have until I drop. Please accept that and give me your love as you always have.' She waited only momentarily before saying, 'You mentioned a heart-to-heart. That's a two-way confidence, Sarah.'

'Mine can wait, darling,' she said with forced briskness as she got to her feet. 'Let's have another cup of coffee while you tell me the latest about the stoats.'

Whilst making the coffee, Sarah watched from the window a squirrel perching on a branch with a slice of apple from Ellie's nature table. Her grandmother had just told her they owed each other no obligations; that the emotional tie had changed to fond independence. It came as a shock; curious considering the way she had abandoned Ellie over the last days, which could have extended to weeks if Rod had not returned her to her senses last night. Coming on top of his advice not to plan a future that included him, Ellie's words made her feel as if those she loved were trying to bow out of her life. The first day of this year had started bleak, and now grew bleaker.

The hissing of milk spilling from the saucepan brought Sarah back from abstract contemplation of the merry squirrels. After mopping up the symbolic spilt milk, she took the coffee back to the parlour with a determined smile. 'Don't let this one grow cool.' She resumed her seat facing her grandmother, but was prevented from further comment by the offer of a newspaper folded to an inside page.

'When I mentioned Alex a moment ago you said nothing about this, so I deduce that the past few days with your Hong Kong friend allowed you no chance to read about it.'

Sarah frowned at Ellie as she took the newspaper. It was true that she and Rod had not seen one, or listened to the radio. The world could have gone mad during those days, for all they had cared. A ringed headline stood out from the rest as she glanced at the folded sheet.

INDUSTRIALIST LEFT NO WILL

Steel Baron, Sir Maurice Tennant, repeatedly ignored his solicitor's advice to set his affairs in order, it was revealed today, when relatives gathered after his funeral to learn who would be the new owner of a company that began as a small foundry in 1906. Sir Maurice, renowned for his pugnacious and relentless approach to business, informed Austin Crabtree that he was 'too busy' to make a will. When Mr Crabtree pressed the point, Sir Maurice replied typically that he had no intention of dying for many years because there was 'a great deal still to be done'. He collapsed and died of a stroke at a board meeting four days ago.

Sir Maurice's entire fortune, his several properties and the giant company he built up with ruthless determination, pass to his widow, formerly one of the de Boucher girls famed for their beauty and vivacity in the Twenties. Lady Tennant is said to have stated that she knows nothing about business. She has therefore bestowed the family steel works on her son, Alexander, who was estranged from his father in 1933. Flight-Lieutenant Tennant, wounded during a courageous effort to land his damaged aircraft after a successful raid on Germany, was released from hospital in order to attend his father's funeral. He declined to comment on his feelings on becoming the head of one of this country's leading industries. Speculation is rife as to whether or not he has inherited the traits which made Sir Maurice one of the most successful but most detested men on the industrial scene.

Sarah read while her skin rose in goose bumps. She glanced up to find Ellie watching her closely. 'Poor Alex! He only went to the dogs because he refused to enter the family firm. Now his spineless mother is forcing it on him.'

'He can always decline.'

'No, he can't,' she protested. 'She's put him in an *impossible* position. All this patriotic gush about his courage won't have wiped out that scandal involving the death of his friend. Unless he treads carefully, they'll revive the details and he'll be pilloried again. The sins of the father – that kind of thing. He's stuck with that damned steel works, whether he likes it or not. The legions who were trodden beneath Maurice's feet will rise up now the blasted man's dead, and the slightest sign of weakness on Alex's part will give them the ammunition to aid their revenge.' She was deeply upset. 'Poor Alex! His father has had the last word from the grave. I meant to write today. Perhaps I'll phone instead.'

Ellie nodded at the mantelpiece. 'Better read his letter first. It came yesterday.'

Sarah took the letter down with several others addressed to her and slit it open. It was very brief.

Sarah,

When you didn't come to the hospital after the concert, I was worried and rang Uncle Charles. He told me what had happened. Durman is the only man who would affect you in such a way, so I'm bowing out gracefully.

Alex

She stared at the page in mounting distress. It was not so much the evidence of a third beloved person declining to share her future, as the absence of his wish that her morning rice bowl be full that brought a return of the cold loneliness she had known when staring into that ravine from the terrace of Echoes.

Chapter Sixteen

Early in February Rod was summoned by Colonel Treems, the senior medical officer at Moxworth Hospital. Greying, exceptionally tall, and full of quiet assurance, his greeting contained the habitual courtesy which made Rod regard his senior as the epitome of 'the English gentleman'.

'Good morning, Captain Durman. Good of you to come. Please sit down. My assistant has just brought tea. Will you have some? This is rather good stuff, actually. My son recently returned from a country I cannot mention, and brought me some practically straight from the plant.' He gave a grave smile. 'That's rather given the secret away, hasn't it? But I'm certain I can rely on your silence.'

Rod nodded. 'For a decent cup of tea, I'd keep quiet about *anything*.'

Treems poured tea and pushed a cup across the desk, along with the sugar bowl. 'Like it pretty potent where you come from, don't you? It lines the gut and toughens the backside, one of your roustabout countrymen once told me.'

Rod helped himself to sugar, heedless of the fact that it was rationed. 'That makes a change from the one about walking upside down.'

The colonel leaned back in the chair to savour his tea. 'Must be difficult for you living in a strange country, separated from those men you came over with. You would normally have been with an Australian contingent, I know, but I suspect you realize why an influx of medical staff was needed to augment our own.'

'I have a fair idea, sir.' He drank some tea. 'This *is* good.

I'm not concerned about being separated from other Australians. The men I worked with in Hong Kong were mostly British and Chinese.'

'*And* Japanese, I understand.'

'I was taken prisoner,' Rod said sharply. 'I saw them only as human beings who needed medical aid.'

'And later?'

He stilled, cup halfway to his mouth. 'What does that mean?'

'We have a copy of the report written by the doctor who sorted you out in Perth. It suggests that your attitude towards the Japanese changed considerably during the term of your imprisonment.'

'So would yours, take my word.'

'So would any man's. As I didn't suffer torture and deprivation at their hands I can't guess how I would have reacted had I been ordered to tend their sick, but I would like your view. Could you have maintained your medical ethics, or would you have seized any chance to kill your patients?'

Rod put his cup and saucer on the desk and leaned back in his chair. 'Sir Kingston Dailey was thrown into jail because he failed to save the life of a Jap wounded in a brothel brawl. He suffered cardiac arrest and died in his cell. Medical murder would have brought my instant decapitation. I was determined to survive. In any case, our creed is to save life, not take it, isn't it?'

'Under any circumstances?' Treems allowed a brief pause. 'If you had found a lone Japanese standing between you and the ship's rail on finally escaping from the hold of the *Lisbon Maru*, would you have let him prevent you from reaching it? If just one soldier had discovered you hiding in the rocks on that island, would you have let him march you off like the rest? Or would you have jumped him and held him beneath the sea until he drowned?'

'Who knows what he'd do in circumstances he's never before faced?' countered Rod. 'I'm not sure what you're trying to get at, but let me tell you this. I once had a hot temper. I was a fighter – with words, not fists. In Shamshuipo I was taught to control my reactions. When you've

402

been tied to a tree with your arms above your head in the full glare of the sun for a day, or been clubbed unconscious for speaking your mind, you think twice before opening your mouth. I no longer have a hot temper. I believe I probably bow to the inevitable too easily now. The fight has gone out of me. But the will to survive is very, very strong . . . and so is the compulsion to help others survive. Does that answer your question?'

Colonel Treems merely pursed his lips before saying, 'To return to our earlier theme of why our medical services need augmenting. It's no secret, even to the Germans, that we shall soon follow our success in North Africa and Italy by an invasion of Europe. When and where this will take place is not our decision but, when it does, there will be very heavy casualties. Medical teams have to arrive with the first wave of troops. These men will have to hold their positions against heavy odds until reinforcements arrive. It will be dangerous.'

'Will I kill, if put to the test – that's what you're trying to find out, isn't it?'

'No, no. You'll be given a revolver, but you don't have to convince anyone that you'll never use it. Men of medicine, like men of God, who put on a uniform land themselves with a moral dilemma. We save lives, padres save souls. Destruction is not our game.' His expression sobered. 'I heard that patients were bayoneted in their beds in Hong Kong. Does a military doctor stand by and do nothing? Does a padre?'

'The latter must, because his calling insists that God's will be done. In Hong Kong, prisoners were frequently tortured, strung up by their toes, locked in for hours without air or water, staked out in the sun – all manner of hideous punishments. We had to let these things happen. No one tried to help me, when I suffered. There *was* no way to help. We had to shut our ears to screams and eyes to suffering. Poisoners used various means to stay sane. Doctors concentrated on helping in the one way we could. Some men became obsessive over a hobby, others played cards from roll-call till curfew. A few ran a black-market business in any commodity useful to prisoners, and concentrated on

403

making a greater profit. A clutch of poets and authors scribbled day after day on any piece of paper they could obtain; budding actors went through their only Shakespeare play over and over again. A very few were unable to forget what was going on, and did go insane.'

'Hence your unease with our mentally disturbed patients?'

'In part, yes, but the point I'm making is that I am well used to controlling my natural urge to hit back at the bully. My job is to tend the victim after the bully has gone. Nothing would make me forget that.'

'What if you were prevented from tending the victim by a second bully, about to fire a gun?'

Rod gave him a frank look. 'I'll give you the answer to that when I've faced such a situation.'

'You've given it, Durman, by assuming that you'd be alive at the end of the war to tell me.'

Rod wagged his head in faint exasperation. 'Now I know how you got where you are. Did you train in psychoanalysis?'

'No, I'm just an ordinary chap who has learned something about human nature.'

Treems continued speaking, but Rod ceased to listen. He was back again in Hong Kong, before the horror of Shamshuipo. Stanley Peninsula was a peaceful finger of green land stretching out across untroubled sea. A girl with blonde hair stranding across her rather wistful face was accusing him of attempting to prise secrets from her; he was declaring himself merely a man who understood her feelings of loneliness.

He had had no contact with Sarah since New Year's Eve. Apart from the significant message contained in her playing of the Rachmaninov Second over the air, as she had promised, he decided things would be better left as they were. She had given him her address; she knew his. What had happened between them in London had been beyond denying. It had satisfied a great many hungers, had even chased away a few devils, but it had shown him the folly of believing deeply in it. Men were leaving widows and fatherless children, and pregnant spinsters, to face life alone. Rod

Durman was no prize for any woman. He was deeply in debt to his father and lived on his army pay; his future was uncertain, his past well and truly chequered. His intention of whisking Sarah to Australia while gaining divorce from Celeste had been born of desperation – his and hers. The horror of the years since then had changed them both. She was afraid of losing him, he was determined not to hold her. Eleanor Fairlie would not live for ever; Sir Peter might not survive captivity. Both he and Alex Tennant – who clearly featured in her life – ran the risk of being killed in a battle. The only certainty in Sarah's life was her music. She must be allowed to immerse herself in that.

'I wish you luck, Captain Durman,' said Colonel Treems, breaking into Rod's thoughts while getting to his feet. 'I'm sorry to be losing a first-rate, dedicated man. Goodbye, and I sincerely hope your ethics are never put to the test in these stormy days ahead.'

The camp at which Rod arrived on a night filled with rolling fog at first inspired a dread sensation of entering another prison. It was a settlement of Nissen huts surrounded by barbed wire, with guards at the gates and others patrolling with dogs. He had been met at the nearest railway station by a shy female lance-corporal driving a jeep. She had contributed monosyllables to the conversation during a half-hour drive through dark, winding lanes. Rod was chilled, hungry and depressed. Australia was never as cold and damp as this country. Even Hong Kong winters had not matched the low temperatures here. Showing his identity papers to a set-faced guard who loomed from the fog with a flashlight, Rod's spirits dropped even lower. The legacy of Shamshuipo was a psychological fear of captivity and barbed wire. He had controlled it, hidden it, but it was still there. Where and what was this place?

Everything these days was a military secret. Place names were painted out. A stranger only identified railway stations by counting them as he passed. There was an increased air of activity now invasion was a certainty. No one knew where or when it would take place, but it must be soon. Rumours suggested Calais in April. It was the obvious target – the nearest port within range of air-fighter cover. It was the obvious month – the start of spring. It was too obvious.' No one believed *that* theory. Rod hazarded no guesses. Even Churchill and Eisenhower had probably not yet decided exact details. When they had, those who needed to, would be told.

They drove through a blacked-out camp until the girl brought the jeep to a halt outside a large wooden hut, whose full extent was hidden by the fog.

'The Officers' Mess, sir,' she announced, coming round to open the door for him, which added to his unease. It was all too military here. He longed for the country elegance of Moxworth. 'You'll be expected,' she added, as he stood hesitantly in the swirling fog. 'The guard will have phoned through to say you've arrived.'

'Yes, thanks.' He returned her smart salute, feeling unhappy about a woman opening car doors for him and behaving with military correctness to a superior. He was a doctor. What was he doing caught up in all this army ritual? She drove off, leaving him in the middle of nowhere; at his feet, a couple of bags containing all he owned in the world. He picked them up and crossed to a door at the end of a short stone path.

A blast of warm air hit him as he went in and around the blackout screen. There was animated conversation emanating from a room to his right, and shouts of laughter. To his left lay another, dimly lit, containing several long tables with rows of chairs, and some heavy sideboards. The dining room, presumably. He dropped his bags and headed for the noise. The room was packed with men in khaki, either sprawling in chairs and settees, or standing in groups. All had glasses in their hands. Clustered in a nearby corner were half a dozen women reading magazines or quietly chatting. One spotted him on the threshold and, after noting that the men were all too absorbed in their conversations, got up and came across with a smile of greeting.

'Hallo. Are we expecting you?'

He took off his cap quickly. 'I reckon so. The girl who brought me said the guard at the gate would have phoned through.'

'I'm sure he did.' She indicated the crowded room. 'They're making such a row they probably didn't hear. Poor you! It's such a foul night. Have you travelled far?'

'Am I allowed to say?'

She laughed. 'You're an Australian, aren't you? You can't travel much further than that. I'm Margaret Rawlings.'

He shook her manicured hand. 'Rod Durman. Don't worry, I stopped off for several months at Moxworth Hospital *en route* from home.'

'You've been ill?'

'No, just looking after those who are.'

'You're a doctor. Oh, Lord, you'll find this lot rather hearty company.' She made a face. 'I'm afraid I have no alternative but to hand you over to them. Although we share a mess, there are rules. If I monopolize you much longer people will start talking. Fraternization is frowned upon.'

Rod liked her frankness. 'They're all so busy being hearty, I imagine we could do a lot more than this before anyone noticed.'

Interest flared in her blue eyes. 'They'll have kept dinner for you. Maybe you'd prefer to eat before plunging into the fray.'

'Right on,' he said.

'I'll take you to the Chief Steward. He'll show you your quarters and organize a meal. Come on.'

They left the noisy room and crossed to a desk where Margaret pressed a bell. While they waited, Rod asked, 'What do you do here?'

'Control the Communications staff – all women, thank God. They're so much easier to deal with than men.'

'The blokes pull rank, do they?'

Her attractive smile broke through again. 'Quite the contrary. They either want to pour out their troubles for some motherly sympathy, or they expect comfort of a different sort.'

'I'll avoid doing either, Miss Rawlings.'

'It's *Captain* Rawlings, actually, but Margaret will be fine, unless we're with others.' She turned to a man wearing a white jacket who appeared from along a corridor. 'This is Captain Durman, Sergeant Reece. He's tired and hungry. I'll leave him in your capable hands.'

'Thanks,' said Rod, as she walked away.

'My pleasure,' came the cheery reply.

Rod's room was very basic. Iron bed, small chest, wardrobe, washbasin, shaving mirror with a crack across the corner, armchair. A far cry from his large comfortable quarters at Moxworth, with their bay window overlooking the river and lawns, but the room was warm and the water hot. He washed swiftly, then made his way back through bare, chilly corridors to the deserted dining room where Sergeant Reece produced thick brown soup, several tiny chops with vegetables, and plum tart with custard. Sitting in that large hall lit only by two lamps above him, Rod felt more lonely than at any time in this country. Margaret Rawlings had reminded him of Sarah – her frankness, her cap of blonde hair, the khaki uniform. The encounter brought longing for the brand of comfort Margaret had spoken of. Was he being a fool over Sarah? Why not contact her and let the future take care of itself?

Sergeant Reece came forward as Rod left the table. 'I'll bring some freshly made coffee to the ante-room for you, sir.'

He shook his head. 'I'll have a whisky instead. Where's the telephone?'

'In an alcove a few yards from the ante-room. Just enter the number and time in the book alongside, sir. Would you like your whisky right away?'

'Yes, please.'

The voice of an elderly woman answered his call, and Rod knew then the source of Sarah's 'cut-glass' accent. He was speaking to her grandmother.

'I was hoping to have a word with Sarah, Mrs Fairlie.'

'Of course. Whom shall I say is calling?'

'Rod Durman.'

'Please wait a moment or two, Mr Durman.'

The moment or two stretched to minutes. The Chief Steward brought his whisky and Rod had drunk half before he heard the rattle of the receiver being picked up.

'Sorry I was so long. I was in the bath. What a time to choose after all these weeks!'

'You're not wet, are you?'

'I have a large towel around me.'

Hearing her voice increased his longing to be with her. 'How are you, Sarah?'

'Very busy. I have four concerts this month, a broadcast tomorrow and a guest appearance in Sheffield at the weekend. When I'm working hard, I don't feel so much of a fat cat licking the cream.'

'Don't be foolish. You shouldn't have taken my words to heart.'

'Which words, Rod?'

Her response contained a challenging note that threw him. He sidestepped the issue. 'I left Moxworth this morning.'

'Where are you now?'

'At a spartan kind of place surrounded by wire and patrolled by armed men with dogs. Rather like a prison, but with food and a few comforts.

'Heavens, that's a funny kind of hospital.'

'It isn't one. I'm here to learn soldiering, I think.'

'Oh, Lord! What does that mean?'

'You can probably guess. I told you about it at Moxworth.'

There was a pause before she said quietly, 'You told me a lot of things there.'

'Yes . . . well, maybe I was wrong on some of them.'

'No, Rod. You were right about everything. I see that now.'

Sensing that he was losing command of the moment, he said, 'Look, once I find out where this place is in relation to you, can we –'

The line went dead, then a female voice said, 'I'm sorry, sir, your time's up.'

'Time? What time?' he demanded.

'You know the rule about personal calls. I've got to open this line for military use now. You could always go to the village and ring her again from the pub.'

Rod put down the receiver and stood for a moment

irresolute. A shout of laughter from the ante-room completed his frustration. He was in no mood for that rowdy mob tonight. They would not miss him. Back in his room he was prey to guilt. He should have walked away from that concert and kept from her the fact that he was in England. It was as well his call had been terminated before he could suggest a meeting. Further snatched hours in hotel rooms would help neither of them, and in no way change the fact that he might never return. Even so, he lay until the early hours thinking of her and how different life could be with love to soften the hard times.

Fog still blanketed the area when Rod was awoken by a girl in khaki bearing a cup of tea. She took his shoes to clean, promising to return them before breakfast at eight. It was bitterly cold. The fire in the stove had gone out during the night. It was even colder in the corridor leading to the main huts. The dining room was now almost full. Rod helped himself to eggs, bacon and sausages, then took his plate to a table where stewards were serving officers with tea or coffee and racks of toast. He sat beside a bright-eyed, muscular subaltern who smelt of carbolic soap and fresh air.

'Good morning, sir,' he said with a smile. 'I see the fog's still with us. No jumping again today.'

Rod frowned. 'Jumping?'

'I was supposed to have gone from an aircraft this time. Fat chance of that.'

'Are you talking about parachuting?'

The youngster looked surprised. 'Well . . . yes. I've done my stint on the hoist, and was looking forward to the real thing today.'

'Rather you than me, lad.'

The bright eyes widened in further surprise. 'We *all* have to do it, sir.'

Rod shook his head. 'I'm a doctor, not an airborne infantryman.'

'I'm an engineer – explosives. That chap over there is an expert at bridging. We're all specialists in some field or other. They're going to drop us with the troops – *before* most of them, probably. Didn't they tell you?'

'Not that I recall,' said Rod with a sense of mild shock.

'That's a bit tough, sir. When did you arrive?'

'Last night.'

'Ah, you'll probably get a briefing this morning when we start on the mock-up over in Hut A.'

'Mock-up of what?'

'As I understand it, they've created a model of the area we're going to be dropped in. They've even constructed full-scale replicas of some of the bridges so people like me can gauge where the Jerries will have placed charges. It's all so that we'll know what we're doing in the darkness when we get there.'

'Where?'

'That's still a military secret. I suspect we won't know until the day before we go.'

'Are we allowed to know where we are now?'

The subaltern smiled uncertainly. 'Sorry, sir?'

'Where is this camp?'

'Well . . . on Salisbury Plain, of course.'

To ease the other's obvious suspicion that he had a madman or simpleton beside him, Rod explained. 'I was sent here from Moxworth Hospital at very short notice. Every bloody directional aid in this country has been painted out, and all I did last night was eat a late meal and get to bed. I hoped I'd see some landmarks this morning, at least.'

The subaltern nodded at a steward waiting to refill his cup, then said, 'This is a pretty big place. The huts are in only one corner of the entire area. There's a landing strip, a tank assault course and a firing range besides this training centre. When the fog clears, you'll be surprised.'

'No more than I am now, I promise you.'

Someone rapped a table for attention. Conversation died as a moustached captain got to his feet. 'Sorry to spoil your breakfasts, gentlemen, but Met has just informed us that the fog will clear by noon. Details of this afternoon's jumps will be on the notice-board at lunchtime. Report in time, please. The RAF chaps have a precise take-off rota and get very ratty if we muck them up.'

A voice shouted. 'The Brylcreem Boys will drop us and come home. We'll have to stop there and fight. We're very ratty about *that*, tell 'em.'

There was a loud cheer as men began getting to their feet with much scraping of chair legs on the floor. Rod and his neighbour finished their tea, then stood to join the general exodus. As they turned into the corridor leading to living quarters, Rod asked if Hut A was within walking distance.

'Turn left outside the mess entrance and keep going. You can't miss it.'

'In this fog, anything's possible,' Rod told him, as he reached the door of his own room. 'Send out a search party if I'm not there by lunchtime. What's your name by the way?'

'Channing, sir.'

Rod stared after him as he walked on to the end room. A relative, or was it just an uncomfortable coincidence? There was an even more uncomfortable one to follow. On entering Hut A, he found a great many men gathered in a partitioned area awaiting the instructors. As Rod halted, trying to assess this situation so foreign to him, his roving glance passed over a group in air-force blue, then raced back to fasten on a face he would never forget. His muscles stiffened with shock. Alex Tennant, looking more than ever like every schoolgirl's hero, was in friendly conversation with a colleague wearing a Canadian flash on his uniform. Then, as if by aggressive magnetism, the other man glanced up. His hovering smile faded. He looked badly shaken as he stared in disbelief at this twist of Fate. Rod was back in Hong Kong hearing that cultured voice telling him what he was doing was 'out of line and pretty bloody despicable'. When a hand fell on his shoulder he swung round as if to fend off an attacker. A beefy black-haired major was beaming at him.

'Sorry, old chap. Didn't mean to startle you. First chance I've had to introduce myself. Understand you were dead beat last night. Quarters all right? Get some breakfast?'

'Yes, yes, thanks,' He had not quite shrugged off the ghosts of Hong Kong and hardly heard the man's words.

'Bit strange, I expect . . . for a medic. Oh, I'm John Killick, the poor sod who has to make a superb force out of a hotch-potch of specialists who've never worked together before, much less dropped from the sky to enemy-held territory at

412

night. You'll go with a complete medical team, of course. Vehicles, tents, medicines, the lot! It'll be up to *you* to get it all together and ready to operate before the main force is dropped. We'll teach you how to jump loaded with equipment, how to break open the cylinders, and so on, what to do if the vehicles land upside down, in a river or are dangling from a church spire when you find them.' He laughed with vigour at that prospect. 'Bit of a shock for the abbé, eh?' He twisted slightly to indicate the far partition. 'Behind that is a scale model of the areas chosen for the landings – dropping zones, enemy artillery sites, bridges, rivers, German command posts, villages, railways, et cetera. It has been constructed from hundreds of aerial photographs, plus a number of snapshots sent in by people who know the coastal belt of Europe. The only thing *we* don't know is where these flaming places are. That won't be revealed until we're practically on our way. But we have to know the area as well as the back of our hands, because it'll be dark when we arrive . . . and the Jerries won't be very welcoming.' He looked at Rod closely. 'Anything wrong?'

'As you said, it's all a bit strange for a medic. I'm more at home in a hospital ward.'

'Never done field work?' Killick asked in surprise.

'Not unless you count treating Jap wounded on Hong Kong's offshore islands . . . more or less at gunpoint.'

The major did not know how to take that piece of information, so resorted to heartiness again. 'You'll soon get used to this. There'll be concentrated training until D-Day. Won't be for a couple of months, at least, so there's plenty of time to sort out any problems or queries, and to get to know your team. Right. I'll leave you to it. Let me know if there's anything you need. I'll introduce you to the camp doc this evening. Make you feel more at ease. Cheers!'

He marched away, shouting in stentorian tones for everyone to follow him behind the partition. Rod moved forward with those around him, all he had been told swimming in his head as he tried to take it seriously. Was he truly expected to jump from an aircraft, weighed down with the tools of his trade, on to an unknown section of Europe held by Germans, there to collect and organize a field dressing station that had also floated down on parachutes? It smacked of fantasy.

One sight of what lay in the huge interior of Hut A was enough to convince Rod it was no fantasy they were contemplating. Occupying most of the space was a section of countryside in miniature, right down to the ditches, turnpikes, barns and telegraph wires. It was a masterpiece of ingenious workmanship. Several hundred men fell silent as they lined the four sides of the gigantic model to stare at their future battlefield. A sensation of coldness flooded his spine as Rod took in the enormity of what was to happen before half the year was out. Casualties were certain to be catastrophic, and it would be nothing like treating Japanese troops on a peaceful primitive island. The prospect was extremely daunting. Small wonder Colonel Treems had probed his possible reaction to coming face to face with the enemy.

Yet again he reminded himself he was pledged to help the suffering, to save lives using every means available. But not in *this* manner. His crusade was to fight disease, not tag along to pick up the victims of mass butchery. He thought of his breakfast companion – no more than twenty-one, muscular, brimming with life, highly intelligent and eager for action. Young Channing could land somewhere on this section of French territory and be blown asunder within minutes. He could face the rest of his life without limbs and sight ... or he could be turned into a poor bewildered creature uncertain of who or where he was. Rod's every instinct protested at this monstrous plan, yet he had offered to don a uniform and thereby placed himself under military orders. Then, even as he recoiled from a vision of the reality while he stared at the mock-up, reason told him someone must help the victims. If he could mentally override personal feelings to treat Japanese, he could surely blot out the greater issues and do this for those fighting evil.

Major Killick and two subalterns began to describe various aspects of the model, saying that it would be studied every day until each man knew the terrain as well as if he had lived there all his life. They would be constantly questioned and required to draw, from memory and without warning,

414

any section of the model. On the camp were life-size reproductions of some bridges and a few of the heavily guarded posts along river banks. Night exercises would be carried out to familiarize every man with the finest details of those vital targets. In short, they would theoretically live in this area of France night and day for the next few months.

They were given tea at ten-thirty, but such was the fascination with the model, most men drank it while walking around the reconstruction of a place where, even as they studied it, life was going on with no notion of what was soon to happen. Rod was still uncomfortably chilled. He had never felt this way when anticipating a cholera or typhoid outbreak, or even a typhoon in Hong Kong. Those had been disasters he knew how to handle. This was all so uncertain, including his ability to jump by parachute.

When Major Killick resumed instruction he was bombarded with questions by men who knew their profession well. Rod grew even colder. What if he let these people down when the night came? He should have stayed in Australia with the Flying Doctor Service, or in a hospital where he knew what he was doing as well as these soldiers did. They would be useless in a ward or operating theatre. Why expect him to adapt to their world?

The sun broke through almost on the stroke of midday, causing a triumphant cheer from the RAF men. Rod glanced across, his attention momentarily distracted from the lecture. A shaft of light through the high window touched the blond hair of the man Rod had temporarily forgotten, drawing his glance. They looked at each other across the mock-up, their feelings now under control. The contact gave Rod food for thought. In Hong Kong, Tennant had earned his contempt as a playboy. If *he* could adapt to this life, then so could any man.

During lunch in the mess, John Killick approached Rod. 'You're scheduled for initial instruction on jumping tomorrow afternoon. One of your medical colleagues has been delayed and won't get here until about four. I want you to do this together.' He grinned. 'Won't seem quite as daunting. I'm sending you out to the airstrip with those who're making their first jump from an aircraft today. You can watch; see where they go wrong and make notes.' He grinned again, like a man sure of his own ability. 'You'll also be on hand to put any Humpty Dumpties together again.'

Young Channing lingered for a while with his after-lunch coffee. 'Hallo, sir. What about that mock-up! Shook the living daylights out of me. Can you recommend a remedy for goosepimples?'

'Yes, Major Killick.'

The subaltern laughed and leaned against the wall prepared to stay. 'Are you on the hoist this afternoon?'

'No, I have the dubious pleasure of watching at the airstrip.'

'That's a relief,' his companion said lightly. 'Scrape up the pieces and put Mike Channing together before anyone notices, will you?'

'It's a promise,' Rod told him. 'By the way, are you related to the banking family?'

'Lord, no. I wish I were. We run a dairy farm in Sussex. Actually, Mother runs it now.' He sobered. 'Guess when the war ends she'll carry on. Dad was killed at Anzio, and I want to stay in engineering.'

'It's a good line. Enjoy your jump this afternoon.'

Rod moved away wishing that he had not asked about the Channing link. When he sat in a truck watching novices tumble from aircraft, he found the experience most alarming and kept thinking about that eager young man making his first jump. Some managed quite well, but a number were clearly intimidated by the real thing and panicked. An ambulance was on hand, with a medical team headed by the camp doctor. They were kept busy with casualties who had landed badly. A vigorous sergeant from the airborne regiment with whom they would be dropped raced about the area in a jeep bawling instructions at the hapless parachutists as they neared the ground, but there were still disasters as men crashed down.

After an hour of being a bystander, Rod climbed from the truck and crossed to the small tent where the Humpty Dumpties were being dealt with. He stood at the entrance watching the medical officer carefully removing a man's boot and thick socks to examine his ankle. The MO was saying, 'Just a bad sprain. Corporal Minns will see to it for you.'

'Will I still be all right to go, sir?' asked the patient anxiously.

'Depends on when we get the green light. If it's next week, no. Next month, maybe. Next year, definitely. Unless you make another bloody awful landing the next time you jump.' The doctor spotted Rod. 'Hallo, what have you done to yourself?'

He entered. 'Nothing . . . yet. I just wondered if you need a hand.'

'Ah, the Doc from Down Under.' He shook Rod's hand. 'Heard you were coming, but I was held up at the hospital last night and didn't get in until after midnight.'

'Can we get it clear straight away that I don't do operations standing on my head?' Rod asked drily.

'Sick of that one, are you?' The other man laughed. 'Anybody yet suggested that you'll go up instead of down when you jump?'

'Give them time.'

Half an hour passed pleasantly in the company of men who shared his profession, then they were informed that jumping had come to an end. Rod left the tent to make his way back to the truck. As he passed a hangar, he saw Alex Tennant in flying-gear. The other saw him at the same time. Both hesitated, then approached each other, unsmiling, knowing the ice must be broken.

'Small world,' said Alex.

'Isn't it.'

'What are you doing here?'

'I'm supposed to be going over with the troops. You?'

'Much the same, except that I'll come back again. I'm learning how to tow a laden glider.' He pointed to a camou-flaged bomber nearby. 'That's my machine.'

Rod was impressed. 'I believe I once told you you must be a pretty good pilot.'

Alex's eyes hardened. 'You told me several things, as I recall.'

'You gave as good as you got.'

After a pause, Alex said, 'A lot of water has passed beneath the bridge. We're supposed to be on the same side now.'

'We were then, if you take into account the Japs.'

'But we didn't, did we? That's how we lost a colony.' Alex pushed back hair blown across his eyes by the rush of air from an aircraft taxiing past. 'How was it when you left at the end of '42?'

'Struggling for survival. I was driven through Victoria to Stanley two months after surrender. There was not a lot left standing. I didn't see much of the island after that.'

'How did you come to be in Shamshuipo? It's a military camp.'

It came out almost as an accusation, and Rod replied swiftly. 'It wasn't by choice, I assure you. I'd transgressed at Stanley and offended the honour of some kinky little bugger who'd decided to befriend me. Shamshuipo was my punishment. They're past masters at invention in that area.'

'I know. I saw what they did at St Stephen's.'

Rod frowned. 'You were *there*? How is it you got away?'

'How is it *you* got away from the *Lisbon Maru*?'

They stood confronting each other as two more aircraft taxied past with engines roaring. When it was once more relatively easy to have a normal conversation, Alex went to the root of their enmity.

'Well, how is she?'

Rod knew whom he meant, but was surprised by the question. 'Don't you know?'

'I haven't been in touch since you appeared without warning after a concert, when she's always emotional, and took up where you left off in Hong Kong.'

'Not exactly. My wife was machine-gunned by the Japs on the second day of the bombardment.' It was clearly something of a shock to the other man. Before Alex gathered his senses, Rod spoke again. 'I have no intention of discussing Sarah with you in the middle of a busy airfield.'

Alex replied promptly. 'Where shall we discuss her, then? Tonight, at a bar? Tomorrow, during the break for tea? In the aircraft as you wait to jump?'

The air had to be cleared between them, Rod knew. They

would be seeing each other day in, day out for the next couple of months.

'You sound as if you claim some kind of ownership?'

'That's right,' Alex snapped. 'We came through China together, and I was there during her inevitable breakdown when we reached India. You and her damned father between you broke her faith in Hong Kong. The ordeal of escape broke her self-confidence. *I* picked up the pieces. She's needed me – in *every* sense – from then on!'

'She didn't give *me* that impression.'

Alex's face darkened with anger. 'You bastard! Are you up to your old game, or playing straight this time?'

'I played straight last time – but you'll never believe that.'

'How right you are,' Alex said savagely.

Rod was as controlled as the other was furious. 'If she's needed you so badly for the past two years, how is it you haven't been in touch since New Year?'

'I wanted to marry her. She was about to say yes when you came on the scene.'

'Thank God I did! What the hell can we offer any woman these days, apart from probable widowhood?'

'You mean . . . you mean you're leaving things as they've been since she first tangled with you?'

'Right on! We're both here preparing for a bloodbath. I'm not going to rush her into something she may pay for for the rest of her life. No man should, knowing he could burden a wife with a travesty of what he once was. I've seen it happen, seen the faces of the women as they try to accept a mutilated stranger. You must have seen it enough times yourself to realize the tragedy of it. Is that what you want to do to *her*, or are you so selfish you thought only of what would be the best for you?'

'Wasn't that what you did in Hong Kong?'

Someone hailed Alex from beside the bomber he piloted, breaking the deadlock.

'Sarah's better off, at the moment, without either of us,' said Rod firmly.

Alex zipped his flying-jacket with excess vigour. 'By the end of the summer she might well be. Who's going to look after her then?'

419

'I reckon she'll manage that herself. There's a third claimant to her devotion. Music will never leave her bereft.'

'It did . . . until she heard you were alive in Chungking,' Alex told him, starting to walk across to his aircraft. 'Bear that in mind when you jump out over France.'

As the truck took Rod and the successful parachutists back to their quarters, he heard the roar of engines as the heavy bomber taxied the runway towards a waiting glider. Damn the man! He had thrown a new complication over the situation, and loaded him with an additional burden where Sarah was concerned.

For the next eight weeks, Rod had little time to think about Sarah. Training was intensive. He learned how to jump from a high tower and land correctly in a sideways roll as he hit the ground. They showed him how to unfasten his parachute, how best to get out of difficult situations like landing in a tree or river, how to break open the heavy canisters that would contain all his medical equipment. He studied the mock-up every morning until he believed he knew every inch of it. They all believed they did, until the day John Killick turned off all the lights, gave them a pencil-thin torch to write by and told them to put on their notepads complete directions of how to get from the village post office to Bridge 21. Seven came through the test with flying colours. The rest either fell into the river, walked into a German guard-post or ended up back at the village post office, totally lost. Rod was among those in the river.

Concentration intensified. They lived, slept and dreamed that unknown part of France until they all made successful mental forays across it in darkness. Rod's first jump from an aircraft was something he would never forget. Used to leaping from a static tower, the challenge of throwing himself from a large gap in the side of a moving 'plane with the airfield a very long way below was considerable. It was the same for everyone, of course. The instructors knew this and practically threw them out in quick-fire succession before they had time to think. The frightening plunge to earth while he counted, the hectic jerk as the parachute opened, the slow drifting descent that would have been pleasant if he had not had to concentrate on counteracting the drift so that he would not miss the landing area – all these Rod would always remember. He was not worried about hitting the ground, knowing the human body well enough to land in a way that gave the least shock to bones and nerves. Apart from being somewhat wide of the mark, he did very well. There were casualties: sprains, cuts and severe bruising; but they all gathered around the bar that evening to celebrate their baptism.

During those eight weeks Rod encountered Alex on numerous occasions. Luckily the RAF personnel were accommodated near the airstrip, so they were not living cheek by jowl, but Alex was frequently nearby during jumping sessions. They spoke briefly to each other, but only on the subject of what they were doing. Sarah was never mentioned. Alex offered to show Rod over his bomber one afternoon. They spent an amiable hour discussing the aircraft, then parted with an arrangement for Alex to have a look at all the equipment that would be dropped with Rod to set up a medical centre. 'God knows what'll happen if it all lands in the river,' he commented with a grimace.

Alex began walking away. 'Set up a *floating* clinic. You've had plenty of practice on one.' He raised a hand. 'Cheers.'

Rod climbed into the truck that would take him back to his own quarters, reflecting that they would probably hit it off well, if it were not for Sarah. They had both changed since Hong Kong ... but so had she. Gazing from the back of the truck at the spread of heathland occupied by thousands of men and women in uniform, he suddenly recalled that garden on the hilltop overlooking China. The girl who had turned to him in a magical dusk no longer existed. She had known bombardment and hunger and danger; Alex Tennant had almost certainly been her lover as well as he; she was carving a distinguished musical career for herself. The Sarah of today bore no resemblance to the lonely, uncertain person who had almost passed out after revealing too much of her inner self to a concert audience in Hong Kong. He was a fool to cling to that image. She was no longer lonely or uncertain, and she now revealed her emotions through music to millions. It occurred to him then

421

that Alex must know her far, far more intimately than he, who was in love with a memory.

The spring landscape passed before unseeing eyes as he took that theme further. Those three days in December had contained little more than delayed passion. Sarah had shied from serious conversation, begging him to put the world aside. Only when he mentioned taking part in the invasion of France had she walked away and gone home. He was not the man she had turned to in Wang's garden. Scarred physically and mentally, he lived each day as it came, discounting the future. Was Sarah also in love with a memory? She had not spoken of Hong Kong, or of their escape across China – nothing which would destroy the visions each had held of the other for two years. If Sarah had been about to agree to marry Alex Tennant, had his own unexpected appearance ruined her chance of happiness? If it were also true that she had forsaken music until she knew he was safe, was he also in danger of ruining that part of her life?

This ran through his mind on and off as the rigorous training continued and spring crept towards summer. Rod was introduced to his team. They spent a great deal of time together, discussing the equipment that would be dropped with them, how best to unpack it and how they would operate. Casualties would occur immediately and would have to be cleared from the area before the main drop commenced. They studied the mock-up and argued over the best places to set up their field dressing station. That there would be hospital ships standing off the coast they did not doubt. Serious cases would have to be driven to beaches that remained anonymous. They were good, knowledgeable men. The sergeant was a regular soldier who had been at Dunkirk, then North Africa. Rod knew he could rely on him in any emergency and that he was the backbone of the team. Once with these men, Rod was at ease, and the operation took on a different slant. He no longer seemed a fish out of water. The sergeant and military orderlies understood his language. He now understood theirs.

Night jumping began with a tragedy. Mike Channing's parachute failed to open. They all saw his body being carried away as they landed, and Rod thought of Mrs Channing running a farm on her own, her husband killed at Anzio and her son now gone. They were all affected by his death. The reality of what was about to happen suddenly overlaid everything they were doing. Night jumping became a frightening ordeal. Throwing oneself into the blackness took even more pluck than doing it when the earth was visible below, and everyone had the additional worry of a parachute failing to open.

Night after night they were put through the routine until the instructor speeded them up so much there was no time for fears. In conjunction with these jumps, the night-time practice in towing and landing gliders continued. April was well advanced; nerves were stretched. How much longer would they wait? RAF crews spoke of seeing convoys of trucks on all roads leading to the south coast, and concentrations of boats along the beaches.

Alex spoke of it to Rod one night when a storm temporarily halted operations. They were sheltering in a hangar while thunder and lightning rent the sky.

'I've never seen so much movement of troops. The south coast towns and villages must be bursting at the seams with Americans as well as British, and the Solent is packed with shipping. The Jerries will have photographed it all and deduced that something's up. Unless, of course, they've dismissed it, as the bloody fools in Hong Kong did when I told them about a fleet of launches in an inlet just north of the New Territories.'

'Several of them captured the islands, and me with them,' said Rod, hunching into his jacket as rain beat in to add further chill. 'I wish you'd convinced everyone to take you seriously.'

'Nobody did in those days, if you remember.'

Rod avoided the pitfall. 'This is different. They know we're going to strike soon, and that the main force must be seaborne. Therefore we must set off from the south coast. Aerial photographs of all this won't tell them anything they don't already guess.' He gazed at lightning fizzing across the sky. 'When do you reckon it'll be?'

'Search me. Not on a night like this, that's certain.'

'How is it, towing those things?'

'All right, once you get used to it. I wouldn't fancy piloting one, especially at night, with heavily equipped troops packed in it. I like engine power, something to control the machine with. I've never flown anything as good as my seaplane. She was fast, graceful, obedient to my slightest touch. That was *real* flying. Compared with her my Halifax is a tortoise to a dragonfly – which was what I named her.'

Rod glanced across at the good-looking face. It bore signs of strain, like them all. 'Will you carry on flying when the war's over?'

Alex remained staring at the rain. 'I never think about it. Life's too short. What about you?'

'I'll get out of this uniform pretty damn quick. It's a mug's game.'

'Is that why you never joined the Volunteers?'

The question was slipped in, betraying the underlying dislike that had not been dispelled, but Rod answered calmly, 'As a doctor, I was exempt from conscription. Our creed is to save life, not take it.'

Alex straightened from his position against the hangar wall. 'Wait until some Jerry runs at you with a bayonet. Creeds are easily forgotten at moments like that.'

'Are they? I was once beaten insensible by a Jap's rifle-butt, but I'd have done what I could for him if he'd been dying.'

Blue eyes challenged him. 'If that's true, *yours* is the mug's game.'

He moved off leaving Rod with a sense of unease he could not entirely identify. Flying was soon afterwards ruled to be over for that night. Rain still fell in sheets. Everyone thankfully went to bed, but Rod found sleep elusive. What lay ahead took on a more monstrous form than before. How much longer were Churchill and Eisenhower going to wait? He wished to God the day would come when that leap into darkness over enemy territory could be made, and he would discover the answer to the challenge everyone kept throwing at him.

*

The village of Kingsmill looked wonderfully peaceful and inviting on a blue day at the start of May. Rod was obliged to admit that England had a beauty and charm all its own, once one left the battered cities. The compact settlements and patchwork fields were so different from the vastness of his homeland, or of the alien appeal of Hong Kong. The sun was gentle here; the creatures much the same. At this instant he fully understood Sarah's longing for all this in the loneliness of her life at Echoes.

Walking along the lane he had been told would lead to Noon Cottage, he could not help thinking of that area he knew so well from the model and imagining *this* patrolled by Germans and about to be torn apart by battle. That other unknown place must once have been serene and charmingly rural. On a morning of birdsong and bleating sheep, of sunshine and the smell of bluebells, he found it difficult to believe in all he had been doing over the past two months. It undermined his resolution, made nonsense of his reason for being here.

When he reached the gate of the house, he paused, taking in every detail to store in his memory. Such a contrast with the grand mansion on the mid-levels, and so much better suited to a romantic artistic personality like Sarah's. Of course, the grandmother was also an artist. He looked forward to meeting her. He had been granted a forty-eight-hour pass because training was completed, and no one doubted that the invasion was imminent. He had had no leave since Christmas, so his application had been approved. Obliged to give an address from which he could be easily recalled, if necessary, he had written Sarah's with the telephone number. There was certain to be a nearby pub with a room for the night, where she could reach him in an emergency.

It was almost noon on Sunday. An acceptable time for unexpected visitors. He rang the bell. Dogs barked within the house. Borzois with Russian names! Sarah had once laughingly likened the Channing relatives to them: long pompous faces. He felt as if he was rediscovering the girl he had known in Hong Kong. The door opened, and she was there in a deep pink skirt and soft cream sweater that emphasized the gentle bloom on her cheeks. That faded as she gazed at him in evident shock, while he gazed back knowing there would for ever be this undeniable electricity when they met.

'Why didn't you let me know?' she asked faintly.

'I wasn't sure I'd ring the bell when I got here.'

'I see.' Her quiet words contrasted with the flaring passion in her eyes. 'However did you find us?'

'After the last ten weeks, I could find my way *anywhere*.'

Still in wondering shock, she said, 'You make a habit of causing an impact, either by descending like a fury to fling typed pages at me or turning up when I think you're miles distant.'

'You're pretty good at that, too. Rachmaninov and a fainting fit, confessions at the foot of the Peak Railway, passing through Chungking when everyone claimed you had been drowned at Stanley.'

'And halting time, for a few enchanted moments in a garden on top of a hill.'

'Ours is that kind of relationship, isn't it?'

As they stood acknowledging something he was here to deny for a second time, an inner door opened and two dogs rushed at him.

'No, no, *down*, Sasha, Vlad! Leave the poor man alone,' cried a grey-haired woman, who emerged into the hall. 'I'm so sorry. I was in the garden and didn't hear the bell. *Behave*, dogs!'

The borzois slunk away in a canine sulk, leaving Rod able to study the woman about whom he had heard so much. The tweed was exactly as he had expected, the voice assured and clear. The grey hair was in a neat bun, no longer in curls around her ears, but he was unprepared for the shrewd, assessing blue eyes which belied the image of a gentle country soul. Yet he should not have been. Sarah had spoken often enough of her philosophies. She now introduced him.

'Darling, this is Rod Durman.'

'The doctor from Hong Kong? Dear me, Captain Durman, you do tend to make a habit of taking Sarah by surprise.'

'He had no time to let us know,' she said quickly.

'I'm delighted to meet you, Mrs Fairlie.' Rod shook her hand. 'You have intrigued me for several years.'

'Good gracious, whatever have you been told?' She turned to Sarah. 'Let's have sherry, dear. You look as though you badly need it. Come through to the parlour, Captain Durman. You'll stay to lunch, of course.'

Rod followed her through to the kind of room his mother used to sigh over when pictured in magazines. The windows gave a view of a garden as neat and orderly as the house. Behind the massed spring flowers was a vegetable plot laid out in ruler-straight rows. An illustrator of books this woman might be, but she clearly possessed none of the artist's passionate, romantic approach to life. Eleanor Fairlie appeared to have it well under control. She sat near a window and invited him to occupy a chair beside a small table.

'Have you come far this morning?'

'I'm not allowed to say where I'm stationed, but it was a fair train ride.'

'It must be difficult for you, living in a strange country,' she said. 'Few friends, different ways.'

'I lived in Hong Kong for several years. I'm used to adapting.'

'Of course. You were a prisoner there.'

'For nine months.'

'And escaped from a sinking ship.'

'Right on.'

'Your wife was killed in an air raid. That must have been the ultimate tragedy for you. You have my sympathy.'

'Thank you.' Rod determined on taking the lead. 'You seem to know a lot about me.'

'As these curious American allies of ours say, that makes us quits,' she replied coolly.

He was driven to smile as Sarah entered with three glasses of pale sherry. She handed one to Ellie, then put the others on the table before sitting on the other side of it. Her composure had returned. There was a relaxed grace to her body; hands that had caressed him with such intense tenderness lay in her lap where sunshine glinted on pale pink fingernails. He momentarily regretted being there. It might

427

have been better to send a letter full of lies about cancelled leave. This was not going to be an easy day.

'Here's to your good health, Captain Durman,' said Ellie before sipping from her glass. 'It's difficult to get hold of good sherry these days, don't you find? I hope this will be to your taste.'

They spoke of inconsequential things until Sarah served the lunch of roast chicken and garden vegetables. Conversation continued in light vein throughout the meal, with Ellie playing the part of ultra-polite hostess to an uninvited guest from the other side of the world. Sarah seemed puzzled by this and kept casting questioning looks across the table. They were ignored. Rod sensed that he was not welcome, despite being invited to lunch, and decided to get to the bottom of the problem when Sarah departed to make coffee.

'I'm very keen to see your garden, Mrs Fairlie. Would you take me through it?'

'With pleasure, Captain Durman. I'm a vain woman when it comes to my garden, because it's all my own work, even the lawns. I suppose I shall have to ease up on *that*. The mower feels heavier every time I use it.'

Rod followed her through the French doors into the afternoon warmth. 'You shouldn't use it at all. Angina needs to be treated sensibly.'

She turned to him as they crossed the rich grass. 'You're very observant.'

'I'm a doctor. The signs are apparent.' He walked on a little further to the first flowerbed before saying, 'Something else is very apparent. Sarah once told me that you're everyone's friend. I believe I'm an exception.'

She stopped and looked up at him. 'May I speak frankly?'

He sighed. 'We don't have gardens much where I come from. I'm not at all interested in them.'

'Oh dear, I do believe if we got to know each other I might discover I had met my match.'

'You can charm anyone, even me, I was told in Hong Kong. You haven't tried and I'm curious to know why.'

'Shall we continue to the orchard, where we shall not be in view of the house?' She walked on. 'I don't want Sarah

428

to suspect that we're having anything but a chat about horticulture.'

'She already suspects something.'

Blue eyes angled up to him. 'Another medical observation?'

'No, the conclusion of a man in love with her.'

They were among blossom trees now. She stopped to face him. 'I do wish you weren't . . . for her sake. Why have you come here?'

'You must have guessed. When we invade France I'll be with the troops.'

'That's exactly why I can't be your friend, young man. I knew nothing of your existence until Sarah turned up here on New Year's Day, looking at breaking point. Unfortunately, the village doctor had given her a lift . . .'

'Dr Barnes, suspected of unprofessional conduct with the butcher's daughter.' Seeing her expression, he said, 'I remember everything she told me about this place. The doctor gave away something you'd kept from Sarah?'

'She questioned me, begged me to coddle myself. I slipped up badly by using the wrong moment to say that my life was purely my own concern now. To soften the blow, I then handed her a letter from Alex Tennant. It delivered another. He had heard of your return and was bowing out of her life. That's when she told me where and with whom she had been for the last three days.'

'You blame me for that?'

'Why revive a destructive relationship? Don't deny that it is. Anything permanent between you is out of the question, you have at least acknowledged that. I believe she could have been happy with Alex. He loves and understands her.'

'He has wealth and he's English – all the perfect qualities.' Rod added heavily, 'But he's also doing a very dangerous job. Luck has been on his side so far. Suppose he ends his war without a limb, or blind, or so badly burned he resembles a monster. Is that what you want for Sarah?' He moved impatiently and knocked a branch that showered petals over him like confetti. 'Marriage is wrong at times like these. It makes no one happy.'

'Your philosophy doesn't, that's certain. On the first day

429

of this year Sarah felt that everyone she loved had rejected her. She's been through too much to weep and wring her hands. She turned to music. Your sudden telephone call unsettled her for a while, but she has grown strong by immersing herself in her career. You shouldn't have come here. It's rather cruel.'

'Mrs Fairlie, I've been an admirer of yours since Sarah first mentioned you, but I feel I've been cheated. Where is that wisdom I heard so much about? Having mistimed your declaration that your life is your own concern, you refuse to allow Sarah the same right. I suspect you've been told only a fraction of the story of Hong Kong. Any woman who went through what Sarah did and then established a flourishing career by performing in cities marked down by enemy bombers, is well able to run her own life. Having denied her any say in yours, I suggest you should keep out of hers.'

The pink-cheeked face worked for a moment or two while absorbing that, then Ellie sighed. 'You're right . . . but I should like you also to apply those last words to yourself.'

'The Germans will ensure that for some while.'

She put her hand on his arm. 'Poor man! You've been through so much already. This dreadful war!'

He slipped a hand beneath her elbow and began leading her back towards the house. 'What happened to Sarah and me in Hong Kong was one of those fatal attractions that can happen to anyone, at any time. She is not the only one to suffer through it. I know I should have smothered it in infancy. I couldn't. When I saw her name on a poster in London, I should have walked in the other direction. I didn't. Now I'm about to embark on a journey from which I may not return, I should simply go without a word. I can't. I'm not a villain, you know, just human.' He paused a moment to look down into a face he would not see again after today. 'Your life is *not* your sole concern. Before long she may need you more than at any time. Be there!'

Ellie gripped his hand. 'If things had been different, I would have enjoyed . . . Good luck, my dear.'

Sarah had renewed her lipstick and brushed her hair. She looked unbearably desirable, Rod thought, but merely said dutifully, 'What a wonderful garden!'

She looked from one to the other. 'You were very serious out there a moment ago.'

'It's the geraniums, dear. I was asking advice on what ails them,' said Ellie calmly.

'Did you provide it, Rod?'

'Sure. The kill-or-cure expert, that's me.'

When they had finished their coffee, Sarah suggested taking the dogs for a walk to show Rod a few landmarks. He collected his cap and went with her back down the garden to a gate in the fence, which gave on to a footpath through the fields. Sasha and Vlad raced ahead. They had to go single file so Rod followed Sarah.

'I'm afraid Ellie's not herself today,' she said over her shoulder. 'She hasn't been well.'

'Angina, that was obvious. Get her to slow down.'

'She won't.' She indicated the church and a huge hill which had once borne a gibbet. 'Did you have highwaymen in Australia?'

'No highways,' he explained. 'But we had Ned Kelly. He was pretty wicked.'

They walked on with the sun hot on their shoulders and the land sleeping peacefully beneath it. Rod was again reminded of that place he was going to at the dead of night; a place like this that would be torn apart by shells and hand grenades. It added to the poignancy of the moment. Sarah reached a stile and stopped, leaning on the warm wood to gaze at a sleeping meadow above the cluster of village cottages. He stopped beside her to admire the scene.

Presently, she said, 'I've known all this in every season since I was four. I came here on the day before I left for Hong Kong and cried for half an hour. My tears should have been for what was to come, not what I was leaving behind.'

He watched the breeze ruffling her shining hair and longed to do it with his fingers. He saw the sun gilding her throat and recalled the sensuous pleasure of kissing it. He heard the sadness in her voice and knew he had brought her little else.

'Sarah, I've spent ten weeks in the same camp as Alex Tennant.'

Her body stilled, but all she said was, 'How is he?'

'Bitter. Still in love with you. He said you were about to be married before I . . . before Christmas. I reckon you two have been pretty close.'

'I owe him everything. When he went out of my life he took a chunk of me with him. He wants and deserves a home like Noon Cottage, a grandmother like Ellie and an adoring wife who'll bring up a batch of his children. I could never give him that.'

'Perhaps he'll settle for less.'

She was quiet for a moment or two, then said, still gazing at the village, 'Do you remember the day beside the Peak Railway, when you told me you'd gone to see Wang Chua after being turned down by the selection board?'

'Of course I remember,' he murmured, tension mounting.

'You said he was very sensitive to mood, like many Chinese. Like me. I also know you've come to say goodbye.' She was making it easier for him, yet so much harder. 'When do you go?'

'I couldn't tell you even if I knew. Soon.'

'Yes, I suppose so. Jakob Myburgh said that only when music became the single love of my life would I be a true artist. Well, it has, and he was right. I've received an offer to tour America. I won't go yet, won't walk out on poor old England a second time. I'll go when the war ends – soon, I suppose. Maybe stay. Vienna, Paris, all the great European centres will need time to recover. Over there everything's thriving and they're hungry for culture.' Words were tumbling over each other and her voice shook. 'That's the place to settle and build a career. Charles wants to be my manager, move over there with his wife. He's the ideal person for the job. He once managed an entire orchestra, you know, and if he can do that he can . . .'

Rod reached for her, but she cried, 'Don't touch me! For God's sake, don't touch me. Just go. Please, *please*, go!'

That narrow path through infant wheat was far longer than he remembered. The sun seemed to give off the beating heat of Hong Kong as he forced himself to walk away. As that field led into another he turned. She was leaning over the stile with the dogs at her feet. That was how he would for ever now see her, with her back turned to him while she cried for what was still to come.

Chapter Seventeen

In the middle of May, Alex and his crew received orders to join a squadron based near the Dorset coast. They were unhappy about the move. Having done all their practising in one place, it was unsettling to join men they did not know on the eve of probably the greatest operation of the war. Hints from both COs that they had been picked for something special was even more unsettling, when no one actually yet knew what it was.

The year had been a difficult one for Alex. The death of his father had shaken him because he had shared Maurice Tennant's belief that he was indestructible. He had attended the funeral only for his mother's sake, and she had rewarded him with a steel works he did not want. He had almost heard his father laughing in his grave. It had been easy enough to delegate responsibility to those already managing the factories, but Alex was now the ultimate authority for decisions on a business about which he knew nothing. Only now was he truly aware of the extent of his father's wealth. He did not rejoice in the affluence it brought him. Maurice's unpopularity would surely pass to his heir. Steel production was at present controlled by the government. When the war ended, Alex would sell his birthright.

The raid on Bremen, which he had been lucky to survive, had heightened his determination to make Sarah his wife, if only for a few months. It would not have meant spending more time together but it would have made their relationship official. Where he had once indulged in sexual conquests without caring, he was unhappy about treating a woman he loved the same way. There was always the faint risk of pregnancy, however careful he was. In addition, he longed to blazen the fact that she was his by giving her his name.

Lying in hospital waiting for her visit after the concert, he had thought of nothing but how and when they would be married, of the congratulations of his fellows, and the joy of knowing their bond had strengthened further. Sarah had not come. Deeply worried, he asked if there had been a raid on London. Reassured on that score, he had then persuaded a nurse to telephone Noon Cottage. On receiving the message that Miss Channing was not at home, he had begged the girl to make another call to Charles Spencer. He had revealed that an Australian captain – a friend from Hong Kong – had appeared backstage and taken Sarah off at the end of the concert.

It was that news which made Alex stop thinking about his future. Sarah had represented that future. Without her it did not seem worth considering. He lost faith in himself and in what he had believed he meant to Sarah. News of the death of his father had then been relayed to him, and he had recalled Maurice saying, '*Are you a man or not? Do the necessary, then tell her it's time you made an honest woman of her.*' He had written Sarah a brief note of farewell which in no way imparted his sense of desolation.

Once back on his feet, he and his squadron had plunged into the build-up to invasion. He had concentrated on the tricky business of towing a heavy load which would abruptly drop away in mid-air, and had drunk rather too much each night. Sarah's failure to respond to his note had convinced him that she was still with Rod Durman. Then the man had walked into Hut A. It had seemed a cruel act of Fate, until Rod had revealed that he had not seen Sarah since New Year. Alex had not known what to think during the subsequent weeks.

On wakeful nights, weakness urged him to contact her. Daylight usually brought resistance. Forced proximity to the Australian had shown him to be equable enough; shared involvement in a forthcoming dangerous operation had revealed areas of understanding. They had inevitably crossed swords over Sarah, when Durman had finally killed all thought of picking up the threads by pointing out the terrible burden marriage to a fighting man could put on his wife. Alex had only considered death at the hands of the enemy. Perhaps his mind had veered from considering limb-lessness, blindness or brain damage. It now considered little else.

No sooner had they arrived at the new airfield amidst a clutch of picturesque villages than all leave was cancelled and the station was virtually sealed off. Even trucks bringing supplies left them by the gates to be taken in later. The secret was about to be revealed to those taking part in the last vital stage of a war which had encompassed the world for almost five years, and a secret it must remain. Hence virtual severance from contact with the outside world.

The squadron assembled in the Ops Room where a map of France was hung. There, they learned that the assault was to be made on the beaches of Normandy, not Calais or any other major port that would seem the obvious choice to the Germans. It meant a much longer sea crossing over waters known to be treacherous, owing to natural nautical hazards, as well as minefields. To offset those disadvantages it was hoped to effect complete surprise. Alex gazed at the map and aerial photographs, his trained eye seeing and identifying every detail of that model he had studied so often in Hut A. The rivers were the Orne and the Dives; the villages Bénouville, Ranville, Bavent and Varaville – all between the coast and Caen.

A ripple of excitement ran through them all. It was a brilliant plan, providing secrecy was maintained. Intelligence reports gave evidence of only light defences being maintained in those areas, the main concentration of enemy troops being around the Channel ports. They would be caught napping, and Allied forces would advance to drive a wedge between the Channel coast and Paris, dividing the Germans' strength. As the team of military and air force officers gradually unfolded details of British assault beaches, and American objectives nearer Cherbourg, the listeners fell silent. It was an operation the scale of which had never before been contemplated, with more men and weapons than could be conceived. The loss of life would be appalling – Allied, enemy and French civilian victims falling in the name of eventual peace.

The squadron would be involved in three separate phases in the invasion of France. The first would be to tow gliders containing troops who would secure vital bridges and put enemy posts out of action before the main force was dropped by parachute. The second, and larger, mission would take further troops and heavy equipment, while a third would concentrate mainly on supplying the force as it advanced on Caen. Crews would be briefed more fully when the invasion date was fixed.

When the meeting ended, crews grouped together to discuss the revelation. Alex was joined by the two-man crew of the glider assigned to his aircraft. Having had no practice as a team, it would be a partnership based on trust – a vital one. The glider pilot had to rely on the captain of his 'tug' to get him to where he had to be; the Halifax pilot had to depend on being given exact instructions on where to release the glider filled with troops or valuable equipment. Success depended on both parties' skills.

Alex wanted to get to know this man better as they both left to walk in the sunshine across to the small Officers' Mess. Norman Briggs was sturdy and dark-haired, with deep brown eyes. Although shorter and less powerfully built, his to-the-point manner and expressive eyes reminded Alex of Rod Durman. Perhaps, because of that, he opened the conversation by going straight to the heart of the matter.

'This is going to be little more than a normal op for us, but you chaps really have the sticky end of it. Once you land, it'll be goodbye and sweet F.A. so far as you're concerned. Your passengers will tumble out and rush away into the night leaving you with an aircraft you can't get off the ground again. What are you expected to do?'

Briggs grinned. 'Hitch a lift to the coast, fighting only if we have to. While khaki-clad sods are all tumbling from landing-craft on to French soil, *we* are supposed to find a vessel willing to take us *off* it and back home.'

'Rather you than me,' said Alex. 'What if some fool imagines you're deserting and shoots you in the back?'

'I shall complain to the Air Ministry.'

They walked on until Briggs stopped and said, 'Listen!'

'I can't hear anything,' Alex replied, also halting.

'Yes, you can. It's called silence,' Briggs murmured, gazing at distant trees forming a bar of vivid green spring foliage. 'Do you realize this is the first day for months we haven't had aircraft roaring overhead?'

'I've only been here two days. I haven't had a chance to investigate my surroundings, much less notice the absence of aircraft. Is it a good station?'

'The village pubs are all first-rate, and the Land Army girls more than friendly. You've no idea what you've missed. We had Ike here last month to see how effective the gliders are. He was impressed.'

'I suppose you were singled out for praise,' Alex said caustically.

'Modesty forbids.'

It was then Alex knew he could work well with this man. 'Care for a beer before lunch?'

'If you're paying, sure.'

They stood with pints and got down to the serious aspect of what they were about to do. Alex told the other pilot the arrangement he had agreed with the man he had imagined he would be working with, and it was accepted by Briggs.

'I guess you've been flying a Halifax long enough to know what you're doing in one. I have to put my faith in you and the poor muggers in my machine have to put theirs in me. When it boils down to carrying the can for us all, I'm looking right at you over this glass.'

'Fair enough,' Alex said equably. 'I shall hightail it home when I've done the deed. Complaints will have to wait until you all get back to Blighty. By then, I'll be an air-marshal and you won't dare say a word.'

Briggs raised his glass. 'Here's mud in your eye!' They drank with enjoyment, then he asked if Alex was married.

'Not likely.'

'Going steady?'

Alex shook his head. 'How about you?'

'Got engaged last summer. Went on Christmas leave to get wed and found she was going to have some Yank's baby. I wanted to wring her neck, then I wanted to wring his. Now, I don't give a damn. The occasional cuddle in a haystack with a Land Girl satisfies the demons, and neither of us gets hurt. That's the only way while this war lasts. Suppose the Lothario from Michigan buys it in this operation? There'll be another flaming little bastard facing whatever mess we leave after it all. I'm bloody thankful she let me down and saved me from making the second greatest mistake of my life.'

'What was the first?' asked Alex with interest.

'Volunteering to be a glider pilot. It's a mug's game.'

His words made Alex think once more of Rod Durman. 'Not half as much as that of a chap I know. He's a doctor going over on D-Day with paratroops. When bullets fly, he'll be running about in the middle of them without returning a single shot. He was tortured by the Japs in Hong Kong, yet maintains he'd have tried to save their lives if they were dying.'

Briggs said, 'He's not a man, he's God!'

That seemed to sum things up nicely, and they wandered in to eat lunch feeling very easy with each other. Over the next few days Alex worked at consolidating camaraderie. They did a number of practice flights in A Apple until Alex was happy with the way they worked together. He towed Norman Briggs to their mutual satisfaction, despite the fact that everyone was starting to get jumpy and quick-tempered.

With the sealing of the station it had been supposed that the invasion was no more than a day or two off. Yet the second half of May dragged past with no green light. The weather turned stormy. All aircraft were grounded, which made tempers worse. There was nothing to do cooped up on the station day after day. Alex wearied of walking his dog, Ben, around the perimeter in pouring rain. He had heard Sarah play Beethoven's 'Pathétique' sonata on the radio, and the tragic flavour of the work depressed him further. He started to brood, telling himself he should have stood his ground when Durman reappeared instead of throwing in the towel. It made him show up in an even worse light against the charismatic doctor – charismatic where she was concerned, apparently. As June arrived with no sign of action, Alex persuaded himself the war would never end: both sides would simply go on dropping bombs even when no building was left standing.

The first few days of June were cold, windy and wet. Everyone knew nothing would happen in that kind of weather, and gloom deepened. The troops who were to occupy the gliders were living in tents clustered over a sodden airfield. Alex felt deeply sorry for them. Once they liberated France, they had to fight their way into Germany. What a prospect! The waiting must be even worse for them. They had been denied contact with the outside world for eighteen days. The WAAFs on the station reputedly barricaded their doors at night. If D-Day did not soon come, *nothing* would save them.

The fifth day of June dawned even wetter and windier. Alex battled his way around the perimeter with Ben after breakfast, and then found he was curiously reluctant to go indoors again. The mess would be full of frustrated men spoiling for a row over nothing. His room was too lonely. He would only think about what a fool he had been over Sarah. As he stood in the lee of a hut, gazing through sheeting rain at the row of huge camouflaged bombers with gliders ranged behind them, he wondered if he would be able to jump from one of them with only a revolver his principles would not allow him to fire, and a pack full of medicines, to face enemy machine-guns and bayonets. He knew the answer. In Hong Kong, the sight of men dying all around him had aroused the fire of revenge on their murderers. If he should be shot down and faced with Germans, he would kill without hesitation. He was his father's son whether he liked it or not – a fighter.

That thought sent him back to his room, where he began a letter to Sarah stating that he would be at Noon Cottage as soon as he was granted leave because there was something he must thrash out with her. Halfway through it, a sharp knock at his door heralded Norman Briggs with an air of excitement. 'Briefing in fifteen minutes. It's on, at last.'

Alex glanced from his window then back to the dark, glowing eyes of his partner. 'Rot! It's slurping down outside.'

'Can't help that. Word is that Met has forecast a lull later on, and it's *then* or not until 1982. Buck up! If it takes your reflexes that long to respond, God help us when we reach our objective.'

Alex told him very politely that he could go fly his glider, *without* a tow, if he would feel happier, then collected his cap and left the half-written letter on the table. He complained all the way to the Ops Room. It was all very well for the Met boys. They sat safely consulting charts and barometers, and never had to take a vulnerable aircraft through a murky night over enemy territory. A 'lull' could mean anything. Surely Churchill and Eisenhower would not give the green light on a day like this.

They had. Tension fairly buzzed through the Ops Room as they were told about a predicted break in the rain pattern that would last long enough to get Operation Overlord under way. Conditions were not ideal, but moon and tides would not be right again until well into July – too long a delay. They had to go tonight. The element of surprise would be all the greater because the Germans would never believe an invasion would be launched in such weather. A burst of sarcastic agreement was accepted good-naturedly by the briefing officers, who then grew serious and outlined the plan divulged eighteen days ago. Crews were nominated for each of the three operations, and flight details were discussed before the final briefing nearer take-off.

Alex and the crew of A Apple were allocated the first sortie to release gliders for attacks on two vital bridges across the River Orne and the Caen Canal, which had to be held until paratroopers arrived in force. It meant a late-night take-off, which would give them the greatest advantage of surprise, but would make identification of the release point difficult in midnight darkness. Accuracy was the hallmark of success: missing the target would give the troops a long march to reach the bridges, by which time the enemy might possibly be alerted and ready to blast away at the descending airborne regiments. A Apple was scheduled for a second run in the afternoon, taking a heavier glider packed with equipment. The sixth day of June was going to be hectic.

They all walked out together across the dark tarmac, dressed in flying-gear and talking quietly to establish that rapport essential before take-off. Norman and his one-man crew seemed calm enough, which reassured Alex. He had never flown operationally with this pair. Some men became different people when it was the real thing. He climbed into the cockpit and began all the necessary checks, feeling a little tenser than usual before a raid. The rain had cleared, although cloud still scudded across the sky in a wind of considerable force. He had worked out his course with Peter Mason, who was tonight showing no hint of nervousness, and knew the wind speeds and cloud ceiling over the sea. Norman had joined them both for further last-minute study of aerial close-ups of the bridges so that they would recognize them and important surrounding landmarks. Their only worry was that cloud would block the moonlight too much to make out anything clearly.

From the cockpit window Alex saw troops marching across the tarmac, so he went through the aircraft and dropped from the hatch to intercept them and wish them all the best of luck.

'Between us, your pilot and I will get you so close to that bridge you'll be able to reach out and grab the guards around the throat,' he promised. Then he shook hands with the men's officers, and with Norman.

'I'll drink a pint for you in the mess tomorrow night, while you're trying to hitch a lift in a boat coming back this way,' he said breezily.

'Hope it chokes you,' was the cheerful response, before they walked in opposite directions.

Apple was the first to take off, so had to circle until the other five combinations were airborne. They then formed a V, with Alex leading, and headed out to sea. The slower speed caused by the drag of the glider irked him tonight. He was worried about finding landmarks in heavy darkness. It was such a tremendous responsibility now he was actually doing it. He kept in touch with Norman through a wire along the tow-rope. The man sounded unworried. But then Alex realized he did too. It was all an act. Beneath it, they were both sick with self-doubt.

442

The sea crossing seemed endless. He always hated flying over water. If they had to ditch, survival was less likely. Finally, a faint paler line below told him they were crossing those Normandy beaches where all hell was poised to break loose within a few hours. Former happy playgrounds would be strewn with the dead and dying – like the beaches of Hong Kong before he left. The expected flak from coastal batteries did not come. Surprise appeared to be complete.

He dropped to seven hundred feet and strained his eyes for the twin glints of the Orne and the parallel canal. 'Do you see anything yet?' he asked Norman anxiously.

'Nope. Oh, hang on! What's that to our right? A sort of glitter that comes and goes.'

Alex looked from the side window. There was water – but was it the river or canal? He changed course, telling the rest of his flight to do the same. When he was above it, he still could not tell which of the waterways he had found. If it was the Orne they were too far east. As he flew on, extremely worried, pale moonlight pierced a break in the cloud to whiten the scene below. That huge model in Hut A leapt into reality. He knew exactly where he was.

'It's the canal,' he yelled to Norman. 'Oh God, we're too close!'

'No, you clever sod, it's exactly right,' came the level reply through the wire. 'I'm parting company with you . . . *now!* Cheers!'

'Good luck.'

His comment came too late. Contact had been broken, leaving a strange sense of loss. Climbing in a wide turn, Alex led his flight towards a course for home. Glancing across at the canal, he found his throat constricting at the sight of an entire flock of silent aircraft gliding downward through dappled moonlight to put British troops on French soil for the first time since Dunkirk, four years ago.

'Blimey!' breathed his rear-gunner over the open intercom, 'I've come over all goosepimples.'

Alex knew he should instruct the wireless-operator to give their 'mission completed' signal, but found it impossible to speak. He was not seeing too clearly, either.

*

They were all quiet as the aircraft droned through the night. Some smoked with nervous puffs, some reread old letters that meant a lot to them, most gazed into space and kept licking their lips. A few had fallen asleep. Rod and his team were not as heavily laden as the rest. They sat at the rear and would be the last to jump. Sergeant Medway was experienced in battle. If he suffered from nervousness, it did not show even to a trained eye. He appeared to be mouthing the words of a poem or song as he stared at a spot above the heads of the men lining the opposite side of the fuselage. The orderlies in the team took their cue from Medway; they liked and trusted him. Each of them, hung with whistles, emergency first-aid packs, water-bottles and wearing distinctive red-cross armbands and steel helmets, sat in apparent relaxation.

Rod was not at all relaxed. It was not the spectre of death or injury that hovered over him. He had endured too much in Shamshuipo for that. What worried him was separation from his equipment during the drop. The most skilful doctor born could do little without medicines and instruments. He carried a knapsack containing morphine, anaesthetics and the basic tools of his trade, but they would not last long. He envied doctors travelling with the assault craft. They would have all they needed right there with them. He had to pray it would float from the heavens and land beside him. What a way to ply his trade!

A veritable armada of aircraft had taken off during late evening, the first having to fly around southern England for an hour while the rest got airborne. Rod's medical team was with the advance guard, which would back up troops arriving in gliders scheduled to land them practically *on* the bridges that must be taken, held, and stripped of explosive charges. Scouts had been parachuted into the area ahead of them. These men would light flares to help glider pilots and airborne troops identify their targets. The lieutenant in command of the paratroopers aboard was in constant conference with the pilot, both searching for the tiny guiding lights below. Diversionary bombing raids were scheduled to take place at about this time, and dummies that emitted sounds resembling gunfire on contact with the ground were being dropped by parachute in another area, to suggest large-scale landings elsewhere. All along England's south coast boats were leaving under cover of darkness with a vast army which, once on Normandy's beaches, would not leave until France was liberated.

In the midst of all that, one lost canister containing plasma, morphia and antiseptic solutions would make little difference. But it could mean the unnecessary death of several men, and that would make a great deal of difference to Rod. He glanced to his left where canisters were piled ready to be pushed out hot on their heels. A last-minute change meant that their vehicles and trailers were being delivered by glider – a much happier scheme. It should be easy enough to identify the glider, once on the ground. The unit Rod had to serve were all armed with high-pitched two-tone whistles resembling a bird's call, so that they could identify each other in the darkness if they became scattered. The man travelling with the freight glider had the same. Rod and his team had simply to home in on the sound.

The young paratrooper officer, named Bedford, appeared before him and squatted to speak quietly against aircraft noise. 'We think we're there, sir. The pilot's circling. He's had a hell of a job finding the flares. It's harder to identify landmarks than we expected, and his compass seems to have a gremlin in it. He was way off course. I was just trying to decide whether to jump and take a chance, when we spotted the lights way out to the east. He's over them now. Will you alert the team? We're rather behind schedule, I'm afraid, so we shall push on to the bridge and leave you to follow as soon as you've collected all your equipment. If you lose us, blow your whistles and we'll reply.'

'Don't worry,' said Rod, with a lightheartedness he did not feel, 'after staring at the flaming model for weeks on end, we won't get lost.'

The subaltern grinned. 'I went in the river twice in practice. Third time lucky, eh?'

He stood and walked between his men, preparing them for the jump and reassuring them on certain success. They were soon in close formation, parachutes hooked up, faces blackened, every nerve tense. A blast of cold air entered as the hatch was opened. The light came on. The first man fell out into the night and they all followed in such quick succession there was no time to think. Rod fought for breath as he plunged through windswept coldness waiting for the jerk that would tell him his parachute had opened. The force of that check in his headlong plunge made him expel breath in a grunt, then he was swinging wildly as the wind got beneath the silken mushroom to blow him sideways. Those who had jumped first were strung out in a long floating line that would certainly scatter the unit on landing. His heart sank. The team would land well apart, and the canisters would be all over the place. A bad start!

He looked down. The flares had been doused or had burnt themselves out. There was uniform darkness below – nothing to suggest a village where it should be. He thought of their pilot being well off course with a dicey compass. Still, the flares had guided them, so everything must be all right. He was sweating inside his heavy uniform, despite the night chill. Straining his eyes to gaze beyond his boots for the first sight of the ground, he dared not risk looking for the rest of his floating comrades. A man could injure himself badly hitting the ground without warning.

Far too late he realized he was almost on French soil. It came up at him in a rush and he prepared to collapse his body in a sideways roll. What he hit was soft and squelchy. His considerable weight, plus the force of his descent, broke the surface so that he sunk below it. Dear God, he must be in the muddy bank of the river – miles from their objective. They were *all* in the wrong place.

Wind was billowing the parachute so the drag on his body was considerable. It was impossible to break his harness as yet, but the pull on it actually helped him fight clear enough of the sucking mud to release himself. He was panting with effort, but his step forward landed him knee-deep again. From all around him came the whistled bird-calls, but it was impossible to home in on one. They came from many different directions. He heard splashing and hearty oaths nearby which could only have come from an Englishman. Germans would hardly be patrolling *this* close to the river, so Rod risked a low call. The response was definitely British.

'That bloody fool pilot dropped us in the wrong place. Trust the bloody RAF to get it wrong! Can't distinguish dropping zones from their backsides. Christ! What a mess.'

'Can you make out the river bank from where you are?'

'I couldn't make out a naked tart from where I am, mate. I'm flaming stuck.'

Rod pulled the torch from his flak jacket and shone it around. About fifteen yards distant a soldier was well and truly sunk into the mud, his parachute still attached. He would never struggle free on his own. Rod told him to stop moving, then circled his torch beam until he thought he saw a small sandy stretch just ahead beside tall reeds.

'Hang on!' he called softly. 'I'll get back to you in a moment.'

'Oh, sure, take your time, mate! I'm not going anywhere,' came the caustic reply.

Dragging his way through stinking mud to the relatively firm surface, Rod divested himself of heavy equipment and his flak jacket before cutting reeds with his knife. Taking an armful, he squelched and struggled back to where he had landed and a short distance beyond that until it was impossible to progress further in an upright position. Spreading the tough reeds across mud, he crawled slowly forward on his stomach until he reached the trapped soldier. Breathing hard, he cut the parachute ropes, then seized hold of the man's shoulder harness. 'Whenever I pull, you wriggle like hell. Understand?'

'Yes, sir,' came the small reply. 'Sorry, I didn't realize it was you.'

'Don't worry. I share your opinion of our pilot. He's on his way home to a large cooked breakfast. I hope it gives him colic for a month.'

Powerful though he was, Rod had to fight to achieve success, and they both lay winded for some time on top of the reeds while bird-calls around them suggested a migrating flock.

'Those bloody whistles!' said Rod. 'Whose clever idea was it to give those out to everyone?'

'General Eisenhower's, I think.'

'He's sure to have a large cooked breakfast, too.

Meanwhile, we have no way of telling who's calling who. They should have been given to officers only, then men would assemble easily. Right, are you ready to move?'

'Yes, sir . . . and thanks.'

Beyond the sandy patch lay what appeared to be an earth lane just wide enough for a farm cart. The concentration of 'birds' appeared to be south of where they were. After Rod retrieved his gear, they set out towards the sound, going carefully in the darkness. They came across others plodding forward, all of whom had been stuck for a while. The general opinion was that they had fallen into marshland – the bog was too extensive to be a river bank – and many had landed too far in to struggle to firm ground. Their combined aroma caused Rod's rescuee to ask if he had a remedy for stinking.

'Right on,' he said grimly. 'A pot shot at the bastard who told us to jump here.'

The lane ended in a field. A group of soldiers had gathered there despite the whistles still audible in large numbers to the north. Lieutenant Bedford was speaking in angry tones to another shadowy figure behind him. Rod went across. 'What the hell's gone wrong?' he demanded.

The other man turned. It was the colonel in charge of the whole operation. 'Every bloody thing, Doc. The scouts were blown too far east and hadn't time to reach the drop zone to light flares for us, so they lit them here. The RAF pilots weren't off course at all. We're on the edge of the River Dives marsh. Half our men and most of the equipment is out there in the middle. I watched two gliders go down in it, and God knows how many canisters.'

'We must get the men out,' said Rod.

'Impossible.'

'You can't leave them to drown.'

'I've no choice. We're four kilometres from the bridge battery we've been ordered to put out of action before the main force drops in two hours' time. We must push on with the little we've got and hope to God we manage to take the Jerries by surprise. We don't have a hope in hell, otherwise.' He turned back to those grouped around him. 'All right, gentlemen, take your men across the fields, skirting any farms in case Germans are billeted there, and make for the bridge as fast as your sodden legs will take you. Rendezvous at Point A, where we should damn well be by now. Good luck.' He had a final word for Rod. 'Search out as many of your team as you can, and any medical canisters within access, then catch us up. We're going to need you badly in the next few hours.'

He went off into the darkness leaving Rod to round up half a dozen orderlies and twelve canisters marked with a red cross. The glider containing their jeep and other vital equipment was somewhere on the marsh, slowly sinking. And so were hundreds of men. As they crossed the field, dragging the canisters behind them, the night was filled with the plaintive sound of bird-calls, growing fewer and fewer. Rod felt sickened. If this was military doctoring he wanted no part of it.

As he ate lunch in the mess, Alex was supremely conscious of many empty places where glider pilots had sat. When he crossed to dress in flying-gear once more, the sound of now-empty tents flapping in the wind added to the desolate air that had descended on the station. All the hopeful warriors had departed. Out on the tarmac stood heavy transport gliders packed with armoury and equipment to resupply troops who had been fighting since midnight. Fifteen hours into the invasion! The BBC news bulletins claimed resounding successes by the legions landing on French soil, and pilots who had returned from the second sortie that morning reported seeing beaches and the roads leading from them black with men and vehicles.

It had not all gone smoothly from the squadron's point of view. They had lost an aircraft and glider on the second mission, during which four additional gliders had broken away soon after take-off and landed in England instead. Surprise had been effective only for the first few hours. German artillery was active: the skies over Normandy were now dangerous. It would be the same story on the ground, where British troops were advancing on Caen and Americans on Cherbourg. Allied aircraft were bombing both areas heavily in support of the army. Naval guns were pounding the shore to destroy fortified enemy positions. No one was getting any sleep today.

Alex had eaten his breakfast after his dawn return, then gone to lie on his bed, too tense to sleep. The thunder of Halifax bombers taking off shortly afterwards had set him thinking about his return to Normandy later in the day. Now he was dressing for it and worrying over the four gliders which had broken away from their tugs. He knew only slightly the pilot he would be taking this afternoon. The precision of this operation was less important because the gliders would be landing on territory held by the Allies, but Alex still felt immensely responsible for getting his men as near the designated area as possible. Yet he knew it was the fault of neither pilot if the towing cable broke.

A Apple had been refuelled and checked over by the engineer and mechanics. His crew looked heavy-eyed: Alex guessed they also had not slept. He shook hands with the glider pilot, wished him luck, then climbed in to begin a ritual which had become a normal part of his life. Peter seemed unusually quiet, but Alex did not think he would be any the less efficient. The rest of the crew sounded normal enough over the intercom. The tricky business of getting a Halifax plus a laden glider off the ground was accomplished without problems and they flew out over the south coast. Alex was conscious of the additional weight of this glider compared with the first he had taken across to Normandy. Apple was heavier to handle. It took a little getting used to, rather like a man who had cycled to work for months suddenly finding he is pulling along a load of bricks. The normal cheery banter over the intercom was missing. Not only were they weary, each man had been sobered by the import of the day. History was in the making.

As he headed out over the choppy, grey sea, Alex wondered how long it would be before the Germans surrendered. The end of the war! What would he do then? Civil flying was an option, but so would it be for thousands like him. What he would really like to do would be to return to seaplanes – lovely, light, graceful machines with speed and agility. He was now a very, very wealthy man. If he sold Tennant's Steel Works and built workshops near a river estuary, he could manufacture seaplanes for rich sportsmen and those who lived in remote lakeland areas. As a future, it could be just what he had always been seeking.

He flew on, elaborating this attractive theme. With peace practically on the doorstep, he could pursue Sarah with everything to offer. He had completed the letter left on the desk. It was stamped ready to go when he got back this evening. He would be more insistent this time. She was certain to capitulate.

'Crikey!' said Peter suddenly, 'look at that!'

Alex returned from his thoughts. Ahead was a concentration of shipping such as he had never before seen. Battleships, cruisers, destroyers, mine-sweepers, tankers, landing-craft, troop-carriers, several well-marked hospital ships and thousands of small craft ranged the sea before the coastal beaches, which were thick with tanks, jeeps, trucks, guns and a moving mass of khaki. A fierce battle was taking place. Smoke hung in drifting layers as invader and defender exchanged shell for shell, bomb for bomb, bullet for bullet.

'Poor bastards,' Alex murmured as they slowly drew nearer.

'Makes you feel a bit guilty, safe up here, doesn't it?' said the wireless-operator

'Not me,' argued Peter. 'When we were going out over Germany night after night, the Yanks were eating cake and ice-cream at home, or were over here stealing our girls with chocolate and silk stockings. Time they had a go at some fighting.'

'Maybe,' said Alex, 'but I wouldn't wish that down there on any man. I know what it's like to storm a position exposed to machine-gunfire. This is a lot safer.'

After a consultation with Peter, Alex decided to change course to avoid most of the flak. He told the glider pilot his reasons, adding that he would approach the release zone from slightly further west than expected. From then on, the crew became completely operational, all personal comments ceasing as flak burst around them before the target came in sight. It was so much easier to identify landmarks now it was daylight. They overflew the Orne and the Caen Canal. The countryside was littered with gliders from earlier missions. Not all had landed safely. Some were in trees or on rooftops. Many had plunged into the water. Alex hoped Norman Briggs had been lucky at midnight.

Roads were busy with vehicles and tanks all heading for Caen. Tents bearing red crosses were in fields along the routes. Many villages seemed little more than clusters of ruins. Marching men waved as they circled to approach the release point. The gliders meant fresh supplies of food, medicines and weaponry. Alex kept his aircraft on course as he dropped to the required height, and a tense exchange with the other pilot as landmarks passed beneath them led to a successful separation. Ready for the sudden loss of dragging weight, Alex put Apple into a climb and asked his navigator for a new course that would get them to the coast avoiding most of the anti-aircraft barrage above the beaches. Ten minutes after he made his request, there was an explosion behind him. Apple bucked and plunged. He fought to hold the machine steady, but another explosion starboard sent them into a violent bank.

'Where the hell's it coming from?' cried Peter beside him. 'I thought *we* controlled this area.'

Alex was too busy trying to prevent the machine falling into a spinning dive to bother about *who* was firing at them. He was a damn good shot.

'Christ, we've lost half a wing,' cried the wireless-operator.

As he spoke, the remaining starboard engine cut out, which unbalanced the machine further. Fighting to right it with all the strength of his arms, legs braced against the floor, Alex shouted to Peter, 'What happened with the first one? Something's wrong with the rudders.'

The rear-gunner failed to answer repeated calls over the intercom, so Peter scrambled back as best he could in the violence of movement.

'Starboard engine on fire, Cap.'

'R/T's gone dead. Can't get a thing out of it.'

'Peter here. Rear gun turret's been shot off. Half the port tailplane's hanging. Looks ready to snap at any minute. Gaping hole where tail should be.'

Messages reached Alex's ears one after the other. They,

plus the fact that he was several hours' flying time from home, most of it over sea, told him they would never make it. He did not hesitate to give the order to bale out. This was so-called friendly territory despite the active enemy battery which had caught them unawares. Jumping now would ensure that they got home eventually – like Norman Briggs.

His crew left one by one, identifying themselves as they did so, until only Peter remained. Alex was drenched in sweat as he continued the fight to remain airborne, very conscious of the flaming engine and missing tail as they dropped lower and lower.

'Well, go on. Jump!' he yelled at his second pilot.

'What about you?' Peter demanded, hesitating.

'I'll come as soon as I glimpse the sea and know this bloody thing'll ditch in the water without killing any poor sods on the beach. They're facing enough as it is.'

'Don't leave it too long,' advised Peter, his face white and shocked.

'Push off!' cried Alex hoarsely, scanning the horizon for the first glint of sea.

'You're all right, Alex ... no matter what your father did,' Peter said as a surprising farewell speech.

'Thanks.'

Peter moved aft and vanished. Alex alternately watched the horizon and the altimeter. A few more minutes and baling out would become risky. Ten and his chance would be lost. Then the sea was there, directly ahead, and so were thousands of troops struggling to survive a death dash across shell-strafed beaches. He stared at them, and recalled those eighteen days of desperate fighting in Hong Kong. He remembered Bunny screaming in agony beside him; Giles marching off never to be seen again. He saw men being mown down on that hopeless assault when he and Jim had been wounded, heard their moans while they lay for ten hours waiting to be collected from that hillside. He was back in St Stephen's College surrounded by casualties, and saw two men sneaking out on Christmas morning to make a raft and leave them to their fate: to be bayoneted in their beds while the men watched, hidden from sight.

He swallowed hard as the altimeter flickered just below

the height necessary to allow a parachute to open in time. Once he abandoned the controls, Apple would plunge. He could not allow that to happen. Something in the past would not let it happen. His arms and body ached from the effort. The starboard window reflected crimson light. The remains of the wing must now be alight. He would not be able to hold the aircraft much longer. The sea was still a way off. He *must* keep airborne until he reached it. It was like a cauldron in the cockpit now. The skin on his cheeks felt as if it were burning, like the wing. He felt no fear. He had had a good run for his money in the RAF. On the Kowloon ferry gazing at Hong Kong Island blacked out for the first time, he had reviewed his life and been afraid of dying without doing anything worthwhile with it. The balance had been redressed, perhaps.

The invasion had met with stronger than expected opposition in some quarters. The Americans had suffered badly in their zones: strong tides had swept boats off course, splitting the landing forces and exposing the troops to fire from fortifications they would not normally have faced. Many landing-craft ran into minefields along the water's edge; tanks and jeeps were blown up by mines on the beaches. All along the invasion front there had been mishaps. A great deal of equipment had been lost through glider crashes, or mistaken drops by aircraft believing troops to have reached areas on schedule, when they had in fact been delayed by misfortune. But most gliders had descended successfully; a very large percentage of parachute drops had been on target. Thousands of men had successfully crossed the exposed beaches and pushed forward along roads leading from them. Thousands had not.

The battle for Caen was proving longer and more costly than expected. A week after the landings, Allied troops had surrounded the city. Bombers were attacking nightly with explosive and incendiary missiles. Fires could be seen miles away; civilians were streaming from Caen with their few belongings. Aerial photographs showed an area in ruins. Yet German resistance in the suburbs was strong enough to prevent possession of the miles of rubble. Advances were followed by withdrawals, so that the ring of Allied forces could not link up for a concerted push.

Ten days after their disastrous descent into the Dives marsh, Rod's unit was reduced to the point of becoming non-effective on its own. It had merged with a larger one and, re-equipped with some supplies dropped practically at their feet by the RAF, they were desperately attempting to hold on to a small rural community along the banks of the Orne. The bridges over the river being mostly destroyed meant that reinforcements could cross only in a few places, and these were congested with vehicles and tanks. They had taken the little market town, lost it two days later, then recaptured it. Intelligence reports told them Panzers were assembling for a fresh drive against them, and their own expected reinforcements had been ordered to by-pass the town and circle to approach the enemy from the rear. Their orders were to hold on until the pincer was ready to trap the Germans in its grip.

In the cellar of the ruins of a small brewery, Rod and a medical team struggled to cope with casualties unable to be sent to the rear because the narrow road was dominated by military traffic driving forward. It had priority over anything going in the opposite direction. The cellar was crowded. The light was poor; dust hung in the air. Wounded and sick lay anywhere a stretcher could be placed. The smell of blood, vomit and urine was strong. Bags of plasma, saline solution and glucose hung from makeshift stands. Soiled dressings, bandages and hypodermic needles were burned on huge bonfires outside, where water brought from the river was also boiled in large cauldrons. As a hospital it was filthy, uncomfortable, too dark, depressing and very unhygienic . . . but it was safe from machine-gunfire. Shells shook the place every so often, bringing down dust and fine debris. Twice, the only entrance had been blocked during a fierce artillery attack, but the wounded were as protected as it was possible for them to be, surrounded as they were by kegs of beer.

Rod had believed himself exhausted during the epidemics or typhoons in Hong Kong, but that had been nothing compared with how he now felt. Doctoring in Hong Kong had been as unlike this as medicine in the Outback had been from work in the Queen Mary Hospital. His skill had been stretched beyond professional limits, but when a man was dying all efforts must be made to save him, so Rod had performed operations he was not qualified to carry out, taken risks that would never be countenanced in a normal situation, used unorthodox methods learned from his Chinese medical colleagues and worked under conditions that most doctors would condemn as dangerous. That was the lot of an army medical officer during a war.

He had had little sleep for ten days. He was dog-tired, his brain working automatically for he seemed beyond rational thought. Sergeant Medway had appeared out of the darkness one night after fighting free of the marsh and following their route. Rod was thankful to see him. Medway took charge of the orderlies and minor casualties, leaving Rod with more time for what he had to tackle. Men died – he could not save them all – and others needed major surgery in order to survive. These cases caused Rod an angry brand of distress. After performing initial life-saving treatment, he knew they were going to die because the road to hospitals at the rear could not be used. The memory of a brother losing his young life because help could not reach him in time lived with Rod during those days. His deep compassion for humanity would not allow him to accept war's rules: it was of greater importance to move fresh troops forward than to move redundant ones to the rear. What was one life among millions? War entailed the sacrifice of lives: medicine entailed the saving of even the most worthless. In those terrible first days of the invasion Rod could not come to terms with those irreconcilable truths.

During the advance he had treated men in ditches, in fields of flattened wheat, on the tables of farm kitchens, in the back of vehicles. A vast number had been left in field dressing stations as the advance continued. Being a front-line medic meant travelling with the spearhead troops. He was used to living rough – it could not have been rougher than in Shamshuipo – but the incredible noise and sight of war was almost more than he could stand. The thunder of heavy guns; the roar of aircraft filling the skies; the explosion

456

of shells; the squeak and rumble of tanks as they crossed the summer countryside; the firecracker rattle of machine-guns; men shouting and screaming; the voluble welcome of some French civilians; the curses and sobs of others whose relatives and homes had been sacrificed to the demands of war. He saw peaceful countryside torn asunder; charming French villages dissolve before his eyes into blackened piles of rubble; fields full of dead cows. He passed burning tanks with charred corpses trapped inside; parachutists still dangling from trees or buildings, their clothes covered in dried blood, their eyes staring sightlessly at whoever had killed them as they hung unable to escape. He watched small boys in villages copying what they had witnessed and making an exciting game of it. The warriors of tomorrow! It was emotionally unacceptable. He thanked God he had made no legal commitment to Sarah. He did not believe he would survive the carnage.

Shaken awake by Sergeant Medway, Rod got to his feet feeling every bone and muscle protest. His watch showed he had slept for only an hour. 'There's a fresh batch coming in,' said Medway grimly. 'Jerry tanks are starting to move forward.'

Rod glanced behind the man to where orderlies in rubber ponchos were bringing in a relay of stretchers. Through gaps in the ceiling he saw rain beating against the cobbles; rivulets were streaking down walls where it overflowed into the cellar. What a day to choose for the annihilation of a small farming community! He gave Medway a nod then went to splash his face and neck with cold water from a nearby barrel. Scrubbing his hands with antiseptic soap seemed superfluous in these conditions, but he did it before going across to see what he had to cope with first.

Two with severe stomach wounds would never see another dawn. Several with half-severed limbs needed vital surgery or they would be gone in a few days. Rod did what he could for them, then concentrated on those whose lives he could save. He and Medway worked silently, surrounded by the gathering tumult of battle above them. The ground began to shake as shells landed on the outskirts of the town and their own guns returned fire from positions almost overhead. More stretchers were carried in, bearers and victims drenched to the skin. Some of the walking wounded began placing receptacles beneath streams of water raining down beside less fortunate comrades. Moans of pain were drowned by increasing thunder outside.

Shells were landing much nearer now. Boots raced over wet cobbles; shiny black tyres splashed through surface water as jeeps dragged guns to positions further back. A frightened dog with fur plastered to its shaking body scuttled past. Farmers' families had started to retreat with the British, pulling on handcarts their most precious possessions along with their children. They had had enough. There was no purpose in remaining. By the end of today the town would have been levelled, fields burnt and cratered. They had been better off before the invasion. Of what use was freedom if everything they possessed had been destroyed?

Rod saw all these telling signs through gaps in the ceiling, but continued giving blood, injecting morphine, extracting fragments of shell casings, suturing and treating shock as if it were not happening. His eyes saw things his mind would not consider. Disaster was commonplace; defeat unacceptable.

By noon, it was clear the German advance could not be stopped. The entrance to the cellar had once again been blocked, and orderlies had been forced to clear a way in with the next batch of wounded. Rod had reached the stage of having to leave the dying to die without comfort. The cellar was so full he could not possibly deal with everyone, so those beyond help were given none.

The cook brought him a plate of stew which he spooned into his mouth without tasting it. The stench of blood and pus tainted everything, including food. He ate only to keep going. By now, the floor was covered in puddles and more of the ceiling had collapsed. He could only regret that the fall had killed four men with a chance of survival rather than four who were not far off death. War was irrational.

The noise of guns had grown so constant it was a while before Rod's attention was caught by a voice shouting his name. He turned from bandaging the stump of a man's arm to find a young officer behind him. Grimy, exuding a strong smell of sweat, face grey and strained, the man looked on the verge of collapse.

'Sorry, Doc,' he began, 'we've got to pull back. It's only until reinforcements are in position to attack the Jerries from the rear, but we're taking too many casualties.'

'Right on,' Rod said with feeling.

'Can you load all your wounded and be ready to move within thirty minutes?'

'No ... and they're *your* wounded, mate,' he replied. 'A number of these men can't be moved. They have a one-in-ten chance of survival. Pick them up and load them in ambulances, and they're dead.' He returned to his bandaging.

'You'll have to leave them, in that case,' the exhausted captain said tetchily. 'Anyone who can be moved must be ready in half an hour. The Germans will look after the others.'

'Like hell they will! I know what happens to wounded when they fall into enemy hands.'

'The Germans are not Japanese. They're civilized,' came the tense reply.

'Except when it comes to Jews, Resistance workers, Russians and anyone who doesn't appreciate their superiority.'

'That's the SS,' the other snapped. 'We're dealing with normal soldiers.'

'I've yet to see the difference,' Rod said heavily. 'All right. Anyone who can travel will be ready to go with you, but I'm not leaving the men who can't. There's no certainty they'll be found here and given treatment. If you're coming back before long, it's possible we could remain undetected until you do.'

'We may need you with us.'

Rod studied the young, ashen face and said quietly, 'Then get back here double quick.'

It was a hazardous business transferring men to waiting ambulances under fire. One vehicle was blown up before it could depart. The German tanks had found their range with unnerving precision. Exactly half an hour later, Rod saw the procession leave. Soon, there was no movement to be viewed through the gaps in the ceiling. The continuous boom of gunfire slowly became spasmodic, then ceased. All Rod could then hear was the distant rattle and squeak of approaching tanks. A German Panzer detachment was taking possession of an area of ruins no longer of use to anyone, at the cost of hundreds of lives.

Rod had sent Sergeant Medway and most of the team back with the unit. Two orderlies had volunteered to stay in the cellar. One brewed tea for them all as the tanks grew nearer.

'Funny old game, sir,' he commented as they drank it. 'Sarge and the lads'll be back here tomorrow or next day, and we'll be back where we started. My old dad was in the first set-to with the Jerries. He said they lost thousands at Passchendaele just to advance a hundred yards. Think of that – dying for the length of a football pitch.'

'I'd rather *not* think of it,' said Rod. 'I just hope they bring our ambulances back tomorrow or the next day, plus fresh supplies.'

He went to check the flow of plasma to one patient only to find the need for it had ended. This one had died for a mountain of rubble.

'Sir, they're here.'

Rod heard metal grinding over cobblestones. Together with the orderly who had touched his arm for attention, he gazed up at the muddied tracks of enemy tanks passing in the street above. Fine dust was shaken over them all as one after the other ground past. They were followed by jeeps and armoured cars, plus a heavy truck containing support staff.

'God knows where they'll stop,' whispered Rod to the orderlies. 'If they're looking for a roof to shelter under, they'll be disappointed.'

Stop they did, and booted feet swung to the ground, turning full circle as their owners surveyed the ruined town. They quickly moved back into the vehicles, which drove off with a shower of muddy water in pursuit of the tanks. Into the relative silence came the sound of tumbling bricks from behind them. All three men swung round. A German corporal stood with a machine-gun at the ready, nervously swinging it in an arc to warn against attack.

'I don't like the look of him,' muttered one orderly.

'Keep quiet,' Rod warned under his breath. 'He's frightened.'

So they stood immobile and silent while the soldier advanced, still swinging the gun from side to side. Rod saw the twitching mouth, the shaking hands, the staring eyes and knew this man was potentially dangerous. One false move and he could shower them all with bullets. He was as much a casualty as those lying on blankets at his feet. Then it became clear that he was seeking food. Descending on the pot containing the cold remains of the stew, he swept the contents up with his hand and ate as if starving while his crazy eyes fastened on the three standing men. Congealed stew hung around his mouth until he scraped if off with his fingers, then licked it from them nervously. The hand had dipped into the pot again when a sudden noise from the entrance made him spin round. The cellar was filled with the deafening chatter of gunfire as he let loose with one hand. Bullets ricocheted from walls into the helpless wounded, bringing screams from them as they writhed in further agony.

Something inside Rod exploded. As if by alien impulse he lunged to the corner where his unfired revolver hung, snatched it from its case and levelled it. A shot rang out; the corporal fell backwards across the stewpot before crashing to the ground. There was a moment of total silence. Then a figure holding a revolver stepped from the shadowed entrance and walked into the light. He spoke in good English.

'I'm certain you did not intend to fire, Doctor. It was *my* duty to stop the poor fellow.' He came forward pocketing the revolver, despite the fact that Rod still held his. 'The wounds of war are not always immediately evident.' He saluted. 'Lieutenant Mehrer, sir. I regret the assault on your wounded. I will arrange for them to be taken to one of our hospitals as soon as possible.'

'But you're surrounded by our troops,' Rod heard himself say, as if from afar.

'We forced a corridor through last night. I assure you your wounded will be given the best available treatment.' He held out his gloved hand. 'I must ask you to surrender

461

your weapon. You and your two orderlies will be put on a train leaving for Germany with other prisoners of war. Please feel no sense of dishonour. I salute your courage in remaining with your patients.'

Rod parted with the revolver, unsure whether or not he would have fired it. His chance to do so was lost. He would spend the rest of the war behind barbed wire once more, deprived of freedom, at the mercy of his enemies.

Chapter Eighteen

'Here's a letter from Alex,' Sarah murmured, scanning the single page, her breakfast toast forgotten.

'Oh, how nice! I do hope he intends to visit. I've missed him.'

Sarah glanced up at Ellie. 'He writes that he'll come as soon as possible because he wants to thrash out something with me. Why now, after six months of silence?'

'When was it written, dear?'

She looked back at the page. 'The fifth.'

'I thought so.' Ellie nodded. 'The day before D-Day. I suspect he wrote it on impulse. Men do. Your father always sent letters to Frances on the eve of a battle. Very frank, soul-baring letters. It must be terrible to contemplate ending one's life within the next twenty-four hours. The compulsion to reach out, confess things that couldn't be said in times of cold reason, must be strong.' A smile lightened her mood. 'Most of them live to regret sending words written when they were not in full command of themselves. The more astute among them leave the letters to be posted only in the event of their failure to return. Then they can happily tear them up before any damage is done.'

Sarah's heart lurched. 'You don't think Alex . . .?'

'Of course not! There would be a covering letter with it. How foolish of me to ramble on. I suppose it's because I've felt so choked with gratitude towards all those poor fellows engaged in the landings . . . and so proud of what they're achieving over there. You know, dear, I am ashamed of my lack of effort in this war. Apart from growing enough vegetables to give to those without gardens of their own, contributing items for parcels for the homeless and knitting socks for sailors, I've done nothing for my country.'

'What nonsense,' Sarah declared, half her mind on the true reason for Alex's letter. 'You've offered children enchantment to offset the horror around them. Dr Barnes says soul therapy is as important as any other. Apart from that, you gave Alex the love and home he'd never had. It was something to return to.'

'Until last Christmas.'

'That was his own decision,' Sarah said firmly. 'But I do wonder what has prompted this letter. I'm not sure your theory applies. He has faced danger too many times, both here and in Hong Kong, to be driven to bare his soul now.'

'Well, you know him far better than I do, dear.' Ellie spread another slice of toast with marmalade. 'I must say this concoction of rhubarb, lemon jelly and a touch of stem ginger substitutes quite well for the real thing. I was extremely sceptical when Violet passed on the recipe, but there's nothing like a shortage to prompt ingenuity.' She sipped coffee. 'Perhaps he wants advice on something to do with his mother. You have met her, and I suppose there's no one else he can ask.'

'There's Diana Spencer. She's a de Boucher, and his aunt.'

'Of course. Well, you'll just have to wait until he comes to get to the bottom of it all.'

'Yes.' Sarah glanced at her watch. 'Heavens, is it that late? Charles will be here before I'm ready. He hates being kept waiting.' She scrambled to her feet, passing another of her letters to her grandmother. 'Here's one from Roma. Do read it, it's so interesting. She's sending another food parcel, and a length of woollen cloth for each of us. It makes me feel guilty about refusing the offer of her husband's friend to organize a concert tour for me.'

'You haven't refused, just deferred it until the war ends. I'm sure Roma understands.'

'Oh, yes,' Sarah smiled. 'She writes that I was always firing up in defence of this little island. I must get my things together, darling. Charm Charles until I'm ready. His car's just turned in through the gate.'

Ellie's charm did not quite succeed in quenching Charles's irritation at having his precious timetable upset. He was quiet during the drive to London, which he took at greater speed than usual. Sarah made allowances for his attitude. Tonight's concert was an extremely important one arranged at very short notice. Announced as a D-Day concert, proceeds from the sale of tickets were to start a fund for French children orphaned during the battle to free their country. A list of distinguished artists exiled from their homelands in Europe, plus several American soloists, Sarah and the obnoxious but brilliant John Vine, with whom she worked in their tiny Cheltenham office, were to be joined by a full orchestra to perform before Princess Elizabeth, Princess Margaret Rose and a number of high-ranking officials.

The concert was to be broadcast the following evening, and Charles had urged Sarah to play the Rachmaninov concerto again. She had refused. Her performance of it at New Year had been for Rod; a message of immense, indestructible love. It could not be repeated when he was somewhere in France, facing the gravest danger, unable to hear that message. The Rachmaninov had gone from her repertoire once more. Her inspiration for it had said farewell beside a stile on a flower-filled May afternoon. She had been unable to give Charles that information, but he had accepted her decision to play the Tchaikovsky First tonight, instead. As every item on the performance was by a composer from the country of an ally, her choice of a fellow Russian was just as suitable.

Sarah was glad of Charles's mood that morning. Nervousness would not begin until after the afternoon rehearsal, but Alex's letter had unsettled her. Having, by his own words, bowed out of her life, what was the point of coming to Noon Cottage? The Normandy landings, although not the unqualified success everyone had wanted, were certain to bring an end to the war before Christmas. Sarah would then go to America to undertake a tour arranged by a friend of Roma, which would consolidate her transatlantic reputation and open new horizons. There was no place in her life for close involvements. Music was all-important to her. It was now her whole life.

During lunch at the hotel where they had rooms booked for the night, Charles worried audibly about his responsibility for the evening's success. Although more approachable now they were on the spot, he clearly would not relax until the whole thing was over. At the end of the concert, the performers were to be presented to the royal sisters and other eminent members of the audience who were donating large sums to the fund. Charles was to officiate, so was understandably anxious that nothing should go wrong. One of London's leading theatres, which had escaped damage, was being used for the concert. Everyone prayed there would be no air raids on the capital tonight.

The rehearsal did not go well. Many of the artists were in temperamental mood, due to their nervousness. The soloists, worried about their own performances, found fault with almost every section of the orchestra, and harsh words were exchanged between them and the conductor, who was quick to defend his musicians before having a token word with the supposed offenders. Sarah was to open the second half and would be followed by Elgar's *Enigma Variations*. The concert finale consisted of a medley of popular war songs led by two distinguished opera singers descending the musical ladder to sing such favourites as '(There'll be bluebirds over) The White Cliffs of Dover'. Sarah planned to leave before the rehearsal for this. There were certain to be fireworks when a great soprano and tenor joined forces to perform something so far from their usual repertoire.

After giving a faultless rehearsal performance, Sarah went back to the hotel, where she lay on the bed and succumbed to nervousness. Playing in the presence of royalty was an accolade. There was no question of the princesses having asked for her inclusion with older, more renowned artists, but Charles had submitted the list of names and they had registered complete approval. She owed Charles so much. She had never yet let him down, and the reason she was so nervous now was because she had played the Tchaikovsky in accord with the conductor from start to finish, the only artist with no temperament this afternoon. She had played like an automaton. The performance had been utterly without feeling. Her fingers had flown across the keys, stretched and arched, her wrists had rippled with fluid movement, the timing had been perfect. But she had felt none of the tragic beauty, the intense heroic themes, the aching triumphant emotion underlying the Russian flavour of the music. Her artistry was technically exceptional but it had no heart or soul. It had been like that since a Sunday in May.

When Sarah dressed in a long gown of emerald slipper satin, fastened the silver chain around her neck and slid over her right wrist the filigree bracelet Alex had given her in Calcutta for her twenty-first birthday, she still felt nervous. Her glance lingered on the bracelet. She must write to Alex. There was no point in his coming to Noon Cottage. The severing of their unique bond had been shockingly sudden, but final. What was the use of attempting to revive something no longer needed by either of them?

The hotel receptionist rang to say Sarah's taxi was waiting. She slipped on a lightweight black coat before taking up her evening purse and leaving the room. The weather was still unsettled and stormy. It had been for most of June. The driver chatted in a friendly manner about his grandson who was having piano lessons. So enthusiastic was he about this apparent child prodigy, Sarah was not obliged to say much during the short drive to the theatre. As she walked through the backstage area towards the small dressing room allocated to her, she heard the soprano and tenor going through vocal scales in theirs. John Vine's hectic violin could be heard further along the corridor, and the Polish flautist was running through some of the more difficult sections of his two-work programme in the room adjacent to her own. Members of the orchestra were tuning up in any corner they could find. The room adequate for a theatre orchestra was not big enough for a full symphony complement.

Charles looked drawn and agitated when he knocked to check that she had arrived. 'My dear, you look so cool and calmly beautiful. That wretched French soprano insulted the conductor so badly, I've had my work cut out stopping him walking off and leaving us all high and dry.'

'He wouldn't, Charles,' she said. 'This evening is too important. He's a Czech, all fire and self-importance, that's all. Just wait. When Madame Temperament has excelled herself and received a standing ovation, she'll blow him very showy kisses to suggest that it was all due to his outstanding accompaniment, and *he* will bow and kiss her hand in homage.'

Charles stared at her. 'You sound very bitter. Are you all right?'

'Of course. Just rather tired of theatrical antics by people overawed by their own consequence. I think they've quite forgotten the cause for which this concert is being held. People are dying in tens of thousands in Europe. The *exact* nuance of a musical phrase is surely not of such importance that insults have to fly and sensibilities be so deeply damaged.'

'Of course it is! They have reputations to protect,' he argued, almost shocked by her point of view. 'The theatre is full of newspaper critics who will be listening for the slightest flaw to comment upon in their columns tomorrow. After the broadcast, there'll be others ready to criticize. Aside from that, there are some very important people out there tonight.'

'*Everyone's* important, Charles, down to the emaciated coolie who rakes through rotting rubbish looking for his next meal.' The words were out before she knew and left her shaken.

'Are you *certain* you're all right?' he asked anxiously.

She crossed to kiss him on the cheek. 'Go and take up your position ready to greet the VIPs. The evening will be a resounding success, you know that very well. You're a genius at organization ... and a very dear friend.' She turned him around. 'Get out there and do your usual best. You also have a reputation to maintain.'

The velvet settee designed for relaxing upon while waiting for stage calls did not fulfil its purpose for Sarah. Tense and curiously apprehensive, she sat on an upright chair throughout the overture to *The Bartered Bride*, arias from *Carmen* and *Boris Godunov*, the 'Peer Gynt' Suite, 'American Hoedown' (a new work with solo flute), John Vine's sensational fingering for three Czech dances, and an orchestral arrangement of Chopin's most flamboyant, patriotic melodies.

Tea was brought to the dressing rooms during an interval extended to cater for the needs of royalty. Sarah normally only sipped before going on stage, but she drank a cupful and had poured another when someone knocked on her door. One of the backstage men entered to tell her that a Flying-Officer Mason was very eager to speak to her.

'I told him you were resting ready to go on next, miss, and that he must wait until the end of the concert. But he won't. He said he had phoned your home and was told where you were. When he went to the hotel you'd already left, so he came here. Says he's due back with his squadron by nine.' The man shifted his weight to the other foot. 'I don't think he's an autograph-hunter, Miss Channing . . . and he insists it's very urgent.'

Coldness was already creeping into Sarah's veins, and her mind was crying 'no' as she got to her feet saying that she would see the officer. He came in swiftly, a slight young man with floppy brown hair and expressive hazel eyes, who looked immensely tired. There was no smile as he thanked her for agreeing to see him, and he got straight to the point.

'I'm a member of Alex Tennant's crew, Miss Channing. I would have contacted you sooner, but it took me a week to get back to England and I've only just learnt the news.'

'Yes?' she heard herself say in a faint voice.

His hands fidgeted with his cap nervously, and he spoke very quickly. 'We bought it over Normandy. The crate was on fire and half blown away. It was obvious we'd never make it. Alex . . . he got us as near the coast as he could before telling us to jump. I thought – we all thought – that he would follow when we were out. Why he didn't isn't clear.'

Sarah was ice-cold now. The young man's face had become a blur. 'I see.'

'I hope I've done the right thing coming to see you about this,' he said awkwardly. 'I know you . . . well, he was pretty cut up because you stopped seeing him after that raid on Bremen at Christmas. But you escaped across China with him, and were very . . . friendly, at one time. I just thought . . . well, he's still pretty much in love with you and I think you ought to go and see him before it's too late,' he ended with a flash of defiance.

'See him?'

'In Moxworth Hospital. Apple crashed in the drink right beside a hospital ship. The crew hauled Alex out. He was admitted to Moxworth along with all serious cases brought over that night. I only heard about this when I telephoned the squadron to let them know I'd got a lift on a supply boat.' He let out his breath on a long sigh. 'He won't make it, I'm afraid. I just thought it would help if he saw you and . . . well, you know what I'm driving at, Miss Channing. The rest of the crew are going to visit as soon as they can, but you're the only one who could make it easier for him.'

A loud knocking on the door was accompanied by a voice calling, 'Five minutes, Miss Channing.'

Sarah gazed at the young officer helplessly. 'I have to play Tchaikovsky. I'm so sorry.'

'I know. I would've waited until afterwards, but I've got to get a train back to the station right away and I wanted to explain in person rather than write it in a note. You see, Alex has brought us back from more than thirty missions. We owe him a lot . . . and coming here to ask you to see him was the biggest gesture of gratitude I could think of. Please go, Miss Channing.'

'Yes . . . yes.'

'Moxworth is down on the coast near –'

'I know where it is.' She saw the house and gardens so clearly.

More knocks on the door. 'Two minutes, Miss Channing.'

Sarah hardly noticed the figure in air-force blue go; heard none of his parting words. She was unaware of leaving the dressing room, walking the long corridor, mounting the steps to the platform, waiting for the final notes of 'Prélude à L'Après-Midi d'un Faune'. There was applause. A face she knew well was staring at her from several feet away. It mouthed words. A man in a starched shirt and tail coat approached, smiling, to take her hand. She was walking with him to a place of immense light. He bowed in the direction of a box. Sarah curtsied. There was a piano. She sat at it and stared at the keyboard while silence slowly settled over the lofty auditorium.

The conductor raised his baton, glanced at her, then loud,

descending chords rang out to fill her ears with stirring sounds she knew well. Her hands moved to the ivory keys. Sudden fire melted the iciness within them, within her whole body, as she struck three ascending chords over and over again with the full power of her wrists, while full-blooded, swirling, heroic melody from the orchestra kept pace with the rhythm of her swaying body. Then her fingers were racing over the keys with swift certain movements, and the music all around was as urgent as the tide rising to engulf her. *If you won't agree to fry my breakfast eggs and darn my socks, for heaven's sake join Charles Spencer's group and do what you're destined to do.* She had! She was! She was doing it for him.

The anguish of protest was in the force of her scales and runs that built to a crescendo, then died, then mounted again. *Why? Why? He had survived those eighteen days in Hong Kong; the destruction of the raft. He had crossed China with poison in his leg, recovered from deadly fever, existed on starvation rations. He had flown safely night after night. Why had he stayed after the rest had jumped. Why? Why?* The notes she played rang out that protest. It echoed in the high-ceilinged hall as the orchestral accompaniment grew in volume to fill her head and heart with throbbing, driving sound. She countered it again and again with explosive retorts from fingers speaking pain she could express in no other way, until a flood of volume burst over her in dramatic orchestral conclusion.

There was sudden silence broken by a few discreet coughs. A bank of black and white musicians rose up on her left. To her right was listening dimness. Beneath her hands, the gleaming green satin skirt rippled down to boards where artists of many generations had hidden their emotions from that listening dimness. Men and women devoted to art above all else. *Let music be the only love in your life.* Was it? Could it be?

Sarah saw the conductor's raised eyebrows and nodded. Softly, quietly, the flute began a lilting melody with the orchestra. Her hands reached out once more. The piano took up the refrain, and Jakob Myburgh was instantly there singing in a quavery tenor to demonstrate what he wanted

471

from her. She gave it to him tonight. She offered her talent as a gift of gratitude he might never receive in this life. Yet she knew it would somehow reach him, that even when he could no longer hear the glorious notes in his head he would retain them in his soul. She saw him, then, saying to a young man in unfamiliar khaki, *I leave you to impress her with some other aspect of your youthful charm*, and the young man declaring, *This uniform disguises the fact that I'm a worthless gambler determined to continue along a dissolute path while others die for my sake. I'm not the only villain masquerading as a hero tonight, so don't be too hard on me.* Had she been?

While her fingers brought from the strings within the well of the piano echoes of nostalgia, hints of melodrama, snatches of patriotic fervour, while the orchestra added power and stirring volume to all three, visions arose of desolate icy landscapes, a hemp boat gliding slowly along a mist-shrouded river, bicycles crossing narrow paths between paddy fields, unkempt, filthy figures shuffling forever onward looking nervously from side to side. One figure was always leading. The villain masquerading as a hero? The scene changed to India. She was sobbing, clinging to him. Hostility was all around her. Only he could provide escape from it; a refuge. Only with him was everything bearable.

The main theme became dreamy, unbearably reminiscent. Her fingers caressed notes; her hands floated above the keyboard with fluid movements as she saw his face smiling encouragement, then glowing with an invitation to surrender body as well as soul. There was a huge moon flooding the bed with cool light. He accepted her so gently, so unselfishly, releasing pain and degradation so that it melted beneath the warmth of his nearness. Without him she was lost. His words made her whole again; breathed life back into a spirit which had been in limbo since that day on Stanley Beach. She owed him her future.

Everything grew strangely quiet. Dreaminess ended as she found herself staring at a different face – round, Slavic, beaded with perspiration. It sailed like a creamy cheese in a void of brilliant light, beyond which was endless darkness. It nodded almost imperceptibly. She returned the nod. A drumbeat resembling a cannon's discharge set her attacking the keys with dedication and vigour. *Of course she'll join your group, Uncle Charles. Give her a few weeks to get back into form, then she'll give you a call. That's a promise.* She had worked hard, spent every moment making her fingers flexible again; had sat at the piano until she felt exhausted and drained. She was working hard now. Her fingers raced the length of the keyboard, then pounded a repetitive theme that spared her no effort. It was what she was destined to do. She must do it.

Next, there arose around her a sweeping, romantic melody to bring a return vision of that dear face smiling as he tenderly touched her in consolation. She longed to stay with it, to stay with other visions of him in her home: his hand caressing the ears of the dogs, his laughter echoing in familiar rooms; of riding with him over the hills, of walking hand in hand through winding lanes, of giving each other the Chinese blessings that said so much. *Do what you were destined to do. Make music the only love of your life.* The compulsion to obey overcame all else and she was back to her solo theme with dogged determination to work, work, work.

It became a battle she slowly lost despite aching back and an aching heart. The irresistible beauty of the rising orchestral melody intruded however hard she tried to combat it. She was gradually overwhelmed by cadences that weakened her resolution, so she made every effort to silence them. She failed. They rose in a yearning crescendo that became unbearable. She still resisted with one last great defiant reprise of her industrious, unemotional theme, but forces within her cried out for recognition, for unrestrained expression. Surrender was dragged from her as she became part of that yearning, passionate melody.

Her cheeks grew wet as she played it with every throb of her heart, every painful breath, every ounce of compassion in her soul. She played it for herself and the truth she could no longer deny. The keyboard blurred. Her head was full of the symphony of regret, of anger and of the sweetest song of all as she was swept onward to the inevitable emotional climax that exposed her anguish for all to see. Then, stirring orchestral clarion calls gave way to utter, deafening silence.

473

Moments later, it was shattered by a tidal wave of applause that rose up to rush towards and break over Sarah with such force, her downbent head lifted to realize what had just occurred. Wave followed upon wave, augmented by cries that burst from throats thickened by emotion. She got to her feet as if in a trance, knowing she had been wrong about the Rachmaninov. *This* had been the sole perfect performance of her lifetime; the never-to-be-repeated instance of complete rapport between artist and composer. Tchaikovsky had written this moment in her life with black dots on white paper. She had recognized that and brought them to glorious life tonight.

After a while, lights came up to reveal pale faces row upon row, and pale hands beating together with wild elation. The tumult of cries rose further when someone arrived beside her to take her hand to his lips in artistic salute. Sarah could not see him clearly through her tears; she was icy and shaking. The man coaxed her from the instrument she clutched to stay upright, putting an arm lightly behind her back in gallant fashion to lead her away.

In the wings, Charles was waiting, unashamed tears on his own lashes. He seized her hands. 'Superb!' he said with difficulty. 'I've seldom heard it played so – so *brilliantly*.'

Sarah was already past him and heading for the steps when he came after her, crying, 'You must go out again – several times. My dear, this is your night. They won't let you go for a long time yet. You have a total triumph on your hands. Make the most of it.'

She hardly heard his words as she descended the steps and began to run along the corridor.

'Sarah! Sarah! You can't do this. Your audience is demanding your presence. What are you thinking of?'

The door of the dressing room crashed open beneath the force of her hands. She snatched up her coat and bag before rushing to the door again. There, she encountered Charles. He blocked her path, his face angry, uncomprehending.

'Are you mad? There are two members of the royal family out there tonight. This is your finest hour. You *must* go and acknowledge the ovation.' He turned slightly to fling out an arm in emphasis. 'Listen! They won't stop until you appear. Then it will be double – treble.'

Sarah was shaking from head to foot. Tears were streaming down her face, and something inside her was threatening to explode. 'I have to go,' she cried. 'Don't try to stop me.'

'Go? Go where? You *can't*,' Charles exclaimed, as she attempted to push past him. 'You're to be presented.' He blocked her way again. 'You can't walk out on *royalty*. It's an insult. It would ruin your career. Tonight has set you up on a plane hundreds strive lifelong to reach. You can't throw it away on a ridiculous show of temperament. I won't allow you to.'

Sarah was fighting against her own total destruction. Words jerked from her as she said, battling for control, 'This is *not* the only love of my life. I know now it can never be. Ellie ... Ellie told me to discover there are people in the world. I did. They're more important than going out to receive homage for what I've just done.' She struggled to remain coherent. '*Alex is dying.* If I get there too late, I'll never play another note so long as I live.'

Charles was thrust aside in her frenzy. She fled to the exit, her coat dragging the floor as it slipped in her grasp, out into the West End, still busy at that hour of ten. Darkness was starting to settle over a chill June evening. Sarah ran heedlessly as she pulled her coat on, urgency lending her feet additional speed as she searched for a taxi, dodging couples arm-in-arm, civilians leaving ministries and service people going on and off duty. Minutes seemed to tick away thunderously in her head. She should have gone immediately and not played the concerto. It would be there for ever; Alex would not.

A taxi loomed from the dusk. She ran into its path waving her arms. It stopped inches from her with a screech of brakes. The driver leaned from his cab. 'Wotchit, miss! I could've run yer dahn.'

Deaf to his protest, she tugged open the door and scrambled inside. 'Waterloo Station! It's very urgent.'

His plain, red-cheeked face glanced at her over the partition. 'You orlright, luv?'

'Hurry! Oh, *please* hurry. I have to get to him before it's too late.'

He put the cab in motion, saying cheerfully, 'Righto! Nah, don't you worry. 'Arry Carter'll get you there orl safe and sahnd.'

Dusk turned to night almost imperceptibly. It was no longer possible to see people on the pavements. Other vehicles were only recognizable by slits of light from their darkened headlamps. Sarah hunched on the seat, still in the grips of the tempest assailing her, urging the man to go faster, faster. Sane thought was elusive. A kaleidoscope of lurid fantasies whirled with one recurring theme. Alex had brought her back from the edge of oblivion in India; she would do the same for him now.

As the taxi raced through unlit streets, Sarah's fevered recollections of two haggard, filthy faces staring through a broken wall while she sang carols mingled with sudden reality. Explosions sent tremors running through the earth in successive pulses. She was under attack in the Halburton Clinic – no, this was a London taxi! The sounds of war were the same anywhere.

'Blimey, there wasn't no siren,' exclaimed the driver. 'What the 'eck's up wiv 'em?'

Bombs were fast falling and yet the familiar deep, concerted drone of heavy aircraft was missing. Instead, there was a curious intermittent chugging sound. Sarah had only one concern, however. 'Keep going! I *must* get to Waterloo.'

'Orlright, orlright. I told yer 'Arry would getcher there, didn't I? Jerry bombs don't frighten me . . . but they makes a mess in streets I want ter drive fru, that's wot. I'll do me werry best, miss, straight I will.'

The wail of warning sirens now swept London, telling the people something they already knew. Mingling with that were the shrill whistles of wardens and rescue workers, while the distant clang of ambulance bells grew nearer. The taxi frequently swerved or braked to avoid people running for the safety of air-raid shelters. The driver was several times turned away by police from the route he was taking. Sarah clutched her coat around her shivering body as she perched on the edge of the seat imploring the man to drive faster, faster. He snapped at her that he was doing his best and she was not helping either of them.

He continued to race and swerve while the earth trembled with each explosion, until he turned a corner and screeched to a halt. Fifty yards ahead, infant fires illuminated a scene of immense destruction. Buildings had been demolished wherever one looked. The street was completely blocked by debris. Tin-helmeted wardens and rescue workers wearing red-cross armbands were shepherding people from the ruins of their homes; others were digging out those who were trapped. As Sarah stared in dismay, a façade standing unsupported folded and crashed on to the fleeing women and children. She thrust open the taxi door and jumped to the ground.

'You can't 'elp 'em, miss,' the driver shouted.

Sarah was running away from the scene, not to it. The taxi would never be allowed through these streets. She must go on foot. Waterloo Station was not far. Ambulances and fire-engines raced by in the darkness, their bells deafening as they passed. Other people were running through that blustery night. She collided with a dark figure and was momentarily winded, but ignored the swift apology in her haste to move on. The air above her was full of an unfamiliar spluttering throb of engines; here and there in the night sky were faint flickers of fire. The pavement shook once more as an ear-shattering explosion occurred nearby. Sarah stopped instinctively, covering her head with her arms, then ran on with labouring heartbeat. Her legs ached, breathing was a painful effort. The heels of her dainty shoes made her unsteady, so she stooped swiftly to abandon them and ran on in stockinged feet.

Up steps and out over the river along a narrow iron bridge. She was almost there. The wind swept the water and that exposed walkway. It billowed the coat to impede her progress. She flung the garment away and continued in the long satin dress, her shoeless feet pounding the metalwork. The night grew even more noisy as guns opened fire at the machines betrayed by their flaming tails. Searchlights swung back and forth in the blackness, seeking aircraft. They fastened on something small, dark and sinister, then another and another. The harsh white beams picked out a sky full of them, darting forward propelled by fire at the rear. The destructive midget aircraft were part of Sarah's nightmare. The sound of their progress seemed to increase until her head was ready to burst; the sight of them added to the fears rioting through her.

Down more steps at the far side of the Thames. The station was in view. Someone caught at her as she ran; held her fast. A voice spoke words she did not hear. She fought restraint like a person possessed; possessed by the need to reach Alex before he departed believing she did not care.

'You can't go there, miss,' a voice insisted. 'It's too dangerous.'

'I must. I must!' she cried, struggling still.

'No, I can't let you through.'

'Yes, yes. Let me go. I must catch the train. Please, *please*, let me go,' she implored.

'What is it, Frank?' A different voice from the dimness.

'Some woman wants to catch a train.'

'There ain't no trains. Tell her the line's been hit.'

'She's hysterical.'

Guns, explosions, bells clanging, whistles and shouts. People running; people dying. Dizzying searchlights. Black evil shapes everywhere. Fire and destruction. Alex may already be dead. Sarah jerked free of the hands gripping her arms and ran forward, the wind whipping her long skirt around her legs and stranding hair over her drenched cheeks.

'Oi, come back!' Boots pounding on stone. Arms imprisoning her. Her clenched fists beating at rough serge. Her whole body racked by distress.

'*You can't go there!*' a voice roared in her ear. Then it called, 'Hey, Maurice, give me some help. She's crazy.'

Additional hands seized her arms. Brilliant light blinded her, then went again. 'Shock!' pronounced a voice. 'Seen it before. Better get her to the first-aid post, pronto. If she won't go, knock her out.'

'I can't do that.'

'I will, then.'

There was high-pitched screaming above her, growing in volume.

'*Look out, here's another!*' roared the voice.

The sound of a million bass drums was accompanied by a wall of heat that slammed against Sarah to knock her off her feet. The night grew blacker than ever. The sound of her own sobbing turned frighteningly hollow and flew away on the wind until she could hear it no longer.

Charles came just as dawn was breaking. His face was grey with anxiety and weariness as he bent over the bed. 'He's holding on. I telephoned half an hour ago.'

Sarah took his hand to her cheek and held it there while mastering herself sufficiently to thank him. Then she struggled up from the pillow. 'I must get down to Moxworth.'

'We'll go together. Train services are badly disrupted, so I'll drive you there. Only because I will, and because you're visiting another hospital, has the doctor agreed to discharge you.'

'And because of Alex's condition,' she said quietly.

'Yes. That, too.' He held up a bag. 'I collected your uniform from the hotel. You'd better find a nurse to help you change into it.'

A cheery girl called May came to pull curtains around the bed and dress Sarah in khaki. She talked all the time. 'I didn't know you were a famous person until Sister found out from the gentleman waiting for you. Fancy playing the piano in front of the princesses! I'd be much too nervous to do anything like that. But what a way to finish up the day! You should've been drinking champagne in a room filled with flowers from admirers, like in the films, instead of lying here all night with air-raid casualties.' She smiled. 'Still, you didn't know much about it, did you? Took you ever so long to come out of it. You still look a bit dreamy. You sure you're all right to go?'

'Yes, I'm fine.'

'Well, be careful. Bomb-blast is funny. It can catch up with you after two or three days. Still, I expect Dr Fleming'll warn you before you leave. Truth is, there were so many brought in last night there's a shortage of beds. I don't think you'd be allowed to leave otherwise.' She stood up from tying Sarah's laces. 'There, that's you all spick and span. Apart from those bruises on your legs no one would know anything had happened to you.' She picked up the green slipper-satin dress, now torn and blackened. 'What a pity about this. It must have been beautiful. Do you want to take it?'

Sarah shook her head, then wished she had not because the curtained space spun around and upside down.

The nurse asked again if she was all right, then reiterated her warning about the unpredictability of bomb-blast. 'You've had a severe shock to your whole system. Let it recover quietly, won't you?'

Within half an hour Sarah was away from the casualty centre in Charles's car. She felt decidedly weak and giddy, but hoped that would wear off as the day progressed. In the vicinity of the hospital destruction was intense. Still only five-thirty a.m., firemen and wardens were searching the rubble for bodies and any lucky survivors. The wind had dropped, the sky was a clear, pale blue: a breathless summer morning, which made the destruction seem even more chilling. Sarah was unclear what had happened and her brain was too tired to puzzle it out. All she remembered clearly was someone telling her to see Alex before it was too late, then going on stage to play a work that had spoken too well of her grief. The period following her performance was no more than a jumble of impressions she had no desire to unravel. She rested back in the passenger seat while Charles sought a navigable route out of London heading south-west. He said nothing, and she very soon drifted into sleep.

They were travelling through pleasant green countryside when Sarah next opened her eyes. She lay back for a while gazing at sunlight flickering through branches of trees lining the road. The song of meadowlarks high in the blue reached her through the open window beside her, and the distant buzz of tractors in surrounding fields reminded her of Kingsmill. Familiar, comforting sounds; a peaceful summer scene. How could last night have happened? Everything was as it should be; all was surely right with the world.

'How are you feeling?'

She glanced at Charles. 'A little unreal, at present.'

'I'll be pleased when we reach Moxworth. Doctors will be on hand should you suddenly collapse.'

'I won't do that,' she assured him. 'How far have we still to go?'

'About twenty-five miles. I guess roads will become congested with military traffic nearer the coast. We're sending massive amounts of supplies across with reinforcements. Trucks are taking it down to the ships, and ambulances are streaming in the opposite direction with the casualties. What a price to pay, to free a country half of which has been collaborating with the Germans anyway.'

'You're thinking of Alex, aren't you?' she asked quietly.

'What a waste. What a tragic waste of life! He fought back from the mess Maurice had made of his youth, and I somehow felt – Diana and Hélène, as well as their mother, thought – that Alex would wipe out the sins of his father with his own worth.'

Sarah sat up carefully and turned to him. 'I know him better than anyone does, Charles. He has no more obligation to compensate for Maurice Tennant than I have to for *my* father. I don't believe in the "sins of the father" creed. We each have one life to be responsible for – our own. Ellie has taught me that. Alex has fought back from the mess of his youth for his own sake, not because Maurice was making money from others' misfortunes. It's the Press, fellow businessmen – yes, and *you* – who follow this ridiculous fashion of burdening him with someone else's wickedness. The child of a heroic father is expected to live up to his parent's shining image; the child of a villain must strive to compensate. It's ludicrous! The child is a person in his or her own right. Parents very easily shrug off their offspring. A child should be entitled to shrug off its parents.'

Charles cast her a shrewd glance. 'You love him?'

'Of course. I've loved him for a long time.'

'That's why I didn't tell you yesterday.'

Sarah stared in disbelief. 'You *knew*?'

'The hospital telephoned Miriam. She collapsed and took to her bed. Diana rang me right away. She agreed that I should wait until after the concert before breaking the news to you.'

Anger flooded her. 'What right had you to make that decision?'

'The right of someone who has your future in mind. Someone who is also a friend, my dear.' His hand closed briefly over one of hers. 'I never thought you would hear minutes before you went out to face the biggest challenge of your infant career.' He concentrated on the road again. 'One of the stagehands later told me that he had taken an RAF officer to your dressing room during the interval. I'm so sorry.'

Deeply upset, Sarah said, 'And when had you planned to reveal that someone very dear to me was lying fatally wounded within my reach? After your precious concert was over, after royalty had been duly fussed and flattered, after compliments had been showered upon you?'

'Yes,' agreed Charles calmly. 'I intended to drive you to Moxworth when you had had time to recover from the emotional pressure of your performance. You are always drained and vulnerable after a concert, Sarah.'

'Alex is Diana's nephew – part of the family! How could you . . . how could you . . .'

'Continue the arrangements for last night as if it had not happened?' he queried. 'Because a great number of people were involved in presenting that concert – artists other than Sarah Channing, and very many backstage helpers who had worked hard for its success. Two members of our royal family were to be in the audience along with important people who could be instrumental in furthering the reputations of each of the performers. The proceeds are to start a fund for children whose parents are killed during the fight for France. You have just now spoken very forcibly in defence of a child's right to his own life. Don't such children deserve your championship as much as Maurice Tennant's son?'

Confused and still upset, Sarah hit out. 'Your own reputation was also in line for enhancement last night.'

'Yes, it was. A great deal was at stake.'

'Enough to counterbalance a young man's life?'

Charles sighed heavily. 'Last night's concert has no connection with Alex. His fate was decided on the afternoon of June 6.'

Silence fell as Sarah tried to accept that this man had kept from her the news she should have been told immediately. Only then did it occur to her that she had no absolute right to that privilege. She had refused to marry Alex, so was neither fiancée nor wife. When he had written so bitter a farewell six months ago, she had made no attempt to contact him, show how devastated she was by the drastic severance. Yet she cried out inwardly that as the person who had shared so much with him, his danger should have been relayed first to her.

'Had you known earlier, would you have gone to Moxworth immediately?'

'Of course. It was only because I was called to the platform at the very moment I was being told something I didn't want to believe that I went on. I was confused, shaken. When I began to play, truth sank in and all I could think of was how much a part of me he was. Every section of that concerto spoke to me of episodes in our lives. My heart was slowly breaking up there.'

'Which enabled you to interpret the music with such intensity and passion you took an entire audience by storm. Alex will be pleased and very proud when I tell him. It was he who persuaded you to join forces with me, wasn't it? He wouldn't have wanted you to toss aside such triumph.'

'Empty triumph.' She turned her head to watch the passing scene, ebbing anger leaving her drained once more. After some minutes, she asked, 'How did you find me?'

'I telephoned Moxworth to ask if you'd arrived there, then rang first-aid posts and casualty centres.' He paused. 'I let your grandmother know the situation. It's the first time I've heard her lose her composure.'

'She loves Alex, too.'

'It was you she was concerned for. And so was I.' Charles waited several moments before saying, 'They won't call it madness in the reviews this morning. They didn't call it that last night. You *are* exceptionally gifted, Sarah.'

She still gazed from the car window. 'How did you explain my absence to the princesses?'

'I told them the truth. They were very sympathetic and asked me to pass on their admiration for your courage in performing for such a worthy cause in the face of personal distress.'

'I've told you why. There was nothing in the least noble about it.'

'Perhaps not ... but you have the soul of an artist, my dear. You could have fled at the eleventh hour, yet something in you responded to a voice calling "Two minutes, Miss Channing".'

She let that pass and merely thanked him for seeking her out to drive her to Moxworth. 'You're very good to me, Charles.'

'That's what a manager is for.'

They were nearing the coast and the war suddenly intruded upon a peaceful England. Trucks, tanks and ambulances made roads busy. In the air, heavy transport planes from numerous local airfields headed out across the Channel with vital supplies. Roads were stained dark by oil, where vehicles had waited for days, ready to be shipped across to France. Grass on village greens had turned yellow beneath tents housing troops awaiting their turn to go over. Tank tracks had left marks across verges and paths. The coastal belt had a tired, shabby air, much like a room after a hectic party.

When Sarah saw the outskirts of Moxworth, there was no sense of returning to a place of vivid memories. She felt too numb for that. Charles drove past The Exciseman and on to the gates of the hospital. They were allowed in on production of identity cards.

'I'll wait here for a while,' said Charles, as he parked in gardens where Sarah had walked six months ago. 'Unless you want my support when you go in?'

'No, I'll be fine.' Before closing the door, she bent to say, 'I'm grateful for all you've done. Forgive me, Charles.'

An orderly conducted Sarah through a corridor, across the place where she had left the New Year's concert, up some stairs and into a small room occupied by a dark-haired army sister. She looked up with a smile.

'I understand you left a sickbed in order to come. A Dr Fleming telephoned and asked us to ensure that you were quite all right when you arrived. Would you like a cup of tea?'

'I'd like to see Alex first.'

She nodded and got to her feet. 'I'll get someone to bring the tea in to you.'

'How is he?'

'Quite bright.' She smiled again. 'He'll be even brighter once he sees you. When I told him you were on your way, it bucked him up no end.'

Sarah put her hand on the woman's arm. 'I helped out in a clinic during the last days of Hong Kong's stand. I know something about injuries. How is he really?'

'His spine is badly crushed and he has serious internal problems we can do nothing about. There's little pain at the moment. When it increases he'll have morphia to combat it.'

'How long does he have?'

'Days rather than weeks, I should guess, but one can never tell.'

'Does he suspect?'

'I think so. Most of them do, you know. They've seen so many of their friends go, they recognize these things. He's calm enough, so keep the atmosphere light, won't you? From what he told me a moment ago, you should be able to handle anything.'

Sarah tried to smile. 'We've always had happy endings.'

'They run out sooner or later,' the woman said gently. 'I'll take you to him, then organize tea for you both.'

Alex was in a side room with a view overlooking the gardens and river. He looked pale and drawn against dazzling white pillows and bedding. There was a traction device above the bed and an oxygen cylinder beside it. In the seconds before he grew aware of her, Sarah felt her resolution falter, and halted. Then he turned his head, saw her, and sent her a look of such intense joy her courage returned.

Taking his outstretched hand, she bent to kiss him and touch his cheek with gentle fingers. 'I've missed you so much.'

His blue eyes grew brighter as they studied her face hungrily. 'When they said you were on your way I couldn't believe it.' His fingers closed painfully over hers. 'I wrote you a letter.'

'I know. It came yesterday.'

Dragging his gaze from her, he looked up at the sister. 'Isn't she as lovely as I said? And as brave, talented, sweet, generous . . .'

'That's enough,' Sister protested with a laugh. 'I'm going before I grow too jealous. I can't possibly compete.'

Left alone they seemed lost for words, and Sarah wondered how she had let him walk out of her life. She sank into a chair, still clasping his hand. He put up the other to touch her hair, let it slide through his fingers.

'You've grown it longer . . . and you're wearing a different lipstick. Sort of orangey. It's nice. Suits that cool look you have.'

'Gracious, you're very observant,' she commented, as lightly as she could.

'Where you're concerned I see everything in minute detail.' His thumb stroked the hand he gripped. 'It's been hell without you. That's why I wrote the letter.'

'I'm glad you did.'

'How's Ellie?'

'Fine. Sends her love.'

'Sasha and Vlad?'

'The same as ever.'

'And Noon Cottage?'

'Just as you remember it.'

'The place I think of as home.'

An orderly came with some tea and toast for Sarah. When she offered Alex a piece, he shook his head. 'It's taboo. I'm feasting my eyes on you instead.'

As she ate, for his benefit, toast she did not want, Sarah asked, 'What happened?'

He knew what she meant. 'We went over at midnight and everything was right. We went back in the afternoon and it all went wrong. Someone fired at us from an area supposedly in our hands. We weren't expecting it. There was so much happening over there. It was incredible, darling. I'll never forget looking down on all those ships, and beaches swarming with men and tanks. You just can't imagine what it was like. That day'll go down in history, and I was part of it.'

As he spoke with enthusiasm about all he had seen and

done on D-Day, it was easy to disbelieve what the sister had said. He was the Alex she knew so well, the man who knew her equally well. When he returned to the point where his bomber had been hit, she then asked why he had not baled out with his men.

'I meant to,' he confessed, taking hold of her hand again, 'but I realized Apple would go down on the poor devils struggling to survive every awful thing a soldier has to endure in battle. I'd done it in Hong Kong, and I just couldn't drop a burning Halifax on them. It seemed so bloody unfair, somehow.' His attractive smile broke through. 'I must have a charmed life. The machine hit the sea right beside a hospital ship. Someone hauled me out, and here I am.' He was silent for a moment or two, then said, 'The last time that happened, your doctor friend did the heroic deed.' He looked right at her to ask, 'How is he?' She was not expecting the question and hesitated. He spoke again quickly, 'We met on Salisbury Plain. He told me he hadn't seen you since New Year.'

'That's right.' She put aside the cup of tea. 'One Sunday he came to Noon Cottage. I wasn't expecting him, so it was something of a shock. It was about a month ago.'

'Did he tell you he was being parachuted into France with an airborne regiment?'

'No, he just came to say goodbye.'

'I see.' His fingers played with hers during the brief silence, then he glanced fully at her again. 'This isn't like the first time I asked you – whacking great moon over Calcutta, balmy rose-tinted night, and holding your beautiful body in my arms. Nor is it like the second or third times. Not in the least romantic, at the moment, but I so much want us to be married. It wouldn't be for long, but giving you my name would tell the world how I feel about you and put you on a plane higher than any other woman I've known. I've wanted to announce that publicly for so long. Will you let me do it?'

Sarah knew then that happy endings had not quite run out. She smiled. 'All the way here I was afraid you'd be terribly noble and not ask.'

He smiled back. 'No fear! I'm not the noble type.'

'When would you like it to be?'

'Tomorrow. Can you be ready by then?'

'Heavens! Yes, I suppose so.'

'I'll make arrangements with the hospital padre, and get Sister to lay on some food fit enough for the occasion. I'm afraid you'll have to get Charles to help you with the rest on my behalf. We'll get him up here in a minute. Listen, darling, I want you to buy the most glamorous dress you can lay your hands on. And all the frilly things that go with it. Please carry red roses. I want this to be the wedding of the year.'

Sarah was determined nothing would mar their wedding day, not even the news that Hitler had loosed on Britain a new deadly weapon – a pilotless flying bomb that dropped on whatever lay beneath when its fuel ran out. The war would be set aside for the duration of her marriage. The 'most glamorous dress she could lay her hands on' was also the most expensive Harrods could provide – lace over creamy satin and a veil held in place by a band of golden pearls.

When she arrived with Charles at six p.m. she carried a bouquet of red roses and lilies of the valley. On her left hand was a ring of clustered diamonds and emeralds chosen that morning. The gold wedding band was given to Jim Maiden when he arrived with minutes to spare, after being granted a special twenty-four-hour pass.

An orderly played the Bridal March on a piano moved to the upper landing while Sarah mounted the stairs, watched by every member of staff and patient who could find a vantage point. When Charles led her into Alex's room, she saw love shining on his pale face and wondered how she had ever doubted its true depth.

It was a very military affair with the best man, the padre, Sister, Colonel Treems, and two doctors all in uniform, but the smart dresses of Jim's wife, Diana Spencer, and Ellie added colour to a sterile room containing a man tied to his bed.

With the gold ring on her finger without mishap, and the register signed by bride and groom, Sarah Tennant was kissed by the guests and her husband congratulated on his great good fortune to win such a beautiful and talented wife. Women from the kitchens then brought up trays of the most tempting buffet selection they and the cook at the Moxworth Arms Hotel could devise at such short notice. Charles had brought champagne for the toasts, and made a short speech concerning his pride and delight in this happy day.

Alex was determined to play his part as fully as he was able, and spoke up from his pillow in a strong voice. 'When I first met Sarah, I was badly in the red and thought it might be a good idea to woo my banker's daughter. The plan failed miserably. She scorned the handsome, debonair, charming, witty . . .' He was interrupted by jeers from Jim and the hospital staff. 'Oh, all right, I'll skip that bit,' he conceded with a grin. 'I only discovered by chance that she was more attracted to unshaven, bleary-eyed, unwashed chaps who shovelled rice into their mouths with their hands and slept in ditches.' There was laughter. 'Like most people today, the war came between us. I was out on the tiles every night, and she was reminding us all of a saner, more human way of life. Fate decided to bring us together again yesterday. Although I'm once more the aforesaid handsome, charming, witty chap, who's forbidden by Sister Pearce and Colonel Treems to shovel rice into his mouth and sleep in a ditch –' more laughter – 'Sarah has agreed to take me on.' He glanced up at her. 'Thank you, darling.' He raised his glass containing a dash of champagne. 'And thank you all for helping to make this the happiest and most worthwhile day of my life.'

Jim Maiden stepped forward clutching a prompt sheet, and induced a laugh with his first line. 'Seeing as how neither bride nor groom saw fit to provide me with a few pretty bridesmaids to keep me happy for an hour or two, I'll have to do what my wife says and say a few words so that we can all have another go at the champagne. I'm here to tell a few tales about this pair. When I set out on that raft from Hong Kong I knew I was in company with a madman. I wouldn't be here now if he had been anything less. During our trek across China, Mr Tennant took charge and spoke up for us without regard for his own safety, and he walked

489

for miles on a leg that was poisoned, without letting on to us. Miss Channing did all *we* did without complaint. It wasn't at all nice for a lady, but she remained one all way through. Each of them nursed the other back from serious illness without taking necessary rest. I thought then that they was made for each other.' He gave an uncertain smile. 'They took their time getting around to realizing it themselves.' There was more laughter. 'Ladies and gentlemen, I've never spoken a truer word than when I say I'm delighted and honoured to be best man to such wonderful people.' He raised his glass. 'May their marriage be happy and their days together be long.'

During the aftermath of that toast, Charles slipped down to his car and brought up a camera for photographs. Telegrams had arrived. Sarah and Alex read them together, blond heads close, exclaiming over each.

'This is from Norman Briggs, the glider pilot I took over the first time that day,' cried Alex. 'Listen to this, darling. *Now you have a bride in tow, don't drop her over the Caen Canal.*' He laughed. 'That's Norman, all right. I'm so glad he got back from France in one piece. And here's one from the chaps in the squadron. How news gets around.'

Sarah smile knowingly. 'Yes, doesn't it?'

'You read the earlier one from Mother, I suppose?'

'She couldn't have come all the way from Sheffield in so short a time,' Sarah suggested gently.

'A mother like Ellie would have managed it, but I didn't want her here, anyway. Everyone I care about is, and that's all that matters.' He glanced up at her. 'Father has got his merger with Channing Mercantile. He invariably got what he wanted.'

She shook her head. 'He had no hand in this ... and anything less like a business merger I couldn't imagine.'

'Funny how things change. There was a time when you couldn't manage without me. Now it's the reverse.'

'Jim was right,' she countered lightly. 'We were meant for each other.'

Everyone left at eight so that Alex could be prepared for the night. They had all booked rooms in the village and went out to the warmth of a midsummer's evening. Sarah saw them off then returned to change from her wedding dress. She had chosen a pale blue silk nightgown and peignoir for the occasion, because Alex liked her in blue. The staff had pushed another bed into the room for this one night. After thanking Sister Pearce for all the hospital had done to make the day memorable, Sarah went in to Alex and closed the door. He looked comfortable and relaxed. Her bouquet had been placed beside his bed.

He lay gazing at her for a long moment and she made no attempt to break his mood. 'And they both lived happily ever after,' he murmured.

'It was a wonderful wedding, Alex.'

Reaching for her hand, he said, 'You look very beautiful in that, but slip it off so that I can see you properly.'

She hesitated. 'I can't. Not here.'

'Don't be silly! It's our wedding night. They put a bed in here because they know what's what.'

When Sarah did as he asked, he finally surrendered to emotion. Tears hung on his lashes as his hand slowly and gently travelled over her warm skin. Later, she lay on the bed beside his and held his hand while they talked.

Night descended unnoticed, until Alex murmured, 'There you are. Ordered it especially for you. A whacking great moon to make things really romantic.'

Silver light washed over them both as they lay quietly for a while. Then Alex turned his face towards her. 'Are you happy, darling?'

'Immensely. Are you?'

'More than words can say.' His hand tightened around hers. 'May your morning rice bowl be full.'

'Sleep well until the moon is covered by the sun,' she replied softly.

'Now you're here, I shan't mind so much when it isn't.'

He was soon asleep, but she continued to hold his hand until her own eyelids closed.

Chapter Nineteen

Christmas 1945. The war in Europe had ended seven months ago; Japan had surrendered in August after the dropping of two atomic bombs. Britain was facing the cost of victory. There were greater than ever shortages, half the nation's cities lay in ruins. Men were starting to return to take up life as civilians; marriages were foundering every day. Husbands had either become strangers through long absences or because of the things they had seen and done. Wives who had coped alone resented handing back the reins. Extra-marital bonds had been formed and persisted; children had mysteriously joined the family last seen several years before. Wives and children who had become homeless and lived in relative peace with parents now found resentful husbands creating insuperable problems in cramped households.

The war widows saw all this with mixed feelings. Many had children to support, but their jobs were being taken to give to men returning from war. The Government was urging a return to normal life, where women cleaned and cooked, and brought up the family, while husbands went to work and ruled the roost. It was a very short-sighted government.

Sarah was one of the more fortunate widows. Her home with Ellie was secure and filled with love, she did not have to depend on a job for her livelihood, and she had no children. The work she had done for Charles had been gladly taken on by a demobbed gunner interested in music. Sarah had equally gladly relinquished it. Although no longer part of ENSA, Charles continued to arrange concerts in a private capacity, with Sarah as one of his most distinguished soloists. The Arts survived any situation, and the British people were more than ever in need of beauty and colour in their drab lives.

The recapture of Hong Kong had released many who had been imprisoned for four terrible years. A number had not lived to gain their freedom. Sir Peter Channing had died of malnutrition and fever early in the year. An ageing uncle of Sarah's was presently attempting to put the bank back on its feet and recover funds appropriated by the Japanese. Sarah had been asked to visit Hong Kong in the New Year to sign a number of legal documents and decide what she wanted to do with Echoes, which had apparently been reasonably well treated by the Japanese officers who had commandeered it.

Tennant's Steel Works had been bombed a few months before the war ended. There would eventually be government compensation for the damage. It was still managed by men who had worked there all their lives, but Sarah's was the ultimate authority on policy decisions. Knowing Alex had wanted it sold, negotiations were under way to comply with his wishes. The deal would make Sarah a very wealthy woman indeed, since Channing Mercantile were handling the sale. More a takeover than a merger. Maurice would have been livid! Miriam Tennant had become a voluntary invalid. Without her domineering husband to order every minute of her day, she had gone to pieces. Rich enough to pay people to wait on her hand and foot, she occupied her days with imagined illnesses and self-pity. Sarah had never visited her mother-in-law.

There had been a great deal to occupy Sarah in the first few months of peace, but once she quit her three-day-a-week job in Charles's Cheltenham office, and he moved to a bigger one in London, she began to feel restless. Practice still took up much of her time, but it was not enough to still a surge of longing within. The relationship with her grandmother had changed subtly. Ellie was growing frail, so caring and advice were now given by Sarah to her. It was not often heeded. Ellie's determination to go out fighting had not wavered. Sasha and Vlad had said their farewells within a few months of each other, but the hearthrug was still occupied each night. Alex's dog, Ben, provided canine compensation. A mongrel with a warm heart and a coat of many colours, Ben had taken to Noon Cottage as swiftly as his former owner, and provided Ellie with devoted company when Sarah was away at concerts.

Restlessness was dispelled when Sarah finally acted on a notion which had been floating in her mind for some time. After talks with the relatives who were selling the steel works, and with RAF administrators, the Alex Tennant Memorial Hospital developed into a feasible project. Combined Tennant–Channing muscle ensured that a crumbling house in extensive grounds on the edge of Kingsmill was bought, cleared and prepared for building within a very short period. Foundations were laid for the impressive mellow-bricked building in which crippled airmen would be given all medical help available to prepare them for rehabilitation. The building rose up with gratifying speed. Sarah wanted a copy of Moxworth and employed landscape gardeners to create lawns, shrubs and flowerbeds which would be easy on pain-filled eyes and provide a pleasant escape from the antiseptic interior.

With the hospital built and ready to be equipped, Sarah arranged an inaugural ceremony to which she invited the Press *en masse*. She was determined to bury the sins of the father, once and for all, in their minds. Her guests included many high-ranking air-force officers, distinguished statesmen and medical practitioners, as well as a number of men from Alex's squadron and several personalities from the world of music. Sarah would have preferred a less flamboyant affair, but that would have been covered by only a junior reporter from Cheltenham. Big names brought top reporters from major publications. Time enough for the people who really mattered when the hospital became operational at the start of February.

It was a crisp, sunny day with a cloudless sky when cars began rolling up the driveway to a courtyard containing a plinth bearing a bronze sculpture of a seaplane – the symbol that would represent the hospital. Inside, caterers had been busy setting out tables and adding floral decorations to the long, white-walled room destined to be used for physiotherapy. A small orchestra played in the lobby, where hot punch was served on arrival. The place soon rang with stentorian conversation, and the windows steamed up. Cameras flashed with satisfying frequency. Sarah willingly repeated details of her amazing escape from Hong Kong with the man destined to become her husband to every reporter who approached. The men of his squadron told of Alex's many successful missions, and of his courage in remaining in his Halifax so that it would not crash on to the crowded beaches of D-Day. There was no doubt in anyone's mind by the end of the day that the hospital was dedicated to a hero.

When lunch ended, the speeches began. Sarah had requested that they be short, but there was ample time for more photographs. When the moment came to uncover the inaugural plaque it was clear Mrs Tennant had obeyed instinct, for it was Jim Maiden, very spruce in his uniform, who stepped up to pull open the short curtains. The stone slab was headed by an engraved seaplane. Beneath it was a simple tribute.

THIS HOSPITAL IS DEDICATED TO AN ORDINARY MAN,
AND ALL THOSE LIKE HIM, WHO SHOWED EXTRAORDINARY
ENDEAVOUR IN DEFENCE OF THEIR COUNTRY
December 23, 1945

The ceremony ended, but the guests were loath to depart. They stood in groups, chatting and smoking, enjoying this lavish start of the first peacetime Christmas for six years. Sarah, in a black costume on whose lapel she had pinned the gold jewelled RAF wings brooch that had been Alex's wedding present, was finally free to join Ellie, Charles and Diana, the Maidens, Marion, Chloë and her khaki-clad fiancé. Marion's adored Bill had been lost in the North Sea in 1943. Time, and the dreadful years of internment, had dulled her sense of loss and she had three-year-old Sarah to compensate. Chloë had fallen in love with one of her liberators and was looking forward to a promising future.

'Charles has been telling us about your American tour,' Marion said. 'When I stood beside you at the Halburton unpacking dressings, I little realized how famous you were to become. Now you're all set to conquer the United States.'

'It hasn't been finally decided,' Sarah told her, avoiding Charles's eyes. 'I have to be here when they equip the hospital, and approve the board of governors. Then I must go to Hong Kong. I've been putting that off too long.'

'The tour isn't due to begin until June,' put in Charles firmly. 'I've already suggested that you sail the Pacific from Hong Kong. It would be easy enough to arrange.'

'Yes . . . I suppose that might be the solution. There's time yet to think about it before . . . oh, excuse me, I must say goodbye to Wing-Commander Clandon. He's been so helpful and enthusiastic.'

Everyone drifted away within the next half-hour, leaving Sarah to drive Ellie back to Noon Cottage as darkness was creeping over the countryside. The village looked so attractive, with lights flooding from cottage windows and the great oak outside the Dog and Duck hung with festive lanterns. A real Christmas again.

'You look tired, dear,' said Ellie suddenly.

'All those flashlights have made my eyes ache, that's all,' she replied. 'It went well, didn't it?'

'That hospital means a great deal to you.'

'Yes. Not only because of Alex, but our fathers. They both used money merely to make more. I want to redress the balance and exchange it for something worthwhile whenever I can. Marion mentioned unpacking dressings at the Halburton. I saw a great deal of suffering during the battle for Hong Kong that could have been alleviated with enough medicines and peacetime conditions. Young people were dying years before their time for lack of the ability to help them. That, plus those few days with Alex at Moxworth, taught me enough to know I want to use my ridiculous wealth in that direction. I'll probably build another hospital later on.'

'The Lady with the Lamp?'

'Why not?'

'And your musical career?'

Sarah glanced at her grandmother. 'That was decided by you when you sent me off to discover there were people in

496

the world. I did, and found they are sometimes more important to me than furthering my musical interests.' She branched on to the road leading home. 'Charles is all set to turn me into an international celebrity, with concert tours all over the world. It would mean I must abandon all else in my pursuit of fame. I would have to mix with all the right people, be seen in all the right places. My life would no longer be my own. Not only do I not want that, I simply couldn't do it. I've always hated social pomp and extravagance; flattery and guile. I like places of natural beauty, like Noon Cottage, and dogs, people who are uncomplicated and sincere. I'm a private kind of person – you know that well enough. When I play, I give too much of myself and almost need to hide away afterwards. To be the kind of shining star Charles has in mind, I would have to surrender everything I value.'

'Except music.'

'I've learned over the years that the price is too high.' She turned the car through the entrance to her home and brought it to a standstill at the front door, where the brass coach lamp threw welcoming light on the gravel. Then she turned to Ellie. 'You taught me how to distinguish dross from gold, and life since Hong Kong has revealed that there are things to do that are more worthwhile than gaining public acclaim.' A reminiscent smile broke through. 'Jakob Myburgh was possessed by music, even though his hands could no longer play it. I'll give concerts only when and where I wish to, but I shall always be possessed by it, too.'

Switching off engine and lights, she said warmly, 'Come on, let's shrug off all that social nonsense laid on for the benefit of the Press, take off our shoes, and sit in front of the fire with a cup of tea.'

Ben rushed to greet them. After returning his affection, Sarah went through to the kitchen to put the kettle on, leaving Ellie to settle in her favourite chair.

When she came back with the tray Sarah gave her grandmother a cup, remarking, 'You're very pensive. Not intending to go off with Robert tomorrow in search of owls, I hope.'

'I was just thinking that this afternoon rounds everything

497

off rather nicely. Your friends from Hong Kong appear to have settled to their new lives after that dreadful internment camp, the newspapers are certain to print what you want in their columns tomorrow, Jim Maiden and his lovely little wife can face a peaceful future with their brood, and the war is over.' She smiled across at Sarah, who had kicked off her shoes and was tickling Ben's fur with her toes. 'Don't you agree there's something warm and satisfying about this Christmas?'

'Mmm . . . and there's something warm and satisfying about sitting here with you and Ben.' She gazed at the burning logs and fir cones for a minute or two. 'You know, I'm not sure I really need to go to Hong Kong. The Channings can send all the documents here for me to go through. I've no real desire to go out there again. I was very unhappy at Echoes. I'll bequeath it to whoever runs the bank for me. It won't be long before intermarriage becomes commonplace, and Chinese start taking over administration of the colony. We "lost face" by surrendering it, Ellie. They won't ever feel the same about us. No, I don't think I'll go.'

They sipped their tea for a while in contented silence. Then Ellie said, 'When Hong Kong fell, I blamed myself for sending you there. When you arrived back and related what you had suffered, I still blamed myself. I don't any longer.'

Sarah smiled. 'What deep thoughts from you today.'

'As a matter of fact, I'm patting myself on the back, dear. Since I packed you off to your father you've worked in a hospital under fire, escaped across primitive, hostile land, survived a nervous breakdown, become a broadcasting celebrity and played to thousands in blitzed cities, made a brave young pilot very happy and eased his passing in the most wonderful way. To cap it all, you've become quite a businesswoman – selling steel companies, settling banking hierarchies and building hospitals. I think I've made rather a good job of rearing the sad, shy four-year-old sent to me twenty years ago.'

'A marvellous job, darling,' Sarah agreed affectionately. 'That's another thing rounded off nicely this Christmas.'

The telephone rang, and Sarah got to her feet with a soft curse. 'I hope that's not Charles to badger me about the

American tour. I could see he wasn't happy when I brushed the subject aside this afternoon.'

'If it's Violet asking about the drawings for Chapter Five, tell her I'll let her have them in the morning,' called Ellie as Sarah went through to the hall to pick up the receiver.

'Hallo. Sarah Tennant speaking.'

There was silence. She repeated her words.

'It's not entirely my fault this time. I didn't know until yesterday that I was being flown over,' said Rod's voice in her ear. 'I'm sorry if this is a shock.'

'Where . . . where are you?' she managed to ask.

'At the Dog and Duck.'

She could see him so clearly it was as if he were there speaking to her. 'How long are you staying?'

'That depends on what you say to me now. Look, I'll make it brief for both our sakes. The landlord has brought me up to date where you're concerned, but I wanted you to know that thinking about you was all that kept me sane through the months in a freezing POW camp in Germany. When we were released, I volunteered to stay with other doctors to help victims of concentration camps. Thinking of you was all that kept me sane through that horror, too.' There was a pause before he said, 'Sarah, I'm no longer the man you knew, and I've learned how the only things that matter are compassion and love of mankind. I need to work for that, so that we never go through hell of this kind again.' She heard his indrawn breath. 'I don't know how things stand between us now. I still believe I was right to walk away from you when I did, but I'm desperately in need of rediscovering things like Rachmaninov, enchanted gardens and the softness of your hair beneath my palms. I'll be here until tomorrow morning. If you don't come, I'll understand and walk out of your life for good.'

If he said any more she did not hear it. The receiver was left swinging on its cord as she ran out to the car in her stockinged feet.

THE BELOVED PEOPLE

Denise Robertson

In the Durham mining village of Belgate, the legacy of World War I has far-reaching consequences for rich and poor, socialist and aristocrat, Jew and gentile alike.

Howard Brenton, heir to the colliery, back from the trenches with a social conscience, but robbed of the confidence to implement it...

Diana, his beautiful, aristocratic wife, afraid of her dour new world and fatally drawn to the jazzy gaiety of twenties London...

Miner **Frank Maguire**, and his bitter wife **Anne**, fired by union fervour as they struggle to survive the slump...

Esther Gulliver, to whom kindly Emmanuel Lansky shows new roads to prosperity beyond the pit...

Linked by place, chance and time, the people of Belgate grapple with the personal and general costs of war, of coal, of childbirth. And in the mid-1930s, face together a new and terrifying crisis in Europe...

'Humour and warmth keep you turning the pages' – *Annabel*

SIGNET

Published or forthcoming

Distant Echoes

Laura Gilmour Bennett

Rachel runs a celebrated French restaurant in California with her glamorous husband, chef Alain Ribard, and is mother to their son Oliver. She seems to have it all – so why does she feel there is some threat to her happiness?

When Alain unexpectedly takes Oliver to France on a sentimental trip to his birthplace, Rachel decides to join them. But upon arrival in Roquelaire, she discovers that they are nowhere to be found – and that rumours abound about her husband's involvement with a mysterious Frenchwoman.

Drawn into village life as she attempts to unravel the mystery of Alain's and Oliver's disappearance, she is befriended by attractive Englishman Michael Lowry, who is writing a chronicle of events in the village in the summer of 1348.

As Rachel's involvement with Michael deepens, she learns of the centuries-old tale of Margaret Prior, who became a pilgrim in order to search for her son and the husband who deserted her in their plague-stricken village – a tale which begins strangely to mirror her own …

The Stars Burn On

Denise Robertson

On New Year's Day 1980, Jenny and seven friends watch the dawn from a northern hill. On the brink of adulthood, confident of their futures, they vow to meet there again at the end of the decade. Just two weeks later, one of the group is dead. The others, irrevocably affected, go on to pursue careers in the law or media, and make new lives for themselves as husbands, wives and parents. Jenny, who establishes herself as a successful journalist in London, remains their linchpin – and only Jenny knows that the secret that binds them is a lie.

'A saga that'll keep you turning the pages . . . told with perception and humour' – *Prima*

'Her prose has a fine flow, her knowledge of the region is deep and instinctive. Above all, her compassion and great understanding of life show in all she writes' – *Evening Chronicle, Newcastle upon Tyne*

SIGNET

Published or forthcoming

THE
WHITE RHINO HOTEL

Bartle Bull

Nanyuki, Kenya, 1920. Desperate to better their fortunes after the suffering of the First World War, two escapees from England are thrown together on a ship bound for Dar es Salaam...

Anton Rider, trained by gypsies to hunt, gamble and read fortunes, comes to Africa seeking gold, freedom and adventure. Courageous Welsh settler Gwenn Llewellyn hopes to rekindle the love of her invalid husband in a farm carved out of the virgin wilderness of the African bush.

Yet bonded for ever by a violent encounter their paths cross once more at Lord Penfold's White Rhino Hotel – last outpost of civilization, and the gambling den that bears silent witness to the death of a thousand dreams. There, pitted against the savage forces of nature and the greed of man, Anton and Gwenn begin their search for a future and a home for their hearts....

SIGNET

Published or forthcoming

SUCH DEVOTED SISTERS

Eileen Goudge

Eve and Dolly are aspiring Hollywood starlets, hungry for fame and success. When one of them betrays the other a tragic chain of events is set in motion that irrevocably changes their lives and the futures of Eve's children, Annie and Laurel.

Forced to leave their home, Annie and her sister run away to New York. There Annie, drawn into the delicious, fragrant world of the chocolate business, determines to become a top chocolatier, while Laurel becomes an artist. Full of unspoken secrets they live for each other – until they fall in love with the same man and the past returns to haunt the future . . .

BEACHES

Iris Rainer Dart

Once in a lifetime you make a friendship that lasts forever ...

From the moment Cee Cee Bloom and Bertie Barron collide on the beach at Atlantic City aged ten and seven, they are friends ... for life. In time Cee Cee, a talented singer and comedienne, successfully pursues Hollywood stardom, while Bertie chooses the conventional life of marriage and motherhood. But despite the striking differences between them, the two women sustain each other through thirty years of careers and children, jealousy and drugs, lovers and divorce. And when they are torn apart by a shattering tragedy, against all odds Cee Cee and Bertie find strength in their extraordinary friendship.

'Well-written, well-constructed and thoroughly enjoyable' – *Daily Telegraph*